AHAB'S WIFE

or,

The Star-Gazer

AHAB'S WIFE

or,

The Star-Gazer

a novel by SENA JETER NASLUND

Illustrations by Christopher Wormell

WILLIAM MORROW AND COMPANY, INC.

New York

It is the policy of William Morrow and Company, Inc., and its imprints and
affiliates, recognizing the importance of preserving what has been written,
to print the books we publish on acid-free paper, and
we exert our best efforts to that end.

Library of Congress Cataloging-in-Publication Data

Naslund, Sena Jeter.
Ahab's wife, or, The star-gazer : a novel / Sena Jeter Naslund.—1st ed.
p.   cm.
A novel inspired by Herman Melville's Moby-Dick.
ISBN 0-688-17187-7
I. Melville, Herman, 1819–1891. Moby-Dick.   II. Title.
III. Title: Ahab's wife.   IV. Title: Star-gazer.
PS3564.A827A76   1999
813'.54—dc21   99-22135
                                                CIP

Printed in the United States of America

First Edition

1 2 3 4 5 6 7 8 9 10

BOOK DESIGN BY MARYSARAH QUINN

www.williammorrow.com

In Token
Of My Admiration and Affection
This Book Is Inscribed
To
John C. Morrison

One must take off her fear like clothing;

One must travel at night;

This is the seeking after God.

—MAUREEN MOREHEAD, *In a Yellow Room*

Contents

Illustrations

Let them be sea-captains—if they will!
—MARGARET FULLER, *Woman in the Nineteenth Century* (1845)

It was now early spring, and the river was swollen and turbulent;
great cakes of floating ice were swinging heavily to and from in
the turbid water. . . . The huge green fragment of ice on which
[Eliza] alighted pitched and creaked as her weight came on it,
but she stayed there not a moment. With wild cries and desperate
energy she leaped to another and still another cake:—stumbling—
leaping—slipping—springing upwards again!
"Yer a brave gal, now, whoever ye ar!"
—HARRIET BEECHER STOWE, *Uncle Tom's Cabin* (1851)

"My God! Mr. Chase, what is the matter?"
I answered, "We have been stove by a whale."
—OWEN CHASE, *Narrative of the Shipwreck*
of the Whale Ship Essex *of Nantucket* (1821)

"Mark ye, be forewarned; Ahab's above the common; Ahab's been
in colleges, as well as 'mong the cannibals; been used to deeper
wonders than the waves; fixed his fiery lance in mightier, stranger
foes than whales. . . . Aye, aye, I know that he was never very
jolly; and I know that on the passage home, he was a little out of
his mind for a spell; but it was the sharp shooting pains in his
bleeding stump that brought that about, as any one might see.
I know, too, that ever since he lost his leg last voyage by that
accursed whale, he's been a kind of moody—desperate moody,
and savage sometimes; but that will all pass off. And once for
all, let me tell thee and assure thee, young man, it's better to sail
with a moody good captain than a laughing bad one. . . .
Besides, my boy, he has a wife—not three voyages wedded—a
sweet, resigned girl. Think of that; by that sweet girl that old
man had a child: hold ye then there can be any utter, hopeless

harm in Ahab? No, no, my lad; stricken, blasted, if he be, Ahab
has his humanities!"

—CAPTAIN PELEG TO ISHMAEL, "The Ship,"
Herman Melville, *Moby-Dick* (1851)

[Starbuck, First Mate of the Pequod:*] "Oh, my Captain! my
Captain! noble soul! grand old heart, after all! why should any
one give chase to that hated fish! . . . —this instant let me alter
the course! How cheerily, how hilariously, O my Captain, would
we bowl on our way to see old Nantucket again! I think, sir, they
have some such mild blue days, even as this, in Nantucket."*

*[Ahab:] "They have, they have. I have seen them—some
summer days in the morning. About this time—yes, it is his noon
nap now—the boy vivaciously wakes; sits up in bed; and his
mother tells him of me, of cannibal old me; how I am abroad
upon the deep, but will yet come back to dance him again."*

*[Starbuck:] ". . . my Mary . . . promised that my boy, every
morning, should be carried to the hill to catch the first glimpse of
his father's sail! . . . Come, my Captain, study out the course,
and let us away! See, see! the boy's face from the window! the
boy's hand on the hill!"*

*But Ahab's glance was averted. . . . "What is it, what
nameless, inscrutable, unearthly thing is it: what cozening, hidden
lord and master, and cruel, remorseless emperor commands me;
that against all natural lovings and longings, I so keep pushing,
and crowding, and jamming myself on all the time . . . ? By
heaven, man, we are turned round and round in this world, like
yonder windlass, and Fate is the handspike. . . . But it is a mild,
mild wind, and a mild looking sky; and the air smells now, as if
it blew from a far-away meadow; they have been making hay
somewhere under the slopes of the Andes, Starbuck, and the
mowers are sleeping among the new-mown hay."*

—STARBUCK AND AHAB, "The Symphony," *Moby-Dick*

*I have fed upon dry salted fare—fit emblem of the dry
nourishment of my soul!—when the poorest landsman has had
fresh fruit to his daily hand, and broken the world's fresh bread to
my mouldy crusts—away, whole oceans away, from that young*

girl-wife I wedded past fifty, and sailed for Cape Horn the next day, leaving but one dent in my marriage pillow—wife? wife?— rather a widow with her husband alive! Aye, I widowed that poor girl when I married her, Starbuck; and then, the madness, the frenzy, the boiling blood and the smoking brow, with which, for a thousand lowerings old Ahab has furiously, foamingly chased his prey—more a demon than a man!—aye, aye! . . . Behold. Oh, Starbuck! is it not hard, that with this weary load I bear, one poor leg should have been snatched from under me? Here, brush this old hair aside; it blinds me, that I seem to weep. Locks so grey did never grow but from out some ashes! . . . I feel deadly faint, bowed, and humped, as though I were Adam, staggering beneath the piled centuries since Paradise. God! God! God!— crack my heart!—stave my brain!—mockery! mockery! bitter, biting mockery of grey hairs . . . Close! stand close to me, Starbuck; let me look into a human eye; it is better than to gaze into sea or sky; better than to gaze upon God. By the green land; by the bright hearth-stone! this is the magic glass, man; I see my wife and my child in thine eye.

—AHAB, "The Symphony," *Moby-Dick*

"There she blows!—there she blows! A hump like a snow-hill! It is Moby Dick!"

—AHAB, "The Chase—First Day," *Moby-Dick*

CHAPTER 1      A Mild Blue Day

C APTAIN AHAB WAS neither my first husband nor my last. Yet, looking up—into the clouds—I conjure him there: his gray-white hair; his gathered brow; and the zaggy mark (I saw it when lying with him by candlelight and, also, taking our bliss on the sunny moor among curly-cup gumweed and lamb's ear). And I see a zaggy shadow now in the rifting clouds. That mark started like lightning at Ahab's temple and ran not all the way to his heel (as some thought) but ended at Ahab's heart.

That pull of cloud—tapered and blunt at one end and frayed at the other—seems the cottony representation of his ivory leg. But I will not see him all dismembered and scattered in heaven's blue—that would be no kind, reconstructive vision; *no,* intact, lofty and sailing, though his shape is changeable. Yesterday, when I tilted my face to the sky, I imaged not the full figure but only his cloudy head, a portrait, glancing back at me over his shoulder.

What weather is in Ahab's face?

For me, now, as it ever was in life, at least when he was looking at me alone and had no other person in view, his visage is mild—with a brightness in it, even be it a wild, white, blown-about brightness. Now, as I look at those billowed clouds, I see the *Pequod.* I half raise my hand to bid good-bye, as it was that last day from the eastmost edge of Nantucket Island, when, with a wave and then a steadfast, longing look, till the sails were only a white dot, and then a blankness of ocean—then a glitter—I wished his ship and him *Godspeed.*

Nantucket! The home where first I found my body, my feet not so much being pulled into this sandy beach as seeking downward, toes better than roots; then my mind, built not to chart this blue swell of heaving ocean, but the night sky, where the stars themselves, I do believe, heave and float and spin in fiery passions of their own; Nantucket!—home, finally, of my soul, found on a platform eight-by-eight, the wooden widow's walk perched like a pulpit atop my house. These three gears of myself—body, mind, and soul—mesh here on this small island—Nantucket! Then, why, when I look into the mild day sky, do the clouds scramble, like letters in the alphabet, and spell not Nantucket, but that first home, *Kentucky?* And those clouds that did bulge with the image of Ahab show me the map of that state, flat across the bottom and all billowed at the top?

As a child of three, lying on my back close to the Ohio River, when I looked up, the puffy clouds formed neither map, nor portrait, nor white animals grazing the sky, but I thought: *Beautiful! This is what they mean by beautiful.*

Even as a child, I wanted to know what words meant and marked those occasions when I did learn as memorable. Once when I sat on a stump in the yard and watched my father drive away in the black buggy, his whip in his hand, I thought, *Sad, I feel sad,* and I knew that it was my first matching of that word and that feeling. I asked my mother to show me the letters for that word, and thus I began to write as well as read at a very early age. "S-s-s," she said. "The letter looks like and sounds like a snake, and *s* begins both *sad* and *snake*." Well might *sad* be matched to my father, for though he was kind to me as a child, he became a moody and then a desperate and violent man, who took his own life.

His ghost rides by in black; standing at his knee, the whip, its lash dangling like a thin banner.

I DID NOT consult Ahab about my decision to spend my pregnancy in a rough Kentucky cabin, with my mother, instead of staying in the gracious home of a captain's wife on Nantucket. But I wrote him, of course, and sent the letter after him on the ship called the *Dove,* so he could imagine me aright.

That time spent with my mother outdoors in the sweet summer and golden Kentucky autumn was augmented by our indoor companionship of sewing baby smocks and cooking and reading again those great works of literature my mother had brought with her to the wilderness, green-bound books I had read as a child or she had read to me.

Sometimes my mother and I stood and looked at our faces together in the oval mirror she had brought with her from the East. Along with her library chest of books, the mirror with its many-stepped molding distinguished our frontier cabin from others. Thus, elegantly framed, my mother and I made a double portrait of ourselves for memory, by looking in the mirror.

WHEN IN MID-DECEMBER the labor began but tried in vain to progress, my mother went from our cabin, driving the old mare in the black buggy through a six-inch crust of snow, for the doctor. In my travail, I scarcely noticed her leaving. When my mother did not come home and did not come home, and the pains were near unbearable and the chill was creeping across the cabin floor and into my feet as I paced, I grasped the feather bed from my bunk and flung it atop her bed. In desperation, between spasms, I gathered all the gaudy quilts in the house, and then, leaving the latchstring out so that I would not have to venture from my nest when she returned, I took to my childbirth bed. There, softness of two mattresses comforted me from beneath and warmth of myriad quilts, a cacophony of colors, warmed me from above, but still I worked my feet and legs and twisted my back.

Despite the heat of my labor, I could feel my nose turning to ice, long and sharp as a church steeple all glazed with frost. *Parsnip!* I thought of; frozen and funny—a vegetable on my face! I chortled and then prayed, wondering if prayer and laughter gurgled up, sometime, from the same spring. *Let nose be parsnip, parsnip be steeple, steeple be nose—whatever that protuberance, it is frozen to the very cartilage. Warm it! Save me, gods and saints!*

Wild and crazed by pain, my thoughts leaped about in antic dance, circling one picture after another. Nose! Steeple! Parsnip! My desperate, laughing prayer from within that quilted hump below its parsnip was only that I should be delivered and nothing at all for the welfare of the rest of the world.

And yet I wanted to wait for my mother's return, and I was afraid because I had little idea of how to catch the baby. So even as I prayed,

I prayed against myself, that time would not pass nor take me any closer to the port of motherhood. I thought of Ahab, as if his ship were wallowing, going neither forward nor drifting back but immobile in a confused sea. Sometimes I slept a little.

During an exhausted respite from the pains that wrung me, and yet amid my anxiety for my too-long-absent mother, I thought I heard the door creak open and an attendant puff of colder cold, but sleep claimed me again. In my sleep Zephyrs roamed the room. Their cheeks were bloated with frosty breath, which they jetted through pursed lips across the tip of my nose, down the part of my hair, and into my ears.

Then there came such a pounding at the door that I thought, *Volcanos! It will burst through!*

"Open the door," they shouted. "Give her up now!" And terrible pounding of closed fists on my boards.

"Pull the latchstring," I called, for terrifying as they sounded, I didn't want my door shattered by their anger, nor did I want to leave the bed. Seeing how humped I was, wouldn't any being attached to human voice pity me? Around me, the cabin was almost black, as I had left no candle burning, and the windows had been shuttered for the winter. The fire was no more than red-glow.

"No latchstring out!" one man called. And gruffer voices growled without human language. So I lifted the covers and stood by the bed, but before I did their bidding, I covered my warm spot atop the two feather beds with my quilts. Slowly I crossed the dim cabin—I imagined a dark ghoul crouching along the wall—harbinger of pain to come?—but I opened the door and faced the snow. As though frozen in the icy air, a group of six, all bundled up in wool and fur, stood around a torch of blazing pine knot.

"Her tracks come to your door, Madam," one said. "Give her up, now."

These bounty hunters seemed to lick their mouths where frost was caked in their long mustaches and beards. They were like ice demons, but my innocence made me brave, for I harbored no runaway slave.

"I am in childbirth at this very moment." They could clearly see my great roundness in my flannel gown. "I'm waiting my mother and the doctor. Have you seen them?"

One of the six was much smaller than a normal man. His head rose only to the waists of the others, and he wore the pelt of a wolf. I would have thought the man a child, but his face was heavily bearded, and the hair of his face joined and blended with the wolf fur. The ears and snout of the wolf hooded his head, and the wolf's ivory teeth were fastened in the man's hair. Were he not diminutive, he would have suggested a frontier Hercules cloaked in skin of wolf instead of Nemean lion. The dwarfish wolf-man held the high-lifted, blazing pine knot, big as a thigh, in the center of the group. As he lifted his torch higher, the pack stretched to see beyond me into my house. Beyond them, in that flickering, orange light, I could see bare footprints in the snow, small ones, such as a woman might make, and indeed they led toward my door, at least to the great mauled patch where their boots were shifting and scratching.

"We must search your house."

The frigid wind swept over my skin like icy water, and then hot water poured from between my legs and wetted my gown and the floor. I stepped back.

"Look, you," I cried. "My water's breaking!" I would use my shame to rebuff them.

"Still, we'll have the wench, and you must yield her up."

"Look in my house, if you like," I replied, resigned. "But I must go to my bed."

And I did, sniffing back my fear, and wanting my mother, and watching them. From the big torch, which they stuck in a snowbank, they each lighted a taper of fat-pine kindling and entered my house, closing the door. They held up the flaming sticks like candles and filled the cabin with light. Deep in my bed, I wondered, *Will these ruffians stay while my sweet babe comes out?* The room glowed, and rosin-scented smoke curled to the ceiling. *Among these demon-angels, is there a father who might help me?* But the thought of their awful paws between my thighs frightened me so much I would not ask. I lay gasping and groaning while they looked around and beneath the furniture. There was little place for concealment in the room.

"Search under the bunk."

The dwarf dropped to all fours, and then he truly looked like a wolf snuffing under the beds. And when he stood up again, he seemed a magic wolf, trained to walk unnaturally in houses, on his hind legs. One hunter opened my sea chest, which I knew to be empty, and peered in.

"You have a hill of cover upon you."

"The lass is a mountain in herself, Jack," another said quietly, and I heard the Scotch burr in his voice.

"Could you bring in wood for me? afore you leave?"

The rough-spoken man put his hand on my cover to jerk it back in his search, but the Scotsman restrained the hand and said, "No, Jack. Be leaving her her warmth now, and let's be off." I have always thought the Scotsman would have brought in wood for me, but because he knew the men to be mean and ready for roughness of unspeakable kinds, he set them on the hunt again.

"Sometimes they walk backward in their trails," the dwarf added persuasively, "to throw us off the chase." I started at his voice—soft as fur. "She's not here," he added, in the same caressing tone. Pivoting in a furry blur, he scampered across the room to the door.

A pack following their leader, the hunters clomped after the wolf-cloaked dwarf, and as they passed through the door, they doused their firebrands, each stick hissing as it entered the snow. From the drift, the Scotsman took up the blazing torch, the pine knot whorled like a hip joint. Then someone eased the door shut, and the cabin was utterly dark again.

My fear seemed to have stilled my labor. I listened to the crunch of the men's boots going toward the river, which was frozen solid. At a distance, they sounded almost merry, like Christmas revelers, rather than a cruel posse on a deadly hunt for a human being.

Their coming and going had let out all the warmth from the fire, which was sunk almost to embers, no bigger than eyes. Though my labor stood still, and I did not knead the covers or corkscrew my back, I quivered and shook—whether with fear that the men might come back or with dread that my baby was to be welcomed only by my ignorance and the winter's cold, I don't know. If I did not die of childbirth, I and my child would likely freeze to death. I knew if I rubbed myself that friction would warm me a bit, but I was too fearful to make the effort. Involunteer, I lay and quivered and shivered. It seemed, after a long time, that the bed itself was cold and also shivering.

Typhoon sleep enswirled my mind and I dreamed—of the dwarf, his eyes brown and warm as ancient amber, beautifully human in his animal face. Did he know the midwife's art? The dream dwarf asked me my name. "Una!" I said sharply and woke myself.

The pain was hard, tight and dark within me. I lay still except for my involuntary shivering and the bedding shivering on its woven ropes in return. The fire had fallen to ash; the last ember eye had closed.

I shivered and the bed shivered, till finally in my delirious state, the bed seemed to be offering a signal, and I thought it was a friendly signal, that it, too, was cold, and I was not alone. Finally, thinking that if *somehow* I *should* live, I should not want to do so without a nose, and if I did not cover it, mine might freeze solid and crack off, falling like a tree cut at its base, I reached up for the edge of the covers and pulled them over my head. Fingering that vulnerable member, I said, *Thou shalt not freeze—not at least if I've brains enough to pull thee under cover!* Then I smiled, to speak to my nose in the voice of Quaker English. *Art turning into Ahab?* I asked. *Nose first?* And, under the quilts, I thumped myself there till I did sting with the feeling, and tears squeezed from my eyes.

But the tears were for the loneliness of the gesture, not for the stinging, but for my longing for my husband. If Dr. Carter was not to be found, what harm or danger prevented my mother's return? I realized cold was but a cloak for the more fearsome specter: aloneness.

As I continued to thump my nose, then it was I heard a voice, coming, it seemed, from my own belly! Or from my back? Within my cave in the bed. I opened my eyes to look down my body, to see if somehow I had, unknown, produced a vocal babe. Under the covers, the blackness of the cabin—the fire having gone totally out—was compounded to the most profound degree.

What had my babe said?

I waited in the dark, but heard nothing. I felt my belly; the babe was yet within. I shivered. Yes, the bed shivered.

"O, Natural Vibration!" I said aloud, but did not know how to further address a Vibration. And so I laughed, an unearthly, merry peal.

Then, it occurred to me to jiggle the bed. I did shake the mattresses upon their web of rope, and in return, from beneath me—a jiggle. Complexing the signal, I jiggled twice—and twice the bed jiggled in return. I skipped ahead in my addition and jiggled seven times for the days in the week. When seven jiggles, to the very count, came back, despite my crazy dilemma, I giggled.

And then the voice, low as though filtered through baffles, said, "We be lots warmer, we put our skins together."

"Lazarus, come forth," I commanded and laughed joyfully, till a birth pain cut me short.

I was not alone.

From between the two mattresses, under my back, I felt her body moving. And though I saw nothing, I imaged with my inward eye her fingers grope the edge, her head and neck thrust through, and then in a smooth lunge—so as not to disturb me on the upper mattress—she slid out onto the floor, her landing muffled by the braided rug. I pictured her quite flat as though passed through the wringers over a wash-tub, and then puffed up to normal, once free of her compression. Lifting up the side of my cover, I welcomed her, emissary of the lost tribe, into my tent.

Though she had run far in the snowy night, she was wearing but a shift, and her body was colder than mine. I turned to her, and she curved her small self, lean and taut, to my belly as though it were a great hot rock. I bent her close to me and she pulled herself yet closer so that our bosoms touched, and I rubbed her back, and *she* rubbed the flat space between my shoulder blades and all down my spine, and what with the friction of it and the two of us constantly moving, we did become warmer. And then I kissed her on the cheek, and she did me, and it was settled that we were sisters and more than that, for the spirits of sisters are not always married.

Before I had seen either her face or the smooth cheek I had kissed, my labor seized me. I needed to turn on my back, and needed to bear down and needed desperately to lift my knees—oh, let some contortion expel this babe!—let me thrust my legs straight. Again, I needed to draw them back and thrust, and coil and uncoil, and again. After much of this labor, during a lull, I learned her name, and she said that she would go out to the woodpile and I said that she must wrap herself in the top two quilts.

She slid out from our bed, and, still not visible in the darkness, carefully drew off the top layers of cover, wrapped herself, crossed the floor, and passed through the door. So quickly did my state vacillate now, between dozing and consciousness, that I am ashamed to say that I kept no vigil for her but awoke when she returned. From the moon-light reflected by the snow, I saw her figure in the door opening, one arm curled up carrying the logs, the other free to reach back. With the closing of the door, her image was lost to me again, but I pictured her by sound. When she straightened her arms, the wood rolled down to the hearth, and the rumble of the pieces jouncing each other, bruising and kissing the bark of their fellows and tumbling onto the hearthstones, was as pleasant and promising as any sound I know.

After she had kindled a blaze for us, in the warm glow of the fire, I could see her—Susan—moving about the room, enfolded by the quilts, the red patch-blocks catching the fireglow with their congenial color. The dark curve of her head and her small pigtails sticking up, which I had known by feel in the bed, I saw in silhouette.

Soon, I discerned her face and believed it to be the color of dark walnut. Her lips, leaning over me, her lips very even in the fullness of the upper and lower lip, and most generous, shaped words: "You be all right, soon now. Push on, now." Her dear lips pushed the air when she said *push* in a soft puff of encouragement. "You sure to live." Her hands briskly rubbed my belly, so fast and light that I could not feel pain where her fingers shimmied.

"You be all right. You be all right."

"You must reach inside me," I said.

"I afeared," Susan answered, but she did not refuse.

"Give me your hands." I took them and kissed her fingertips. "Now," I said, "reach in."

Susan nodded yes and, between my tented knees, bent her head to the work; her short pigtails marched in a single row over the top of her head. Quicker than a gasp, I saw ancient helmets with their row of short, stiff horsehair, line drawings of warriors in Mother's *Iliad for Boys*.

"I not want to hurt you." Her voice was a sweet whisper of kindness. Through it ran the silver vein of intelligence.

I told her I couldn't feel. I smiled as I lied. That the feeling was elsewhere.

We screamed together. The screams tore out of us.

She tore the baby out of me.

"Aloft! Aloft!" I shouted, and she held him up by his heels, the purple cord spiraling down.

When he cried, our screams sank to silence, and each of us snuffled back tears. Together we sounded like a quiet surf. Spent.

"You be all right."

And I was.

We named the baby Liberty, but he was listless and did not try to suckle me. Though I had no belief, I bargained with God, offered my life instead, but the universe did not listen. I planned how Susan could have taken my baby with her, had I died. Found sanctuary from the cold as soon as they crossed into freedom. But my baby died.

Susan stayed with me.

That night with the wind howling above the snow-laden roof, I thought of wind in canvas, at sea, and of Ahab, sailing the South Seas. Standing at the rail each morning, Ahab surely would think that each new day the sun might be message-boy with news of a child for his old age. Sleepless, lying on my back, with both hands and groping fingers, I searched the loose flesh of my belly—a husk, my fruit stolen away. I had only disappointment and an empty womb to offer. In his age, with passion, Ahab had given me seed; I in my youth had failed to birth a thriving child.

The only comfort was to turn and curl toward the warmth of Susan's dark body, radiant beside me in the bed. I nestled against her as though she were my husband, mother, sister, shadow, angel.

CHAPTER 2   The Dirge

IN THREE DAYS, the snow had still not melted, but the river had begun to break up. Those days! I will not tell of them now. Imagine Christ crucified and not yet risen.

Imagine him *comforted* in the bowels of hell by an angel, who was neither named nor imaged in the Gospels. But such a one was she who was small and dark, her hair standing up in pigtails. We wrapped the baby in soft white lamb's wool and placed him tenderly under the snow not far from the mound where the men had stuck their torch.

When neighbors came across the snowy yard, I quickly hid Susan in the sea chest I had used to transport my goods from Nantucket to Kentucky. These neighbors said that my father's old buggy, driven by my mother, had turned over through the office of a deep rut hidden under the snow; and my mother had frozen before anyone found her. Her skin had turned black from the freezing. Black, like a cinder, one neighbor said, before they could stop her describing.

I heard Susan sob once from inside the green-painted chest, so great was her sympathy for me. For myself, the quick and caring and grieving part of me already frozen beyond feeling, I wanted not my mother so much as that hidden person who could sob for her.

"Take the baby," I wailed, "for he's dead, too!"

The neighbors and I agreed that the ground would surely thaw enough to dig in three days, whereupon someone would come for me, and we would have the funerals.

"You and your news of death, leave me!" I blazed at them. "Take the second corpse and leave me!"

When they had reluctantly gone—I stood before the closed door and watched their progress in the snow—then, as I turned, up from the sea-green trunk rose Susan, like a dark waterspout unwinding grief for me. I watched the flowing of her tears, but my own were unshed. Instead, I felt my thudding heart, a pump whose shaft was sunk in a dry well.

In her gush of tears, Susan said though she had never had a child, she had had a loving mother, left behind in slavery.

"Your mama be black like my mam," she sobbed.

I reached out my hands and arms to enclose and comfort her, while she yet stood in the chest. I envisioned my mother's cheek—leather-slick as well as black. Feeling myself to be a jointed doll, stiff and unnatural in my movement, a wooden thing, I reached for Susan.

"Your mother lives," I said.

My bodice was soaked with her weeping, and though I could not cry, my swollen breasts unloosed my milk, which mingled with her tears.

"We ain't got but one mam," she wailed. "Never be no other."

Standing knee-deep in the chest, like a spent jack-in-the-box, she leaned on me and sobbed—for her mother, not mine.

SUSAN HAD LEFT her mam for the sake of freedom, but for my sake she lingered, even though the river ice was thawing.

"You stay with 'em?" she asked anxiously, referring to when the neighbors would return.

"No. I'll stay here."

"You don't care for them folks?"

"I don't know them."

"But they be good to you."

"I know."

I got slowly out of bed and held out my hand to her. I took her to the mirror and framed both our faces. She looked solemnly at us.

"I think we look alike," I said.

She did not laugh. "How that?"

"I think we both will go where we will go and do what we will do."

For three days, we prepared for Susan's journey. When the neighbors returned, she folded herself back into the Nantucket sea chest.

LIKE A STONE STATUE I walked away from my cabin with them. Like a juggernaut, that stone car pulled forward relentlessly by the Hindi, I was pulled forward, arms outstretched, by my neighbors. I do not know how my adamantine body was able to bend enough to sit in the wagon.

The world was a vast whiteness barred by the black trunks and limbs of trees. Half a world away, did Ahab stand on the wooden deck, feet firmly planted, watching some mournful scene? Perhaps a sailor, fallen, sewn into canvas, was sinking into the water. I seemed to feel the pitching of the *Pequod*. Did Ahab also mourn? I fastened my gaze on the brown haunches of the two horses, and their color was a relief from the world of alabaster and ebony.

BESIDE THE COFFIN of my mother I held the body of my boy in my arms. Susan and I had cocooned him in wool, and the neighbors had added batts of cotton to try to soften him for me, and they had wrapped him again in white crochetwork, and so he seemed larger, as though he had grown. Yet I could feel the stiff, unbending hardness. Slaunchwise, across my bosom, his little fleecy oblong looked the picture of a cloud. His face was covered. They had bound this cloudy shape with string, a little parcel of mortality.

I laid him down beside that bundle of sheet-shroud they said was my mother. I committed him to her care, and them both, their coffin lidded, down into a muddy grave.

Anger that she should have died lay in my left hand and sorrow, for him, in my right. Someone had knitted black mittens for me, and within their muffling wool, over the mud-stained grave, sorrow clasped anger and anger sorrow, with all their might, till they were the same. I would not move from my clenching till they shoveled clean snow over the brown smear.

After that, I looked skyward. I wondered if the universe was punishing me.

CHAPTER 3   The Crossing

THAT NIGHT, Susan and I stood on the banks of the river, which was moving blackly with its load of white ice floes. The floes were flat on the top and big as the floor of my cabin. Some were as big as a river barge. They all moved downstream in a ghostly procession, separated by jagged black lines where the water was bare. The edges crunched when they touched and hissed when they swept by. In the center of the river, where the current ran swifter, a band of floes moved much more quickly than those near the sides.

The moon was full, which would make the footing easier for Susan, for she must jump from floe to floe to cross the river. We stood alone—hand in hand at the edge of the water, our skin separated by the wool of our mittens. No other eyes, no other soul, would watch her go. Silence, stillness, cold. They chimed about us as one snowy chord.

Susan and I had fashioned her a coat from a quilt, and called it a Joseph's coat, because it was truly of many colors, and I had given her my own knitted cap and, under the patchwork coat, an oat-colored sweater. In a cloth bag, she carried some cooked potatoes and johnnycake and a pair of my mother's shoes. She wore another pair of Mother's shoes, and we had driven nails from the inside so that the soles would prick into the slippery ice and keep her feet from sliding.

Around her neck, in a tiny gathered bag, she carried a lock of my baby's hair, for he was born with hair and it was red as flame. I have a lock of it, too, intertwined with one of Susan's, but I do not have a lock of my mother's hair. I'd given Susan my red mittens; I wore the new black ones. We loosened our grip on one another's hand.

When I saw Susan step upon the ice, I bit my lower lip till the blood flowed down my chin and crusted in the cold. Here the riverbank was no higher than a step, as from house to yard. In the moonlight, new snow like sugar glittered atop the sheet of ice lying along the bank. Behind her, in a lengthening path, Susan's footprints indented the sparkling snow. She moved toward the center of the river as calmly as though crossing a broad moonlit road cut through the brush and trees of the wilderness.

When she came to the first black edge, she stepped across the open water as though it were a mere stream. The next floe was smaller, and the next even smaller; they dipped or tilted slightly when she stepped onto them. The spans of open water between them seemed wider and wider, and sometimes she waited for the current to bring the ice rafts closer together. Then she leapt the narrowed fissure and walked on.

It seemed to me Susan was walking on clouds in a black sky. There *were* clouds in the sky, but they stayed far from the moon and did not block her benevolent light. I blessed the moon that held up her lantern for us. Over the water, from seeming cloud to cloud, some silvery, some gray, some white and bright as mirrors for the moon, Susan stepped across the black water.

As the current accelerated and the spaces between floes widened, Susan ran and jumped from raft to raft; my heart hung in the air with her. In the center of the river, the swifter current zipped the ice rafts downstream, with Susan standing on one of them. Her arms fluttered once for balance, twice.

I began to walk downstream and then to run to keep up with the central river as it swept Susan's floe downstream. She never turned to look at me, nor did I want to distract her, and I never called any words of encouragement except as the mind blazes out messages brighter than a lighthouse.

Fly! Fly! as she leapt and landed, the floe she landed on already taking her downstream.

"The Crossing"

At last the treacherous midsection of river was traversed. She was far from me now—a dark upright using the flatness: flying and landing, running and leaping, from floe to floe. I saw shapes in the ice rafts, mostly like enormous animals, flat, not like a natural swan or bear but flat as a cookie animal or a tin weathervane. Near the other side, approaching a bend, she had to wait for her floe to come close to the bank. Holding the stitch in my side, I continued walking as rapidly downstream as I could till I came to a high but tangled shoreline that thwarted me. Soon the current would sweep Susan's floe beyond my sight. *O, carry her close, carry her close, now,* I prayed to the ice, and I prayed that Susan would not feel herself passing beyond my sight and take the risk of trying to jump ashore when the gulf remained too great. The floe that wheeled her toward the far shore was like the palm of a hand, open and presentational.

Patient Susan! Her ice raft nudged the shore, and she jumped. Even as her shoes landed on the snowy bank, she turned and looked exactly where I stood. Together we lifted our arms, blowing each other a kiss across the water, for we had not kissed on parting, saving it till she should be safe, and trusting the sweet air to be our go-between. And then one shout, though it was small from the distance, from Susan: *Freedom!*

IT WAS DURING Ahab's first voyage after our marriage that I had and lost my first baby, and when Ahab came home, in much kindness, he did get me with child a second time, and that is our boy together, whom I borned in Nantucket, there being no reason to go back to Kentucky and many reasons not to. When he returned from the second voyage, though yet in agony from the loss of his leg in the Sea of Japan, Ahab loved Justice as soon as he saw him, and said he liked the name right well.

The night before he shipped again, Ahab asked the boy to touch his ivory leg, and said, "What would you trade for that, my little Justice?" And the boy ran and brought back in his hand a small rocking horse, also all carved from ivory and decorated in scrimshaw drawing with a curly mane and saddle and reins. "Nay, lad," my husband said. "Bring me the white whale." And the boy went and fetched that ghastly thing from the window ledge. I called it gruesomely carved because when you turned it over, the sailor had hollowed out the chest and left there a heart like a dove's egg, all rounded, and through it an ivory splinter, toothpick-size, a lance.

CHAPTER 4   Reverie

THIS TIME of reverie I have spent lounging on a golden sand dune. Such a mild blue day it is here in Nantucket, where the breeze sometimes whips me, sometimes caresses me! Yet intact Ahab, back from his first voyage, once said of just such a changeable breeze, *This contrast is the way of life itself.* All playfully, he added, *But were I God, then would every day be invariantly good.* Then he asked me if he might be the god of my world.

I teased back and denied him that *Never,* I said, *as long as sky arches over or earth lies under.* Once, out of guilt and grief, I had given my will away, but ever after, I kept my soul for myself.

And Ahab asked, *Thou wouldst have me unvault the firmament to prove my godhood? Exalt the valleys? And what dost thou require that I demand of the sea?*

Then I spoke with more conviction and said, *Certainly you are not lord of that, for the sea takes you from me, and am I not your heaven?* Here I traced the zaggy mark that began at his temple. *How can you be lord of an element having the power to take you from your heaven?* Ahab scooped up sand, and in a warm trickle, he poured it on the back of my other hand. *The sea has brought me back. Once, to thee.*

O, Ahab's smile! rare and shy. Precious then and now to my constricting heart. For even on that balmy day, I would have thought what if those lapping waters should not bring him back the second time, or the third time? Perhaps I swallowed and said to Ahab, *If the sea bring you back a second time and a third time, then truly will I make you lord of me and of our bed.*

But he was already that. In our happy leisure, I might have thought indolently of the brown people, so far away on the Pacific Islands, perhaps lounging on their own sand, which Ahab said was white as sugar, not golden like these grains. I saw Ahab as a young man going to them. I did not begrudge him his happiness there. In imagination, I became one of them. From the women on the islands, he had learned how to touch the magic places on my body. If there were children left behind in the South Seas—well, I would people the world with Ahab's. Once I asked him, what would a girl-child be with his spirit? And he answered, *Una, thou art she.* If there were children begot in the South Seas, they would be my older sisters and brothers in age, for in his middle years, Ahab went to the island women no longer, saying it was not right for a captain. (He had no prejudice against the mingling of brown and white.)

I teased him, home from that short first voyage, as we picnicked on the Nantucket moor, said that certainly Captain Peleg, and probably Captain Bildad, used to sport in the grass huts, but even during that first, idyllic homecoming, if I saw the moral fervor was on his brow, I desisted. It would not be kindness to tease Ahab on the subject of good or evil, and whether simply custom makes it so.

He believed the moral powers—demonic and heaven-generated—are separate things, *must* be separate to be themselves; eternal. But I see them as all nested and layered together, sometimes with no clear seam between, but a gradation; transient. He wanted something ultimate and absolute. If there be reality beyond the appearance—be that reality ultimately good, or evil, or indifferent—then it must be so always.

That second homecoming brought him home dismasted, one-legged, raging; yet he would go forth again to war upon the deep.

Before he left, he, seated, called me to stand between his knees, one leg bent naturally, the other outthrust in tapering ivory. He twisted the sculpted nuptial bracelet on my wrist and made the whales depicted there swim round.

Wouldst thou have an ornate ivory cross? he asked me. And the flicker of rebellion and wildness galloped across his face.

I do not hold well with the Christian symbols, and he knew it.

Nay, my wife, he said (for he could ever read my thought). The storm gathered in his mien. *My girl-wife shall have a crown, and I will carve it myself from the jawbone of Moby Dick!*

He reached up, placed his hands on my hair, surrounded my skull, and squeezed till he trembled, his force caught statically between his knowledge of my human frailty and his power.

Yet, I thought how I might yield, unharmed, and I knelt till my knees were on the carpet and I looked up at him. Then he left off squeezing my head, but those strong hands had bequeathed the pressure of a crown that never was to be, except as memory and imagination conjoin to circumscribe my scalp.

Art thou afraid?

When I shook my head no, he kissed me upon the lips, passionately, and then upon the brow, in tender blessing.

O SUNNY DAY, O golden sand, O loving breeze—I would lounge and loaf forever, my spirit basking in your clear goodness, if I could. From how far away does the sunlight come to fall upon this one glittering grain I hold between my forefinger and my thumb? This grain is square as a quilt block, its edges straight as any carpenter cuts wood or glazier scores glass. Perhaps it *is* glass, or salt—a crystal left by the water. I put it on the tip of my tongue and taste nothing salty. I push it sideways with my tongue and it is grit between my molars. I take it out again, all wet from my mouth. My stubborn sand grain lies drowned on the whorls of my forefinger. It can tell its fellows that it has been in a strange place. A wet, pink cave.

Perhaps the mind as well as the mouth is a glistening, pink cave. As a child that image was available to me, for my mother read aloud how Plato likened his mind to a cave. But his was dark instead of pink. With this writing I wish to enter that opalescence and inhabit the pearly chamber of memory. Hindsight, retrospective wisdom, I leave, to the extent I can, at the threshold. But as a child, I was given much of the language of adults, and I continue to use it, even to describe my youth. I court the freshness, the immediacy, and all the resources of language that make the past tense strangely shine as though it were the present.

OH, MY LOST AHAB. I had my prayer then, if not my God: *Let the green land and the warm hearth call you home. As surely as after our first night in the marriage bed, the sea called you away.*

If I turn back the years, Justice is standing in the water, but he hears me over the surf and turns to wave. He is five years old, his hair black as soot. Though the hair of your head, Ahab, was gray and white, yet you were still sooty in the loins, as young as my first husband when he was eighteen and I was seventeen.

I met my first husband when he visited my aunt and uncle, who kept an island Lighthouse out from New Bedford, but first I must turn back more years to say how it was that I who was born in Kentucky on the banks of the Ohio came to be with Aunt and Uncle near New Bedford. When I was twelve, my mother sent me there to save my life, for she was afraid that my father would kill me.

CHAPTER 5　📷　The Window

WHAT INCITED my father to fury was my lack of Christian belief. I wanted no part of the church because I could not believe its dogma. Perhaps there was some imbalance in my brain—I don't know. But the belief that was imbibed by everyone I knew, with scarcely a moment of skepticism, seemed to me most unlikely. Whether there was God or not, I admitted I did not know, but it was Jesus as God, or the Son of God, that seemed to me highly unlikely.

How do you know it's true? I asked. One would say that the Bible was God's holy word and that it said so, but I saw no reason to think it holy just because that was the custom. Did I not feel myself a sinner? they would ask. Readily did I acknowledge I had many shortcomings, but why should I think there was a hell waiting to swallow me? And what was the evidence that any part of me was immortal? Perhaps I just wished it so. And how could belief that one good man, long ago, was actually the incarnation of God wipe away my sins? What possible connection could there be between the two ideas?

"If you believe the sky is red," I said to my father, for I had a small paring knife in my hand and was peeling the waxy red skin from an apple, "would it make the corn grow?"

At this, my father struck my face with his open hand. "Believe!" he shouted.

"Neither you nor I can command belief," I replied, though I was only twelve. I was shocked not so much at the blow but by the calmness of my own voice. But tears had jumped into my eyes.

He harnessed the buggy and rode away into the woods, lashing the horse.

I watched through the cabin front window, which had just been unboarded from the winter. Often, as a younger child, I had followed him into the yard, sat upon the stump, lamented his leaving. No longer! Now, from the house I read him, crossing the window left to right, how the harried buggy and his flailing arm moved as a unit from the left pane of glass to the right pane of glass, and out of sight. How undisturbed the trees seemed in their dark uprightness, how intact in their neatly fitting bark. My father had seemed so till his recent conversion.

I ceased looking through the window in order to contemplate the wavy glass itself. What was a window but a machine for making the opaque transparent? Then I regarded the window framing, which divided the four small lights by a slender, equal-armed cross between the panes.

My mother came to sit at the table. She remained unconverted. Why did his wrath not fall on her? With her hand and arm she swept her dress to one side from beneath her bottom as she sat. I registered that competent, automatic gesture, and the way her face shone at me in sympathy. With a light stroke, her fingers acknowledged the smarting of my cheek.

"What are we to do with your unbelief?" my gentle mother asked.

"Let him accept me as I am. As you do. As we both are."

"It's through my blood that tolerance and unbelief have run to you." She gestured that, twelve-year-old girl though I was, I should come and sit on her lap. "My father was a Quaker of Rhode Island," she said. "And my sister is a Unitarian."

I had never heard the word *Unitarian* before, for all about me were Methodists, like my father, and Presbyterians and German Lutherans; I had heard them speak of Catholics, but I had never seen one.

"Do you believe in Jesus as God?" I asked my mother.

"Most do," she said.

"But you yourself?"

"It does not matter to me if Jesus was God or not."

"It does not matter if a person can really be God?"

"It would have been a long time ago."

I sat on her knee and listened to a bird sing. Mine was a darting mind, and it darted after the bird and its world, while I partly talked with my mother. With its song of *Pretty, Pretty, Pretty,* I imagined its crested red among the high green leaves of the tulip poplar, and then, again diverted, imagined the way light shone through leaf so that you can see compartments and veins within the thin flatness.

"Think," she said. "Does it matter to you whether Caesar captured Gaul or not? If you think, 'Why, yes, he did,' are you not the very same girl sitting on her mother's lap? And if you think, 'No, I don't believe he did,' don't you love me just the same as before and hear the same bird singing?"

Her eyes were dark brown, and she never spoke seriously without a sheen of love over her eyes.

"It might be quite a different thing about God," I said.

"If it makes you happy, believe it."

"But I want to know the truth."

Again she was silent, then she sighed. "The truth about the unseen makes little difference to me."

"It would make a difference to me," I answered. "But I do not believe that a man was God."

"Perhaps we each adopt or create our truth."

When my father returned, he was morose. "Struggle with the devil," he told me. "I will ask you again in a week."

The next day the dog, King, playfully chased a pullet, and when my father called the dog, he disobeyed. Reaching over the door for his long rifle, my father stood on the threshold and shot the dog.

He said, "The Lord has given man dominion over the creatures of the earth."

I climbed the tallest white pine I could find.

Nonetheless, when he next asked about my belief, he found that the week was to no avail. Nor the months, though my father's rage at his helplessness compounded, and each time he struck me, he added a blow. "Children, obey your parents," he thundered. Each time I watched him drive away in a fury, lashing the horse, the buggy rattling across the yard. I watched him through the window, the cross of its mullions interpreting the scene, as he drove from the left side of the window to the right, and out of sight. I thought of him as a crusader; I saw his head as though it were encased in a gleaming helmet. I saw him as zeal-driven as those warriors of old, violent in their love of Christ, approaching unbelief with raised sword. I had read *Ivanhoe,* one of two or three dozen books my mother kept in the humped trunk.

Once my father did not drive away, but stood in the cabin door holding the buggy whip. My mother stepped before him and said only "No."

He went into the yard and lashed the little stump where I liked to sit till foam came to the corners of his mouth, and he fell in a faint. Then my mother tore a strip from the hem of her green dress, wet the cloth, went to him, and bathed his forehead. She crooned his name, *Ulysses, Ulysses.*

That night my mother asked me if I would consent to live with her sister. "She is a Unitarian," she said again. And when I asked my mother what that meant, she said, "With her, you can believe what you will. Only your behavior must be according to what is commonly held to be good. You must be kind. As you always have been."

And that is how I came to live at the Lighthouse.

The Lighthouse itself became my church, my single tall tree trunk, my faith in stone and earth, and, eventually, my conduit to the sky.

CHAPTER 6   The Steamboat

M Y M O T H E R and I journeyed downriver by buggy to start our voyage up. (Is it not the case that many a life journey starts out in the opposite direction to its destiny?) Our land was located some twelve miles north of the Falls of the Ohio, where the city of Louisville had sprung up at the portage. Steamboat travelers, as well as freight, were obliged to disembark on the upriver course and to change boats, Louisville being the northernmost port for those who had traveled up the Mississippi and then branched to the right, leaving the muddy waters of the Mississippi for the clearer water of the Ohio. Though the falls were rather low, they were unnavigable.

The night before our journey, our trunks standing like dark twins before the small summer fire, my mother had negotiated with my father that she alone would drive us to the Falls and then hire a boy to return the buggy, as she would travel with me all the way to her sister's home.

"Certainly you will return, Bertha?" An anguish masked my father's eyes—not that I was being escorted to a tiny island populated by only one family but that my mother might decide not to return to him.

For a moment I dared hope that she would *not* return, but a glance at her loving, loyal face, even before she spoke the words *he* needed to hear, told me otherwise.

The morning of our departure, after loading the trunks, he seated himself on my stump in the yard. I almost passed him without looking at him—for I loved my Kentucky home that I was being forced to leave—but I could not. He loomed like a black rock whose size and shape I must register in order to pass safely around. But I looked in his eye, and it was as though lightning leapt from both of us! Instant and powerful, undeniable connection!

"Una!" He ejaculated my name, and I ran to him for a farewell embrace.

His hands on both my shoulders, he pushed me back to look again into my eyes. His voice choked, he croaked, "Doubt not that I love you." I made one quick nod and fled to the buggy.

From my seat I looked back at him as the wheels began to turn. I waved, one quick pass of the palm through the air—*his* style of wave—and thought now we were reversed, now he sat on the stump and I rode away in the buggy. I knew that he was *sad*. And much more.

AS WE PASSED through the woods, though it was a warm day, my body felt cold, especially my hands, which were clinched tight into fists. On either side of me I pressed my cold knuckles against the buggy bench for balance. Before long, my mother transferred both reins to one hand and with the other covered my cold fist. My hands felt as though they had turned into toads or stones. Her palm was warm and comforted me, but it was also damp as though her hand had been crying.

Because I did not want her to think I was indifferent to her comfort,

I uncurled my fingers, turned my hand over, and returned her clasp. Still, my torso felt petrified, the fibers of my being turned insentient.

As we stood on the street admiring the steamboat, a plume rose from her and immediately a blasting sound that reverberated up from my feet, through viscera, and out the top of my head. I was surprised it did not lift my scalp and attendant hair as though I wore a wig. And with this mighty noise gush, I was blasted from numbness back to life. Like gunpowder clearing the river of ice, the sound cleared me and life flowed again, seeking its own expression and adventure.

I gasped, my mother looked down at me, we exchanged excitement, wonder, hope, even happiness at our decision, and stepped forward. Thus began our upstream journey. When I looked down at the giant wheel turning, I thought of Don Quixote's windmill.

A STEAMBOAT is a pretty thing, trailing its black cloud; to tour its tiers, to look out at the slowly passing landscape are activities so purely recreational that one feels deliciously leisured. Sometimes a drab barge, headed west, would pass us. We gloried in the white-glazed gingerbread of our railings and our knowledge of the appointments within, the shined brass and the velvet seat covers. We felt valuable and prome-naded the balconies daintily, stopping at the railing first on the Kentucky side and then on the Indiana side to admire the vistas.

We walked past one gloomy section. On a bulletin board affixed to the cabin were tacked several Wanted posters, advertising Rewards for runaway slaves. I yet remember three of these declamations and the Value they attached to Property:

> *Wanted*
>
> *Large, strong, coal-black $800 male Shifty eyed,*
> *bit-broke teeth on left*
> *Clover-leaf brand left shoulder*
> *Dangerous and Desperate*
> *$50 for information*
> *$500 for return to Sweet Clover Farm*
> *Tidewater, Virginia*

```
WANTED

CLEVER SMALL MALE MULATTO, CAN MEND SHOES AND

DO OTHER LEATHER SEWING. SCARS IN LEFT PALM.

MAY TRY TO PASS FOR FREE WITH FORGED PAPERS.

CAN READ SOME AND IS VERY TRICKY.

STABBED OWNER TO DEATH.

RETURN LEFT HAND FOR REWARD

$1,000

SHERIFF AND CITIZENS OF CHOCTAW COUNTY, ALABAMA

GONE SINCE EASTER 1820
```

```
Negro Wench and Daughter
$1,200 Reward for Both Unharmed
Mother is Pecan-colored; daughter almost white
but with broad nose and dark freckles, gold eyes
Mother may be in family-way; daughter about 12, unbroke
Last seen New Year's Day 1822
Take to New Orleans Dock: Mr. Beauchamp
```

When I walked with my mother I did not look at the posters because it seemed degrading to even glance at the offering of blood money. Whenever I promenaded the deck alone, I stopped and read the notices in horrible fascination. The girl with the golden eyes was my own age. There were three notices with sketches of men who looked through me at the passing Kentucky shore, but I did not think the pictures would be of much use in apprehending any particular slave. The runaways had been drawn so as to look more or less alike, as though to be a Negro were simply to have certain lips and hair. All the eyes looked haunted and frightened.

After supper but before we retired to our sleeping berths, Mother said, "Come, Una," and took me for another stroll on the deck. The sun was setting and breezes had come up. Most women and children had gone straight to bed and the men to the card room. The stench of cigars polluted one section of our walk. Mother pointed out how the smokestack blew a dramatic black plume across the red of the western sky. Someone played an accordion from within. I peeked in to see an old black man with tight-curled, snow-white hair hunched over the squeeze-box, an unvarying smile carved into his face, his eyes focused on the floor. Sometimes he closed his eyes as his fingers flew over the buttons and keys.

Mother walked me around to the rear, on the Kentucky side, where the posters hung. Without hesitation she grasped the edge of the paper bearing one of the sketches and ripped it from the cork. The tacks burst out. She dropped the page over the side into the river. My heart leapt, for in small print on each sign was the instruction: Do not remove.

I grasped the one from Sweet Clover Farm and mailed it over the side and into the water. I ripped off the poster concerning the Mother and Daughter and would have cast it into the wheel to be churned into bits, but Mother stayed my hand.

"Over the side! It might be bad luck to grind them in the mill."

So I cast the heinous advertisement over the side. It curled and rode the water a bit. I was glad when it swamped and sank, its message never again to be read.

"Would I had the nerve to do it," my mother said, "by light of day."

We were both agitated and walked to the prow of the boat so that the breeze might cool our faces. We liked having our backs turned to that infamy. I fancied the boat moved more swiftly against the current as though unburdened not of ounces but of tons and weighty years of guilt. My mother spoke through her teeth: *We hold these truths to be self-evident, that all men are created equal, that they are endowed by their creator with certain inalienable rights, that among these are life, liberty and the pursuit of happiness.* In my feet, I felt the vibrations of the heavy, turning wheel, propelling us forward.

WHEN MORNING CAME, I felt it still, the rhythmic, powerful turning of the wheel, and I decided to spend part of the day with it.

Painted a glossy, bright red, the wheel made me think at once of my own heart that beat my blood so that I might have life and movement. The wheel's red paint was so thick as to look like enamel; the sturdy lathes were slick-armored against the ravages of water-wear. The wheel's method was to gain purchase against the surface and to push itself forward as it encountered the resistance of the submerging water, but also it lifted the water in the rear and seemed to purify it. Cascades of bubbles, made all the whiter for pouring over the red paddles, sang of rushing glory. More powerful than any Kentucky stream splashing and dashing over smooth rocks, this turbulence shouted Red and White, White and Air, Splash and Foam till I was dizzy with it.

For an hour I watched the powerful, mechanical lifting of water and its immediate rush and fall back to the river, white foam yielding to the dun flow. Our wake was white-churned for only a short distance and then the seam we constantly opened was sealed over as though we had not passed. To myself as a young girl our passage seemed significant and momentous, as though it told me important things.

When we reached Cincinnati, the wheel turned more slowly and more slowly with less and less foam and splash till it stopped. My feet tingled after the vibration of the pistons ceased. In quietness we drifted a few feet till we were close enough to the shore for lines to be thrown and secured on the pilings. The gangplank was lowered, and Mother and I took a brief walk on the shore. I looked back at the giant paddlewheel, wet and dripping, reared up, immobile as a statue. A gray engraving of a rose in a book came to mind, but enormous now and bloodred. It made me catch my breath—the paddlewheel—a gigantic rose, brilliant, red, perfect, still as eternity.

My MOTHER, who had been to the Island once before, first pointed out the Lighthouse to me from the ferry. The Lighthouse seemed only a line. A short vertical line, with one end in the sea and one end in the sky. How unaspiring it seemed! Such a puny human effort to draw a mark an inch up the dome of the great sky. A mere budge of the pencil, a dash of graphite, gray against pale blue. But suddenly, at the top of that stubby thing, there was a glint!

"It's on!" The exclamation broke from me.

"No," she answered, pressing my hand, for she, too, was excited. "It shines only at night. The sunlight has caught the windowpane like a mirror."

Then a wave of homesickness lapped within me, for I thought of my forest and the shiny objects my mother hung among the dark trees.

"Why did you hang the mirrors in the woods?" I asked.

But she didn't answer.

Instead, she asked me how was my stomach and did the motion of the water make me queasy. When I looked at the water, I felt contempt. The color was more green than the dark blue of the English poets, and the waves were small and choppy.

"It's not wild enough," I said.

"You always loved a storm," she said. And she told me again how when I was a small girl, only freshly equipped with language, when it rained I had said, "Harder," and begged her to make the rain bigger and more extreme.

"How do you like the Lighthouse?" she asked.

"I wish that it were taller."

She laughed. "Accept the world, Una. It is what it is."

Gradually, the vertical line of Lighthouse widened, so that the Lighthouse seemed not like a mere pencil line but a brush stroke with width as well as height, inching up the sky. For a time, the sunlight on its high glass glared steadily, but as our angle of approach changed, the whole column went gray and lightless. It grew taller and more satisfactory.

I could see the shaft was made of stone, and some of the stone jutted out so that it appeared knobby as a spine instead of smooth-sided. It tapered like a candle as it grew taller, and at its base was a stone house, the roof of which was shake shingles, covered with a splash of pink roses.

"Oh, the roses," I said.

"They lie on the roof in the sun all day."

"And the goats!"

"They're nimble enough not to fall off the island rocks into the ocean."

"Did they swim here?"

"The goats were brought by boat. Like us."

I admired their dark, spiky horns and their big, dark udders.

"My sister shovels up their manure to feed the roses. Perhaps you can help her."

In Kentucky, small white roses grew in sunny places in the woods, and I loved them well, but these were pink and so profuse, I could scarcely believe in them. The roses climbed up to the roof on wooden trellises, and on the roof lay another trellis which roses' stems wove under and over. Those roses were the first time nature surprised me; for the first time she exceeded not only what I wanted but what I had imagined possible.

"We'll have goat cheese for supper, I imagine, and toast, and rose-hip tea."

At the corner of my eye, I saw a goat jumping, jumping as though to greet us. And then when I looked closer, it was a white apron flapping, and a little girl, jumping and jumping—Cousin Frannie. And I remembered that Aunt Agatha had written I would be good company for her little girl, isolated on the Island. She was four, and I loved her at once for her joyful jumping.

Soon we were disembarked, and when I hugged Frannie, I felt I was hugging a sturdy little churn. The moment I let go of her, the dasher inside made her jump and jump again with joy. Her hair was the color of nutmeg, between red and brown, and across her nose and cheeks were scattered freckles of the same nutmeg color. Her eyes were as green as the sea, and forever I forgave the sea for not appearing blue.

Oh Una, oh Una, oh Una, you're here was all she said, over and over, in a voice like little bells jangling—with that same pleasant discord. And I held her hands, and big girl that I was, jumped up and down with her. Breathlessly, I asked could we pick the roses and could we pet the goats, and my aunt sent us off to do whichever we preferred without demanding so much as the semblance of proper introductions.

We scampered away, through a gate, up rocks till I knelt to pet a little white goat, and its hairs were very distinct, long and wiry, not nearly so soft as a cow's, but less sharp than a pig's. With its insistent, solid little head, the kid nuzzled hard against my chest and hurt me where my bosom was beginning. I looked up from my kneeling to Frannie and, laughing, said, "Make her stop butting."

"You can't make her do anything," Frannie answered. "You yourself must stand up."

But she took the goat by her shoulders and pulled her back. I stood up, and then the goat butted at my knees.

"Does she have a name?"

"You can name her."

"She's 'Apron,' then, because she is white as your apron."

Then I looked up and, for the first time since our landing, noticed the Lighthouse, which was, indeed, a great gray tower so stern and austere in its height that I let my gaze slide down to the cottage.

"I've named the Lighthouse," Frannie said.

"What?"

"His name is 'the Giant.'"

I thought it fit him perfectly, and I took Frannie's hand, and we walked rather soberly back to our mothers, who, from that little distance, appeared as blotches of windblown color. My mother's dress was ocher, as was my own, and Aunt Agatha's dress was deepest indigo. I was startled that here on the bare rock of the Island, colors suddenly had meaning, as though the light itself were defining. Only the stone of the Lighthouse seemed sullen, as though there was no color there to be brought out by even the strongest sunlight. My mind went dizzy with abstraction—the great gray upward sweep, and at its base, a blotch of yellow, a blotch of blue: mothers.

"He can't move," Frannie said confidentially. "He can't step on us."

OUR MOTHERS' NAMES were complementary—Agatha and Bertha. Their names belonged together. I wished my mother would not go back to Kentucky, but she planned to stay with us on the Island only a week.

My mother was slightly taller than her sister, and her dark brown hair tended more toward black than red; it was parted smoothly in the middle and soft wings framed her lovely forehead. Aunt Agatha was shorter, and rounder, like her daughter; her brown hair tended toward red, and it was frizzy. She pulled it straight back from her forehead, but a cloud of fine frizz hovered at all the edges. About Agatha, who was the older, there was a certainty, while about my mother, the dominant air was gentleness. I later came to think that they both knew the foolishness of the world, to which Agatha remained unyielding while my mother, less certain that any view could be absolute, responded with pliant accommodation.

For our first meal, they sat together on one side of the rough table, Frannie and I sat together on the other, and Uncle sat at the end of the table facing a small window. From my bench, it was easy to watch the two sisters, and I rather regretted that I did not myself have a sister who was a friend and with whom I could compare myself, the better to understand both my singularity and our commonality. But I had Frannie.

I saw that little Frannie was mostly a replica of her mother, though she had Uncle's green green eyes. I had Agatha's eye color, which was the same deep blue as her dress, but my hair color was dark, like my mother's. The texture of my hair was even more wavy and frizzy than Agatha's, and everyone who saw it in Kentucky said I had gypsy hair. My body was and is slender, like my mother's. I was glad of that, as I didn't like large breasts on women, though they fascinated me on cows and on the goats and seemed quite comely there.

My uncle Jonathan had crisp red hair, and freckles, like Frannie, all over his face and arms to match. He was clean-shaven, and his hair stood up thick and tall and bright. I wondered if he could get a cap down over his hair, but perhaps he didn't need one.

When he caught me staring at his head, he said, "All lighthouse keepers must have red hair, you know."

I gasped.

"Should the light go out, I myself would stand at the high window and glow."

I bowed my head in confusion.

The white goat cheese bubbled in a wrought-copper chafing dish, in the center of the table where we could all reach it. "Now, take your toast," Uncle said, "and spoon the cheese on it. Here are the herb leaves—dill, sage, and thyme—roll the herb you like best between your fingers"—he did so to illustrate—"and sprinkle it over the cheese. Careful not to burn your tongue."

I did burn my tongue the first time, but then I noted how they all held the toast and melted cheese before their mouths and blew on it before biting. So between the talking, sometimes in the middle of the sentences, there were little huffs and puffs of breath. In a blue bowl there was a pile of stiff, dark green vegetable, all dried, and Aunt told me it was seaweed and good for me.

Glancing toward the small window at the end of the table, I saw twilight was coming on. Uncle Jonathan and Aunt Agatha and Frannie, with my mother joining in, began to sing a song about a lighthouse keeper, but I did not know the words. While they sang, Uncle put a hurricane glass over the candle, the glass settling nicely into a circular groove in the wood of the candlestick holder. I could well imagine that he would not want to climb all the way to the top only to have his candle extinguished accidentally. Then he went to a low door in the side of the room and opened it. The stone steps, quite steep, began at once and bent around the inner wall of the tower.

"The steps are blocks of Belgium granite," my mother said through the singing, "brought over as ballast in the ships."

Uncle bent down and passed from the house to the shaft. His voice took on an echo in the tower, and I saw the circle of light disappear.

"Sing *la*," my aunt commanded, "till you know the words," and so I did, with loud and lusty LAs, for it was nicer to join in than to hang back. We seemed most peculiarly snug, we two girls and two women, with the colorful driftwood fire—red, blue, green, yellow flames like feathers—the strange food on the table, and the pretty copper chafing dish. Even the window through which I could see the graying sky was peculiar, for its walls were stone and very thick-sided. I watched the light outside gray until it matched the stone.

Soon we could not hear Uncle's voice at all, he was so high up. A chilly wind blew down the tower, and Aunt told Frannie to close the door, but I felt uneasy that the door be closed behind him while he was ascending the stone vault.

Then Mother and I sang them a slave song, "Go Down, Moses"—rapt, Frannie breathed, *I want to learn it*—so we sang it again till she had the words and her eyes glowed with the heroism of Moses. Then Agatha and Frannie sang "Loch Lomond" with a jaunty Scottish accent. After a while, we sang marching music, and Uncle came through the wall, or rather the wooden door in the wall, blowing a harmonica. The notes came and went with his breathing, and his mouth slid back and forth.

"Make a square," he called, and we all hopped up and circled and danced, Aunt Agatha making the call. What a jolly evening, my first at the Lighthouse, and how my mother's eyes sparkled beyond their loving glow!

That was not all. Tired out, we sat before the fire, and Frannie passed around saltwater taffy, and Aunt Agatha read Lord Byron aloud. In Kentucky, only the Bible was read aloud when we gathered, but Mother had always read me her poetry books from the trunk when Father was away. When bedtime came to the Lighthouse, my mother went to her traveling locker and took out a quilt she had made for a gift. My aunt exclaimed, "Twelve stitches to the inch, Bertha," and Uncle asked the name of the pattern.

"Log-cabin," my mother said, "light and shadow." It was a very beautiful quilt, pieced with strips, like logs of different lengths, instead of blocks, except there was a small square block in the center, and the section as a whole formed a square before the pattern repeated.

"The red square in the center represents the hearth," I said, my mother having explained it to me in Kentucky. "Because it is the center of the house." Actually, the fireplace was in one end of our cabin at home, and not in the center, but I had known that my mother was speaking symbolically.

"The dark green tones are for the forest all around us," Mother said. "The brown tones are for the deer and the bear and the trunks of the trees."

"And everything pale is the light, when it can get through."

"We will let Una have it on her bed," my aunt said, "and it will remind her of home."

"I should very much like Una to keep up her own sewing," my mother said.

"I'll make you a quilt," I promised, and I went to stand beside her, feeling again that it would be hard to let her go home. I thought of my father and his black beard and long black hair. And the whip with a handle of black, braided leather, and its long black lash.

"Bertha and I used to run races with our needles," Aunt Agatha told me.

"Frannie," her father said, "show your auntie and cousin your sea-shells now." I knew that he had seen the shadow of memory darkening my mood; he would defer bedtime till ocean charms occupied my thoughts.

After Frannie fetched her collection, housed in a basket woven of sea grass, with a woven lid, Uncle took out shells one by one and explained that many had come from far away. As I touched their whorls and knobs and spines and admired their spots and shadings of brown, pink, purple, he described to me what oceans the shells had lived in, and what kinds of people and what languages were spoken in those distant places, and what the people wore and ate. It was the most marvelous telling I had ever heard, and yet I grew sleepy listening. Sometimes Uncle himself was in the stories, for he had been a sailor to the South Seas.

I was nodding when he said, "The mouth organ is a proper sailor's instrument because it slips in a pocket. There's no room to spare on a ship. Would you like to learn to play, Una?"

I said yes, but then I thought of sliding my mouth in the same place as his, and I did not like the idea.

"We'll wash it off with good strong soap," he said, "and then you can play with it." I stole a shy glance at him, that he should have known my secret thought, that he should have responded so kindly!

"Now," Auntie said, "let's go outside so you can see the light. Close your eyes, Una, and we'll lead you down to the point, and then you can look back." I got up, half asleep, and Uncle took one elbow and Aunt the other.

"I'll tie a scarf over her eyes," my mother said.

So they led me out. My feet felt afraid of the unfamiliar slants and textures. I felt the night's chill on my arms. Ocean waves were splashing against the rocks, and I heard a goat nicker. I listened to our pairs of feet, sometimes on stone, sometimes on grass, and then on crunchy sand.

"Now there's a large rock behind you, to sit on," Aunt Agatha said.

Someone untied the blindfold, and there it was—so high in the night my heart flew into hiding. The light seemed to cut the blackness. It was as though a star had come down to speak to us. The sides of the light flared like a megaphone, and what the light said was *Loud, Loud, Loud.*

"My senses are confused," I said.

"It is a wondrous thing," my mother said.

CHAPTER 9   🐚   **A Difficult Farewell**

A T H O M E, in Kentucky, I had liked to stand my paper dolls against the windowpane so that they were surrounded by light. On the Lighthouse, as we moved in the morning of the first day, my mother, uncle, aunt, and cousin seemed similarly defined to my eye, as though they stood always against brightness. Though the cabin window's light had seemed to elevate the dolls and make them more important than mere flats of paper, here the light almost overwhelmed the human figures— my mother, my aunt and uncle, my little cousin. Four-take-away-one would leave but three to populate the moated Lighthouse. No, add one. Me.

We all worked outdoors that day. Mother and Aunt Agatha sat in chairs on the little pier and mended fishing nets. Frannie and I frolicked about, at Aunt's particular command, which countermanded my mother's suggestion that we take up the hoes—Frannie had a small one—and cultivate the soil between the rows of onions and radishes. To please Frannie, I consented to splashing water on the ground to make mud pies. From a dirty little basket, she promptly lifted a nest of cunning tin dishes with fluted edges just for the purpose of holding mud dainties. Frannie informed me one of the flat rocks was the oven-rock, and there we would leave the pies to bake.

I noted that Frannie, like myself when I was younger, used far too much water in the mixing of her pies, so that they were unnecessarily soupy, and would surely take a prolonged time to firm. But I said nothing. At one point, I noticed some small, purplish rocks, and I said that we might pretend they were currants and raisins and add them to the batter, but Frannie objected. "I save them for him," she said.

"For whom?"

She gestured toward the tower, and I noted Uncle up on the encircling platform washing the windows of the lantern house.

"For your father?"

"No. For him." She gestured again, as before. "For the Giant. I'm making him a collar of all the prettiest stones."

Still I felt confused.

"I'll show you. The collar is on the ground around him. Like a path."

She scampered up the flat rocks till she reached the base of the tower, and there I saw several patches of stones, some dun, some purplish.

"The colors show up best when they're wet." She picked up a small dun rock. "These turn golden." She licked the rock and held it toward me, and it was like a smooth lump of gold. "And those purple are red as rubies"—I reached out and took her hand to restrain her—"when they're wet."

"Why do you do this?" I replaced the golden stone among its dull fellows.

She shrugged. "I like to." And she ran back down the boulders to our mud kitchen on the edge of the garden.

I sensed that I would be strangely caught between the adults and the child. But as I spooned my pie into its mold, I knew there was pleasure in the idea. I would be who I liked here. No one wished to constrain or define me. And I liked my kinfolk.

I walked down to the pier where my aunt and mother were sitting, their laps covered with nets, and asked, "What kind of light is this, here on the Island?"

Both women looked at me with open mouths. Then Aunt reached out her arm and swooped me on top of her lap onto the net.

"Why, look! I've caught me an Una!" she exclaimed, and she kissed my cheek heartily.

I wondered where the needle was, and she held it out, as though to answer my question, at arm's length, and the sunshine caught its tip like a star.

"This is the light of unbridled Nature," my mother answered.

"Of unveiled Nature," Aunt put in. "But sometimes we're veiled in mists and fogs that last all day."

"You have a splotch of mud on your cheek," my mother said, and she reached out and, slipping her nail under the edge of the dried mud, flicked it off. "Like a teardrop." With the ball of her thumb, she rubbed away the last crumbs of the blemish.

"Go down the shore," Aunt said, "you and Frannie, and wade."

When I conveyed the instruction to Frannie, she was delighted, for she was forbidden to put so much as a toe in the water without an accompanying adult. On the little beach, we slid out of our pantaloons and held up our skirts. Our toes giggled in the cold water, but we were bold and made them go deeper and root in the mushy sand while the water splashed around our ankles and then up our calves. The sheer cleanness of the waves! The cold freshness!

"Ocean water makes you want to drink it," Frannie said.

"It does! It does!" I bent and cupped up the foam.

"But you mustn't. It will make you sick."

That first day set the pattern for our relationships. Frannie and I shared what we knew—I not to go too deep; Frannie not to drink the salt sea—and followed each other's desires, and played and chatted, comfortable always, yet always with careful respect. Young as she was, Frannie often pointed to the ships far out to sea and told me their names.

The last sensation each night, in my bed across the little room from Frannie in her bed, and the first awareness when I awoke was dread that soon my mother would leave. But each day of her presence was licked by light, glowed like mellow gold.

The last evening, my mother and I sat on the pier alone and watched the western sun slide toward the sea. My mother remarked that in Kentucky we never had so clear a view of the sunset, and then she asked me if I liked it, on the Island.

"Could you not stay?" I asked stiffly, because the question was too important not to articulate, and yet I knew the answer.

"Let your aunt represent me."

"But she's not you."

"I think it is a mistake, Una, to insist on having only one particular person near you. And we will be close together whenever we think of one another. And we will write." She leaned toward me. "And your father and I will come to visit."

I squirmed in my chair. "Shouldn't we be helping Aunt in the kitchen?"

"She shooed me out. Because you and I will not be able to sit together again for many afternoons."

So we sat quietly in our chairs and did not help with supper, or sing Uncle aloft, but watched the smooth red slide of the sun toward the restless water. Even before the sun slipped into the slot of the horizon, the beam from the Lighthouse shone out in the dusk, and the cool, westerly breezes caped our shoulders. When the last red arc disappeared, my mother stood and said, "And so we eat again."

Our dinner was beautiful fillets of cod, simmered in goat butter, and sprinkled over with toasted bread crumbs. Afterward, Uncle set up a chessboard and invited my mother to play, while Aunt set up a second board and said she would show Frannie and me the moves.

"O, I love the horses," Frannie exclaimed. She picked up a brown one and a white one and mated their green-felt bases.

To sweeten the time with the boards, Aunt served us dried-apple cobbler, with brown sugar, like sand, on top.

None of us seemed to like the bishops. Aunt showed Frannie and me the diagonal cut across their faces, and said that was a sign as to how they moved—always on the slant. But even more than the bishops, I disliked the pawns with their stupid, hobbled conformity each to each. My mother asked what the pieces were made of, and Uncle said the white were ivory, carved from whalebone, and the dark were walnut, which was a very hard wood for carving. "So they represent the sea and the land," he added.

"And the board is the beach where they meet." I spoke so quickly. Thoughts never fell from my lips like that at home, before the words were in my brain.

What with watching the other board out of the corner of my eye, I could barely pay attention to the moves Aunt set up for Frannie and me. I terribly wanted my mother to win, and she did. "Bold move," Uncle said, as he laid down his king in defeat, "to sacrifice your queen."

"Bertha always knows what she's doing," Aunt Agatha commented.

I thought that was true, and if my mother wanted to return to Kentucky though I was to live at the Lighthouse, she surely had good reason. Though I had not been safe with my father, she would be. But I knew her only motive could be love of my father and loyalty to him—a priority that was difficult to swallow.

AFTER OUR WEEK of radiant, expanded domesticity, she did, indeed, depart. The small cargo boat (the *Camel*) came to fetch her, and I watched her seat herself beside a water keg; she tucked her skirts around her and looked pleased and excited to be going somewhere. Her skirts bunched smoothly from her waist; her hair fell serenely from the part. Her eyes glistened. The two men quickly unfurled the single sail, and she was off. How quickly they skimmed my mother away from us. Without variation, she steadfastly smiled and waved at us till her features became indistinct with the distance, and they all four—mother, men, and boat—were but color upon the water.

At that moment, I felt a shadow fall across me. I looked up, yet I saw no cloud.

Frannie took my hand.

Aunt said, "It's the shadow of the Lighthouse."

"Do you know what a gnomon is?" Uncle asked.

"It is the stylus of a sundial."

And I saw that a long bar of shadow began at the base of the tower and fell like a slat across the face of the Island, across us, upon the close-in water, into the chaos of the waves.

CHAPTER 10   The Giant

BY DAY, the Lighthouse stood like a great, gray stalk, and that first summer Frannie and I contracted to worship it together. I had been exiled for my unbelief—but that was for the ready-made mythology I inherited. Left to myself, like an innocent savage or a younger child, I toyed with objects of veneration, sought constancy and comfort in some dominant force.

Who else gazed skyward? The roses, whose exuberance had given me satisfaction with the extremity of nature, had first attracted my admiration with their profuse beauty. The mass of roses lay supine atop the cottage roof. Each rose had at its center a yellow eye, gazing upward. "Do the roses worship His Highness?" I asked Frannie, as I indicated the great, gray tower. "Or do they merely take his measure?"

Frannie gaped at me and gave no answer.

"Those yellow eyes are *saucy*," I opined. "They *use* the tower like a highway to take their gaze to heaven."

While Frannie and I hoed and tended the early summer garden, she suddenly said, "Una, the roses worship the sun."

"Yes," I agreed. "Those rose-eyes see the sun as a distant kinsman. He's yellow, like them, and the roses take from him whatever they need."

But the goats led me back to a contemplation of the tower, for I observed how warily they glanced at it. There were six goats, one billy, three nannies, and two kids—one of which was brown and one white. Apron was the white kid. The billy was also white, with strong curved horns the color of slate. Once, in late summer, when Frannie and I were taking a walk on the high land just above the Lighthouse, we saw the billy run across the hill and butt the tower.

"The color of his horns matches the granite," Frannie said.

"He is the minion of the tower," I replied. "The roses are of the sun's congregation."

At supper, as we enjoyed the squash and sweet red peppers from our garden, Frannie asked her mother, "Why does Billy butt the tower?"

Agatha laughed and told us that he did it once each year, at the end of summer. "He rebels against Authority."

"He tests the tower when he himself is fattest and strongest," Uncle said.

"It must give Billy some satisfaction," Agatha went on ruefully, "to crack his head against rock."

"What do you think of God," I asked, "for testing the loyalty of Job?"

"I think it is wrong for the strong to test the weak, though it is natural for the weak to test the strong."

"Agatha, Agatha," Uncle said, looking up from the sweet potato gashed richly open on his plate, "how can you lay down such ready maxims?"

"Billy is much weaker than the Giant," Frannie said.

"You call the tower the Giant?" her father asked.

"I think of it sometimes as Jack's beanstalk," Aunt Agatha said.

"It looks like a chimney," I said. "It's snug against the house like a chimney. Like a chimney that grew out of control."

But in my heart, I adopted Frannie's idea—that the tower was a Giant, and I would use all my senses to know him, and then, I would offer him a challenge.

SIGHT

That night, as I lay in my bed, I wondered what it would be like to live under a mountain instead of a lighthouse tower. (*Condense* the plot, my mother used to instruct me, after I had lived the experience of reading a novel. Can you *abstract* meaning, she would ask with a smile, after the pleasure of poetry.) I wondered if the Lighthouse were not just a condensed and abstracted mountain. *Height* was the feature they shared, and *stone*. But had I leaned a shoulder against a mountainside, it was likely that close at hand there would have been other mountains to look at, for nature rarely throws down just one of a kind.

Part of the power of the Lighthouse, however, derived from its singularity.

In Kentucky, I had lived next to a river, and sometimes the Ohio was indeed a running of gray, though more often brown with mud, or, occasionally, reflective blue of the sky, and sometimes all aglitter with sunlit silver spangles. At this time of year, the river water would be floated by autumn leaves, especially the sycamore, which liked to grow near water. Did it matter so much that the river's gray was horizontal and the stony Other vertical? I thought not. Or that the river if marked off stretched for miles, and the tower, after all, rose only in feet and yards? In its length, the river curved and bent, and while that had a graciousness, some credit had to be given to the Lighthouse for his straightness. Perhaps if there were no gravity, he would stretch up for miles, curving sinuously as smoke, as he climbed the sky. As my consciousness rarefied toward sleep, I decided that when I compared the spectacle of the Lighthouse to the river, it was His Highness's *Stillness* that ought to be emphasized and capitalized. And did stillness mean *permanence?* Eternity?

THE LETTERS my mother sent from Kentucky arrived that fall in a bundle, brought out to us on the *Camel*. I half dreaded to open them. I did not like to think about the life I was missing in Kentucky. Her letters, though, were almost boring. They described the animals heard or seen in the woods and the gatherings of neighbors for church or harvesting. I used the corner of one of the envelopes to clean under my nails, as I sat beside the hearth.

"Don't do that," Aunt suddenly said.

"Why?" I was surprised by her tone.

"It's not respectful to your mother."

"Get a toothpick," Uncle said kindly, "if the garden dirt is under your nails."

When winter fell, the river would be frozen and closed to steamboats, and there would be no letters. The last letter in the stack was a short note from my father, full of wishes for me: he hoped I enjoyed the food of the Lighthouse, he wished he could send me a pumpkin from their garden patch, he hoped I enjoyed my sewing as my mother did. *I suppose that sometimes you and your little cousin enjoy tossing a yarn ball between you. Does your uncle take time to explain the workings of the Lighthouse to you? Will you take time to write to your father who loves you? Both your mother and I miss you.*

TOUCH

The winter gales on the Island resulted in our bringing out caps and coats and scarfs and mittens, but sometimes Frannie and I took off our mittens to touch the rounding of the Giant. And what did the sense of touch tell us about the Giant? He too had his temperature, and that was changeable. He had his sunny side. It was recalcitrant during the morning hours, retaining its night coolness, but by afternoon, if you spread your hand on the stone, it gave back warmth greater than your own, and so, noticeable. The stone could really grow quite warm, warmer, say, than the udder of a goat, when you laid your hand against that hairy bag.

So, we stepped, feeling with our hands as though we had gone blind and the tower were the shaft of our giant cane, around the base.

Yes, when we rounded the turn to due north, the Giant's skin became cooler to the touch and finally cold and clammy. He had a pelt of rough lichens there, flat, scaly, and branching like gray fire. After we knew him well, we became sorry for his north side and its perpetual cold. We warmed stones in the sun, carried them to his backside, and nestled them up against him. True, it was like warming no more than a few toes of a person; still it was something. (And, Frannie and I agreed, we very much liked having a warm brick for our toes when we slid into our beds those cold nights.)

And so we got to know the Lighthouse by touch (both texture and temperature) as well as by sight.

SMELL

He did have an *odor*—we noticed it in the thawing of spring—as all rocks do. It is the moisture in them that gives them an aroma, and we believed that if the Giant had no moisture he would crumble into a great pile of dust. We agreed on that, but I said there was really no danger of dilapidation, for he was something like a wick. He was rooted in the Island, so its spring-fed fresh water was available in abundance and could be wicked up from the lower stones to the higher ones, as needed.

If there were many bright days with no rain, sometimes we splashed a pail of fresh water from the cistern against his lower stones.

TASTE

Did we *taste* the Giant? Frannie proposed it. No, I replied, for I was fastidious about my mouth. But, I allowed Frannie to kiss the lichen-crusted stone with her lips, as though he were an holy icon, the mighty thighbone of God, and I stood beside her and sang a hymn, such as they sang in my father's church, *God of Wisdom, God of Power,* changing the words to suit me: *Sign of Safety, Sign of Silence, Sing we to Thy Speaking of the Light,* and thanked him many times for his palpable being.

WHEN FRANNIE jumped into her father's arms and thrust her hands boldly into the burning hair atop his head, the sensation I felt was *envy*. O, to be so little!

"You're like a *torch*, Papa," she said, tugging at his topknot.

He smiled down at me. "What do you say, Una? Am I now your Uncle Torchy?"

Frannie pulled a tuft of his red hair, as though to test how well it was rooted to his head, but he made no move to stop her. I smiled at them.

I remembered my father, sitting on a stump, holding me on his lap. "Now, I'll put on your golden gloves," he had coaxed; he slid his fingers over each of mine, starting with the thumb and saying with each stroke, a word: "Do-unto-others-as-you"—changing hands—"would-have-them-to-do"—and then he buttoned the fanciful gloves, having run out of fingers—"unto-you." Then he cautioned me, holding both my hands tightly, "Whenever you do wrong, Una, the gloves come off. You must then say the verse again and put them on with new resolve." I also remembered his hand, when I was twelve, swooping for my cheek, and the impact that turned my head. And after that picture, another appeared, unwanted, of him framed in the narrow door, his whip in his hand, of my mother rising, standing between us, saying, "No."

Uncle Torchy began to hum and to waltz around, holding his little daughter against his chest.

SOUND

That night when I lay in bed, I listened to the wind humming in the tower. Did the Giant emit sounds? Along with *Stillness* one of his great attributes was *Silence*. Yet when the wind, like a horsehair bow, rubbed him as though he were a long stone string, he sang.

Or did the breath of God make the Giant into a lone Pan-pipe? I fingered the hard stone wall beside my bed. As the velocity of the high wind increased, the column of air inside the Giant's long hollow throat was set to mournful vibrating. I wailed back till I woke Frannie, and she left her warm bed to crawl in with me to offer comfort. *Don't be homesick*, she whispered. *I'm here.*

"I EXPECT the *Camel* to appear any day," Uncle said to me at breakfast. "Are your letters ready?"

"I have one for every month for my mother."

"And for your father?"

"I'll write him at the end of summer."

Uncle only slightly frowned, but he looked away.

Aunt said quietly, "We understand."

ABOVE ALL, Aunt Agatha was a pacifist who was unyielding in her abhorrence for violence. She labeled war not only the greatest of human evils but also the silliest. One summer evening, while we stood on the beach to enjoy the sunset colors, she told us—she seemed blushing, in that light—of women in ancient Greece, who had withheld their bodies from their husbands as long as they pursued war. That, she believed, was probably the only effective way to end strife among men.

Uncle Torchy put in the statement that sometimes the Greek men loved each other, like sailors at sea without women. Not only his red hair but the skin of his face and bare arms reflected red.

Auntie said firmly, "Wait till she's sixteen, Torch." She took Frannie's hand and walked back toward the cottage.

Since there were so few of us on the Island, Aunt Agatha's views about war were of remote importance to me—our peace, marked off by the inevitable shadow of the Giant, seemed unending—but Aunt's attitude toward education was an immediate matter—one from which my spirit, if not my mind, benefited greatly. She said that Plato believed children should not learn to read till they were ten, but instead spend their time with music and exercise—so Frannie was exempt from formal instruction. Since I came to the Island at age twelve, my reading (and I did a lot of it) was acceptable. But Frannie, now age five, lived a life as free as the goats', and more so, for she could come inside, or thrust her nose in the roses, if she liked. Of course, she was curious about her small island world, and whatever questions she asked, at five, at six, at seven, were promptly and kindly answered by both my uncle and aunt, but they volunteered no information whatsoever, as far as I could make out.

This seemed a bit of a lapse to me, and that second summer with Frannie on the Island, I endeavored to tell Frannie everything I knew so that she would not grow up ignorant. On June 1, I told her that I was a University of One, Una University, and that all day she should listen to me talk. I traced the letter U in the sand and said it had two sounds, when the U was like the vowels in *moon,* or in Una, and, in that U-sound in *university,* when the U-sound was like *you.* Promptly I moved on to what I likened to the contents of an encyclopedia. But when I began to expatiate, it amazed me how little I knew, and that, really, it did not require the day, but only the morning to get through it all. That afternoon, in the shade of the cottage, we pretended to eat from our pantry of mud pies and gossiped about the goats as though they were people.

More glorious than the gulls, the clouds alone dominated the tower. If it was stolid permanence, they were playful change. They filled my head even as they filled the great dome of sky, and when I thought of sewing my mother the promised quilt, I wanted to fill it full of clouds. "Patched Clouds" my aunt and I called it, and the quilt was such variations of white and blue, and a full year in the fashioning, that Auntie almost cried to say good-bye to it and to fold it in the box to send back to Kentucky. I promised Aunt to make her a quilt representing the waves, which would be easy triangles, tipped with red at sunset. Aunt said that I learned much of geometry in making quilts, and that a proper tessellation took a kind of imagination. I did like to control the colors. My first sewing in Kentucky, which my mother had commenced in the same effortless way as my reading, had been a sampler of the alphabet, with the motto *Love One Another.*

As the summer reached its conclusion, Uncle Torchy asked if I had my letters ready for the *Camel* and if there was one for my father. I surprised myself by saying I would write it that evening.

Dear Father, you asked if Uncle has explained the workings of the Lighthouse to me, and the answer is that he has not, for I have not asked. Nor have I yet climbed up into the Lighthouse. But I have contemplated it in many different ways. Perhaps it is a Trojan

*horse—it appears to be a gift from the gods, but really it harbors
death and destruction?*

Why, when I tried to write to my father, did my thoughts turn
dark? I had never thought that before.

I have been reading the Iliad *and the* Odyssey *this summer, and
whenever I come to the name Ulysses, for he is given the Roman
variant of his name in this translation, I think of you. But it is I
and not you who has gone from home.*

I sighed and looked unhappily at my letter. He had written a kinder
letter to me, of pumpkins and yarn balls. Again, I saw his hand diving
for my cheek. I thought of how the sea eagle smites the sea and comes
away with a fish in its talons.

*Uncle has taken me fishing many times, and I can manage a small
boat by myself. Of the fish we catch, scrod is my favorite to eat. I
help Uncle keep his log of passing ships, as the government requires.
He says my eyes are very keen. We keep a very large garden here
so that the packet boat will not have to bring too many groceries
when it comes. Probably the boat will come tomorrow, but if it does
not I will add to this letter. Please ask Mother to read those of hers
to you. In the meantime, I remain, your daughter, Una.*

The *Camel* did come the next day, but she had a new master, and
he had not known to gather our letters from the post office in New
Bedford. We were able to send out letters, and our groceries and fire-
wood were aboard, but there was no news from Kentucky to savor.
My second summer on the Lighthouse closed sadly.

THAT SECOND WINTER, bereft of the letters from my parents, I
became gray with isolation and loneliness for the world. That winter
was fiercer than the one before, and when I went around to the backside
of the tower in the late afternoon, I found that spray had been blown
all the way up the hundred-foot cliff, and it coated the stones with
silver rime. We saw only a few ships a week plying the rough ocean.

That second November I felt especially hemmed in by grayness, for not only the tower but also the sea and sky were paler shades of gray. It occurred to me one evening when I knew it was time for sunset, though the sky had been a uniform colorless hue the whole day, that if I could elevate myself, I might get above the gray ceiling and see some color before sundown. How welcome a flash of crimson would be, a billow of pink. I determined to try to climb up the tower to get a better view.

Without asking permission, I creaked open the door to the Lighthouse and disappeared. I carried a candle with me, and its weak light shone on a world more dismal than that outside. The barren gloominess of stone and steps presented a silent indifference to my presence. I climbed only to the slot of the western-facing window. The sky held no blush of sunset for me, but I sat down and waited. Perhaps the sky would change.

When it did change, it was to darken from gray to black, and then all at once there were hosts of stars. I felt afraid, as though a swarm of yellow jackets had appeared in the distance. Behind glass, encased in stone a hundred times thicker than an elephant's hide, what did I have to fear, even if they had been a host of stinging wasps? But they entered my mind, through my eyes, and buzzed of my loneliness and insignificance. Disconcerted, I sprang up, slapped first one cheek and then the other, as though to swat insect pests, and hurried down the steps.

As I descended, I heard Uncle opening the door, carrying up his light for the Argand lamps.

"I'm late tonight," he said. "Without the sunset, I was careless."

Then he asked me if I wanted to go up with him. I quickly declined, and as I went down carefully, I heard him hurrying up the steps, higher and higher. I wanted to shout up for him to look out for the star swarm, but I knew my November fancy was bleaker than the reality. Stars were only stars, but I shuddered at the thought of them.

That Christmastime, sweet Frannie, to distract my depression, suggested we make a holiday wreath to encircle the Giant. Then she asked Uncle if we might cut some branches from the cedars—trees and wood being scarce enough on the Island so that no one would ever thoughtlessly mutilate any of the trees. Uncle replied that a full, encircling wreath would require too much greenery, but we might make a small wreath to place on the side, and he would drive a hook, or we might make a garland.

I chose a garland, and all four of us stood in the afternoon wind, while Uncle hammered two iron nails into crevices at either end of one of the five-foot granite blocks. I winced at the sound of the blows. How could one stand such nails going through the palms of his hands? The ends of the garland tossed freely in the wind, and the swag of the midsection luffed out.

That night, after Uncle had come down from lighting the high lantern, I suggested that we all come out to see the garland. Aunt suggested that we each carry our own lantern, and we did. As we stood in the cold, my eye traveled from the holiday greenery up the gray tower to the top. "Now it looks like the Star of Bethlehem," I said, with satisfaction, and Aunt hugged me with her free arm.

And the year turned round the tower again.

DURING ALL THAT TIME, my aunt, and my uncle, too, proved as liberal in their attitudes toward religious belief as ever my mother had described. During the third and fourth winters on the Island, we celebrated Christmas royally, with much preparatory baking, and the making of gifts as fall gave way to the blowing cold. We sang Christmas songs, and each did as he or she wished in terms of exact belief.

Aunt Agatha renamed Billy the goat "Liberal," for challenging the preeminence of the Giant. She herself challenged not only the narrowness of the prevalent Christianity but also the rigidity of education, the inhumanity of the slave economy, and the position of women.

For me, Aunt's liberality in education meant essentially that I, like Frannie, might learn what I liked when I liked. I learned at least one new word every day, and all kinds of random facts springing from the words adjacent in the dictionary. Aunt encouraged me to write in tiny print beside any word I looked up my initials US (for Una Spenser) and the date.

I have already mentioned that Aunt herself had a collection of the poems of Byron, and she also had *Lyrical Ballads* by Wordsworth and Coleridge, which had been published in 1798. Her volume was the twin of one my mother had in Kentucky. Another collection, in a small green binding, was by the Scottish poet Robert Burns, though Uncle always affectionately called him Bobby Burns, as though he knew him. I should like to say sometime what those poems meant to me, line by line. When I read Wordsworth in the hammock, tended by the summer breeze, the poet's reverence for Nature helped to fill the vacancy left by my father's toppled God.

Giles and Kit had yet to materialize out of thin air.

WHEN I THINK of Kit and Giles, I think of the summer birds that wheeled through the sky all the daylight hours. The Lighthouse seemed to organize us—the house and garden, the larger scallop of the Island. Those of us who lived there—four years for me—had our paths, our predictable rounds, all referenced to the Lighthouse. And these were lovely paths, for Torchy and Agatha had set about to make something of a little paradise of their Island, our Arcadia.

But the summer gulls! The air was freedom for them, and they might come in close, or weave out of sight over the water. None flew so high as to fly over the Lighthouse, but once I saw a sea eagle stand on the knob above the lantern.

Giles and Kit soared into our lives one warm day when I was sixteen, as freely as the ever-roving gulls. Though they came by water and not by air, of course, the sail of their tiny boat was like the wing of a gull. The dark boat itself was named the *Petrel*, because, they said, like Saint Peter, it could walk on water.

But I would not skip over the time when I was fourteen, and for a week on the mainland I was reunited with both of my parents for the last time.

Like the gnomon of a sundial, the tower did cast a shadow, as I had observed the day my mother left for Kentucky. We were under its measure of time, and many a day, since that first one when my mother embarked, was marked off as its shadow moved like the slat of a fan over the goats' hill, and then down the boulder steps on the east, until the shadow-shaft again grew chaotic with the waves.

ONCE EVERY SEASON, as I have implied, the packet boat came to us, but the winter boat came at the beginning of winter, and the spring boat came after mid-spring, so it was sometimes five months that we were alone on the Lighthouse with our books, with nature, and with ourselves. During the summer when I was fourteen it was successfully arranged for a June Saturday that my mother and father would come up from Kentucky to meet us.

When I saw them at the New Bedford wharf from the deck of the *Camel,* naturally they looked smaller to me. But even when the boat was bumping the wood, to my surprise, they still seemed shorter than I remembered. My mother and I fell into each other's arms immediately. She was the same, though smaller, with the same serenely parted, glossy-smooth hair. She fingered my curls tumbling over my shoulders in front and down my back and said, "My gypsy girl."

My father said, "Una, at fourteen, young women braid their hair." He did not touch me and he stood like a column of darkness.

"Does not the scripture somewhere forbid women to braid their hair, brother Ulysses?" my aunt said subversively.

My father's eyes flashed black darts, but he spoke mildly. "I'm not such a literalist as that, sister Agatha."

Suddenly I wanted my two families to get along, and I leaned forward and shyly kissed my father high on the cheek, on the skin above where his black beard began. Aunt Agatha was right behind me, but she said with a note of merry mocking, "Clearly the scripture says to greet one another with an holy kiss."

Uncle loaded our valises onto a hand truck and paid the boy to trundle them to our hotel, while Mother and Father greeted Frannie, whom Father had never seen before. Frannie was unafraid, and she shook my father's hand as though she were as tall as he was.

Then my mother put her arm through my father's elbow and held out her hand to me. As we started toward the hotel, I joined with them. Then I held back my free hand for Frannie. She took it and grabbed her mother, who in turn playfully took Uncle's hand, so that we made a chain with six links in it as we walked along.

I think my father had eyes only for the churches of New Bedford, for as we passed them, he stopped to read the sermon topics tacked to the doors. We all stood patiently, still holding hands, while he read. He looked like a dark minister seeking a home for his little flock.

"We could play crack the whip," Frannie said, all smiles, for that was a game that all four of us sometimes played on the beach. I shook my head solemnly at her.

At Seamen's Bethel Chapel, after Father read the sermon notice tacked on a blue-painted door, he announced, "This will do." My mother moved beside him in front of the door also to read. Then we moved on, but we did not take up our linking of hands again.

When I had the chance, I inquired of my mother what was the promised sermon topic. She said that the next day we were to hear a discourse on loving obedience and loyalty. Her eyes looked into mine with such love and loyalty that the protest which rose to my tongue subsided. All evening, I felt fixed in the admonition of her gaze, and I tried to please my father as the six of us ate supper. I asked him about the horse that pulled the buggy and about his fishing in the Ohio, of catfish and bass and bluegill, and I reminded him of when I had fished with him, and as I spoke of these things, I discovered that I did indeed care about them. But I felt as I imagined an old person might, reminiscing about times long gone and far away.

Sunday morning found the six of us entering the Seamen's Bethel, an odd church with a pulpit shaped like the prow of a ship. No sooner had we seated ourselves in a pew about halfway down, on the left, than the minister ascended the pulpit. To do so, he climbed up a rope ladder, then hauled the rope up into the prow. He began by reading from the Book of Ruth. During the night, I had slept off my acquiescence to the tyranny of religion and paternity. I listened to the reading grudgingly, sitting between my parents, instantly in hot rebellion. When, in the sermon, the minister began to generalize on the application of Ruth's words—*Thy people shall be my people and thy God, my God*—the words hit my heart as the sea hits the headland rocks—to be turned away with its own force. I thought, *Thy people shall not be my people—I choose my own—and thy God shall certainly not be mine, for I have my own allegiances.* I seemed to grow taller, as though my shoulders had shot up to the level of my parents' ears. I felt fiercely gigantic, and I knew that I could begin to roar, if I chose, that neither they, who sat so close, nor the congregation as a whole could keep me from roaring one gigantic No! in the face of the high minister. After that, they might drag me out, true, but really I could say whatever I pleased.

Yet I knew my words themselves would dash senselessly against the pulpit. That ship would sail right over me. Instead of roaring my dissent, I studied the minister, who was tall, lined, and battered in appearance, as though he himself had often been to sea. While his words seemed foreign and offensive to me, he himself was a pillar of dignity. I could not help but like him. His figure contrasted with that of my father, who was short and powerfully compact. The minister was silver like driftwood, not the certain black of my father.

Down the pew was the blazing head of Torchy. Suddenly I wished that I had climbed to the top of the Lighthouse and stood there, beside Uncle Torch. Soon after I had come to the Lighthouse I had asked Frannie if she ever went up in the Lighthouse, and she had replied that she was not big enough. This had set me to thinking if I was big enough. After a month on the Island, with no one having suggested I might climb the tower, I asked at the supper table if I might and added, lamely, that the view from the top was probably wonderful—as though I needed some reason for ascending.

"I think your legs turn into steel," Frannie had said solemnly, "if you climb the steps often. Papa's have."

Laughing, Torchy pushed back his chair and straightened out his leg. (My mind left the sermon.)

"Feel, Una," he had said, pointing to his thigh muscle.

I put my fingers lightly on the corduroy cloth of his trousers. "Press down," he said. When I obeyed, I felt, indeed, a muscle as hard as a steel plate under the cloth.

"But this is fifteen years of climbing," he said. "You won't turn into steel right away."

I had thought it might not be too bad to turn into steel if it made one the happy, self-assured person that my uncle was. But I had never climbed the tower with him. My partial ascent had taken me only to the level of fear.

All of this came into my mind when I but glanced down the church pew and saw the red hair of my uncle, as though his brain were erupted in flame. It pleased me to think that he was in fact no blood kin, but a stranger who liked me. I regarded my aunt beside him. Then I contemplated my parents together and thought it might be very nice to marry a man with red hair.

When we left the Seamen's Bethel Chapel, my father looked straight into my eyes—we were the same height—and said that it had pleased him to sit beside me in church, as we had done when I was a little girl. There was a glitter in his black eyes and a soft nostalgia swept over his face, and I was glad that I had not bellowed No! at the pulpit.

I resolved that I would not provoke him. The two families stayed more than a week in New Bedford (the government having provided a substitute for us at the Lighthouse), and, as my mother suggested, we visited many different places of work while we were there. How lovely to have my mother beside me, often touching my shoulder or hugging my waist, pointing for me to look at this or that. I saw men making barrels and candles and items of metal. I saw harpoons forged and rope braided by the mile. I saw great pans of hardtack baked and then packed into barrels—all of those items that a whaler, gone to sea for two or three years, would need for the lengthy voyage. My mother said that she would have me to notice what kind of man did what kind of work. *I want you to learn,* she said, *how men differ from each other.* Mainly I noticed how my gloomy father differed from Torchy's cheer, from the silver minister's serenity.

During these excursions around New Bedford, the sense of the six of us gradually became a sense of five, as my father drew more and more to the periphery. Once I said to my mother, "He looks like an ember smoldering, over there."

"You don't need to be afraid," she said quickly.

I had not really felt afraid, only observant, though in the woods he *had* seemed dangerous. I remembered the retort of his gun as he stood on the threshold and King's blood in the dust. Then I thought of the shaft of the great white pine I had climbed. At intervals, the branches shot out from the trunk like the spokes from the hub of a wheel. And the sprays of yellow-green needles were limber and redolent.

When we went again to church the next Sunday, I studied the faces of the men who were returned from sea or who were likely to go there soon. It seemed to me there was an alertness to them that I seldom saw among the landsmen, and a knowing. And I thought of Uncle, who had been many places in his youth and now seemed so content with his small family on the small Island with the tower, plus one niece, myself, and how he was cheerful for weeks and months and years. And I wondered for the first time where I myself would go next, and, if I went there, if that path might branch as elm trees do and as rivers do and go elsewhere. Would I ever come back to the place where I started? What portion of my lot would be choice and what part accident?

That night, at a New Bedford tavern named the Hollyhock, I was surprised that during our last dinner together before my parents returned to Kentucky, my father asked me a question along these very lines.

"Una," he said directly to me, "do you hold that our lives are determined for us or that we are free to choose?" It was as though the dark case of a coal lump had split open, and I saw the fire within, like a wound.

I glanced uneasily at my mother and felt afraid that their nice visit might end in contention. I had tried to conform! I had concealed my growing unease! My mother nodded yes at me, ever so slightly.

"I think we are free," I said. I helped myself to another portion of beef stew, as though it were a normal question and my answer a casual one. "We don't eat so much red meat on the Island," I said, "do we, Aunt?" But she made no reply.

"Until recently," my father intoned, "I thought so, too. I thought you, daughter, were free to choose to believe, but now I think that fate, or God, determines it all."

I was afraid to speak, because it seemed to me that again fanaticism was contracting and smoldering within him. I studied my napkin and the hastily done embroidery on it—a pink hollyhock, to remind one of the name of the place. I could have said, *I believe in neither God nor Fate*, and the conflagration would have been upon us.

Uncle asked in a kindly way, "What caused you to change your mind, Ulysses?"

My father ignored my uncle and focused on me. "I thought you, daughter, were free to choose and that you freely disobeyed. It was my solemn duty to punish you." He spoke all on one pitch, an intoning, as though he were mesmerized. "I have changed, by the will of God!" Suddenly his voice blared, and the word *God* was almost a shout. The other diners at the Hollyhock turned to look at us. My mother put her white hand on my father's dark shoulder, but she said nothing.

In a lower voice, he continued, "I was in church. You know there is a great debate in Kentucky, south of us, near Tennessee, between those who believe in free will and those who hold with predestination. I have always believed I was free. Look at this hand," he said. "It will not rise from the table unless I will that it do so. No, it lies inert."

Suddenly his hand shot up in a definitive gesture. He held it aloft over us. "I choose," he said.

We stared at him. Aunt Agatha frowned and looked away.

"Am I as a body so different from my hand?" he went on. "That is what I thought, and my minister with me. If I choose whether my hand should rest or move about, can I not make the same decision concerning the entirety of the body? I went to hear my minister say, far better than I could ever formulate, what my soul clung to—autonomy, self-governance. I seemed to need the idea. Was I not like God, in my own world? Were not things done as I ordered them to be done? How could God be less than I?"

He rose slowly from his chair. It was as though he were in a trance, as though his high hand held a rope that pulled him from his seat. He was not noisy or dramatic, but he began to circle the table. Once when I was out fishing with Uncle, a shark circled our boat just in that way, its fin held out of the water up in the air and quietly gliding.

"In his sermon, my minister summarized the arguments of our opponents. As he is an honest man, each argument was given its full weight and its attractiveness. Those predestinating views claimed such as this: that if God were all-powerful, as he must be to be God, then what mattered our puny human will? Could not God have had the power to prevent the crucifixion of his only son? Did not Jesus say, 'Not my will be done, but the will of my father who is in heaven'?"

When my father circled round to his empty chair, I pulled it out and said softly, "Father, won't you sit down again?"

He rushed back his hand as though to strike me. Though the hand did not flash, in the gasp that ran round the table, I was sucked back to Kentucky, back to when his palm smote my cheek, and he thundered, *Believe!* But now he slowly brought the hand before the dark cloth covering his chest, he turned the hand palm up, as though he were testing the air of the room for some interior rain. He looked up questioningly at the low, beamed ceiling. Then he placed his hands together in the attitude of prayer. Slowly he rubbed them against each other, as though to let the one warm the other. The sound was like sheets of fine sandpaper abrading one another.

"And if Jesus, God's own son," he spoke softly, "was determined by a will greater than his own, would it not be blasphemy to think that we mere mortals were not so governed? Our minister presented that thinking and many other arguments against us free-willers as forcefully as if they were his own. And, amazingly, as though through sheer sympathy"—he scrubbed his hands furiously together—"he became convinced of our opponents' reasoning. And I with him." He opened his hands and his arms as though to embrace us. In a normal voice, he uttered a single sentence: "In the middle of the sermon, my minister did change his mind." Then my father whispered, "Never have I seen a man so transfigured."

Again, my father's hand rose above his head, as though suspended by a rope. The hand went before him, leading him, leashed, in the circle around our table. "In that godly man, the light of truth shone brighter and brighter as he spoke. And its reflection in me, and in half of the congregation. Truly, all was determined by the will of God Almighty. We were not like him. He was entirely Other. At the end of the sermon, the minister said, 'All who believe as I have this day been led to believe, follow me through the western door,' and almost half of us stood up and walked out of the old church, and there on the grounds at Mulkey, we formed a new church."

As my father finished his story, he stopped in his circling of us and lowered his arm. Still, I did not so much see him as that brave minister who had started with one idea and through the paths of his own mind found a new place. *Yes!* He had done this in public, not giving blind allegiance to the position that all knew him to have, but daring to think and to change before their very eyes.

"Your pudding grows cold, Ulysses," my mother said.

My father sat down and took up his spoon, but then he glanced around at each of us. He seemed lost, disoriented, and my heart swelled in pity for him. I had no idea what to do. I started to reach out, to cover his hand with mine, but when I saw the hairs growing there, like black, frost-bitten grass bent by a breeze, I did not.

I looked at my own dish and realized I had not seen the serving girl bring dessert. Half-tranced myself, I made myself recognize it as the Indian pudding I loved so well—a cornmeal mush flavored through and through with molasses. I took a spoonful to my mouth and enjoyed the sweet, still slightly warm graininess of the flavored cornmeal. I pressed the mush against the roof of my mouth, as though to extract more warmth from it.

WHEN I EMBRACED my parents in parting the next day, my mother seemed encased in glass—fragile and brittle. My father's hug seemed dangerous as a bear's. My body wanted other sensations. Yet I loved them and was glad to have seen them. I wanted a noble perch, a place to flap my wings.

Upon our return from New Bedford, I climbed the Lighthouse, at noon, by myself. Boldly, I passed the gloomy western window. Halfway up I became tired. An eastern window pierced the stonework, and I looked down. The height made my stomach toss. I looked out to sea, where the waves moved only as lines of white foam; the water appeared as blue as though a bag of indigo had been dropped in it. There were depths in it. I saw a school of fish move like a dark cloud. My knees were shaking with fatigue, and I felt all jellylike and queasy, but I climbed again.

As I climbed, I was anxious that the door at the top might be too much for my strength, but it yielded to me. And then! The glory of the sky! Light and air all about me! The earth and the enormous sea at my feet. "Mine!" I shouted, and flung open my arms to embrace it.

CHAPTER 13   Boston

FROM THAT MOMENT, my appreciation of the Lighthouse changed from reverence for its imposing presence, as we below moved around it, to affection. It admitted me to its interior. With the work of my own legs, it elevated me. I shared the splendor of its view. Knowing the structure from the inside, I loved it and counted it more friend than father. Thus, the book of my life on the Island fell into two testaments.

In my sixteenth year and my fourth year on the Island, but before

Kit and Giles came to visit, Torch and Agatha and Frannie and I went to Boston instead of to New Bedford, for they wanted me to know something of the variety of the cities and also the variety within Boston. Perhaps Aunt Agatha detected in me a certain restlessness.

When we approached the city, by sea, I saw a sweep of structures from one side of the horizon to the other, and out of this mass of buildings arose six sharp steeples, and also, on their right and apparently built on a hill, a dome, which I soon learned was the State House. The steeples and the dome seemed to me like fingers and a thumb reaching impiously from humanity to the heavens. I could not but gasp at such a display of human achievement and thought that if there was a God with eyes, he was surely impressed with this.

Frannie was also impressed with this hive of humanity and sensibly asked, "Where do they grow their food?"

Torchy promised to show us not where it was grown but where it was marketed, and as soon as our bowsprit crossed Commercial Street, we all cried out at an enormous and harmonious community of buildings fashioned of glittering white granite. Our Lighthouse was granite, but it was gray, single, and devoted to the vertical. Here the horizontal, the sheer amount of land covered by three structures stretching back and back with long streets between, awed us almost to tears. A gleaming central building, adorned with a dome and a portico of four columns, resembled a temple. However, this was a market building, and the two long granite buildings on either side were warehouses for the produce, which we saw being delivered in an endless line of wagons. Even Torchy was impressed, for the Quincy Market, as it was called, had been constructed only in the last few years. He speculated that the three buildings stretched back for at least five hundred feet. Everything was new and fabulous; even the vegetables were carted in shining heaps of all one color. I thought of the word *Xanadu*.

When we began to walk the streets of Boston, I saw many rectangular buildings fronted by columns, and Aunt Agatha pointed out that their architecture was similar to that of the Greek Parthenon.

"Are we in Greece then?" Frannie asked.

"Everyone has read Lord Byron, who died fighting for Greek independence from Turkey," she said. "We honor him by reviving the Greek style."

I was astonished that a poet who dealt in airy words should have influenced the shape of substantial structures. But when we visited the Bunker Hill Monument, Aunt said it was in the Egyptian mode. I smiled and echoing Frannie said, "Then perhaps we've come to Egypt." But Aunt, explaining they were the residue of Napoleon's famous Egyptian campaigns of 1798, pointed out a number of obelisks and cemetery gateways of post-and-lintel construction. We also saw something of the Gothic medieval influence.

After much walking around, Frannie and I both developed a desire to see inside. What I loved most, perhaps because of the way the sun was streaming in the high arched windows above the balcony, was King's Chapel. Within its vast volume, fluted columns stood in pairs, like a queen and king, and each was crowned equally in an ornate Corinthian capital. The columns stood companionably together, two by two around the sun-filled room, and I thought if ever I should marry so would I like to stand with someone so like myself that we had a certain majesty.

In a curiosity shop, we saw more of the wonders of the world. The window and counters displayed gods and goddesses—an ivory Buddha with a tummy like a keg and elongated earlobes; hairy faces made of coconut shells with eyes of inlaid mother-of-pearl. Aunt pointed out an Egyptian god, Bastet, in the form of a cat with a tiny silver hoop in her ceramic cat ear.

"Do you know why sailors wear gold in their ears?" Uncle asked me. "It was the law, long ago, that a sailor had to have on his person enough gold to bury him should he wash ashore. So the seaside folk wouldn't be out of pocket at the funeral expense."

I shuddered, and Frannie said she would like to have a cat, like Bastet, someday, as a pet. I was most pleased with a bronze statuette of many-armed Shiva dancing in a circle of fire.

The streets themselves unfolded like an argument of question and answer. Where were we now and where would we go? they asked. Street ran squarely into street till I felt fatigued with the rectangular geometry of it and was pleased when an avenue swooped or curved in a more natural or streamlike way. We walked through an area called the Crescent where all the dwellings linked onto each other, and in front they shared a common park.

While we tramped about Boston, at the mariner's supply, Uncle Torch saw a model of a new sort of lens for the Lighthouse lantern.

Our light had produced a steady star, which was, to me, of astonishing brightness, but the new lens, which was called a Fresnel lens for the French physicist who had invented it, promised luminosity of far greater magnitude. Furthermore, the new light would rotate.

All expenses connected with the Lighthouse had to be approved by the Nation, and so that evening Uncle spent several hours at a desk in our hotel room composing the letter to the Governor asking him to recommend to Congress the new lens. He tried out his sentences on Aunt and me and Frannie. He said that sentences were like blubber and that you must send them to the try works to render out the fat.

"It must be so clearly written," he said, "that an eight-year-old will comprehend how the invention works." He looked at Frannie to enlist her greater attention. "Then there is some hope that the lawmakers will understand the logic and science of it."

"Perhaps you had best leave out the science, Uncle, and write only in terms of the economic logic," I said.

"Could we have dinner sent up?" Frannie asked. She had seen a wheeled cart, on which lay a tray loaded with food, being pushed down the corridor, and I was sure she wanted just such a magical and unexpected conveyance to enter our room.

I told her, "Under the small silver dome on the cart we saw is the hotel mouse. And we are supposed to let it eat up our crumbs when we've finished because it is very dainty and leaves nothing to be scraped off."

"Really?" Frannie said.

"Una has quite taken up your brand of teasing," Aunt said to Uncle. "Under the small silver dome, Frannie, there is a round of butter."

" 'Honored Sirs,' " Uncle read from his position at the desk, " 'Today I have become newly acquainted with an apparatus, invented by Augustin Fresnel, that is vastly superior to the Argand Fountain Lamp, currently used in most lighthouses in this country. The apparatus has been duly tested in France, having been installed on July 25, 1823, at the great Cordouan Lighthouse—' "

Aunt put in quietly, "Torchy, you'd best tell the Governor about the Fresnel's efficiency."

Uncle referred to his notes jotted down at the mariner's supply and reported that with the best parabolic reflectors set in the Argand lamp, 17 percent of the light was used, whereas with the dioptric apparatus

83 percent was saved. What with his numbers and a patriotic appeal not to let our country lag behind France, Uncle wrote a splendid and, as it later proved, convincing letter. Although, for reasons not entirely clear to me, subsequent historical accounts credit New York with installing the first Fresnel lens in this country, in 1842, let the record show that, in fact, the first Fresnel, when I was sixteen, became the blinking eye of our Lighthouse.

The first night we were back on the Island, we moved chairs out onto the dock and admired the steadiness of our light. I felt half in a trance—that Boston was gone, and it was replaced with our own simple vista. Aunt Agatha nodded at the beam and said, "How strange that sometimes things as well as people deserve some formal farewell."

Uncle agreed. "Once I heard a sailor sing good-bye to the crow's nest, the last night he stood watch."

"May I be as constant as that good light," Aunt said.

"You are, dear wife." Uncle reached out and stroked her cheek with the curl of his finger.

ALL THE NEXT WEEK, Frannie and I took an old, worn quilt to the elbow of beach and lay on the sand to watch the steadfast light. Its sides widened, like a megaphone, as it shone out and finally diffused itself into the dark with no boundary definition.

How would we feel to have that steady illumination replaced by something intermittent? Something that swooped and darted far above our heads? Lying on the quilt on our strip of sand, I felt subdued, as people sometimes do, at the end of an era.

Suddenly Frannie said, "Feel my forehead, Una. I'm glowing."

I touched her skin with my fingertips and felt the extraordinary heat immediately.

"We must go in."

FRANNIE WAS rapidly very sick with the fever and blisters. They were so tight with fluid that they seemed to shine. In her delirium, she imagined the Giant to be walking. Once her eyes opened wide while I sat with her, and I quickly told her there was no such thing as the Giant. She nodded her head feebly and whispered through parched lips,

"I know. He's only a leg." Quickly I gave her a spoonful of water. Then she shouted, "He has a hinge at the knee!"

When one night we saw she might die of the smallpox, a terror gripped me such as I had never experienced. Helpless, I stood aside while Aunt bathed her forehead and Uncle held both of her hands. I wanted him to hold on to her forever. Once he let go, and I feared Frannie had died, but then he reached farther up and held her arms. Suddenly for myself I had to break the stasis of our waiting.

I slipped outside and climbed up the stone boulders to the tower. I leaned my head against the stone. A hundred feet below the waves crashed against the headland, but the breeze was soft on my back, like a kindly touch. I didn't know why I went there, but quiet words formed on my lips. With my forehead pressed against the stone, I prayed, "O Tower, who joinest earth and sky, O Lighthouse, who warnest of the danger of the sea, impart Thy cool temperature to Thy little servant Frannie, who hast served Thee well in the past. Be our Friend now. And guard over her and keep her safe from death."

I recalled the small religious objects from around the world I had seen in the shop window in Boston. I imaged and prayed to them all—Buddha, Bastet, Shiva, the wooden mask—to preserve the life of Frannie. To the sunlight bathing the interior of King's Chapel.

When I returned to our bedroom, I pressed my forehead against Frannie's, as though to transfer coolness. Then I sat down and held her vacant hands, while Uncle grasped her arms. Aunt brushed her lips with a wet rag, bathed her forehead, pulled up her nightgown to bathe her blistered ankles and shins.

Frannie lived, though the skin of her face was left forever pock-marked. After her illness, her body elongated and lost its delightfully sturdy and churnlike appearance. I couldn't help noticing that some of the pits on her skin were just like those in the stone of the tower, and, thus, through her illness, she had come to look a bit more kin to our Friend.

Before the government sent out the Fresnel lens and the dozen men to install it—how strange it was to see our Island population so inflated, to see foreign ropes and pulleys dangling from the tower, to hear shouts more shrill than gulls, and to regard the jackets and cast-off gloves of the installation crew lying on our rocks and grass, to glance shyly at their mouths chewing above the extended board of our table—before all that, the government sent two young men to survey the scene. They arrived in a small dark boat named the *Petrel:* Giles Bonebright and Kit Sparrow.

CHAPTER 14 🐚 **The *Petrel***

THE SKY being white that day, their sail was not the first I saw of Kit and Giles, but the dark wooden curve of the *Petrel.* I called to Uncle and Aunt, who were weeding and cultivating the garden, and Uncle, leaning against the long hoe handle and shading his eyes to see better into the morning sun, said it must be the advance guard of the Fresnel.

It had been a month since our Boston trip and Frannie's contracting of pox, and I had almost come to believe that our light would not be changed after all. Now I glanced up anxiously at the tower. I wondered if my inanimate friend shuddered at the thought of having his eye changed. I was sure that I would.

Whenever the world of the Island seemed too small for me, his steps provided the route that lifted me up to the freedom of the air. Up there, the gulls flew below me, the sea crawled at my feet, and only the vastness of the sky was above me. I relished it. If I stepped outside, on the high platform, the wind blew around my body till I was cold, and I would retreat into the lantern room or around to the lee. Many times it was the sun shining on me with unfiltered force that moved me to the curve of shadow. But I loved the sunlight, and, at that height, my blood seemed to fizz and evanesce, and I opened my arms to it many times.

Since the high platform of openwork iron ringed the lantern, sometimes I challenged myself to skip around and around till I was dizzy. Then I lay down on the grill in a rapture. With the clouds spinning around my head, I was the center of a benign and exhilarating universe.

THERE THEY CAME, while we stood in the vegetable garden, and the dark form of the *Petrel* and the straight way they came put me in mind of how the shark had approached Uncle and me in the fishing boat, before the beast began to circle. I projected an imaginary line drawn from their boat to us. In a linear, unhesitant way, they would come forward till the prow bumped our dock.

"I'm going up in the Lighthouse," I announced. I knew that these visitors would not yet be changing the lens, but I needed to say good-bye to the old order. I left my relatives standing among the planted rows to walk inside. The stone house seemed dim as I moved around the familiar objects, touching them, or speaking to them.

If the lens was changed, would not everything be changed?

I opened the door to the tower, where the stairs up to the height of the house were fashioned of stone but beyond that level changed to the same open grillwork as the encircling platform at the top. I stepped hard and fast, dared myself to climb faster, and increased the tempo. My feet resounded on the iron stairs. I created my own wind and roar. I thought myself to be a tornado.

When I passed the first window in the tower—the sunlight piercing through it—breath was still strong in my lungs, and I raced on up, as fast as my feet could lift me. Never had I run up the tower with such speed, and I imagined the tower itself was proud of me and enjoyed the passion of my rising knees and feet.

I let myself through the iron door into the lantern room. There was the old Argand apparatus, the fountain lamps, and their parabolic re-flectors. Uncle kept them polished to perfection and had told me that some ignorant lightmen rubbed the reflector too abrasively and ruined their surfaces. I stood beside the lamps and looked through the glass to sea. Yes, there was the small dark boat, and now I could see the white sail and two men tending the boat. They were the size of ants, and their arms and legs seemed no thicker than a hair.

If they looked up, they would not guess that a girl was standing among the lamps. My chest was heaving, and I thought of how com-pletely concealed from the world I was now and had been when inside the tube of stone, myself rising in the sky by the power of my own legs. While they sailed closer, they may have looked at the long column, but they had no idea of a girl within it winding up the spiral stairs.

Suddenly I wanted to startle them. I opened the door of the lantern compartment to the encircling grillwork, and as I had done perhaps a hundred times, I stepped into the open air. The wind washed my skin immediately and flattened my long broadcloth skirt against my legs and made it toss and ripple behind me. My dress was dark blue. If they looked up, they would surely notice me against so white a sky. I grasped and spread my skirts to make myself broader. Perhaps I would appear as an indigo angel, if they were the superstitious type who believed in mermaids and angels and the like. Perhaps if I stood still, they would count us as eccentrics who had a figurehead for our Lighthouse as most ships had for their prow, and they would wonder whether I was real or carved.

Now their boat was as large as a large toy, and I could read on its side in red script the word *Petrel*. They wore broad-brimmed hats, fastened, no doubt, under the chin, and I could see nothing of their faces, but I liked the way they moved about their boat—neither lazy nor hurried in their movements—and I thought of how in New Bedford my mother had encouraged me to watch and make judgments about the way people went about their work. Between these two, I could draw no contrasts. They seemed to move in harmony.

Just then I was startled by a sea eagle swooping close. It was a fearsome thing, with cruel beak and talons the size of clenched fingers, but it was only looking for a lofty place to rest. Nonetheless, I jerked away from it and lunged toward the abyss. The railing caught me, the gasp still in my throat. With a raucous cry, the eagle veered toward me. I snatched off my bonnet and struck out at the bird, and it squawked angrily back at me. Now it attacked, hovering, pinning me against the railing. The great wings beat furiously up and down.

I raised one hand to protect my eyes and face, and with the other, holding my bonnet by the strings, I swung at it. Again, it squawked, a shrill and piercing cry. Its flapping wings spread out much fuller than my skirts, and I could see the broadness of the pinions and their rugged brown color. Never had I seen such a cruel face. Its mouth was open with its screaming at me, and I saw the sharp, horny edges of the beak and, near its base, black nostrils. The eagle was a flurry of feathers and harsh noise. I beat at it with my bonnet, and the bird curved off into

"The eagle was a flurry of feathers. . . ."

the air, at first flying below me and then circling over both me and the Lighthouse, and flying up till it was nothing but a speck.

The back of my hand was cut. Not wishing to drip blood on my dress, I held my hand over the railing into the wind till it was numb in the wash of moving air. My knees were trembling. I did not like doing battle. A flap of fabric had been ripped loose on my bonnet, and threads had been caught and pulled in many places. One of the ties had come off and floated away. I was lucky the eagle had not flown off with my bonnet as his trophy. I smiled a little at the thought of such an empty victory for a bird. But for once I was too much shaken to enjoy the humor of my own pictures.

"Hal-looo." The sound seemed to puff all around me. A human voice rising on an updraft. "Hal-looo." I looked out to sea. One of the sailors was waving his hat at me and calling. The other stood still with his hands on his hips, but he looked at me.

I felt too weak to return the salute. I opened the door to the lantern room and retreated inside. I sat down on the floor, and I was glad to be encased in glass, out of the moving air, safe. Inside enclosing glass there is a warmth, sent there by the sun, and held while it compiles. I sniffed, but I did not cry. The still warmth comforted me. I drew up my knees and folded my arms across their top and laid my head there. The back of my hand smarted where the eagle's toenail had passed. I felt dazed, my eyes open but unseeing, but I could feel my heartbeat slowing, and I was glad for the peace. Outside, around the window above my ears, the wind softly played, as it often did. But it had hosted those wings.

At length, I noticed the reflection of my body in the parabolic surface of one of the lamps. I was distorted, of course, so that I was little more than a stretch of color. But the blue was the blue of my dress, even if it was all bent. I looked for my face and the color of my flesh. My features were so warped and ugly that I felt offended by my accidental mirror.

My hair, which had been braided and coiled under my bonnet, had come down. The reflection showed it as a mat of darkness. With both hands, I began to divide it into sections and replait it neatly. I had lost my pins, but I made the braids neat and bound them with a thread pulled from the frayed bonnet. Mine were fat braids and long enough to hang over my breasts to my waist. I took my time with the braiding.

My cheeks were hot, and I did not like the way the contest with the eagle stayed in my muscles. I felt nervous and troubled. I remembered how, unbalanced, my body had lurched out toward the abyss. Placing my hand at the top of the girdling hipbone, I could feel the sore place where the top railing had caught me and kept me from charging over. I looked at the blood-crusty line drawn over the back of my hand. It had wanted my cheek, but I wouldn't allow that.

When my hands were little, and my mother was teaching me to sew, she placed her hands over mine. She put her middle finger, encased in a pitted silver thimble, at the end of the needle and pushed for me. *This finger, with the thimble, is a little engine,* she said. *It makes the needle go.*

I thought of the miles and miles of thread that her thimble had pulled through cloth. What song had the needle sung to the fibers of the fabric? When she quilted, the needle passed through three layers: the pieced top, the inner batting, and the sturdy muslin underlayer. If all the thread from all her quilts were measured, would it stretch a thousand miles? Had her needle trudged, as a man's foot might trudge, over a journey of a thousand miles?

She sat still, I thought, and yet she traveled. And when one stitches, the mind travels, not the way men do, with ax and oxen through the wilderness, but surely our traveling counted too, as motion. And I thought of the patience of the stitches. Writing a book, I thought, which men often do, but women only rarely, has the posture of sewing. One hand leads, and the other hand helps. And books, like quilts, are made, one word at a time, one stitch at a time.

I did not know how long I had stayed aloft, nursing my right hand and musing, but with that last thought, I unfolded myself and stood up; felt ready to go down. I spiraled slowly down the steps, the soft way a milkweed seed sometimes twirls to earth. I wanted time for any vague thought to come to mind that mind should want. No new ones came, but the pace seemed a meditative winding, and what I was winding was like yarn on an oblong skein, softly enfolding a quiet center that was myself.

My feet passed from the metal steps to the sixteen stone ones, and then I came through the wall into the common room. They sat at the table together, my adopted family and the two strange men, who were young; the odor of fish chowder laced with onion and celery filled the room.

"This is Una," my aunt said, "our niece and cousin."

Both sailors stood up, as though they were the best-bred gentlemen in the world.

"Battler of eagles," one said.

"As brave as a dragon," the other said.

"Then this heap of stones is my treasure," I replied to the second one, thinking how in legends a dragon nested atop its pile of gold goblets and chains and stolen coin.

He replied, "My name is Giles Beowulf."

I looked at him skeptically, for I knew Beowulf had fought the fire dragon for his treasure.

"Bonebright," he corrected. "Giles Bonebright."

"You have a magic name," I said, "if not a legendary one." I looked closely, as though his bones should be shining through him. He was tall and fair. His nose was unusually large, rather a disfigurement, but his eyes, also, were unusually large, blue, and wide-open, with nicely arched black brows, though his hair was light.

The other sailor, shorter with dark hair, comely, merely said, "Kit Sparrow."

"I must wash my hand," I said, and I went to the water pitcher and poured into the china bowl. I hoped that washing over the scab would not renew the bleeding.

Frannie began exclaiming about the sounds of the eagle and how it had looked as big as I was, that she hadn't known they had such long wings till she'd seen them *in comparison,* that a feather had floated down. The feather itself was ten inches long—she had measured it—and the shaft was almost as thick as her little finger.

"You must have it as a pen, Una," Uncle Torchy put in.

I knew from her voice that Frannie wanted the feather, and almost I said that she could have it, but, instead, heard myself say to her, "You can use it, too. To write with. Whenever you like."

By chance, my seat fell across from Kit Sparrow. Giles helped himself to more chowder, though his bowl was not yet empty, and at once, I knew he was busying himself so he wouldn't have to speak. There was a shyness in Giles. Despite the storehouse that must be in his mind, if he was able so quickly to allude to Old English tales of kings and dragons, now he didn't know what to say and filled his bowl instead.

Kit looked at me straight, through eyes dark as my father's, and said with a kind of breathless burning, "I hope you will not wash your hands so quickly of *us?*"

It was an impertinence, and Aunt looked at him acutely, but there was a kind of suspension in both his breath and face that suggested the question mattered to him. I forgave his impertinence and met his boldness. "No," I answered, but I looked down at my own food and had no other words. Then I flashed up, "Besides, I only washed one hand."

Uncle and Aunt, who were pleased to have visitors, talked very freely and encouraged the sailors to talk, for it was a treat to have company. Kit Sparrow was never at a loss for words, and he himself asked questions and talked to little Frannie as much as to anyone and teased her. He said she should begin by fighting with the gulls on the dock so that she would be ready for eagles when she was a young lady. He made us laugh, and I thought his last name suited him, for he skittered from one topic to another like a land sparrow—we had none on the Island—with no shyness about landing on whatever idea he liked.

His boldness was infectious to Frannie. I was glad to see her so animated and uncareful, for since her illness, I had thought her never so exuberant as she had been before. She asked Kit if he went to church on the mainland. I was old enough to know such a question was a degree rude, for people did not always want to reveal their religion, but Kit answered promptly and simply: No.

Frannie asked him why, but this time he avoided a direct answer, though he said that once he had tried visiting the AME.

"What was that?" Frannie queried.

Giles said, "African Methodist Episcopal. The slave church."

"Did they accept you?" Aunt asked Kit.

"Yes, but they asked me what I was doing there."

"What did you say?" Frannie asked.

"I said my skin was white but my heart was black."

We laughed together, all but Kit. Though there was a trace of amusement in his eye, at the end of his statement there was that breathless suspension again, a strange intensity, as though he had revealed something that was of import to himself, beyond the way he spoke.

"You make a wonderful chowder," Giles said to my aunt, as though to change the conversation.

"It tastes like home," Kit said, quick to follow his friend's lead.

"And where is home?" Uncle asked.

"For me," Kit answered, "Nantucket."

"Then it may indeed be like home," Aunt said, "for I got the receipt from Mrs. Hosea Hussey of the Try Pots Tavern."

"A very fishy woman," Kit said. "Guess, Frannie, what her necklace is made of."

"Seashells."

"Codfish vertebrae, all polished up."

"And Mr. Hussey," Giles added, "has his five account books bound in sharkskin."

My aunt turned to Giles and asked sweetly if he, too, then, hailed from Nantucket, but he said he was from Alabama.

"I don't hear the South in your speech," Uncle said.

"I've knocked about enough to lose the accent."

"I hear it in the long *i*," I said. "*Five* account books."

"I'm still working on that," he answered.

"Giles thinks he sounds more educated," Kit said evenly, "if he doesn't sound Southern."

I thought Kit's statement, again, to be an impertinence, but Giles took it perfectly at ease. When I knew Kit better, I asked him about his public explanation of Giles's motives, and Kit said that he and Giles had a pact between them never to be inhibited in what they said to or of each other. I had never heard of people consciously making such an arrangement, and it increased my sense at the time that Kit and Giles were rather special young men, many cuts above the ordinary.

"Once I was walking on the Madaket Road," Kit said, "and I saw the Husseys' cow. She was a brindled cow, and she fed on fish remnants behind the Try Pots. And when she walked down the road to get something green to eat, she wore a cod's head on each foot."

"She did not," Frannie said.

"Yes, she did," Kit answered. "It was to protect her feet from the sand."

Giles looked up. "Sand soon files down a cow's hooves," he said solemnly. And then we all laughed again. If the conversation had lagged, at a graceful moment, Uncle would have taken out his harmonica and played for us till our talking fires had been rekindled. But so well went our chat together, or *gam* as our sailormen taught us, that Torchy never checked his shirt pocket to be sure that the mouth organ (which I had not learned to play) was there. After a bit we left the table and went outside to sit on the eastern rocks, which were now in the tower's shade but gave off a comfortable heat. Kit asked if we sometimes had seal families up to lounge with us on the rocks, and I saw how our relaxed postures did suggest that we ourselves were a seal clan in love with warmth. But Aunt and Uncle did not consider it a bit lazy, when company came, to talk away the afternoon, as we worked hard every day.

At dusk, Uncle left us to light the lantern, and Giles went with him, but Kit said he would look at the stairs and lantern room later, and he stayed on the rocks to talk with Aunt and Frannie and me. I thought Giles was relieved to get away a bit, for his shyness swept him like the tides, even as mine did, coming and going at intervals, and he at the mercy of it.

With the other men gone, Kit talked more at length in his speeches. Very considerate, I thought, his not wanting the weight of the conversation to fall on us. He asked me, quite unexpectedly, if I thought to live forever on the Lighthouse Island and become a keeper myself. What with Aunt there, and the question implying some distant demise of Uncle, I felt embarrassed. Kit, seeing this, but not divining the cause, assured me that some women did, indeed, keep lighthouses. I saw Frannie gazing at him as though he were a Greek god visiting mortals.

"Tell us of your own mother," Aunt said.

While he talked, I watched how the low wind over the waves was catching and pushing against the gulls. Though they flapped their wings vigorously, sometimes they seemed to stand in the air, neither falling into the surf nor making forward progress. Kit said his mother, whose name was Hester, had become a baker, standing in for his father, who had made a trip back to England to see his aged parents. He said many women of Nantucket had the jobs of men, since theirs were often gone to sea as whalemen or on merchant vessels. His mother had been up before daylight and had baked many kinds of bread, with nuts and raisins and cinnamon, sometimes with dill or pumpkin flavorings such that the whole of Nantucket talked of it, and the stagecoach took orders of the bread out on the eastern end of the island as far as 'Sconset.

One time, Kit told Frannie in particular, the stagecoach driver had been so obsessed by the wonderful aroma of the still-warm rolls that he stopped the coach. The driver stood beside the horses and shamelessly devoured the whole basketful, though the passengers all taunted him. "I couldn't stand it," he had said—Frannie's face shone with glee— and the driver got back up on the box and drove on as though nothing unusual had happened. Such was the fame of Mistress Sparrow's baking. Kit said he had been an apt boy of eleven when his mother was a baker for his father and that if Aunt would show him her flour and yeast and things he would bake yeast rolls for us in the morning.

"Is your mother still a baker then?" Aunt asked.

Kit said that when his father came back from England, he had wanted the bread made in the plain, old way, devoid of special flavorings. "They didn't get along so well," Kit explained, "after he came home." And it turned out that his mother had an affliction of the mind. "One time," he said, "in anger, she defiled the bread. Afterward, he sent her out on the moors to a family that kept sheep and also kept the mad people of the town."

We were all stunned by this. The conversation had been all sunny and generous, and here was this dark and inappropriate cloud. Kit sat silently, as though he had fallen into a bog.

"What is a defilement of the bread?" Frannie asked, but in a small voice.

"She urinated in the dough."

"Goodness!" Aunt exclaimed. She was disgusted that Kit would say such a thing to a child. For the first time, to me, the contours of my aunt's mind seemed less broad. It was as though what I had deemed an unbounded plain was, after all, a road, mostly broad, but with narrow places in it. Still I knew my own face was flushed red. I knew what *urination* was, but I thought Frannie did not, and I thought she would not ask.

"How did they care for her madness?" I stammered.

"They gave her dried-berry teas—huckleberry, which grows on Nantucket, and blueberries and cranberries. And rose-hip tea."

We ourselves, on our Island, drank rose-hip tea, our cottage being covered with roses, and we were not mad.

"Did the teas help?" I asked.

"Sometimes they took the madwomen to the sea, in winter, and made them bathe. They thought the shock of the icy water might cure them." He added, "All of their patients were women."

"How many were there?" Aunt asked.

"Just four."

"What happened to your mother?" I asked. All the color had drained from Frannie's face, and the rims of the pox marks cast shadows so that her face was all cratered. She looked almost ill.

For a moment Kit said nothing, and then he said, "She died."

"I'm sorry, Kit," my aunt said.

"See how the wind beats back the gulls?" Kit said to Frannie. "And the low clouds on the horizon? Likely we'll have a rainstorm after supper."

Not accustomed to scientific observations about weather, or any cause and distant effect, Frannie looked at him with wonder. She seemed in awe of Kit, who talked so freely and told in one day both the funniest tale of a cod-shod cow and the saddest story of a mad-stricken mother that she had ever heard. I could see that Frannie, who was only eight, already idolized Kit. Never having practiced guile, Frannie now asked Kit if when they changed the lens, he would come back with the crew.

He smiled at her, a happy glance with no trace of condescension, and only said, "Would you like that?" Suddenly I wished he would smile just so at me.

I saw that Frannie regarded the Lighthouse only as a tower and a lantern, and the changing of the lens was a desirable event that would perhaps occasion the return of Kit. Indeed, since that trip to Boston, or was it since her illness—at any rate, since Kit came, she never spoke again of the Giant as though he were a person.

OVER THE SUPPER TABLE, there was much talk of lenses, and Giles explained very well, lifting his expressive blue eyes to ours, to check our understanding, how prisms were arranged around the light source, and how the prisms fit around each other, with spaces in between, but with the outside curve of one prism being consistent with the inner curve of the next prism so that the whole apparatus focused and concentrated the light into a powerful beam. He drew on a piece of paper while he talked, and he was just as considerate as Kit in making sure that Frannie, as much as Uncle or anyone, could see the illustration and understand the physics of light. I noticed again Giles's lovely eyes and how intelligence shone from them.

In explaining the light, Giles spoke with confidence and happy animation. I said I would like to learn more about the "physics of light"— a phrase I had never heard or said before. "It gives me goose bumps," I told him.

"Then I will teach you what I know of optics."

"We will all learn," my aunt said.

Turning the paper over, Giles said, "Here is a law of light to remember: 'The angle of incidence equals the angle of refraction.' "

Frannie interrupted, "But what is light?"

Giles looked at her and smiled, but said nothing.

"I think," I said, "that it is a process in the air, like fire."

"No one really knows," Giles said.

"What is wrong with my idea?" I asked, for I was truly curious and knew that it must be in some way inadequate.

"Light can shine through water," he said.

"Then let light be," I said, "a process, a movement of brightness through whatever it passes through."

"Yes," Uncle said. "It passes through glass. It must be incorporeal, a process."

"But it cannot pass through wood," Giles said. "Why is that?"

"I know, I know," Frannie said, her face glowing. "Wood is too thick."

"If you pick up a bucket full of wood and a bucket full of water, which is heavier?" Giles asked.

"Water is heavier," I said.

"And there is an experiment," Giles went on, "where a glass bottle is pumped out so that it is a vacuum. Nothing at all is in it, neither air nor water. Yet light passes through a vacuum with no trouble at all. Can a process occur when there is no medium?"

"How," I asked, "can we know laws about light, and yet we don't know what it is?"

"But perhaps we should go on with the laws, anyway," Giles said. He looked at me appreciatively, and again I liked his face, which seemed more poetical than rational.

During our scientific lesson over the supper table, Kit listened, but he left all the explaining to Giles. I liked that Kit knew when to be silent, as well as when to talk.

Suddenly rain was thrown against the small window at the end of the table. It came at first in hard little particles, and then the glass wavered with streams of water. The stone walls of the cottage were thick, but the rain did a muted dance on the shake roof. At a certain point, Frannie walked round the table to Kit, stood beside his chair, and asked if he would like to see her seashells, and I remembered how, during my first night at the Lighthouse, Uncle had had her show me the shells as a step in our getting to know each other.

Kit quietly went with her to the fireplace; so as not to distract us at the table, he replied softly as she took the shells one by one out of the basket for him to see. I admired his courtesy, and I heard him tell Frannie about a shell he knew called the Venus comb. He sent Frannie to the table to beg a scrap of paper, and on it he drew a picture for her of the Venus comb, which I saw later, as she kept the picture of the shell in the basket with the real shells. The Venus comb was a shell with a row of long, parallel spines, like a comb.

Giles must have been listening, too, because he looked up from the lens he was drawing and asked me if I knew who Venus was.

"She was the Roman goddess of love," I answered.

"Was she?" Kit asked from the fireplace. "I didn't know that."

"What did you think, then, that the name 'Venus comb' meant?" Giles asked him.

"That the shell was to be found in the vicinity of Venus. That Venus was a place."

"So it is," Giles answered, "but it is a place in the night sky. The place you mean is Venice, in Italy. Venus is a planet. The evening star. I don't think anyone has collected seashells there. How was Venus born?" he asked me.

"From the foam of the sea."

"Very good," Giles said. "Now, Una, look at this."

Eventually, Aunt went to wash the dishes, and much later Uncle withdrew to a corner. He took out the mouth organ, but he played it softly and privately, as though he were making music with the rain and wind and not with us. Only Giles and I remained at the table bending our heads over the drawings. Giles's pleasant voice explained on and on.

He talked not just about light, but also about many laws of motion, that one could calculate the exact force it took to move an object up an inclined plane, that a screw was itself a kind of twisted inclined plane, and, in the tower, the spiral stairs whereby a person lifted himself in air were a special case of inclined plane. He explained how, through tacking, which I had often observed but never fully understood, a ship could sail into the wind. There was nothing he did not know about pulleys and ropes and how they could be assembled to reverse the direction of the force applied or to make the pulling easier.

"Would you like to be a sea captain someday?" I asked him. Giles seemed so sweetly sure of what he knew that it was easy to imagine him as a remarkable captain, gentle and dignified.

"It would be an enormous responsibility."

"You know so much."

He looked embarrassed, but pleased. "Nobody knows how to make the wind blow, or the sun shine, or how to ward off disease. A whole crew can fall too ill to move the sails."

"No one expects a captain to control the waves."

"You have a nimble mind, Una."

Now it was my turn to be embarrassed with pleasure.

"Do you know how a wave really works? It only appears to bring water from far out to sea into the shore. The motion is really up and down, not transverse." And he drew wavy lines to show me.

But my mind was full of waves as I knew them—splendid walls of water, long swells and humps traveling to the shore with perfect weight and inevitability. The crash of foam unceasing. " 'Roll on, thou deep and dark blue ocean—roll,' " I quoted.

"Byron," he said. *"Childe Harold."*

"Una," my uncle said, "if you will bring your eagle feather, I'll sharpen it into a quill for you. Then we'll have a song together and off to bed."

While he sat by the dying fire, wielding his ivory-handled knife, Uncle told the visitors about fishing around our Island, speaking of the mackerel close in and the great schools of cod farther out, on their way to Cape Cod, which was named for them.

When he had finished cutting the quill, Uncle handed it to Aunt and said, "What do you think? Will it do for Una to write with?"

My aunt examined the point and then playfully stuck the feather in my hair.

"You look like an Indian," Kit said, "with your dark braids and feather."

Many families would have been offended by the comparison, but I knew that Kit had decided we were a group without the usual mainland prejudices.

Out of a similar thought, Aunt remarked, "You are a liberal fallen among liberals, Kit." But she looked serious and did not smile when she said it.

"Our billy goat is a liberal," Frannie said.

At that we all chuckled, and Kit's riposte, though he did not know that she was referring to the goat's name, was quick: "I am probably as hardheaded as any goat, Fran."

Bestowed with Kit's new, shortened name for her, Fran-Frannie turned quickly away with a hasty "Good night" to all, toward the little room she and I shared. Aunt and Uncle climbed up the ladder to their attic bedroom, and I left the men spreading quilts over the braided rug before the embers.

WHO DOES NOT like to fall asleep with the rain beating on the roof and the wind rubbing the outer walls, while oneself is dry and warm in a comfortable bed? My narrow bunk, covered amply with the log-cabin quilt my mother had made, was a home within home. Frannie's bunk, since she was younger and more tender, lay along the backside of the rock fireplace, as a winter comfort—though this being summer our cook fire had been too small to heat the chimney rock. By my choice, my bunk was placed so that I could see out the small east window. When the moon was full, there was enough light to make out the colors of the quilt—the red square for the hearth in the center and the surrounding "logs" shading across a diagonal from dark to light.

But with the driving rain, my window was a blackness, and I had pulled the door tight shut, since visitors were sleeping before the fireplace. With my fingertips, I ran the seams and stitches and waited for sleep to fall.

But it would not. The day had been too full. Again I heard the eagle scream and my eye went to the dark nostril-dashes at the base of its yellow, horny beak. How, within the egg, when nostrils formed on the eagle chick, how had the horn of the beak known to leave an opening in its smoothness there, so that the bird could breathe? And why did a bird need to breathe?—fishes did not, except whales, which were not truly fish though everyone called them fish.

Birds may require light for life, not air: usually when my thoughts scrambled unreasonably it was a sign that I was sliding into sleep. But not so that night. I thought of Giles and Kit. It was they, more than the eagle, who had made the day full and remarkable, and yet hanging over all the day there seemed that warning, warring scream and the open beak. I traced the thread of scab across the back of my hand. The fan-shaped tendons could have been cut through, the delicate, long bones exposed. *Giles Bonebright, Kit Sparrow!*

There was an evanescence in me when I thought of Kit and Giles, of either of them, of both together. Kit was easier to talk to, but I felt a kinship, an understanding, between Giles and myself, and Kit—there seemed something I couldn't know about his thinking. They were both kind to Frannie, and I liked that very well. Were they sorry for her pockmarked face? Would that be an impediment for her, if she left the Island and sought a home on the mainland? Surely it was fortuitous that the first men she met after her illness did in no way scorn her but sought her out with questions in conversation. Kit seemed almost too familiar with her, and he had called her Fran. He seemed fascinated with her because she was odd, with her scars. And I seemed unusual to him, too, because I had fought with an eagle, but that had nothing to do with who I was. It was only an accidental circumstance. I perceived, though, that Kit was drawn to what was unusual, for whatever reason, either accidental or intrinsic. Probably he was drawn to Giles because of his unusual mind. Never had I spoken with a person who seemed to have so bright a mind as Giles. He was well named—Giles Bonebright—but his last name should have been Brainbright.

Thus, while I thought, and the rain beat on the roof, I turned and rolled many times, looking for the posture of sleep. Finally, the bed grew tiresome, and the rain and wind sounded dull and muffled. I listened to the surf booming against the rocks and the slush and suck of it running on the sandy beach, and even those sounds that I loved as an everlasting comfort entered my ears monotonously.

I threw off the quilt and went to the door. I would peek through the crack at the visitors. There was a form lying before the fireplace. But the other man was up and standing at the door to the stairs! His figure was long and draped, hooded, in one of the quilts—was it the height of Giles, or did the long quilt make Kit look tall? I couldn't tell. The standing figure disappeared through the wall. With the wind and rain and sound of surf, I could not hear footsteps on the stair, but as I waited, and he did not emerge, I could only conclude that he was climbing the tower.

I stood uncertain in the crack of the door. I never climbed the Lighthouse at night. Uncle Torchy tended the lamps in the night, but when? I had never asked. I felt annoyed with the dictum of the house—that one must ask in order to know. I remembered my father's sayings from the Bible: ask and ye shall receive; knock and it shall be opened to you.

I closed the door and returned to bed. I listened intently to wind and rain, and they began to stir my senses. I would have liked for the moaning of the wind to be louder; I would have liked for the rain to drum more furiously. I wanted to be closer to those living elements.

If one were up in the lantern room now, would not one be truly in the midst of nature's storm? The lantern itself would be an awesome power. I wondered if my friend—whichever one—had reached the top. Probably he climbed with his hand on the stone wall to guide him up. It was always dim in the tower, and the night outside would be as black against those windows as against my own. Had the figure carried a candle? I had seen his hands holding only the quilt about him.

Was it Giles or Kit? I rummaged my mind to know what reasons could compel either of them to make that dark ascent, but no reason came to mind. If I climbed to the top, which of them would I *rather* see? Again, I found no answer in me, just a puzzlement at the question. But one of them was climbing the tower and one lay sleeping by the fire, and it ought to make a difference.

It would be startling to find out which one it was. What a strange moment, I thought, when possibility changes to certainty. I realized that my life itself was then all a matter of possibility. Who knew where I would go next or with whom, or whom I would meet? Yet some one thing would happen and not another. Did it mean that things were predestined, as my father thought? I could not accept that, for all seemed free and open to me, with only my own mind to consult as to what I hoped or chose.

Yet I did not know what I hoped or whom I would choose, and suppose one chose but was not chosen back? A deep shame rolled through me at the thought of that. To be unworthy! Not to be chosen! Perhaps one should not hope or want or plan at all.

With that, I sat up and swung my feet over the bedside and determined to find out simply who it was who chose to climb the tower. I was in my nightgown, so I took a quilt from my bed to wrap in, but not the precious one from Kentucky. I passed six feet from the form at the fireplace. I could stop and stoop and look, but suppose he, whoever he was, awoke suddenly to find me peering in his face? And besides, the blood of the storm was in me now, and I wanted to be in it.

On the table, Aunt had left Giles's drawings of angles and pulleys and lenses. The Fresnel lens looked like an anatomical drawing of a huge gem, a layering of facets. Giles had said that the cavity at its center was large enough for me to stand in. It seemed that my heart was a hard little diamond, sharp and curious, standing in the center of me.

The window at the end of the table framed perfect black. I wanted the darkness to clap its hands. And yes, there *was* a low growl of thunder. I opened the door in the wall, stepped through, and closed the door, carefully, behind me.

The utter blackness of the tower! Here there was no sense of form at all. Perhaps there was a curving wall only an arm's length away, but my eyes could not tell me this. The wall might be a mile beyond my reach, there might be no wall at all. Only my feet knew. What they touched was familiar stone, smooth and hard, but even the existence of my feet became for my eyes an act of faith, for I could not see toes or ankles or any part of them. Perhaps I had entered a land where I had no body. Yet my feet felt the stone. My legs, calf and thighs, bent and pushed, lifted me, just as they had in daylight. Though I could not measure my progress with my eyes, I was climbing. The ordinary muscles worked, and I rose, but it was like a dream of flying.

Suppose, I thought, he has stopped someplace along the steps and I bump against him in the dark. He cannot hear me coming. He might think me a demon and wrestle me, hurl me down the steps. And I thought how horribly I had been startled by the sudden being of the eagle. If I was thrown down the steps, as God cast Lucifer out of heaven, I would bruise in a most palpable and purple way. My body cringed at the thought of a descent in stony darkness. Better to have fallen through the daylight and air. My hip hurt where the railing had caught me.

Now the steps were iron, not stone. Metal would scrape and gash as much as bruise. I could have touched the wall as a guide—I had imagined him doing that—but I wanted to trust my legs, let them be the leaders instead of fingertip and touch. And partly, I loved the nothingness. Kit had said that his heart was black—was this what he meant? A blackness like nothingness?

Then there was a sheet of lightning, and I saw that I was in the middle of the ascent, the portion of the Lighthouse between the windows. For a garish moment, all was familiar, though there was a strange gloominess to the stone walls and the grillwork. In the cities, people moved through the streets—perhaps they were doing it now—but they were as unknown to me as I to them. I tried to think of a girl, sixteen, like myself, a resident of Boston. I pictured her: in a shoulder cape; her shoes fit well, beautifully buttoned and snug above her ankle. Her hands were in a muff, a velvet muff, and they held each other. With my left hand, I touched the scab across the back of my hand. My toes were naked and cold.

The moment I saw one of them, it would seem that I had known forever. In a sense, my life would be changed, for I could not return to a moment on a stormy night, in the summer when we changed the Lighthouse light, when two ideas were equally possible.

Yet one visitor was above and one was below, and what difference did that make? In a moment I would talk with one, and tomorrow I would chat with the other. They were both available for conversation.

As I ascended the tower, I began to climb into vague light. Whoever was in the lantern room had left the iron door open, and light was spilling down the stairs. At first it was only a haze, and then as I climbed higher, ever brighter. The light seemed to fill my ears and the sounds of the storm were muffled. Surely if there was a heaven, one might ascend just this way toward incredible brightness. I no longer thought of my feet or of my body; I myself seemed as vaporous as light. I had left weight with the earth, and I had stepped from corporeal being to that of spirit.

The figure stood opposite the door. His arms were outspread as though he were a priest or a bird such as a condor. He was spitting on the lamps! It was Kit. The room was a world of light, but at that moment, lightning struck the rod atop and split down the grounding wire on the outside behind Kit so that it seemed to strike his head, and I shrieked as I have never shrieked.

Blinded, I felt him enfold me, and I knew he was alive.

"We're safe," he said. He loosed me.

The optics in my brain were swimming in dazzle. "I can't see," I said, in a shaky voice.

"Wait."

My eyesight gone, my hearing returned to the boom of thunder and the roar of wind.

"We're safe here," he said again.

"I know," I said, for Uncle had explained to me, when I asked, the function of the lightning rod and the wire bradded down the length of the tower. Nonetheless, I could neither see nor stop my quaking.

"My eyes are seared!" I began to cry.

"Is it bright or dark?" he asked.

"Bright! Nothing but bright!"

He held me again while I sobbed for my eyes. The brightness was all swimming and wild.

"Can you see?" I wailed.

"Not well, yet. But my eyes were closed when it passed. My back was turned." Then he told me that he believed my eyes would be all right and to calm myself if I could. "Smell," he said. "There's an odor that lightning leaves."

"My father says it's the odor of the devil."

"Why not the odor of God?" Kit asked.

I breathed it deeply, for I knew it would soon be gone.

"Have you seen the footprint of the whale from up here?" Kit asked.

"No."

"Do you know about that?"

"No."

"Let's sit down," he said. And we slid down, he with his arm still about me. A greater comfort than his unfamiliar arm was the wall I had so often sat against. The thunder clapped and rumbled away from us.

"Was there lightning again?" I asked.

"Nothing much."

"I couldn't see it."

"You have to wait, Una."

We sat quietly. I told myself it was not Kit's fault. I told myself that surely all would be well with my eyes. Yet I could not see. Still, the world did not seem absent, because I could hear the storm, and its sounds conjured up images to my mind's eye. Just as when a person reads aloud to you, you see the world suggested by the words, so did the elements read aloud to me.

At length, I wished to hear Kit's voice. I asked why he was silent, and at once I knew that he did not wish to intrude on my adjusting. What a strangely tactful man! It seemed almost a reverence for my experiencing. And so he seemed to treat everyone. I had but to speak, and he would speak back to me.

"What is the whale's footprint?" I asked.

"I've sailed only merchant ships—though I'd like to go whaling— but once a whale came to the surface close to us, when there was a whaleman aboard. He and I stood at the deck together and watched. The blowhole is as big as your waist. These were humpbacks, neither sperm nor right whale, such as are hunted, but still the whaleman wished he had a harpoon. I tossed a penny to see if I could ring the blowhole, but I missed, and the penny slid off its back into the water, and, right away, the whale submerged. When it went down, the whale-man pointed to a patch of water that had a shape rather like the print of an enormous shoe. 'It's the whale's footprint,' he said. We watched the print move along the surface of the water. The print just glided along, a patch with a different surface and a distinct form. Gradually the margins of the form gave way, and the footprint slowly dissolved into the greater ocean."

If I were blind, yet if people talked to me as Kit did, then yet would I see. But I thought of myself groping along. I could perhaps memorize the Island but not the world. Still, I had not been unhappy on the Island. Almost it was enough, I told myself. But then such an urge to travel independently came upon me that the sentence burst out, "I should like to go whaling!"

"Why not?" Kit answered. "You could dress as a boy."

"You could go with Kit and me," another voice said.

"Giles!" I had known who spoke! "Giles, I can't see!"

"The lightning blinded her."

"And you?" Giles asked.

"I can see fairly well. There's a spot in the center of my vision. I didn't see you till you spoke."

"I see nothing but brightness," I said.

"It's the afterimage," Giles said.

"Should we go down?" Kit asked.

Giles said that he and Kit would guide me down the stairs. And he thought my sight would gradually return. He asked us why we had gone up in the Lighthouse.

"I followed Kit," I said.

"I wanted to be in the storm," Kit said.

"Why were you spitting on the lamps?" I asked Kit.

He laughed, but his explanation was brief: "An experiment."

The descent was careful. I trusted my guides, and the steps were familiar, but still I was afraid. I made myself trust in a mechanical way, and my brain seemed to go numb with it. Was this brightness any more blinding than the darkness through which I had ascended? Yes, for now I had the sense of injury. They held me under the elbow, on each side—Kit with a consistent firmness, Giles as though he were sometimes uncertain of the propriety of holding on to me.

At first my body held back from stepping: I wanted to run my foot to the edge of the tread and feel down with my toes before I trusted my weight. But gradually, I did become more confident and trusting. When I judged us to be halfway down, I proposed that we run the rest of the way.

"We can't see either," Giles reminded me, "in this darkness."

"Then I'll lead you both," I proposed. "The blind leading the blind."

"No," Giles said simply.

I could hear Giles's feet, for he had put on his shoes, and I could hear the low swish of Kit's fingertips along the stone wall, as he was on the outside of our turning.

"Do you know the seashell called the precious wentletrap?" Giles asked. "Its name in German is *Wendeltrappe,* which means 'spiral staircase.' "

"Do you know German?" I asked.

"No. But I would like to."

"Why?" Kit asked. His short question sounded cramped, clenched.

"To read *Faust,* in the original."

"I don't know about *Faust,*" I admitted bravely. Where there should have been darkness against my eyes, my mind was filled with the blinding brightness.

"Goethe's *Faust.*"

When Kit asked Giles why he had an interest in that story, Giles explained that there had been a medieval version of the same folktale, and many other versions as well. "It cautions against intellectual pride."

We continued our descent in silence, till I asked Giles why he had gone up in the tower.

"To find you two," he answered.

Then I felt happy, and I wondered if it would be possible to leave the Island with them. I could go in disguise. When my bare foot felt the first of the sixteen stone steps, I was sorry. I wanted us to go on together forever, even if I could not see.

CHAPTER 16   🐚   The Brightness of Brightness

Unending brightness! Surely at the point when I passed from the tower into the familiar chamber, colors would return—at least, the customary dimness in the corners of the room? the small glowing lump in the middle of the hearth? At least, when I passed through that room, guided by Giles and Kit, into my bedroom, then I would cross a border into the ordinary? Here, in my bedroom, would reside a familiar darkness? But it was not so. My mind swam in brightness.

Kit asked me if I should like my aunt to be awakened. I felt my bed bump against my legs and groped my way under the covers. No, I told him; I would wait for morning. Perhaps by morning there would be nothing to confess. I did not want my aunt to know that I and our guests had walked about together in the night. How quickly her critical glance had shot out at Kit when he told Frannie of his mother's defilement of the bread dough.

"Good night," they told me.

I pulled the quilt up under my chin and fervently hoped for morning and for the world to reappear to my eyes even as it was already reappearing for Kit. But his eyes had been closed, his back turned away from the lightning bolt, and I had looked at it straight. I listened for Frannie's gentle breathing, and there it was. I pictured her curled away from me, her face to the rock of the chimney. I thought of Aunt and Uncle up in their attic above the big room. Such a private room they had—I had been in it only a few times during my four years on the Island. Did the odor of the roses on the shingles above Aunt and Uncle visit them as they lay in bed? In the summer, were their dreams rose-scented? The rain droned on, and I thought of it tearing off petals from the flowers. But all in my mind was veiled in brightness.

What is the brightness of brightness? A sizzle of the nerves? At first it had seemed a scalding of the sense of sight, but now there was no more sense of seeing anything. It was as though the imprint of brightness was directly in my brain. I did not see it. I dwelt in brightness.

When I was a small child, I had asked my father to describe heaven, and he had said it was eternal light. There, there was no more pain and no more death; he had lifted his eyes as though they were focused on an invisible realm. With my brightness, there was no pain. Was this brightness but a forerunner of the eternal light of heaven? Was not bliss an implied component of that brightness? My world—not bliss—was very much with me; still, I could die into brightness. For Father's heaven, there was the counterbalance of eternal darkness, of hell. This brightness was absolute.

The contours of my universe were altered. It was as though I lived in a star. Or a star had come to fill me.

How could I, Una, become blind? What trajectory intended for me, determined by me, could include the subtracting of sight from the sense of me? It was as though I were climbing the tower but instead of the reliable next step, I stepped into nothingness.

All the underbelly of my soul seemed falling, plunging down an abyss whose limit I had not yet found. I shrieked as I fell. The noise of the storm outside seemed distant and muffled. Would something in me scream all my life if I was forever cursed with this blinding brightness?

I heard a step in the room. And Kit's voice saying quietly, "Una?"

"Kit?" I whispered.

"You're not asleep?" he asked.

I felt him sit on the edge of the bed, and I reached my hand toward him. His clothing was wet.

"I went outside," he explained. "I wanted to make some clay."

I had no understanding of what he wanted, but I was glad he was with me. Clay? He began to speak again—gently, coaxingly, but with some strange and steely imperative.

"When Jesus made the blind to see, he spat on the ground. He reached down and took up the clay and mixed it with his spittle into a paste." He paused, then said, "Feel what I have," and he took my fingers and put them in the cup of his hand. Kit had brought in mud.

"The paste he used to anoint the eyes of the afflicted."

The scream within me turned to ice. As calmly as I could, I said, "I do not believe in miracles. Nor in Jesus." I felt afraid for Kit. Did he hope to work a miracle?

"Probably some of the miracles happened," he said with unusual intensity. "Or some form of them. Would people make things up out of absolutely nothing? Maybe there was a healing element within the clay. Maybe it could be widespread as dirt itself, and we but have to reach down to the earth and take what she offers us."

"Kit?" Frannie's little voice spoke. "Kit, is it you?"

"Don't be afraid," he said.

"I'm not afraid," she answered. "Are you awake, too, Una?"

"The lightning hurt her eyes. She can't see."

"Una?" Her voice swooped up in alarm. "Una, you can't see?"

"My sight will come back," I said.

She rushed to me and flung herself on me, her arms around me, softly calling my name.

"I think it will be all right," Kit said. He told her how his own vision had returned. "I was going to put some mud on her eyes, to speed their healing."

"Your clothes are wet," she said.

"That doesn't matter," he said evenly.

"I want to wait, Kit," I said.

Kit stood up and walked to the door. "Good night," he said. His voice was stiff.

"Can I get in with you?" Frannie asked me, as soon as Kit left.

She slid in beside me, and, cuddled together, we both fell asleep.

IN THE MORNING, I woke to a visibly returning world. First there was a rim of movement around a central blankness. When color became discernible in patches around the rim, I felt a bit reassured.

I said no more to Aunt and Uncle than that the lightning had blinded me. Uncle said that he had heard the bolt come down the tower to the ground. They were both full of tender concern for me. Uncle said he had known a sailor who had been temporarily blinded in a lightning storm off the coast of New Zealand.

Of climbing the tower, of seeking the company of one of our visitors, I said nothing. Even deeper in my heart, I buried the idea that Kit had gone out into the rainstorm, found some muddy place, and gathered the mud into the palm of his hand, with the intent of healing me. Had spoken of Jesus and miracles. I asked Aunt if she thought any sort of poultice would help my eyes.

She suggested that we protect them with a thin cloth, that we let the light back in only gradually. So that day, I lay much of the time with a double thickness of cheesecloth over my face. Giles visited me briefly and explained that he and Kit would be taking measurements of the space in the lantern house, and of the stairwell, and of the tower itself, to see what lengths of ropes and beams and pulleys they would need if the new lens was hoisted up rather than carried up. He said he would come and read to me, if he had time, and we agreed on Wordsworth. But the day passed without his return.

Kit also visited, and he spoke cheerfully for a time, but then he said, "We have not brought you luck, Una."

"I think I am lucky to know you both," I said.

"Your life was more peaceful before we came."

"I could die of peacefulness."

"I used to wonder what it would be like to grow up with very few other people, no society. One of the things I admire about all of you is your contentment."

"What do you like about content?"

"I have so little of it."

"Giles, too?"

"We're very different."

As I lay under the cheesecloth, I asked myself if this was true. I could not tell. They both seemed wondrous to me, and that wonder was like the brightness. Within it, there were no distinctions. On my bedsheet, my fingertips felt a crust of dried mud, and I picked at it and flaked it, and brushed it away. Then I asked Frannie to bring me a damp cloth so that I might clean my fingers.

By dusk, I could see in a broader circle around a bull's-eye of blindness. It seemed like an unwanted sun masking the humans who were dear to me. When I tried to look into a face, there was only abstract brightness, but if they raised their arms and hands to gesture, I could see that my bright spot had human appendages.

Kit said that the phenomenon had been the same for him, but more short-lived. "I wanted it to last longer," he said, and I asked him why. "People are always composed of a combination of the real and the abstract," he said. "We make each other up."

I WAS NOT SICK, but there was a weakness about me, and a timidity. I moved as though I were recovering from an illness. Uncertainty seemed to me a kind of illness, and I felt as though I wanted special food to strengthen me. Aunt was wonderfully sensitive to this and asked me what I would enjoy eating, and I asked for rose-hip jelly on toast. My mother had made jelly from calves' hooves, which I did not like, but Aunt's jelly seemed to bring to me all the clear goodness of the sun and the rooftop roses.

For supper, I particularly enjoyed a mess of herring fish. Every person at the table picked out the tiny bones of a herring for me, since my sight would not permit such fine work, and I enjoyed the flavor and meat of the fish without any of the tedious labor. Then Giles brought out a sack of pecans that someone in Alabama had sent, and the adults separated the meat of the nut from the pith for Frannie as well as for me, Aunt saying that the pith was so bitter it would turn your mouth inside out. Though I could not see it, she placed the nut-meat in my hand to feel and told me that some people thought that pecans nourished the brain, because half a pecan resembled the human brain.

"And some people believe," Kit put in, "that if you eat cucumbers, your nose will grow long. Or other parts."

"What parts?" Frannie asked.

"Your feet," Aunt said. Then she asked Giles when the measurements and plans would be complete.

Giles said they would stay but one more day and leave the next morning, if the weather held.

"Then I'll certainly bake the famous rolls in the morning," Kit said. "If I may."

"I want to help," Frannie said.

"And I'll help, too," Aunt said.

But I had no fondness for cooking and merely looked forward to the eating.

After the lanterns were lit in the Lighthouse, Giles read from Wordsworth, "It is a beauteous evening, calm and free," and the image of the narrator standing above the great city of London came before us. How the speaker looked down on all the buildings and all the life that they contained and felt a kind of love and awe for our lives and our multitudinousness.

My own response included the thought that should my eyesight not have returned, never would I have seen for myself such an expanse of city. Yet, again, I thought how the mind's eye sees, and if it was as Kit said that halfway we make up what we see, then already, through the words of Wordsworth, I was seeing.

Then Giles read the poem about the daffodils that begins "I wandered lonely as a cloud" and how, suddenly, the poet came upon "a crowd, a host, of golden daffodils," which were "tossing their heads in sprightly dance." The sight became a mental treasure for Wordsworth, to which he could return in memory, and when he did, then his heart once again, Giles read, "dances with the daffodils." I thought how the two poems fit together—one of the city with compassion for humanity and our composite creation, and the other about the beauty of nature and one's individual joy of it.

Giles read in such a manner as to increase my understanding of the poems. It was as though with his own mind, his tempo, and where he made the emphasis fall he presented the lines with more clarity than they might have had in themselves. The cadence of his voice curved the thought of the poem, and we were enriched by Giles's interpretation as well as by the words composed by Wordsworth. Then he read "Tintern Abbey."

I had always felt kin to Dorothy, Wordsworth's sister, who often accompanied him on his rambles through the English countryside, who relished the wildness of nature, its "dizzy rapture." But there was a phrase in the poem that I had overlooked before. The line put me in mind of Kit's theory—Wordsworth said that nature was half created, half perceived. I glanced at Kit, but his body made no movement of recognition. It was as though, for Kit, the idea had only his own particular twist to it, and if the twist was not there, he did not recognize it as a kindred thought. Or so I read his stillness. I could not yet see his face.

Were many people in the world cut from the same cloth as Kit and Giles? I wondered. Were there many men like Giles with such a gentleness and wide learning about them and who were yet sailors? Or those like Kit, with such a strange originality to their minds that they left mine reeling? There was a kind of dizzy rapture for me in talking with Kit. With Giles, his thought was not so much original as deep and complete; I did not think many people could know so much about such different things—certainly not I. But I thought I knew how Giles felt.

I AWOKE in the morning to the odor of yeast rolls and baking pecans, and for breakfast we indulged ourselves in such tender bread, such tasty buttered nuts lodged between the turns of the spiral, such a caramelized sweetness crowning the rolls, that no one could thank Kit enough.

The bright blank spot in my vision had shrunk to the size of a nose. People had their ears again and their cheeks and the outer corners of their eyes, and only in the center of their faces a candle seemed to burn. The colors of the world delighted my looking as much as the sweet rolls delighted my eating. The simple colors I knew with their names and incarnations—the pink of the roses; the yellow crown at their center; the white, wiry hair of the goats; the cerulean, azure, and periwinkle blue of the sky; and the green and white of the ocean rolling in and breaking on our shore—delighted me. The hues that have no name even more charmed my eyes. I saw tones of gray, when a cheek was in shadow, or tones of yellow, or pink at the flanges of the nose; I noted the way the violet of my aunt's blouse reflected under her chin. The many colors in our food spoke to me with joyful voices. It was as though there were landscape and vista enough to have pleased a Wordsworth in a spoonful of vegetable soup or in the stretched tent of shiny, whitish skin over a bent knuckle.

I did not want to miss any conversation I might have with our visitors, yet I wanted even more to reclaim my Island, my world, to my sight. Not from the lofty height of the tower, but close to things. Antlike, I wanted to travel our paths, to look long and hard at the design of Queen Anne's lace, the long spurs of columbine. Even the yellow cap of a dandelion delighted me, and how there was something greeny in its yellow. The beach was littered with mussels, and I loved the bruised blue and the ridges of their shells. When I heard a sound, I wanted to look directly at whatever thing it was that caused that sound and know its color. The light poured over the world like honey, and I wanted to see the breeze as well as feel it. I watched the tiny hairs on my forearm ripple like the sea grass. Whenever a wave withdrew, the million bubbles left behind, sinking rapidly into sand, tickled the corners of my eyes with iridescence.

I would store it all up; I would reclaim it if I ever was blind. As I looked, I planned that in my bed, that very night, I would remember these colors and shapes, the distinctiveness of every part of nature. Then I would rejoice again, like Wordsworth, with "that inward eye, which is the bliss of solitude." I was full of love for all that I saw.

THEIR LAST NIGHT with us, Giles read many parts of Coleridge's "Rime of the Ancient Mariner." I had more taste for it than Frannie, who said, after a while, that she felt too sleepy to stay up. All day she had followed Kit at every step, even up to the first window in the tower, where she stopped and waited for someone to come back down. Even though she truncated her journey up, being afraid of the height, her legs and lungs were not used to climbing the tower. "Feel how hard my heart is beating"—she had come to me down on the beach after one of her descents and placed my hand on her delicate chest.

Uncle and Aunt retired as Frannie did, and Kit decided to go out and look at the stars, so only Giles and I were left before the fire. Some of Coleridge's lines, though solemn in their intention, seemed funny to me in their rhyming: "Water, water, everywhere,/And all the boards did shrink,/Water, water, everywhere,/Nor any drop to drink."

When I giggled, Giles asked me solemnly if I thought I could endure the guilt of the Mariner.

"His crime seems so symbolic," I answered. "Shooting a bird with a crossbow."

"Yes, it is a crossbow." Giles's lovely blue eyes gazed at mine. He had *speaking eyes,* as my aunt said, yet I could not discern the meaning of his emphasis. "He could have decided to *die* for the crime."

When I responded, I tried to match Giles's tone, for I felt that the issue was important to him. "His *telling* about it, the *way* he tells, seems like expiation to me."

"I suppose." Giles did not quite agree.

He continued to read, tucking in the overly obvious rimes so that they were less humorous. At length, Giles said, "I think that's enough, Una, even for us."

"But Kit hasn't come back." I looked at the mantel clock. How relentlessly the pendulum disk swept back and forth!

"He's probably communing with the spirits of darkness."

To my surprise, Giles held out his hand to me. When I took it, very happy, he squeezed my fingers and, at the distance of both our outstretched arms, smiled at me.

"Don't worry. I'll go look for him."

AS I PUT ON my nightgown, my fingers tingling, it was as though all the million beach bubbles were inside me, evanescing.

But I dreamed that as I gazed out my window, Kit's face, like a disturbing full moon, rose in the darkness. I reached out, first with my right hand and then, strangely, with my left, and the moon became a circular pendulum such as wagged in our mantel clock. Held awkwardly in my hand, the pendulum had a sinister weight, heavy beyond expectation.

CHAPTER 17   A Rose

WHEN I AWOKE, my back turned to the window, and my eyes registering the gray stones of the backside of the fireplace and chimney, I thought of the sentence I must say to Giles before he left: *I hope that you are an indefatigable letter-writer.* Thus he would know that I wanted my mind forever to be in contact with his. Thus he would see that I put no undue claim upon his physical presence—only letters; thus he would know that my own appetite for exchange could not be exhausted.

When I said my sentence, as Giles and I stood beside the cascade of roses on the roof and side of the cottage, my heart fluttering, he corrected my pronunciation: indeFATigable. But he smiled.

I blushed, but smiled, too, to think that I was admitted to the brotherhood of honesty that existed between him and Kit. *We* need not stand on any ceremonies of courtesy.

Giles went on to say he would write to me, but it would probably be only Kit who would return with the crew for mounting the Fresnel. I did not know why he would not return, and I felt that I could not ask him why—that question would cross some unspoken boundary having on one side the freedom to say anything and on the other the restriction of an extraordinary respect for privacy, an extreme of trust. Giles said that if he could not be with us, he hoped Kit and I would talk often and enjoy each other's company, for him.

This last seemed an odd request to me. But I dipped my head in acquiescence—just the way I have seen a thousand terns dip their heads under the water to catch small fish.

"Shall I pick a rose for you, Una?" He said it as though amused at himself, but wanting to please me.

"I'd like that."

Quickly he touched one or two, discriminating among them, then pronounced, "This one will do. Not too perfect for earthly use." He snapped the slender green stem and handed it to me. Despite words that seemed determinedly unromantic, his eyes were as innocent and tender as the sky. Later I would put fresh water in a seashell and keep the rose on my windowsill. When the pink browned and fell, I saved the petals in a loose heap in the corner of my drawer, and when I left the Island, I folded them in a piece of paper to take with me.

The *Petrel* before us ready to sail, all of us stood on the dock in the sunshine for a last good-bye. Aunt shook hands with Kit and thanked him again for the wonderful rolls, but Giles she hugged. Uncle, his hair blazing in the sunlight, was a tower of goodwill to all. He was taller than anybody. Frannie hid her hands under her apron to squeeze and wring them.

When they jumped into the boat, Kit turned and said his final adieu: "Farewell, Fran."

"Come back soon. Come back soon," she said, wringing her hands. I could tell that she wanted to jump up and down, as was her usual childish way of saying both hello and good-bye, but she restrained herself, wanting to be taken for more dignified than a mere age eight.

After they had cast off and sailed nearly to the horizon, I turned to Frannie and asked if she wanted to climb to the top of the Lighthouse and see them again.

"Yes!" she said, though Frannie had never completely mounted the air before.

We had to stop so many times in the ascent, for her to catch her breath, that I was afraid they would have sailed beyond even the vantage point of the Lighthouse. "Hurry, hurry," I urged her, and she tried her best. At the higher of the slit windows, I had her stop and look out, and we did see them, sailing quickly toward the horizon. The sight revitalized Frannie's feet, and we scampered up the rest of the way like two squirrels spiraling up a tree. Frannie would not go out on the grillwork, but we could see them well from behind the glass.

I wondered if they knew that we yet watched them. Frannie slowly waved her hand and said aloud, "Farewell, Kit; good-bye, Giles."

It looked as though they sailed off the edge of the world.

Before we left the lantern room, Frannie first took my hand and then said solemnly, "I'd like to be called Fran, now."

"But I love you as Frannie," I protested.

She smiled her full childish smile at me, for the first time since her illness, and said, ready to please and accommodate, "Then I'm still Frannie."

She herself looked pleased and comforted.

CHAPTER 18   ✦   Our Lady of the Rocks

ON THE TOP FLAT ROCK of the natural boulder steps Frannie and I made a calendar of stones, seven in a line to count the days and weeks till Kit and the workmen returned. I wondered if we should keep two calendars, since, after all, we were separate people, but Frannie wanted the companionship of keeping the same calendar. We agreed that we would take turns selecting the stones. They were mostly dark gray ovals with some sparkle to the surface, and they were about the size of Uncle's pocket watch.

From her small chest of books—so like my mother's—Aunt left a new book on the settle beside the fireplace. As was her wont, she did not suggest I read it, but I understood that I might if I wished. It was a novel titled *Robinson Crusoe,* and I soon saw why she might think it appropriate for me to read. Poor Robinson was marooned on an island with no one to talk to except his parrot and his man Friday. Yet he was ingenious with provisions for his convenience and safety, and I knew the suggestion was that I, too, should be ingenious in filling my time. We had not been told any definite span of days, though four weeks was the absence mentioned to Fran by Kit. Sometimes I now thought of her as Fran.

About six weeks into our vigil, Aunt suddenly told me that the next day she wanted to take a walk with me to the far part of the Island. She said we would take a picnic basket and make our lunch there and that Frannie would stay with her father. This seemed unusual to me, and I realized that was just the point. Kind Aunt was trying to introduce some variety into the monotony of my days. She had told me a day ahead of time so that I might have it to look forward to. And it was a definite appointment. After she spoke to me, she commenced baking the dark rye bread I like so well, pumpernickel flavored with molasses. She sent me to the garden with the instruction to pick the two prettiest of any vegetable that I would like to eat raw the next day, and I picked two small cucumbers and two bell peppers. Of course I could not see into the ground before pulling two carrots, but I picked the two with the most luxuriant ferny tops.

WE STARTED our walk in the morning ceremoniously, with Uncle and Frannie standing together at the door of the cottage, holding hands and waving to us. Aunt carried the picnic basket, and she had made up a bundle of sewing work and knitting for us. Good work during digestion, she said. The bundle was wrapped in a tablecloth, and this pouch was suspended from the end of a stick which I was to carry over my shoulder. In her skirt pocket, Aunt brought along a copy of Bunyan's *Pilgrim's Progress* for us to read aloud; she said it taught virtues that transcended its theology. My bundle on the stick and her basket, she said merrily, would make us feel the more like pilgrims journeying on the path of life.

I thought it quaint of her, and she did seem particularly girlish. Perhaps I was passing into the realm of adulthood where Aunt, more than Frannie, would be my natural playmate.

Our destination was a sort of rocky cave or grotto at the foot of the high cliff. It was a place quite close to home, as the mole burrows, for all one had to do was climb the hill behind the Lighthouse, and then go straight down a hundred feet! Rather than accomplish this precipitously, we would walk over the gentler hump of the Island and gradually work our way halfway around the Island, closer and closer to the water.

Our entourage included at first the goats, but we both knew they would tire of us at some point and pursue their own goatish curiosity or appetite. Apron, all grown up, was among their number, and for the first time, she was going to have kids of her own. She had hidden the first year the *Camel* had brought over a special breeding billy, and the next year she had not "taken" from that goat or from our resident Billy Liberal.

It was a lovely-feeling day. The warmth of the sun penetrated the cloth of my dress on my back; our forearms were bare and we wore straw hats like fishermen. We exclaimed at what we saw—a ruby-throated hummingbird drinking five times from the compartments of a columbine; a cluster of tiger swallowtail butterflies on a patch of goat manure. Some of the seeds of the grass heads were ripe, and there was the faint odor of baking in the air. My feet crunched on the grass.

When I was ten, my mother and I had walked through the woods, once, to a mossy boulder to have a picnic. We had had the pumpernickel bread, too. Probably the sisters had cooked from the same recipe, but because we had several beef cattle, the main fare for Mother and me in Kentucky had been thick slices of roast beef flavored with wild garlic. Aunt and I carried no beef in the bottom of our basket but two bowls of herring and hard-boiled eggs soaked in vinegar and thin slices of onion. In Kentucky there had been much shadow in the sheltering woods, and here, on the exposed Big Meadow, there was much light.

I wondered if my mother was lonely. Why was it that they had never sent for me to come home? My father had been willing to visit me in New Bedford. Whenever the supply boat came or we went to the mainland, there were letters from Mother, and Father often wrote me a few lines. Sometimes he quoted a bit of scripture. The gulf between my father and me had been partially traversed, during our visit together when I was fourteen, but since then our spirits had not progressed much toward one another. In his brief letters—mine, too, were brief—he always told me to mind my aunt and uncle and be dutiful. He had no idea of what it was to live on the Island. There was scarcely any idea of dutifulness here. Everyone was simply kind. If we had a duty, it was only to make each other happier, to provide our daily needs and, for Uncle, to care for the light.

I glanced back over my shoulder and saw just the head of the light, for now the terrain was starting to slope downward, and here was the first of the little cedar trees that stood up like green bottle brushes. The aroma of cedar always reminds me of books, for Uncle had fashioned the chest for Aunt's library out of the wood of one of these trees that had blown over in a storm. He never cut the trees down, saying their roots helped to keep the Island from being washed down into the sea. The wood we burned was driftwood, and, of course, the lumps of coal and cords of wood that were part of the lighthouse keeper's allotment from the government.

Now Aunt pointed out another tree that lay on its side, the jagged stump with its red heartwood still rooted among the small rocks.

"We must tell Torchy," she said. "Perhaps he will make you a chest, after the wood cures."

"But I don't own a single book."

"Some girls keep their embroidered pillowcases and their knitted lace in chests, apart from the family's goods."

"Why?"

"To take with them when they marry."

Marriage—what a strange and thrilling word. Not at all like the pairs of crowned columns in King's Chapel, Boston. Not now. The color of our picnic modulated. It had been the pure yellow found next to the black in a tiger swallowtail's wing; it became the red of cedar heartwood, something gashed.

"How long does it take the wood to cure?" I found myself asking.

"About a year." She picked up a red splinter and held it to her nose. "It is sooo aromatic," she said, and sounded like Frannie taking her delight.

What would it be like to have a daughter with one's own delight, or skin, or mind? I remembered Frannie, when she was five, sitting in the wooden tub—also fashioned from staves of cedar—before the hearth. I was unfolding a piece of sheeting to warm at the fire before drying her. She was sturdy then, neither plump nor thin. As I was turning my back to her to spread the sheet to the warmth, she spoke. "I love you, Una," she chirped, as she often had before. As always, I told her that I loved her, too. "No," she said, "this is different this time." I turned and asked, a little amused, "How is it different?" She answered, "I love the way you think." I swooped down and kissed her damp cheek. It was not Frannie who was naked before me, but I, accepted and naked, before her.

Could my own child ever surprise and know me so well as Frannie?

"Aunt," I asked, "is Frannie quite well now?"

"Yes," she answered. She smiled at me with full confidence both in the fact and in her knowledge of it. "I am sure of it. We do not need to fear losing her, Una."

I nodded.

"And your eyes? Do you see perfectly well now?"

"Yes."

"It is the same with Frannie. Feel assured. As you came close to blindness, but escaped, so she came close to death and escaped."

Strange to say, I shuddered. Aunt looked curiously at me. I remembered the uncertainty I had felt as my eyesight returned. It seemed to me that perhaps Aunt was wrong in her certainty, though I liked it quite well. Perhaps between sickness nigh-to-death and health lay the region of vulnerability, and perhaps Frannie was in it. Perhaps I, too, was in it. Perhaps Vulnerability was a land that, for some people, could never be entirely traversed.

"Let's go on to the plum grove," she suggested.

On a terrace of particularly fertile soil (washed down from the slope where the cedars gripped what was left of thin, rocky soil) grew six little plum trees, all weighted with fruit. *Ripe early, this year!* Aunt exclaimed. My palm hefted the sweet weight of a plum, relished its exotic purple skin. My teeth broached the tight plum skin into the warm, golden meat. Juice and flavor gushed into my mouth. I sealed my lips on the rupture, thought myself a bee, and sucked. I devoured the plum and all its globed delight of Now. Both Aunt and I picked another to carry along, and we ate our way down to the shore and tossed the pits into the sea.

I listened to the slurping of the surf and the screeching of gulls. Access to the sand was a mere step down at this point, but as we walked along, the bank on the right grew ever higher and steeper. Sometimes it was a reddish clay, sometimes cracked rocks faced the ocean. At the top of the embankment lay a thin line of dark soil from which rose blades of grasses, small against the sky. This was a forbidden area for Frannie and me, for one must know the ways of the tides to walk safely here. The margin of sand upon which we walked could be covered with water, and the bank too high to climb up. For knowledge of the tides, I trusted to Aunt. The bank on my right rose to thirty feet and then fifty and then beyond my easy calculating. The ocean curdled in a low, white froth beside us. Though my legs were strong, it requires different muscles from climbing ones to walk in sand: one could not run fast in sand, even if one needed to. Aunt stopped twice to rest before we reached the cave.

This was not a dark and dank cave. It was filled with sunlight and was very high and wide. It seemed big enough for a ship to sail into, and I said so to Aunt. She said that could never happen because there were many large and treacherous rocks under the water in front of the cave. Over time, great rocks and tons of soil had fallen out of the cliff face, and the cliff itself was always moving back. In two hundred years, Aunt said, the cliff would be so undercut by the waves that the Lighthouse itself would topple into the sea. But that was not now. Of course, we could not see the Lighthouse, but it delighted me to think that it was someplace not far away, standing tall above us on the cliff.

Thrusting up from the floor of the cave rose many pitted and sea-carved columns of stone. When the tide was high, it rushed in among these pillars and wore at their sides and tops so that they were polished as well as pitted. A few rocks were more flat and tablelike. Their surfaces sloped toward the sea, but they were flat enough to sit on. One of these was almost the color of an eggplant, a deep purple with black in the purple, and this was the one we chose for our picnic. A coolness came from the back of the cave, even though it was shallow, but the sun shone full on us when we faced the sea, and the water sparkled and glittered before us.

I asked Aunt how it was that she knew the cave so well, and she said that she and Torchy, when they were first married and newly moved to the Island, often came here.

"Before Frannie was born?" I asked.

"Oh, many years before Frannie." There was a shyness in her voice. "Like Apron Goat," she said, "I was beyond the usual time after marriage in conceiving."

I wanted to ask her how long, but it did not seem my place to inquire about something so private.

Unasked, she said, "I was eight years married before Frannie."

"Was it lonely for you and Uncle to live on the Island?"

"Not in the least. We talked from sunup till bedtime, and read to each other, and sang, and worked."

I thought bitterly that my father was probably no such companion to my mother. "Do you think that being on the Island helped to make you happy?"

"Often lighthouse keepers and their families are thought to be strange, because they are so much alone. Do you suppose we are, Una?"

"No," I said stoutly. Of this, I was sure. "I feel very normal and natural here."

"Normal may not be the same as natural."

"You don't want to leave?" I asked.

"Not at all," she said. "But you?"

I looked long at my dear aunt's soft face. Usually there was a vivacity about her that masked the softness, but lately there had been a touch of my mother about her. From the reflection on the sea, a greenish light quivered over us. Occasionally I had looked down from the fishing boat and seen a tuna hang unmoving in the water; so at that moment I felt suspended in that greenish light and in my uncertainty.

"Some of 'yes' and some of 'no'?" my aunt said for me.

I slid off the purple rock and walked among the fantastic formations, a forest of stone gnomes and dwarfs. When I walked to the edge of the cave, the rock cracked in a clean line and stepped into the sea in terraces.

"Where the waterline is now," Aunt said, "is a definite steep drop for many feet. When it covers the next step, we must leave, because it will also start to cover the beach."

I thought of the vicissitudes of time, of the early ripening of the plums. "How consistent is the timetable?" I asked, smiling.

"The tides keep a better clock than the seasons."

"Are we only a part of a great clockwork?" I asked.

"Usually that argument leads to belief in God," she said.

"How does it go?"

"Imagine a man walking on a beach. He finds a watch. It works in an intricate and perfect way. He asks himself if such a thing was made by accident. He answers that there cannot be a watch without a watchmaker. It is called the Argument from Design."

"But is our world really like a watch?" I asked.

"With such a question, so do all analogies fail," she said. "Come, let's eat."

The slippery white part, the dry yolk, the rinse of vinegar—is anything more delicious than that layered orb, a hard-boiled egg? And a carrot to munch, and the juice to chew out of a cucumber. I wanted more salt, and I stuck the cucumber into the sea before sucking it. Aunt asked me to so salt hers as well. I handed it back to her with a bow: "For My Lady of the Rocks."

Many years later, a learned lady in Boston, Margaret Fuller, invited me to her home—for conversation, she said—and showed all the women there, most very finely dressed, engravings of famous works of art. One was called *The Virgin of the Rocks*. Then I remembered my aunt and my presentation of a cucumber, and with the Boston women about me and the steelpoint engraving before me, I pictured my aunt's face, and I saw that her countenance had been no less beautiful than that of da Vinci's Mary.

How the mind flies forward and backward when writing, and forward again to Margaret Fuller's invitation to join her parlor gathering. I had been standing at a stall before the shop of a bookseller on Newbury Street when a strange woman stopped beside me, also to page the books. "You're reading Montaigne's *Essays*?" she noted. I replied, "I like the reality he assigns to thought." The sentence just slipped out; I hadn't known I thought it till I looked into her asking eyes. "Thus epic journeys are made," she answered, "in the mind." I nodded. "But we need to see new things," she went on, "to have new thoughts. This Tuesday, I will show a group of women pictures they may not have seen before. I invite you."

In that way, I came to see the static picture that now, in my telling, I have superimposed on that moving, eating, talking memory of my aunt and me picnicking, seated in a cathedral of a cave, steeped in the light reflected from the sea.

"I feel more chill than I thought I would," Aunt said. "I don't want to stay here to knit."

I was not reluctant to start back.

"Do you mistrust my sense of the tide?" Aunt asked.

"No, but I want a softer seat."

"We'll sit in the grass for a while. But first I want to show you something." She untied the bundle. Then she held up a square of knitting, sea-green and edged with a scallop of white, worked on tiny needles. "What is it?" she asked.

"A little blanket?"

"A blanket for a new baby." And she laid it over her stomach.

I am sure my mouth fell open, for Aunt laughed.

"In perhaps seven months, there will be a new baby."

I saw that she was happy, and I told her I was happy for her, but I was more full of surprise than happiness.

"Do you know how it is, Una, that a woman comes to be with child?"

I told her I had deduced something of it from the animals. As we walked back along the margin of sand, she told me I might ask her anything I was curious about in the ways of married folk. She talked anew of tides, those of our female body, and of the cave within.

THE NEXT DAY, Aunt took Frannie on a walk just to the plum trees, with a basket between them. When they came home, Frannie, seeing me in the garden, released her side of the handle and ran to me. She took both my hands and jumped up and down. "You know, you know, too, don't you, Una? Isn't it wonderful?"

Aunt sent her to get a piece of string and a wisp of yarn.

"Belt the string around me," she said, "where I'm biggest." Frannie circled her waist. "A little lower," Auntie instructed. "And, Una, tie tight the piece of yarn." I did so, pulling hard and making a square knot so that it wouldn't slide down the string. "Now," she said, "every week you can measure me to see how baby and I increase." And so, in addition to the lines of stones, Frannie and I had another calendar with which to mark the time.

CHAPTER 19

The Return of the *Petrel*,
with Three Letters

Sometimes when we look forward to an event with great and happy anticipation, the event itself may disappoint, or be in import so different from what we have expected that we can say the anticipated event did not occur at all but some other experience. When the *Petrel* returned, rather overloaded, Uncle said, bearing Kit, five workmen, and the Fresnel lens, all disassembled and packed in straw in crates of various sizes, it also transported two letters of much import from my mother.

The first of my mother's letters was a matter of joy. Like her sister (though unbeknownst to her in Kentucky), my mother wrote that she, too, was again with child. She was feeling well, though quickly tired and often sleepy. My aunt thought it was a marvel almost of frightening proportions that she and her sister were pregnant at the same time, expecting their babies, indeed, in the same month. Uncle put in that, after all, women all over the globe would be having babies on the same day and perhaps even at the same hour, minute, and second, though they commonly had no knowledge of their sisters also in labor. It seemed a pretty thought to me, one that made all the women of the world more kin to each other, whether really sisters or not.

Between Agatha and Bertha there was often a congruence: the sisters shared the same plum trees, the same recipe for pumpernickel bread, a love of Lord Byron. The very stitches in the quilts were so similar that one could start a seam and the other finish it, and no one could tell where the needle had been passed off. I myself had been passed, I thought ruefully, from one sister to the other, with no loss of nurturing. Well might they be pregnant at the same time. The simultaneity of their pregnancies seemed less surprising than the mere fact that my mother was with child.

It was our custom when several letters fell into our hands to open only one a day. We waited so long for news; this practice spread out the tidings and extended our pleasure. From Giles, Kit handed me but one letter. I was surprised—I had ten letters, one for each week, saved up to send back to the mainland—and wondered at first if Kit was teasing me. He smiled mischievously at me and said, "There is only one letter to be delivered, but he said also to give you this——" And with that, before everyone, he hugged me quickly.

Naturally we had opened the letter from my mother first, and the news was such a sunburst on our world that we basked in it for several hours. It was a sewing day for Aunt and Frannie and me, and we sat outside in the good light. The men were unloading the boat and stacking the crates in the big room near the tower door, so we had the diversion of watching them come and go. Gradually each of the five became distinctive in his shape and clothing and face. I was smocking the bodice piece for a little dress for Aunt's baby, and I thought happily that I would make its twin for my own little brother or sister. Occasionally, despite the glow from my mother's announcement and the pleasure there is in drawing up and puckering the fabric when smocking, and the interesting parade of five new people, the waiting letter from Giles would make my breath catch. And after a while, Aunt, being perhaps cognizant of my little gasps, said we would break the rule of a letter a day and I should go ahead and read my Giles letter. "Take it to your room, Una, and enjoy your letter."

I saw Kit, who happened to be passing with a tool for unfastening the old lens, look curiously at Aunt, and I wondered if he could tell that she was going to have a baby. Perhaps he had noticed that I was smocking a tiny garment. A blush rose in my cheeks.

What if he *had* written only one letter? A letter from Giles would be worth its weight in gold. I sat on the side of my bed, took a hairpin from my coil of braids, and slit the envelope. It was short, I saw with dismay—the front and back of a page, and only the front of the second sheet.

In his writing, there was a kind of clipped and precise quality, more so than in his speech, though Giles always seemed to choose words with care. I thought that there must be an abundance of feeling pressing against the restraint of his language. In some ways, his restraint was more enthralling to me than a franker expression of feeling might have been. He asked me had our parting rose withered and had I made dried-petal soup of it, as the Chinese were said to do with abandoned birds' nests!

I determined to write back that I had (yet it was not true) and thought the flavor of guano was perhaps more stimulating than garlic.

I puzzled at the idea of such an exchange—of course he would have known that I had not made a soup of his rose, flavored with garlic or onion or with nothing; it was as though we were blowing a bubble world between us—he with a pipe embedded in one membrane of the bubble, and I on the opposite side with my own pipe slowly pushing air into a thin-sided reality. I pictured our bubble—a kind of pregnancy of the air; iridescent and shimmering as it bent and trembled to exist.

In a serious paragraph, he wrote that he had presented himself at Harvard College with the question what must he do to be admitted. The rector had asked him of his family and told him it was unlikely he could ever study there. "I think, perhaps, I'll ship for broader waters, sail the Atlantic, instead of the coastal merchant service. I want to see more. You, Una, probably understand this very well? At my request, the rector indulged my hubris by asking me ten questions of his choosing, all of which I answered, but it made no difference in the matter of my admission."

A fury rose in me for my friend. How philosophically he took his rejection! "Amuse me, Una, by sending ten questions you would like to ask the rector!" At that I smiled. But the letter was running out, and still my soul hungered.

Then he said he had been reading the First Book of *The Faerie Queene*. "I presume that you are named Una for the lady of the Red Cross Knight, for you, like her, are pure of heart, steadfast, and clear of mind. What dragons are there for me to slay so that I might be worthy of my lady?" There! I held the page to my bosom.

And yet it was so quaint and old-fashioned! There was little of chivalry in our century! He closed by saying, as he had said on parting, that I must keep my promise to make Kit's stay as pleasant as if we were all three together.

Of course, I read the letter over and over; each turn of phrase was squeezed for its juice. Squeeze, squeeze, squeeze—here was a bit of flattery, here some evidence of trust, there the flavor of affection; surely admiration was close to love. Squeeze, squeeze, squeeze the sentences: was he putting on a brave front? did he want me to say I would miss him if he set out for broader waters? did he want me to encourage his wanderlust? would his letters be longer if he traveled farther from the familiar? A bitter note to the flavor of the juice: was he trying to give me away to Kit? Perhaps Aunt had a copy of *The Faerie Queene* that

I could read. The last day Kit and I would bake rolls and send them back to Giles.

So did I milk Giles's letter for meaning till the fingers of my brain could scarcely close, and that night, I dreamed it was my task to milk a line of a thousand white goats till my fingers and their udders seemed all the same and aweary of pulling. I awoke to find myself milking my own fingers.

BEFORE the Fresnel crew arrived, since Uncle knew that the lantern in the Lighthouse would necessarily go dark, he had gathered driftwood and constructed a great pile of it on the highest part of the headland to serve as a primitive beacon. By the second night, the Argand apparatus being dismantled, the crew lighted the bonfire and made their camp around it, and we had our privacy again. In the cottage around our hearth fire, in the bosom of my Island family, I opened the second letter from my mother. I was grateful our visitors were not about, for the letter contained dreadful news.

My mother's second letter, written a week after the first one, told that my father had fallen into a despair. He feared that he would *fail*—"again," she wrote, again! as though I had not forgiven him—in both mercy and justice toward any child that embodied his own passion and rebellion—he, rebellious!—and he had gone to the barn and hanged himself from the beam, among the sides of beef.

HIS BLACK SUIT, his straight black hair hanging to his shoulders, his beard the same hue as coal but crinkly, all of him a blackness of cloth and hair—I saw him suspended in the air with a rope around his neck, his head pulled to one side.

No!

My mother opens the wide barn door. It drags in the soft dirt. Her eyes dart to the rafters, where cracks of light flood the dusty air. There! Among the curing beef!

No!

She runs to embrace his knees. Lifts the sagged weight of him.

No! I screamed till the stones of the cottage screamed back.

She looks for any sharp thing and sees the scythe. She pushes a bale of hay close to his legs. (He stood on nothing.) (He jumped from the rafters.) *With the scythe, she chops at the rope. It frays, breaks, and he crumples to the barn floor.*

Aunt held me, an enormous baby, in her lap. Uncle knelt before us, Aunt sobbing, too, and bathed our eyes and hands with a damp cloth. The cloth he handed to Frannie, who ran with it to the china bowl and then wrung it out as she crossed the floor. Repeatedly, she handed the rag to Uncle and then put both arms around her mother's shoulders and then about me.

My father dead: the black hair, his pale skin, the blush of pink on his high cheekbones. Even his eyes, flashing blackly. The long braid of black leather dangling from his hand. But what was his essential part that I loved in utter conviction, with my own black heart? *That smoldering.* The smoldering power. The strength across his heavy shoulders.

Now Frannie was instructed to make us tea, to bring shawls for our chilly trembling.

Sad. Sad. And torn with grief. I saw myself, age three or four, sitting on the stump in the yard. *He flicks the lash harmlessly, harmlessly on the rump of the horse; the black buggy rolls forward, and the spokes of the wheels turn to blurs. Over his shoulder, he looks back at me, his teeth smile and he says, "Be back soon, child." He leaves the smile hanging in the air to look straight ahead. He parts the air with his nose, his arm reaches out, but he does not look down to house the whip forward, in its holster.*

That night, no one went to bed. We sat around the fire wrapped in our quilts, though it was late summer. Uncle kept a big blaze in the fireplace, and still we were cold.

"It's the mortal cold," Aunt said.

"Didn't he want his baby?" Frannie asked in a voice so small I fancied a mouse had spoken.

"Poor man," Uncle said. "Poor, driven soul."

But there was a part of the terrible letter that presented a line of consolation. My mother had written that she would come to the Island to have her baby. In September, I would see my mother, and she would stay through spring. And then?

Once Uncle went out for lumps of coal, which was stored against the outer wall of the house under a canvas. When he came back in, he asked us to come out with him, said that he wanted to show Frannie and me something, that it would be good, too, for Aunt to walk around a little. Outside, he pointed to the bonfire on the cliff head. Two black figures were silhouetted there. The fire glowed red around their bodies. They seemed to stand at ease, with their hands in their pockets, chatting and watching the flames. How peaceful they seemed! They knew nothing of our misery.

One turned and picked up a length of driftwood. It, too, was silhouetted, like a stiff, black snake. He poked the fire with its end and dots of sparks rose like a fountain many feet into the air. Then the silhouette man cast the silhouette snake into the flames.

I thought of the great bonfire more than a thousand years before, at Alexandria, and how its light had served the ships of that time. Though this fire was on the ground, the headland elevated it a hundred feet above the sea.

In our cliff's face was a cavity shaped like a ship itself, or the print of a ship. That was the place where one talked of babies waiting to be born.

"The fire puts me in mind," Uncle said, "of times we passed whaling ships, when I was in the merchant service." He stood between Aunt and me and put a hand on each of our shoulders. Both he and Frannie feared that the shocking news might injure my aunt in a bodily way, or the babe she carried.

"After they kill a whale and begin harvesting the blubber, they fire up the tryworks. At night, when you pass such a ship, it looks like a frigate from hell. The fires under the pots are blazing away, and you can see the dark figures of the men moving back and forth to bring blubber to the pots. The whole ship glows, and the stench and heat of it can be felt as you pass. They frantically feed the flames with rinds of whale, then dip off the oil into cooling tubs, and all is done in a fury because the sharks are always working the carcass. Once I felt a shark, in his haste, I suppose, for the carcass chained shipside to the whaler, run headlong against the hull of the ship I stood on. Not a night for falling overboard."

We stood some minutes watching the much more peaceful scene beyond the Lighthouse of the beacon bonfire. At a short distance from the fire sat the pile of driftwood, almost the same shape and size as the burning pyre. Unhurried, from time to time a figure would pass between the waiting stack and the burning one.

As we watched, I heard an unfamiliar sound behind me, a line flapping against the stone column of the Lighthouse. Turning to look, I saw high up, extending from the lantern house, a projecting wooden brace, which the men used with rope and pulley to raise and lower large parts of the lenses. The rope dangled and swayed indolently beside the long stone side of the tower. Suddenly it seemed to me like a gallows. I put my hand to my throat.

"Let's go in," Frannie said, as though she knew my thought.

AS WE SAT beside our tame and friendly fire inside, I thought of the frenzied spectacle of the whale ship's tryworks. I knew the furnaces were built of brick on brick on the wooden deck, and I thought of the men furiously working as though to contain and appease the flames. From the passing merchant vessel, the fiery whaler must have seemed the living image of nightmare—a ship aflame. I remembered Kit's saying that he should like to try whaling. There was in Kit himself something smoldering, if not bursting into flames.

Finally I fell asleep in my chair, till, too soon, I saw the dawn and felt Aunt shake me, saying that soon the men would come in for breakfast, and I should go to my bed.

I lay in my room and listened to them come in, their voices strange except for Kit's. Why should they be alive and not my father? Who were they to me? And yet each of these workmen was son or father or friend, I knew, to some person whose grief would be as real as mine if their bodies fell lifeless.

They ate with right goodwill, but after a time I heard Kit asking my aunt if something was wrong and where were Frannie and I. "Really?" I heard him say, when she answered. "Really?" with a sharp sympathy and surprise in his voice. He said no more.

When the others rose from the table to set about the day's work, I heard Aunt tell Kit that he might look in on me, that she was sure I was awake. So Kit came and sat on the bed. I turned my back to him and looked out my window, and he rubbed my back in kind circles and said over and over that he was sorry, in a low voice so as not to awaken Frannie.

He often spoke my name.

THE NEXT DAY, Kit had careful and hard work to accomplish. I had no heart for watching, but several times he sought me out and passed a few cheerful words with me. It was balm to me. He had the gift of tact, and always I knew that he had my loss in mind, that he respected my grief, and yet—his tone of speaking seemed to say— here's life, here's someone who cares that you grieve, here is affirmation for who you are, Una.

Aunt often stopped to kiss my cheek, and Frannie hugged me almost till I dreaded her approach. Uncle was always there with his quiet understanding, but Kit with his newness diverted me. At one point, he put a small box of maple candy on the table, simply saying, "I brought this for all of you, from Boston." Then later, he stopped to tell me the candy had come from Vermont, and how they tapped the maple trees and boiled down the sap.

That evening, he asked Aunt if he and I might walk together down by the water. While Aunt hesitated, Uncle spoke up and said that it would do me good, and I felt grateful to Uncle.

IT WAS THE FIRST NIGHT of the Fresnel lens, and I was astonished by the boldness of its beam. It appeared to flash round and round, like a reaching arm. The swoop of it bothered the edges of my mind, and yet there was a determination about it that I felt myself drawn to and that I admired.

Kit averred that the new light could be seen as far as twenty miles out to sea. The old light had come to seem as familiar and restful to me as a fire in our fireplace, but this one had a relentless energy. Powered by clockworks, which Uncle wound, a "revolving eclipser," or shield, rhythmically moved in front of the lamp.

"It seems to say," I remarked, " 'I shall rule the sky.' "

Kit laughed.

The beam actually seemed to push against the clouds, to stroke them back. I was glad for the familiar plashing of the waves, and we sat on the dock with our legs hanging over the edge.

Suddenly Kit pretended to shove me off.

"What would you do if I did?" he asked.

"Come back and push you," I answered.

"I believe you would." He was pleased with me. "Can you swim?"

"No," I admitted.

Finally he asked me if I was cold, and when I said that I was a little cold, he asked if I wanted to go inside. When I said no, he loosely put his arm about me.

Here was comfort, I thought. If Giles had been with me, he would have done the same to warm and comfort me.

Then Kit asked me a strange question: "What do you think of your body?"

Something curled inside me. "No one has ever asked me that," I said.

He waited. What was I to say?

"What do you mean?" I asked.

"I wonder how a girl, a young woman really, regards herself."

"With uncertainty," I answered.

"You move as though you were uncertain of nothing."

"What do you think of the soul?" I asked. Despite the light above us, the water was dark.

"I am certain that I have none. I have a mind. People mistake it for the soul."

"Does Giles agree?" The waves kissed one another, a sweet and friendly sound.

He sighed. "Giles is an agnostic."

"Why aren't you an agnostic?"

"I don't always agree with Giles's ideas." There was a studied neutrality to his voice.

"I don't mean you depended on Giles to think for you."

"Nor do you. You have your own mind and body."

I looked back at the lighted house. I would have liked that night to believe that my father had a soul and that it dwelt in the heaven he espoused. "Do you think we are nothing after death?" Kit did not reply. I felt he was sad to have no comfort to offer on that score.

"Did your mother describe the funeral?" he finally asked.

"She's bringing his ashes with her."

"That's morbid enough," Kit said.

I had no reply. Who was to criticize anyone's funeral practice? My father had left an instruction in his pocket to burn his body as though he were a pagan Greek. But I did not tell Kit. Could my father have given up his God for gods?

"I suppose we should go," I finally said.

"Wait." He took a small package from the pocket of his jacket. "A gift. Don't let it fall out."

I peeled off the crumpled newspaper and there was a spiny shell.

"It's a Venus comb," he said. "Remember I drew a picture of one for Frannie. I bought it in Boston."

It was sharp-pointed, delicate and beautiful. "Could I really comb my hair with it?" I asked.

"Let's try," he said, and reached up and boldly pulled out a hairpin.

"No, I don't want to," I said quickly.

"Well then, I get to keep the pin," he said and put it in his pocket. "Do you like the shell?"

I did and, remembering my manners, told him so.

"I'll try it in my room," I said.

"If it works, I want you to show me sometime."

I stood up, remembering my father was dead, by his own hand. The Fresnel light swept and swept the sky.

CHAPTER 21   🐚   The Fourth Letter

THE NEXT DAY presented a mien of unusual fragility, a blue much more pale and washed than a robin's-egg blue but with that uniformity of hue. It started with a dewy freshness, and, as the sun climbed higher, the day grew hotter and hotter, till even with the sea breezes there was a baking quality to the heat. In Kentucky, such an August day is called a scorcher, and it did seem that some implacable flatiron was upended near one's body. In the face of the heat, we were all helping to load the *Petrel*.

Pearls of sweat hung in a line across Frannie's forehead. Finally Aunt told her she must rest in the shade. She herself retreated to the cool of the stone cottage, but she left the door open to watch us. When I glanced her way, I saw Aunt leaning on the table and fanning herself. Uncle swabbed his forehead and announced that *there* was enough water to quench the fire of his hair.

Inside each of us, I am sure, was the dreadful hollowness of my father's death, but outside, the world and its weather went on and felt free to burn and scorch us. That I would never see my father again seemed an impossible idea. (And how strange to carry a mere basket to a boat while my mind was haunted with death, was reeling from the suddenness of the reality of death.) Even more impossible: that I probably could, if I chose, look at a container of ashes and think that that once was he. *Ashes to ashes, dust to dust.* It was a quotation he liked, an idea to make one humble. But he himself had always borne his body with pride.

What do you think of your body? Kit had asked.

That it's melting, I could have said today. I heard one of the men say he wished for lemonade. The packing finished, but the wind and tide being wrong for sailing, we were all rather at loose ends in the heat. The crew were young, and some of them went wading where the sea was shallow, and others dug for clams and promised us a clambake for supper.

Uncle came into the cottage (whose stony walls, I thought, made it seem humid and confining instead of cool) and said to Aunt that he had half a mind to send Kit and me to pick plums for a cobbler. Aunt said rather sharply, "Send her if you like, Torch. It's on your head."

Torchy looked at her quizzically. "What do you mean, Agatha?"

"I don't like his eyes. I never have."

Uncle glanced at me apologetically. "If you like, Una, you can go."

"Wear a hat," Aunt called after me, and I snagged one of the straw ones hanging from the pegboard beside the door. I closed the door carefully to keep the heat out and quietly so as not to jar Aunt's nerves.

My eye found Kit immediately, sitting barefooted on the dock, with his trouser legs rolled up. The hairiness of men's legs appalled me, being inexperienced. I expected Kit to stand up when I approached, but instead he lay backward on the boards and looked up at me, squinting.

"You have a plan," he said.

"We could walk over the meadow and pick plums."

"Fran, too?"

"We can ask her."

So we took a basket and started out, but first I sent Fran back for a hat, and when she went in, her mother told her to stay home. It seemed capricious on Aunt's part, and Frannie was much disappointed when she came back to tell us.

"Don't worry," Kit said. "This evening I'll pick out a whole cupful of pecans just for you to eat."

Nonetheless, Frannie's head dropped.

"And," he went on, "I have a present for you, Fran. Three buttons, and one has ruby glass in it."

Now Fran looked up happily, and I thought highly of Kit for his kindness to her.

"I like your hat," he said to me as we walked single file along the path. I could feel his eyes on my back, and I held my shoulders straight.

If I had been walking with Giles, it would probably have been a silent walk. Each would have left the other to enjoy what there was to see. But Kit kept up a steady line of patter, and I found myself amused and laughing and paying almost no attention to where I was. We were on some high road together, going to some giddy place.

It was too hot for butterflies or hummingbirds, but we saw a cottontail scuttling through the grass. And then the fringed shadow of a hawk.

"Is that your friend?" Kit asked.

I knew he meant the eagle I had battled. "My eagle fishes the sea," I said. "That's just a redtail. Uncle says there are too many rabbits here."

"I should bring you my fox," Kit said.

I hadn't known he had a pet, but he told me he had raised a vixen and a friend back on Nantucket kept it for him.

"What's your friend's name?" I didn't know why I was suddenly curious.

"Charlotte," he answered.

I felt my heart stop. My face grew hot, and I was glad I was in front. Quickly I knew I must say something.

"Are you old friends?" I asked.

"I knew her before I went to sea for the first time."

"And how did you meet Giles?" Giles, after all, was the person I had chosen. I felt unsteady.

"He was also on his first voyage out."

"Do you still think of going on a whale ship?" I pictured the blazing tryworks.

"Do you?" he asked.

I did not answer. How could I be a passenger on a whaler? It had only been an impulse to say I wanted to go a-whaling. And now my mother was coming. Perhaps she would want me to return to Kentucky with her. Surely she would. Suppose she let me choose?

We walked past the scrub cedars. There was the jagged stump, but Uncle had sawed up the trunk and taken it home to cure in the attic. Small piles of sawdust lay on the ground where he had worked.

"Maybe you'll go back to Kentucky," Kit said, as though he read my thoughts. "You could always marry a pig farmer," he added impishly.

I put my hands on my hips. "How dare you, Kit Sparrow! You'll just say anything, won't you? Somebody ought to gag you."

"Gag or tag? You couldn't tag me if you tried." He danced on his toes and darted away.

I chased him hard, but I couldn't catch him. He followed the path to the plum grove, and then turned and yelled, "King's X! Home free!"

Holding my side and panting, I dropped my speed to a walk. My hair had come loose and I was sweating rivulets. By the time I reached the grove, he had half eaten a plum.

"Side hurt?" he asked. "You could run better if the whalebone didn't pinch you."

A laugh burst from me, and that hurt my side, too. "Kit!" I said. "Don't." But he was smiling merrily, and I couldn't be angry with him.

He gave me a plum, and we sat down together in the shade of the trees. Though some breeze came up from the water, the heat was still smothering. The juicy plum seemed sweet and wet as sin. What was sin?

"You remind me of my father," I suddenly said.

"A handsome man," Kit said solemnly.

"Restless. Full of energy." I thought, but did not say, the word *smoldering*. Not an apt description for the moment, anyway, because Kit seemed at his leisure, assured and happy.

As though to affirm my appraisal, he said, "I feel happy to be with you."

"Giles said we ought to enjoy talking."

He snorted. "When I first saw you, Una, fighting the eagle over your bonnet, I thought I had never seen such a woman. But there are some very conventional aspects to you."

"Was it you or Giles who called to me?"

"I did."

"I have a scar on my hand." I held it out to him.

He slowly took my hand. Slowly bent and kissed it.

I felt myself dissolve in brightness.

Slowly he placed my honored hand on the grass and gazed out to sea.

I wanted him to say something. Where were his manners and his gift of gab? But he would not. There was a perversity about him, a stubbornness. Why had Giles written me only one letter if he was fond of me?

"Is—is . . ." I stammered. "Is Charlotte a special friend to you?"

"Yes," he said.

Heaviness settled over me.

"But she is not as special as you."

I wanted him to say more. Now I would wait.

Finally he said, "Giles is the most unusual person I know."

"Yes," I answered, content with simple agreement. Later, as we picked the fruit for the cobbler, I wished that I had said, *You, too, are the most unusual person I know.*

Why should one want the unusual? I asked myself. The exotic seashell, the arresting phrase? Concerning Giles, these were not real questions, at least for Kit or for me. I knew that Giles was a person to be cherished. He had some gift of spirit, not just of mind, that marked him as rare and valuable. Aunt had seen it. To Uncle and Frannie, it made less difference.

But never with Giles had I felt so simply happy as I did picking plums with Kit. It was not Frannie but I who felt his allure. I slipped the pit of the plum he had given me into my apron pocket.

When we started back along the path, I asked Kit to help me find my lost hairpins.

"No," he said.

"Why not?"

"Una," he asked, "are you really so conventional that you cannot return with your braid hanging down your back?"

"I could if I chose," I said.

"No. You can't choose. You can't just say, 'I was running and my hair came down.' It doesn't look respectable to you. They don't expect you to come back any different from when you left."

"I'll find the pins by myself."

He shrugged. I did find my pins, or enough of them. Beside the path I found my straw hat, too, which I hadn't even known I'd lost.

Kit laughed at me. I felt his will wash over me. I remembered his comforting arm across my shoulders. I expected him to tease me now about how the hat must have been unnecessary if I never registered its loss.

But instead he grew serious and said, "That's the way it is in life. You let go of what is beautiful and unique. You pursue something new and don't even know that the wind of your own running is a thief."

BEFORE we reached home, I asked Kit to wait. I took off my hat and placed it beside my foot. I took out the pins and let my braid dangle below my waist. Then I took my fingers and loosed the braid so that all the hair spread wild and free. "I wear my hair as I wish," I announced. "I'll tell them so."

"Good for you," he said. But he did not walk in with me.

Aunt gave me a sharp glance, but she only said, "You'll die of heatstroke if you don't put your hair up."

"Let me, let me," Frannie clamored, for she loved to brush and braid my hair. And so up it went. But I did not fail to note: the sky does not fall if you choose to let down your hair.

AS IT TURNED OUT, both Kit and Giles had had the same idea that we might bake bread for the mainland. Giles had sent a bag of nuts for that purpose, and we cracked them that night, the sweep of the new Fresnel lens swishing above us. When we packed the fragrant rolls in the morning, after first serving each of the crew and the family, I asked Kit, a little petulantly, how Giles had known to send the nuts.

"He sent you something else, too, Una. But he made me promise not to give it to you till the morning of my leaving, and for you not to open it till the next day." He produced another envelope.

I was hurt. I tried to cover my feeling, but together they had tricked and tested me.

"He made me promise," Kit said.

I held back my tears.

"Then place it on the mantel," I said. I would not give them the image of my greedy hand reaching for the letter.

Though Frannie was all eagerness to climb the tower, as soon as the *Petrel* left our dock, I fetched the letter. I told Frannie to climb alone, and I went to my room with tears barely held in abeyance. With a trembling hand, I plucked a hairpin from my hair and slit open the top of the envelope.

The letter was like a honeycomb of sweetness. This time I did not need to crush the words to extract their flavor. His affection for me was direct and his hope for our future unstinting. But he said he wished to sail the Atlantic first. "I do not doubt that felicity lies not on the sea, or on the other side of the sea, but in the hearth and in the heart, yet I want to know the broader world, and ask you, darling, for patience and content."

Felicity! How glad I was that I had given only a part of my heart to Kit and surely could reclaim it. Kit must have judged us so himself, or he would not have delivered the second letter. But perhaps he had been instructed to deliver it in any case. Darling. Had Giles and Kit made it up between them to test my steadfastness? Or had Kit's admiration for me been genuine and of his own heart?

If they had tested me, it was a shabby thing to do.

CHAPTER 22   The *Camel*

T HAT NIGHT, I tried to comb my hair with the Venus comb, and I borrowed a small looking glass from Aunt. But my hair was too thick and curly for the spiny shell, and before I knew it, a prong had snapped off. I contented myself with combing only the more airy ends of my hair, instead of the whole mass. Since my hair hung to the curve of my buttocks, it was easy for me to see how pretty the unusual comb looked (and my hand holding it) feathering the ends.

As I combed my hair, I asked Frannie to fetch me a damp cloth to wash my face. As always, she was happy to serve me. If I were a true lady, should I not wait loyally for the Red Cross Knight? I looked at my dark hair and thought of the beautiful tinted picture of "Rebecca, the Jewess" in *Ivanhoe*. Then I thought of another story, of Lancelot, and he had Kit's face, Kit's dark-eyed interest in the body.

Giles, it seemed to me, was like a Parsifal. His eyes saw some holy grail, even if they looked at me. I sighed, because in my heart, I knew it was a matter not of loyalty but of preference. And my preference was for the lofty vision of Giles. Let it leave silences in our commerce; let me suffer less than satisfaction. I could not help it. There was in Giles that which I was bound to love, because I aspired to it myself.

But Kit had loved my hair. And Lancelot had seduced the Lady.

I doubt not that true felicity lies in the hearth and the heart. Giles had known that his letter would engulf me, for he knew me. I knew he knew. My thoughts wheeled round again: perhaps Kit was a means of giving my life broader experience, a breadth that Giles sought for his own life with the longer voyage of the Atlantic crossing. Uncle had already had his life on the sea. For my aunt and my mother, journeying lay in their fingers for the most part. They knew the landscape of colored patches, the rivulets and tributaries of stitchery. They knew the voyage of reading. It seemed an inward journey. But the sea! the sea! How could it not seem freer, wider, more uncharted than anything else one could know?

I wanted it for Giles. For any man I loved. Perhaps in sending Kit to play the part of companion, Giles wished me to learn that many men could love me, that choice and not inevitability were the lot of both woman and man.

For my mother and my aunt, the thought of babies revitalized their beings. And yet, I did not just want babies, or men who went to sea. I wanted something for myself.

In the drawer of my little table, close to the corner of rose petals, I put Giles's two letters. In the other front corner of the drawer, I put a plum pit. I knew where it came from. I knew the joy of its flavor.

THE HOT WEATHER PASSED. Frannie and I did not start a new line-of-stone calendar, but we measured Aunt, who grew not only larger but more agreeable as the cooler weather came on. Her measuring string was festooned with knots of colored yarn, and it seemed amazing to all of us that Aunt had once been so small.

One day Frannie surprised me by saying, "You're growing, too, Una."

"Where?" I asked.

"Here," and she swept her hand across her chest.

Once I had thought breasts would be nothing but an encumbrance, but now I knew I was pleased. And I knew that I was changing.

Once I heard Uncle say to Frannie, "It will be nice for you to have the company of the baby. And soon it will be a real playfellow for you and not just a doll."

"I have Una," she said.

"But Una is starting to find the Island small."

"Really?" Frannie questioned her father.

"Well, I don't know. Perhaps she'll go back to Kentucky to help her mother."

"Couldn't everybody live here forever? There's lots of room."

"We can invite them."

"Kit and Giles, too."

"So you are a Utopian, Frannie. You'd have a world apart with only those of like mind?"

"Why not?"

"Many have tried it, or dreamed of it. Why not you, indeed?"

THAT NIGHT when I wrote to Giles I asked him what he knew of Utopia. I wanted to ask if there was not a society where even among grown men and women there were to be found threesomes, instead of twosomes, but this last seemed a dangerous idea, and one that might hurt Giles's feelings. For Giles's ideal world seemed chivalric, and in the castle of the heart stood two.

We had told Kit (and thus Giles) that we expected to meet my mother in New Bedford on September 15 at the inn named the Sea-Fancy and that we would be glad to see them, too, if their schedules permitted. Kit had said immediately that he knew the Sea-Fancy, it being distaff to the Spouter-Inn, a somewhat rougher inn where he and Giles often stayed, and if at all possible they would visit with us.

As Aunt grew larger, she decided that not all of us but only I was to go to New Bedford to meet my mother. Uncle thought it would be a fine excursion—after all, I was sixteen—for me to go alone to meet my mother, and I could tell that Aunt believed my mother and I would benefit from a private encounter. When I asked Uncle if Frannie might go with me, he said he thought she was too young, and she would add unnecessarily to the expense.

One cannot be a happy traveler, I think, without taking pleasure in her clothes. It is not her rod and her staff that comfort her—indeed, she carries no such implements—it is her clothes that comfort the female pilgrim, when she fares forth alone for the first time. I know no color so satisfactory for travel as navy blue. There's a color to contain one! It calms the soul and lends respectability to the most wildly beating heart. And if one has re-covered her bonnet frame to match, and if it happens that there are sharp green grosgrain ribbons in the house to sew onto that bonnet, and if those luckily found ribbons have never been creased with tying till the very morning of departure, then one is new and complete indeed. And so I was.

I collected the dried rose petals into a small drawstring pouch. The plum pit I took to the edge of the water. I set the pit, like a small boat, adrift, and turned my back on its fate. And when the supply boat, the *Camel*, turned her bow back toward New Bedford, I alone was aboard, with the captain and mate who manned her.

When the *Camel* was in the middle of her crossing, and I could see neither the mainland ahead nor the Lighthouse behind, I felt myself a regular sailor. The slap-slap of the water on the keel was hypnotic. Almost I forgot where I was going and whence I came—I was simply myself, moving swiftly on a friendly sea, under a kindly sky. Slap-slap. *Forward!* Perhaps Giles was wrong to believe that felicity lay in the home and hearth. I felt it lay in the open sea and the adventure of discovery. I lifted up my eyes to it.

I was so enamored with the vastness of my independence—how high the sky, how wide the sea, how white the foam, how brisk the breeze—that at first I did not notice the fittings of the *Camel* or the crew that made my pleasant speed possible. At length, humming my internal song of independence, I looked more carefully at the captain. This captain (a new one) of the *Camel* had the most enormous gray, wiry mustache I had ever seen. Its sidebars were the thickness of my wrist. First it swooped horizontally from the parting between the nostrils, and then it made a right-angle turn and grew and hung straight down, well below his jaw, in points like twin awls. He carried his head—probably to display his magnificent mustache—at a thrust-forward angle, and his shoulders seemed a frail yoke to support such a head that supported such a mustache!

Of course, I sat in the open air, as near the prow of the ship as possible. Though I was as proper and contained as any bonneted-with-new-grosgrain-ribbons young lady could be, I fancied myself a kind of mermaid, a figurehead of a free spirit.

WHEN THE *CAMEL* came into New Bedford port, I was swept with sorrow for the forests, for here, it seemed, in the multitudinous masts of ships, stood all the straightest, tallest, most majestic trunks of North America. But their branches were all broken off and stripped away, their roots planted only in the barren pots of boats. Sails might have suggested the cloak of leaf-filled branches, but sails were furled, and the nakedness of the timbers stood in jumbled display. The standing rigging was in place, to be sure, but would you drape the mighty spine of a tree in cobwebs and call it clothed? Bare as crucifixes, the ships at rest seemed nothing like the unfurled fairy-swans that skimmed the oceans.

Is there always, under the glory of white wings and graceful speed, the scaffolding of a cross? This is not a Christian question but one applicable to India and China and Africa. If you meet a woman of whatever complexion who sails her life with strength and grace and assurance, talk to her! And what you will find is that there has been a suffering, that at some time she has left herself for hanging dead.

CHAPTER 23   🐚   The Sea-Fancy Inn

No SOONER did I enter the Sea-Fancy Inn than I met such a woman. But first, my mustachioed captain upon disembarking, took me by the elbow, saying I was but a young lady, and steered me past the inn named the Crossed Harpoons and past the Sword-Fish Inn, and beyond a place called the Trap, where many finely dressed black people were congregating as though for church, to the Spouter-Inn, of which Kit spoke, and to the inn across, on the left side of the street.

Rebekkah Swain, round as a world, stood behind the desk of the Sea-Fancy. I knew her name because it was written in ribbonlike script, below the name of the inn itself, on the oval board hanging in the street. No sylphlike creature was Rebekkah Swain. She would have been a treasure trove for a whole gang of cannibals, and I suspected she knew some—though her English was of the finest—for her black hair, greased up into a small crownlike knot atop her head, was held by a sharpened bone. Her complexion, though, was more yellow and Chinese-like than black—see how in her person she gathers in the nations? In the middle of her forehead was a red dot, which I since learned was characteristic of a Hindu woman and denoted her caste. Rebekkah Swain's clothing, like her last name, seemed to bespeak the Renaissance, for such silken puffs sat on each side on her hips that she seemed to step from an engraving of the court of Elizabeth, though later—oh how convenient is *later* in the halls of knowledge—I saw that these expanses of cloth were nothing like decorations of fabric over some basketlike contraption of fashion, but necessities! to clothe her ample, rolling flesh. In that moment, she seemed a woman of all time as well as the melded personification of the geographically diverse human race.

Her shoes, mere foldings of brute leather, were of the earliest time: no cobbler's nail or needle had penetrated there; such foot coverings might a cave dweller have bound with the self-same thong and sinew.

Her eyes, tilted up at the corners—the Chinese again!—the lips, full and negroid, and the words they shaped: as I have already said, there was her kinship with the kings and queens of England.

Zest for discovery! Zest! I had but started my odyssey and here already, all exotically, was the world! What next!

"I have had a letter from your mother weeks ago. I expect her in a day or so," Mrs. Swain said, as soon as she saw me. She had no need of my name. Her voice was rich and full, yet there was a sweetness to it usually reserved for higher, lighter voices. "And I will show you your room."

Then her great bulk sailed or rather rolled out from behind the counter.

"She is now in my care, Monsieur Whiskers," she said, dismissing my escort.

She went before me. Her silken-robed girth completely filled the width of the stairs, and I could see that they posed a difficulty for her. She grasped rather than held the handrail, which was itself a beam rather than a rail, and hand over hand hoisted herself up. I slowly followed behind. At the landing elbow, she rotated rather than turned to present her yellow-brown face glistening in sweat, her features wreathed in a smile.

"If you like, you may skitter up to the next level. Wait for me there. Your room is yet beyond, on the top."

How to say the assurance with which these words filled me: *your room*. There was a friendly calm in her voice. Not an equality but a comprehensiveness in her tone.

My legs long trained in stair-climbing fairly whizzed me to the second floor; my guide-who-came-behind labored a full minute in elevating to the same height. I was not sorry, for her delay gave me ample time to study the scene before me.

The second floor presented a hall, spacious as a lobby and all the more restful for its removal from the bustle of the passing carriages and pedestrians. The wall colors here were pastel such as I had never seen before. The fragile colors of dawn hung here—pale blue, fluffed with paler pink on the ceiling, and woodwork a yellow, the color of a new chick. In various chairs, seeming to be collected from around the world—some from the courts of Europe, others leather and wood slings from the Congo, a lacquered Japanese affair ornamented with a golden dragon—sat women of various colors and origins. It was as though Rebekkah Swain had come apart into her components. But here were the pure types of which she was the amazing composite.

And each sat with some handiwork. The African was stringing beads so tiny they seemed a blur of silver in her dark basket. A woman whom I felt to be an Eskimo worked a pelt with a bone needle, and while she sewed she chewed! Out came a whole slimy mass, like an awful tobacco wad. My stomach fairly rose in disgust, but I knew she was softening the leather with her teeth. I glimpsed the latter item—her teeth—and saw they were tan and much worn down with their work. A stylish young woman with black ringlets held a cushion full of pins and a web of lacework, an example of which film overlay her blouse collar; I doubted not that she was making Brussels lace. And there were many others: an American Indian woman with the saddest face of all was cutting fringe with a steel razor that I knew was not indigenous with her people. Each worked, each made something beautiful, and then the world rolled up again and said for me to climb to the next level.

All the heat of the building seemed to have come up before me to the third floor, and I wondered if I might raise a window. Did people raise windows in other people's hotels? I did not know. This level's landing was deserted, but on the wall hung a painting of a ship with two keels; I could not say whether it was headed to one side or the other. On one side was a sun-drenched scene, rather like New Bedford. There were pretty houses and iron lace fences, flowers and fruit trees both blooming and ready to harvest (which, of course, one does not find in nature). On the other side, broached by the second keel of the ship, the world was a black void filled with swirling stars. Some were shaped like pinwheels, others were glowing spheres and spirals. One was so large that only an arc of its curve fitted in the frame, and some stars were painted so tiny that the artist must have touched the canvas with the point of a needle dipped in paint, mere pricks of gold—no, there was a silver one, there a red.

The two-fronted ship, Januslike, straddled the middle of the picture, and the whole thing had a naive, fabulous effect, as though it weren't meant to be believed, but rather thought about.

"Now," sighed Rebekkah Swain, "here is the room reserved for you and your mother."

I sat on the edge of the bed.

Rebekkah went directly to the window and sent the sash skyward. What power she harbored in her arms! (And legs, too, to be able to transport her bulk!) In my little bedroom, there was but one spindly chair. She gave it not a glance but seated herself in the windowsill, hundreds of pounds of her silken backside hanging over the edge into the out-of-doors. What a sight, should a passerby look up! It would seem that someone was trying to stuff a feather bed out the window. A woman who used a house as her chair!

Alas, she so completely filled the sole window that very little of the hot air could escape, and none of the cool breeze bypassed the mighty cork of her being.

"Raise the window in the hall," she told me pleasantly.

So I passed onto the landing again, glanced at the two-keeled boat, and raised the window overlooking the street. The cobblestones below lined up like the tops of endless loaves of bread. However, their hard, curved surfaces seemed ill suited to the rattling wheels of the wagons. The horses were shod in steel, and often sparks flew out as their hooves grazed or nicked the stones.

At home, I knew well that if Uncle started down the path with his creel he was likely going to put out for fishing, or if Aunt moved her chair close to the window in the winter, then likely she would soon start to sew. Here in New Bedford, everything was a meaningless bustle. I chose one couple to watch, but they turned a corner together, with me left none the wiser about where they were going or why. In another street, a black child, dressed like a prince in red with gold braid, zipped from a closed carriage to a tobacco shop. He did not even go into the shop before the door was open and a box thrust into his hands, and the boy ran back to his carriage. A box of cigars, I thought. But was the child a slave, a servant, the scion of a wealthy freeman? His manner was one of alacrity and cheer, and so I thought he could not be a slave. But then through the carriage window I saw a white-gloved hand strike his cheek and the contorting of his previously happy face. With a shake of the reins, the horses pulled away, and if there was a cry from the slaveboy, the clatter of the hooves and the bumping of wheels over the cobblestones drowned out his distress.

"Una," the musical voice called me, and I left my view from the hall window to sit on the edge of the bed. From her throne in the window, Rebekkah Swain regarded me, a hand resting on each of her knees.

"What would you most like to know?" she asked.

It was a strange question. Like a school of minnows, questions flew through my mind: How long will I wait for my mother? Will I see Giles and Kit? Are people happy here? Why did my father die? Whom will I marry? What will happen to Frannie? Where are Giles and Kit now? None of the questions seemed right, and then a bigger question swam, mouth open, toward all the others as though to swallow them up. "Why do you ask?" I asked Rebekkah Swain.

"I ask because I would like to know your mind." Her expression was so merry that I began to wonder if she was mad. But would my mother send me to a madwoman? And could a madwoman own a house and run a business such as a hotel?

"How did you come to be here?" I asked.

And at once, she began to tell her story.

"Your bed was once my bed," she said. "This house was a great house for one family, not a hotel, and I was a maid. I came from India"—she touched the caste mark on her forehead—"abducted by a whaling captain. I was as tall as you, and like you, as slender as a reed. The captain kept me locked in his cabin, and sometimes I was tied into the bed, which itself was suspended from the ceiling on gimbals. He treated me as a whore."

Whore. I watched her mouth go round as she said the harsh word. The world as I knew it seemed sucked into that mouth. With the sound of the word, whose meaning I knew by instinct and the puckered rounding of her thick lips, I lost my innocence.

"Then my face," she went on, "was sweet as the moon, and my eyes like almonds."

Certainly her face was still round, her eyes still slanted up at the corners.

"I was very quiet. I did not have the language to speak to my captor. My father was an African, from the great grasslands, a killer of lions. My mother was from Tonga—Polynesia. They met in India, and I spoke their languages, and Hindi, and the language of my part of India, Calcutta, which is Bengali. And English, of course."

Yes, the flow of her speaking was natural, as though she'd always known it, but her language had a lilt to it, a slight crispness—as though her words had a thin, silver edge.

She rolled up the sleeves of her dress. Her very body was imprinted with pictures of strange people, of spears and crisp hair, the mane of a lion and a long tasseled tail.

"Was the captain the owner of this house?"

"He was not, but his friend was. 'She is a sweet, resigned girl,' he told his friend. 'Take her as a servant, for my wife will not want to see her.' They were Quaker captains, and their wives believed them moral."

"Quakers do not believe in war, at least," I said.

"There is no axis on which all turns," she said. She rolled her hands over each other, round and round, as though her hands were a ball of yarn rolling loose across the floor.

"Did you ever go home?"

"Home?" she chuckled. "I have made my home wherever I am. A gimbaled bed, a maid's room, the howdah atop an elephant." She stopped smiling, tilted her head back, and looked majestically at me over the bulges of her cheeks. "And I advise you to do the same."

"I have lived in a lighthouse."

"I know."

"Before that, I lived in the woods, in Kentucky, close to the Ohio."

"I know."

"I don't know which is more nearly home."

"I know." With that, she heaved herself up from the windowsill. Her skirts whispered their silk secrets as she passed, but I thought them to say, *Welcome to the world.*

THUS I BEGAN my wait for my mother at the Sea-Fancy Inn of New Bedford. I positioned the spindly chair close to the window of my room and watched the street. I wondered if I would ever hear the rest of the innkeeper's story—how she rose from maid to proprietor—and I can say now that I never did.

The afternoon light began to fade, and lamplighters lit up the street. I did not want my mother to have to travel in the dark, and I began to grow anxious and hungry. I pictured her as yet contained in a stage-coach, her trunk tied up on the rack, and a box on her knee full of the ashes of my father. When a knock came at my door, it was a maid with a small basket and a cup of milk in her hand, saying that Mistress Swain had sent up some victuals.

I thought of all the other women in the house and wondered if I should join the common table. I imagined them a happy group, convivial, but I wanted to stay at my window and look out. I was watching for Giles and for Kit, as well as for my mother. As night drew on, I expected more to see the men than to see her, for surely she was too tired to travel at night. Now I could see shops go dark, and I saw a store owner thrust the key into the lock of his chandlery and then shake the knob to be sure it was fast.

The street lamps burned whale oil, and the odor of it wafted about on the late-summer air. My own candle I extinguished so that I might watch the street unseen by those below. I seemed a kind of Rapunzel, though my hair was dark and gypsylike and by no means long enough to let down as a golden ladder for my suitor. If Giles but saw me at the window, though, he would have thought of Rapunzel. And Kit? I could not guess. He was as likely to see me as a sea witch, wild and free—not an imprisoned princess. Again, I asked myself whose vision I preferred. And this time, I was not sure.

Still, it was Giles who stirred my own depths. When I wrote the letters to him, I found thoughts and feelings that were hidden to me until I conjured up his mind as attentive. Suppose he was not attentive, and I only imagined him so? *Darling*—he had written the word. I did not imagine it. How had it been between Uncle and Aunt when they were courting? What was their degree of certainty? And my own parents?

The flash of my father's teeth between the black of his mustache and the black hairs of his beard. Sometimes that smile had been kind and jolly. Is our life determined for us, or do we choose? Some of both. Some of both—the answer came clean and simple to my mind.

My father himself: perhaps two handfuls of ashes—perhaps six. Contained in a wooden box? some of him in the corners? some sifted into the crevices? *We take him to the Lighthouse, and there, on the end of the island dock, we slip him back to the sea so that he might reassemble his grains of dust as a fish, a small black fish, perhaps with golden bars on his sides, a gold ring around his eye, a transparent tail.* No. *I take him high in the tower. I fling his dust in the air. Eagles! Here is one of your own. Let him float and soar with you. Let the sun, like a magnet, draw him to its fiery heart.*

What did one do with one's father when he was dead?

Full fathom five, my father lies,
And are those pearls that were his eyes?

If I spoke such modified Shakespeare to Giles, I was sure that his glance would be quick and liquid.

But what was it that Giles *wanted* of me? *That* I could not imagine. *He does not want anything of me. He simply sees a congruence in our shapes, knows our rightful, luckily found matching.* And Kit? *Oh, he wants. He wants what he cannot have of me. But I like his wanting and am drawn toward it.*

WHEN NIGHT was almost settled on New Bedford, when the street was illumined by only the nimbuses of light surrounding the lamps and by the chunks of light falling through the windows of the Spouter-Inn across the street and from the windows of the Sword-Fish down the way, I saw them walking, arm in arm. Without a glance at the Sea-Fancy, they shoved open the door of the Spouter and disappeared. Now I was glad! Now the tempo of my heart accelerated. Now I would see them in the morning.

And so to bed.

Under the woven counterpane, green and white, a pattern of houses, my fingers found a quilt. I explored the puckers around the stitches, found the edges of the pieces as they were seamed together, but I could make no sense by touch alone of the pattern. I could not compose an overview of the design. I watched my thoughts unhinge from logic and reality. So it always is for me, before sleep—if I care to observe the passage. Some part of the mind slips into error and distortion—like a moving face on the curve of a shiny surface, and some higher part of the mind observes the melting away of pattern. *The whale's footprint.* I thought of Torchy's image. No, it was Kit who told me that.

WHEN MORNING LIGHT like happiness filled my room, I hurried to the window in my nightgown to look across at the Spouter-Inn. Silly me. It was but a building like a wooden box, just the same as yesterday, only sitting in early sunlight. Ah, in that box were my friends! How could life have seemed complete at the Lighthouse, on the Island, for four years! And I had had no knowledge even that Giles and Kit existed. Here was the great world! And it was full of houses and streets and people hurrying about their business, and Giles and Kit. Probably yet asleep.

The bong of a church bell shook the air. Where was that sound yesterday? Dimly I could pull it out of memory, but yesterday I had been only eyes. No, the rattling of the carriages, I had heard that. And the melodious voice of Mrs. Swain. Now I heard my own feet crossing the painted boards, a pearly gray those boards, to the nail where hung my navy dress. And my bonnet. Today the grosgrain ribbons showed a crimp where they had been tied yesterday. For the first time they were tied yesterday. Never again for the first time. I thought it gaily. I was in the city. I might do as I liked.

I could go out! If my mother came while I walked the sidewalks which yesterday had belonged to other women and men, she would find a note or message. Today I could not stay high up and waiting. I must be among the world. It was the new sunlight that told me so. And that single clap—*bong! That* was what had smacked my heart awake.

Quickly I put on my dress. Why wash my hands and face? They weren't dirty. My comb glided, glided, and my fingers found the old curves of the last braids and wove all together so nimbly and smoothly that I thought New Bedford should hold a contest for which maiden could braid her hair the quickest, and I would win!

Silly me! Why, I liked myself best when silliest!

But would Giles? I didn't know. But would Kit? Yes!

"Breakfast all! Breakfast all!" It was the voice of Mrs. Swain from two stories below. I pictured great piles of fluffy eggs. Sunshine incarnate! Sunshine beaten with milk and piled high in a china bowl. All of us women, all the women of the world feasting on scrambled sunshine! And toast! Yes, the rough-sided, crunchy-edged toast in my mouth, with a slick of butter.

I went to the window to inhale the world. Why was there this pane of glass between me and it? Then, through the wavy glass, I saw Giles and Kit step out of the Spouter. I raised my hand to wave hello, but they did not so much as glance at the Sea-Fancy. Were they confused of the day? Didn't they know this was September 16, and I had already been waiting a day? I raised the sash, dropped to my knees, and angled my head and body out into space. But now their backs were to me, and they were walking away!

Should I shout? A cry rose in the column of my throat and then sank down again. No. I withdrew from the crisp morning air. It had had a wetness to it. I lowered the window. I hesitated. Then all at once, I decided to follow them and know their business.

Down the steps—I tried not to clatter, but only to hurry. Mrs. Swain was at her post behind the receiving desk.

"Breakfast in the dining room, Una."

"I'll eat later."

"Then you must eat out."

"Tell my mother I've arrived."

And out I went. Behind my head floated some impression of Mrs. Swain, a large purple orb this morning. Were her fabrics always of a slippery texture? Perhaps it helped her to slide through the air—less friction! There! Ahead—Kit and Giles. And carrying sailor's duffels on their shoulders. But they would not ship without seeing me. Of this I was absolutely certain.

They turned the corner, and I hurried along. When I turned the corner, I saw the street led downward, and at the bottom of the street were the docks, the water, and the forest of sailing ships. The street was like a chute leading to the sea.

How well dressed I was! I smoothed the good cloth of my navy dress. But the soles of my shoes seemed thin on the hard cobblestones. Our island paths were softer. Soon I would be hungry, and I half regretted having never seen a breakfast table that perhaps held besides the golden eggs a platter of pancakes, a tureen of grainy grits. Surely Mrs. Swain's table would hold most that was delicious and nutritious in the world. I passed a meat shop, but the uncooked meat hanging from the rafters had no appeal for me. There was the smooth, glistening end of a knucklebone. *My father, hanging! A rope around his neck.*

No.

And where was my mother? I thought of her jostling and jouncing in a carriage. Perhaps she, too, was hungry. I knew she was anxious, fretful that she was tardy. I looked ahead at Giles and Kit and wished that I could walk between them. I did not want to choose between them.

The voice of my mother said to me, *Then, Una, perhaps neither of them is really for you.* But who else was there in the world? I meant who else that I would want.

The docks of New Bedford held much of the world, for here were sailors with all manner of complexion and hair and clothing, according to the custom of their homeland. I saw men so black their skin had a tinge of purple to it, like an eggplant, and I saw Chinese and heard languages that were guttural, or slippery, and some with clicks and sounds heaved up from the chest, or *r*'s rolled in the back of the mouth. One face was pockmarked, and I thought again of Frannie. I saw a man with a lifted lip, as though an invisible hook were pulling it upward.

Kit and Giles walked across the plank leading to a ship named *Sussex.* I waited beside a wagon of barrels—there seemed to be thousands of barrels around the dock, and their shape preoccupied me this morning the way the cobblestones of the streets had when I first arrived.

The *Sussex,* I knew, was a whaling ship. Its smaller whaleboats hung from the davits, three on a side. The shape of the *Sussex* was boxy, built for strength and stability more than speed, for she must be able to withstand the strain of hoisting a whale enough out of the water to be stripped of blubber. Could I do such work? I thought not. But I could mop the deck, or climb to a masthead. Yes, the Giant had trained my legs for any amount of climbing, but how would it be to step up the openwork of ropes? I remembered the minister's nimble ladder-run to the pulpit of Seamen's Bethel Chapel. And would my eyes serve as sailor's eyes? Surely they were among the keenest. Had I not seen to push a needle through miles and miles of fabric, a twelfth of an inch at a purchase? Could not these same eyes see far as well as near? Might

The Harbor of New Bedford

not the head of a whale surface for an instant from the water the way the tip of a needle broke through fabric? If a ship had furnaces for trying out, could not one boil her monthly rags, the same as at home? And the men could look away, as they did on land.

Thus absentmindedly did I grumble to myself as I stood beside the wagon of barrels and wondered about my friends and the *Sussex*. When one is feeling fine and free, sometimes a grumble seems to express it, or to provide a necessary brake on a feeling that might run pell-mell downhill, off the edge and into the water, if something didn't check it.

To think no one in the world knew exactly where I was on that fine morning! And here I was! in my navy blue dress, wearing my bonnet, and now, in this moment, I fingered the little ridges in my grosgrain ribbon.

When Giles and Kit left the *Sussex*, they walked without their bags, and thus I knew that she would be the means whereby Kit would satisfy his ambition to go a-whaling and Giles would gratify the part of him that needed to sail wide waters before settling at the hearth. I felt sobered by the idea that they knew so definitely what they wanted and knew so clearly the means to fulfill those ambitions. My life had not been like that.

I moved in a way that kept me hidden when they passed. A shop behind me had a sign in the window: Seamen's clothes, mended and made. The window displayed a pair of canvas trousers, and a sewing kit such as a sailor might purchase for his own use on a voyage. I turned to risk a glance at my friends. I checked the shapes of their noses and cheeks for familiarity, the texture of their skin to match my memories from the Island. They were chatting to each other, pleased, good comrades. What did they need of me?

Nonetheless, I followed them up the cobbled hill. But at the corner, when they did not turn back toward the Spouter, I pointed myself toward home. *Home?* Was I as portable as that? The room I had stayed in for one night now might be called home? I thought of Mrs. Swain's advice. There had been a first day for her, too, in New Bedford. *I slept in the bed that will be yours. I was once as slender as you.* I was hungry.

When I walked under the oval sign and into the Sea-Fancy, I smelled the aroma of cloves and sage. The Indian woman passed through the lobby, the fringe of her buckskin skirt hanging below the calves of her legs, her moccasins also fringed and decorated with tiny beads. Behind her swept the world—I mean Rebekkah Swain.

"Una, your mother has not come, but here is a new letter from her." Mrs. Swain's face was smooth with seriousness. "I knew your mother when she was your age, and your auntie."

I took the letter and ran lightly to my room. It seemed I hardly touched the risers of the steps but hummed up like a bumblebee.

Again, the heat had gathered at the top of the house, but I passed into my room to sit on the unmade bed to read:

Pittsburgh
My Sweet Daughter,
  Do not be alarmed that you hold this piece of paper and not myself in fond embrace. With my heart and with my words I do embrace you. This, my representative, is as real as I myself.
  Yet I know you are alarmed. Be assured I am living and shall continue to live. Here, at Pittsburgh, though, I turn back for home. The dear babe that I carried is no more. I have suffered a miscarriage, yet I myself will soon gain strength and be the same again. Why I have miscarried I cannot say. Was it all a fancy, I ask myself. So it seems to me too, sometimes, when I think of your father. I have parted with his ashes. I scattered them here where the three rivers come together to form the Ohio. Thus his ashes will flow back home, and perhaps that is for the best. He shall accompany me, whisper beside the steamboat.
  Home seems closer and most of all easier to access than New Bedford. Do not think to come home. You are too young to make this much of a journey by yourself, and, of course, no one from the Island could bring you at this time. Give my love to my sister, Torchy, and Frannie. Send me a letter by return as soon as possible so that I will not worry longer about our missed connection.
  I miss you, oh my daughter. Shed a tear for your lost brother or sister, even as I do. But my nature is to be strong, and I shall be so. I promise it, darling one. You, Una, at sixteen, must be sturdy enough to hear the grieving words of your mother, as one woman listens to another. Perhaps someday I shall sit with you and your

own dear newborn babe. There is no joy like that of being a mother. You have been the joy of my life.

Bertha Spenser, your loving mother

I wept. So this was what it came to! For the first time I felt that life was a cheat. My mother robbed!

I read her page again. The lines of writing seemed bleeding cuts. If our joy was motherhood and that was taken from us, then what was the point? What was the point at all?

My father was dead—that I could understand, or, at least, puzzle. I could worry and spin the idea till it had meaning. But my mother disappointed! That I could not abide.

When she—Mrs. Swain—heaved herself into my room, I am not sure, but I felt the bed dip and her hand on my back.

"There now, there now," she said. "Let's see," and she read the letter. "Too bad. That's too bad. Poor lambs," she muttered. "Poor, poor lambs." I knew that she, too, as a woman was outraged and smoldering with it.

Between my sobs, I managed to ask Mrs. Swain if she thought my mother would be all right.

She sighed as though all the air were leaving her gigantic lungs. She thumped the bed. "In this bed," she said, her voice a sudden rage, "I gave birth ten times, each too soon, each lost. Miscarriage after miscarriage. Bertha will live. She knows it can be done."

CHAPTER 25   The Cabin Boy

NEVER WHILE I was at the Sea-Fancy did I sit down at the table with my sisters. I feared hearing more stories, uniquely female, uniquely painful. I wanted shed of such stories.

I wanted my own life. And I wanted it to be different.

Choice lies in the purse. In mine, a denim bag with a drawstring, I had had the foresight to place, besides the money, my needle and thread, for those implements, for a woman, can be transformed into money, or as good as money. And I had in my purse also the dried petals of Giles's rose, but they were coins of the heart. The money intended for hiring the *Camel* to ferry Mother and me to the Island I quickly spent on coarse clothing and a larger needle at a shop near the wharf. And I bought one gold-plated earring.

Then back to the Sea-Fancy. Scissors I borrowed from Mrs. Swain for cutting my hair, which I stuffed into the kitchen garbage under some potato peels. I also used the scissors to cut two other pairs of trousers and their linings, using the bought ones as a pattern, from my navy dress. Lightweight, for the tropics, I thought. How my needle flew up and down those flat-felled seams; men's britches must be firmly stitched. A loose jacket, with warmth, was a necessity—and that afternoon I found one at a pawnshop, cheap, because both sleeves were partly torn away from the armholes, but again my sewing skill prevailed. With the large needle I pierced one earlobe, and then inserted the golden hoop.

Then I told, or rather wrote, the necessary lies. To Uncle and Aunt and Frannie I conveyed the news of the miscarriage and claimed that I had gone to Kentucky. To Mother I wrote that I had returned to the Island. The fall supply boat would leave tomorrow for the Island, and it would be months more before any news would pass among my family. When I was safely at sea, I would send back a letter with more truth in it. Since Mrs. Swain had read the letter from my mother telling me not to come to Kentucky, I left on the receiving desk a note saying I had gone back to the Island. And should Giles Bonebright or Kit Sparrow call for me, to tell them I had gone home!

A loosely filled duffel sagging on my shoulder, I strode all-boyish under the elliptical sign, *Mrs. Rebekkah Swain, Proprietress—The Sea-Fancy—Hotel for Ladies,* and set out for the wharf, to see what job I could procure. Suppose, having done so much, no ship would have me? I posed the question as I descended the street toward the boats, my feet shod in men's shoes, for which I had swapped my button boots. Would I ship with whatever vessel would take me? Yes. Yes, I would.

I found a red cap in the street, with a dusty footprint on one side, but I took it as a good omen, brushed it off, and put it on my head. How light and free it is to have short hair! My neck felt bare, and longer, as though it had grown up out of my shoulders.

How full of scurry had been the taking of definitive action! But when I reached the wharf and looked up at the *Sussex,* I stopped as though a stick had been stuck among the spokes of my wheel. I saw standing on the deck the very picture of what I myself would be: a cabin boy. His hair, too, was dark and curly, and he was as pretty a chap as any girl. I judged him to be about ten years old. His jacket fit tightly while mine was loose, but aside from that, we were almost the mirror image of each other.

"Hi, there," I shouted, with all the confidence of an older boy. How much older? I decided to be thirteen and a half.

"Hi, yourself," he said. "Come aboard." He spoke as though he were the captain. Later I learned that this was his usual manner of speaking, and for this much of the crew disliked him, since, of course, no captain was he; but he was the captain's son, Chester Fry.

He rightly divined that I was looking for a berth, and I found out from him that the *Sussex* was due to embark on the morrow. How little time Giles and Kit had allotted for me! I was angry at them both.

The *Sussex* was British-made and christened, I learned, but now she flew an American flag. I had never walked the deck of a big ship before, let alone a whaler. There were the brick furnaces for trying out! Cold, of course, now.

When I asked the boy how he liked serving the ship, he said it was boring.

I laughed at him. "I've never been bored in my life," I told him.

This surprised him. At once, he took me for an inventive, entertaining chap—a valuable one to have at sea. He ushered me directly to his father, a man with kindly eyes and somewhat older than I would have expected. Before I could open my mouth to account for myself (in the tradition of lies I had newly taken up), the boy explained that I wished to be a cabin boy, second to himself!

The captain inquiring my name, on the spot I took my father's: "Ulysses Spenser." The captain said he really had no need of a second cabin boy, but his son would be happier for a companion, and what else could I do? Quickly I said that I could be cook's help as well and could mend as well as a girl. On the last, I felt particularly audacious.

Captain Fry replied that all sailors sewed well and would this be my first voyage.

I readily admitted my greenness.

"But what can you do for a whaler?" he said. His manner was so sweet and meditative, his tone so conversational and eschewing of authoritativeness, that I thought of Giles. Just such a quiet captain could he make!

I told the captain I had remarkable eyes.

"But can you climb the rigging? The height might make you sick."

Then I said that I could stand a hundred feet high and not be sick, for I was a lighthouse boy, but that I would have to learn to go up the ropes.

"A hundred feet? What lighthouse, Ulysses?"

Here I was in trouble, for I did not want to name my own. I could not say Alexandria or Cordouan or Eddystone—historical and foreign! I knew but one at all likely and named it: "Sandy Neck. The light at Sandy Neck across from Barnstable."

"Sandy Neck is scarcely a hundred feet, boy."

I said that was true, but I *could* stand at a hundred feet.

"Then you must show me," he said. "But take your time climbing. I'll not have you splattered on the deck."

Chester hugged his dad as though he were a child of six, and the captain's gnarled hand rested lovingly in the boy's curls. I saw why the boy was aboard; his father could not bear to part with him. I wondered if Chester did any work at all.

"What do you see, Ulysses, that you stare so at us?" my captain asked.

Ah, he was quick as Torchy had been, when first I met him, to read my face for my thoughts, or, at least, for their shadow.

"Would there not be, Captain Fry, quite enough of the usual cabin boy work to spread out between the two of us?"

The captain glanced up the mast as though to check its height.

"You are afraid?" he said.

With that I turned to the lower footings and began my ascent of the rigging. I went willingly, for I was not afraid and he misquestioned me there, but I was careful.

"Sailors go faster, Ulysses," Chester called to me.

Promptly his father called up an amendment: "Take your care. As you are."

Thus instructed by my captain, I climbed with a light heart, for surely I was a girl who could climb. Now I remembered climbing white pine trees in Kentucky, for the mast of a ship reminded me more naturally of a tree trunk than of the innards of my old friend the Giant. After climbing the standing rigging, I passed the lower of the furled sails and looked sternward to the mainmast and beyond that to the timber pole of our third mast. Beyond that I looked into the rigging and masts of other ships, and the horizon of the waterline began to be perceived at a different angle. I could see down into the whaleboats hoisted on the davits of the whalers, and the aspects of items left on their decks were now a matter of an above-perspective. From this height, a coil of rope looked like a button with a spiral design, and a bundle of lances, standing like a shock of wheat, were seen mostly as their bright tips, the rest of the head and their staffs being foreshortened. Here was the wind! Here was the sense of sky and air, and this I recognized from standing on the platform of the Giant more than being among the white pine, for in the woods the view was obstructed. The rigging seemed like cobwebs before my eyes that I would brush aside because I was used to the view of utter clarity the Giant afforded.

Now my body spoke to me—my arms trembled. To climb rigging, the legs are not enough, and my arms were all weak and unpracticed in comparison. Yet my legs were so extra-strong that they compensated without complaint. It was more for balance that I wished my arms to be stronger, and I vowed to exercise them till they were the fit companions for my wonderful legs.

Legs like springs! I would glance down at the tops of my shoes occasionally to be sure that I purchased the rope at the ball of my foot and did not work dangerously toward inserting only the toe into the rigging. Though these shoe soles were thick and less sensitive than my button boots would have been, still I could feel the sagged rope of the ratlines underfoot. Below my toes, I saw once or twice the upturned faces of Captain Fry and Chester, and how their bodies disappeared so that they were only faces floating like face-fishes some yard or two above the planking of the deck. Surprised fish, they. But with kindly eyes and smiling mouths. Excitement on Chester's face, that I could do such a thing. Pleasure on the captain's face, caused by the same reason. Then I climbed higher.

Up and up! How to tell you about it? You have looked from the edge of a cliff? Climbed your own trees? Those efforts suggest a whiff of rigging-climbing—as the volatile oil from an orange peel suggests the full flavor of its ecstatic juice.

Think of a kite. You know the pleasure in that, I am sure. It is you who are up there dancing, riding the wind. Yes, those who really love to fly the kite no longer have two feet planted firmly on earth. Though there is pleasure in the horselike, alive-seeming pull on that elongated rein of kite string, if you soar airborne with the kite, then perhaps you rejoice with me in the eagerness and liberty of my sky-climbing.

I hope so, for this physical thrill—as wise Wordsworth knew—is but prelude to the symphony of soaring that I would show you and share with you before this tale is done, for it is of the spirit.

I reached my goal—the palms of my hands imprinted with the twisted and tarred hemp. I threaded my body through the opening that is the eye of that tall, upright needle of the mast. And immediately, I began to use my eyes, for of what use is a lookout if she can only climb? There must be some advantage for the ship; it must profit. I looked to sea.

Ah, training of the eye! How many ships had I spotted from the Island? High in my tower at home had I not seen specks in the air and come to know them as the precursors of birds? I could tell by the shape of the speck, the proportion of horizontal dash to vertical depth, by the flying habit of dipping or curving, by its very speed of approach, whether I was looking at a gull or sea eagle or tern or puffin or lone goose blown off course. Likewise the distant bodies of whales strung on the line where water meets sky; that shape was long known to my eye and distinctive as to species. Take the plumes they made—well, that had been my ocean-fashion show, a parade of parasols, and as surely as some girls might say "made in Paris" or "domed up in the English manner" of city sunshades so could I say, noting the distant promenade of whale spouts, "a finback" (whose origin I knew—having asked—from Uncle to be the Azores) or "a right whale" (swum up from Cape Horn). If the beast was a humpback sounding, I knew it by its flukes, and the sperm whale by its gigantic battering-ram head.

(But more of that last quality anon—and doubly more of that, and tragically. How the excitement comes upon me to tell it all! In the quest of writing, the heart can speed up with anticipation—as it does, indeed, during the chase itself of whales. I can swear it, having done both, and I will tell *you* though other writers may not. My heart is beating fast; I am in pursuit; I want my victory—that you should see and hear and above all feel the reality behind these words. For they are but a mask.

Not the mask that conceals, not a mask that I would have you strike through as mere appearance, or, worse, deceitful appearance. Words need not be that kind of mask, but a mask such as the ancient Greek actors wore, a mask that expresses rather than conceals the inner drama.

(But do you know me? Una? You have shipped long with me in the boat that is this book. Let me assure you and tell you that I know you, even something of your pain and joy, for you are much like me. The contract of writing and reading requires that we know each other. Did you know that I try on your mask from time to time? I become a reader, too, reading over what I have just written. If I am your shipbuilder and captain, from time to time I am also your comrade. Feel me now, standing beside you, just behind your shoulder?)

When I reached the crow's nest, I heard a faint "Bravo" waft up. A strong, good, male voice: Captain Fry extending congratulations. But I could not let myself be distracted by that.

My well-trained eyes swept past the harbor—there was someone manning the masthead of our sister ship the *Essex*, for what reason I didn't stop to imagine—and my gaze roved out to sea and on to the horizon. But stop. Back up. Well before the horizon, just three eye-steps out to sea—say, three thousand feet—what was that submerged shadow? Did I see a treacherous rock waiting to scrape out the hull of some harbor-bound ship? No, it moved. There it was again. A dark gliding. Rapid.

I looked down to aim my voice at my captain. "Whale, ahoy!" I sang out. All triumphant now.

But his words climbed slowly up: "Not possible, boy."

I doubted not my vision, or my judgment, but I looked again to make it more precise. "Killer whale, sir!"

"If you see a whale," he shouted, pausing, "shout 'There she blows!' "

"There she blows!" I yelled with all my heart to all the world, and pointed. And at that moment, the lookout on the *Essex* who had happened to be aloft turned like a surprised automaton, and the whale breached.

"There she blows," the *Essex* shouted, as though his cry were echo of my own.

The whale was elegantly patterned all black and white, as neat as a penguin. Its black glistened in the sun, and its white flagged pennant-like. It arched skyward, birdlike, but hefty, wet and sleek, with so much power in his curve that it took your breath. And then it landed, spray flying as though a palm had smacked water, and the sound of smacking, too, and then tucked itself back into the deep.

"There she leaps!" I yelled. And then the killer whale emerged again, farther away. "There she flies! There she runs! There she sails!"

Suddenly the decks of all the whalers and some of the merchant ships were alive. Up their rigging they scrambled, till every masthead was manned, and the harbor rang with their cries like a disorderly choir—"There she blows!" They could not quit, but repeated my original cry compulsively, as a cluster of hills will announce in many rebounds the first shout.

She was not spouting, but sewing the water with her body, headed for the open sea. The lookouts strained forward in their perches, but, of course, the boats could not give chase. Sails were furled, anchors were down. The ships were like tethered dogs, penned up and scrambling at the gate to race after prey that has innocently crossed their yard. The lookouts could only look. The rhythm of her breaching and diving proved regular and ordered the cries of the men (and myself) so that we did begin to sing in unison; and there was a kind of harmony, too, for our voices were at different pitches.

I ceased in my shouting.

Noble Woman, I silently apostrophized the killer whale. I leaned my breasts forward, as though I, too, were breasting the water. Why did I call her Noble, when her name was Killer? I muttered, *She kills no more than any creature of the sea.* Her nobility lay in her freedom.

Gradually, all the voices grew quiet. The last one, like the last pitch in a game of horseshoes, sailed out, clanked down. I watched the other sailors descend one by one. Some nimbly; some carefully; some sliding down, their feet cupped outside the lines. In the mastheads, they had been like bright birds, now flown down out of sight, songs silenced. Still I stood and looked to sea.

"Ulysses!" It was Captain Fry. "Stay there."

Then he began to climb, with little Chester climbing, too, in front of him, but with the captain's body providing a kind of movable cradle in that Chester climbed within the captain's hands and body and feet. They climbed very slowly, and I could see by his glances and conjecture from his moving mouth that the captain was gently encouraging his boy.

I began to be cold, exposed as I was to the September air, as I waited for them. No doubt little Chester had insisted that he, too, as superior cabin boy, must go aloft. I was sorry I had not bought a regular pea jacket, for I felt I would freeze in a wintry sea. Yet I trusted my ingenuity to provide when need arrived. I would quilt a lining from sailors' scraps.

At length, first Chester, who reached up for my hand, and then the captain threaded into the loop. Some whalers do not have this safety device, but just a tiny open platform to stand on. It was typical of good Captain Fry that he provided safety insofar as it was mortally possible to do so. Ah! the limits of mortality. But that comes later. If only writing were like music with many strands in many layers progressing at once! Da Vinci was said to be able to write different messages simultaneously with each hand! But can anyone read that way? Da Vinci himself, I suppose.

Standing all three together, Fry said to me, "Now, boy, let me look at your eyes."

Obligingly, I looked straight into his, and we commenced to read each other shamelessly.

"So these are eyes that can see under water?" he asked.

"There was a shadow. A moving shadow. Moving at the speed of small whales."

"Looking into your eyes, I do not know what I am seeing," he mused. "But I know that I have never seen it before."

"Nor I, sir," I answered somewhat shakily. For the first time, I felt a little afraid. Here was an impertinence, as is any utterance from the heart.

"Can you teach me to see so keen?" Chester asked.

I looked at the father to see his wish.

"Yes," I said. "Partly, at least. I'll teach you from the deck."

But we three stood some time longer in the masthead, and both the captain and I pointed out boats and currents and clouds to Chester.

After a few moments the captain said kindly, "You're cold, Ulysses. Your cheek is flushed. We should go down."

I went first, and they followed after. We all moved slowly, like crippled ants. As children try to tell their pet cats, climbing down is harder than climbing up. But I vowed to practice.

I was assured my berth on the *Sussex*. There was no need to talk further of that. I felt most unusual, most lucky.

That night in my hammock, slung next to Chester's in the stateroom which opened into the captain's cabin, I thought of the three of us aloft in the crow's nest, with volumes of air about us. The present chamber spoke confidingly of close wooden walls, white-painted, a low wooden ceiling. My breath seemed enclosed. I was hung all netted up like a leg of mutton in a string sack. I felt feverish from too much wind. Beyond his closed door, I could hear the captain snoring. A homey sound. The wind had all but blown through me when I was aloft. Did I inhabit the wind, or the wind inhabit me?

I thought of my searching in Captain Fry's blue eyes—steady, penetrant. Kind. What had I thought I saw? All reflective in my hammock, I knew at once. I had seen the eyes of a true father.

CHAPTER 26   The Companion

WHY HAD I never thought of Uncle Torch that way? He had stood in for four years as dear as any parent. And Aunt, too. My hammock swayed with the natural rising and falling of the ship on its bed of waves, but I could not sleep. Had my mother reached home again? Perhaps the Kentucky cabin door was even now swinging open on its hinges. What an emptiness for her! My father gone. The emptiness inside her body. Perhaps a neighbor woman stood beside her, both of them with web shawls across their shoulders.

My conscience smote me for the lies I had sent to the Island and to Kentucky. But those lies would give them peace of mind—each home believing I was at the other. Was it not clever and kind of me to lie?

The Kentucky cabin—so far away. Here, in Captain Fry's day room, the enclosing space was smaller, the boards planed and painted; there we had huge logs, brown almost to black, with chinking betwixt. I wished for my mother's hand on my hot forehead. *I had lied to my mother*. Or Aunt, who would check on me unobtrusively but whose will I would feel, impelling me to health, strength, even to sensible thoughts! *I had lied to my aunt.*

That night I dreamt of that peculiar pressure of the ratlines under my foot and of how I pushed up and off with each step.

In the morning, Chester and I took our breakfast at his father's table. What a bounty it was! Mrs. Swain's board could not have been much better. Captain Fry explained breakfast was celebratory, as we sailed right after. He told us to listen and we would hear the handspikes turning the windlass to haul up the anchor, even as we cut our ham.

There was fresh cow's milk and butter for our toast. Chester had a cut-crystal pot of a mixture of white sugar and cinnamon which he was allowed to spoon liberally over his toast. He enjoined me to try it, and I did, finding it to be a heavenly condiment. The captain urged us both to eat more and more, reminding us that we were growing boys and needed to eat heartily. In the center of the table sat a golden brick of cheddar cheese. We had large bowls of oatmeal—molasses on that— and we each had a hard-boiled egg sprinkled with black pepper. Chester informed me that when the chickens aboard stopped laying eggs, we ate the chickens.

Last voyage the chickens had stopped doing their duty on the morning after the *Sussex* crossed the equator. The captain and mates had had fried chicken, baked chicken, poached chicken, and finally chicken stew—four mainland meals in the middle of the South Atlantic.

I inquired how many chickens we had among us this time. Thirteen in the crate under the carpenter's bench. "Last time there were twelve," Chester said cheerfully. "So one chicken is a veteran, like me." (The last voyage had been his first.)

"What do you mean?"

"She never stopped laying eggs. So we didn't eat her. She gets to sail again."

I could think of a better reward for that productive bird, like a berth in a land-rooted coop at home. I glanced at the captain to see if he entertained any such thought, but I noted a placid justice on his brow— not mercy. However, as I immediately learned, I could not always read my captain accurately.

"Perhaps we'll just keep her as a pet in any case," he said, with that extreme of mercy, pardon, in his voice. He smiled at his boy. "A companion."

Little did they guess that Chester's human companion was also female. Involuntarily I cleared my throat.

Chester looked at me impishly. "Are you my human hen?"

"Chester," his father said, "leash your tongue. He means no harm, Ulysses."

"Ulysses!" Chester said. "That's a clumsy name."

"A classical name. Ulysses survived the Trojan War," his father said. "He was a sailor, a voyager of many years before he returned to his wife. His son, Telemachus, grew up while he was away."

"I shall call you Billy."

The memory of our old goat charging the Lighthouse tower came to mind, and I laughed.

"Billy has a pleasant temper," the captain said. "It's a good thing for you, Chester."

At that moment, the ship gave a lurch. It came up through my feet on the floor and into my bottom on the chair; my shoulders, neck, and head swayed with it. My body knew! We were moving! I, a girl, was going to sea.

I'm sure my happiness was made visible to the captain. I could not help but beam at my new family at the breakfast table.

Retrospectively, I flagellate myself. How could I have so callously left my old family? Sixteen thinks the joy of adventure is her natural right. Sixteen thinks that because all is well—temporarily—with her, those who love her must mystically be assured.

"How does it feel, Billy?" Captain Fry asked me. What a surprising question! It was as though he *were* my mother but invested with power. And what a quietness those two qualities made in combining. Power and sympathy equal quietness. What an equation!

"Your mind moves in flashes," Captain Fry said. "Thoughts shimmer like sheet lightning on your countenance."

"What do you mean?" Chester demanded.

I dodged my head and was silent. No one had ever made me dodge before! Certainly not my own father. Chin up! That was the necessary attitude for defiance. But now my head drooped.

"I feel happy and excited," I mumbled.

"And don't you look it?" The captain laughed. "Chester, go up and stand by the pilot."

"Is he the same as last time?" Chester made a gesture with both hands as though to smooth a gigantic mustache parallel to the floor. Then his hands made abrupt, right-angle turns toward the floor.

"I've seen that man," I said. "He owns the sloop *Camel*."

"He was so *hairy*," Chester pronounced.

"No," his father answered. "One of the new crew, Giles, is a licensed harbor pilot. He's taking us out. We save the pilot fee."

"But how will he get back?" Chester asked.

"He's with us for the voyage. Go and talk with him. Learn what you can of piloting. Billy will be cabin boy and straighten for you this time."

Chester licked his finger and stuck it straight in the cinnamon-sugar pot.

"Come along," his father said to Chester.

I liked it right well when they both quit our chambers. I left the dining table to enter the stateroom, to peer through the portholes. Yes, we were moving. And it was Giles who guided us. This last gave me a special thrill of pleasure. Giles had no knowledge that his ship was pregnant with me. I was a kind of Jonah in the whale's belly. While he guided above, I was picking up cups and plates. I was making a neat stack and wondering if it was my duty to wash them, as cabin boy, or was that work assigned to cook or to the steward? And perhaps still I would wash them, as cook's help? Doubtless I was to straighten the captain's bed. I walked toward the door of his cabin, along the starboard side. My feet moved in the direction we sailed. It seemed a true walking away from New Bedford.

I smiled. Perhaps I could stay hidden from Giles and Kit till we crossed the equator. Surely that line was the boundary of another realm? How smoothly we moved. Giles was at the helm! I dropped into the captain's chair at the head of the table, his stateroom door behind me. The stack of dishes sat on my left, and I could see the ring of toast crumbs left around the spot where Chester's plate had been.

Not curly-headed Chester but big-nosed Giles was the natural heir to a sailing ship—let it be merchant or whaler. But not a battleship. There was too much Quaker in me to imagine that. Harvard would not have Giles for all his perfect answers to their questions. And better than perfect, too, I would warrant. Telling things they themselves did not know. Yes, though they learned from him, they would not have him. "That which the builders rejected hath become the cornerstone of the building." Was that my father's voice intoning scripture? For Giles might, indeed, be the president of Harvard College. His mind and character were fit for it.

They were not worthy of him! What had they shown of true integrity? But Captain Fry would see Giles's promise. I smiled to think that the man who had recognized me with such alacrity would surely see the same and more in Giles. The captain had already passed the first test—for he had hired Giles and Kit.

But it would have been Kit who talked at their interview. Something in me knew that Giles would have arranged it thus. He would himself have stood silently, a little taller, behind Kit. Giles would have folded his arms across his chest with his hands in his armpits. It was Kit who would think of what would persuade another. Giles's thought was tethered by what signified to himself.

How could Uncle Torch have given up the sea? I listened. I heard the rush of water passing my wooden wall.

Ulysses I was, and no Billy!

I got up to tidy the master's room. The captain's stateroom, where Chester and I slept, fitted all across the stern. Three round windows looked out at the wake of the ship. Across the water, I could still see the harbor of New Bedford. I took down the two hammocks and folded them so that the captain might use his sofa and table if he liked, then I returned to his bedroom, adjoining. The bed was suspended in the center of the room, on gimbals, as the captain's had been in Mrs. Swain's story. "I became the captain's whore," she had said. But my captain was not of that sort—so the good daughter in me said. But the woman part of me asked, "What do you know of men?"

Suppose Giles and I were to marry? (I forgot I was angry with him.) Then would I be sent back home like a bad girl? But if I were a passenger and we paid my way with his salary? How quickly I laid hold on my spouse's purse! Well, I could sew and earn my passage.

What is a gimbaled bed? Imagine a bed such as you ordinarily see in a well-appointed house: a wooden frame strung across with rope, a mattress, a headboard—Queen Anne with two arabesques of waves crashing toward a central spindle—but do not imagine legs on the bed.

Instead it is suspended. From the tops of its posters, lines lead to a central gimbal, which device digests the rolling and the pitching of the ship so that the passage of the bed is more smooth than that of the vessel transporting it.

In short, a gimbaled bed was one that could be made up like any other bed, and I set to doing it. The captain's linens were the finest I had ever seen or touched.

The captain had left none of his clothing lying about, but against one wall was a high cherry chest of drawers topped with the same spindle-and-waves design of the headboard. The spindle was the abstraction of a lighthouse, I mused. On either side of the cabin door hung a decoration. On the right was the skin of a zebra—I recognized the jagged bars of black and white, and the tail hung down with a black hairy tassel at the end. It hung on the short wall that separated the bedroom from the head, or toilet, jammed in the corner formed by the perpendicular of the bedroom and the stateroom. On the other side of the bedroom door hung a cutlass in a silver scabbard which was worked all over with a scrolling line. Like the zebra skin, the cutlass sported a tassel, but this one, hanging from the hilt, was made of an aquamarine blue silk. I did not know why, but I shuddered when I saw this weapon displayed as something pretty.

I returned to the stateroom to have a last glimpse of land. Now New Bedford was small out the stern portholes; the mighty masts of harbored ships became the size of scratches on window glass. Did I view reality or merely random marks across my lens?

One book lay on the desk, a thickish one. There were no other books about. None at all. This surprised me, for the captain had read, I knew, the Greeks, at least. I hoped the book would not prove to be a Bible. It was bound in dark green cloth boards, frayed at the edges. I read the single word stamped in gold on the cover: SHAKESPEARE. I hefted the tome and opened the book to the flyleaf. Here was written, in a firm hand, the sentence *Shakespeare is my Harvard and my Yale.* And then the captain had signed his name, *Clifford Fry,* and a date some twenty years before.

The pages were soft to the turning. *The Tempest,* a play I myself knew well, seemed the most read and annotated. Yes, it suited the temperament of Clifford Fry. A world kept safe by a benign despot. I felt like Miranda: "O brave new world, that has such people in it!"

He had also much read *King Lear,* but I did not like it so well. The scenes with the cruel daughters bit at me. I had not been so rejecting of my paternity as Goneril and Regan had been. But neither had I proved a Cordelia.

I was interrupted by the abrupt opening of the door. A very red-faced man informed me that the captain wanted me on deck, that he himself was the cook, and that after the captain was done with me, I was to report to him in the galley. Now my heart was fearful. Would I walk straight into Giles and we scarcely beyond land? There was no possibility that he would look at me and not know me. How had those heroines of Shakespeare appeared so convincingly as boys to those who knew them already as girls? It was a ludicrous convention of drama. But Deborah Sampson, a woman in history, had fought in the War for Independence dressed as a man. Could I signal with a wink that Giles was not to betray me? If he understood, would he obey? I made my feet climb up the companionway to the deck. Even through my worry, I was pleased at once at the sunshine and brilliance of the open deck and by its size. After the cramped rooms below, there seemed a platform presenting a whole world, clear, bright, and trembling with uncertainty. If only I did not have to hide from two men instead of one.

I walked gingerly along, trying to keep my head down. I had put on the red cap with the long bill I had found in the street to the wharf, and I hoped that that would mask my features from a downward glance were Kit or Giles aloft. My shorn curls stuck out from the cap, and I was sure that I did not look like myself, from above. I found the captain at the wheel, with Chester at his elbow, and no sign of Giles. Could a month? a week? be made up of such lucky non-encounters?

It was the captain's desire that each morning after breakfast Chester and I should walk the deck round about for a distance that I judged equal to a mile. During this time we were to converse. "Tell him what you know," the captain said to me.

"I think it is not much," I said, for I remembered when I had undertaken to educate Frannie.

Again I congratulated myself that at neither of my homes had any-one been left worrying about me and my whereabouts, though both letters had been shameful lies. I asked Chester how soon he thought our course would cross that of a homebound ship. I would tell them the truth now. Now I couldn't be reclaimed. Now I could say that my disguise had worked with the captain, and I was perfectly safe. I had begun to see my own life as a story and myself as the author of it.

As Chester and I talked, my eyes sometimes shifted to the sea and sky and sometimes dwelt upon the gear and fittings and architecture of the ship. I wanted Chester to name every single part to me. My eye sorted out rails and ropes, masts and booms and barrels and brooms, where there were doors and windows, how the small boats were suspended and what was stored in them. I noted the smell of tar, the slide of water against wood. In the distance I heard the sea's natural sounds, the shifting of unspeakable tons of heaving water—sounds which the world would make whether any boat sailed or not.

And there was the urine barrel. I turned my eyes away. The pressure on myself for relief was sudden.

"I must go below," I said, thinking of the captain's private head. I should have used it sooner. I told Chester he should let his thoughts wander while I was gone and then give me an account of how one thought had led to another. I knew it was a strange assignment, a kind of game almost, but one I had played whenever I lay awake on the Island, wanting home.

I was lucky again in that the captain was not in our quarters, and I started my return with the satisfaction of feeling comfortable and safe, when whose passing shoulder should I bump on the deck but Kit's. For a moment his tan-gold eyes, his mountain lion eyes, looked straight into mine. I hurried on.

CHAPTER 27   Captain Coffin's Story—
Secondhand

I WAS GLAD whenever I was cloistered in the steward's pantry belowdecks, peeling potatoes, for in there I would be entirely safe from encounters with Kit and Giles. They being common seamen, their quarters were the forecastle, in the bow of the *Sussex*, and though both their quarters and those kept by the captain, the mates, and the carpenter, cook, etc., were all belowdecks, they were separated by a bulkhead with no door in it and also by the huge, low-ceilinged blubber room. We entered our separate quarters from entirely separate staircases; even on deck we were unlikely to meet, as they were consigned to that area entirely "before the mast." There were only two occasions when my realm and that of Kit and Giles might overlap. The galley was aft of the mast, and they did come there to get the victuals passed out by the cook. And in our morning perambulation Chester and I circled around the entire deck, including around the carpenter's bench and the abutting tryworks, and around the quarterdeck. In order to stay cloistered in the pantry, at least till we had crossed the Line, I resolved to make myself agreeable. As I slipped my knife along under the brown skins of the potatoes, which were of a fine quality except for being uncommonly knobby, I glanced around to see what other tasks I might volunteer to do.

The cook, whose red face had startled me in the captain's bedroom, was shy of middle age but he had the comportment of an older man, one with crotchets and manners that seemed the habit of many years. Perhaps living and working in so confined a space as a ship's galley had condensed his mannerisms prematurely. Yet, as it turned out, the content of his speech, if not his style, was unpredictable, and he surprised me almost every time he spoke.

Wooden boxes, many drawers and cabinets, crockery pots, barrels, hinged wooden boxes were stored all around the cook's larger galley and its pantry on deck. The smaller steward's pantry (belowdecks, next to the captain's dining room) overflowed with storage boxes of the nicer foodstuffs, some labeled as strawberry jam, capers, crackers, fig preserves, smoked herring, tinned beef tongue. Positioned on a high shelf so that the contents would flow down were two large casks, both labeled water.

One of the casks, toward which he seemed to gesture, had a sealed bunghole at the bottom.

"Have you a taste for wine, my lad?" he asked.

"I don't know. I've not had any."

"Not had wine," he said. "Not even the communion wine?"

"No."

"Are you not a Christian?"

He seemed so full of wonder that I decided not to shock him. "My family did not hold with wine."

"But now," he said, "you have aught of *them* a-looking over your shoulder."

Then he took a small pail and told me to hold it under the bunghole. From a kitchen drawer he produced a spigot. In short order, he broached the tun, losing not a precious drop, and installed the spigot.

"Now I must draw a sample," he said. "We must drink to the wind. A proper toast guarantees good winds. Neither weak nor overly strong. Isn't that what you pray for, lad?"

Two cups were whisked out, the spigot was opened, a wine of lovely golden color flowed out. "Muscatel," he announced.

I watched him take a tiny sip, his eyes fastened on mine over the rim of the cup. "Taste it, lad. It's the gift of the gods. What was the first miracle of Jesus? He turned water into wine. Well, not meaning to blaspheme—oh, no, not that at all—I have done the same."

I took a sip and found it good.

"Not too fast, lad. But this is the drinking time of day. I've been waiting for you. No one drinks in the morning—oh, no—and no one suspects anyone else to imbibe then. Oh, there are secrets on a ship, lad. Make no doubt about that. And this is the finest one I know."

I quickly resolved that he should not know my secret.

"Now, say it with me: To the winds! All of 'em, bless 'em." Then he solemnly took a sip. "Now, to the North Wind. Let him love us like an old man—not too often. Heh!" We drank. "To the East Wind. Let her blow warm and smiling from Africa." For each of the four cardinal winds, we sipped our wine cups. What can I say—by the time we reached the West Wind a glow was spreading through me like a golden sunset. The flavor of the grape was in this muscatel wine, and I thought of the berry teas and jellies I had so enjoyed on the Island and how Aunt had said they were good for the body.

"Now to the ordinal winds," he said. And after toasts to the nor'east, the sou'east, the sou'west, and the nor'west (I had begun to giggle, which delighted the cook, for he felt I was happy), he proposed that he drink to our names. "I didn't proper introduce myself: Prince Harry, I am. That's what the captain calls me."

"He calls me Billy. But my name is Ulysses."

"Is it really?" he said. "A Bible name, I believe. And which do you prefer?"

"Which do *you* prefer?" I asked with silly deference.

"I think Billy is the preferable name," he answered. "And here's to you, Billy Green, for I've never seen a lad so green as you."

"And here's to you, Prince Harry, for I've never seen a cook so red as you." And we laughed as though the idea made some sense. I felt full of swagger. So this is what it was to be a man! Well, a certain kind of sailor man. One who was help to a drunken steward.

"Now, above all," Harry said, "we must get the captain's lunch ready on time. And it won't do to keep the crew waiting either. What, my Billy Grin, do you think is the watchword of my kitchen?"

"Punctuality," I answered confidently.

"No, no," he said. "Economy. Economy. So what does it mean we do with the peels you've accumulated?"

"Put in crew's stew," I pronounced.

"Now you catch my drift. That's the way I always uses the peels. Now that being the case, lad, you can peel more generously in regard to what's left with the skin. You see this potato?"

All the time we sipped. He seemed the most entertaining companion I had ever had.

"What's your opinion of him?"

"A fine potato."

"Yes, but ain't he a bit unusual?"

"Very unusual."

"In what regard, lad?"

"Well, in regard to lumps and bumps."

"Well spoke. Now, we peel him straight. The knife just slips along, and, you see, it's quicker that way and what's left under the bump, well, that's good potato meat for the crew's stew. Now you understand me."

"Tell me," I said confidentially, "are there ever any women among the crew?"

His face became very solemn, his eyes spread round as pennies. "Not so as I've heard," he said. "Have you heard of any?"

"Well, where is Chester's mother?"

"New Bedford! Not the captain's bed. Oh, no. New Bedford, lad. Her bed's the grave. She gave her life for Chester of the darling curls."

He paused to see how I was taking all this in. I lowered my eyes to the rim of my cup. "The next Chester's mother? The old mother's sister, housekeeper to the captain. Look for her in Union Street in the shops that's got the bounty of the world. Look for her on the wide avenues of County Street, where the mansions are. Never look on board the *Sussex*."

"They have a fine and happy house?"

"À la mode, lad. Absolutely à la mode. Only one thing—when you go in the gate you must walk through the jawbones of a sperm whale 'cause he's got them reared up there like an arch. Otherwise, strictly à la mode, à la Paris, France. You've felt his sheets?"

I nodded affirmation.

"Aha, that's good. Don't try to tell me you haven't."

"Have you sailed long with Captain Fry?"

"I was his cabin boy. Like you. You might turn into *me*, lad, given patience."

"What else for the stew, Harry? And should we start the water boiling?"

He opened a cabinet door and threw out a bouquet of dirty spinach and two large bunches of carrots, again remarkably knobby. "Now you know how to peel 'em, don't you?"

"Which 'water' do I use to wash the spinach?"

Again, he stopped stock-still, as he had when I asked about women aboard. His eyes grew round. Finally he sucked in his breath in a wet whoosh and began to laugh. "You surprise me, boy," he finally said. "I like that in a buddy. Well, my surprising boy, never waste the better water. That's my advice to you."

I busied myself washing the gritty spinach leaves. Harry seated himself on a low three-legged stool, his cup—replenished with the better water—in his hand.

"You ask about women. I'll tell you a story of women. Of one who went a-whaling with her captain husband and what became of her."

"What happened to her?" I kept my back to him. I felt my attention focus. It was as though I drew myself up from wading in a pool of golden, grapey nectar. I lugged my mind onto a hospitable slanting rock.

"She survived. That's what. Not her husband, not a single member of the crew. She proved the adage: a woman on board is bad luck. She had no need of a cook, I can tell you that. But let me tell the story right. This I heard from Captain Roland Coffin, which happened to him in the South Seas."

"Captain Coffin?"

"The name startles you. You've not been yet to Nantucket. It's populated with Coffins. When you get to Nantucket, note that I told you so. Remember this very moment when I taught you how to enjoy the golden syrup of life. Muscatel. I drink no other. I have my own vineyard, or I will someday. Oh, you'll go to Nantucket. Have no doubt of that. When you see Coffin, when you see Starbuck and Swain, think how I told you it would be so."

"I met a woman with Swain in her name in New Bedford."

"Yes. They spread about. But that's mainly what's in Nantucket."

Content that I had washed out the grit and the little black beetles from the spinach, I began to peel the carrots. I had always been taught to cut a peel paper-thin, and it went against the grain to take long swipes with the knife and leave the carrot square-edged, but I meant to do as I was told, and for the crew, whose stew would be stocked with peelings, there was an advantage.

"Let me tell the story right." He plopped upon a high stool, his red face shining.

"Captain Coffin was a young man, and as a youth, he was in a whaleboat towed off by a whale. Yes, they do that. A Nantucket sleigh ride. Slap, slap, slap—you fly over the waves like the whale was a horse and you was in a runaway sleigh. But a whale ain't no little horse, is he, lad? Put a hundred horses together, put ten elephants together—then you have a whale. So off this harpooned whale runs, like a hundred horses, off from the ship. Off goes Captain Coffin in the whaleboat, till there's no ship to be seen.

"Now's the time to cut free. Yes, there comes a time, and he did. So they in the whaleboat wait for the ship. They wait a day. After that, lad, don't wait. Set sail. That's what they did, provisions being low. They set sail and made a lucky island. Why lucky, lad? Because there was water, fresh water, on the island, and there ain't on every South Sea island—oh, no. And even better, there's no horde of howling savages ready to eat them.

"The cannibal stories are real. I'll tell you some myself sometime. Let me tell you, it's a relief not to live amongst cannibals. But this island with its pleasant spring, it appeared deserted. There's some sort of little scurrying animal around the spring pool, but that's not cannibals.

"But, hark ye, there's a native. But it ain't no native.

"It's a tattered-up, suntanned American woman, a Nantucket woman, wife of a whaling captain. She sailed with him, but no luck brought she. Oh, no. Where are they? Dead. All lost on a reef. But how long has she been on the island a-making do? Five years, lad. Five years. Could you or I live on an island five years?"

Of course I had lived on an island four years, but, I had to admit, the circumstances were very different.

"She gathers up boards and bits from the wreck and she makes do."

"Like Robinson Crusoe," I say. I am delighted, for this is a true story, and of a woman.

"You can believe she was excited. Captain Coffin said she commenced to hollering, 'It ain't no dream, you're real, you're real!' and to pinching each of them to make sure. 'Thank God Almighty, I'm saved!' After a bit, she promises to cook for them a stew, a capital stew.

"She was good as her word. These is Captain Coffin's words: 'She looked on quite delighted for to see us eat, and a-fillin' each chap's dish as fast as it was empty. After she done helped us round for the fifth or sixth time, says she, "Now you don't any of you know, I'll warrant, what you been eatin' up so hearty." '

"The captain says again how powerful good it was, but, no, he couldn't say what was in it. Says she, 'That there was a rat stew.'

"The rats from the ship had come ashore. They, like the woman, survived that wreck. They had bred, and for five years that is the meat she lived on.

"Now the captain and the crew had admitted she made them rats taste good. I don't know what she found on the island to make 'em sweet. The men would have preferred not to eat more rat, but their vessel was slow in finding them, and they must keep body and soul together. She was a cooking woman, and Captain Coffin said they had rat fixed every which way—roast rat, broiled rat, fried rat, rat fricassee, and rat stew. Finally the vessel did come, and the woman and all the men, well fed, went aboard, leaving the island to the rule of the rats."

"I should hope," I said, "that if we wreck on a reef and get marooned on an island, it's chickens that come with us."

CHAPTER 28   A Whaleboat by Moonlight

T HAT NIGHT, as I lay in my hammock, I couldn't sleep for thinking of Aunt and Uncle and how good they were. And Frannie, who loved me. And how was my mother? Finally, I was almost asleep when Chester announced impatiently that he could not sleep.

"Let's pretend," he said.

"In what way?"

"Follow me."

Without putting on his shoes, he tiptoed to the small staircase called the companionway, and I followed him, sleepily. On deck, Chester made his way to one of the whaleboats, which was not hoisted on its davits, but sat open in braces on the deck. He stepped inside. I hesitated.

"Pretend we're on the water," he whispered. "We're on the chase."

"I've never been on the chase," I replied.

"I'll tell you how. I, the harpooner, stand in the bow. You, the mate, in the stern." Chester waited imperially for me to join his drama. Somewhat reluctantly I climbed into the stern, grasping first the upright brace for the steering oar to support me and then a sort of stubby post. "What's this?" I asked.

"The loggerhead. The line from the large line tub"—I saw the tub lodged between the near seats of the whaleboat—"goes aft to the loggerhead, circles round, and then goes forward toward the harpoons. They connect by their own cords to the line."

From nowhere Chester lifted a harpoon. He almost staggered under the weight of it. The implement consists of a very stout wooden holster and an iron. In later years, the irons were developed with a toggle point, but ours were barbed like a simple arrowhead.

"Pretend we're at sea," he said, rocking the boat a bit for realism.

"The harpoon should rest here," and he erected a stick, divided at its top into two compartments, perpendicularly into the starboard gunwale. Through one compartment he rested his harpoon, the barb leaning out beyond the prow, like a projection eager to do its duty. "Usually, there're two," he said. And he lifted another harpoon to rest in the second compartment of the upright *crotch,* for so this harpoon stand was named. "The first iron, and the second iron."

The whaleboat was some sixteen feet long, with struts across the width to reinforce the boat and serve as seats for the six oarsmen, two on each.

"What must I do?" I asked, being a rather ignorant mate.

"You must sing out, 'Break your backs! Break your backs, my hearties!' For that's what the mate says to the crew."

"Break your backs! Break your wrists, and arms!" I improvised, and, like Chester, made the boat rock in the moonlight. Our pretense did not seem to progress much. Maybe Chester envisioned whales ahead, and we were approaching them. He stood crouched and ready. Abruptly I asked, in a normal tone, "What are these other casks and implements?"

Chester relaxed his posture. "I'll tell you about it," he said. And he proceeded to name parts methodically, from bow to stern, in a clear and authoritative manner. He leaned forward and put a finger in a small vertical groove near the chocks; the cut was used for straightening harpoons. Another larger notch, like the half-moon that sailed in the sky above us, cut into the horizontal bracing across the prow, was called the clumsy cleat, and there the harpooner might wedge his thigh as he reared back to heave the iron. Besides the harpoons the whaleboat carried other sharp implements: a boat spade, a boat hook, and lances and knives. "Suppose we were towed away?" Chester asked. "We have our supplies." Standing on the gunwale, he pointed out the lantern keg, used to carry candles and hardtack, which had its own line to retrieve it, should so precious an item be swept overboard; we also had a water keg and a compass aboard. There was a bucket for bailing.

Chester showed me a hinge that could be let down to receive a single sail, which lay furled with its mast beside the oars. In some ways, the whaleboat was like a miniature of the ship, though of course it had no layering of decks and was entirely open. "Each oar has its name," he said earnestly. They were named for the men who wielded them, and those men were so named for their position and function in the whaleboat. The large steering oar was easy to remember. "You would wield that," he said, since I stood in the stern. And next came the oars known as stroke, tub, midship, bow, and boat steerer.

"Here is the waif pole," he said and waved a small flag about. "If we can't tow in our whale, we tag him with this"—I noted the dart at the end for entering the whale's flesh—"and then he's claimed as ours." I thought how vast must be the bulk of a whale, and how great in value, for him to be claimed exactly the same way Columbus might have claimed America, with a flag.

Chester stood for a moment, regarding the sixteen feet of boat between us. Finding nothing left to explain, he turned, saying, "Now you say, 'Give it to him!'"

"Give it to him," I whispered, my heart not in the game.

Chester did not lift either the first or second iron from the crotch, but instead pretended to heave a harpoon. "Now we must change places," he said, and he began to walk toward me and I toward him. "The mate steers us in and we beach on his back!"

"Whose?" I whispered as I passed Chester, he taking one direction around the line tub and I the other.

"The whale's back! You beach us onto his back. Pretend you hold on to their heads, like knobs. The boat is rocking crazy! crazy!"

"Whose?"

"The heads of the crew. Steady yourself, or it will be 'man overboard' and no stopping. Here's a wave!"

I obediently groped the air for invisible heads. When I reached the bow, Chester urged, "Take up the lance, take up the lance," and so I pretended to do so. Then Chester added, "I shouldn't have to tell you what to do." He sighed.

A real member of the crew materialized. "Ye'd best go back below, Master Chester," he said. To me he spoke not at all, as though I didn't exist. Silent as moonlight in our bare feet, we padded across the deck and down the companionway.

  Captain Morrell's Story—
Thirdhand

W HEN THE WATER was boiling briskly on the galley stove,
Harry told me to set out a smaller pot, for the captain's soup later. It
turned out that Harry was both cook and steward, and that fact probably accounted in part for my getting to come aboard.

"The captain don't eat the regular stew, then?" I asked, corrupting
my English to better fit in with Harry.

"The captain requested the egg-drop soup. It's a Chinese recipe. I'll
show ye how it's made—just by dropping the raw egg into the boiling
water, a pat of butter, the way Captain likes it, and a sprinkle of green
onion tops, cut fine. Break the eggs now, ahead of time, into a bowl."

I did so and was about to chunk the shells into the garbage when
Harry stopped me.

"What's the watchword of the galley, lad?"

"Economy."

"And what be ye about to do? Throw out shells? What's sticking
to the inside of the shell, boy?"

"Well, it's no more than a wet slime," I said.

"There's nutrition there," Harry said. "Don't doubt nature, or nature's God. Grind up those shells in my mortar. Use the pestle till
they're fine as cracker crumbs. Then we sprinkle 'em in the stew. It
makes a nice crunchiness for the crew. But this we do in the pantry,
belowdecks. Come along."

"Perhaps I shouldn't have washed away the grit and bugs," I said,
following him down the companionway. How many times was I to run
up and down those little steps? I had the legs for it!

"Oh, bugs. If we had to, we could eat 'em. I know an island where
the Tasaday people live. It's a paradise. They eat all morning, turn up
leaves and eat whatever's under till they're full. Bugs is strong meat, Billy.
All afternoon, these Tasaday sit together. They have seats in the side of
a rocky cliff. It's like a theater. Only there ain't no show except as what's
in their heads. They hold hands and daydream all afternoon. The night's
for fornication. All together, anybody with anybody, I've heard."

I felt shaken by this. Fornication—yes, I knew the word, for my father's Bible prescribed against it. But the island peoples, having no Bible, apparently had no prohibition. They had our ways neither in diet nor in married life. I did not comment.

"The egg-drop soup should be served fresh-made, so we'll wait for that," Harry said, "till you're ready to go in for lunch yourself and you shall serve it."

"Will I ever help to serve the crew?" I asked, for there I would certainly see Kit and Giles. But again it seemed I was lucky. I was to serve the captain and the officers, who sometimes ate at the captain's dining table, sometimes apart, as the captain liked some time with just his boy at meals. Harry fed the crew.

"Now the elderly Chinese gentlemen that can afford it have a special soup beyond egg-drop," Harry said.

"What's that?"

Harry commenced to prepare pans to fry freshwater fish that he had bought on shore and that must be cooked right up. We had stores of fish in brine and smoked fish, and as we sailed, we would catch dolphin from time to time, and cod and tuna and other saltwater fish, which we would eat, but that was all haphazard, our main mission being to chase the whale, of course.

"For rejuvenating, when their old peters hang limp, they eat *bêche-de-mer.*"

"What's that?"

"Sea slugs."

My stomach unseated itself and danced a jig.

"Some white captains make a good profit on sea slugs," Harry went on. "You gather them among the reefs. You cure and dry them and take them back to China. You sell them high for the soup."

"Do only men eat the soup?"

"There's no need for rejuvenating old women. Oh, no. They've got plenty of young women."

"You've been to China, Harry?"

"There's not much I haven't been to. The sea goes everywhere. There's sperm whale in every sea, and where the whale swims, there swims the *Sussex,* with me cooking on her deck and chopping in her bowels. But I'll tell you a story of Captain Benjamin Morrell, captain of the ship *Antarctic,* which sailed out of New Zealand for the Fiji Islands, him intending to harvest sea slugs for *bêche-de-mer.*

"Now here again is a true story that happened recently, and it's all quite true, he having kept a record himself, and his wife, whose name was Abby Jane, she having kept account, too, of the tale he told her."

"A tale of sea slugs?"

"Oh, sea slugs is just the jumping-off point. Sea slugs is not at all the main thing. Sea slugs is but the trigger. Let me send out the bullet for ye."

"Harry, are the lunches on schedule?" For I did not want to be thought a corrupting influence and lose my job in the pantry, though it was a close, small place, as all places on ship must be. The sunny, open deck flashed in my mind. There was a world of difference between its open sea and sky, and the cabinets and drawers and work spaces of belowdecks. We did get a trickle of sunlight, for two greenish prisms were set in through the floor of the deck, the work of these prisms being to collect light and funnel it, much weakened, below. The greenish light gave our place a certain eerie, underwater, wavering kind of glow.

"Carry these up to the galley," he directed. And when we arrived: "Another stick for the fire, Billy-boy." He opened the oven door, and heat poured into the galley. " 'Tis a story of the fires of hell, I'll tell ye. Certainly it was hell for some. Americans, too, though they set out, Captain Morrell and his crew, from New Zealand.

"Well, they left Abby Jane off in Manila, and they sailed not to Fiji, but to the Bismarck Archipelago, which lies north of New Guinea. The crew went ashore to build a curing house for the snails. There was natives there, men as black as ebony, but they seemed tame enough. For a time. For a time. Morrell was on board when the savages let out their war whoops and started to massacre the men ashore. For they were black cannibals, every one. The sound of their whoops, Captain Morrell said, was 'lifeblood-curdling' to his heart. Many a black savage fell, but their numbers was legion compared to the fourteen crew ashore. Morrell and his men aboard were forced to do little but watch. The savages took the crew's own cutlasses out of their scabbards and used them to cut and carve, to butcher. Yes, it was butchering. And some used their own spears, sticking and tormenting any who still had life. They built fires, and there on the beach with Morrell looking on, grinding his teeth no doubt, they roasted pieces of human flesh and ate it half raw with blood, fresh blood, running over their black chins. So Captain Morrell could only sail away that time, which was in May, back to Manila, where he told Abby Jane the story.

"But that weren't the end. No. He told the story, yes, but he also told he would have revenge. I do not know why he would take Abby Jane back with him. I don't know why he would have taken her whaling in the first place, but he did do both. Well, she wrote about it.

"September and back to the archipelago. Three hundred cannibals attacked the *Antarctic* as soon as she appeared. But now Captain Morrell was ready, and he opened fire. But that wasn't enough. Not enough revenge at all. He put ashore and built a garrison. There was another battle, with war canoes coming in from all the islands in the archipelago. They had the devil in them, but without the guns—well, Captain and his men, with Missus looking on, mowed them right down. The whole village was destroyed under the cannon fire. Then the crew and all struck up 'Yankee Doodle' and after that 'Rule, Britannia' for the Brits among them.

"A whaleman can be a fighting soldier, lad. In a whale there's enough blood and strength for three hundred cannibals. Captain Morrell and his men had whatever courage you'd want to see in the best military man. Now I'll tell you what Mrs. Morrell had to say. She wrote her feelings out: 'I saw all this without any sensation of fear, so easy is it for a woman to catch the spirit of those near her.' "

I was troubled to hear that Abby Jane had been caught up in the spirit of revenge and war. My aunt was right to say that war was the worst of evils, but what of cannibalism? Aunt had called war silly, but it was linked by blood to cannibalism, and I asked myself, Should not civilized folk be able to mourn their dead and not require blood for blood? Did not Jesus himself admonish Christians to "turn the other cheek"?

"It's all fresh for me," Harry went on, "for I bought her book onshore." Then he opened two of the cabinet doors, and to my surprise, there was a regular library stored there. "It's the library of the sea," Harry said. "My second secret." Again, Harry surprised me, for while I expected my captain to have a little library, he had only Shakespeare. Harry's books were a library of the sea in two senses, the second being that all the books he owned dealt only with life at sea. I must have looked surprised. "Being so much below," he said, "I miss a good bit of the action above. Sometimes, I cook and have my muscatel and read a bit. The ship rocks and plows and I'm a part of it all."

Suddenly Harry seemed to me about the age of Chester.

"Here, listen," and he opened Abby Jane Morrell's *Narrative of a Voyage* to a place marked with a scrap of leather and read:

" 'If I had, a few months before this time, read of such a battle' "— Harry pitched his voice high as he read, like a woman's—" 'I should have trembled at the detail of the incidents; but seeing all the animation and courage which were displayed, and noticing, at the same time, how coolly all was done, every particle of fear left me, and I stood collected as any heroine of former days.' "

Harry softly closed the book, carefully returned it to its upright position among the other books, closed and locked the cabinet. "What do you think of that, Billy?" he asked me. "The language of it? A 'heroine of former days'? There's a romance, ain't it?"

"Have you yourself ever seen such a carnage?" I asked.

He shook his head in the negative.

"I think it might be a quite different thing than the way she writes about it."

"Her account," Harry said, "is the same as her husband's. His came out the year before. They corroborate each other."

"I don't mean so much in terms of the facts," I said. "But the feeling. Or the lack of feeling."

"Do you think she was afraid after all?"

"That is not my point," I said. I felt very impatient with Harry.

"Do you think, Billy, you understand it better than her or him, you who was never at sea till this voyage?"

I could tell that Harry, in turn, as is often the response to impatience, was becoming annoyed with me. *That* I could not afford. "A soft answer turneth away wrath, but grievous words stir up anger." So my father's book said, and he had often quoted it, to quench my childish fiery temper. But then, temper had gotten the better of him when I was twelve, no matter what words he knew. I swallowed my desire to argue with Harry and said, "You have a fine collection of books, Harry."

"So I do," he said. He meditatively sipped his wine (I had decided to leave the muscatel for Harry), and his manner proved the truth of my father's adage, for Harry's anger was all turned away when my tone was soft. "I'll read a bit to you from time to time."

He did not offer me the key to his collection. I thought that ungenerous of him, but perhaps he believed me unable to read.

"It was the reading of sea books that made me want to run away to sea," he said. His voice took on the naive quality of a young and wondering boy. "I had been a good scholar in my school days. I was apprentice to a glover. I could still make you a pair of gloves fit to wear to a coronation."

"How old were you when you went to sea?" I asked.

"Sixteen."

And suddenly I had a fellow feeling with Harry.

CHAPTER 30   Captain Ahab's Story—
My First Acquaintance with Him

THE TABLES SET and the cooking ready, except for the egg-drop soup for Captain Fry, which was to be last-minute, Harry and I returned to the steward's pantry and continued to talk. I soon learned that he was forever between the two places, and that he really did have too much to do. Hence I was not a mere companion to Chester but a sort of apprentice to Harry. As we settled ourselves, he on the high stool, I on a box, he pointed to a small bell, which was wired to be rung by a tug from the captain at his table. He lighted a tiny spirit lamp under an iron plate in the galley to keep the water boiling for the captain's soup. When we heard the ding, Harry would drop the raw egg into the boiling water, leave the serving, which would be almost immediate, up to me, and himself go up on deck to set out platters for the crew, which numbered about thirty.

Harry having shared so much with me, I thought I would tell him of some of the landscape of Kentucky. I felt confident that my description of mere landscape would not signal that I might be female. I seemed to owe him something true and real for all the pictures he had made to dance before my eyes. But almost at once the little silver bell dinged, and I postponed a narrative of Kentucky.

Today's setting was one in which the officers ate at the captain's dining table, which had a rail called a "Scotsman" to save the dishes from sliding off in rough seas. The captain's table was flanked by padded benches bolted to the floor. At the head of the table was the armchair for the captain, but today, he and Chester (and I) were to lunch in the more private stateroom. In fact, this arrangement continued for almost the whole first week of the voyage, so my acquaintance with the first, second, and third mates was delayed.

I did hear the third mate, who was new, remark on the unusual arrangement of the crew's meals being prepared in the pantry instead of on a deck galley. Harboring something of Harry's secrets, particularly the first one of the "better" water, I knew, I thought, exactly why this arrangement prevailed on the *Sussex*.

The second mate explained to the third that it was a matter of Harry's serving as both the cook and steward to the captain.

"And why is that?" the third asked.

"Economy," answered the second.

The first put in that this way the crew ate not so much worse than the officers, as there was overlap in the food preparations.

It seemed to me that Harry having been with his captain for probably half his life, longer perhaps, and, in a sense, more intimately, than the captain's future wife in New Bedford, he had earned the right to a few adaptations. Certainly he was sincere in his belief in the economy of overlap, even to the purchase of knobby vegetables. I did not know what most crews ate on whaling vessels, but I would warrant that those manning the *Sussex* were exceptionally well fed. This seemed to me a credit not only to Harry but to Captain Fry, who had the wisdom to allow an unconventional organization on the vessel where he ruled supreme.

Both the captain and Chester seemed glad to see me, and I resolved to make myself agreeable company to both, once I got the food on the tables. During those hours when I helped Harry and was entertained by his stories of savory rats and Fiji cannibals, Chester had been assigned to read Shakespeare. He seemed not to have made joyful headway with the bard. I entered their presence bearing the Chinese soup, and I must say it had an enticing aroma, and I felt proud of it even if it had been mostly Harry's doing. Though I had set the table earlier with bowls and spoons, they had been replaced with small China ones with oriental designs painted on their sides—cunning little red dragons—and the spoon itself was made of porcelain and had a little bowl and tonguelike handle so that it seemed more like a small ladle than a spoon.

The oriental spoon served very well when I finally did sit down at our charming table. My soup was good, but a little tepid in temperature, and I felt that Harry had been right in presenting the soup as hot as possible. The captain told me whimsically that the soup tasted better served in tableware of similar origin. Transported by the accouterments of exotica, I felt as though I were already experiencing China, though the captain said our longitude was about that of New York.

"Look yonder," he said, gesturing toward the porthole. "It's the *Balance* out of Bristol."

I looked through the round porthole and saw the vessel in full sail, head-on, slender and leaning. Framed by the circle, it is my mind's prettiest, most untroubled image of a whaling ship.

"The skipper is a drunk," put in Chester.

Captain Fry looked at me and smiled. "From Samoa, he put out so drunk that he sailed the ship in circles. Tacked the ship some thirty times till she was like a duck going round in a puddle. He was out of his mind from drinking so hard, and so the crew took him back to Samoa, to the port of Apia. He and Captain Smith from New London had drunk two barrels of rum the few days before they set sail."

I thought the *Balance* a lovely name for a ship; too bad the captain was so unworthy of her. I remarked that racehorses in Kentucky, like ships of all types, had beautiful names, and sometimes odd ones. "I knew of a horse," I said, "named Beware-the-Demon-Drink. It was a filly and owned by a woman and her husband who believed in temperance."

"Take the motto to heart, Billy," Captain Fry said. I wondered if he could smell Harry's muscatel on me. "Many a promising man has been ruined by drink."

"Tell about Captain Swain," Chester said.

This was a name that interested me, though I now knew that many a person from Nantucket was named Swain and it might not be Rebekkah Swain's husband.

"Out of Nantucket, on the *Globe,*" Captain Fry began.

Again I thought it a lovely name, and remembering the captain's book, I said, "Shakespeare's theater was named the Globe."

"How did you know that?" the captain asked.

I felt unveiled. I shrugged, dropped my head, and tried to look ordinary.

Getting no answer, the captain spoke again: "And, Chester, do you remember the name of Swain's monkey?" But Captain Fry aborted the tale to get out his telescope and to report on another ship crossing the portholes.

"Out of Nantucket, the *Pequod,*" he said, "and Captain Ahab, I'll warrant."

I trained the spyglass as best I could. Uncle Torch had said they ruined the eyes and did not keep one at the Lighthouse, and, further, he said that he did not care to see farther out than nature had intended. But I was shocked at how the device made the ship in much detail appear before me. I reached out my hand as though to touch it and heard the captain chuckle.

"Everyone makes the same gesture," he said, "looking the first time. Even a Shakespeare scholar. What do you see?"

"Ivory. Polished ivory hangs round the bulwarks. And she's all fastened up with whale teeth for pins. Even the blocks for the tackle appear carved of ivory."

"Let me see," said Chester, and I handed him the glass. He ran to the second porthole to look. "There's no wheel. They use an ivory tiller, and it's the lower jawbone of the sperm."

"The *Pequod* is called the cannibal craft," the captain said.

I could see why, for she was all bones and teeth wherever such material could be used in place of wood. Her mien was that of a grinning, toothy jaw.

"It was Peleg decorated her thus, but Ahab likes it well enough."

"Who is Ahab?" I asked.

I expected a jocular story, a narrative of drunken escapades such as that told of the captains of the *Balance* and the *Globe,* but Clifford Fry shook his head and did not smile. "They say he's lived among the cannibals."

"Fought the cannibals?" I asked timidly.

The captain said nothing else but shook his head in the negative and looked grim. "They say he's been to colleges, too, as a young man," he added. "Harvard and Yale."

Those last names were uttered with bitterness, and I thought of the inscription in the flyleaf of his book, *Shakespeare is my Harvard and my Yale*. If Giles ever had to make such a statement, the list of authors would be very long, not confined to a single name, no matter how singularly worthy. I was troubled, as I pulled the bones from my fried catfish, that my perfect Captain Fry had in him an element of discontent, even of regret. I thought of Kit saying that he had been fascinated with the contentment he had found among us at the Island. How lightly I had thrown away content for adventure, but I could not imagine regret. And soon I would write letters explaining everything.

"What age man is Captain Ahab now?" I asked.

"Over fifty and still sailing. With iron-gray hair and the mark of lightning down his cheek."

I went to Chester and took the glass from him. At the tiller, I inscribed Ahab, for surely it was he, his legs planted, his trousers rippling. Hatless, his gray-almost-to-white hair feathered in the breeze. All puissance, he held the ivory tiller against his hip, and it seemed to spring out from him like a third leg, a superfluous ivory one. I looked hard, focusing both my excellent natural eye and the extended one to see what expression figured the face of this associate of cannibals and colleges.

I saw there *joy!* Fierce joy and pride.

P EOPLE CROSS our paths casually, when trumpets should blast. So it was with my first sighting of the *Pequod* and the man who would become a husband. Had I met Ahab face-to-face and not across a wilderness of water with him all unaware that his face had become a cameo—had I done so my first days at sea, I would have had only a vague response. I was not then ready for Ahab. Yet, I did feel kin to him when I saw his exultation in wind and water and speed, his pleasure in his own preeminence. High in the Lighthouse, though motion lay around me in the wind, the traveler-clouds, the fluid sea, the pilgrim birds—there, close to the sun, alone, I myself had known strange joy and the strength that attends such joy.

He, too, has stood next to lightning, I thought, remarking the brand on his face. I touched my own cheek, glad that it was not marked, remembered Frannie, the permanent pitting of her face. Remembered my gratitude that my prayer for her recovery had been granted. My hope that she played contentedly. *No.* Frannie was lonely. And it was my fault.

Aboard the *Sussex,* we went on with our luncheon, and Captain Fry told me I should begin in the post meridiem to learn to climb the rigging. "We want to be able to send those fine eyes aloft," he said, "safely." Then he asked Chester and me what program we could devise to achieve that end.

The answer was as obvious to Chester as it was to me—that I should practice climbing to low altitudes and then, by degrees, climb higher.

"Mounting under full sail is quite a different thing from a climb in port."

"You'll be cold," Chester said.

"And what's the remedy—nay, the preventive?" the father asked.

Chester volunteered the use of his own thick peacoat, which was too big for him now. They had purchased it in anticipation of still being at sea some two years hence when Chester should have grown into it.

The coat was fetched, and it was large even for me. They must have prophesied prodigious growth for Chester. It was the most tailored and expensive garment I had ever put on—a thick, navy wool, top-stitched on the collar, double-breasted, ornamented with a double row of brass buttons stamped with a smiling anchor. The lining was a slippery silk, also navy blue but figured with small gold anchors. I was profuse in my thanks and could not help but exclaim in ways that might have been considered girlish. But nothing was interpreted from my enthusiasm.

When I climbed, I required my arms to do perhaps more than their fair share of lifting my weight aloft in order to develop them. The muscles in my arms could not, of course, take on that definition that is characteristic of males, but my arms did grow much stronger. The palms of my hands blistered and then callused. When I went to sleep at night I felt again the pressure of the ropes across the balls of my feet. After a week had passed, when we were skirting the wide Sargasso Sea in the regions of the Caribbean, I climbed, with the ship under full sail, all the way to the masthead.

The *Sussex* began to feel like home. For the most part, Kit and Giles had been avoided. I deduced that they had been given nightwatch duty, and that reduced the risk considerably of encountering them. Though I held no particle of anger toward them (for having neglected to call at the Sea-Fancy Inn in New Bedford), I found that I did not need them. Tucking into my own duties, listening to stories from Harry and the captain, tutoring Chester in a random, peripatetic manner, all this filled my hours in an interesting and comfortable way. Sometimes when I lay in my hammock at night, I thought about Kit and Giles, just as I did about my parents and my folk on the Island, but my friends seemed almost as remote to my present existence as my family. Should I ever become bored on ship, I decided, I would enliven my existence at that point by speaking with Kit or Giles. Yet, as I had told Chester upon meeting, I was a person very rarely bored.

I did learn that Harry had made the acquaintance of Giles, for Harry passed on sometimes the interesting things he had learned and his wonder at Giles's wide reading. My own days fell out along these lines: breakfast and an hour's walk with Chester; in the pantry with Harry preparing the noon meal; trips to the galley, where the food was cooked; my service and meal with the captain and sometimes the mates; the cleanup aftermath of lunch; tidying of the captain's quarters, sometimes assisted by Chester (this seemed his only duty as cabin boy; his father attended to most of his own needs). My time aloft fell in midafternoon.

"Aloft"

Surely it was the best time to be aloft. Especially as we sailed closer and closer to the equator, the air was so warm that I unbuttoned the peacoat and let the air bathe me. As the weather grew warmer and then hot, Harry moved his food preparation out of the pantry area and to the galley deck. Even the food for the captain and mates, who ate together now, was prepared there, and I took it below.

The possibility of sighting whales began to excite the atmosphere on board, and the sound of hasps honing the steel of lances and harpoons filled our ears throughout the day. Many a sailor sat on the deck, his back propped against any upright structure, his legs spread, and his whetstone moving back and forth against the edge of his harpoon, or lance, or cutting spade. These edges were stroked to the point of flashing silver, and all over the deck when I was above, I could see the short reflective dashline of a sharpened steel edge. High above the din, the sound put me in mind of a pack of demons patiently filing their teeth. Another lookout saw a whale, a right whale, and we gave chase, though the sperm whale was preferred. The beast escaped us. Nonetheless, the sighting sharpened the edge of excitement the way the whetstones sharpened the killing tools.

I once spied another ship in the offing and called down the news, but Captain felt we could not stop to gam until we had taken a whale. That night, I resolved, I would write my mother and my aunt the true story of my whereabouts.

For more than a month, we saw neither whales nor ships. We seemed suspended in time; our killing tools grew sharper and sharper.

CHAPTER 32   "Pardon Me"

PERHAPS I SHOULD admit that the prospect of actually harpooning a whale (though I was not assigned a boat), bringing it shipside, and butchering it appealed to me less and less. All the while everyone else grew more eager. Beginning to feel like an *isolato* in my new home, I tried to talk only to my most immediate "family." When exchanges were required of me with the larger crew, I looked down and mumbled, hoping to make less of an impression that way. Once someone had said in a teasing way that rounding the cape would put hair on my chest and whiskers on my face, but Harry, hearing the remark, said sharply to let me alone. The cook is a rather placated member of a ship's company, and Harry's injunction was obeyed.

He had told me about the butchering, with language full of blood and gore. Harry spared no details: the peeling away of the blanket of blubber; the cutting of that into horse pieces in the blubber room, which was between decks in the waist of the ship; the mincing of the horse-sized pieces into pages connected by a black spine of whale skin, these pieces being called "Bible leaves" because they were thin like pages; next the continuous pitching of the Bible leaves into the boiling try-pots. According to Harry, the stench was beyond description from the try-pots and also from the decaying animal, which oozed a black tar tracked all over the ship, the decks so oily and splattered with gobs of black blood everywhere it was difficult to walk.

Because we had been at sea a long time without taking a whale, all the mastheads were furnished with lookouts, and we took short turns to be sure our eyes were fresh. A whale ship being much overmanned in comparison to a merchant ship, there was no shortage of people to send aloft, though Captain was certainly as selective about the task as he could be. He seemed to feel that my eyes were both sharp and lucky, and often he would ask me if I felt like taking a second or third duty. Even my morning walk with Chester was shortened so that I might spend more time aloft.

Surely the captain could sense that I was reluctant to target a whale for butchering. Yet, he trusted me to do so, and, in good faith, I would not have let one of the brutes go his innocent way unheralded.

One other detail of life on the *Sussex* I feel compelled to mention—being on the subject of innocent blood—because it is never a part of men's narratives, they having little reason to think of it. How did I manage my monthlies, since I did not dare to put my own bloody rags in a washpot? I had brought a supply of rags in my duffel, some of them left over from the cutting up of my eight-yard blue dress. And whenever there was any stray rag about the ship, I snatched it up and laundered it clean, then stowed it away against the time of the month when I should have need of it. My monthlies ran with the moon quite regularly, and when the crescent moon appeared over the masts, then

I knew to look to my needs. Innovative Aunt had shown me how to contrive a kind of oilcloth diaper to hold my rags and contain any accident, so I never had the embarrassment of bleeding through on my outer clothing. As for my bloody rags, I simply crept out to the stern at night and tossed them overboard. It was a waste of good cotton cloth, but the public washpot was out of the question.

As for the innocent blood of the whale, it was, indeed, through my cry from the masthead, off the coast of Brazil, that the *Sussex* made her first kill of the voyage.

I did but do my duty.

I suppose many a soldier tells himself the same, and thus assuages guilt.

Having stayed aloft after my sighting, I was already sorry as I watched the lowering of our sixteen-foot whaleboats and the frantic chase with men bowing their backs so rapidly they seemed in danger of permanent injury. I watched the strange dance when the mate changes places down the length of the boat, grabbing heads as handholds, with his harpooner, just as Chester and I had pretended by moonlight in the decked whaleboat.

The way the harpooner stood there poised to hurl at the gigantic animal reminded me of stories of knights and dragons—so unequally matched they seemed. But, as in the fairy tales of monsters and men, the man prevailed—in this case assisted by other men and his conveyance to the battle place first by mighty whale ship and finally by lesser whaleboat. But I do not think dragons drained such sad blood. Nor were dragons ever female, and this whale evidently was, for I saw her calf, who had been hiding under her like a dark chick, grow frightened and swim away.

At last Harry hailed me to descend. Before I did, I turned and looked straight across at the lookout in the next mast over. The tawny mountain-lion eyes of Kit locked with mine. He did not seem to recognize me, or rather, the recognition between us was focused on only the ungendered sadness that we saw in each other's eyes. The whale discovered, his death was sure to follow. Had Kit, too, spied the whale, but chosen not to sound the cry? Already Kit anticipated that a bloody reality would replace his fantasy of whaling. We descended our masts at a parallel rate. When my feet touched the deck I quickly moved to the companionway and effected my disappearance.

My whale was estimated at sixty barrels. The labor of reducing, or literally *rendering*, the living animal with lungs and bones and heart and skin down to an essence of whale oil, stored in casks and barrels stacked in the hold of the ship, occupied us all, myself included, for two weeks.

What was my job in all of this? It was I who held the bucket when after the severed head of the beast was divided into the case and the junk, and after a hole was bored into the case, it was time to scoop out the clear, fine oil. It was I, posted with Chester in a whaleboat slung from the starboard quarter, who watched for particularly aggressive sharks. Yes, the sharks came almost at once. They watched the man on the monkey rope thread the heavy blubber hook into the end of the scarf that must be hoisted off and boiled for its load of oil. They watched his feet in particular, as we did, for he stood on the slippery carcass of the whale. The corpse was broader than the bole of the mightiest oak, but it was completely greased by the blood and slime exuded by the animal. And we watched the feet of the mates, too, who were all lined up on a kind of narrow stage pivoted down beside the animal. Standing on that board, they poked and prodded at the juncture between the detaching blanket piece, pulled up through the action of the windlass and chains, and the place where the layer of blubber still adhered to the animal.

And it was I, as well as other slight crew members, who kept empty tubs supplied at the edge of the hatch to receive the horse pieces cut in the blubber room. I watched those full tubs dragged to the mincing board to be fine-sliced into Bible leaves, the horse pieces dripping blood and oil set free by the between-decks heat trapped in the blubber room. Oil poured in fountains from the horse pieces and partly filled the tubs and dripped all over the deck.

Captain Fry did not have me tend the tryworks flames, but I ladled oil from the boiling cauldrons into cooling tanks. From these the storage casks were filled, and the casks were then lowered on massive chains into the hold, but again, I was spared the heavier work.

Who was who in all this work? We were all so covered in grease and blood and dirt that I recognized men only by their voices.

It was this circumstance, Kit told me later, that led to his discovering me. He was standing at the tryworks (though I did not know it was he) taking out the rinds left from the rendering and using these portions of the whale to feed the flames (which rendered oil from new Bible leaves) when I, at my job of ladling off the oil, bumped Kit and without thought said the phrase "Pardon me."

Only two words, but there it was, he said, unmistakably, the voice of his female friend from the Lighthouse, though the speaker be covered with black grease, even the face a mask of soot.

We finished the rendering and storing of oil, we finished cleaning the ship, using the whale's ashes from the tryworks to concoct a strong lye for the job, before Kit made himself known to me.

The crew had cleaned the ship of its guilt; the hold cradled the purified, barreled-up profit. I was asleep in my hammock only a few feet away from Chester when I was awakened by a whisper in my ear. "Una!" My name sank through layers of consciousness, past all the fatigue of the last two weeks, to rouse me. It was a happy awakening. I rolled silently from the hammock and silently but wholeheartedly embraced Kit.

Summoned by my own true name, it was not in me to deny my identity.

"It's my watch, but never mind," he said. "Come aloft with me."

CHAPTER 33 🐚 **Reunion**

K IT SLIPPED his hand into mine and led us upstairs and across the deck.

"The mizzenmast," he muttered. "Let others take the lead in this bloody business."

Although we were as attached together as could be, hand in hand, I felt a distance from him, and I shuddered. His hand itself was smooth as moonlight, as soft as milk.

"Your hand?" I said.

"I was set to squeezing spermaceti at the end. Giles and I."

The boards of the deck, scrubbed down to a creamy color with the lye from the tryworks ashes, gleamed in the light of the full moon. Shadows fell westward from the three masts, from the rigging, from the deckhouse, the davits, and the waiting whaleboats so that we seemed to walk through a jumble, but it was insubstantial shadow. The deck itself was clear, and to my bare feet the planking had the nap of brushed denim.

"The spermaceti is like a ladies' emollient." He stopped and took his hand, still clasping mine, to my nose, with the urging "Smell."

I did, and breathed in sweetness like violets. Over his knuckles, I glanced at him, with the moonlight in his eyes. Had I ever seen such hurt? There was no physical wound on Kit, but it was as though there were a gash behind his eyes. Instinctively I took his hand to my lips and kissed it.

He burst into a suppressed but spontaneous laugh.

"You make a good gentleman," he said. He turned to the rigging and said, "But do you want to go first?"

I commenced ascending for an answer. I had never climbed at night before. It happened that the full moon was lodged near the top of the mast, and I fancied that I was climbing to it, with Kit as shadow to me, for he was dressed darkly. First I, then he, popped through the hatch to the crow's nest. He did not ask permission but encircled me in his arms. His breathing changed to deep and hoarse. It was not frightening, in fact I enjoyed the sense of his proximity, but there was something distraught about him.

"As sure as you are a woman, Una, tell me you were repelled by that butchery."

"I was."

"I pardon you, Una. Now you must pardon me."

"I, Una, pardon you, Kit."

"Say it again. And hold me."

I did both. His mien was full of streaming stars. *Are those stars that were your tears?* I thought.

"Crouch down," he said, "so no one will see us."

We closed the hatch and sank down on it, I kneeling, Kit squatting on his haunches.

"This is the devil's ship," he said.

"No," I answered. I would not be quiet for such a wrong reckoning. "Captain Fry is a good captain."

"He's not good at finding whales. We should have taken at least one before we crossed the Line. Now there's no going back."

"Would you go back, Kit?"

He snorted that thorough, spontaneous suppressed laugh.

"Wouldn't you?" he asked.

I thought before I answered. I thought of the immensity of the Pacific, of Japan and China and India beyond. "No," I said. "No, I would not go back."

He laughed again. "They've made a man of you, and they've tried to make a woman of me."

He spoke with such contempt of being a woman that again I tried to steady his thinking. "I have always loved—"

"—being who you are," he insisted. But there he stopped and, squatting, merely stared at me. In a moment he held out his hand to me again. "So you like a soft paw?"

I stroked the back of his hand. "Kit, Kit, you know your hands will return to their natural way."

"How many days have we been now scraping with the jackknives, scrubbing with the lye?" His voice was a low hiss.

"Three," I said. I didn't know what to make of his question.

" 'The third day he rose again from the dead . . .' "

" 'He ascended into heaven—' "

"Do you think, Una, that we are in the ascendant? Is this heaven?"

"Kit," I said, full of alarm. "It was only the blood of an animal."

"I walked in it. Didn't you?"

I remembered too vividly. I had felt that I was rolled in blood and grease.

"Every night I soak my hands in a jar of spermaceti," he said. "No, I wash my hands in it. I wring my hands in it. If I had salvaged the heart of the whale, I would curl up in it as though it were my coffin case."

Was his reason unseated? I answered as sensibly as I could, "The unction is keeping your hands soft." When he made no reply, I asked, "How do you come by your own spermaceti?"

"I stole it."

The words seemed to drop downward like three stones into a well. They made a hollowness surround their fall.

"I want to stand up," I said. "My legs are cramping." So I stood and felt the rocking of the ship come up my legs. Even a gentle swaying below is amplified by the long lever of the mast, so that the crow's nest transcribes a sizable arc. "Stand with me," I said, for I hated seeing him all huddled and crouched.

We stood there together; Kit's breathing gradually became normal, lulled by the swaying and the calm of the night. "It's beautiful," I said. The light from the full moon suffused a portion of the sky and obliterated the stars; beyond that glowing haze, tiny stars studded the blackness.

Kit put his soft hand over mine and whispered, "You're beautiful."

In that moment, I felt myself a part of the night, and as a part of the night, it seemed true: that I was beautiful. Attendant on that notion came the conviction that I had chosen and would choose my own life. Yet I was afraid. I was afraid of Kit's passion for me, so apparent.

"You mustn't tell my secret," I said.

"I won't."

"Giles?"

"Giles and I are no longer friends."

I felt dashed with cold water. "What happened?"

"I don't want to say."

"You'll make up. Surely, Kit, you'll make up?"

"No."

I was cold. The night that seemed so full of light was smitten.

"Don't tell him I'm here, then," I said, angry at them both. "If I want him to know, I'll tell him myself."

"You have to promise to meet me every night. Just for a little while. After I fix my hands. To talk."

"Every night?"

"No, I'll come wake you up when I want you."

"Suppose you're discovered out of the forecastle?"

He laughed again, that surprising, too-thorough laugh. "I'll say I was lost."

When I returned to my hammock, I lay awake. I was still cold, and I got Chester's peacoat and determined to sleep in it. I thought about one of my recent tasks, the bailing of the case. You let the bucket down again and again into the severed head, and again and again it comes up brimful of the clear oil. But finally you let it down, and there is no sense of the bottom of the pail resting on a surface of liquid. No, it has bumped all the way to the bottom, and the well is empty. As you retrieve the pail you feel its brim knocking against the sides of the fleshy cavity, occasionally catching there. The pressure of the little scooping collisions causes a few drops more to be forced from the walls of the case, but the retrieved container is pitifully empty. So it was with Kit's laughter. It went down to the bottom of his being, but it brought up precious little mirth.

BECAUSE I HAD difficulty sleeping when I needed it most, after those weeks of straining labor, I felt tired and deprived during the day after my moonlight reunion with Kit. But there were duties to resume. All morning I wondered what had occasioned so serious a falling-out between Kit and Giles. When I could not solve the conundrum by thinking, I decided to leave their quarrel to them. It seemed childish to me that adults who knew each other well and who had been devoted friends could allow a breach in their friendship. But I was too sleepy to think of it further, and my bewilderment itself seemed to be soporific.

During the afternoon stint in the crow's nest, I almost fell asleep. Here I had stood with Kit, and now Kit was not here. Here were light and air and sunshine, and Kit's mind was enwrapped in a cloak darker than night. I thought of my having been blinded with the brightness of the lightning—but that was a temporary, physical condition, healed by time. Perhaps Kit's spirit had been drowned by blood. Perhaps time away from the carnage would restore Kit just as naturally.

I resolved to see no new whales that afternoon. When a plume arose far to the east, I closed my eyes and then turned my back. I numbed myself to the idea that I was cheating my captain. When I saw another whaler from New Bedford, the *Reconciliation*, I did sing out, and Captain Fry consented to a gam, since we had now taken a whale. I asked to be relieved of my station and scurried down to add a paragraph to my letters to the Lighthouse and to home. I added again how sorry I was to have deceived them. I asserted again how much I loved them. I assured everyone that I was safe, that Kit and Giles were also aboard the *Sussex* and would help me, if I ever needed it.

That night I hoped that Kit would not call on me. Would my confession to my loved ones be enough? The question wrung me. The whale butchery haunted me.

Perhaps Kit read my thoughts, for I slept undisturbed that night and the next one, too. The next night, I wanted him to come, and I lay awake waiting for him.

CHAPTER 34 ◐ Revelation

SINCE MY TIME on the *Sussex*, I have ever feared the weathervane in me. Sometimes I point toward Independence, isolation. Sometimes I rotate—my back to Independence—and I need and want my friends, my family, with a force like a gale. I have in me a spinnaker sail that finds the breeze and leads all my sails in that direction. I do not count myself fickle, for I have much of loyalty in me, but I am changeable.

Before the taking of the whale, I had had no need of Kit or Giles. Now I longed for them, and I felt that Kit, at least, had need of me. But he did not seek me out.

Now when I passed Giles boldly on the deck, I *hoped* he would glance into my face and know me. Kit's mind was in danger; I knew no remedy; I needed Giles to help me save Kit. *Lust* was a word I knew, and I knew it was all mingled with my anxiety for Kit. Yet I hesitated to make myself known to Giles. I had new connections— Chester, his father.

As we approached Cape Horn, Harry conveyed to the captain that Giles was a person of learning, and Captain Fry asked Giles to serve as Chester's tutor for an hour in the afternoon. This circumstance provided me with an opportunity: playfully—ah, that was the way to unveil myself to Giles—playfully. I told my little ward, one morning when the sky was piling up with gray clouds and the wind was freshening, to ask his afternoon tutor to tell him the name of the lady of the Red Cross Knight. "The right answer, Chester, is Una. If he gives you the right answer, tell him he may send back a question for your morning tutor."

When I saw Chester next, he said Giles had answered the question and sent his own: What French physicist had invented a new kind of lens for lighthouses?

"Fresnel!"

"Did you go to the same school?" Chester asked.

"I think we did."

I found Giles leaning against the bulwarks, looking out at the waves. I, too, placed my elbows and looked out. Without turning his head, he said, "You are a remarkable woman."

I laughed. "Are you surprised?"

"Una, Una. How did you do it? When did you do it? You've contrived a sky trapeze and dropped down from it, I know. But how?"

"First I lured the eagles to come into the Lighthouse. When I had ten, I began to teach them to follow directions—all flap south, all veer east. I made harnesses out of braided kelp, and off we flew."

Very quietly, with long pleasure, he pushed the word through his lips: "No-o-o-o-o."

"I've found a way," I said, "to wish till things happen. The very atoms I'm made of come apart in a kind of sparkle. A cloud of sparkle propelled by will. When I crossed Cuba—it was night—they thought I was a comet. At Rio they said gnats—a strange phosphorescent pod of gnats on the move. During the last rain—whenever that was—has it rained?—I attached myself to individual drops, fell into a puddle in a low place on the deck, and reconstituted myself as a male, and here I am."

"Are you male, now?" For the first time he looked at me.

"No. I am purest female. Virginal, virtuous, and . . . and . . . voluptuous."

"You are bold, inventive, unconventional, and . . . ambitious."

"So are you—ambitious! 'Quantities equal to the same or equal quantities are equal to each other'—Euclid. I am your equal."

"No. I am not your equal. I pity the man who is."

"Giles!" Reproof, though quiet, was in my voice.

"How lovely, Una, to hear you say my name."

"Then you're happy that I'm here. You'll meet with Kit and me in the masthead at night; we'll talk the dark away; and you'll always keep my secret."

"You're much less shy. Full of directives."

"They have made a man of me. I say what I want."

In what sense, I asked myself, was my jest true? The words were Kit's, who had said them bitterly, as though my thoughts and feelings were unnatural.

"I believe you are the second cabin boy," Giles went on. "These last two weeks—how have you worked?"

"Like everyone else. I may have stood beside you—I don't know. We were all disguised in soot and grease."

"Ankle-deep in blood. I threw my shoes to the sharks." He shuddered the way a horse does after the race is over. "Won't Kit be startled," he added more cheerfully.

"No."

"No?"

"He already knows."

"You told him first?"

I laughed. "He discovered me. He recognized my voice, at the try-works."

"Kit is angry with me just now."

"I know," I said soberly. "But I don't know why."

"I'll talk with him. With you here, with all of us together—maybe he'll forgive. So you two meet aloft for midnight confabs?"

"We did once."

"Tonight, then. I'll tell him you'll be there."

It pleased me to think that I was the bridge over their discord.

I decided to make us a picnic treat. From Harry's larder, I stole a flask of wine, a slab of cheese, a jar of raspberry preserves, a small loaf of bread. I was a whirligig of joy.

CHAPTER 35   **Sea Storms**

BY NIGHTFALL, the ship was tossing. Swells rose like hills—I did not know the sea could be so high, a gray wall moving toward us. It broke over the sides and ran on the deck. The most experienced men were sent up to trim sails. The mainsail was struck and furled. Night came early. The ship's bell clanged continuously till Captain Fry caught the clapper and throttled it. He sent me to be companion to Chester, who had crawled into his father's gimbaled bed and tucked his face under the covers.

When I saw him there, the bed swaying and gyrating above the floor as though possessed, with only his brown curls visible over the spread, I sympathetically put my hand on his head.

He jerked the covers from his little pale face and commanded, "Don't touch me."

"I'm sorry," I said.

"I'd let Giles pat me. But not you."

How quickly had I been demoted in preference!

"Do you feel sick?" I asked. "I am, a bit."

"I hate the storm," he declared vehemently.

"You've made this passage before, Chester."

"It's too soon. I was to have another day of tutoring. It will be nothing but mountains of water and everything wet for days." He wailed. "And I'll be in jail, in bed!"

"So the fire to learn burns in you now?"

"Billy, you should talk to Giles." Chester's tone changed from petulance to wonder. "He knows everything. Truly, he knows everything. He likes every idea in his head."

Chester's enthusiasm, like his fear, made him seem younger than Frannie.

"I *have* talked with Giles. I agree with you."

"Suppose Giles should get washed overboard!"

"Giles is too smart for that," I said.

"It's only luck," Chester wailed back. He was sitting up in the bed now. He looked like a little prince, coddled but needing a promise beyond human control. "In war, it's only luck—the sailors told me so—who comes back and who doesn't. A whale holds an army's worth of blood. Then it's only luck for us, too, like soldiers."

"I don't believe that," I said. But I was shaken. "It's partly luck. Not entirely. Your alertness, your intelligence, what you know about wind—or the ways of war: these can save you over and over."

"Giles deserves to survive," Chester said, suddenly calmed. "You can earn being safe?"

"Sometimes," I said, trying to take back any measure of comfort that seemed false.

"During storms, I always sleep in here. Father never comes down." He sighed heavily. "It's almost Christmas."

"Your father'll be on deck," I said. Though I had not weathered a bad storm with Captain Fry, I had no doubt that he would be at the helm till he dropped or the sun shone.

"You can sleep here with me. Come tonight."

"Not all night," I said. "Maybe for a while. Maybe I could bring Giles and another friend, Kit—do you know him? We could picnic."

In retrospect, it seems odd to me that I should have wanted the first meeting of us three to include Chester. I can only say that my happiness seemed elastic. If three friends, why not four? I had had something of the same feeling when I turned the tap to steal Harry's muscatel: that it was a shame not to include Harry. The theft itself seemed natural enough. Do not all people who live together intimately use each other's goods? It is a sign of solidarity more than a matter of robbery. At least it had been that way at the Lighthouse. Even as I rationalized, conscience reminded me I had stolen from Harry: *This is not the Lighthouse.* Conscience added: *There will never be another place like the Lighthouse.* I envisioned my letters in their hands. I wanted forgiveness. I wanted them not to be afraid for me.

When I went on deck, rain lashed every surface. I had forgotten that rain could be added to swelling sea. Yet able to discern the form of Giles, I stretched up to his ear and yelled the plan.

"No," he said definitely, glancing down at me.

"Then come for me to the captain's stateroom after Chester is asleep. Bring Kit."

As long as possible, the crew would keep its usual hours, but when storm compounded around the Cape, then double duty would be ordered.

THEY ARRIVED TOGETHER—Giles with pleased triumph, Kit with dignity but less than happy, as though he had unwillingly acquiesced to a plan not in his own best interests. But I was jubilant, and I insisted on a three-way hug—they were quite wet—and babbled about the food I'd stolen.

Giles nodded toward the door to the captain's chamber. "It's too close. Follow me. Bring a quilt to sit on. Wrap it in oilcloth."

He led us out into the storm and back down to the blubber room in the waist of the ship. The hatch banged closed on us and muffled the storm sounds. Once the stage of butchery, the room, like all the ship, now proclaimed its neatness and called that innocence. Giles told Kit to lean over—I thought his tone dangerously peremptory—and then Giles stood on Kit's back to check the fastening on the hatch. We could still hear the muted sea crashing down on top of us and washing across the deck above.

The blubber room seemed cavernous. There was another level, the hold, below us, where the casks of oil were stored. I spread the quilt— snitched from the captain's chest—in the middle of the empty blubber room and felt the kind of excitement born not of storm but of the more subtle adventure of a party, with augmenting or diminishing of friend- ships at stake. I willed my stomach to settle itself against the pitching of the ship. I was not much afraid of the storm. Let a ton of water crash against us! Laugh at its impotence! The ship was made to with- stand.

"Does Chester worry about his father?" Kit asked.

Though I did not speak, I doubted that Chester worried about his father; Chester perceived him as invincible. It was Giles who seemed so strangely precious or so newly discovered by Chester as to be vul- nerable.

With light irony, Giles said, "Ah, shall we discuss our fathers?"

"Let's have some wine," I said.

Kit laughed his hollow laugh, but there was some echo of pleasure in it: "You've started drinking wine?" Aberration was meat and drink to him.

"Why not?" I said. "I'm sure royalty of both sexes drink wine." I turned the flask up to my mouth, drank, and swallowed manfully. "To the Royal Friends," I said. "To us."

"To us." Each of them took the flask, toasted, and drank.

"Sit down," I said. "Sit down," and when they did I proudly cen- tered the bread and cheese and jam. "Compliments of Harry, unaware."

"Ah, Harry," Giles said. And again that mocking tone. "Kit, how would you rank Harry?"

"With the rats."

"We don't have rats on the *Sussex*," I said.

"The Innocence of Una," Giles said.

"You haven't been in the fo'c'sle," Kit said.

"I believe I found a rat in my hammock," Giles said. "But never mind. Here's cheese that rats will only dream of." He chomped off the corner, and his teeth left slide marks in the yellow. "I guess fo'c'sle folk are not so dainty as the second cabin boy would like." He passed the cheese to Kit, who decorously broke off a corner for himself. "Oh, bite it like a man, Kit," Giles said.

"Let's not bait each other," I said.

"All right," Giles replied, subdued and serious. "Harry? Cover your charms, Una, when you're around Harry."

I was stunned. What could Giles mean? A quiet fell among us. I felt as hostess that I should make things smooth, but I had little practice in that art. On the Island, conversation had seemed a natural act. Yet, I recalled how sometimes awkward silences had fallen between Giles and me. "Why are we quiet?" I suddenly blurted.

"Perhaps we don't have so much to say," Kit answered.

"Well, we could speak of our charming fathers," Giles said again.

"You know that mine is dead?" I asked.

"Yes, Kit told me. I'm sorry. Suicide."

Another silence fell upon us till Kit laughed. "I suggest we change the subject."

"Mothers?" Giles said.

"Not a good subject for me," Kit said.

"We know nothing of either your mother or father," I said to Giles.

"Mother, a saint. An ignorant, strong, good saint. Father, a reprobate. A drunk. Deserted us on my twelfth birthday."

"What else?" I asked gently. Giles seemed to have sprung like Athena—even with her blue-gray eyes—from the head of some Zeus. "Where did you live in Alabama?"

"Winston County. The Free State. No slaves."

Yes. Giles did not have that taint about him.

"Soil?" he continued, as though catechizing himself. "Red."

"Red as blood?" Kit asked.

"No. Ferric red. Iron-ore red. At Elyton, at the very southern tip of the Appalachian chain, they cook the iron ore with coal and limestone—all found right there—and make iron."

"Did you ever work there?" Kit asked.

"No. My work, and Mother's, was behind the ass of a mule. But we plowed the last cotton fields with me in harness."

"No!" I said.

"No, that's not true," he laughed. "I think you two would believe anything I told you."

I thought that Giles was too arrogant for his own good, but I held my tongue. I thought he had some purpose or some need I could not divine.

"What, in nature," Kit asked, "is the most beautiful thing you've seen? Or the most terrible?"

"The Dismals," Giles answered promptly. "A beautiful aberration in the lay of the land—north Alabama. A section mysteriously lowered, strewn with boulders, ferny, mossy, cooler—the vegetation, they say, typical of Canada. There the creek runs clear, but all other Alabama rivers and waterways are muddy with sediment. I even like the name— the Dismals. An eternal place, disjunct with the climate, the time, and its location."

"You think being dismal is an attractive association with eternity?" I asked.

"It is a cool Eden in the Southern summer heat. What's yours, Una?"

"The Kentucky hills in spring. Layers of pink and white—redbud and dogwood."

"And you?" Giles asked Kit.

"Stars," he said. That was all.

A pencil of water streamed through the hatch.

"Heaven is pissing on you," Giles said to Kit.

Why did I allow Giles to say anything and consider it holy writ? I trusted him, with a trust beyond trust.

I snatched up the captain's quilt from the puddle. A board on the hatch broke and a splash of water fell through.

So there was a world beyond our egg of a world. A stormy place, strong enough to crack our shell. Fear stirred. I held the quilt to my bosom.

"What pattern is that?" Giles asked, pointing.

I suspected that he was pointing at my breasts, but I answered, "The forest." The quilt pieces were stacks of triangles fitted together like pine trees, a rectangle of brown at the base to suggest a trunk. "Mostly green triangles," I said, as though Giles could not see the pattern for himself. "An occasional brown, on a white field."

"Fry, like most sea captains, thinks he pines after the land," Giles said dryly.

Our picnic lacked ease, lacked kindness. Our fare was irony and cynicism.

CHAPTER 36   The Frost Wind

THE *SUSSEX* sailed into the storms. The ocean bulged itself first into rounded hills and then into mountains, jagged, crested with foam and wind. The *Sussex* sailed up these slopes by staggering increments, almost as though she climbed an endless staircase. We jerked upward to a symphony of creaking and snarling wood, of wild screeching of wind, of canvas straining, sometimes bursting. The height of a mountainous wave obtained, the bow crashed and the ocean swept the deck.

Strung in lifelines, the men attempted the necessary work. Their faces were blue with cold, and their drenched clothing was shiny with water. I saw one man slammed against a rail, but it held, while the man was caught like a fragment against a strainer, the sea streaming over the wood. "Paul," he cried out, and his mate was there with his arm extended. Far to starboard, I saw a wave as high as my old Giant, all movement and forward-falling weight, but we rode our own mountain, and the monster passed at our side. When I opened the galley door, the two men heaved themselves inside, to safety.

One morning, the gale increasing, I felt Captain Fry's wet mouth at my ear. "Our object is to get to latitude sixty. Take the wind on the larboard tack. Go round." At ten, he double-reefed the topsails and soon furled the jib and mainsail. When I carried coffee to the door at eleven, I saw the main topsail was close-reefed, the foresail furled. Still that day, and each day, we progressed a little. But the fury and tumult of the gales escalated, and the men moved among torn sails, broken spars, and damaged rigging. Bit by bit, I feared, we were being torn apart. Each hour, I hoped to glimpse Giles and Kit, to know they were alive. If the interval between sightings was long, I was frantic with anxiety. Not allowed to cross the deck myself except by Captain Fry's express permission, I sometimes stood in the portal of the galley and tossed bread to the men.

Once, there never being a safe time to get below, I stayed miserable and wet in the hurricane house all day. In the morning, the storm wind came from north-northwest, and poor sailors had to climb the tattered rigging to take in the mainsail and mizzen topsail. By noon, the blast increased to a gale from the west-northwest, and the fore topsail was taken in, and the foresail reefed. Around four, two men were sent to furl the foresail. As I watched, a wave reached up, shoved against their backs, and swept them into the boiling sea. I screamed and screamed, but my puny sound went unheard in the storm. Exhausted, I rolled myself into the driest corner of the house and cried, till I felt Captain Fry's hand on my shoulder. He tied me to himself and took my hand as well to escort me to the hatch. As we walked, he pointed out to sea, and I saw building there the most gigantic wall of water I had ever witnessed. We ran across the slippery deck.

Together, we scurried below. He ordered me to go to Chester at once and to stay with him, but I was mesmerized by that vision of what seemed our doom. Together, beneath the closed hatch, we listed to the storm and waited. The ship climbed up and up—I knew the wheel was lashed—we were lifted and lifted and then dropped and dropped till I thought us descended to the floor of the sea. So much water poured over us, fore to aft, that I knew the hull of the ship rode submerged for long moments.

The day came, Chester and I swaying and spinning in the gimbaled bed, in the dark, when we heard the ship scream. The fibers in the mainmast screeched and were torn asunder. The mast flew away from us, the captain said later, trailing her rigging with her, leaving a stump broken six feet above the deck. It was a miracle that the loosed mast did not become the battering ram of our destruction.

Chester told me that his father could sail with two masts or even one or none if he had to. And that masts were replaceable. But mostly there in the dark Chester talked of the beautiful Pacific, and how he would slip overboard and swim when we got there, with half the crew about him to watch for sharks. Some ships, Chester said, hurled themselves against the headwinds for three weeks, but his father had navigated last time in two. When I questioned Chester closely, he said this rounding was no worse than the last, except for the loss of the mast. I added quietly, "And two men gone."

Just as there had been several days in which the storms gradually intensified, so were there several days during which they diminished.

One day, the captain, carrying a candle, hurried through the door of the bedroom and told Chester and me to come topside—the sun was shining. All disheveled and sleepy—for we had confused night and day in our hideaway—we emerged blinking, and there was the sea, blue and sparkling as though she had never brooded a gray moment in her life.

And then, in as strange a sight as ever I saw, birds blew over us. Gulls, hundreds of them, as though they were pushed by a current of air that streamed across us, flowing rapidly toward the west. "The frost wind! The frost wind!" the captain shouted, and he gave orders to unfurl all the sails, should the wind descend to our masts. Chester and I watched the slack sails hang while high above the ship streamed the birds, pell-mell, using their wings for balance rather than speed. Then we heard the sails begin to stir.

It was a creaky, stiff sound, but the canvases were beginning to fill with wind. The captain called down the lookouts. Then I felt the stream of air lowering to us on the deck and passing around our bodies with a clean, clear, sunny chill. The wind was unremitting. In the two remaining masts, the sails luffed, then strained at their tethers, and we were off!

Like a magic ship we flowed with the wind in our sails toward the South Pacific. The sea surface itself was calm and unruffled, a steady, normal movement. How could the air be so divided and layered? I did not know. We stood like statues on the deck, our clothes, our hair catching, too, in the breeze as though we each had become masts hung with skimpy sails, and we, too, helped to move the ship.

"Let no man go aloft," the captain said. He lifted his head to look up at our luck, but no one knew the force of the wind in the big-bellied sails. It seemed to me that the two remaining masts almost leaned forward, out of the vertical, so great was the pressure of wind in sails. Nothing broke, nothing tore—so beautiful was our position and so constant the current of air. It made the blood sing in my veins, and I knew I could be a sailor for life, if I chose. Yes, I could gladly wait a lifetime, a full sixteen years more, for such a sensation again. Without our effort, grace moved us forward.

Before the wind blew all the heat out of our bodies, the captain sent Chester and me below. All night we felt our speed humming in the boards of the hull and heard the water zinging past our ears. When we went up in the morning, the airflow had warmed, and, I thought, slowed a bit, but we were covering a great distance.

As the day wore on, the airstream could no longer be felt on the deck, though it still moved at the level of the sails. Toward dusk, I noted that the wind was far less in the lower sails than in the higher ones. At midnight—Giles came to get me—the sails were slack, but we were still gently moved in the current. "How far have we come?" I asked Giles. He thought hundreds of miles.

I asked him what had created that extraordinary wind, but he did not know. He answered whimsically, rather than scientifically. He said there was a flute player in the Andes, and he breathed a note purer and higher than the earth had ever heard before. Earth took the note and made it into a scarf of wind.

"The captain called it 'the frost wind,' " I said.

Giles smiled at me puckishly. "That is because the scarf of the high Andes is always fringed with frost."

CHAPTER 37   Collision

THE NEXT MORNING, an ordinary wind blew for us, on course, increasing and decreasing, in puffs and pauses, under sunny, subtropical skies. The deck was crowded with cheerful sailors. Whatever task could be done on deck was performed there rather than belowdecks. Harry set up his deck galley again, and I helped him with hearty goodwill. He asked every idle sailor to fish, in the hope of a feast, but even the porpoises that jumped in the spray from the bows eluded us. He did snag a gigantic turtle. We were obliged to haul it up with a chain and tackle usually used to strip off the whale's blanket, and the captain speculated that the sea turtle weighed a thousand pounds. To kill the beast, the captain shot him cleanly in the head with a pistol as we hauled him up the side.

Harry was a genius of seasonings. I think he even added some of his hoarded wine to sharpen the piquancy of the flavor. The turtle meat itself was savory and soft.

Oddly, Kit refused to eat it. "It's a curse to eat turtle meat," he said, but I coaxed him to try the broth.

The shell was enough of a wonder to us that the captain allowed it to remain on deck. It would have made a nice boat for a child on a pond. Chester and I sometimes lounged against the greenish turtle back after we had finished our morning constitutional. Many days passed thus pleasantly. The two masts served us well, and we were in no great hurry, for we were again in cruising territory for whales. Chester told me it was his father's intention to put in at Hawaii, though it was still a very far distance. If the "frost wind" had not caught us in its breath, we would have put in on the coast of Chile, at Santiago, for repairs and supplies. But, really, we felt the need of nothing. Giles had suggested to Harry that he capture some of the torrents of rainwater to replenish our supply, and he had done so during the storm. The splintered stub of the mainmast stood like a totem over serene seas.

Nonetheless, we were a whaling ship, and to complete our completeness, if that is a possible idea, we began to watch eagerly, again, for a whale.

Aloft once more, I felt seasoned and relaxed. The height and the motion of my roost seemed natural to the world in which I lived. Since both Kit and Giles knew my identity, my very bones felt more comfortable and free of dread: the precautions I took with the other men and with Harry, Chester, and Captain Fry were habitual now. Sometimes I even thought of myself as a man and was proud of my manliness.

The question of the horror of killing and butchering another leviathan I tried to defer. I looked at the near and far heaving of the green sea and loved and relished the sight. Should a dark shape, moving— perhaps spouting—appear, I supposed that I would look carefully and then sound the expected cry. It was not my job to ride in a whaleboat, to row in pursuit, to dart the harpoon, to plunge in the lance. No. I was a pair of eyes. And when I tired of the sea, there was the cloud-laden sky inviting my soul into its blue expanse. If I gazed there, why, then there was no chance of sighting a whale.

Sometimes I saw other ships at a great distance—I had new letters ready in their envelopes—but Captain Fry was not interested in gamming. He had his Shakespeare and his son; now he had Giles to converse with, too, and he did not wish to stop his work to entertain himself. Perhaps the broken mainmast embarrassed him, too. The mates were so quiet and content on board the *Sussex* that I asked Harry if they were opium eaters. To my surprise, he said he did think they took a few grains occasionally.

As for Giles and Kit, we were friendly, but it seemed for Giles that conversations with us were perhaps less interesting than molding the young mind of Chester, or benefiting from the captain's broad nautical experience. Giles made little effort to talk with Kit or me since our stormy picnic in the blubber room.

Kit seemed to me a person apart simply because he was melancholy. Whatever pain had alienated him from Giles he never spoke of. He seemed to try to assume an air of normality. The other crew members enjoyed Kit's quick and unlikely wit, like the spurt of a match in darkness. The ship was not paradise, but there was order and goodwill to be found there, if not the vitalizing force of love or the pleasure of intimacy. And besides, we were in motion. New regions would appear. Weeks passed. I did my duty and waited for change.

From my perch aloft, I thought the smudge on the horizon betwixt the green sea and the pale sky too large to be a whale. Its shape reminded me a bit of the Island at home, for there was a steepness on one side like the headland under the Lighthouse and from that there was a gradual long slope into the sea. There was no tinge of green to this South Pacific island, such as one usually sees in mild climes. Instead it had a blackish appearance, and I wondered if it might be the eroded tip of an underwater volcano, basalt often having a deep blackness to it.

Then there was a small eruption—a short plume of smoke went up, strangely familiar in shape. Could the sterile isle be inhabited? Had I seen a sort of smoke signal such as the Indians of the American West were said to use? Surely it was a signal or a sign, but my brain refused to interpret it. Then the island sank from sight. I rubbed my eyes. Could it be so near to sea level that sometimes the waves covered it?

Surely there were some islands somewhere even now being built up from their bases at the bottom of the sea. Was I to be privy to such a land-forming process?

It was a drowsy day, and patience came easily. I thought of the six little plum trees at home and wished that I had a plum. I thought of Uncle and Aunt and Frannie. I pictured them around their new baby. I looked down to the deck. I saw Kit clap Giles on the shoulder in quite a natural and friendly way, and I was glad. Surely this was real friendship and not just gesture. Then I looked again for the black island.

Perhaps I had only dreamed. It would be nice to have a pet in the crow's nest—a little mouse would be fine, or a bumblebee that buzzed just for me. What kind of pet would a ship rat make if it was handled frequently and lovingly from birth? The knobby, hairy white knees of Apron came to mind, when she was a little goat. I sighed. I wanted to fold my arms on the edge of the crow's nest, close my eyes, and dream, lulled by the sea.

How was it that I had received a loving rose from a man who walked the deck below me but who now treated me like the man I pretended to be? How was it that another man had lusted for my body and now found little delight in looking at me? Was it a pact between them not to compete when the arena was so small? And what was the cause of the coolness between them? Had they quarreled about me?

I wanted no quarrels, but here in the Pacific, I had rather expected to return to the intense communion we had all had on the Island. They, on the other hand, having been so little expectant of seeing me, now seemed to discount the reality of my presence. I didn't care, I decided. I would marry Captain Fry! That would show them. And then I smiled at my childish petulance and felt lazier than ever.

I would not marry anyone anytime anywhere. I would sail as a man and live ashore as a woman. I would do just as I pleased. So long as I hurt no other being, why not do exactly as I pleased?

The black island was back. I had not realized that we had come round. I checked the azimuth. We had not come round; the island had.

"Shoals ahead!" I shouted down, for who knew how close our keel was to submerged rock or what new formation of land might rise hidden under our keel and scrape us out?

"Thar she blows!" shouted the other lookout.

No island, but an enormous black sperm whale, with a head steep as a cliff, erupting not volcanic smoke but a huge spume of water vapor.

"Lower way!" Captain Fry himself shouted the command, and there was a boyish crackling of excitement in his order. I didn't like such jejune glee. Instantly the crew rushed to the boats and piled in, and they began to be lowered into the rocking sea. The black whale seemed unaware of us. He lay on the water like a slope of coal. I imagined his tiny eye, the wrinkles around the socket. *King!* the word came strangely to mind, startling as the retort of a rifle. King of all lunged creatures, this whale; king, thus, of mankind? And then this dark idea spelled its way across my mind: *We shall never take him.*

I had seen bulls in the fields of Kentucky, and in their shoulders there was always such a concentration of unintelligent power that I always thought the word *brute*. Well, here was the Brute of Brutes. Though he had no shoulders in the bovine sense, there where shoulders are was that same concentration of force. How feminine we, the ship, seemed in comparison—how white and swanlike, despite our jagged stub, we had moved before the stream of frost wind. No wind would move his mass. Black and dense, completely powered only by his own will and muscle, he lolled before us. Who was Captain Fry to let his men attempt to dismantle this? Let them rather choose to assault a volcanic rock such as I had thought that I was seeing! Let them take little spoons and try to dent hardened lava! Let them try to shovel up an Alp and fling it into the Mediterranean! I wanted to tell him so, from aloft.

Bring them back aboard, I wanted to say. *Keep them safe*. I saw the captain at the helm, and I knew that he but waited for the small whale-boats to clear the ship before he himself would use the ship as the largest whaleboat and sail directly upon the beast.

The whale's eye was like a star embedded in a night with only one light. Suddenly the great beast dove. Such a volume of water did he displace that I felt the ship rock with his passage downward. How could anything alive be so large? He was nearly twice the size of my sixty-barrel whale. Could the animal really be stowed below as small casks of oil? *At your own death*, I asked myself, *can the vastness of your own experience be buried in the ground, funneled into nothing but the shape of a grave?* For how long could those gigantic lungs sustain him under-

"He rose in the vertical, jaw agape. . . ."

water? And if this leviathan did fall to us, despite all his hugeness, what would be the quality of the oil?

He rose in the vertical, jaw agape under the lead whaleboat. It rose in the air with him, men falling into the sea, the boat shivering into planks and splinters. The men were tiny in the water. Foam and splash and bubbles washed over them. Immediately a boat turned to pick up its comrades. I watched as the eagle watches—high and detached. There was no blood. The black boulder dropped again; the foam subsided. The swimmers were pulled aboard.

Now we waited. I peered into the depths but saw no movement.

Captain Fry called up, "Cry out, Billy, if you see him flutter."

I waited and watched. Like a mass of kelp, the wavering began deep in the sea, and I shouted out his position. He was going to come up under the double-laden whaleboat. Not waiting for the captain to direct, I yelled, "Pull for the ship!"

And they did. The shadow of the tip of my mizzenmast fell across them as they neared the boat. It was a pointer for the demon. This time he butted the boat into the air, and the men flew out like moisture along the curving lash of a whipline, their backs and necks flexed beyond endurance.

Again I saw no blood, but only a few souls came up swimming— three of sixteen. These flailed their arms and kicked their legs, swam straight for the safety of the ship, and my eyes filled with pity's tears.

From my perch I could see underwater where the whale changed the angle of his ascent, slanting outward. Glad-hearted, I called down to Captain Fry: "He's going away!" Could something so massive move with such speed? Underwater, the great tail muscle worked up and down, causing the dark body to leap ahead through the depths, angling away from us.

Dimly I heard the captain order me to come down, but I could not remove my gaze from the swimming monster. His outline was distorted by the water, of course, so I saw him as a great inkiness as though exuded from an octopus, an amorphous blackness. But he had been close enough for me to see the wrinkles in his skin, and I knew the intimacy of his eye. Now I saw a human body floating, facedown, and I called to the remaining boat and pointed out the form, but they did not hear me, for they were pulling for the ship.

The whale continued to move underwater like a dark, misshapen comet swinging out of our universe.

"What ho?" the captain yelled up.

"In retreat," I replied. "Southwest." I wanted to speak of his speed, but the number of knots he made I thought to be beyond credibility.

The captain went to the side and yelled to the approaching boat to turn and pursue the whale. To my amazement they continued to come mutinously home, and yet it was what I would have advised them to do.

"Southwest!" Captain Fry bellowed, stabbing the air with an impotent finger.

The whale was swimming with unbelievable velocity; no human crew could catch that torpedo of destruction. Then I saw the whale deviate from his trajectory, a curling round. He dashed at us, as though he intended to ram the ship. The crown of the massive head emerged.

"Reversed! Reversed! He closes on us!" I shrieked.

Then I stood still in mute disbelief. Whales attacked small whaleboats. Never the ship. Yet he closed on us. His blunt forehead, high-seeming as a headland, plowed toward us. Then he submerged.

"Billy!" Captain Fry roared. "Come down! Come down! You'll be tossed!"

Immediately I understood his logic, but there was no logic in what I beheld. A natural whale would not ram a ship. My body weakened at the uncanny wonder of it. Across the void over the broken mainmast, the legs of the other lookout gave way, and he clutched at the yardarm.

I was so horrified by the whale's deliberate charge that I could not move. Then my own name flew up from below like a spear: "Una!" Giles's voice broke my trance, and I scrambled down the rigging. No sooner did my foot touch the deck than there was such a lurch that I fell to my face. I heard and felt the boards break below the waterline, the copper sheathing nothing but decorative foil. The whole ship shuddered. A death throe. I looked up; the other lookout had disappeared. As soon as he could stand, Captain Fry ran below to assess the damage.

When he reappeared, he shouted, "The pantry's full of water," and I saw by his eyes that Harry was gone, but Chester was at his father's side. Both were wet to the knees. The captain carried the saber that I had seen on the wall alongside his bed. Chester clutched the zebra skin.

Giles and Kit were already loading the spare whaleboat. To look at

Giles's face was to see question and catalog move through his brain—what was most needed, what next in priority, and where was it? Captain Fry ordered me to sit in the boat with Chester, neither of us to leave it for any reason. A barrel of biscuits was put aboard. Giles would have loaded a bundle of knives, but the captain rejected the idea; then he gave me the saber to put under our seat. Rope, fishhooks, tarps, three kegs of water.

The *Sussex* was listing badly now, and those who crossed the deck ran uphill. "My dagger!" "My slicker!" "My letter!" Men cried out for their possessions. "Food! Bring only food!" a frantic voice directed. The other spare boat was readied. A lantern smashed as it was thrown against a bailing piggin, and the crew scrambled into the second boat atop the disordered gear. In the offing, the whaleboat which had not reached the ship waited. "Stay back! Stay clear!" Two whaleboats already sunk, one in the water, two coming down.

As soon as the other boat was lowered, we followed, smacking hard onto the water. "Row for life!" Our oars were put into service and we joined the other two boats at a distance. A sad pod of three whaleboats, we focused our gazes across the green water to watch the *Sussex* sink.

No sign of her assailant surfaced. Perhaps that murderous forehead had been so wounded that the whale sank and would soon lie a few rods from the ship on the ocean floor. But not a drop of blood reddened the water. Perhaps he swam underwater unscathed, to masquerade again in black ambush.

Thus began, amid such speculations, the ordeal of being at sea in an open boat.

CHAPTER 38   The Course

WHEN CAPTAIN FRY said we must set our sails for Tahiti, a murmur went up from the other two boats. Men in those boats had heard that Tahiti was a habitat for cannibals. In our boat, at that word, we all looked questioningly at the captain. I felt myself fill with fear, but I only stared at the water.

The captain explained that we must choose between Tahiti and Chile, which latter lay to the east many thousands of miles.

When this idea of the great distance to the South American coast did not convince them to prefer Tahiti as destination, Giles said he knew that Tahiti had been purged of cannibals by the Christian missionaries. All the men had developed, through Harry's open admiration, an idea of Giles's great store of knowledge and of his intellectual abilities in general, and his statement gave them pause.

But one of the men in the fartherest boat called, "What was the name of the missionary?"

Giles replied that the names of missionaries were not something that interested him. And with this admission of ignorance all his credibility evaporated.

"Hammersmith," I shouted out. "His name is Hammersmith." I did not know why I made up that name on the spot, but it was to no avail. I was only a pair of eyes, a redundant cabin boy, small of stature.

"Christopher Jones," Kit called out. "Solomon Brown."

The men in the far whaleboat took up their oars, and their boat began to turn away. They were lightly manned compared to us.

The captain ordered them to remain with us, but they did not obey. The boat between us and them, carrying only four men, also took up oars and moved to join the rebels, pulling for the east.

From his belt, the captain drew out his pistol. He stood, and again he ordered the two boats to turn.

"Fire!" Giles yelled.

Captain Fry did fire, but he aimed into the air.

The shot was ignored.

Quietly Giles asked, "Will you reload?"

"I cannot fire on my own men," the captain said.

Aboard our overcrowded boat, a man with pointed shoes stood on one of the seats and said, "We'll not sail to Tahiti either." He stood with his hands on his hips, leaning belligerently toward the captain. Kit tensed as though he might spring on the man, but his companions rose beside him. The boat rocked dangerously. Captain Fry looked sadly at the men and slowly lowered the pistol.

I looked to Giles, but he said nothing.

With a sweep of his arm, Captain Fry flung the pistol into the sea. "As you will," he said and sat down.

And our boat, too, began the long journey, in the face of the prevailing wind, toward Chile.

Captain Fry draped his arm around his son and bowed his head. Chester fastened his eyes on Giles.

All day we rowed in dejection toward the east. Only a few words were spoken. Giles moved beside me and said the course was well aimed, though ill-chosen. I was heartened by this, for it had seemed to me that we were merely following the other boats.

During the first night, we lost sight of the other boats. Perhaps they slipped away on purpose. We had lit candles from the lantern keg to signal our whereabouts, but they had not.

In the morning, when I awoke, I saw that we faced the rising sun and that our boat was alone. The captain still slept in the prow, his arm still about his son. I counted twelve of us, clustered around the three rowing benches and at the prow and stern. During the night, when the wind changed, someone had hoisted the single sail. The barrels of our provisions circled the mast; we rode low in the water, slowly tacking. A sixteen-foot open whaleboat is a small country for a population of twelve, but already the territory was subdivided into districts, fore and aft of the provisions. The man with the pointed shoes was the center of the group next to ours. We were at the stern, with Giles's hand on the big steering oar.

Giles bent to whisper in my ear that during the night he had tried to persuade the men to turn west toward Tahiti, still only two days' sailing behind us, but so great was their fear of cannibals—I myself was still afraid, though I did not admit it—that they would not be persuaded. Giles had pointed out the rations, ample for three days, even for the overnumbered crew, but inadequate for a longer voyage. He had stocked the boat with Tahiti in mind.

I did not and do not know what to think of Captain Fry and his capitulation of power. But from that moment when I saw him asleep, he seemed to me a part of the wood of the boat. He seemed inert. What is the opposite of one of those pretty female figureheads at the prow of proud ships? It is a captain, turned around, curled in the prow with his back to destiny. I could not bear to look at him.

His face seemed blotted out, as when I had been blinded by lightning. And Chester? I could focus on his face, alert and frightened, nestled in the crook of his too benign father's arm.

CHAPTER 39   🐚   The Distance of the Stars

D AYS PASSED, and nights.

"How far away, then," Giles mused, "are the stars?"

I shifted myself in the boat and put my cheek on his thigh.

"Kit is asleep," he said.

"And the others, too."

Our boat rocked from side to side at the same speed, it seemed, with which we progressed. There was a harmony in our movement then, though the pace of it—for our survival—served us ill. One man's cheek lay against the hard rib of the boat, yet he slept as though pillowed on his mother's breast.

I remember the next morning that the man's face still bore the wide red welt across his cheek as though he'd been struck by the flat of a sword. But I do not want to remember any of their faces too vividly. I have forgotten their names, though certes, I once knew the names of all thirty with whom I sailed on the *Sussex*. I remember the slight man who fanned his fingers low on the broomstick when each sunset he swept the deck of the *Sussex;* he was with us. The man who wore shoes of dark suede with an unusual tapering and point in the toe—he was with us. It was he who had stood to defy the captain. The image of his feet, standing on the rowing seat, seared into my memory. For a long time I could not recall who else was with us in the light boat, neither names nor faces.

Giles steered us into the wind, and I thought of our zagging on the water as a kind of decorative stitch. And I knew that such a stitch takes a fourth again as much thread, and time, as a straight stitch, and if the angle of the back-and-forths is too acute, it may take twice the labor to reach the other side. And if the angle is acute and the stitch is long, and lengthening, then one sews, I think, with infinity.

Moonless, the sky was an utter darkness (as was the sea, which met it seamlessly), strewn with stars, as was the sea occasionally, when the swell of some wave before me would bulge up to reflect briefly the light of some star behind me, before rolling it under the water. Can the sea thus swallow even the stars? Do seas toss on any other world? In that other place, does some girl from a desperate boat see the reflection of a distant planet twinkle an oar's length away from her? Does she watch that spark roll down into the black? Would she, perforce, imagine me, the moment I imagine her? Am I not her? and, thus, far removed from here?

How far away are the stars, Giles asked, but I replied, "How far away is Chile?"

"A thousand miles. Or more."

Much more, I thought, but did not say. "And that would be as the crow flies," I said.

"This is a night for black birds."

"Think of one the size of our boat," I said. "A black bird hovers over us, with a circle of gold for an eye. Its wings are shaggy at the end. When he sees us, he spreads them individually, like black fingers, to brake his passing."

"He would not brake."

"Why is that, Giles?"

"Crows love only shiny objects, and we are a dull crew."

It is true: our boat is more dull than black. Black, after all, is a color and can have its glory and sheen. All around us in the sea and the sky, there is a black glory we do not share. We are a blemish on it, a spot of rust. When obsidian is hit with a rock, it may split off into sharp and useful flakes, but hit athwart, it blemishes—a crazed spot, a wound. Athwart was our world smacked.

"My mother loved shiny things. She hung them among the trees, to light up the darkness of the forest," I said.

"She must have loved the stars."

"In Kentucky, we were so ringed with trees that you saw the stars only by peeps through branches or in small clearings for houses." I thought a moment, listened to the waves against the wood, and remembered the small dock my father had extended like a timid finger into the Ohio.

"Perhaps over the Ohio, you could have seen a highway of stars. I was never there at night."

It was a fishing dock, and once he had taken me there during the day, when I was a small child, and fixed me a pole and let me fish like any boy. After a while, I had laid down the pole and had lain down beside it. I remember yet that azure, cloudless sky, that lulling sound of the river's water against wood. It was not so different a sound from that which now sang lullaby to all the crew but Giles and me. The river swept the dock away in spring flood, and my father said that he could fish as well from the bank, if he needed to fish, and would not rebuild.

"We would have been in Tahiti," I said, "if we had sailed west." I thought that Giles should have made up the name of some missionary. What point of honor in him had dammed up his throat? A thousand names could have come twinkling out of my mouth, as numerous as stars. But mine was not to question Giles. I believed and do believe that there was a nobleness in him.

"Who but Una," Giles said, "would imagine a crow over the dark Pacific?"

"A giant crow," I put in, with a glint of pride. But had Kit been awake he would have thought of outlandishness beyond any of my imagining, and it would have been deeper. Crows flew out of him as from the depth of a coal mine shaft. From the bowels came his thoughts. "Kit scares me sometimes." My voice was all tenderness—their pact as friends was older than mine with either of them.

"Kit loves you."

How simply we were speaking. All unguarded and soft. Giles traced his fingertips across my forehead. He spoke again: "Kit loves you, and he would never hurt you."

Suddenly, I was all discomfort. It passed through me that Giles was looking into blackness and seeing the future. "We should have sailed for Tahiti," I said again.

"They should have feared the cannibal within." His voice was tight with impatience and judging.

"What do you mean?"

"You're not without math, Una. Count the biscuits. Count the miles. Count the days."

"I don't know how many biscuits are in the barrel." I looked at it— the upright cask, the metal bands like two equators. The altar of our salvation. "Maybe it should lie on its side?"

"You know the size of a biscuit. How tall is the barrel? Estimate its average diameter. Figure the volume." He snorted through his superior nose.

Disdain is becoming to no one. We would be found—some crossing ship would see us. Perhaps the hulk of the *Sussex* had ascended, floated derelict, and someone would look for us. Which way? those people would wonder. East or west? Perhaps there would be two ships, and one would go toward Tahiti and one toward Chile. Yet, it was possible that time after time a ship would choose to search toward Tahiti. What was to prevent that choice being always made?

"Giles, if you were to flip a coin, and ten times it came down heads, the eleventh time, would there be good chance, excellent chance, improved chance, that now you would get tails?"

"No." I could feel the sigh and tenseness run out of his body. His leg stirred under my cheek. "Think of it yourself. Each time you flip the coin, there is an equal chance that the coin may land either way."

"But if you try over and over?"

"I think the law of the coin is the same."

"But that is not the world we live in."

"Can you really say"—he stroked my forehead—"what world we live in?"

I thought of my fantasy of the woman rowing in a region far away among the distant stars. But he could not have known I'd thought that. It was not so much a thought as a picture.

"Here," he said. "I saved my biscuit today. Let's eat it."

His disdain had been but the irritation of hunger.

He took it from within his shirt, quickly broke it in half, and handed me my portion, which was still warm in a tepid way from being against his flesh. "Eat quickly," he said. "The odor might wake them up."

"Why did you save your share, Giles?"

"I wanted to see what it was like to miss a day."

I could hear him faintly as he quickly, almost delicately, ground the biscuit with his molars. He was making a kind of soup of it in his mouth, to make it go further, to crack every crumb and sub-crumb, to liberate all the potential of its nourishment.

I said stoutly, "I don't think they smell in their sleep."

"Really? Haven't you heard a bell ring in your sleep, and immediately fashioned a dream around it?"

"Yes," I said. "And the odd thing is that the drama manages to *precede* the sound, to lead up to it so that there is a notch for the sound in the narrative."

"I've noticed that, too."

"What do you make of it?"

"I think that in the dream the sound is but a memory of the original sound."

"But you don't hear the bell twice."

"The trick would be to time the real sound and the sound within the dream."

"But you cannot place a clock in the unreal world of dreaming."

Now my biscuit was but a memory. Suddenly Giles leaned over the side and vomited. He did not let the upheaval fall into the water, but caught it, as best he could, in his hand.

"Are you very sick?"

He shook his head, but could not speak again for a moment. Still he held the vomitus in his hand, and I could smell the bile from his stomach.

"Wash off your hand," I said.

He held it toward me. "Would you like to eat it?"

"Eat it yourself!"

"I cannot. I'd only vomit again."

"So would I!"

"I drank a little seawater today, and that's why I'm sick. Not the biscuit."

"It's already part digested!"

"Wolves regurgitate for their young. Birds, too." Still, he continued to offer me his hand like a cup, as though the mess were broth. He sat like a Chinese idol, straight-backed, dignified.

"No."

He rinsed his hand. "The day may come, Una, when you will long for anything you can offer your stomach. You may imagine my hand as a Christian pictures the chalice holding the blood of his salvation."

"Wine," I said.

"Choose your salvation—Catholic or Protestant?" And now he was teasing me.

"Give me goat milk, and let Nature be my god," I said. Six goats clambered over a magic island, in the shadow of something large and armlike.

"An impersonal god, Nature," Giles said.

"Oh, I don't know about that," I said. Perhaps I had a secret, could think a thought, image my own universe that was beyond Giles himself.

"What do you mean?" he asked.

I would have answered, but I had no words for the idea, nor any image either. Yet I could not retract. "I don't know."

Again we were quiet. I watched the brief lives of the star reflections in the sea. Some bulged out on a swell, gushing refraction as they went down. Some in the concavities grew harder and smaller, sharply focused before they disappeared inside themselves. Or so I imagined. Perhaps they were really only spots of light. My head seemed swaying and unstable.

"Shall we calculate the number of biscuits in the barrel?" I asked.

"No," Giles answered. "Look up. How far away do you think the stars are?"

CHAPTER 40   🐚   **The Sentence**

A<small>T FIRST</small> the men stood often and pissed over the gunwale. I waited till night when the watch was ours. Then Giles and Kit held my arms as I sat on the side and lowered myself till my bare bottom was just above the water. They always turned their faces and waited till I came up, pulled on my trousers, and said, "All right." As the crew ate and drank less and less there was less necessity for anyone to relieve himself.

Our days were spent in glitter, dazzle. Sometimes the cups of light were small as thimbles, sometimes big as bowls. They rocked, they danced, they could not stand still. No. Not when I thought as loudly as I could *Be still!* did they cease their clapping of hands, their kicking up of heels.

Ceaselessly moving, endlessly spreading water.

Colors: green, blue, slate, gold. Pink at sunset.

Us: groaning. Feeble. Angry with a smoldering more malignant than the try-pots.

One afternoon Captain Fry said, "This is the last biscuit. I divide it equally among us, regardless of our size or condition." I could not look at his shining face, that abstract goodness that refused to fire on the disobedient, that flashed our human doom.

My crumb was the size of my little fingernail.

CHAPTER 41   🐚   **What Do You Fetch for Your Mouth?**

ON THE ISLAND, Una, what did you eat?"

The question came from Kit, with mischief in his eye. In New Bedford, in front of the Seamen's Chapel—not on the Sabbath—I saw a boy toss a stick over and over for his wolfish dog to fetch. So the question seemed to me: a stick tossed for me to fetch back, for no reason but the distraction of it.

"We never killed our animals. We had goats, and we milked them and made cheese, and we had chickens." *This is the last biscuit.*

"Did you eat the eggs?"

"Yes."

"And isn't an egg some form of a chick?"

"Still, we didn't kill the chickens or the goats." *I divide it equally among us.*

"And what if a goat died? Did they ever die?"

While the memory was not pleasant, I liked being pressed against it. Here, in memory, was some other reality than sparkling blue water, sick, weak, slumbering men, a dark fin cutting round and round the boat. I thought of the shark that had circled Uncle and me, but that was not the memory I wanted—that moment was one both too near to the present scene and too totally different in degree of desperation.

"My favorite goat, Apron, a little white nanny, died in birthing. It was twins on her first time." Was this history true? Or had the nightmare swamp within me spawned ghostly gas, independent of fact? Yes, Apron had died, between the installation of the Fresnel and my trip to New Bedford.

"Did the kids live?" *Regardless of our size or condition.*

"We hand-fed them at first. One lived and one died. We made another nanny claim the brown one that lived."

"How did you get them to claim up?"

"You build a small pen so the nanny can't get away from the kid. The proximity kindles the nanny's maternity."

"What happened to the carcass of Apron?"

"I'm not sure."

"Well, did you have goat stew soon after?"

"Yes."

"But no one spoke of Apron?" *This is the last biscuit.*

I thought of the stew, thick with innocent vegetables—onions, potatoes, celery, carrots, spiced very hot with black pepper. "Shall I describe the stew?"

Kit laughed. More a cackle, because his throat was dry. "I'll pass," he said, and mischief burned in his glance. "What else did you eat?"

"Fish. Tons and tons of fish. Mackerel, cod, small tuna . . . But you see, we pulled them out of the water around the Island. They didn't live on the Island."

"What about the creatures on the shore—sometimes in the water, sometimes out?"

"We counted the shoreline as part of the sea."

"And so, you ate?"

"Our little Island was a complete world. It had every kind of shore. The Lighthouse was not at the crest of the headland, but about two-thirds of the way up. The hill behind it continued to rise on one side, almost a little mountain, all meadow, then at the crest, there was a drop of a hundred feet to the sea. The sea battered away at this bulwark, ate off big chunks of it in bad winter storms. That was why the Lighthouse was not built at the top of the crest."

"I was there."

"What?"

"Remember, Giles and I came to the Island in the *Petrel*."

Why had I spoken to Kit as though he were a stranger who had never seen my home? I was embarrassed. My face burned in the sun. I shaded my eyes, looking for the tower.

"You said there were many kinds of shore." Kit's voice was soft, almost a murmur. Perhaps he had not asked. Perhaps I was fishing with Uncle Torch.

"I'm thinking of the eelgrass."

"Where?"

"In the inlet. The leaves are green, like long ribbons. It's rooted in the mud, and when it's ripped up in the fall storms, it sinks to the bottom and decays into a rich, brown muck. The top of the grass floats on the surface. It's always swaying. A strand may be as long as a man."

Once I measured Torchy with a strand of eelgrass. He lay on the beach, and I stretched it out beside him. It was the measure of a tall man, six feet tall. Or perhaps it measured him. "What's measuring is also measured by what it measures," I said aloud.

"What did you find in the eelgrass to eat?"

"Mussels, scallops." *Regardless of our size or condition.*

"Cats that eat scallops drop off their tails and ears."

"It's not true."

"Probably a myth perpetrated by cats who talk to people in their sleep. The cats want all the scallops themselves."

"Why do you think, Kit, that if you hear a bell when you're sleeping, you can dream so fast that you make a place for the bell to sound in the story, and then it sounds right in its niche?"

"In dreams, the arrow of time is reversible."

My mouth was dry. If you speak the air comes in, and the mouth dries. My lips were cracking, and the flesh in the cracks was tender. I moved my hip, though it was numb and continued numb against the boards in the bottom. My eyes were closing.

"Uncle planted dead trees to farm the mussels. Like the French do. These are dead trees, and you make them stand up, and the mussels cling to the branches. They festoon it. Every dead branch is a shelf with mussels clinging above and below."

"How does a mussel clamp on?"

"It doesn't open up and clamp on. Each mussel spins out binding thread."

"Like a spider?"

"A clam just spins out one thread, but the mussels spin and spin. Their threads are golden, called byssus threads."

The sheen of gold seemed before my eyes. Cloth of gold can be woven from byssus threads, but Kit would not have believed that so I didn't tell him. Aunt treasured such a cloth she herself had woven of threads spun by pen shells. Her cloth was narrow, and at Christmastime she laid it on the table, and it stretched from Uncle at the head of the table to the small, thick-sided window cut through the stone wall. On the runner of gold cloth she placed the Christmas candles, held by a curl of driftwood, and the candles were colored with cranberry and scented with bayberry, which grew, like everything else in the world, on the safe Island.

"I've thought of the true name of the Island," I said. "Its name is childhood."

"Not everybody has such a childhood."

This is the last biscuit.

"Remember, Kit, when you made the yeast rolls in the morning?"

"You could have gotten along with my mother. Most people couldn't, but I think you could have."

"Why?"

"Sometimes you can think like her."

But I thought of a madwoman urinating in bread dough. I knew Kit was not thinking of that. I loved to be praised. The comparison to a madwoman was made with approval, affectionately. I opened my eyes and looked at Kit. His nose had a long blister down it, and the skin from his cheeks was peeling. His skin seemed charged with brick dust. The sail hung listless.

"We're lucky it's not storming," I said.

"Yes."

I looked at the heads of the ten others. Each wore some sort of hat fastened under his chin. Discolored, bumpy, their faces looked like gourds blistering in the sun.

ONCE WHEN I sat at the head of the table, I looked down the shining cloth to the window, and I saw a ship, in full sail, centered in the square. It was the very picture of a ship, framed in stone. Leaning over the table, I pointed and said, *Look!* Aunt had said, *A merchant ship,* and Uncle said, *It will make Nantucket by Christmas Eve.* Aunt had asked if Boston was not the likely port—all laden with goods as she must have been, and Uncle agreed with her.

Kit and I fell from talk to silent memory.

THAT EVENING, toward our discomfort and our growing fear in the small boat, the setting sun, dropping into the sea, threw out a cloth of gold from him to us.

I noted, but disregarded, such glory. Sleep sealed my senses like a black bandage.

In my dream, a starfish and a mussel. At low tide, the eelgrass lies flattened, combed down by the retreated tide, and piled on the eelgrass are starfish, all sizes and colors, lying limpsy. I am a starfish, and I fasten my five arms to the mussel I want to eat. *You shouldn't be here in the eelgrass; you should be safe in the farmer's tree,* I think to the mussel, though I know my logic is faulty. At first I cannot open the mussel, but I use only two of my arms at a time, and when they weary, I pry with two fresh ones. The mussel, exhausted, opens. Now I must get my stomach to it. My stomach is a thin sack. Turning my stomach wrong side out, I eject it from my body. I send my stomach inside the mussel shell, and it secretes its juices. I digest. When I am nourished, I pull my stomach back inside to the center of my starry body.

CHAPTER 42   The Beginning of the Debate

SUCH DREAMS began to fill my days as well as nights.

My eyes were swollen, but through a slit I checked from time to time to see if it was night or day.

Once I looked at Chester, unmoving, and wondered if he was dead.

Captain Fry—his face visible again since it had turned gaunt, blistered, and scabby as any of ours—sat beside his son like a heathen idol. No, he moved! He took off his hat and laid it over the boy's face.

ONCE I saw Giles take a jackknife and score the gunwale.

"What for?" I asked.

"Each mark is for a day passed since the last food."

"All around us in the sea and the sky,
there is a black glory we do not share."

There were four upright marks. With his knife he crossed them with a diagonal.

THERE SIMPLY is no more water.

WAS THAT a voice? It seemed like a flag. *No water* was the flapping flag under which we sailed.

Each man sat with a string in his hand. The strings passed over the sides and down into the water. I understood. We were fishing for water.

THE MURDERING. *We shouldn't.* Voices cracked as lips and tongues. *We must.* Who wanted to wait, to debate at night? *Wait.* Night was the time to sleep. *Not yet.* I still knew that. There was the Big Dipper anyway, bringing me water. *Soon.*

CHAPTER 43   **Father and Son**

WE DECIDED. They said.

Why, what could we even use as lots?

"I have paper, Captain." Giles.

"Let it be on your head."

We decided in the night.

"Suppose we're rescued? It could be next hour."

"Do you see a ship?"

"Would you have everybody draw? Even the cabin boys?"

Regardless of size or condition.

MY FINGERS are in a hat sorting cracker crumbs thin as paper, but I am glad. How slowly my hand moves to my mouth. Someone impedes me. "Wait," he says. I try to disobey. "Wait!" Kit commands, and he holds my wrist so that I cannot eat. Unfolds paper.

"IT'S THE little boy!" The voice is Giles's, and it is a wild, despairing shriek.

The captain is standing in the boat, his saber in his hand. "Let no one touch him!"

Kit asks Chester, "What would you?"

Chester responds, piping, "It is as good a fate as any."

The captain brings the blunt, knobbed hilt of his saber down on Chester's head. A measured blow. To stun. He holds the saber low, and with its tip he opens his own throat. Opens extravagantly. Without restraint. He tosses the saber the length of the boat to Giles, who catches it and stands. The captain falls among the men. He falls straight, like a cut tree. Like a fountain. Only he is a bone among dogs.

CHAPTER 44 ◈ The Human Animal

SOMEONE RELEASES my wrist. I get to chew my paper.

Someone puts a finger in my mouth. I suckle. But I know. I will always know. I am drinking blood.

CHAPTER 45 ◈ The *Alba Albatross*

WE DRANK and ate. We slept. We dreamed, and believed reality was dream. I crooned the song of the Lighthouse, as though torture were sung in a long, stone throat. It seemed that as days passed, other people left. And why was that?

My cheek on the gunwale, I saw so many scratches. The point of a jackknife making another. What does a steel tooth like to eat? Wood. Just some shavings. Another calendar, Frannie?

Giles pulling my head up by the hair.

"Do you want my throat?" I asked.

"Look! Look!"

Why, I could still read, and yet be a cannibal!

A ship. The *Alba Albatross*. Distant. Closer. Closing. A merchant vessel, the *Albatross*. She swooped down for us, appearing not at all like her namesake with wings spread out and out on both sides fifteen times in length the width of the bird's own body, but like a white mother hen, feathers all heaped and ruffled, ready to settle over her chicks.

Six sailors came over the side and down the ropes like six seraphs, though they were weather-brown and whiskered, one in a shirt of broad red and white stripes, looking jolly as Christmas or St. Valentine's Day, though I did not believe such days existed anymore. Two on each side, they helped Kit and Giles into the slings, but Red-and-White, whose name I later learned was Bob, sat in the sling himself, saying of me, "This one is so slight, I'll hold him before me, lest he fall."

He folded his arms across my stomach and chest, and I did not care that one thick forearm surely felt the shape of my breasts, for he adjusted his arm so that it rode under and not across me. But he said nothing except, lifting his face toward the deck, "Heave away."

Our miserable state was so urgent to them that I saw the hands of one sailor tremble as he worked to secure Kit in the sling. He moved away, in fact, too rapidly, and did a poor job. Kit was scarcely three feet above the water before he toppled into the sea. Another sailor dove after him immediately. I watched them both disappear under the waves. I watched with interest, but it was a slow interest. I wondered if they would emerge, what beasts under the water they might encounter if they continued to descend. But I made no cry and felt nothing. I looked away.

Giles, who was rising beside me, was in a swoon. I looked up at the cloud of sails hovering above us. Surely the Second Coming! Our Savior and his clouds had come, and even as it was written in Revelation, we quick, we dead—whichever one we were—were caught up to meet him in the clouds, halfway to heaven.

When we lay in the makeshift sickbay, I saw there were three of us, and a woman with a wadded white cloth gently bathed the salt water off Giles's naked body. So must the women have bathed the body of Christ, taken down from the cross. Behind a black curtain of my mind, it was as though my father read the scriptures to me that I needed in order to interpret my experience. The sailor who had borne me up swabbed my own lips with blessed water. I could not open them, but with a large wet finger he most gently went into my mouth. I could feel him prying past my teeth, but even this was done with no more force than was necessary to accomplish the saving of my life. He did this over and over. It seemed an eternity, and throughout the corridors of timelessness, I heard him say to others, "No, no. I'll attend."

Likewise the woman would not leave her post with Giles. I wanted to turn to see if Kindness Incarnate, a human of one sex or the other, had also come to Kit, but there was no part of me that might turn, or bend, or twist, or fold, or glance, not even so much as to shift my eyes in their socket-beds. But I could hear. And that part of me worked that counted and shuffled numbers. I had seen Kit go under the waves, but Kit was beside me; at some point I had counted us Three upon the cots. Blessed Three, take away Two Known, and the Unknown must be, was most surely, Kit.

Giles should have lain in the center, for surely he was the Christ upon Golgotha, and Kit and I were but thieves in comparison. But it was I who lay in the center, and blasphemy came with the position, for on my right hand of myself, God the Daughter Almighty, was Kit. What sinister meaning was hidden in having Giles to the left? Whose promised place was on the left?

Abide with me; fast falls the eventide.

Da da da-da.

Three halves divided by zero: Won't go. Won't go.

MY SAILOR painted in blood. My lips are at the veins. Not his, her, your, their veins. Just the veins. Veins removed from the body, miles like thread. Stitch a quilt with veins, pocket full of sixpence.

Your penance lies in your fingers. The graveyard quilt. That morbid thing stretched from one corner of my mind to all its corners and covered the floor of thinking. All colors are gray or brown or charcoal, burnt wood, blackened fish, glistening coal, octopus ink, the black of the pupil of an eye. All dark fabric, crossed or paisleyed only with like darkness, or darker. We stitch the coffins, the names in black thread on their lids. All the coffins go like boats, but they are out of their element, for this is on land, a graveyard near a church, perhaps. And there is a gray fence. Inside are the already dead. Outside are all whom we know, waiting to die. There's a crowd of us—too many ships in the offing waiting, crowding, jostling each other for the narrow neck and the spacious harbor within.

Gray squirrels run over the tombstones, and the stones are white and sparkling marble. The squirrels cavort and one runs up the magnolia, in full white blossom, and there twitches its tail, a flurry of gray air. And Giles's voice tells me Sanskrit—that *squirrel* in Sanskrit means "ass-flasher."

It is Uncle Torchy, head flashing like a lighthouse. He takes the needle from my fingers. Ah, the dear needle. I want it. Its sides are smoothest steel, smoother than any silk. Let me prick my fingertip, the very bull's-eye of the whorl, let blood soak into the graveyard quilt, for everyone weeps blood when making such a quilt. I must make a graveyard quilt for penance. He puts an eagle feather in my hand.

Surely blunt, but no: it is a quill, his knife has sheared it slanted and sharp for me.

I SUCK the finger in my mouth. I am Apron's child, Apron Young Nanny dead in birthing, and the little thing made to suckle on my fingers. *Ah, yeah,* the flag over me says, red and white unfurled. The squirrel turns the magnolia cone under its paws; the cone turns like a wheel. Handspikes turn the windlass. The squirrel seeks one red seed left neglected in the dark honeycombs. The windlass winds the chains; the anchor lifts from the bottom. *Ah, yeah,* the angel croons, and my tongue seeks around the fatty pad of his finger and *wants.*

Now I would hold his finger tight with my teeth, but he slides past my clamping, and comes again, dripping water. And again. *Wait now.* But he puts his finger in my fist to hold. The part of me that sends out numbers knows the dripping water came three times, and when it comes again, it will be three times. It will not be less, but the same, the same, I sing it, or *more!*

Abide with me; fast falls the eventide.
Together our mouths tell the news; yours first:
Thy friends are yet living.
It was poor Tom who dived for him.
We sent the anchor down, and Tom found it.
But when we hauled them up, poor Tom's ears were burst for it.
And his lungs—we squeezed the water from yonder's and hisen's.
They lay aside each other on the deck, the sea pouring out of their
  mouths.
Poor Tom's the fourth cot here.

When I counted on the road to Emmaus, were there not four of us, though we had started three on the road? Had I not secretly counted four, though logic told me three? Tom's ears were burst for it. Mine worked. I was the thief who robbed ears. I could hear creaking, the safe slow creaking of the timbers of the ship. And I safe inside. And the cradling timbers brown and thick, once of the forest. And this timber, brown and sturdy, shaped, artfully turned, a scroll, an arabesque. Turned not for the strength of it, though it was strong, but for the beauty. And then, with open eye, through the slit of it, I saw also Red-and-White who had lofted me, that flaglike shirt, the brown scroll of the ship timber beside his head.

His eye must have been ever fastened to mine, for through that slit, his stared back at me, and again he gave me water on his finger, though the interval had not passed, but to reward me.

Next, thee will be having it by the spoonful. Very soon now. Rest now.

THE PRISM light focused a dim and greeny light upon Kit's attendant. I had no doubt that he was attended by a kindly woman, for there was her long hair pinned up, and she wore a dress with a wide lace collar.

"Mrs. Swain," my Red-and-White said in a low voice. He laid aside a flap of my shirt and rose.

What was that small huff, that inward sucking of life? It was the surprise of another woman. And after that, she leaned to me, her cheek against mine. "Oh, my dear," she said.

It was Sallie Swain, the wife of the captain of the *Alba Albatross*, a merchant ship, who became my devoted nurse. From Swain to Swain,

I thought, remembering the proprietress of the Sea-Fancy Inn. In life, do we but swim from pole to pole? Do we seek our origin in our destination? Though I felt much gratitude to Sallie, it was old Red-and-White who saved my life, and I wanted him now. The red men have a custom, I've been told, that if you save a man's life then you are responsible for him. It would seem to me more fair the other way around. But, in any case, though he had been all gentleness and consideration to me, Red-and-White retreated to the edges of my recovery. One time he approached me on the deck, when I was sitting with Sallie in our chairs, I wearing a plaid dress she had taken in so it would not hang on me too loosely, and said, "I'm glad to see thee filling out. I'll catch you a little dolphin for supper, over yonder."

I must say, I wetted my lips and smiled, for my appetite had become wolfish. I would not think of what I had eaten. I was alive. And hungry. And the *Alba Albatross,* despite her kind rescue, had a scarcity of food, many barrels having been ruined when the ship had sprung a leak several weeks before it rescued us. Despite his good promise, Bob never presented me with the dolphin, and he did not often cross my path, even in such a small world as the ship.

The first real food I ate was a kind of miracle, though. A flying fish jumped through the open porthole of Sallie's cabin and landed in her lap! She seized the fish and called the cook. My recovery was somewhat faster than that of Giles and Kit—they still could drink only broth—so I got to eat most of the fish myself. Sallie generously declined, saying I needed it more than she. Thus she became my savior, and the love I would have given to Bob of the striped shirt I transferred to Sallie Swain. Bob had no use for my female devotion anyway.

I preferred to spend all my days with Sallie. This may seem like an odd betrayal of Kit and Giles; indeed, I would have thought it so myself, if my mind had pondered my conduct, but I preferred not to think of it at all. I know why I wished not to see them, though. I did not want to see in their eyes the reflection of what we had done together. Sallie was delighted simply with my sisterhood. Once she asked me about the ordeal; I began to tremble, and she put her pretty hand on my wrist and said, "Never mind." She had had no companion woman for many weeks, and then came the gift from the sea of me. Her pet name for me was Undine, and it made me smile in a smug and crafty way. Such a sea-clean name.

Perhaps I should have felt only shame. But let any of you suffer damnation and return to the living! Put a plaid dress or butternut trousers upon you, and I defy you not to feel a smidgen of smug. We survivors! There is a cult of pride among us—as surely as there are demons who come for us just when we think we deserve some good fortune or peaceful moment.

Did you survive at your fellow's expense and not have the demons at your throat? No inexplicable rage? No blackest melancholy? No fear that the cosmos was a mouth ready to swallow you? No terror of Nothingness itself? The wrath of God? Then you are a blessed angel, or an automatic man made of blacksmith's iron and less than human. Or a demon yourself.

I had had enough of this: mouths like that of the moray eel. In nightmare, a boat full of eels, some slipping over the side, some devouring others. Some falling with fountains of blood before the sword. Till we were only three, and Giles threw the saber into the sea. *Through the air, the saber spins on itself, climbs in hyperbolic ascent, faster and steeper than the sun.* That picture: *the saber spins, climbs like a wheel between strings, fast and steep till it joins the sun.* That picture: always in the present tense, always available.

To survive again, on the *Alba Albatross*, I felt I must clear my being of Kit and Giles. I must sit beside Sallie and learn to tat.

Lace must fall from our fingers—a blunt shuttle, no sharp needle, thread not piercing fiber, not binding cloth to cloth, but purest thread knotting on itself. Thread mixed with air, the lace of snowflakes. My lap rising with the purity and lightness of new-fallen snow.

CHAPTER 46   Ganglion

TAKE SOME thread of yourself—say it is your ability to love—put your finger on it and trace it back in time. Not far, and your finger finds a lump, a bump, a tangle, a ganglion. Here the thread loops back on itself, encircles and chokes itself, convolutes till you know: it is a knot.

Now you can begin to pull, and you learn (say you are six now) how the limpsy string becomes a nubbin, a recalcitrant, tiny, in-laced rock, and with each impatient tug you convert energy into a minute hardness. You cannot make a knot unloose itself with this external force; no, you can make it smaller, but you cannot make it disappear. Perhaps all matter is really made of knots! Perhaps fire, like love, can unloose a knot of coal into a free and dancing heat.

So it was with Giles and Kit and me. We three had become a strand with three plies. We embraced only ourself: a firm knot. Oh, there's much that is good to say about a knot—its security, its steadfastness, its strength. Its mysterious overs and unders—the way it occupies three dimensions in space, unlike the lowly two-dimensional line. We looped ourselves together in the cannibal boat. Our loyalty to each other firmed us against the world of other men and nature. But who was who and what was what in that knot of love?

Oh, mankind, you must learn to tat if you would live content. The thread of yourself must form a knobby loop that takes in a larger, growing shape: where you make your home and who is at your hearth and whatever you do for a livelihood, from whaling to mending roads, from raising roof beams to baking bread. Three cannot tie together, turn their backs on all else. Tuck it all in, toward the center! And then let that loop join hands with other loops till the structure is intricate, multifaceted, predictable but growing as a cathedral. Yes, for that piece of stone lace studded with colored glass is the work of centuries. Don't think you belong only to your own time! To your moment of survival. What you do or don't do is left behind.

There was a clinching in the knot we three made—Giles and Kit and I. We could say, "I did it for him," "I did it for her." If we held each other close, there was justification. *There* was love. Oh, let me knot my thread of life in grace and beauty; let me not be entangled by accident, desperation, hopelessness.

But so we were, I felt. Having survived, our spirits demanded *that which we granted to the other* but could not grant ourselves. What's that? This little phrase *that which*—what's the meat encased in those two halves of a walnut shell? We would come to want, entangled again, from each other the love that we could not grant ourselves.

Pardon me, I needed to say to myself, not hear in touch and glance and word from Kit or Giles. *Pardon me, dear human self, capable of the most heinous degradation, capable of soaring.*

Let me know that into the knot of self comes the thread called time, and that what I am, disgraced or blessed, came from what I was, goes to what I yet may be.

CHAPTER 47   **Postscript on the Above**

*I*SOLATO! Do you think yourself a string too short to save? Do you think that you are lank and straight, a linear bit with no connection fore or aft? Fear not your insignificance. Nature has a drawer for you. Yes, nature garners all the string too short to save, and mice visit that drawer. Here's nesting material! Yes, you will be interwoven, be it now or later.

CHAPTER 48   **Soaring**

D ID I PROMISE myself soaring? It has been a long time coming.

As the lace fell from my fingertips, as I wove the thread-loaded shuttle into and out of its own creation, a skeleton came walking across the deck.

He came as a shadow. A flicker at the corner of the eye. Sallie had left me there, seated in her deckhouse, a small room with all its windows open to the ever warming, ever lightening day. Cape Horn had been rounded eastward in my delirium. We were sailing north toward the temperate zone, to Spain. We were not headed home.

Why was it that he seemed blown toward me, puffed along by air? Because he was himself insubstantial, light as milkweed fluff, except he was gray, not bright white. And the filaments had no seedlike center. No, he hung like gray smoke.

"Una," he said. "We walk now. Kit and I."

"Do you?"

"You're looking well."

He rested his hand on the windowsill. His bony fingers, his blue veins, the transparent encasing skin, lay half inside the deck cabin with me.

He spoke again, his voice frail but the words lined up, certain of themselves: "What are you making?"

"Beauty. Yards and yards of beauty. Edging for a bride's pillow. No, no, no. For her sheet, for her shroud."

"For a bride. May she walk in beauty."

" 'Like the night,' " I finished the phrase for him.

"At night," he said. "Practice climbing the rigging. I want us all to go aloft together. It's as close to heaven as we ever came, isn't it?"

"There is not much to eat here." Then I covered my lips with my hands, horrified, as though blood had dripped from my mouth. Then I reached for his skeletal hand. "I only mean it's hard to gain strength without food."

"I will steal some extra."

He turned to go, but I stopped him with my voice. *Ask, if you would know:* the dictum from the Lighthouse prompted me. "And Kit?"

"It will benefit Kit to ride high—up there. With us."

We both looked up to the topsail of the *Albatross*.

"She has no crow's nest," I said.

"But you can stand a yardarm, Ulysses. I've seen you do it."

"It's like having your own wings up there," I said.

Giles's attention focused sharply on me, then curiously. "Whose wings, Una? For I had the same thought."

But I hadn't a sure picture in my mind. I tried to get it, willed yardarms and flapping cloth to emanate from my shoulder blades.

"The albatross herself?"

"Wrong. Guess again."

"Raphael, the archangel?"

"Which one was he?"

Was this the only thing in the world that I knew that Giles did not? Thanks be to my father!

"The angel who appeared to Mary, the angel of the Annunciation."

"Wrong wings again." He ducked his head through the open window into my deck cabin. He put his lips close to my ear. "Guess right this time, and I'll give you a kiss."

Did I want a kiss? Behind the lips are teeth. His were tenacious, I remembered.

"On the cheek, goose. Tenderly."

The whaleboat! "You swung the blade too high. You missed the neck. The cheek was laid open. To the bone."

"Hush."

"Heathen!" I labeled him. "What wings do you want?"

"Close. Much closer. Try pagan. Try Icarus."

He withdrew himself from my interior. He stood upright a moment looking in at me and then stooped his body through the opening again. He touched my ear.

"This earring," he said. "Would you give it to me?"

I slid the hoop out of my earlobe and handed it to him. My fingernails brushed his palm as I left the hoop in his hand.

"Generous Una." He lowered the sash.

I watched him go, the glass between us.

In the west, the yellow-yoked sun broke bloody, like a bad egg.

I clinched my eyes shut. *Now let me see an eagle. Let me see an eagle soaring above the Lighthouse that elevated me in my youth. Let some steady pedestal rise up from the earth herself, stone of her stone. Let clouds swirl, let the tides heave up the sea incessantly, but let me find stillness again.*

And let it be a high platform for viewing eagles.

CHAPTER 49   **Portrait of a Virgin Listening**

O NE NIGHT my stomach troubled me so that I got up and went to knock at Sallie's door, for she kept the ship's medicine chest. Before my knuckle touched the wood, I heard the sounds of the captain knowing his wife. What else could it be? It took my breath. *My love,* Sallie whispered, her voice as lovely as a wisp of lace, but silky. *My darling,* I heard him gasp, his voice suffused with passion.

Turning away from their door, I heard an urgent clicking, like a clock rushing to make up time, as the gimbal moved in its socket.

CHAPTER 50   **Icarus**

A RAINY DAY, and I sat in the stateroom belowdecks, at Sallie's invitation, watching the raindrops fall into the sea. *So some mystics say it is with the soul: we are the individual drops; at death, our boundaries all dissolved, we join the oneness. Salvation, home, is universal; as natural as rain joining the ocean.* Whose voice? My aunt? My mother?

The idea pleased me because it seemed independent of belief. That belief makes anything happen was discordant with all my experience of nature. If I dispensed with belief, did all the feelings go? Trust and hope and love? I thought that they were all lenses, which were indispensable to the human condition. *Even the natural eye is a lens. And Shakespeare is right again! Nothing is a heaven or a hell but believing makes it so.*

But I defy you, Shakespeare, and all the other gods—Milton, Bunyan, Homer (not you, Byron; you can be heroic, but that's only half-god)—to make a heaven of that hell-boat of Three.

The rain, so innocent and unhesitant, pattered down into the sea.

Frequently it rained on us. For three days, Giles's new calendar showed, there had been nothing of them with us. But stains. We had cups. Giles had insisted that we make cups. I think we were adrift three months altogether. When it did rain, we had a way to catch water. The ship's keg had been broken in some of the fighting. During the night, sometimes Giles held the sword to keep the others at bay, sometimes Kit. The others were not allowed to move. One cried that we would not torture him with waiting his turn and slipped over the side.

Does it make any difference if I swear that neither Giles nor Kit nor I ever enjoyed a moment of what we did? It was torture for us, too.

So we had cups. And when it rained we did catch water. And drank it. It rained three days before the *Alba Albatross* swooped into view. There had been so much rain that it had puddled in the bottom of the boat. We bathed in it by turns. We were clean. Each of us naked. There are worse embarrassments than nakedness. This was not a cold rain and yet it was a long rain. Giles called it the Impossible Rain.

Perhaps believing made it so, and warm was really cold! I'll never know.

Then we put our clothes down in our tub, and we used the convex of our cups to scrub at stains. We bailed out the dirty water—the color of wine. And still it rained. Nature's ablution, nature's absolution. Well, doesn't it rain on wolves and wash their maws clean?

Our clothes dried out, so lovely in their crumpled cleanliness. We put them on. We waited. I laid my cheek on the gunwale. Look!

At first she seemed a cloud on the horizon. We smiled. When her coming was a clear matter of square sails and wooden hull, of prow and jib, Giles took our cups from our hands. He stacked them together and plunged the hideous stack beneath the water. I watched him wait to be sure they filled, and then he let them sink.

And then he swooned.

Thanks be to rain.

"YOUR FRIENDS want you to promenade." It is Sallie, down from the deck, water beads caught in her brown curls, her cheek pink and fresh. *My love, my darling,* they had said, and the gimbal ticking like a clock.

"In the rain?"

"They have borrowed umbrellas!"

A WALK in the rain on ship's deck has a touch of home about it. There is a pleasant incongruity, too. Here we are afloat on water, high above that enormous wetness. And do we escape? No, the heavens open and say: Here's rain, just as it is on land. And it can make you wet. (Even under umbrellas, there's a bit of drip and blow.)

Walking between Giles and Kit, my hands lodged in the crooks of their elbows—was it not the echo of an idyll? I asked them what story they had told Captain Swain of our survival. They had said our whale-boat had become separated from the other two. (Giles fingered his earring, as he recounted the tale for me.) We knew nothing of their fate. In our boat, the captain and his son, and all the others, had died.

We were getting stronger. When the larder got distressingly low, Captain Swain sent out a small fishing boat, and after a day of anxious waiting, she returned to us with an enormous marlin lashed to the side. His sword was as long as a walking stick, and the captain later nailed it to his cabin wall as a decoration. The fish's flesh was fixed in all the ways imaginable while it was fresh, and the rest put down in vinegar or dried and salted.

During our rainy promenade, when we came to a puddle on the boards, they swung me over it. "Fragonard!" I exclaimed, for he once painted a happy girl in a swing, her shoe kicked high in the air. I had seen a copy in Boston when Frannie caught the pox.

"Watteau," Giles corrected. With what dry self-irony he spoke— as though it were his distasteful duty to make things right.

The pendulum in me swung back to wanting their company and connection, under Sallie's borrowed umbrella. Afterward, I wrote letters to the Island and to Kentucky, and a few days later we met with the *Thistle*, New Bedford–bound, to convey my reassuring letters.

Far from scorning Kit and Giles, now I loved their company so much that I could scarcely abide sweet Sallie's, though our time to-gether was always pleasant. She felt that my clothes (borrowed from her) must fit, and so there was much taking in of seams, and then gradually letting out. "Look," she'd say, holding up a new-pinned seam, "it's going out an entire half inch!"

That I climbed the rigging at night I concealed from Sallie. At the foot of the mast, I unhooked my skirt. Giles brought me trousers, and I pulled them up over my long pantalettes. I think there was no more modesty about the body left in me.

What did we do those nights? We climbed to a low yardarm and stood there, talking, like convivial birds perching on a limb. But, of course, our fingers were laced into the rigging, and we were perpetually adjusting our balance with the plowing of the ship.

As we gradually climbed higher, our talk became freer, for there was less chance of being overheard. And it became darker.

What do you remember? was often the question. Usually it was asked by Giles, of Kit. Without fail, he had some new and ghoulish image to relate. Once I asked him to stop, but Giles admonished me to let him talk.

But I think I may have been right in trying to dam up that black river. As we climbed higher by night, and memory compiled, Giles's own face became sadder by day.

One night, when we were truly aloft, perhaps a week's sail from the Azores, where new groceries would be purchased, Giles said simply, "Perhaps we made the wrong decision to live."

"I think not," I said promptly. I surveyed the quiet night around me—the ship below, serene water encircling us. I was glad to be there.

"Dulce et decorum est, pro patria mori," Giles quoted.

"Translation?" Kit asked.

" 'It is sweet and decorous to die for one's country.' It's the motto for a Roman soldier."

"We were not soldiers," Kit said.

"A ship is always the ship of state," Giles said quietly. The night breeze gently flapped our sleeves and trousers. I gloried in my strength, that I was well enough and still uncowed enough to stand in the mast.

"There was one sweet and decorous death." Kit gripped our shoulders.

We hung there silently, Giles and I, till I asked, "Which?"

"The captain for his son," Kit answered.

"Ah," Giles uttered.

"That was the answer to Christianity."

I felt a dread in me. I did not like Kit's speculations on reality or religion. They seemed to me to be a snarl of words. What should be said metaphorically he thought of as truth. I had visited those dislocated realms myself.

"In Christianity," Kit went on, "the father sent his son to die. Captain Fry, the father, died to save his son."

The idea had some appeal. "It's why war is a mockery of Christianity," I said. "The old generals send the young men to die."

"No," Kit said. "War is an enactment of Christianity, not its mockery."

" 'Love your neighbor as yourself'?" Giles asked.

" 'I come not to bring peace, but a sword,' " Kit replied.

"The devil can quote scripture," I said. It was something my father used to say to me when I used Biblical words to defy him.

"What do you think," Giles asked Kit, "of *pro patria mori?*"

"I prefer friends to countrymen."

"Yes," Giles answered. " 'Friends, Romans, countrymen'—even Marc Antony put friends ahead of countrymen."

I chuckled.

"But then," Giles added, "he was a traitor."

"I need to piss," Kit announced.

"Go ahead," I said. I had seen the act often enough.

"You'd not piss on the heads of our saviors, would you?" Giles asked.

"No."

"I would," Giles answered. "But I have no need."

"Urine in the bread dough—do you remember when you said that to Frannie, and Aunt was shocked?"

"I shouldn't have said it," Kit said.

"Why not?" I asked.

"It upset your aunt, and she'd been hospitable to us. It probably disturbed little Frannie."

"You could wait a few years and marry little Frannie," I said.

Here I knew I had overstepped. I felt Giles on one side and Kit on the other stiffen. I shuffled my feet on the masthead platform.

"I intend to marry you," Kit said. Then he laughed. "Both of you."

"Sometimes I feel that way," I said shakily.

"In case you want to know," Kit said across me, the words like the threat of a spear, to Giles, "I forgive you for what you did to me."

"You can't," Giles replied. An utterance like a pebble dropping forever down a well.

We waited for Giles to speak again. Finally, his tone all changed, he said, "I think we are all already married." He sounded happy and ironic. "If that's possible."

"How do you say in Latin," Kit asked, "that it is sweet and fitting to die for your son?"

"In King James's English. 'Greater love hath no man than this. That he lay down his life for his friend.' "

"Do you think we could have killed each other?" Kit asked. "If you hadn't thrown away the sword?"

"No," Giles answered.

"Do you think that we would die for each other?" I asked.

"Yes," Giles said. "Or live. You might find that harder."

After we had climbed down, and I had shucked my trousers and donned my billowing skirt, Giles spoke to me privately.

"Una, 'my words fly up, my thoughts remain below. Words without thoughts never to heaven go.' "

"Claudius," I said. *"Hamlet."*

"Who was Claudius?" Why did Giles ask? To test me?

"Hamlet's uncle, Hamlet's mother's husband, the new king of Denmark."

"No. Claudius was a murderer. So am I."

"We all ate."

"But I was the one who decided, wasn't I? I was the captain."

I saw the sword flying above the boat from Captain Fry to Giles. He caught it so solidly. It had been as though nature put the sword in his hand. And the captain already bleeding, quickly falling forward as though to prostrate himself before the new captain. I knew what he was doing there. He was asking for the life of his son.

"He didn't want Chester to see, of course," I said. But Chester had never seen anything again. The blow, meant by his father only to drop his boy into a sleep, sent him into a level of unconsciousness from which he never awoke. Chester's burial in the sea had been decent.

"I had made a ladder of reasons," Giles said. "I thought I was justified, but I was only arrogant. I didn't want to die."

"I will never give up my arrogance," I said. "I want to live." I said it to encourage him. Having suffered so much for our lives, we needed to value them.

THE NEXT DAY at noon, I watched Giles go up the rigging. He'd offered to check a sail, Captain Swain said. I don't know for what reason I stopped, looked up from my tatting, and watched him go. He seemed to climb toward the sun the way I had once climbed toward the moon with Kit.

There was no cry at all. His foot seemed to tangle. He tumbled down the sky and, with hardly a splash, disappeared into the indifferent sea.

CHAPTER 51   **The Test**

HOW DO YOU become a trumpet? Heart and throat open in blaring. Their heads—the heads of the men on deck—unbent innocently from the ordinary, for no one but me had screamed Giles down the sky. While they polished the capstan or trimmed the wick of the binnacle lamp or while a man lowered his eyes to whittle a new belaying pin—that was when the catastrophic superimposed itself on the ordinary: a conundrum that soldiers and sailors knew well. All those tasks and more were abandoned, and a line of men crowded up to the taffrail beside me. We saw only the heaving sea, the small whitecaps where water built and broke. And my pointing, my shrieks, the chattering of my teeth.

A boat was lowered: *Albatross* turned into the wind to wait. Though the sailors rowed the small boat all around the spot where I had seen Giles enter the sea, a place I had watched with unbending eye from that moment, Giles never surfaced, nor any article of his clothing. The glassy green water lifted only itself, and fell, and rose again. The small boat rode the rise and fall of the green swells. Sometimes they rowed, and bits of foam, little necklaces, floated and dissipated.

If only the boat would not return—we could wait for eternity. Let him not be irrevocably gone! My heart beat with the strokes of their oars. I willed my heart to stop, but the boat came closer to the ship. Wood against wood. Returned. Six men with arms and legs and moving life. Not even the husk of Giles, not even a sodden, lifeless, drooping form.

Sallie stood with me at the rail, guided me to her cabin, sat beside me on her bed, wept for me. I could find no tears. I stared. I felt her braided rug under the sole of my shoe.

Had his body finished its descent to the floor of the ocean, or would it slowly sink for hours, wafted by the currents? Was a marlin passing, parting the water with his spear? Did the water grow dim and cold as he sank deeper? Did some giant squid with undulating arms wait at the bottom, opening its beak?

Surely Giles died at the moment of hitting the water, hard as iron. Death quick as the smack of a hand. No harder. He *felt* nothing harder than that. Had he been afraid as he rushed toward the water? When his foot missed the spar and stepped on air, did he think, *It's just as well*?

I imagined a slight smile.

Was it falling or letting go? Or some of both?

I FOUND KIT sleeping in the forecastle, his cheek pressed into the netting. I shook his shoulder. He gazed at me without acknowledging the oddity of my presence, but his hand reached over the edge of his hammock, and he gently put his finger in my curls and then brushed the weave of Sallie's piqué collar with his fingertips.

"Giles is dead."

"What?"

"He fell from the topgallant sail into the water."

"I don't believe you."

"Giles is dead, Kit."

"You and he have made it up to test me."

"No."

Then I sat down on the floor beside him, to wait. Giles would have wanted my undivided love to go to Kit. *Console.* That was my pure injunction.

He lay slung in the hammock, staring up. After many minutes the tears began to seep from the corners of his eyes. I knew he knew, and I began to sob. Even the linings of my mouth wept and filled it with water.

Then Kit got up from his hammock and sat on the floor beside me. He put his arm across my shoulder and drew my face against his bony chest. "Poor Una." He, too, had consolation to offer, but I felt numb as stone.

The ship rocked us, sometimes my weight bearing toward Kit, sometimes his body leaning into mine. Only my skin was alive. I was a rock covered with a tissue of flesh.

Kit put his hand under my skirt and touched my thigh through the cloth of my drawers. When he said, "May I?" I said "Yes," and unloosed the drawstring and lifted my skirt so that we might be more together.

CHAPTER 52   The Funeral

WHEN I SAW SALLIE, I told her that my menses had commenced again and asked if I might have some rags of her.

Her face cleared a moment at this "news" of returning health, for my body had been so dried out, so starved and tried by many weeks in the open boat, that the womanly functions had ceased. Sallie spoke sympathetically. "Your friend gone, and this, too. I'll get you a clean dress."

I would have spent the night in Kit's embrace and in my embrace of him, but he and I both had known that soon other sailors would come to the forecastle, and we must not be found upon the floor. My shoulders remembered the hardness of the boards. There had been gladness and pain, purging pain, and desperate comfort in joining with a man whose heart knew my heart's sorrow.

"My mother," Sallie went on, "often told me that some great shock in life could either start or stop the monthlies."

She handed me a navy-blue skirt and waist, and I thought ironically of how bravely and naively I had left my childhood Island in just such a frock. After she poured fresh water in the china bowl, Sallie hugged me again and kindly left me to bathe in private.

I was scarcely changed—some dried blood on my legs. The loss of the label "Virgin" signified nothing compared to the real loss of Giles.

Signified joining—that neither Kit nor I was alone. The world was utterly changed.

When she returned, she said that her husband would read scripture on deck as a funeral service for the soul of Giles, but we were under sail again, headed for the Azores, and would not stop. The crew, or many of them, would assemble for the brief memorial. As soon as I felt I could come, I was to appear on the quarterdeck.

Wearing a dress saber, Captain Swain placed a black Bible on the gleaming head of the capstan and proceeded to read from the Twenty-third Psalm. Only the phrase "He maketh me to lie down beside the still waters" reached my brain, as I regarded, beside the brim of the captain's hat, the incessant dancing of the waves.

After he had finished his reading, without any thought or decision, I said the poem of Wordsworth that begins "I wandered lonely as a cloud . . . / A host, of golden daffodils; / Beside the lake, beneath the trees . . . And then my heart with pleasure fills, / And dances with the daffodils." But my heart was a still lake of sorrow.

Kit abruptly said, "We went through a lot together. There were some happy times." Then his face became angry, and he added, "He was a great man, greatly flawed."

Here Sallie came to put her hand, restrainingly, on Kit's shoulder. *Great man?* There was a lie in Kit's statement. Were we not *boys and a girl?* Sallie's white fingers, curling around Kit's shoulder, gleamed as innocently as seashells. There was a spark of iridescence on her hand—an opal ring. I thought of Frannie innocently tipping the basket of shells, their inner surfaces, some of them, splashed with iridescence, for Kit to see as they sat before the hearth that night of first acquaintance.

Kit brushed away Sallie's hand and squeezed shut his eyes and proclaimed, "He would never have fulfilled the potential of his youth."

It was a stunningly inappropriate statement, but I accepted it as quickly as I used to accept Giles's own quiet outrageousness. Quickly the captain loudly began, "Our Father, who art in Heaven . . ." and the crew mumbled loudly along, but Kit growled obscenities.

I would not listen to what Kit was saying. I had given Kit my body. I smoothed the skirt of my dress with my hand. *Our Father.* I thought of Captain Fry standing hatless in the prow of the boat, his sweat-wet hair adhering to his forehead, and then, as though it were a mere envelope, opening the flesh of his neck, penetrating the jugular with the tip of his sword. Offering himself—*my body and blood*—in the hope that his son might live. I would have given mine for Giles's life.

CHAPTER 53   The Contest

H ADN'T OUR PACT been to stay alive for each other?

I would not have died for the man with the pointed shoes or his mates.

There was no sleep that night. I lay on my back and fought down the memories of the whaleboat. Legs, trousers, swollen hands—not their faces; I would not envisage faces—yellow trousers, a ripped sleeve lay strewn among the seat struts of the whaleboat. Exhausted, recumbent, the crew sprawled. Intact. We had hoped for rescue.

Their faces were wiped of features, as though I had been blinded by brightness again. Kit, Kit! If only I had Kit to hold me.

THE NEXT MORNING Sallie brought me a fried piece of marlin, a slice of toast, and an orange that she had been saving for herself. She watched me eat, and I tried to do so with some show of pleasure, for I wished her troubled countenance to brighten at some small enjoyment, directly or vicariously experienced, as was her habit. She collected the orange peels, nesting the fragments one inside the other, and said that they would be ground up to flavor a sauce for another dish. Then I thought of poor Harry and his endless economy.

"I knew a cook who saved eggshells," I said. And then it struck me that these were the only words ever said in eulogy of Harry.

Sallie did not reply to this, though usually she was full of pert and prompting questions. After I had finished, she said that during the night Kit had begun to rave and rage so loudly that no one else could sleep, and that they had taken him up and chained him to the foremast. *No! We should have been together.*

In a blink, I rushed to Kit and found the steward pouring water over him. My Kit was chained, by a wrist. His eyes were glazed and unblinking. I saw that his body was brownly smeared.

"He befouled himself," the boy said, embarrassed. "I be helping him to wash."

In fact, he was washing Kit by himself, as Kit sat cross-legged on the deck, stripped to the waist, one hand chained up and the other lying idly in his lap. Terror swept through me. I shook his wet shoulder and called his name, but Kit continued to stare.

Finally he said, "We've eaten everything else. Why not? That's what Giles said."

"No, he didn't say that," I said.

"Yes, he did. You didn't hear, Una."

"Stop it," I said. I could feel hysteria rising in my voice. "Stop this!"

"Una. Come closer. I want to whisper to you."

I leaned over to listen. The wash boy retreated.

"Bake me a pie, Una, and in the pie, hide a rasp. A file. Bring me the pie at dusk when they can't see well. I'll saw free—very quietly—in the night."

"Una!" It was Sallie calling me. "Una, come away now. Let the men take care of him."

I looked at the brownish puddle on the deck, a foul-smelling and shallow sea. What tiny, invisible creatures swam there? A degraded universe.

AS THE DAYS passed, Kit's dementia deepened, and he imagined me to be his mad mother. "Let's bake bread," he would say. He spoke of seasonings, of raisins and cinnamon and cardamom, as though they were magical in their powers. He spoke of eyes as witching stones and said that mine were lapis and his were agate. He said the wind smelled of blood. He tried to unfasten his trousers.

My grief for Giles became displaced by anxiety for Kit.

Sometimes he was quiet, and then he was allowed to walk about if

I or another accompanied him. One day, he ran for the rigging and tried to climb up, to look for Giles. After that he was chained, and again there was talk of pies and rasps when I visited him. Once he asked Sallie where was his wife?

I had a cold dread that he would point an accusing finger at me and tell that we had coupled or how we had survived. But so many of his words were wild and whirling that I doubted his stories would be taken as anything but madness. Yet I dreaded to hear those true words uttered in the open air. I dreaded to have to pretend that the idea was shocking.

I would have sat with Kit all the live-long day, and night, too, in spite of this dread, but Sallie and her Captain Swain firmly asked me not to do this. Sometimes in the night I fancied I heard him shrieking *Una, Una, Una* and the jerking of a short chain. There were no potions or herbs for treating madness aboard the *Albatross*. "We can only try to keep his body safe," Sallie said. His mind sank, like the wrecked *Sussex,* beneath waves of melancholy and dementia.

Now it was my time again to stand at the rail and look to sea. With the sun warming me, I strove to concentrate its goodness in my person. Often I felt I gathered strength and resolve till I was brimming with it. Then I went to see Kit, to try through sheer dint of cheerfulness to plant him with the seed of a happy thought.

Once he was standing manacled to the foremast with his hat off, staring at the sea. When I came nigh, I could not cause him to look at me.

"We will resurrect him," Kit said.

"It can't be done." I answered as judiciously as though he had said that we would merely climb a mountain.

"Under the right conditions," Kit spoke intensely, "anything is possible. Giles called it the Theory of the Impossibility of Impossibility." Kit did not look at me, but he put his hand on my shoulder. "I want us to marry."

Was I as mad as he? I simply said *yes*.

For a moment, it seemed everything stopped.

I TOLD KIT not to stare so at the water, that the glare would hurt his eyes. I glanced up. Clouds moved again. Slowly Kit lifted his eyes to the sky.

"It's a contest," he said. "I'm going to make it stop."

"What?" Hadn't our lives already stopped? And started again?

"I will make the sun stand still." He spoke and stared with riveted gaze at the sun. "Then Giles will rise from the water."

And so he stood all day while the sun passed over his head and down the sky into the western waters.

I was not mad, yet Kit's madness seemed woven into me. His steadfastness, his devotion, sang through his pain of our great loss. How could I ease Kit's pain? My own I could scarcely face.

CHAPTER 54   🐚   I Am Married

As we approached the Azores, a whaling ship that once I had watched through a spyglass came into view—the *Pequod*, out of Nantucket. I knew that whaling ships did not often stop to gam with merchant ships such as the *Alba Albatross*, but when the *Pequod* hove into view, I got the scent of home—Kit's island home—and I asked my captain if he would not try to hail the *Pequod* and prevail upon its captain to take Kit to Nantucket, if they should be homeward bound, as they appeared to be.

"What of yourself?" Sallie asked. "Will you stay with me?"

"I doubt the captain yonder would board Kit without a caretaker."

"But if he will . . ."

My mind would not knead the question.

I did not tell Sallie that I had agreed to marry my Kit. Perhaps Kit himself had forgotten. Let it be as Kit willed, but I knew that if I was married to him then I would have some say in his care. Who would care for him if not I? Charlotte, that name, came to me—his friend who had kept his pet vixen. But he never spoke of her. And he had lain with me.

And I had had enough of trying to live at sea.

THEN THE WORLD was full of sails as the *Pequod* and the *Albatross* drew together. I saw the ivory tackle of the squarish *Pequod*, built so much more sturdily than the clipper *Albatross*. And the captain—Ahab with the zaggy mark down the side of his face. I thought of how, when I was still a girl at the Lighthouse, the lightning had come close to me. Ahab had an eagle's face; he wore no hat, and his gray-white hair streamed back from his brow.

He was of medium height, and though he was not young, his body had an extraordinary hardness to it, as though he had endured much. Whatever the gods had hurled at him he had withstood, I reasoned. Time might blanch his hair, calamity might mark his face, but he strode the deck as though every nail belonged to him. His hands had a peculiar reddish hue, as though they had reached into a fire and snatched out whatever it was that Ahab wanted.

His foot in a rope loop, Captain Swain was swung by the cargo crane to the *Pequod*, which then moved off a short distance. With the calm certainty that my life had come to another crossroads, I watched the two captains talking on the deck. Captain Swain gestured back to the *Albatross*, and Captain Ahab looked at me.

At once Ahab walked to the rail of his *Pequod* toward us, speaking to Captain Swain as he moved. They boarded a whaleboat, were lowered and ferried back toward the *Albatross*. I stood still and waited. Someone brought Kit to stand beside me. He seemed to know that some judgment was to be rendered on us, and he stood quietly, though I could sense the contraction of tension in him. I knew he would insist on being judged aright.

As Captain Ahab strode toward us, I heard him mutter, "I never liked the tread of a merchant vessel."

"Nor I," Kit suddenly said.

Ahab eyed him closely. "Ye'd go to Nantucket on a whaler then? With Ahab, would ye? With cannibal old Ahab?"

"Brother," Kit said, unsmiling, challenging. He stared at Ahab as though he were the sun.

"Brother?" Ahab questioned. "Ye'd better count me on fingers and toes and teeth as well. I'd say 'Father,' were I ye, before I said 'Brother.' "

"With my wife."

I felt my head jerk up with surprise.

"Captain," Sallie said, "they're not married."

"Marry us," Kit said, turning to Captain Swain.

"I won't," he answered. "It's not fitting."

"Marry us," Kit said to Ahab, "on your ship."

"The man's mind spins like a weathervane," Captain Swain said.

"What would ye?" Ahab asked me, and as he asked, there was a softening of his tone, imperceptible to the others perhaps, but soft as dew to me.

Kit grasped my hand and squeezed till it hurt. "I will not go," Kit said to me, "if you fail in your promise."

"Una!" Sallie exclaimed, gently taking my hand away from Kit. He let go and watched. Sallie led me aside. She spoke softly, directly into my ear; she implored me to consider the seriousness of marriage.

"I did say that I would," I answered.

"A promise to a madman cannot be binding," she said. "You were probably half gone yourself. Did you think of what you were saying? Answer truly."

I told her no, that I had not thought. I had only said the word that seemed inevitable.

"Inevitable?"

"The universe prepared us for each other."

She put her gentle hands on my shoulders and shook me.

What sentences could I speak that would seem meliorating and reasonable? I told her that I had loved Kit for many months, that I was not afraid, that I believed that he would never hurt me, that we had an old understanding.

"It was Giles you loved."

"Sir," I called to Ahab, "will you marry us?"

"If ye wish it," he said.

"You are a barbarian," Captain Swain said to Captain Ahab.

"She chooses her fate," Ahab said. "Look at her." Something like a smile passed his face.

So I turned to Sallie and asked if I might take a few things with me.

"Whatever you like," she said, true to her generous nature to the end. But she did not accompany me belowdecks.

In going toward my cabin, I passed one of the merchant sailors whom I had seen before only at a distance. Though I was preoccupied,

I looked at his eyes, and he stopped and looked deeply at me for a moment as we passed in the corridor. A voice within me spoke: *He is the most interesting man I have ever seen.* In an abstract, detached part of my mind, Giles and Kit grew pale. *Interesting*—why that cold word? Did I mean *promising?* And promising *what?* As I walked into the room to pack a few dresses, my inner voice added with regret: *But now is a time when I must leave this place.*

I had said I would go with Kit, and I would. I wanted to be *truthful* and *loyal.*

I was wearing a navy dress, and I was glad of it, for marriage, like leaving the Island, had the feel of beginning a journey, even though I had already put my foot upon the path. I selected two of Sallie's older dresses, folded and placed them in a pillowcase along with a few other items. A sad little part of me thought of the dried rose petals, the gift of Giles, that had accompanied me onto the *Sussex* and sunk with her. I threw the pillowcase over my shoulder like the sailor boy I had tried to be and hurried to the deck.

Ahab and Kit had already crossed over to the *Pequod,* and Ahab, his hand at a long bone of a tiller, was bringing his ship close beside the *Albatross.* In Ahab's stance—legs spread, body balanced—I thought there was something wild, outside the usual laws of risk and chance. At the corner of my eye, I saw Bob in his red-and-white-striped shirt. I crossed to Bob, held out both hands to him, but the words of thanks would not come.

"I was glad to help ye," he said simply, his face red, his eyes teary.

I kissed Sallie through her weeping, tried to thank Captain Swain, and settled myself into the half-barrel chair, upholstered in red oilcloth, with which the *Albatross* had equipped itself for the sake of comfortably transporting Sallie onto or off the vessel. Thus, seated in the barrel chair, I was swung by a crane from one ship to the other, though Ahab had brought the *Pequod* so close I could have walked a plank between the ships.

Kit came to me with that gallantry I had noted so long ago on my Island, to help me from my seat. There we stood together on the deck of the *Pequod,* holding hands, not looking back at our kind friends. We sailed west. When we were at a distance safe from accidental collision with the *Albatross* and yet again some—far enough to feel our free-

dom—Ahab gave the tiller to the first mate—Starbuck, he called him—
and approached us.

"Now be it true," he asked, "be it true still that ye both would be
married?"

When we both answered yes, Ahab reached for our hands. He held
them between both of his—rocky hands, like the kind of outcropping
that could scrape the hull out of a ship, but forming for our nuptial a
natural cathedral, one flinty hand for our floor and another for our
ceiling. Within that strong vise, he pressed our hands together. "Now
ye be married," he said.

CHAPTER 55   🜨   **Aboard the *Pequod***

GINGER COOKIES," Kit said. "One pint molasses, one cup sugar,
one of butter, one-half cup water, two cups flour, one of saleratus, and
one of ginger."

"His mother was a baker," I said to Ahab. "Of Nantucket. Their
name is Sparrow."

"Ye have the name, too, now," Ahab said.

I felt surprised, a nudge, as when the search boat, bearing nothing
of Giles and all of a new reality, had nudged against the *Albatross*.

"She has the ginger in her," Kit said to Ahab.

"Man, take your little wife below," Ahab said. "I'll give ye and her
my quarters. I'll sleep with the mates."

I was astonished that a captain would casually give up his quarters,
but Kit gestured toward the hurricane house built on the deck. "Who
lives there?"

"Naught. Naught but time and weather. That little house is reserved
for winter wind. We'll meet him as we sail. He'll be stamping his foot
on deck in a week or two." Ahab stared at Kit with the fixed gaze of
a man mesmerized by fireplace embers. "Take your wife and go below,"
Ahab repeated.

Kit pointed up the mizzenmast. "Who inhabits the heights?"

"Lightning and thunder, sea hawks and wind."

"My wife would like that."

"Go below. Take your sweet wife. She's married you, man."

WHAT KIT dreaded most was to be locked up belowdecks, but I coaxed him into Ahab's chamber, a room very spartan compared to the other two samples of captain's quarters I had known so well aboard the *Sussex* as a boy and aboard the *Albatross* as a woman. The captain of the *Pequod* slept in a hammock, not a gimbaled bed. He had slung the hammock in the stateroom.

Ahab had an enormous library of maps, with shelves built vertical to stand them in, and a very large table upon which to spread them. His clothes had been relegated to an ivory-plated sea chest, with scrim-shaw ovals and rectangles. These decorative lozenges, of varied styles and motifs carved by many hands, were fastened with tiny screws to the wood of the chest so that it looked shaggy, covered with a congeries of whitish scabs. In the corner stood bundles of harpoons and lances wired to the wall so that they could not shift in some swell and strike the hand or person of him who should have wielded them. When I opened the door to the chamber usually used by captains as a bedroom, I found an extra storage space stacked to the ceiling with small casks of spermaceti.

Kit peered out one after another of Ahab's three aft portholes. Anxiety swept his countenance. "Where have we been?" he asked. "And where are we going?"

"Home," I said. "To Nantucket."

"We'd best study the way." He reached up into the vertical shelves and clutched the gilt spine of a map book. Spreading the map on the table, he remarked, "I'll copy this. This time we'll know the right way."

I put my hand on his shoulder, a bit timidly. "We're married now."

"If you say so."

A knock at the door, and a rough-and-ready steward appeared with a stack of covers. He stammered that they were "for a pallet" and retreated, red with embarrassment.

I arranged our bed and called Kit to come and sit, but he replied that he needed to copy a map, before the ship sank and we were adrift, chartless in an open boat. "Which is this?" he asked. "The South Pacific or the North Atlantic?" When I told him, he set to work, making free use of Ahab's pens and paper and Ahab's broad table.

As Kit worked, my eye visited the shaggy chest decorated with little ivory plates. Among the scrimshaw pictures was a particularly fine row of whales, a kind of encyclopedia, including narwhals with their unicorn horns, the right whale with his ironic smile, the finback, the great blue with his mammoth pleated baleen hanging like a basket under his mouth, the sperm whale whose body is one-third head, the orca shaded in black and white, and many others.

Through the porthole, I watched dusk and then night come on, but ere nightfall, after a knock, I found left at our door a burning candle and a platter of food. Ahab had had sent to us a common salver, assuming that I and my husband were one. But at night Kit climbed into the hammock and I slept on the pallet.

I could not sleep for wanting the comfort of my husband. Gladly would I repeat the pain for the sake of his warm embrace. Perhaps in his mind we were not even married. But we had lain together on a hard bed. That forecastle floor of the *Albatross* was the hard fact of Giles's death. Kit and I were married then more than by words uttered and hands pressed together on the *Pequod*. Had he forgotten the *Albatross*? Suppose he did not want me, but dreamed of Charlotte? But he *had* wanted the pleasures of the flesh, with a natural, male wanting, on the Island. And my body had yearned in response.

Certainly he dreamed, for he mumbled continually in his sleep, but the words were misshapen and incomprehensible. Not English words, nor words in any language, but syllables cut loose from sensible words. From his fitful slumber, sounds rose and fell, in volume and in pitch, as though his tongue were a sea-tossed ship.

But Shakespeare counsels that sleep can knit up the raveled sleeve of care, so I let Kit be. The babbling might have come from a babe rocking in his cradle.

At length, I rose and stood at the porthole and looked at the starry sky. I was grateful for the glass between us. What did I know of madness? Only what the poets taught. I knew Lady Macbeth, Hamlet and Ophelia, Lear. None of them ate dung. I knew a bit of my own madness from the boat. Now the stars were sturdily framed by Ahab's porthole, but then they had been loose in the sky and diving into the sea. There had been another universe, one in my mind, so lonely and distant that its presence was an absence.

What would I do with my mad husband? Here all was in suspension. But when we came to port in Nantucket? Then life would be real. It would be no transition from one state to another. Nantucket would be my lot. It would be my penance. Had not Giles commanded Kit and me to love one another?

I turned and looked at Kit, trussed up in his hammock. He had a bonny face, though now it looked hurt even though there was no mark upon his skin. Gazing at his lowered lids, I knew that a strange universe lay behind a veil I could not lift. I wished there were a sound I could make, a bell to ring, that would make time rewind behind his veiny eyelids.

We would go back to New Bedford. I would lean out Mrs. Swain's third-story window and yell at them. Giles was there! We would not go to sea at all, but westward, wanderers walking to the heart of the land.

I began to pace the cabin, and finding it confining, I took up the candle and slipped up the companionway to the deck.

As I walked to the prow of the ship, the candle guttered and went out in the breeze. Before us, in the west, hung the crescent moon. When I was a little child, my father had said, "There, you see, God has been paring his fingernails."

But then, why wasn't the sky full of crescent moons—ten of them? Did God have only one finger? Yes. It was the one he used to smite us with.

I listened to the wind smacking and flapping the sails. Someone was aloft, two men, taking in canvas. Not Giles and Kit. I did not look.

The moon was enough to see. She was like a shuttle. I smiled to think of my tatting. I had left the yards and yards of lace under Sallie's pillow. By this time, her fingertips had found the strange mass of threads, had pulled out the lacy wad, had exclaimed to her husband. Perhaps, missing me, she had cried, and he had comforted her. And in her grief, perhaps, she unleashed passion warm and free.

Certainly for me, grief had flung open the doors of passion.

I had been a welcome companion to Sallie, though I had felt myself apart from her in spirit because she knew nothing of the human capacity for savagery, the inevitable animal within.

Now there was no one who could ever tell that I had lived on human flesh. All of the others were perished; Giles dead; Kit mad. *Nobody knew.* Though I could think of a smug safeness, I could not enter it. What was safety? A room, but I was without that room; I could stand in the open door and look in at its boxy comfort. Or I could look in at windows and see those cozy rooms where others lived, but I was forever unhoused. And yet I was intact.

"*Mrs. Sparrow,*" a voice whispered in my ear.

It was Kit. Kit's eyes—wounded—but knowing me, calling me by my name, his arms open. I entered their haven, was guided downstairs to our pallet.

SO, IN SOME MEASURE, I had my Kit. For a fortnight, aboard the *Pequod,* his mind was with him, and my body was wife to his body. Then he seemed like the Kit of the Lighthouse. The kindness he had shown to Frannie he showed to me. The passion he had had for me, then much suppressed, he expressed freely. I had not had a woman's sensitive response till Kit loved me.

The nights gave us to each other. We often left the candle burning, and in its glow his skin and eyes and hair were radiant for me, and all of me, he said, for him. That candle glowing on the floor beside our pallet seemed to have a double, for I swear there was a glowing within my body. Glory—flesh of thigh, of breast, of buttocks, and humbler flesh of palm and ear and cheek and tongue—all existed to rhapsodize! Their song had only two words: *Kit Sparrow, Kit Sparrow, Kit Sparrow.*

If Giles had to die, then let him have died to give us this joy. I think he would have smiled to see us.

When Kit and I were not together, even when I walked about on the deck, I felt him physically within me. This was a new fulfilling, a new secret about my body. The shape of him had a ghost, and it haunted my flesh. He seemed yet palpably with me when I leaned my elbows on the taffrail, hands clasped, skirt billowing. And there, under my skirt, the shape of Kit yet, within my womanness.

The crew seldom spoke to us—I saw Ahab occasionally at the bony tiller, but he, too, was unobtrusive. They seemed to let Kit and me live in a giant bubble. We might walk as we would, sleep and eat as we wished. Food was left at the door twice a day—coarse, hard fare, but the hard biscuit had beside it a bit of pickled herring, or mackerel in mustard, or a pot of honey, so we had our flavors. I did not imagine our captain ate any better; he had thrived on hardship.

During that honeymoon fortnight, Kit seemed to give his mind to me to steer, and when the wild sentence came—"Now we eat our fingernails. Now the spiny stars"—I turned abruptly, shook my head, and said, "No, Kit." He would fall silent for a time. Then I would ask some innocent, simple question. "Do you see that school of cod, starboard?" With his careful reply, we'd be on course again.

But one night, he boxed the compass with his mind. No statement or question of mine could stop the whirling. He could not stop his mind or feet, and as we walked round and round the deck, he touched the railings and pins and cables we passed. Many times we passed Ahab, and he stood like a statue, his hair white in the full moonlight. The sailors we skirted in our rounds were as phantoms who offered no interference, but each paused in his task, suspended by the wonder of our journeying.

Finally, Kit stopped beside a hinged chest and opened it. Within, piled to the top, were coils of thick rope.

"You," he said. "I don't want you. I'm going to bed. You stay here."

Placing his hands atop my shoulders, he forced me to sit on the coil of ropes.

"You are a she-eagle. Sleep in your nest." He gashed my heart.

"No, Kit. I am a woman and your wife," I said quietly.

"It takes a beak to strip flesh from bone. As you did." My soul gushed from my heart.

"Hush." He risked me with the sailors.

My heart ran out of me, up the mizzenmast. From that height, it looked down at my shame. I wanted to throw out the ropes, to hide in the chest and pull the lid down after me. I wilted on the hard nest of ropes, and he left me. I felt frozen there. Certainly I could not follow him. And what he had implied was true. Had they heard?

I had no strength to move. Though Kit had gone below, I was now haunted as though by his whole physical being, standing beside me with an accusing finger. I felt as though I could not remember when last I ate, so little strength came to my limbs.

What could I do but wait for dawn? The disk of the moon went high and small. Our fortnight of honeymoon had waned as the real moon waxed. Without a word, a sailor placed a prickly blanket around my shoulders, and with that act of kindness the looming sense of Kit left me. Still I sat immobilized. When daylight came, someone brought me a plate of food and placed it in a shallow box at my feet. Through much of that day the ghost of the full moon was visible in the blue.

I saw nothing of Kit, and the sailors moved about me as though I did not exist. To them, I was free to sit or walk or go. I sat on the coils of rope in the chest. I sat in a misery of rejection, of utmost anxiety and loneliness.

At noon, Ahab came and squatted down beside me. He looked only once in my face and then said, "I've put a padlock on your husband's door. He flings himself about in the room."

"Your maps?" I said dully.

"We took them out. There's no great damage done. He ate some strips of paper."

Then I turned to look at him. *No great damage?* I thought, but did not speak.

He read my gaze, and he looked down. "Ye cause me to look away," he muttered. "Is it possible that ye, a mere girl, have seen as deep as Ahab?"

"What is the stuff a mind is made of?" I asked.

Ahab rose and walked away. His tread was steady, but slow, as though he felt his age.

CHAPTER 56   The Hurricane House

W HAT IS THE WEIGHT of a cat's meow?" Kit asked.

Looking as cheerful as a man on a Sunday stroll, happily smoking his pipe, Mr. Stubb, the second mate, led Kit past me on a chain.

"Those are cats meowing in your trees," he said, glancing up in the yardarms.

Behind Kit, a sailor carried the blankets and covers that had been our bed, and a hammer in his hand.

"Here, kitty, kitty. Here, Topgallant. Here, Royals. Here, Sky-Catcher." Kit called the names of the uppermost sails.

The men entered the hurricane house. Hammering within. Kit moored inside. Then the sailor nailed a blanket on the inside, over the window. But he did not nail fast the bottom, for Kit lifted it and looked steadily out at me, as though he had lifted the curtain at the window of a passing coach. I could not meet the detachment of his gaze.

When I looked down, I saw the feet of Ahab.

"It's been three days he's been below," Ahab said. "Time enough for the soul to go to hell and back again."

I heard the yardarms meowing against the masts. "A cat will come down if you leave out a bowl of milk," I said.

"Mrs. Sparrow," he said. "Listen to me." He touched my shoulder to get my attention. I looked at his fiery eye and the long hair, here snowy, there gray as old snow. With an act of will, he seemed to dampen the blaze of his eyes like closing the door to the tryworks oven.

"Chained belowdecks would make a sane man mad, a mad man madder."

I said nothing.

"Ye should go down now, Mrs. Sparrow. Take the hammock. Ye've been as chained up here as he down there. Go sleep and rest. Ye'll be sick yourself, if ye don't."

"May I not keep my husband company in the hurricane house?"

Ahab muttered, " 'Tis aptly named, for his mind is a hurricane."

"I know him."

"When did the madness come?"

"We were at sea in an open boat. Many weeks."

"Aye, that may do it." But he looked at me as though I might tell him more, if I chose.

"The *Sussex*." My mouth went dry.

"A whaler! And rammed by a whale."

"Yes. A whale large and dark as a promontory or a new island pushing up from the sea. Black as lava."

"Ye were not married then? To someone else?"

"No."

Ahab paused in his interrogation. Indeed, he abandoned the factual path altogether. When he spoke again, it was in a gentler tone, one something akin to fatherly compassion. "Ye have a curiosity about the sea, then?"

"I have a curiosity about all of life," I said.

He laughed. "But ye are nothing of chatterbox. Where are the questions?"

I saw Kit let the curtain fall. What was he looking at now? The board walls inside of an empty box. The hurricane house had been unfurnished for the coming winter weather. Perhaps Kit liked it so. Perhaps he invented furnishings fit for a king in his mind. It was kind of them to leave the blanket curtain unnailed; and it would add warmth to the little room.

"He asked to be taken up here, then?"

"Aye."

"You have been good to us, Captain Ahab."

"What is your first name, Mrs. Sparrow?"

"Una."

"Then, Una," he said, and his tone was like a cove, tranquil and protective, "obey your captain and go below to rest."

CHAPTER 57   Ahab's Jottings

WHY, WHEN I SPEAK to this poor girl, flesh of the flesh of a madman, is my soul all peace? Is it the latent father-part of me? Even God wanted himself called Father. There might have been children of mine scattered in the isles of paradise. And is she one of them, grown-up?

There's something of me in her.

WHEN THE CURTAIN'S DRAWN, then, that's the time to whisper confession. On your knees. What's in a knee? Cartilage and gristle. A knee's a kind of bone knot. And my throat's another knot. Untie that lacing in my neck. The neck is tied off, wrapped round and round with inner cords I cannot loose, though I would speak, whisper, confess.

She forbids it. Let us confess to each other, she says. As though she were the world. No. I should put my mouth into the sea, press my lips against its great watery belly. Blubber my secrets there to Mother.

Perhaps Giles would hear me. We did it for love of one another, he would say again. I see his lips moving underwater. What soldier has done less? he would say. Don't soldiers kill to preserve those they love? Don't they kill for the sake of the men who stand beside them? And if all of their comrades have fallen, they kill for their own sweet sake. It's natural.

She would say I'm glad to be alive. Glad. She did not see herself with rubies on her mouth. What would it benefit the world, she asked, if we were also dead?

He used his knee to crack their long bones, and out of the splinters, his finger lifted the fat marrow and took it to her lips, and all in a smack and a swallow, it was gone. But she closed her eyes, and Giles fed her the horror, and spared her.

He didn't spare me.

"Kit Sparrow," he said to me, the last thing he said to me. "Kit Sparrow, change your name to Kit Sorrow." As though a new name could give me a new life.

Cursing him would be as good as confessing.

Yet, there he is all bright at the bottom of the sea. A phosphorescent skeleton-angel. Something wondrously strange that though I see I cannot see, for he's a bleary light. He wants me to use him like a lantern, to find my way through the midnight depths, my movements wavy, slow, cold. Uncertain and unreal.

CHAPTER 59

🜨 Starbuck Introduces Himself

I N A M A N N E R particularly upright, with a careful humanity, Starbuck said, "Ye ought not sit in the wind, Mrs. Sparrow. Move to the
lee. I'd not let my Mary take so much wind."

"Have you and Mary children, Mr. Starbuck?" I asked.

He patted his shirt, and I heard the crinkle of paper.

"I durst not take it out lest the thieving wind make off with it," he
said. He smoothed his chest with the palm of his hand.

"She writes you of your children, then?"

"My boy."

"When did you see them last?"

"Two years ago I waved good-bye to Mary. Him, I see him only
through her words, first and last."

I was shocked to think of the young mother so long without her
husband. "Have many letters found you?"

"This is the second, in as many years."

No wonder he treasured it next to his skin!

"All at once, I have a son, and he is one year, four months of age."

"What's his name?"

Here he laughed. "She does not tell his name but calls him 'Baby,'
and 'Beloved Child,' and 'Puck,' but she would not name him Puck—
there's nothing of Quaker in that, or Christian even."

"There's Shakespeare in it, or it is in Shakespeare."

"Sometimes she writes 'our son.' He recited: 'I bought our son a
little boat, and yesterday we sailed it on a puddle before the door, the
puddle-water was all crimson with the setting sun, and I sent the boat,
about the size of my flatiron, across to him and he to me till the sun
was down and a star shone in our puddle.' "

"Not for naught, then, is your name Starbuck."

"Eh? But she doesn't say that."

All of Mistress Mary's words in the letter had been memorized by
her husband. Sacred writ to him, and he would not have added one jot
or tittle.

"It's strange," I said, "that she doesn't give the child's name."

"Sometimes my Mary will tease a bit. But I'd rather have the babe
himself with no name than a name and no dear babe."

I wondered what kind of woman Mary was who could tease so upright a man as Mr. Starbuck. He seemed to have no fun in him, but was filled to the brim with a sweet seriousness.

"In what part of Nantucket do you live, Mr. Starbuck, if I may ask?"

"Ah, Mary will not have any place but 'Sconset."

"And what is particular to 'Sconset?"

"It's against the open water. It's as close to coming to sea with me as she can get. Our house is almost of the beach. It's a hard, lonely, eastern end of the island, where the waves from the open sea pound the land."

"Kit's mother—she was a baker—used to send buns to 'Sconset, by the coach."

"You must come out to see us when you get Mr. Sparrow settled."

Mr. Starbuck's eyes gazed into mine, and I saw there sadness for us, and pity, that our landfall would be far less joyous than his.

"Where do you suppose Mr. Sparrow and I might best live on the island?" I asked.

His blue gaze held mine steadily, but he shifted his feet though the ship had not rolled under us. He hesitated and then spoke calmly. "I expect Mr. Sparrow will have to stay in the madhouse."

CHAPTER 60   Ahab Overheard

I HAD JUST come to the top of the companionway when I noted Ahab standing on deck, gazing north. One hand rested on a deadeye in the standing rigging. He was alone, his back to me, but speaking.

"So, Old Winter, where art thou? Ten times, nearing home in November, we've shaken hands over these gray waters. What news of the polar bear? and the Lapman herding his reindeer? And hast thou tucked in the nation of Canada?"

Ahab paused as though he were waiting for the North to answer.

"What! would make Ahab wait? Well, Thou art older, 'tis thy privilege." He fetched a sigh. "Older even than Ahab. Will Time hump my back as well as whiten my hair?" He grasped into the rigging, seeming to flex his back. Then he spoke too loudly. I hoped no one else would hear. "Where is thy rude blast, Winter?"

He clasped both hands behind his head, stretched his back again, lifted his chest, and spoke lightly and rapidly. "Thou hast donned thy spectacles? Panes of ice, I'm sure. But they sharpen thy eyesight, for all of that, and mine as well. For now I see why thou waitest. There's Spring aboard the *Pequod*. There's no place for Winter, where Spring is, and her name is Una."

Quickly I fled down the companionway, amazed that his thoughts had turned toward me. And pleased, too. *Somebody* aboard the ship was glad I was there.

CHAPTER 61   A Letter to the Lighthouse

Dear Uncle Torch, dear Aunt Agatha, dearest Fran,

I write to you from the stormy North Atlantic, aboard the Pequod, *headed home—which now I name Nantucket. For it is Kit's home, and Kit is my husband. Before this letter, I hope you received my earlier letters, one sent by the* Reconciliation; *in the second writ aboard the* Albatross, *I described the terrible mishap. That letter was given over to a passing ship, the* Thistle, *New Bedford–bound, but I know full well that letters often lie moldering in the hulls of ships themselves sunk, without so much as a surviving scrap. I have often wondered how many fond letters sank with the* Sussex.

Nonetheless, I cannot bring myself to repeat those details; I hope to see you soon, and then I will answer any question. Knowing now what I did not when I decided to run to sea, that it is agony to be anxious about the welfare of a loved one, I do want to repeat that I am sure I caused you much anxiety on my behalf, dear family; and if I prayed, I would pray that you forgive me. I have heard nothing from you or from my mother, yet for a letter to find me on the high seas would itself be a kind of miracle. I must ask my heart what your disposition toward me is. And there I find pain, but little anger. There I find your sincere hope that all has gone well. I grope within my own heart to find that you wish we may all see each other again, you three and your new babe. Perhaps if you make another trip to Boston, you will put in at Nantucket Harbor?

The Pequod arcs north, then home, for Ahab would have one more whale.

Exactly how Kit and I shall make our way, I do not know. Perhaps Kit will wish to take up his mother's trade of baking, and I will help him, yet hat requires some capital, and our wages went down with the Sussex.

I must tell you with heavy heart that Kit is not well. You may recall his saying his mother sometimes suffered mental infirmities, and with the duress of our ordeal something of that instability has surfaced in Kit. Yet, when he was able, he was, indeed, the most loving and kind of husbands to me, and I intend to see him through what is surely only a temporary indisposition.

There is a part of the first ordeal of which, even if you received my earlier letter, you have no knowledge, Giles's accident having occurred aboard the Albatross but after my letter was taken off by the Thistle. Even now, sitting at the broad map table in the cabin lent me by Captain Ahab, my fingers grip and grip the quill but do not want to form the letters. I would give those fingers, hand, and arm to sand out what Fate has already written. Though these words appear formed with ink, my pen is really dipped into heart's blood. Giles fell from the topgallant mast into the sea. I saw him fall. Nevermore will we see him again.

My letter to you has sat unsent a week, but now there is a west-bound clipper sail in the distance. Perhaps we will draw together, before it passes us, though the sea is rough and the wind blows very chill. So I say good-bye, with love and hope, to you whose names wring my heart—Torchy, Agatha, and Frannie.

P.S. The clipper breezed by the Pequod with just a polite dip and nod, and so I shall post this when we come to Nantucket, and you will know that Kit and I arrived safely. Ahab has sailed north to take a final whale. The cooper prepares new barrels.

I saw a strange, low, white ship in the north today and asked Mr. Starbuck, the first mate, what manner of craft she was. He replied that what I saw was an ice floe driven down from the Arctic. Tonight, he said, the Pequod would meet the first of her winter gales.

THERE WAS sunshine here a moment ago. Yesterday? I lifted the corner of the blanket curtain and sunshine came in like a wedge and lodged on the floor there, just beyond the toe of my shoe. I'll touch the spot. Well, it's a blank of cold now against my palm. Yesterday, the sunshine left a warm triangle like the kiss of an iron.

My wife says Starbuck's wife and child sailed a wooden boat the size of an iron. She says she's my wife. I don't remember any church or any ceremony. Maybe she's a whore. There's something repulsive about her. Likely she's a whore and thinks that's nothing to a madman. They say I'm a madman.

But I feel the cold like a normal man. I shiver in the dark, like a normal man, like that Starbuck. I guess Starbuck is a normal man. He has a wife and child. I have a wife, they say. But I'm not the same as Starbuck. I have no child. I think I would like to have a child, though. Their child sailed a boat, Una said, in a puddle in their front yard. How would she know? Wonder any water wouldn't be frozen this time of year.

That's all the news I know. It used to be, when I worked on the ships, I would say to Giles, "Tell me something I don't already know." And he would. When I said to Una that I was bored next to madness, she would laugh and point at the clouds. "They're always new," she'd say. "Look up."

She's a kind of bird. She only wants air and clouds and sky. It's not enough. If you could get your hand around it, if you could squeeze some meaning from it! My fingers are almost too stiff to close. But there's nothing to the air. Try it, I should tell her. I'll try with the other hand. Nay, neither right nor left can get anything out of air. Enough of science. I'll put these hands together, like praying hands, and clamp them between my thighs.

Starbuck wanted me to pray. Why not? Our Father, who art— where? In the clouds? No. I'll tell you who's been in clouds. Ahab, with thunder and lightning in his face, with storms piled on his brow. He gathers all electric to him, and there's only one discharging. That's with the harpoon. That's for the whales, gray and massive as clouds, but substantial. Blubber-thick. Blood-filled.

They keep me here to freeze the same way a hunter hangs up a haunch of venison in a tree. That old captain is naught but a hunter. All the whales of the sea run before him and this ivory-tusked ship. Oh, the innocence of the whales! We hung them outside the ship, peeled their flesh like a rind from an orange. Squeeze a whale! There's more than plenty in a whale. It oozes and bubbles and bleeds into every cranny of the ship. If I licked these boards, there'd be some taste of whale in the tiny cracks. I could lick it up.

No, the wind says. No, don't do that, it wails. The wind tries to make me behave. He says he'll whip me. Yes, right through my clothes. He says he'll blast me. He says he'll freeze my tears into beads. He says he'll devour me with cold.

But he won't catch me, for now I'll run. I'll run and I'll run and I'll run, like the baked brown man! And those were raisins that are his eyes!

CHAPTER 63   Arctic

FROM WITHIN Ahab's cabin, I heard, of course, the wind, buffeting all the boards of the ship, but I heard, too, a sound like running, and then a rhythmic thud, as though a body and not the wind had slammed against a wall. Was some sail loose? A barrel rolling about the deck? Yet the sound was not the continuous scrambling over and over of a barrel, but distinct like feet. And only four steps and then the thud.

I adjusted my shoulders in the hammock, and I pulled up the covers. There was sleet in the wind, and the sleet slung against the glass of the portholes like endless needles. I thought of the two bright needles that Sallie had given me. In that tool was my livelihood! I could sew on Nantucket as well as anywhere! Yes, I preferred that to baking, for then one's work was consumed in a flash, but needlework was something that might last. *My seams would be the strongest, if it was clothes I made. The town would talk of Una's seams. A shirt I sewed might last a man and his growing son, and the next and next brother in line. One must pay attention to the fibers and the weave in cloth and make the stitches compatible with their firmness.*

The wind grew weary and bammed itself about less frequently. They had said Nantucket was a stormy place—low and open to the ocean winds, few trees, much sand, and inland, the moors undulating like large swells on the sea, but laced with small shrubs and plants, heathers, heath, gorse. Starbuck said there was a grayness there—the twigs of the shrubs, the shingles of the houses, sometimes the sky and sea were all a quiet Quaker gray. He liked that peace. There was longing for it in his eye. I asked him was it never blue and bright, and he had said all summer it basked in the sun. We would be arriving, Kit and I, in cold weather, but I would have the sparkling summer to look forward to.

Winter or summer, I never doubted I'd make Nantucket into home. Already this place, Ahab's cabin, so borrowed and temporary, was for me a home. At the Lighthouse, in Rebekkah Swain's New Bedford boardinghouse, aboard the *Sussex* with Chester, and on the *Albatross* with Sallie, given a bed, or even just a hammock—any small center that was my own and some person at hand to exchange affections with—then I had seemed adaptively at home. But the place must have some coziness about it. I was no animal content to burrow. I wanted some artifact about me.

In Ahab's cabin, there was much of clever joinery, in cabinets and drawers, and a long piece of wood overhead, curved and carved like a simple arch, curled decoratively into a knot. Like the knot of a cinnamon roll. "Oh, reason not the need," King Lear said. As he needed something of ceremonious retinue, so I needed something of beauty. If all around me went dull with familiarity, then I would pick up my needle and make something new.

There was no time to make a quilt for Ahab, but if I had, it would have been in shades of white, for his hair, and the ivory-plated sea chest, and the *Pequod* herself all sheathed and decorated with ivory fittings, and the gray-white sails. It would have looked like a bride's quilt, but with the feeling not of freshness but of something weathered, stark like bone.

And all the time I lay in the hammock listening to the wind and the creak of timbers, I thought of the future. Everything about the

Pequod was headed for home. Every man (and woman) aboard her longed for Nantucket. Perhaps even the whale oil stored in great barrels below yearned toward its own destiny—bright burning in lamps and candles. But Ahab would have one more whale.

There was a gentle knock at Ahab's door, and when I opened it, Ahab, all wet and a little breathless, stood there.

"We are bringing your husband here."

"How is he?" If about to be brought to me, Kit was surely better?

"He's not conscious. He's bruised himself against the walls of the hurricane house. He's a man who's run beyond his limit." The excitement in Ahab's voice dropped to sadness. "He's run like a blind mind through a thick forest, punishing his body."

I was too appalled to speak.

"You must look to him. We need all hands."

What was this excitement, this practiced joy, returning to Ahab's face?

"A whale. A right whale off the starboard bow," he answered my puzzlement.

"Who would raise the cry in this gale?" I knew that I would not.

Ahab looked at me curiously. "Starbuck. Upright Starbuck."

As Ahab left, I asked to his empty place, "Do ye even have room below for oil?"

Two sailors, Stubb in front, with his pipe clenched in his teeth, and one I did not know behind, carried Kit, eyes closed, between them, his body sagging like a hammock. His head was bruised and bloody, but not broke open. Had he used his head against the wall, like Billy the goat against the Lighthouse? His sleeve was torn and blood stained the fabric.

After they laid him in the hammock, I bathed his bruised head and cooed, *Oh Kit, oh Kit*. Peace was in his face. Would it be better if Kit were dead? How bitter the idea broke in my heart; like a bad, foul egg, the shell of that idea shattered and drained out gall. What world was this to let Kit's pain drive him to nonbeing? And yet there was peace, quiet, rest, in his countenance—as though he had got through to something better.

I could not believe that. This world was our arena. This place was where we had to look for any happiness. And yet his mind was gone from me, and that place—his expression was undeniable—offered comfort. Only the skin of his brow was scraped, and in one place cross-hatched with little cuts.

"Una." His eyelids were open, his lips parted. Again, he spoke my name and lay perfectly still.

"You've hurt your head."

"Not very much, I think."

"How do you feel?"

"Peaceful."

The tears spilled down my face. He seemed himself.

"Don't cry," he said.

But I could not help myself. I sobbed and knelt beside him and placed my head on his chest. Before long, I felt his fingers gently on my face. "Don't cry," he repeated softly.

"Giles is dead," I blurted out. "We can't ever get him back."

"I know." Only Kit's fingers moved about my face, as though he would know me by feel.

"Kit, can you see?" I asked.

"Oh, yes. Sometimes I dream. When I see Giles in my dreams, he's hurt. He's hurt his head. His head is always bowed, held to the side as though to avoid me. But he's alive, and I call to him."

I could not stop crying. I thought of my mother, who had lost her baby. I thought of my father, dressed in black, hanging in the barn. I thought of the fear on my behalf that must have squeezed the hearts of Agatha and Frannie when they knew me to be gone and to have deceived them.

Both Kit and I heard a boat banging against the hull and then splashing into the sea.

"They've lost a boat to the storm," he said.

"No, they're lowering for a whale."

Kit stirred. "I should help," he said.

"Captain Ahab ordered you here. To be here and let me care for you."

I lifted my face and looked into his puffy eyes. He smiled at me. "You like that, don't you?" But he was not angry. "I'm almost too stiff to move."

I noticed the backs of his knuckles, which were whorled with abrasions and new scabs.

"I think you tried to beat down the walls of your jail," I said.

"No. I liked the hurricane house. It was a home. All mine."

My heart seized up at my exclusion. But had I not called Ahab's cabin my temporary home?

"It was the Almighty Wind," he went on. "The Wind wanted to whip me. I wouldn't let him. My mother used to whip me. I always ran away from her, too."

"Why would the wind want to whip you, Kit?" Surely gentle reason would guide him back. It had, a number of times, during our honeymoon. But now he did not seem mad but only recounting how his thoughts had run then.

He turned his head a bit to look squarely with both eyes into both of mine. His hands looked for my hands. How glad I was to give them!

"Because," he said, "of what we ate. We must be scourged."

I would not have that nightmare reassert itself.

"I've distressed you," he said.

I stammered and looked away. "The wind has no volition, Kit. The wind is only a mindless force of nature."

"I felt that something palpably wanted to whip me."

"Suppose it had? You've paid enough. You've bruised yourself over and over."

"Yes."

"You yourself are the Eumenides who scourge you."

"Perhaps if God forgave me, I could forgive myself."

"Let me forgive you," I exhorted. "Let me, a fellow sinner, forgive you. Who better?"

"You have a powerful love of yourself."

"Why not?" I said, strangely angry. "I am glad. I'm glad that we have each other and a life to share between us."

"I think you'd better find someone else." How neutral his tone! Neither compassionate nor offending.

"I won't," I said. "You are my husband."

"Oh, well," he said and closed his eyes.

"Kit! Kit!" I shook his hurt shoulder and cared little if I pained him. "Wake up!"

"I am awake," he said, with his eyes closed. "But sleep is coming over me. I want it."

He slid away from me. I took his hands and cleaned them with a wet cloth, rubbing the blood from around his knuckles. I looked for salve among Ahab's drawers and found a pot whose contents were yellow and waxy, which I spread on Kit's knuckles and head. His shoulder wound could not be easily accessed, except through the torn sleeve. It was chill in the room, and I did not want to risk trying to remove Kit's jacket. I longed to take up my needle to repair the rent even while Kit lay sleeping in the hammock, but then I would have no entry to the wound.

He had known me and called me by name. He had conversed with me, strangely but pleasantly, been considerate of my feelings. But— this part I wished had not happened—he had dismissed the fact of our marriage as though it were nothing at all.

I leant over and kissed him on the mouth, but he did not awaken. Then I thought it was a violation to kiss him while he slept, for all that we were married. He had not held out his arms to hold me as a husband. No, he had soothed me like a friend.

Why should we not be happy on Nantucket, baking and sewing? Warm together in our bed at night. Suppose his mind were to come and go. There would always be a moment when he called me— "Una!"—and again our minds would meet. His beloved body would be with me in the bed. That was not an honest hope. When his mind wandered abroad, he seemed unsexed, aware neither of himself as man nor me as woman.

"Mrs. Sparrow," the cook called through the door, which I opened to receive a tray of food. A hot soup as well as the hard biscuits and some fingers of herring from the barrel.

"There were birds," the cook said. "Their feet frozen down to the yards. I clumb up and got them. There's almost the last of the onions in that. The men will want warmth, I says to myself, after the chase."

"How goes the chase?" I asked, glancing back to be sure our talk did not disturb Kit.

"All spray and cold. Mr. Starbuck has gone for a Nantucket sleigh ride. Well, there's snow in the air if not under him. It may be a wrong whale, Mrs. Sparrow, instead of a right whale that Mr. Starbuck sung out."

"I hear the wind howling."

"Aye. It's bad luck to lower in a gale, but Captain Ahab has lowered in a stronger gale than this. It's the cold, though. It's their hands I worry about."

"It was good to think of the soup, Cook."

"Aye, and the blessed birds frozen fast in the masts. A flock must have blown in together from the north and roosted with us. In the pot now. Every one."

"You might have let one or two escape."

"What would be the point in that?"

"Perhaps to tell the tale."

"Now, Mrs. Sparrow. Eat your soup. Wake him up to have some while it's hot. Too much sleep is bad for a brain injury."

I DID TRY to waken Kit, and failing that, pulled his body more upright, and with a spoon took the broth to his mouth. I hoped he might yet swallow while he slept, but the liquid only puddled on his lower lip and then spilled down his chin. I did not want to choke or drown him in soup, so I fitted down a lid on the dish and put it aside. I took my own bowl and sat on the long narrow sofa under the port-holes and tried to look out as I ate.

For Mary Starbuck's sake, I thought, let the whale tire that dragged Mr. Starbuck's whaleboat over the winter water. Let them not fall into this cold, I thought, for bundled as they were, swimming would be difficult. I could see the water rising in great swoops. Sometimes the wind dug bowls in the ocean, slope-sided, just like the bowl from which I ate, but all unstable, collapsing and reappearing. Even the large *Pequod* swayed and wallowed in the wild water. And yes, those were snow-flakes, only a few, beating at the porthole.

My own comfort seemed sinful to me: men I knew out in the winter fury. I sat with my feet on a brown leather cushion. I sat with my stomach full of warm and savory soup. My clothes were dry; my welfare certain, for I had no doubt that Ahab would pilot me safely to Nan-tucket.

And what of Ahab's whaleboat? It, too, I knew was down on the water, lifted high on the waves and then dragged low. They would be rowing, though half the time the oars might strike only air. Ahab would have them rowing in the direction of the fleeing whale and the harpoon-tethered boat. Starbuck would not cut the line, knowing the whaleboat's weight dragged strength from the fleeing whale.

Eventually, I fell asleep, tossed and tossed by the storm; eventually it seemed to rock me. It seemed reliable.

WHEN I AWOKE in the morning, sunshine came into the portholes, and the cabin was illumined with it. Kit was still sleeping; his face was flushed, and a great black bruise darkened his forehead. When I called to him, there was no response.

Despite the sunshine and the pale blue of the sky out the porthole and the calm in the movement of the boat, I felt restless. Borrowing one of Ahab's coats, I prepared myself for the cold and sped up the companionway to the deck. The *Pequod* was covered with snow! We were frosted, pristine, inviolate. We sparkled and glittered. Scarcely marked with footprints, snow ankle-deep lay drifted across the deck; above me, icicles hung from the yardarms.

And out to sea, I saw three boats towing the slain whale—a right whale after all—and the gap of water between us and them was rapidly closing. How pretty it all was in that moment. Mr. Flask, the young third mate, came in the lead; he was very short and his chest was swelled out with pride at having conquered another whale. Both Starbuck and Ahab stood relaxed and pleased in the prows of their boats, with a full company of men. They were smiling at us on the *Pequod* all covered with snow.

I waved and shouted, "Hooray! Hooray!" though it was no husband of mine who returned in standing triumph. But none were lost! All returned! Let me wave them home anyway, as wife of all—welcoming and glad-hearted for dangers survived and safe return. Joy did leap to all their faces, and they waved back and returned the hooray. Cook grabbed the bell and added its din to the victory. From below, two men carried up the great steaming, gleaming pot of bird-and-onion soup, and a third in the parade came with a high stack of bowls, and a fourth carried fistfuls of spoons. From the porters' feet rose small clouds of snow that caught the glint of sunshine and were suspended lightly in the cold air like swarms of glitter.

Lines were thrown over, and Ahab and Starbuck came up the sides of the boat more nimbly than goats—monkeys or apes, rather, all hands and feet engaged. Ahab was pleased with himself, pleased to be noticed, though still his face bore something of the mask of his usual dignity and reserve. And in Starbuck I saw relief as well as joy. His honest sighting of the prey had brought neither disaster nor undue delay.

Now the process began again of bringing the whale alongside the ship, the lowering of the cutting stage, the peeling away of the blanket blubber, the ooze of fat and the flow of blood as the ship became a factory. Already, the first kindling wood was being placed in the try-works. The men hurried like ants over the deck, but in my woman's garb, I was excused and excluded.

Ahab had gone to the taffrail, where he stood looking steadfastly about, first to the north and then before us to the east. His brow was contracted, and he shaded his eyes with his hand.

"What do you see, Captain Ahab?" I asked.

He pointed, and my gaze followed the line of his finger to an iceberg. It floated like an enormous tooth, like a molar upside down with the jagged roots thrust up.

"There's much more below the waterline," he said.

I glanced about and saw that there was a whole flotilla of icebergs. But they seemed safely distant. They looked almost like distant clouds, low on the horizon, but cloud shapes have more roundedness and less jaggedness to their shape. The maverick iceberg, Ahab said, had a great white frozen mass below it. Like a ghost ship, but solid ice, it traveled the water submerged.

"It has great power," Ahab said. "We are less than the thin shell of a pecan to that jaw."

"But we can avoid collision," I said quickly.

"Aye, Una, we can, given that we keep keen watch. That we get well to south before night."

The day was so bright, the morning so youthful, that I thought to myself that there was little worry. But I checked this dismissal, knowing that Ahab's experience was vast, and unwarranted caution impossible for such a man.

"I could stand lookout," I said.

Ahab's head pivoted swiftly. "It requires a trained eye and standing aloft."

I hesitated. Should I cite my experience? I looked seaward. I only said, "The glare requires a patch of soot under the eyes."

"Aye."

Again I hesitated.

"How fares Mr. Sparrow?" Ahab asked.

"He is asleep. But last night, he spoke to me."

"Lucidly?"

"Yes." And I shivered. Not only lucidly but tactfully—referring to our crime, but not calling its name lest we be overheard. Careful and tactful, like the Kit of old.

I turned my back to the sea and regarded the deck. The snow had been ruined by trampling. The icicles were dripping water from their tips and falling.

"It would not be safe for any man to go aloft yet," I said.

"Aye."

I regarded the little hurricane house. Its roof still wore an unsullied cap of snow. It looked like a small deserted house in the countryside. A slope of snow leaned against the windward side.

"In men's clothing," I said, "I can climb as well as any man. On the *Sussex*, there was no man with either keener eyesight or better brain for imaging the form of a distant whale." I dared not look at Ahab as I spoke even that very truncated version of my history.

"I've thought that ye were Ahab's daughter," he said. His hands swept the top of the taffrail, and ice sputtered loose.

CHAPTER 64   Ahab in His Cabin

WEAR WHAT YE *think suitable,* I said to her. *Go aloft when ye think it less than foolish.*

Almost I added, *Watch not only north and east.* But I looked in her eye and saw beyond a brain nimble enough to know already or to deduce in an instant the wiliness of icebergs, how they may ride a deep current to emerge far south of any expected appearance.

Will she play the fool and scamper up prematurely on some female whim? No, not Una. She's seen too much.

She's seen him, lying trussed up in my hammock here like a Kentucky ham. The hectic flush lies on him. There may be pneumonia in him. But he's young. He could fight that. If there's fight in an addled brain.

Despite the hectic, there's a comeliness about his features. She loves him well. He's blessed, I think, in such a wife. If people jeer his madness, her nose will be up at the topgallant level. Still, she's little more than a girl.

Last night in the storm, I thought of her safely within this room, and I was glad of it. She'll find some hut in Nantucket and make it home. And him? Will he be swung from the rafters as he is here? Perpetually nursed? Should he survive this, then what for Kit Sparrow?

The Madaket Road, with the Indians, that would be the place. The Indians have a tolerance for madness that the Quakers of the town lack. I have a fellow feeling with Abram Quary. But what sort of life for her? Well, she's not usual. It might suit her.

All is scurry above my head. Again the whale: the chase, the butchering, the casks and barrels stowed below. We'll come in full. The carpenter can build bins in the blubber room. We needed only this, and Starbuck sounded the cry. Starbuck, whose only desire is to move like a shooting star to the doorway of his home. Starbuck enters there to the glow of homecoming, to a warm hearth and a warmer wife. He said he has a son. But they've given him no name. Not likely they'd call him Ahab.

So, where's my tom-girl? Aloft, or feet still firm on deck? I've left it to her, as though she were sensible as Starbuck. She's not awash in men's clothing. No. While the ice melted, she came here and ran up seams and seams from his trousers and jacket, till all was neat. Her hair tucked inside the collar, a kerchief tied over the crown of her head, she looked a boy. As likely a cabin boy as anyone could sign.

Starbuck might think it sin—a woman in man's clothes—but I care naught for that. Even Starbuck will give chase on the Sabbath. He is a man who bends only enough not to break.

This poor wretch, hung swinging like a babe in my cabin—he's known too much of both bending and breaking. She would put her needle to his brain to seam him up where all is tatters.

THE SEA is silver as far as eye can see. Soft silver, bending and bluish, sometimes brushed with mist above the swells. And in the distance to the far north, yes, a white expanse of iceberg. Here's its breath, all about me. I feel the little hairs in my nose trying to freeze for all the light of the sun. Light with scant heat up here. Time to pull out the red mittens.

Beneath my feet the ship moves more smoothly than any horse could canter. We slide south, and the sails below me are bellied out but unstraining. Ah, to be a sail! To be a pair of wings! I would name this ship not *Pequod* but *Pegasus* of the strong, white wings.

When I turn south, the silver water flashes mirrorlike. There is a perfection of the color today. It's been too long since I stood this high. What is the world but water and sky? Did Kit ever love it as I do? I do not think so. I do not think his heart unfurled and filled with it like this. For he could have it now. He could stand here, higher than all he surveys, for today there are neither birds nor clouds. Only the sun insists on his sovereign height. But he is a friend of mine.

Below me, the deck flows with blood. Their shoes and the cuffs of their pant legs are stained and dyed with it. From the tryworks issue twin curls of smoke. The hatch cover is removed and I can see down into the cutting room. Off comes the first of the blanket strips; swung across the deck from the whale by the great hook, the piece oozes oil and fats that congeal in the cold in yellowed fists.

Now I look at our prow. We cleave the water, and the foam and spray sweep back. What a whiteness we turn up from the silver-blue. The rising and falling I see of the prow I can feel in my feet. A smooth, triumphant rhythm of our riding. Here, let me watch most carefully for the floe beneath the water. But I see no appalling mass. The way is clear. The way is ours. Nantucket! I can all but breathe it into my nostrils.

Let there be help, and kindness and patience, in Nantucket.

And to the north again. A vast, what is that form? It slides under the water all square in front and tapering. How came that iceberg so rapidly, so close? Not ice. Living flesh. A sperm whale the color of ice!

He turns and swims parallel to us. He is like a ghostly shimmer under the blue-white water. He could be a mass of bubbles, a cloud. Would any eyes but mine ever have discerned his shape? He melts now into something bluish. I know there is a great blue whale, but I have never seen it. This white one is of enormous size, but his shape is clearly sperm. Is? I must say was, for he dissolves.

Why should I cry out? He doesn't spout his presence. He is all submerged, peaceful, a warm-blooded part of the blue-white-silver of this day. No, Starbuck shall not be harnessed up again to give chase. Nor any of them. Let them complete the bloody work on deck. Let us clean ourselves as we sail ever closer to Nantucket Harbor, arrive like a honeycomb, every cell filled.

Ah, Ahab, you assigned me to sing out for icebergs only. I will bless you, this voyage, with silence on the subject of a white whale and all his massive innocence.

So I subverted the trust of my captain. But instead of guilt, I felt an invigorated peacefulness. Let nothing deter our forward progress. The ghostly whale had disappeared, and we alone moved at the center of a crystalline, encircling sea and sky. Surely in such a pure, blue-white world there was hope for Kit. The sheer expansiveness of the ring around me seemed to suggest it.

I stood the watch for two hours, while the sun was at its zenith. My cheeks, my fingers and toes, became stiff with cold. Gradually, the icebergs to the north became a mere line, a blur of white. In my descent, at the height of the main yard, I could see nothing of the Arctic ice. At that low altitude, my nose filled with the foul clouds of smoke roiling up from the tryworks.

Putting my feet on the greasy and bloody deck seemed a defilement. The joking and swearing of the men—to which I had become perfectly accustomed on the *Sussex*—annoyed me now. But as I walked among them in men's clothing, they mistook me as one of them, and no one curbed his tongue. Perhaps there was a kind of music I had forgotten in their rough rhythms and gritty syllables.

I felt convinced that no ice floes had broken loose to pursue us, and I told Ahab as much. Since he sent no one else aloft, I surmised that he trusted my judgment, and this pleased me more than a little. With the stench and soot in my nose, the fat and slime underfoot, the swearing in my ears, I felt descended from angelic heights to the realities of earth, albeit the *Pequod,* as a ship upon the water, was but a chip of the mainland.

As I went below, yet another level down, the closeness of the quarters, the wooden walls, and the despair I felt about Kit's condition combined to suggest that now I traversed a dismal and confining underworld. Before I entered Ahab's chamber, I removed my gory shoes and left them by the door.

Kit had turned on his side while I was aloft, and I took this to be a good sign.

"Kit. Darling," I called him, and he opened his eyes. *Darling*—there is magic in that word. Giles once addressed me as darling, in his letter to the Lighthouse, and the world changed its hue.

Clouds seemed to float before Kit, so hazy his gaze.

"I'd like to talk to Giles," he said.

"In a bit, love," I answered. "Talk to me now, won't you? How do you feel?"

"Hot. Sick. Have I been sick long?"

"Not so very long. You seem better, don't you think so?"

"There are things that are wrong."

"It's an imperfect world, love." I smiled.

His eyes blinked, and a fear washed over me that he would sink again to sleep. "But just now," I went on, "I was aloft. And such a day it is, Kit. All silvery, brushed with blue. And white at all the edges, just behind or beyond."

"Or below," he said.

"What do you mean?" Did the mad have an uncanny ability to read the minds of others? Could he picture the white shadow under the waves?

"Why are you afraid, Una?"

"I am only afraid," I said, "because you are not completely well."

"And so," he said, stirring in the hammock and glancing around as though he would see for himself, "tell me more of the day."

"We've been far to the north. There was a winter storm—"

"Yes. The wind will give chase to us even as we give chase to the whale."

"But today," I went on hurriedly, for I did not want him to remember how it was he himself, within the hurricane house, who had bruised his body and bloodied his head. "Today, there's only a good wind, and it blows us south and west, back to Nantucket. The sky is the palest, most fragile of blues, and the air seems purified with cold. We had snow on deck this morning, and the yardarms hung with icicles. We were a fairy boat, Kit. As far as I could see, there was nothing but beauty."

"Were you aloft, then?"

"I was. The captain let me. To watch for icebergs."

"Can you tell an iceberg from a whale?" There was a twinkle in his voice. Something of the old teasing Kit.

"I think so," I said, but I wondered if I had been wrong about the white whale. Trying to be chipper, I amended, "At least we've not been stove by whale or floe."

I could have bitten away my tongue. Once, of course, we *were* rammed by a whale, and all our dark history had funneled through the hole created by that black monster. That horror came back to Kit like a black tidal wave. I saw it crash on his brow and swamp his brain as surely as I saw any occurrence.

"Why do you want to lie?" he said nastily.

"I didn't mean that time," I faltered. "I meant now. Now we are safe. This ship is intact."

"Isn't this a ship like any other ship?" he said. He was angry. "The only safety's here!" And he smote his forehead with the palm of his hand. When he drew his hand away, having dislodged the scab, his palm was smeared with blood. "I'm stove," he muttered.

At that moment, I heard someone pass in the hall. That man's voice, too, muttered, and he muttered the cry of the whaleboats: "A stove boat or a dead whale."

"Was that Giles?" Kit asked.

"No."

And from outside, the voice murmured, "Break your backs, boys. Why don't ye row till you break your backs?"

"I'll inspect your lovely day," Kit said.

So I gave him my hand and helped him to stand up and then to walk to the door. I was afraid to speak.

"Lady Una," he said as he moved uncertainly, "for you are a lady, Una. Giles always said so."

When we opened the door, the dark smoke of the tryworks and its awful stench puffed in. The hallway before us was awash in whale blood. Kit grabbed the door and slammed it shut. "You are a witch from hell!" he said. "For you, hell is heaven! But you'll not take me there. I'll 'bide with you no more!'"

"It's only the trying out," I said. "They've taken a whale."

" 'They've taken a whale,' " he mocked me. "It's you with your she-eagle eye who took the whale. You feast on blood and flesh. You have the fangs of a wolf. I don't want you. I have never wanted you. He was the one who wanted you."

"You did want me," I said.

Then he lifted his hand and struck my cheek.

I ran from the room.

I would not go up to that butchery.

There was nowhere to go but deeper down. My head rang like a struck bell. Trembling with outrage, I could hardly run, my knees wobbled. *You did want me. You did.* I pressed my cheek with the palm of my hand to quiet the throbbing. I descended to the hold.

In that dim space, dominated by the unadorned ribs of the ship, I climbed into a pen of barrels. I sat on the flank of one and cried upon the curve of another.

Giving Kit the name "love" had no magic power. He hated me. At least at times. The cup of my heart overbrimmed with bitterness, sorrow, pity, anger.

CHAPTER 66   **Starbuck: Ship's Log**

MONDAY, November 15. Having taken a right whale yesterday, of 40 barrels est., in the midst of the trying out, a naked madman, one Kit Sparrow of Nantucket, ran amongst us in the freezing air. He offered his flesh, in particular his manly member, to us to butcher and rend for oil, if we would but spare the whale. At my order, Mr. Stubb has dressed him and manacled him to the far side of this cabin where I sit writing. I do not know what he has done with his wife. Pray God he has not thrown her overboard, for he raves and curses her. Mr. Stubb is to supply him rum until he falls into a stupor. We are but three days out of Nantucket, if this fair weather hold. All of us lean toward our homes and hearths.

CHAPTER 67   Starbuck Communes with Mary, His Wife

EVENING STAR, forever when I sail, your name is not Venus the pagan goddess, but Mary. Though I be no Papist, that name is sacred. That name is all gentleness, steadfastness, affection. Mary means home. If ever Starbuck sink beneath the waves, may the evening star be the last of my beholding. If it be daylight, may imagination, though in me it is sluggish slow, bring to my mind this star. Gentle Mary, would that I could have spoken with your voice today! Would that I could have soothed with your hand.

I stand in the prow of the *Pequod,* blessing the sails that billow above my head, for they bring me, Mary, to you.

The madman's wife had been missing an hour—let me think it accurately—Captain Ahab said he'd waited an hour for her to reappear (he did not consider turning back the ship, though he thought Mrs. Sparrow might have been thrown over)—Ahab called me to his quarters. Kit Sparrow lay all slumped against the wall, and the odor of liquor was thick in the room. Captain Ahab rarely drinks liquor, but his aspect was nearly as disheveled as that of Mr. Sparrow.

"Look for her," he ordered me.

"Where shall I look?" I asked.

"You know the ship. You have a wife," he said.

I must have been quite blank. I could not imagine you, my Mary, on a whaling ship, nor where on the ship you might sequester yourself.

"Look in the hold!" he suddenly exclaimed.

The Hold

Strangely, Ahab's intuition was entirely right. I found her amongst the barrels, blind with tears, her shoulders and back heaving with grief. It was then, Mary, that I wished for a woman's touch upon her shoulder and womanly comfort to come from my tongue. "Mrs. Sparrow," I said. "It's Starbuck. We . . . the captain . . . has inquired after ye. He wishes ye to rise up now, to come back to the cabin."

Mary, Ahab had said nothing of the sort. I knew being in the cabin, confined with her mad husband, was no place at all for the woman. So I amended myself. "Ye are to rest in my berth," I said. "I'll just go tidy it for ye." And I started to leave, but she made no move at all to follow me.

I felt an utter fool. With all my heart, I was sorry for her and wanted to give her comfort. You, with a touch and a word, would have let her know she was not alone in her misery. But where is my tongue for speaking to any woman save my own dear wife? So I only stood and waited at the bottom of the ladder.

Eventually, she began to speak, starting with the idea "He has cast me off." I quickly said that was not possible and I was sure she had done nothing to deserve such treatment. Indeed, Mary, she has always tried to coax him from his derangement and to cheer him, accompanying him in his mad whirls about the deck. She has asked for nothing for herself, she has never scolded him nor addressed him in anger. In all things, I have seen her to be a sweet, resigned wife. And one with courage.

If there had been the power in me to console, I would have added to her store of courage. But, dearest Mary, sympathetic discourse is as much a skill, a learned and trained one, as standing in the keel of a whaleboat pulled by a bull whale faster than any sleigh on land. I haven't the legs for it. I haven't the tongue for it. The urge is there in my heart. I do not think that it is unnatural for men to speak from the heart, but I do not know how. If in this moment, bright star, with your heavenly glitter, you could loose these lips, I would go to that poor woman, kneel beside her, and pour out your benisons.

But then as now, as I pound my fist on the taffrail, imploring thee, what is there for me to say? The words! The appropriate words!

Let imagination re-create the scene. In *hindsight,* what would I have said, as she sat on the barrel, dressed I see now, though it made no impression then, dressed in men's attire! *Brother,* I would say. *I would help you. Dwell not in the inner hell which is always of our own making. Inside yourself you must give up the illusion of power. That is God's realm. Your life is like a vast ocean. Can you control the tempest? Can you make the sun to shine? 'Twere naught but folly to think so. Your despair comes from your struggle, from your vain belief that you order the sea of feeling. But despair is like the tempest, and joy is like the sun. God gives us rules for living in nature. Take shelter from the storm; stay not too long in the sun. Prayer is the shelter from despair; good works for others is the obligation of joy at home. Meditate only on the glory of God, his magnificence, his kindness in the most ultimate sense, his ever-flowing forgiveness, his warm love. Admit your lowliness before his plan. Give up the illusion that you can order either your own life or Kit's turmoil. Trust that Kit can find his way, according to the plan of God. Look you only to your own way, which is in God.*

So it is for me, Mary, when my loins ache with loneliness, with unspent love of thee. In my berth, I close my eyes, and with one hand I squeeze the bridge of my nose. Thus, I pray, sometimes till I hear Ahab stir and know that it is dawn.

But soon, Mary, you will hear my knock. Soon I will open my arms to you. Already I have the taste of honey in my mouth, for you are all sweetness, all goodness.

And this sigh? This long exuding of human frustration. It floats over the taffrail—drops into the sea? rises in the atmosphere? What difference does it make? Those were words I could have said. Yes. And so should I go now to Mrs. Sparrow and say them? They are my exhortation, but are they comfort? She has not much of the Quaker mien. I think she prefers adventuring to calm, activity to quiet. But she does not prefer pain to joy.

Certainly she is a good, true person. And I believe that she once had hope. What I saw in her was the sudden departure of hope. So it is about hope that I should have addressed her?

And what did I say in actuality? "Come, Mrs. Sparrow," I said. "It is always darkest before the dawn." Those worn-out words. But she did look up, and she did follow me to my berth, where now she lies.

I'll make her rose-hip tea. In the square tin with the lovely tight lid ye gave me, there is yet a spoonful of crushed hip. It lasted me till home, just as ye promised.

But do I blaspheme, Dear Star, to talk to my wife instead of to my God? I believe that in Thee, both are joined. Thou be small and isolate like my wife; Thou art ever-luminous like God.

CHAPTER 68   🐚   **In the Steward's Pantry**

AHAB: What, Starbuck? I thought I heard a mouse in here.

STARBUCK: It's tea water. I'm heating tea for Mrs. Sparrow.

AHAB: Ye've found a bunk for yourself?

STARBUCK: Nay. I've been on deck. I'll take his old one in the hurricane house.

AHAB: There might be contagion there. Who knows how madness works?

STARBUCK: My mind is clear.

AHAB: As it ever is. Would I had thy clarity, Starbuck. . . . No answer? What do you use, then, for tea?

STARBUCK: There's still a bit of my wife's garden in the tin.

AHAB: After a two-year voyage?

STARBUCK: I've doled it out. My wife swore it would last.

AHAB: Not even Ahab knows the length of a voyage.

STARBUCK: She knows I have a sense of things. If there were but one teaspoon to start with and she bade me make it last, I would do so.

AHAB: Ye are in all things moderate.

STARBUCK: How fares Mr. Sparrow?

AHAB: I'll keep him drunk till harbor.

STARBUCK: Will his wife like that?

AHAB: Who knows? I've not talked to her. Her life is pleated—there's more gathered up and stored behind than one can see.

STARBUCK: Aye. There's a fullness to her sail that surprises me.

AHAB: So those brown flakes are of a rose from old Nantucket?

STARBUCK: Aye.

AHAB: Let me sniff it. (Puts his nose in the tin.) Rose of Nantucket. *Rosa rugosa.*

STARBUCK: Sir?

AHAB: 'Tis but the Latin name for what is all familiar. I grew up, as did ye, with that fragrance in my lungs. All summer, how the roses bloom in Nantucket, Starbuck.

STARBUCK: I know it well.

AHAB: Perhaps I'll take a house with a garden plot this homecoming.

STARBUCK: Every man needs a hearth.

AHAB: The water boils.

STARBUCK: So, I scoop it out—the last shreds of home in a teaspoon. (He makes the tea.)

AHAB: Don't lie in the hurricane house. There're blankets galore in my quarters. He's drugged and quiet, manacled on the larboard side. Ye'll not disturb me. Take the starboard wall.

STARBUCK: Aye, my captain. And thanks to ye.

AHAB: Give me the cup. I'll tell her 'tis from home.

CHAPTER 69   Ahab's Comfort

THOUGH HE HAD taken to calling me Una, as if I were his daughter, when he appeared in the doorway of Starbuck's tiny cabin, he spoke formally, calling me Mrs. Sparrow and saying he'd brought me a cup of tea. I could scarcely see him because my eyelids were nearly swollen shut with weeping. Nonetheless, the steam of the cup tickled my nose and seemed to open me to breathing. Not even a syllable of courtesy came to my mind, but I sat up and held out my hand.

He stood no more on ceremony than I, but without invitation seated himself in the one small chair, which he pulled into the doorway. Leaving his shoes in the passageway, Ahab wore only socks on his feet, so as not to soil Starbuck's cabin with the gore of trying out. As though he were a gentleman caller, Ahab promptly asked a conversation question, whether I had ever been to Nantucket.

I could only shake my head. My cheek still pulsed with the blow Kit had dealt me.

"Not so," Ahab said. "For that's Nantucket in the cup. Rose hips from Mrs. Starbuck's garden at 'Sconset."

I sipped the brew. I did not want to enter into a polite exchange. But he waited, as though I must now make some civil reply.

"What friends on Nantucket has Mr. Sparrow spoken of to ye?"

I cleared my throat. "Charlotte," I said. The word sounded like a croak.

"I think that Mary Starbuck would be a true friend to ye."

"They are Quakers," I said.

"So is half of Nantucket. And ye are not?"

"I have no religion," I said, gratingly pleased to be unsociable.

"Nor I," he said pleasantly. "Though the Quaker speech wags my tongue."

It was my turn to speak, but I sipped my tea. He stirred his feet on the floorboards. At last, I'd made him uncomfortable.

"My husband regrets his marriage," I said.

"But he's married all the same." Again, Ahab's feet scraped about on the floor. "What do ye know of the world?" Ahab asked.

"Enough," I answered. Feeling spiteful and audacious, I returned his question: "And what do ye know, Captain Ahab?" I was not angry with him but with my lot in life.

"Like ye," he answered mildly, "enough."

Then we sat in silence, mistrusting one another. He sat still and gave me no more satisfaction by fidgeting. I drank the tea. In its taste and fragrance was the hint to my own Island, not Nantucket but our Island, our stone home with its roof spread for roses. I thought of the day when up in the Lighthouse the bird attacked me and I fought with it. Then I thought of Giles's long plunge into the ocean.

"Our best friend," I said, "fell, or maybe jumped, from the mainmast of the *Albatross*."

"Was it night or day?"

"Broad daylight. I was looking at him. The sun stood at his shoulder."

"An Icarus," Ahab said.

Then I looked full at Ahab—his gray-white hair, his ruddy and weathered but handsome face, his strong, hard body. He seemed himself a kind of sea hawk. Had that comparison really fallen from his lips? My own label—Icarus—for Giles?

"What did ye say?" I asked.

"Icarus." He looked full at me. "Our minds fit tongue-and-groove."

"So it seemed with Giles and me," I said.

"And when he died, ye married the other."

"I loved Kit for himself."

"Aye, ye would."

"How do ye know?"

"If I think of the high, snow-capped peaks of Chile, rising straight up from the sea, I see ye there. If I think of the troughs of water, plowed by a gale, there, too, I've seen ye, strong-winged. Ye have the sea hawk in ye."

I felt afraid. Who was this captain? A male version of myself?

Starbuck's cabin seemed a too-close cage for Ahab and me. Birds with such terrible wings should not be confined together so closely. Here, we were both sent to school, imprisoned, a tiny, cramping classroom. Sea hawks, we wanted the sky, maybe some rough rock as a roost, outcropping, spray-dashed. I saw cruel beaks preening feathers, causing each other to shine.

"I should be alone," I said.

"Ye've finished your taste of Nantucket?"

"Aye." His language came to my lips.

"Your pinions are not held with wax. They are rooted deeply in thy very flesh, they clothe a structure delicate and strong as bird wing-bone, native to thine own constitution and being. Bird bone is a lattice inside, a honeycomb filled with air. Ye know that, don't ye?"

"Yes," I said, feeling stronger. The muscles tightened between my shoulder blades, and I sat straighter, readying myself to the effort that was before me.

"Thy husband's mind—" he said. "Do ye also know the ship's compass, housed in the binnacle, may, if lightning strikes, reverse itself? It points wildly, has no idea of north. So it is with Kit Sparrow's mind. But the compass needle can be taken out. It can be placed on iron, it can be struck till the shock reorganizes the element of the magnet. And again it points truly, knows itself. So it may be with Kit Sparrow. His mind could unscramble, point true again."

"On what anvil could Kit's mind be laid?"

"Land. Nantucket. Home."

The sea captain looked strangely excited. I did not know if land would prove an anvil for Kit, but clearly for Ahab, the idea of land, and of himself upon it, was strange and stirring. So might some landbound man appear if you spoke to him of the sea and distant voyaging.

CHAPTER 70   Nantucket—the Faraway Isle

FOR THE NEXT three days, I kept myself in Starbuck's tiny cell, or I went below and sat among the barrels. The crew brought down the newly filled casks, nodded to me as they went about their work, and I watched the bins filled to their tops and more barrels stored in the walking spaces between. I did not inquire of Kit. My assumption was that he was much the same; that he lay quietly manacled to Ahab's cabin's wall. I was sure that Ahab had food and drink delivered to Kit, just as he had to me.

I felt like a mole constantly belowdecks. Against the November chill, I wore a heap of coats and scarfs, and I never changed my clothes. When I went to the hold, I carried a candle, and sometimes I warmed my fingers on it. I could not question myself as to why I wanted to sequester myself with the cargo. It seemed the place for me. Had Kit really struck my face? I could not bring myself to think of it, to question its meaning or to contemplate the future.

Often I thought of Uncle Torch and his kindness to me, and of Aunt Agatha and of Cousin Frannie. I pictured myself and my mother at our quilts, the sound of buggy wheels and my father passing the window, leaving the yard. I thought of the night sounds in Kentucky, especially of owls—perhaps because of the dimness of the hold and because the creaking of the *Pequod*'s timbers reminded me of those soft, persistent sounds.

And I remembered my father striking my face. One blow as Kit had done. Then twice—a blow for each cheek. Then thrice. The left cheek left swollen and bruised.

Once, when I made my way to Starbuck's cabin for supper, I noted that the corridor had been scrubbed. The next day, no new barrels were delivered below, and so I knew that trying out was complete and that cleaning had begun. In two nights, I found pinned to my door a note from Ahab, stating that this was the last night at sea and would I join him and the mates that evening at the captain's table. My hand went to my hair, which I knew was disheveled. Then I bethought me of my clothes, which were Kit's trousers I had stitched up for climbing aloft.

Upon entering Starbuck's tiny room, I found one of my dresses spread on the bunk, and on it a small round mirror framed in beechnut, and a tortoiseshell comb. On the chair had been set a china bowl and water pitcher for my toilet. I would not have known if this was Ahab's kindness or Starbuck's, except for the fact that I saw these items later in Mary Starbuck's home.

And so the mole emerged and tried her best to become a human being again. When I entered the room, Ahab rose, as did Starbuck and Stubb and Flask, the second and third mates. All were wearing clean clothes and were fresh-shaven and wetly combed.

"Pardon my tardiness," I said demurely.

"To Mrs. Sparrow," Ahab replied and raised his cup.

"It's but a rum *punch*," Starbuck said, as though he questioned the propriety of serving me strong liquor.

"Thank you," I said, and then tasted and appreciated the hot libation, composed of rum and molasses; a sliver of lemon cut thin as a window glass floated on top and bore a sprinkling of cinnamon powder.

The dinner itself was a meager one. The cook had toasted a slab of the usual ship's biscuit, and each of us had upon it a nice portion of pickled herring with shreds of onion, which was a great treat in terms of flavor, though the ratio of herring to onion could have been vastly increased in favor of the onion.

"What can you tell me of Nantucket?" I asked the company.

"A place to raise a turnip," Mr. Stubb said, and they all laughed.

"How's that?" I asked.

" 'Twas William Rawson's turnip," he said. "Measured three feet two inches in circumference. And berries! None that size, but in abundance—huckleberry, elderberry, blackberry on the moor, cranberries in the bog."

"There are entertainments," Mr. Flask put in. He being a very short man, his face was close to his plate. Nicknamed Little King Post by the crew, he commanded great respect. A king post was the hub of radiating spokes which buttressed from the inside the sides of whalers plying iceberg-laden waters. "There's a bowling alley at 'Sconset, at Bunker Hill on the South Side," Flask continued politely. "And Peleg Macy's got a bathing establishment on South Wharf."

"What is the barrel record?" Ahab asked Starbuck.

"That of Captain Frederic Arthur stood for a while. He and the *Swift* brought in over three thousand barrels of sperm. 'Twas in October 1825. Then he topped himself in 1830, on the *Sarah* with almost thirty-five hundred."

"Did it bring a good price?" I asked, for I knew nothing of the money end of whaling.

"Valued at ninety-eight thousand dollars," Flask said. He had finished his dinner first and sat clutching his knife in one hand and the fork in the other, as though those wands could conjure up more victuals for their employ.

"There are many churches," Starbuck said.

"HELL!" It was Kit's voice roaring from behind the wall.

"The Unitarians," Ahab answered as though deaf, "have added a tower tall as a mast—one hundred and nine feet."

"With a Portugee bell," Starbuck added.

"HELL!"

I took a gulp of air and tried to remove my ears and mind from my circumstance. Though I knew only a little of the Unitarians, I remembered that both my mother and my aunt had spoken well of them. Yes, it interested me that they prospered on Nantucket. "What other sects are on the island?" I asked.

Starbuck seemed the church authority and named the African Church on West York Street, the Congregationalists, and the Orthodox body of Quakers.

"There's more choices than that, Mrs. Sparrow," Mr. Stubb put in. "All in the process of organizing—the Baptists are on Nantucket, the Episcopal, the Methodists with all their disruptions amongst the members. Somebody brought over an elephant and there's some that want to build a church for him!" Stubb laughed. "The Elephantists!" The second mate had a rare sense of humor.

"Nay, it's the Universalist Society," Mr. Flask corrected.

"What is their belief?" I asked.

"That ye cannot be damned. It makes no difference if ye worship elephant Hindu gods or the crescent moon. There's no hell, they say, and ye can't go to it. Salvation is universal."

"Hell," Kit groaned, and I half rose to go to him.

"Mr. Flask," Ahab addressed the third mate, "earn your name and give him something to soothe his mind till morning. Keep your seat, Mrs. Sparrow."

The steward appeared and cleared away our dishes. I felt most miserable that I had partaken of company, had eaten and drunk and tried my best to make merry, while my husband lay in chains. But in my feeling guilty, an issue became clear to me. Amongst the barrels in the hold, my face burning from the blow, I had pondered what to think of Kit, of our marriage. When my father struck my face, I slammed shut the door to my heart. Let him knock, it would not be opened. But Kit was mad, suffered in his madness, and that fact lent him innocence, inspired my pity.

"Tonight, Captain Ahab," I asked, "might I watch over my husband?"

"Ye'll need your strength tomorrow," he said—not unkindly, but firmly. "Wait till we're ready to quit the ship. We'll have him up and ready. Then walk him off as if he were a normal man and go seek out your friend."

I blushed with shame, for I knew neither Charlotte's last name nor where on the isle she was to be found. But perhaps Kit's mind would be clear. I would wait and hope. And if he struck me again—well, I would ponder again.

"Now," Ahab announced, reaching into his coat and drawing out a cloth pouch. "We have five pieces of maple hard candy. Let us taste the mainland! I give you Vermont!" And he rolled out the candy onto the table the way one might roll dice. We all reached over for one of the amber lozenges and quietly tucked them in our mouths. At first, mine tasted of the cloth, but when that layer had melted off, pure sweetness filled my mouth, and I thought of maple trees all scarlet and gold in the fall, for we grew this tree in Kentucky, too.

"I do thank you, Captain Ahab, for your dinner, and for all your hospitality to Kit and me."

"I wish ye well. Cover your head and hands and walk up on the deck with me. 'Tis the last night ye'll ever stroll the *Pequod*."

Not having been in the open air for several days, I found Ahab's invitation agreeable. On deck, I was surprised by the cleanliness and tidiness of the ship, all pinked by the sunset. The tryworks had been dismantled and the carpenter's bench taken below, so there was a spaciousness to the boards. The ship moved along smartly, and while the wind was steady and chill, it had no meanness to it. I listened to the slapping of the water against the hull and found the sound familiar and reassuring.

"Ye have sailed the Pacific," Ahab said, "with the *Sussex*."

"Yes," I said—not at all eager to go into detail.

"It's strange to me," he said, "that though we are this moment completely encircled with water, and it is the same in the Pacific, yet the Pacific always seems to my senses larger, more ultimate. The mind infects the senses, I think, casts an aura over them."

"And which sensation do you prefer? The little round or the greater one?"

"When I am one place, I remember the other and want it."

" 'Tis a character flaw," I said and smiled.

"If I develop none worse than that, I will feel that God is pleased with me."

His answer surprised me, for it contradicted his claim to having no religion. But I said nothing. The end of the pink light caught the ivory fittings of the *Pequod*. The belaying pins, which were in fact the teeth of sperm whale, made me somewhat uneasy, as though I stood not on a deck but upon a tongue inside a great flat jaw.

"When I sat in the hold of the ship, the ribs curving up around me, I thought of Jonah."

"Many times I've felt the same."

For perhaps a quarter of an hour, we simply stood silently at the rail. A few dim stars appeared against the sky that still held some sunlight up in their domain. Out of nowhere, I heard my voice again. It rose naturally to the surface, the way I have seen some fish rise from the depth.

"I associate you, Captain Ahab, with the color white," I said.

"My hair almost gone to white; the bits of ivory about the *Pequod*."

"You seem the opposite of my father, who always wore black, had black hair, carried a black buggy whip whenever he drove out of the yard."

"Well, the *Pequod* always sails under white canvas."

"Do you know of any instance in the whalery when that is not true?" I asked.

"Not in the whalery, but it is an ancient sign. When the Greeks came home in the wooden walls, if the news be bad, they sailed under black. And in medieval times as well."

I remembered that Starbuck had said Ahab was a learned man, though Starbuck's own reading was confined to the Bible.

"But there is a way that you and my father are much alike."

"Aye?"

"You both have a wild eye, a fiery eye. I saw yours when you set out to hunt the whale."

"And what did your father pursue?"

"God."

"I could chase him, too."

Ahab's eye roamed the newly starry sky, regarded the wind in the sails, then he bent his eye to the plowing prow of the ship.

"But," Ahab added, "where is he?"

I was surprised at the pain in his question. "Are you, then, religious after all?" I felt disappointed. He had seemed a fellow skeptic, like Giles, like Kit.

"Religion and God usually have very little to do with each other," he said. "What do you think of the wind, Mrs. Sparrow? What Arctic news does it blow to Nantucket for the season?"

"What does the word mean, 'Nantucket'?"

"It's the Indians' name: the faraway land, for its distance from the mainland. And Kentucky—its meaning?"

"Also an Indian word—the dark and bloody land."

"Beware the treachery of words, Mrs. Sparrow. They mean one thing to one person and the opposite to another. They are like all conventional, land-born habits. Words seem to be well-woven baskets ready to hold your meaning, but they betray you with rotted corners and splintered stays."

"You mistrust all that is of the land."

"It pretends to permanence, but even mountains wear away, and the river finds a new bed, deserting the old though it may have served a millennium. So it is with humans."

"I think it is possible to be at home," I said. "I have been there."

"The sea promises nothing, and so it is more to be trusted."

The night had grown cold, and I decided to terminate my time outside in the wind, but first taking courtesy leave of Captain Ahab, for I knew he would be busy the next day.

He paid no attention to my heartfelt gratitude. Perhaps I expressed it too conventionally.

"The sea," he finished his comparison, "bears all her changeability on her face, and so is more kind."

"In her cruelty," I added as I turned away.

The glitter of the stars discomforted me.

OF ALL THE BERTHS I'd had on ships, I preferred Starbuck's. It had all the comforts of a coffin. The bed itself was wooden, only a bit wider than myself, but clean. There was an aisle to stand in which was the width of the bed. In it, beside the head of the bed, sat the one small chair, a convenient place to put one's clothes or to set a candle. Beside the door was a tiny writing shelf that could be folded down and suspended on one side by a small-linked chain, for his writing in the ship's log, and the chair could be pulled up under the shelf. Where to put the clothes, if one turned scribe? Well, there were three pegs along the wall, and a chest slipped under the bed. In the ceiling was set a green-glass bull's-eye for funneling down the daylight. A sort of net was fastened against the wall alongside the bed. There Starbuck kept his Bible, and in its leaves there were a few dried grasses, some violets, and a pencil sketch of a woman who was certainly Mary.

A very narrow red rag rug covered the strip of floor so exactly that it surely had been manufactured to its dimension. It was the color of cranberries and likely dyed with them. Probably Starbuck had been comforted hundreds of times by the color, but never with any conscious association to the cranberry bogs of Nantucket. I thought well of Mary for making her husband a red rug. If he could not have a hearth fire to cheer him, at least he could have the color red.

I thought of my mother's log-cabin quilt, with the red square in the center, though that was a redder red—a red the color of blood. And I had never associated the color with the idea of the bloody land. Nor could she have intended me to.

To lie on this bed was like lying in the drawer of a well-made cabinet. Here I was contained. And the container ordered my confusion. Far too small for two people, for the lone person the room fit almost as well as a shell fits a turtle. It seemed protective. And my toes found a hot brick wrapped in flannel.

I blew out the candle that I had set on my chair, and I listened. Would I ever hear these sounds of wooden ship, of passage through the waves, of night wind in the sails, again? Would I ever make my way alone over the sea again? What had happened was terrible beyond anything I could have imagined, and yet . . . and yet . . . I had lived. I would manage. I touched my face, the still-sore cheekbone. I would not be struck again.

I listened far into the night. Then I rose, dressed, and tiptoed to Ahab's cabin. Ahab and Starbuck snored peacefully; from Kit there came a low, continuous moan, at the same pitch as the wind in the sails, but with a human timbre. One wrist was manacled to the wall in a low place, and he was lying down. I sat beside his head with my back supported by the wall and lifted his head and shoulders into my lap. I cradled and comforted him and kissed his face.

I shall take care of you, Kit, my lovely, I promised. *I shall pick you berries and plums. You shall have a radish as big as a washtub. I'll get fishhooks and stand on a smooth rock beside the ocean and fish for you. I'll dry fish and I'll pickle them. I'll sew plain and fancy while I wait for fish to bite. We shall have jams and jellies, quince and elder-berry. We will harvest seaweed till we have a great stiff stack of it. I shall get us a sheep and shear her and spin and knit from her. What needs anyone a large house? Ours will be like a double cupboard, built warm and hugely thick. And you shall do just as you please all day long.*

WHEN I AWOKE, both Ahab's hammock and Starbuck's pallet were empty. Kit still slept in my lap. Gently I slid from under him. As quickly as I could tidy myself, I ran to the deck.

Land! A hundred masts in the harbor! Buildings! The high tower of the Unitarian Church, its dome wrapped in gold leaf!

" 'Morning, Mrs. Sparrow," Starbuck called out.

" 'Tis no longer the far land," Ahab called, "but the near land— Nantucket!"

CHAPTER 71　📿　Ahab Prepares for the
Next Voyage

KIT AND I packed our clothes inside the pillowcase I had borrowed from Sallie and the *Albatross*. Standing at the prow with Kit, among the sailors, I watched the island festooned with buildings grow larger. Ahead of us sailed another whaler, the *Boar,* and the airstream behind her bore a horrible odor. It seemed a combination of rotted fish and rancid grease.

"She's coming in dirty," one of the sailors said.

"Her flag flies lowered," another said.

And others spoke disparagingly of the filth, till Starbuck put in an explanation: the captain must have died during the voyage, and the first mate had lacked the authority to make the crew clean up as they should have. He pointed out, too, that she was from Australia, and it made little sense for her to be docking here.

They seemed scarcely competent to steer the ship, and we closed on her. The deck was in disarray with ropes and spare sails, harpoons; even a dangerous cutting spade lay in the rubble.

"Look up," I said to Kit, "at the church spire."

He quietly took my hand. Then he meekly asked, "What do you notice, Una?"

I had only noted the sunlight on the golden dome, but quickly I supplied ideas for Kit to chew. "See, the clock portion is a cube, a square, but the next level, the one all louvered, is hexagonal, and there the square is moving toward curving. And the third level is the round drum of the cupola, and that is topped with the dome, which is almost a hemisphere."

"You would have me transform like that building?"

Some unintended correspondence had dashed up in his mind. I tried to ride the wave. "I only mean we all change by degrees," I said. "Neither in good architecture nor in nature is there any abruptness, but gradual modulation, requiring planning and patience."

"Would you lecture me, Una?"

The land approached, ever nearer, and nearer. When I looked at the water day after day from the masthead, the ocean had seemed to go on forever. Yet any journey across the widest sea led to land, and the limitlessness of the sea was illusion.

Now I half regretted the ending of my journey. Again I savored the rise and fall of the boat beneath me. As I have often done, I watched a black-backed gull riding the waves, up and down, exactly fitted to the sea. I watched how the small whitecaps folded over, just as the fingers of a raised hand may fold down over the palm. Little foam good-byes, they waved to me.

Suddenly two men, one black and one red, leapt from the stern of the *Boar*. Huge men, their arms were stretched over their heads, their bodies taut as harpoons. They entered the water without a splash, and then they breached and hallooed at us.

"Throw lines," came Ahab's command. There was relish in his voice.

He was obeyed at once, and soon the two giants had pulled themselves like twins over the railing, where they stood half naked and dripping before Ahab.

"So, Pisces," Ahab addressed them. "We have fished you up from the ocean, and you are ours."

"Daggoo," said the black man, the water glistening in his tight black curls.

"Tashtego," said the Indian, with a voice that seemed to come from the bottom of a muddy river. His muscles lay long and flat in his upper arms. "We harpoon whale for you." The Indian spoke in a sullen manner, suggesting it was his right.

With excited vitality, the black man repeated the sentence exactly: "We harpoon whale for you."

"Who am I?" The captain of the *Pequod* spoke as though he were God before whom appeared two souls petitioning admission to heaven.

"Ahab sails *Pequod*," the Indian said.

"You be the Ahab?" the black man said, squinting and lifting his chin.

"Cut round the *Boar*!" Ahab commanded. "Starbuck, bring the book. We'll sign them on." Ahab was all erect pride, vainglorious in his power. Indeed, he was lord of the *Pequod*.

The crew stood back, in some awe of the red giant and the black giant. Daggoo's nostrils flared as we passed the *Boar*.

"Him stink," he said, jerking his head to indicate his former ship.

Mr. Flask was passing out chits to a few of the sailors—apparently extra pay for having seen whales or other accomplishments. "What's this?" he asked, reading a name. "Mr. Sparrow?"

Ahab took the chit from Flask's hand and stuffed it into Kit's pocket.

"Your pay," Ahab said.

"Did I work here?" Kit asked. I saw the confusion in his face.

"Aye," Ahab answered. "I say ye did. Put in at Captain Peleg's office to redeem your wage."

I was dumbstruck.

"What did I do?" Kit asked.

"Ye swept the winter wind out of the hurricane house."

"I sold you a pound of my flesh for your dinner table, didn't I, brother?"

"Sir," Starbuck said, "there's not a jot in the log of his work."

"I say there is," Ahab thundered. "Give me my book."

He took the pen and the book from Starbuck, and before us all, wrote several lines in it.

"Now, Tashtego, now, Daggoo," Ahab said more calmly, "ye are entered here, too. We sail again in the early spring."

"You sail close to Africa," the black man said, "Daggoo swim home."

"When we sail next," Ahab said, all mildness, " 'twill be for the Sea of Japan."

"Tashtego home now," the Indian said.

He turned and raised both arms ceremoniously, as though to embrace the island.

"Are ye?" asked Ahab. "I took ye for a Gay Header."

"Yes," Tashtego said. "Vineyard is home."

Then he turned again and walked across the deck, as though he owned it, to us. Placing his fingers on Kit's brow and hair, he stooped his tall head and looked wonderingly into Kit's eyes. Kit held his gaze.

"Mad," Tashtego said reverently. "Indians to the west, very far west, great Rockies. Duwamish. Their word. Mad—'I am going home.' Tashtego also mad."

Tashtego reached behind his own head and unfastened an ornament from his hair. With a movement so swift and sure that I never saw it, he placed something in my right hand and turned away. When I looked down, I saw that he had given me an eagle feather.

I felt that something lost had been restored to me. I opened the drawstring I had sewn into the mouth of the pillowcase and dropped in the feather. Tashtego's feather was naturally rounded on the tip, but a few slashes of a knife would quickly fashion a point for my new pen.

I TOOK KIT by the hand and together we walked the gangplank that bridged the sea with the land. How strange to walk upon the earth herself again! After the fluid sea, land seemed stiff and unyielding. My muscles strove to adjust to this new rigidity, and I whispered to Kit, "Walking seems so odd," but he walked straight ahead without speaking. I was glad that he moved with authority and purpose.

In five minutes, walking down the wharf and onto the streets of Nantucket, I saw more people than I had seen in over a year's time upon the sea. As in New Bedford, here were people of the most varied sort—every race and every shade of color, some with mahogany and purple tints to their skin. Their horse conveyances, too, people's shoes and clothes, even their languages, existed in bewildering multiplicity. I felt overcome by this multitudinousness—what did my single self matter in a world so crowded and varied? I looked for a place to mail my letters to my loved ones. *I was safe. I was back.*

"Look at that man," Kit said, and I followed his nod to a well-dressed black man. "That is Absalom Boston. A success."

"Kit Sparrow," Mr. Boston called. "You've come home."

"Aye," Kit answered in a way that seemed wonderfully normal, "with my wife."

"You need a place to stay," he said, "come over to my side. I have a rooming-inn."

"Thank you," Kit said. He put his hand under my elbow for us to journey on, but I lingered.

"Sir," I said, "will you help me?"

Mr. Boston answered slowly and carefully, "In any way I can, madam."

"I need to mail my letters," I said urgently.

"If Madam would honor me with her trust, Absalom Boston will see to it."

I gave him the letters. Good, I thought. Our first test, and we have passed for normal.

We walked on a bit farther and saw an old Indian holding a bunch of fishing poles. His gray hair was parted over the crown of his head and softly braided beside his cheekbones. He stepped into the path in front of us and asked if his son had landed.

I said we had but one Indian aboard, and he was from the Vineyard.

In the old days, he told us, his cloudy eyes fixed on the sky as though it held another time, the whales came to men. Men did not go to the whales. The blackfish, he said, washed ashore to die and be butchered.

"What is your name?" Kit asked.

"I knew you when you were a boy. You never noticed me. Abram Quary."

"That is not possible," Kit said.

"Maybe I forget," the man answered, immediately humble. He looked down as though ashamed.

"Take this to Sailor's Pay," Kit said, reaching for the chit in his pocket. "The *Pequod* paymaster. Tell him you are my representative."

I remonstrated, for it was all the money we had.

"Was it pay for my work, or for yours?" Kit asked me.

I felt uncertain of his meaning and could not answer.

Taking pity on me, he added mysteriously, "It was my pay for sweeping." And to the Indian, he added, "Maybe we forget."

Again Kit put his arm to my elbow, and we continued down the street of Nantucket and on beyond to the outskirts.

The third person who hailed us was walking toward town along the Madaket Road. This was a man who smelled most wonderfully of fish and who commenced to rub his eyes with the backs of his hands when he saw us.

"Are you real?" he asked. "My eyes says, 'Why, that's Kit Sparrow!' and my mind says, 'But he went down with the *Sussex*.' "

"Mr. Hussey, smelling of the Try Pots Tavern," Kit said, whereupon Kit was wonderfully embraced by his old friend, who had a face as deeply grooved as a steamed prune. I was duly introduced, and the man swept off his hat, out of which flew a few fishbones.

"We'll go back, we'll go back," Mr. Hussey exclaimed, "and Mrs. Hussey will feed you chowder till it flows from your ears. Why should I go to town when Kit Sparrow has rose from the dead with a mermaid for a wife? All lost, the *Hemlock* said. Nothing but flotsam. A floating chest. But here you are!" He continued to marvel over us, repeating several times, "But here you are!"

"And how is your cow?" I asked Mr. Hussey, in an effort to divert him.

"My cow, alas, the fish have gotten the better of her." His face changed from genuine joy to mock tragedy. "She coughed up the whole skeleton of a sole, and perhaps it was her soul, for she fell on her side and expired after that." He poked Kit with his elbow. "But why does she ask after my cow?"

"I told her once," Kit said, in perfect equilibrium, "that your cow was shod with the heads of codfish."

"But who would shoe a cow?" Hussey asked. "Especially one that is part dog?"

Then I noted that trotting down the road to meet us, just as a dog would follow her master, was a brindled cow. She came right up to Hussey and with her giant head gently butted against him and nuzzled his chest, all the while turning her head on one side and being most considerate of not hooking him with her horn.

"So you, too, are rose from the dead, Bessy," he said softly. "Maybe she has as many souls as she does stomachs, and there's a sole swimming in each of them." The man narrowed his eyes, pretended to peer into the mysteries of philosophy.

"What makes your cow so affectionate?" I asked.

"Why, Mrs. Sparrow, don't you know the laws of nature yet, and you being a wife? She is affectionate to me because I am affectionate to her. And why shouldn't I be? It's her milk that makes the chowder famous. Oh, never mind the fish. They are quite secondary, in my opinion, though Mrs. Hussey would say otherwise."

On the right side of the road, I could now see the Try Pots Tavern, built with actual try-pots steaming in the front yard. A woman stirred the chowder. Smoke and fragrance rose off the pots in the November air, and the aroma was just as wonderful as that of Mr. Hussey, for when I said that he smelt wonderfully of fish, I meant no irony. Here was the mother of his fragrance. I cannot say how cheerful I felt. Perhaps we were home.

But no sooner did my body relax in that aroma as though it were a warm bath than I felt Kit convulsively grab my hand.

"That is not Mrs. Hussey," he said. "That is Charlotte!"

"Yes," Mr. Hussey said. "The first Mrs. Hussey did strangle on a fishbone. I missed her terrible. But later, when the *Hemlock* reported the *Sussex* gone down, Charlotte cried her eyes out, and then she married me."

"Charlotte!" Kit called and ran toward her.

She brought her hands, spoon and all, to her face, which registered first disbelief and fright and then pure pleasure. She had a round, kind face with pretty pink cheeks and dark hair like mine, but her curls were short and well controlled.

"Kit, you've come home! You've come home!" she cried in a lovely, high, sweet voice. "And I am married to Mr. Hussey." This last statement seemed to her no grief but a source of merriment.

"And I am married to Una," Kit said, indicating me.

And then they both laughed, and Mr. Hussey joined in, as though the very best of cosmic jokes had been played upon them.

I managed to smile, since *they* all took our circumstance with such good humor. Perhaps it was because of the odor of heavenly chowder that constituted our most immediate atmosphere, for the wind had shifted so that we all stood in the midst of airborne chowder particles.

Charlotte held out her hand to me and said happily, "You are Una of the Lighthouse then. Kit spoke so fondly of you."

Her hand was sure and kind as she pulled me closer to their circle. I don't know whether it was her mention of the Lighthouse or the generosity of her greeting that made me think of Frannie and how she had welcomed me when I was twelve. But this was a woman's greeting, not a child's, and it included a mature measure of content that I could not but wish were mine. Yet it was I who was married to Kit, whom doubtless she had loved, and not she.

"Lad, you must have some ale," Mr. Hussey put in.

"We all must," Charlotte said cordially, "and I have bread ready to take from the oven."

"Shall I stir here for you?" I asked.

"Nay," she said, laying the spoon on the brickwork next to the bubbling pot. "If it needs stirring, Bess will come and do it for me." She laughed and pulled me toward the tavern. As we passed through the door, I could not help but imagine the affectionate cow taking up a post before the pots. I envisioned her holding the spoon in her soft lips and commencing to stir away as she switched her tasseled tail.

It was, indeed, the very moment for taking out the bread, and Charlotte pulled it out on her long-handled bread spade exhibiting a breadcrust as brown as any could be without a speck of black or bit of burn on it. With her knuckles she knocked on the crust, and the good hollow sound came back.

"Bread and butter?" she said, indicating a golden pat as big as my fist on the long tavern table.

"I've told the world about Mrs. Hussey's chowder," Kit said.

"She makes it just as good as the last one did," Mr. Hussey said appreciatively.

"Sit you down, sit you down," Charlotte urged, and thick-sided, heat-holding bowls of thick, creamy chowder appeared before us.

And so we ate our first shore meal, in every way enjoying every crumb and swallow of the food, and with my feeling, too, for the first time, that Kit and I were a proper husband and wife.

In every exchange, Kit was as cordial and convivial as ever he had been at the Lighthouse. I thought myself that perhaps he was, more than most, a person defined by his society, and when good cheer and hospitality surrounded him, the inner weather became for him a reflection of that outer glow. Perhaps that tendency accounted some for his absorbing the horror of what had happened in the open whaleboat.

"I saw a shadow pass your face just now, Mrs. Sparrow," Charlotte said.

"Let it begone." But in my mind, even in my body, I felt a ceaseless rocking, the motion of a small, frail boat floating on a vast sea. It seemed that nothing but a whim kept us afloat. Then under the table fur brushed my ankle, and then a short sharp nip!

"Ouch!" I jumped.

In a flash, Charlotte was under the table. She came up with a vixen cradled in her arms, its long bushy tail hanging down before her apron.

"She's more mine than yours now," she said to Kit.

The fox lifted her lip and showed me her needlelike teeth, but she did not growl.

"She won't have forgotten me," Kit said. "I nursed her when she was a kitten." He held out his arms to take her, and, in fact, the vixen went right to him. In a quick motion that scared me, lest she bite, the fox stretched her head up and licked Kit's chin. Then she turned and settled into his arm, just as she had with Charlotte. She looked quickly at me, and again, she showed her teeth.

"We'll have none of that," Charlotte said, and she reached over to hold the sharp little muzzle and jaw together. "She's jealous of you," Charlotte said.

"She's very pretty," I said. "What's her name?"

"Giles named her Folly," Charlotte said.

"Did you know Giles, then?" A dart tipped with pleasure and feathered with pain passed through me.

"And Giles gave Charlotte the nickname of Miss Jolly," Kit went on. "It's easy to see why, isn't it?"

I thought that our hostess would then surely ask about Giles, but she did not. Instead, she contemplated the scene before her as though it were complete and perfect and there were neither past nor future.

"You must stay with us," Charlotte said.

"We've an extra room," Mr. Hussey added, "if you'd like to stay, Kit."

I thought that perhaps Kit and Charlotte had truly been nothing but friends, since her invitation was so without misgivings. I didn't find her exactly jolly, but she was certainly lively and of good cheer.

"Will you tell us, Kit, how you survived the *Sussex*?" Mr. Hussey inquired. "What caused her to be lost?"

"Only if you'll let me make a short story of it," Kit answered.

"Perhaps he'd rather not tell," Charlotte said.

"Hush now," Mr. Hussey said. "I want to hear."

"The *Sussex* was rammed by a whale. I floated in a boat for ten days, with five others—where they are now I couldn't say. Then we were picked up by the *Albatross*."

"When did you marry?" Charlotte asked me.

"We are but newly wed."

"She was a passenger on the *Albatross*," Kit said, "and the captain married us."

I let Kit lie without contradiction. Perhaps he was ashamed I'd dressed as a boy, sailed with the *Sussex*.

"But you are Una of the Lighthouse, aren't you?" Charlotte asked.

"Well, it was a coincidence," Kit said. "As so much of life is. As you have always said, Charlotte. Were others found?"

"There was a whaleboat of the *Sussex*," Mr. Hussey said, "adrift near the Galapagos. A boat of bones and human rot. They starved."

A silence fell for a moment, but Kit was far too sociable to let it settle in a heavy way. "Have you taught Folly any tricks?"

Charlotte put the little fox on a stool before the fire. "Sing, Folly," she said, and the little fox lifted her nose and yipped two syllables. "Higher," Charlotte commanded and pointed to the ceiling, and the animal howled at a higher pitch. "And higher." Was she approximating a tune? Was I hearing the old church tune my father liked, "Holy, Holy, Holy"? I held my breath. Would the uncanny animal be able to continue? Following the jabbing of Charlotte's finger in the air, the fox stretched her mouth open and yawned a syllable rather like "Lord," but the entirety of the next phrase, "Lord God Almighty," was beyond her. Or beyond my imagining. Then Charlotte held open her arms, and the fox leapt into them. With her bare fingers, Charlotte fished right into her bowl and brought out a nice piece of milky cod to reward her pet.

"Now go outside," Charlotte commanded. The vixen ran like a streak across the floor, under the table, where we sat, toward the door, at the bottom of which was cut a small hole hung with a flap of leather.

"When the real cold comes," Mr. Hussey said, "I'll have to stopper it up, but she knows how to ask to go out."

I nodded appreciation and smiled. I did not tattle on Folly, who as she passed under the table had taken just time to nip my ankle again, but that night as we got into bed, I showed the punctured place to Kit and whispered what had happened.

"You shouldn't complain," he said and looked at me strangely.

The remark made me shudder, but I was happy to be on land, so beautifully fed and kindly received. And we were about to lie in a real bed together, on land, for the first time.

"I want to take you from behind," he said.

I was uncertain of his meaning, but I quickly said, "No."

"You don't understand. You need to let me."

"No," I said. "I don't want that." And I thought of what I had heard of the practices of some soldiers and sailors long without women.

"I need you to let me. It's what Giles did to me."

"Giles?"

"Giles wanted me. It surprises you, doesn't it? I hadn't meant to tell. It was why we couldn't be friends any longer."

I would have thought he was delusional, except for the last sentence. The hiatus in their friendship, while we were on the *Sussex*, had stood an open question. Kit's explanation did not so much answer the question as engulf it.

"Giles said for me to pretend I was you."

"Stop," I cried, almost too loudly.

"Now you must be you for me."

My defense, smaller than a child's sand wall, seemed swept away, and I rolled onto my stomach. I began to cry into my pillow as he lifted my gown.

"Now you are my friend," he said.

My body was not made for this, and it was cruel. Kit gnashed his teeth behind my ear and groaned. *Giles?* Was that the word I heard? When Kit lay spent upon me, he whispered in my ear, "I love you. Rest now."

Who was that "you" to whom he spoke? And of what rest?

AS WE AWOKE in the morning, he pulled my head to his chest tenderly and held me there. "Thank you, Una," he breathed. "Sometimes when a husband and wife don't want to conceive, they love each other like that."

I did not believe this notion had motivated Kit in the least, but still I kept my ear against the soft thuds of his heart. My body contracted with the painful shame Kit had inflicted on me in that bed.

Kit stroked my hair as though I were his pet. Perhaps he would be less tortured now. Perhaps he needed to pass on the pain, to do to me what had been done to him. How was it that he knew I could not refuse if he told me Giles had wronged him? No, not for Giles had I lain with my face in the pillow. Because I knew the depth of Kit's injury, I could not deny him.

I heard the Husseys stirring in the next room. Suppose life had sent a Mr. Hussey to me as a spouse? I would have said no to that. But because Kit spoke to me from the land of pain, I could not say no to him. I hoped he would not ask that of me again and wondered if Giles had asked him many times.

I was glad in our stillness together, but our thoughts were separate. Yet he held me as though I were dear to him. My letters home! Inadequate apologies, pale explanations! But Absalom Boston had posted them.

I wished it were night and we could now fit together with the passion of husband and wife. Should we have a child, might we name him Giles and thus seal up a wound and a loss that each of us bore? We three might form a healed and healthy unity. But when I sat up in bed and looked into Kit's eyes in the morning sunlight, I saw on their horizon the sure storm clouds of gathering madness.

CHAPTER 72   Breakfast

SUPPOSE there were an assemblage of musicians whom one was used to hearing in the front chamber of such-and-such a house. And suppose you were a thousand miles, no, leagues, a whole *ocean width* away, and you yet heard those same instruments tuning up. Without going to look, as first a low note and then a squawk and next a toot came to your ears, then, no matter how unlikely it was, you would entertain the hypothesis that these so familiar sounds must be emanating from that same group that you thought yourself to have left in another life.

So it was that when I heard a great stamping of feet and an entering of certain voices into the Try Pots Tavern, I concluded fifteen bulls must resolve themselves into something like the able-bodied seamen of the *Pequod*.

And so also concluded Kit.

"The devils have followed us," he said.

I came close to laughing, but instead I replied, "That's the hortatory tone of Mr. Flask. Only instead of urging the men to break their backs a-rowing, he's demanding a swift passage of porridge and codfish gravy."

"I think they're speaking of us. Or they're going to."

"Not unless we have assumed the names of porridge and gravy."

"What do names matter? They're only code."

I thought of how Captain Ahab, a man far saner than Kit, had said much the same of words. My ears had detected no evidence that Ahab was with his former crew, and, indeed, I was sure that he did not hobnob with them, for all of his respect for, say, Mr. Starbuck (whose voice was also missing from the company).

"That's Mr. Stubb's pipe I smell. Come, Kit, let's go down and have breakfast, too."

"We won't be able to stay here if they talk about us."

"What's to say?" I asked defiantly, though I knew an answer: *Ye have Kit Sparrow, do ye, Mr. Hussey? Had to be chained to Ahab's wall. And his wife . . .*

"They don't know anything about me." I was surprised to hear my defense, as though I were afraid.

"I think you told Captain Ahab. I heard you at his dinner table. You drank blood together, didn't you?"

A plume rose from my heart. Red, as from a whale harpooned in a vital organ. "No, Kit," I stammered.

"I won't see them." His voice was growing louder.

"Let's, then, take a walk. They'll leave and then we'll breakfast with the Husseys."

And holding him by the hand, I coaxed him out of the room and down the stairs. It had seemed warm upstairs, but when we stepped out the back door, the November chill of Nantucket washed over us, and I did not dare suggest we go back for coats. "Let's run," I said, and we rushed down a small hill behind the tavern.

The distant, hushed sucking of the surf charmed my ear, and before long I had led us to a desolate beach and to the sea, which we had but so shortly quitted. We walked beside that heaving, and it was a gray heaving that day, though the waves turned over in whiteness. Close to our feet, it was as though pitchers and pitchers of foaming milk were being poured out on the sand.

What colossal, relentless waste it all was—this pouring and pouring, this rush to nothing, a few bubbles sinking into the ground. And the heave and fling of it, till I wanted to tell it to hush, to rest. Sometimes I chose a surge and thought to myself, "There, that was the last." And there would be a deceptive pause, as though my will had worked.

"I'm trying to stop the waves," I said.

"I wouldn't," Kit said.

"You tried to stop the sun."

"Well, it is gone," Kit said quietly, "today."

I felt his warm hand in mine, and I wondered if I would go mad with him this time.

"Try to be well," I said to Kit urgently.

"I *am* all right now."

I stopped our walking and inspected him. "Shall we have breakfast then?" While I waited for his reply, I watched the sea and its processes. In long gray rolls the water built itself higher, and then at one end, the shape broke over into foam, and the froth came traveling across the top of the roll, and all went to flatness, flowing white fringes. As though they had pushing knuckles of water behind them, the fringy white fingers came scampering up the sand.

Kit knelt down. With both hands, he formed the sand into a little mound, a cake. "Una?" he said, looking up at me shyly. "Will you squat down with me?"

I did, wrapping my skirt across the tops of my knees.

He stuck his finger in the little sand heap and held some grains toward me. "Would you try my cake? Cinnamon and sugar."

"No, Kit," I answered gently, as one might to a child whose fantasy of mud pies had carried him away.

Kit slowly put his finger in his own mouth.

"It's gritty," he said.

I stood up and held my hand out to him. "Let's walk again. I'm cold when we stay still."

We stood up and walked. In answer to my need for warmth, he put his arm across my shoulders.

"Look at all the skate egg cases," I said. The beach was littered with the small black, leathery rectangles, from each corner of which extended a kind of hook. "My uncle called them mermaid's purses."

"I liked your uncle. He was a merman himself."

"Why do you say so?"

"He escaped the ordinary."

"So have you, Kit."

He did not dispute me, nor speak at all, but kissed my cheek. I felt a bit of pride; at last I had given him something good.

CHAPTER 73   Shame

THOSE LATE FALL DAYS, I *managed* him. He could be guided. He did not get better. Charlotte remained hopeful. "He's not had time enough," she said, "only a month or so—it's not enough time."

I took him Christmas Day into the town, thinking perhaps some of the Christmas cheer, the sight of happy faces and families, the aroma of stewing fowl and roasting joint, might conspire to raise his spirits. Charlotte and Mr. Hussey I left to their endless chowder making, though Charlotte was also steaming a pudding. Kit came with me docilely, but he insisted on walking just at my heel. Finally, he said, "Call me Fido, Una, for I am your faithful dog."

I stopped at once. "You are my beloved husband, my best friend."

"But scratch behind my ears, anyway," he replied with the light of teasing in his eye.

"Gladly."

But as I scratched in his hair, his expression changed and suddenly he snapped at my fingers.

"Let's walk on now," I said, turning my face so that he would not see my tears. My cheek remembered the terrible slap he had given me on the *Pequod*. A chill went through me, but surely I was not afraid.

And how was my mother spending Christmas? And had Torchy pinned a wreath to the tower?

The Nantucket weather alone was cause enough to shiver. All is gray in Nantucket in winter: the sea, the sky, even the earth is matted with low-growing, twiggy plants, all gray and stark, and the shingles covering not only the roof but also the sides of the houses have weathered a matching shade of gloom.

In the town, the gray doors were bedecked with wreaths of bayberry. Several times we saw a red candle burning in a window, though it was still afternoon. I wanted to walk to the bake shop to buy a cranberry-and-nut cake to share with Kit, and while we walked down Vestal Street, I heard piano music tumbling from one of the houses. At the keyboard sat a young woman of about my own age. Younger brothers and sisters were about her, and a gray-haired man, doubtless her father, turned the pages of the music for her.

"William Mitchell," Kit suddenly said. "He sets the chronometers for the captains."

There was something in Mitchell's face, wreathed by his family as he was, that very much pleased me. I wished that Kit and I might have been members of that circle—not as husband and wife, but as children, being instructed and provided for. Just then, the family dog rose up from the door stoop to greet us, wagging his tail as though we were cousins. He seemed to smile in the way that bulldogs sometimes have. Kit dropped to one knee and stroked the massive, wrinkled forehead.

"Here's an inscription on his collar," Kit said. He read: " 'I am His Highness' dog at Kew, / Pray tell me, sir, whose dog are you?' "

"It's a quotation from some eighteenth-century wit," I quickly said.

"A philosophical dog," Kit said.

"He doesn't know what his collar says."

"Did I say he did? You make mountains out of molehills, Una. It's something I don't like about you."

I stood quietly for a moment. Yet I felt angry. Was I to be criticized whensoever he liked? Who does not sometimes have a critical judgment of a companion? But we do not have to inflict our thoughts on those who try to be pleasant with us.

Kit stood up, and the Mitchell dog lost interest in us. He walked to a stump and lifted his leg. "Ha," Kit sneered. "Natural philosophy, unbridled." The dog scratched the earth a few times with his hind legs and walked back to his own threshold. As though quoting the dog, Kit muttered, "I piss where I please." Again the beast's face seemed to smile, but not particularly at us. All the while, the young woman played the piano. "Deck the halls with boughs of holly," they sang lustily. Her father turned another page and then smoothed it with his hand.

"Shall we get our cake now?" I asked.

"I thirst," Kit said.

Were those not some of Jesus' own words? Did I now hear portent in every utterance of Kit's? But I followed him as he walked toward the town pump.

Kit worked the handle and bent to drink. After that he walked three times around the pump, eyeing it all the while. With just such a baleful eye, long ago, he had regarded the Argand lamps and spat on the light, just before I was blinded by lightning. Suddenly Kit unbuttoned his trousers, took himself out into the air, and directed a stream of urine onto the pump. I saw that another woman was approaching the pump, and I hurried to stand between her and Kit, to shield him from view. I spread wide my skirt.

"You'll not ruin this," Kit said.

Then he doused my skirt on one side where I held it out. In a low voice, I urgently admonished him to stop, but it was too late. At the sight of a man pissing on a woman's skirt, the unknown woman let out a shriek. I covered my face with my hands and cried bitterly and publicly.

When next I looked at my husband, two men stood on either side of him. For a moment, he seemed to embrace their waists—all the time with his trousers unloosed and his member bare and nakedly hanging down before him. One of them grasped Kit's trousers, and the other adroitly tucked in his member.

Someone tried to put her arms around me, but I ran away a little distance and stood there and watched, sobbing, almost hysterical, all the while. I would not abandon Kit, but I could not bring myself to stand beside him. The odor of his urine rose from my skirt. A number of women did come to surround me loosely, hiding me in their midst. The constable was summoned, and after some short talk with Kit, he came to me and said Kit must spend the night in gaol, for his acts of exposure and defilement of the public pump, till the judge might be consulted. With that I broke from the group and ran, half blinded with tears, back toward the Try Pots, my wetted skirt flapping against my knee. I stank with his urine. As I struggled through the streets toward the road, I thought, *I can leave it all behind*—run faster—*I can leave it behind in the town.*

The Christmas Day sun was beginning to set before me—all gold around the sun itself and mauve and purple to the north. Scarcely noticing the roadbed, I stumbled and cried and rushed myself most miserably westward.

When I reached home, Charlotte saw my wet skirt and that I was distraught. She followed me up to my room, and, my own hands shaking too much to unfasten my skirt, Charlotte unhooked the waistband.

"A dog?" she asked. Her nose prompted the question.

"No. Kit did it."

"Kit?" A stillness descended upon her. "Where is Kit?"

"Gaol. They saw him."

She gathered up the garment, and my stockings, and said I was to "never mind." She would wash my clothes for me. I was to get in bed. But I took a rag first, and water and soap from my washstand, and bathed my leg. My skin felt scalded from the urine. Then I did crawl into bed, biting my thumb to keep from wailing.

Why had I yoked myself to a madman? Because he had given me a seashell comb for my hair? *Experimentally,* he had wondered if the Venus comb would fulfill the function promised by its name. Giles had given me a rose in the tradition of high romance and assumed its decay.

Again I saw the yellow stream directed at my skirt, the rosy head of his penis held in his hand. Once I found a dead tortoise and reached for the shell to make buttons or tortoiseshell hair combs. But when I turned it over, the shell was unbearable with maggots. Just so my hand drew back now, when I imagined reaching out to Kit. My body shivered.

Before long, Charlotte appeared with a tray, lighted by a red candle. Thus she brought me a serving of plum pudding, covered with white hard sauce. Between her arm and her body, she carried a square of folded cloth. After Charlotte had me sit up and put the tray across my lap, she shook out the fabric.

"As Providence would have it," she said, "I made you a new skirt for Christmas." It was dark, forest green, and I thought of the cedar trees of Kentucky. Charlotte sat on the bed and chatted with me, never mentioning Kit. My mother had remained loyal to my father, but he had not hit *her*. He had not made water on her.

Charlotte's kindness, as always, soothed and healed me. Before long, she was telling me a light story that she had heard in the inn. She wanted us to be friends. The plum pudding was in itself so sweet, so rich, so savory and plump with figs and currants, that it seemed we were indeed having a bit of Christmas. I ate slowly. The dark, strangely rewarding flavor, the rectangle of my bed, my new skirt, never worn and darkly green, fanned over the counterpane; Charlotte and I together on the bed, her gentle, entertaining talk—taken all together these composed a little world of our own making. Here safety and order, a rich sweetness, reigned.

CHAPTER 74   🐚   **B'twixt**

LATE IN THE YEAR, between Christmas Day and the beginning of the New Year, late in the afternoon, I sat in my room, so generously provided by Charlotte Hussey above the Try Pots, and stared out the window at the pale gray sky and the darker, slate gray of the sea. Even the form of the sea resembled slate, striated with small, rigid-appearing ripples. A flock of gray shorebirds flew by in the distance—a gray blur. " 'How weary, stale, flat, and unprofitable,' " I thought, quoting Shakespeare, of my existence. Kit would be released in a few days.

I was having my period—at least I was not pregnant—but the monthly condition contributed to my mood of woe and dejection. No letter had come either from the Island or from Kentucky, and I felt completely alone in the world while Kit lay in gaol. The prospect of his release did nothing to brighten the seascape.

Staring out at the drably rolling ocean, I heard a soft plunk. I turned around to see Charlotte's vixen, Folly, making a nest for herself in the middle of my bed. The fox covered her black, pointed nose with a single wrap of her bushy tail, and then peeked out over the ruff with her glittering eyes. It made me mad.

"Shoo," I cried at her and clapped my hands together. "Get off! Go!" I commanded.

But the vixen contemptuously closed her eyes as though to sleep.

I put my knee on the bed and clapped loudly right at her ear. She did not move. I was afraid to lift her. Well did I remember the sharp nips she had given my ankle. I lifted up an edge of the counterpane to roll her off. Her eyes opened, and she seemed indignant that at a remove, I with my human wit could yet dislodge her.

"With this soft and bending plane," I told the fox, grasping the counterpane on one side, "I lever you out of my spot."

I stood high on the bed, lifted up on the coverlet, and thus contrived to roll Folly to the edge. She, being not without her own intelligence, foresaw her fate, jumped down, and quickly ran under the bed. There she hunched. She lifted her lip to show her teeth. Then I wrenched off my shoe and threw it at her. As my aim proved poor, I quickly pulled off the other. She yelped when it hit her and adjusted her position, but she did not leave. The little beast should have selected someone else to harass.

I looked around for something to throw and found a rusty flatiron used to prop the door in summer. I checked under the bedskirt to see which side Folly was closer to, and then I circled. She was not dumb, and as I circled the bed, she again moved. I took the flatiron and beat on the floor with it and yelled.

At this racket, Charlotte soon appeared in the door.

"She was in my bed!" I exclaimed.

"Was she?" Charlotte asked. She snapped her fingers, and to my amazement the fox immediately came out from under the bed and jumped onto it.

"Just like that," I said.

Then, in the air, Charlotte drew a number of circles, loops like an airy lariat, and then stuck a pointing finger through the invisible figure, toward the door. The fox leapt off the bed and went briskly out the door.

My lip trembling, I turned to the window so that Charlotte would not see my distress. It was her control, her mastery over her world, even the animals in it, that shamed me to tears. "Thank you," I said.

I heard her walking around the bed to join me. She put her hand on my shoulder.

"You did not see Kit yesterday?" she said.

"No."

"Nor the day before."

"There is no use to see him. He lies in his filth. He curses me."

"But he is mad."

"And will be so again. And then? He'll be gaoled again. When he raves his worst, he asks me to marry him. When his dementia clears, he tells me he has changed his mind."

"Was it not a proper wedding, Una?"

"It was at sea."

"Perhaps then a sea wedding does not bind on land?" she went on. Was her point a legal one, or sarcasm?

"We have shared a bed," I said. "That binds."

She took her hand from my shoulder. Suddenly she made strange clicking sounds with her tongue, and instantly the fox ran in and nipped my ankle!

"You caused your Folly to bite me!" I exclaimed. "And to claim my bed."

"Yes." Her face was serene and composed. "Would you like to hear her sing again to the glory of God?"

"Charlotte," I said, "I marvel at you."

"Your mind is like a bright light, Una. Unable to shine on itself."

Her serenity and her beauty kept me from labeling her a witch with a fox for a familiar. Perhaps she had worked a witch cure: perhaps I needed to be nipped out of my self-pity and isolation. I put my hand on Charlotte's shoulder, and in touching the point of her collarbone, I knew she was as thoroughly mortal as myself, a woman coping with what life brought her. "Would you explain yourself?" I asked my friend, for she had befriended me.

"Yes," she said. "But let it be with tea and scones and not in your room." She turned her gaze and her body from the window, avoided my eyes, and led me out of the room. "Sometimes I like the public space," she said. "It's where the most private things can be said, confidentially."

There were, in fact, customers in the tavern, three large men whom I took to be from the South Pacific basin, for they had the kind of blue tattoos on their cheeks that I had seen on wooden artifacts from that region. They themselves, in the color of their skin, had a kind of mellow, wooden appearance, like sandalwood. Charlotte smiled at her husband and told him she would not be getting up to help with the service. She handed me two brown mugs to carry; she plucked two large scones from the warming oven, wrapped them in a cloth, and set them on a woven tray beside a large brown teapot. She led us to a booth where the backs of the facing seats were so high that we had something of a private alcove, though to my left the business of the tavern continued and to my right, through a small, diamond-mullioned window, lay a patch of the gray world. My eye noted the carvings on the table before me, for one of them was a sailor's name and the word "Sussex" with the date of her last sailing. I sat in the place where a man now dead, one I had surely known, as it was the year of my own passage, had sat.

"Did you know him?" I asked, putting my finger on the incised name.

"Yes. He was from Nantucket. He sailed three times from New Bedford with the *Sussex*. But the last time, of course, he did not return."

"I suppose then," I said, thinking that my husband had grown up also on Nantucket though he shipped out of New Bedford, "that Kit knew him."

"Yes," she said. "Did you?"

"Yes, but not well." I felt sad and weak.

"Then you met him in New Bedford before the ship sailed?"

Immediately I saw that she had trapped me, that I had made an error, for Kit had said that he and I had met by chance on the *Albatross*. Charlotte eyed me closely.

"You're not going to make Folly nip me, are you?" I said.

"Do you deserve it?"

"Who are you to judge?" I tried to defend myself.

Our questions were not aggressive, but they were on the edge of it. She unwrapped the warm scone and handed it to me, along with a small crock of butter and a spreading knife.

I tasted the fragrant bread—it was baked with plump, soft raisins in it—and told her sincerely what a wonderful cook she was.

"Mr. Hussey would not have married me otherwise," she answered. "The first Mrs. Hussey was well known as a cook, and he did not want someone who would bring him down in the world."

"You bring Mr. Hussey down?" I glanced at him: spry, amiable, certainly, but wrinkled—much older—bowlegged. Above all, he seemed *ordinary*. Another part of me smiled to think that I had adopted one of Kit's measures for a human.

"Youth doesn't last," Charlotte said, with a bit of edge in her voice. "I could not through any act of will make my youth last. Cooking recommended me with more assurance."

"I look to sewing," I said. "It's how I'd earn our keep."

"Sewing has no aroma," Charlotte said, smiling.

"But it lasts longer than a scone," I answered. I took another appreciative bite of mine, following it with a slosh of tea. "Cinnamon," I said.

"Yes, with a grate of dried orange peel."

"I doubt that anyone in the world is a better cook than you, Charlotte."

"I thought that Kit would marry me," she said.

"How can you not hate me?"

"Look at Kit."

"Still he is Kit."

"And, you're thinking, so is Mr. Hussey yet Mr. Hussey." Her face turned crimson all of a sudden. It was a tide of blushing swept over her, and I knew she would reveal something remarkable. "Mr. Hussey loves me in such a way, in our bed where it is dark, that I can imagine him to be whomsoever I choose. For he is all men in one. Every night, there is nothing but newness in his touch. His imagination is beyond bounds. He speaks to me, and he never says the same words twice. He touches me in ways that I beg him to remember and do again, but the next night, again, all is new. Mr. Hussey is kind and loving even to my toes. I did not know, could not have known, that yonder nimble, deep-creased man could be such—both servant and king. And most odd is that he says he did not know it himself, that never in his life has it been so before, but he says it is me alone who makes him full of glory, and that it will always be so, as long as I can cook."

Someplace in the midst of this astonishing speech, she had reached out her hand and held mine. How urgently, how vivaciously, she wanted me to know the quality of her marriage. Could it be so? Involuntarily, I glanced at Mr. Hussey, who was carrying a large tray of chowder bowls up on his shoulder, and at that moment he looked at his wife, and his tongue licked just the corner of his mouth and his grooved face was washed with—yes, I may as well name it—glory. I saw that it was true. They were inflamed with each other.

"Kit is a good cook," burst from me.

"Yes. He was. He courted me with buns."

"And me as well."

"I thought that Kit was dead. Gone down with the *Sussex*. Una, how he startled me, materializing beyond the steam from the chowder."

Now it was my turn to reveal the truth. "I was on the *Sussex*, disguised as a cabin boy."

"You went to sea!"

"Yes."

"How could you?"

I laughed. "Since I was a cabin boy, no great strength was expected of me."

"You ran away to sea?"

I thought she had never been so astounded in her life. It pleased me. I nodded.

"Just like a boy?"

I nodded.

"I can't believe it."

I sipped my tea. "So why do you have Folly-fox bite me?"

"You deserve it, for your disloyalty to Kit."

"Disloyal?"

Her face, which had blushed with thoughts of her marriage bed, now drained of color to a milky white. As she spoke it seemed to me her teeth grew more pointed and foxlike.

"You let yourself grow discouraged. You neglect to visit him. This is the time between Christmas and the New Year, a bland, waiting time that you could fill with possibility. Kit is your husband. Kit Sparrow, Kit Sparrow! I would have died for Kit Sparrow."

"I have tried to be a good wife. No, it was not trying. It was my heart's desire."

"If you leave him, leave him to me."

"What do you mean?"

"Mr. Hussey will equip him a room here, with barred windows, and I will tend him. It would be a less lonely cell than the one he lies in."

"Would Mr. Hussey let you keep Kit?"

Now she looked at me with fury. "Do you doubt my loyalty to Mr. Hussey? *He* would not. He knows me too well. I know myself too well. I've promised him. There is nothing in heaven or earth that could come between Mr. Hussey and myself. The world is not closed off, Una, because a man and his wife make a small, inviolate circle at the center of it."

"Certainly," I replied, "you have let me, let Kit and me, hang on to the edge of your world."

"No, I have made you welcome, and Kit as well, though Kit betrayed me."

"You were not engaged, I think."

"I thought him dead and vowed to myself I would give to any husband all the passion that could not be given to Kit. But Kit had no reason to think me dead. And yet he married you. Before he ever came back to Nantucket."

"His life had changed."

"As you know well, he was yet Kit; I was yet myself."

"When the *Sussex* went down, a few of us survived, for a time, in a whaleboat. Giles was there, too."

"Giles had a volcano in him. I never knew what it was."

"I don't know if Giles fell by accident or if he killed himself."

Some of the natural color returned to Charlotte's face. She considered the idea, and, finding no explanation in her own thinking, asked me why Giles might have decided to end his life.

"At the end, in the whaleboat, it was only we three who survived." But then I stopped. I feared that if I continued the story, she would never look at me again with the same trust in my humanity. We had broken a tabu for which there could be no forgiveness. I regarded the innocence of her face, her plump, chinalike cheeks, her vibrant black eyes and glossy curls.

"You can say," she said.

"We lived off their flesh and blood—the others."

"Did you?" She drew back, her eyes round.

I would not say it again.

"Him too?" She put her finger nervously on the name cut in the table.

"I don't know. My mind refuses to remember who. Sometimes I see a pair of pointed shoes. Somebody's watch cap."

With both hands, she reached across and took mine, my fingers still curled around the scone, though I had ceased to eat.

"I'm glad," she said. "Whatever it took to bring you here and alive. I'm glad, Una Sparrow. And I will never tell."

I felt the tears fall down my cheeks.

"Stop now," she said. "Or Folly will bite you."

But I could not stop. I put my head down on my folded arms and commenced to sob.

She sat there, across from me in the booth, for a while, patted my head. And then she slipped away. Dimly, I heard her go about the business of the tavern. She did not send the fox to nip me. After a while, a great stillness came over me. It was as though the sea had ceased her heaving, and she lay a motionless plane of gray.

From my mind's eye, I turned to the actual window, across which flew a flock of blackbirds. They flew as a group, but the size of their shape constantly contracted and expanded. What held their flying together, what allowed its varying? They were gone, and I did not know. Yet here came another flock even larger, and after that a third, moving swiftly but enlarging and contracting like breathing lungs.

Some light was left in the afternoon, and gradually the idea formed in my mind that I should go again to the gaol to visit Kit. I went up to my room to fetch a shawl, for I knew night would come on, and it would be cold on the walk home.

Charlotte seemed to know my mind and where I was off to. Before I went out the door, she hugged me and kissed me on the cheek. I was surprised to find that all the time I had clutched the scone, even to taking it outside with me.

CHAPTER 75   Enter: The Gaoler and the Judge

THE COLD AIR invigorated me, and I walked hard and fast, hoping to gain the streets of Nantucket before nightfall. With the clearing of my head, I ate the raisin-studded bread as I walked.

The wind was penetrant, and I wished I had cloaked myself in two shawls. I walked fast to heat my blood. I had told Charlotte. I had told. Whatever had been in her recoil initially, she had accepted me on the rebounding. She had said she was glad I was alive. She had wanted to take care of Kit. My mind whirled between these points, but most important—she had not labeled me a monster. Not a brute. Not an animal.

I wanted to tell Kit—we were acceptable. At least to Charlotte. Charlotte, who had never left Nantucket but yet had a generosity, a largeness of heart, that encircled us. Kit might not be fit to hear the news. I would have to wait. I felt health pouring into me as I walked. I felt my own strength. Charlotte, Charlotte the healer. Perhaps Kit should have married her. Perhaps she had health and passion far beyond my own to offer. And her loyalty. She had shamed me there. Yet, Kit had chosen me—had married his guilt? When I thought of Kit, hope died quickly.

THERE WERE STREAKS of pink in the gray sky when I reached Nantucket town, and an inky blackness was gathering in the northeast over the rooftops. Inside the homes, a few candles and lamps already burned. People on the streets seemed homeward bound, scurrying to escape nightfall and the intensifying cold. I opened the wooden door to the gaol without knocking and stepped into the room. To my surprise, the keeper was not in attendance. To my greater surprise, instead of seeing Kit, I found his cell occupied by the old Indian Abram Quary, dressed in Kit's clothes.

Upon recognizing me, Quary said, "He help me—I help him."

I was speechless, but my mind filled with dread and anxiety. Unsupervised, Kit would surely fall into a terrible state. He wouldn't think to eat or to find shelter. Quary meant well, no doubt, but his "help" was nothing but endangering.

"Tashtego," Quary began again.

"Tashtego?" Yes, I knew the name—the Indian harpooner who had hired on with the *Pequod*.

Quary's mind wandered back to the old times when schools of blackfish had beached themselves, and a person could walk for half a mile without foot ever touching sand by stepping from one whale to another.

Quary and Tashtego had built a small boat and taken a small whale. They had gorged themselves for days.

He had brought Kit a basketful of dried strips of the whale meat and a bowl of beach-plum preserves to dress it with. To the keeper, the Indian had also given meat and jam, but that jam had been infused with powerful sleeping herbs. When the drug had done its work, Quary undressed Kit and redressed him in his own clothes. In his simplicity, he seemed to assume that a mere change of clothes constituted an adequate deception and that color of skin or arrangement of hair would go unnoticed. He had led Kit out of his cell and out the front door of the gaol.

"He will be lost!" I exclaimed. "And cold!"

But Quary unfolded for me the rest of his planning. Tashtego, waiting with warm clothing, would row Kit first to the Vineyard—Tash's own home—in the boat and then from the Vineyard to the mainland. Not to a city, no, but through the countryside. Tashtego knew some of the Penobscot of Maine, to whom he would entrust Kit. Those friends would, in turn, guide Kit to Canada. Tribe by tribe, Kit would be guided west until he came to the people who believed that to be mad was the same as to have arrived at home.

A cold fire raced through my brain. It was a good plan. What better could have been done? In Nantucket, his name was already Lunatic. His life might become a series of incarcerations. But I thought of the weary miles, the cruelty of the weather. Then I saw Kit inside some Indian shelter, a hogan thickly insulated as a beaver's house. I imagined him eating venison stew, his ravings incomprehensible, but, for the Indians, in a language they did not understand. *Don't foul yourself! Honor their home.* I heard myself offering these injunctions. In reality, they were in the small boat, skirting the island. Quary said that when the gaoler awoke after an hour's sleep, he had quickly discovered Kit's absence.

"Gold, gold," Quary said, inexplicably swirling his forearm around his head. But he made me to understand that the gaoler would soon return.

Then Quary asked me to take the key from the drawer of the table and release him. I could not refuse, no matter what the consequence. Once liberated, he moved as quickly as the shadow of a bird, across the room and out. Almost as quickly, I laid the key on the table and followed Quary.

In the street, he had already disappeared. I began my walk home, my body rigid with anxiety. With each step I feared being arrested by a shout or a firm hand grasping my arm. But neither shout nor restraint came. From a tavern burst a group of bundled-up citizens, led by the turnkey. Their voices were excited, but not angry. Quickly they rushed past me, clustering around the gaoler. I reversed my direction and made myself follow after them toward the gaol. I went unnoticed.

When they disappeared into the log building, no doubt expecting to question Quary, a boldness came upon me. I waited, then watched them emerge, splitting in groups of two or three and going in many directions.

I approached the gaoler. He wore a good coat and cap, and a scarf wrapped across the lower half of his face, but his nose had a clean cut to it, and his eyes, too, suggested clarity.

"I came to visit Kit," I said. "He was gone. The cell was empty, and the key upon the table."

"The Indian took him," the gaoler said. "Old Abram Quary."

"He is as addled as Kit," I said.

"Abram Quary does not disrespect the town pump."

"Kit was to have been released at the New Year. It's but three days early."

"You would have me not to search for him, Mrs. Sparrow?"

"He has no place to go but home. You could come for him there tomorrow."

The gaoler, being a reasonable man, proposed we should talk with the judge, and together we walked without further conversation toward his house.

Guard him, guide him: my prayer was to Tashtego. Again I felt the tip of his feather slide against my scalp. I had saved the feather, in a drawer in our room, at home.

THIS WAS A HOUSE—the abode of Judge Austin Lord—as large as three ships. When we stepped into the parlor, its warmth and rich furnishings amazed me. How completely, just beyond a door, beyond a screening wall, may lie an undreamt-of reality in this world!

When the gaoler took off his cap and scarf, he revealed a cap of golden curls. His beard was composed of wiry, red-gold hairs bent around like rings. The judge had us sit upon a sofa upholstered in dark red velvet, the wooden portions being of polished mahogany. He sent a servant for tea, which came in a pot of blue and white such as captains brought back from China or Japan. Meat sandwiches on small plates were handed us. I was so warm, so sheltered by the beauty of it all, that I found it hard to speak. Nervous, I wanted only *to be* in that luxurious place.

Judge Lord himself was a pudgy, balding man; the crown of his head gleamed pink. From just above one ear, a ruff of black hair circled the back of his head to the other ear. A pair of spectacles clamped into the flesh of his nose. His plump hands moved dexterously among his fine things, and he seemed much inclined to listen. Judge Lord addressed Cap-o-curls by name, but at the time I paid no attention. The judge asked the gaoler many questions about Kit's deportment in jail, what had been the subject of Kit's conversations, what the frequency of his agitations, and if there were discernible causes. Of me, he asked very little. The turnkey, who relished the comfort and honor of our circumstance, talked very fluently, with few errors in grammar.

His account of my husband branded new pictures in my mind. Kit had gnawed at the bars. " 'You'll but injure your teeth,' I told him. Then he pronounced that I was an honest man, but things sometimes had to be tested, that the common wisdom could be false."

At length, but not before we had all finished our sandwiches and tea, and a hot dried-peach cobbler had been summoned and eaten, the judge said he saw no real reason to pursue Kit farther. "I hope, Mrs. Sparrow, that you will find him at home and that you will be able to keep him away from the town."

"What of Abram Quary?" I asked. I did not want the judge to punish a man who meant so well.

"When you see Quary, tell him he is to knock at the back door for a chat with me."

I turned to the gaoler and said I was sorry people were put to trouble because of Kit. There being nothing else to be said, I stood up and thanked the judge for his hospitality. He graciously responded that he was glad it was in his power to resolve legalities, but he wished that something therapeutic could help Kit.

"You do help him, Judge Lord, by not pursuing him, by not confining him further." (I wondered if Kit and Tashtego had reached the stretch of water between the two islands.)

With that the world of luxury and light closed behind us. Though the kindly gaoler offered to walk with me out to the Try Pots, I declined. While he was pulling his cap over his hair, I remembered Quary's description of the gaoler as "gold, gold."

Across the street, from a dark portal of a dark house, my eye caught two other flashes of gold. I saw the African harpooner, Daggoo, step forward. The light had caught on the hoops of his large golden earrings. He walked toward the wharf.

CHAPTER 76   On the Moor

THUS, I commenced to traverse the road alone. After I passed the last lighted house, I listened, for company, to the familiar sound of my feet on the roadbed. Certainly there was a map in my mind of my route, but the usual sense of sight could not serve as a check to that plan. The night was starless and utterly black. The brushing and quiet placement of my shoe soles reassured me, but steady cold invaded my face and chest. I thought of the pressure of an apple press bearing down against the flesh of the apples—so it was the cold bore down and squeezed me of my warmth.

I searched the sky for some star's gleam, but the blackness was utterly complete. Stars offered little comfort anyway. I felt my lips growing numb. Licking them only gave the frigid night moisture to freeze. My fingertips, too, grew numb, and my toes within my boots.

The warmth of the judge's tea had completely left me. His soft home seemed a kind of delusion. So might one imagine heaven. I wondered what lay beyond his parlor and how Judge Austin Lord had come to his station in life.

I began to hear a creaking, groaning sound. It reminded me of the straining of a ship's mast in a wind, but I knew myself to be far from the harbor. Still, these timbers sounded massive in their adjusting. Suddenly, the fear came to me that though I was upon a road, it could not be the right road! There was no natural or artificial structure on all the deserted road to yield up this particular creaking, turning sound. A wheeling.

A wheeling with a pattern to it. I might smash into some gigantic wagon. Perhaps some vehicle had overturned, and its mammoth wheel now turned in the wind, and if I walked into it, my flesh would be abraded away in an instant. Yet it did not sound close by. There might be an abyss before me.

I was afraid to step forward, and yet I made myself do so. Where I had walked confidently before, I now sent out a foot like a probe. Uncertainty compounded fear till I stopped, considered crawling so that I could feel ahead of myself with my more intelligent hand.

I would not crawl, but I palmed the air before me.

My body tilted, which meant the path was turning upward. And the groaning, turning sound seemed nearer. I knew where I was. I had taken the road to the mill hill. Dazzled by the judge's house, I had been disoriented. I would come to the mill, whose wooden blades must have come unbraked and were now turning in the wind. I thought of Don Quixote. *I will not tilt with you, but I will take a moment's shelter under your arms.*

So I climbed the hill. Though I still could not see in the darkness, I felt my way to the door, but it was locked. I leaned against the structure. The great gears turned and rumbled inside. Trailing my fingertips around the tower, I moved to the lee side, sat down, and rested myself. Though the mill was wooden, the height and cylindrical shape reminded me of the Lighthouse. The mill shuddered in the wind as though it would unscrew itself from its moorings and tumble arms over root down the hill.

My father had given me a whirligig, carved of wild black cherry wood, one Christmas. The blades were twisted, and he had said that with birds the tips of their feathers could twist in the wind. I was reluctant to leave the mill, whose internal motion gave it a kind of aliveness. I was growing sick from the exposure.

I imagined Kit stumbling in the wind. With every second the gulf between my life and Kit's widened. The mill arms churned the night;

the grinding gears within whirled and gnashed. I wished Kit shelter and happiness among the wild tribes, who, after all, did not think of themselves as wild. Kit was a wild man at heart.

Stiffening with cold, I struggled up and set out again in the blackness. The mill was for me a giant compass, for I knew its door faced east. If I went north over the moor, I would come to my road. My feet would tell me it was a road. I would go left, westward, perhaps a mile farther to the Try Pots. I would see the lights. My mind cleared of confusion, I had but to confront my fatigue and the cold.

These were not easy to face. The low shrubs of the moor caught at my clothes. I stumbled many times. Sometimes the land was strewn with rocks. Once I stepped into a declivity and fell. I could feel my slow tears as cold as snail trails on my cheeks. Still there was naught to do but go forward. I schooled my mind to be alert, not to miss the change underfoot from moor to road. I crossed a few more open places, but these could not be road, for I heard and felt that I trod on ground-hugging heath and brittle moss, desiccated by the cold.

When my feet did step into the roadbed, I knew it at once for what it was. I consciously made my turn to the left. Now the walking was not so hard. As the physical exertion lessened, the darkness of the night closed closer about my soul. I thought of Charlotte, and I dreaded to tell her that she was not, no more than I, destined to care for Kit. But Charlotte would adjust to that. She had her Mr. Hussey. She would always have him. I was alone, and my heart cried out for some sense that I was cared for.

Kit would think himself lucky to be rid of me. A she-wolf, he had called me. Yes, in this utter blackness, I could remember the taste of human blood in my mouth.

But I could not condemn myself again for it. I panted in the cold air. The life I now had was condemnation. Against the gunwale of the whaleboat I saw the burnt face, the parched lips, of a sailor. I gasped, for I knew him! His face recognizable, his name known! No! *Willard Wilson!* I willed the vision to dissolve. My life! My life! Surely that was enough of condemnation. I panted harder, afraid of my conscience as well as the night. I conjured up a comforting face and name: *Charlotte Hussey*—had she not acquitted me, called me human, welcomed me to living? Charlotte cared for me. She would forgive me.

I might be made of grosser stuff than Giles or Kit. Nothing in me bent toward my own death or desired the expiation of madness. Marriage was my expiation. I had assumed the harness. Of those who had died in the open boat, I would not think. And yet, if Kit was gone, then their dark specters would have his place. *Thomas Rodgers! Oscar Brian! Livingston! Joseph!* Their names echoed in my brain till other words pushed through my cold lips into the blackness: *I am sorry. I am sorry.* I uttered and repeated this sentence as though the intensity of my speaking could engrave it on air. And I was afraid.

I prayed to those whalemen. *Spare me! Spare me because you were not spared.* Logic left me, and I stepped from the road back onto the moor. If I could wander the moor till daybreak and absolution—then I could go home. I fled cross-country, dry gorse pulling at my skirt. Driven by fear of who I was and of what kind of world I lived in, I heard behind me the sound of other footsteps.

Perhaps it is Kit! Perhaps Kit had decided to come home to me. I paused to listen. The steps continued toward me, quickly. This was not Kit's gait. I was stalked. Demonic forces walked the moor.

I moved as fast as I dared in the darkness, the way a fish might plunge through the depths of the ocean. Blackness streamed about me. Still, I heard the approaching footsteps. My eyes strained for glow from the Try Pots Tavern, but there was none.

Some harmless townsperson, I told myself. No one would wish me harm, surely. Yet the town was full of unknown people, and sailors from ports around the world. The steps were closing on me. Small rocks fired from under the soles of his boots.

I would not run, I would not run, I told myself, but fear ran through me. The pursuer was at my shoulder. *Let him pass by. Oh, let him pass.*

Then a large, flinty-hard hand took my hand. That was all. The man took my hand. There was naught but kindness in it.

I did not speak. He did not speak. He led us back to the road. Occasionally the side of my arm brushed some part of his clothing. Some human consciousness had seen my aloneness. He had offered comfort. I held that hand gratefully. Flinty and hard in terms of the texture of his callused skin, the pressure from that hand only reassured. *I am here too,* it said.

So we walked together. My heart boiled and brimmed. My lips

parted as though parched. Some human had shown me compassion—simply because I was a human. Perhaps I would get letters from Mother and Aunt. Perhaps they, too, forgave my cruel desertion.

At length, in the distance I saw the lights of the Try Pots. We walked on together but a short piece. It was as though my companion wished to make sure that my eyes had registered the evidence of a haven. Without a word, his hand slipped from mine. I walked on. I listened for his footsteps, but he either stood still in the road or had stepped onto the felted moor.

My hand remained warm from his comfort, and I tucked it under the cloak, up under my armpit, to keep it so.

THAT NIGHT in my bed, with a warm brick to my feet—Charlotte had been all kindness—I clasped my hands together. I relived my journey on the moor. Again I was comforted by the dark stranger.

My body seemed to whisper that there was something familiar about that hand. Kit? No. But I thought of Kit's hands and mine when we clasped together in our marriage vow. Both Kit's hands had been between mine, and *my* hands covered both above and beneath by palms as hard as stone. That rocklike hand from the night! Why, it was the hand of Captain Ahab.

CHAPTER 77   A Slow Spring

As I HAD suspected that bleak night upon the moor, the exertion and cold made me sick, and I stayed abed till after the arrival of the New Year. Charlotte brought me bowls of chowder—cod or clam—and one evening a plate of steaming root vegetables—carrots, beets, a turnip, a parsnip, a whole cooked onion which fell apart in concentric, translucent shells. She made my bed, causing me to sit wrapped up in a quilt in a chair while she smoothed the sheets; she carried out my slops; she gathered up my nightclothes and undergarments for the wash pot.

When I told her of Kit's flight with the help of Quary and Tashtego, I concluded, "So his care falls to neither of us, Charlotte."

"Then I shall take care of you, instead," she said.

What a system of substitutes she had! If not Kit to meet her passion, then Mr. Hussey. If not Kit to care for, then his wife. It was in her nature to love and to nurture; she would not leave those feelings within herself to fester and sour, but instead she chose someone who would receive her gifts gladly. She did not hold herself to be so special that only one special person could she find satisfactory.

I was not truly *glad* to be the object of her concern, but I was grateful. Being sick in bed from exposure gave my mind and spirit as well as my body time to heal. It was good for me to be confined and cared for.

Charlotte had many questions to ask me about my life aboard the *Sussex,* the *Albatross,* and the *Pequod,* and as soon as I was well enough I gave her many details of the various ships, including descriptions of their captains and crews. She asked me nothing about the time on the open sea in the whaleboat, and we rarely spoke of Kit.

The twelfth day after Kit's departure, an extremely bright and crisp winter day, Charlotte said she was walking into town, and perhaps I could help Mr. Hussey a bit in the tavern. The bright day brought many sailors who boarded in town walking out the Madaket Road to us, and I quickly saw that Mr. Hussey had real need of my help. Merely dishing up and delivering the chowder kept me on the trot, and I developed an admiration not only for Charlotte's cheerful ability to organize the serving but also for her physical stamina. I was still weak from my illness.

Among the clientele of mostly sailors I was surprised to see Kit's gaoler, who asked to speak with me when I grew less busy. Such a moment was hard to come by, and I was sorry to make the man wait. After nearly an hour, I sat down in the vacant chair at the small table.

"You're pillar to post, aren't you, Mrs. Sparrow?" he began.

"It's been very busy, to be sure."

"I'll say quickly then that I spoke with Abram Quary myself, after Judge Lord had had his chat. Kit stole Quary's boat and rowed to the mainland, but another Indian has brought it back."

"And how is Kit himself? Does anyone know?"

"I asked Quary if he thought Kit would make his way back to Nantucket."

"What did he say?"

"He said no. I expect he's right. I'm sorry, Mrs. Sparrow."

The man's eyes more than his words told me he was sympathetic. I thought of the hard, unspeaking hand that had consoled mine on the dark road. Then I had said nothing at all, but this time I had the presence of mind to say thank you.

"My name is Isaac Starbuck. If I can assist you in any way, let me know."

"I knew a Mr. Starbuck, first mate of the *Pequod*." But the gaoler was not connected to that good Quaker whaleman. Still I associated them.

Afterward, I went up to my room to rest. As I was turning back the bedcovers, the little vixen walked in, her toenails clicking on the floor. I was too tired to care. I closed the door, and when I climbed into bed, Folly jumped in beside me. She made a nest next to me, and I let her stay. Thus it was that I acknowledged Folly as my rightful bedfellow. I went comfortably off to sleep with the fervent hope that Charlotte would return in time to wait the tables at the evening meal.

When Charlotte came into the room, I had napped for more than an hour, and the sunset was at the window. "See what I have," Charlotte said, setting a bundle on the bed and turning to light the lamp. Folly instantly came and stuck her nose in the bundle.

"It's sailors' mending," she said. "You like that better than cooking and serving, don't you? After you've sewn up the tears and holes, we'll launder and press them. Mrs. Hilda Macy isn't expecting that. This way you'll soon be quite in demand. Something extra, you see. You must offer something extra to be noticed."

"You've gotten me mending work!"

She chatted on, as though the sizable walk, the conversations in the town on my behalf, the lugging home of the load of clothes had all been nothing but a welcome change in her usual routines. She emphasized how surely the "something extra" would cause my new business to prosper, just as she had known that not just milk but cream and butter must be added to make a chowder distinctively delicious.

And so it was that during that slow spring when I stayed with the Husseys, I earned my keep with my needle. Soon I delivered the shirts and trousers and coats myself, and, indeed, Mrs. Macy, a bubbling, voluble woman, was charmed by the neatness and strength of my stitchery and by our laundry work. Mrs. Macy herself was the best-pressed woman I had ever seen. Perhaps she never sat down, for the back of her cotton skirt was as smooth as the front bib and straps of her apron. The cloth had a subdued, perfectly behaved surface. As she sorted out the shirts and trousers I returned to her, Mrs. Macy declared, "Why, these clothes could almost pass for new! You've a gift for the mending, girl." She gave me a new bundle, one as large as I could carry.

As I made many journeys there, I began to speak to the people of the town, and once I walked in merely to attend a lecture at the Atheneum. Nantucket town was a pleasant place, with many independent and intelligent women. When men were home from the sea, they were happy to socialize along with their wives. I much liked the gabbiness of the town, for the talk was not mere gossip but of ideas and politics, spiced with the customs and sights from all around the globe.

CHAPTER 78   🏛   Churches

I T WAS DURING this time that I began to attend first the Universalist Association and, later, the Unitarian Church on Orange Street, the gilt dome of which Kit and I had admired as we approached Nantucket aboard the *Pequod*. The message of both groups was much more hospitable to the human spirit than that of the Kentucky Christians, whose emphasis was on human sin and God's wrath. I came to the Universalists through Charlotte, and with that context, I understood much better her unwillingness to cast me into outer darkness for my unspeakable sin. The Universalists believed, quite simply, in universal salvation: no soul was eternally damned, as Mr. Stubb had reported during the maple-candy dinner that last night on the *Pequod*.

They argued that if Jesus was the Savior of mankind, then this was a fact, universally true, and whether one believed the fact or not did not matter, Christ having died for all. Further, the minister explained that while there might be some punishment for sin after death it was not of eternal duration, the word *eternal* having been mistranslated from the Greek in many scriptures. Their position was that everlasting punishment was entirely inconsistent with the idea of a benevolent Father, since even earthly fathers could and did forgive their offspring for criminal acts. All their tenets were refreshing ideas to me. At meeting I found the congregation, simple farming people, to be a kindly group, slow to cast even verbal stones at one another. I cannot say how they might have responded, specifically, to my own crime, for I had had enough of confession for a while.

When I was with the Universalists, I felt a kind of peace, and I wished that both Kit and Giles had heard their message. To believe it was not necessary. Merely to know that some people had invented a more liberal view of Christianity loosed the bonds of the old dogma and its dependence on damnation. I had thought there to be only one Christian Way, straight, narrow, exclusive. And here was a road that went off at right angles, that could bend and double back, that was open to whatever sheep might wander onto it.

Though I did not think of Kit as dead, during the long-coming spring, there was a finality to his leaving. I did not expect him ever to come back. Yet my heart held a quiet hope for him. If there was hardship in the wilderness, it would distract him from his mental travail. If he was strange among the Indians, so long as he was not violent, then that strangeness itself might protect him. Elaborations of language had been a snare and a delusion for his thinking. The words that were the names of animals, of nuts and berries, those for fire and for shelter, would suffice.

Once, walking home from meeting, Charlotte asked me, "Do you not wonder where Kit is, fret for him?" Her question surprised me. She had kept silent till she judged I was strong enough to speak of Kit.

"I have taken a page from your book," I replied. "I live the life that is before me."

The gray moor about me, bathed in sunshine, was comfortably unprepossessing. I remembered that long, cold nighttime crossing of this same moor with a small shudder.

"Does your heart not search for Kit?" Her voice took on urgency.

"I loved Kit, but I count him gone." I spoke slowly, wanting to speak truthfully. "My consolation is that I believe him to be alive. If I cannot be with him, I can bear that." I paused and saw the windmill, its arms fitted with canvas now, slowly turning. "Gladly would I have said good-bye to Giles, if it meant that he could live and walk the earth, though I never see him again."

"Sometimes my heart yearns for Kit."

"I am surprised to hear you say so."

"I've sensed your letting go of him. As you let go, I miss him more. We grew up together. I had always thought to marry Kit Sparrow."

I was astonished: because of her account of life with Mr. Hussey, I had counted Charlotte to be the most contented of women. "Kit is not fit to be any woman's husband."

"Sometimes I think that he has met an Indian woman. In my mind's eye, he crawls under a deerskin with her." She swept her hand about— the Try Pots lay ahead. "All this I would give up to be that wild woman, traveling with Kit."

"Charlotte, your life is too full of chowder making. But there's no romance in being pissed upon. He slapped me once. He has reviled me many times."

Here Charlotte fell silent. Finally she said, taking my hand first, "But, dear Una, I have not done what you have done."

It was as though I had been slapped again. The taste of blood flooded my mouth.

"*Your* unforgivable sin would be adultery," I said to her, for I knew Kit would find something unforgivable about any person who dwelt in a world that was itself unforgivable in its cruelty. "We all are unforgivable to him, and he punished us."

"I think that I would lie," she said. "He wouldn't know. I would tell him that Mr. Hussey had died."

DURING THE WEEK that followed, while we worked together serving the tables or stirring the great pots, Charlotte questioned me about the onset of Kit's madness. She rightly guessed that I had seen a glimpse of aberration on the *Sussex*. I told her how, at the Lighthouse, I had come upon Kit high in the lantern room worshiping the lamps or trying to work some magic over them, and then how he had made mud for my lightning-blinded eyes, hoping to reenact the miracle of Jesus. I asked Charlotte about Kit's mother, who surely was the root of his madness.

"The urine!" she exclaimed. "His mother liked to squat behind a bush, only half shielded. She wanted to make the private into the public." And then Charlotte hurried on with her serving.

That night when Mr. Hussey was snoring loudly, Charlotte came and knocked on my door. I was almost asleep, but she climbed up onto the bed with scarcely an invitation and commenced to talk.

"When I was just a little girl, I saw Mrs. Sparrow squatting at the privy ditch, this one well out of view, but she said to me, 'Come, little one, come and confess with me.' I never knew what she meant by confession, but today it came to me. For them to take what is usually secret and hidden, shameful even, and make it public is to confess. They want to confess the animal side of their nature. To be as nonchalant and natural as animals."

Charlotte was much excited about her reflections on the logic of madness. "Each night I shall tell you his history before you knew him, and then you shall tell me the history afterward, and together we will make sense of it—where the ideas come from, what they mean to him."

I had not heard her speak in such a rush since the time we sat in the booth and she had told me Mr. Hussey was all lovers in one. That revelation had made me happy to hear, but now Charlotte herself seemed obsessed. After her season of patient silence, she was ababble with questions. "Will talk of Kit be too painful for you?" she asked.

"No," I said. I sat up in bed. What I felt was not pain. "Charlotte, I doubt that we shall ever see Kit again. He will walk west. I know him. Even an addled brain can walk toward the setting sun. With a fierce determination. To what end do we plow up his history from our brains?"

"After he has reached the edge of the continent"—her eager face reminded me of Frannie and her fascination with Kit—"what will he find there?"

"The Pacific Ocean," I answered.

"But Kit will have the habit of walking. When his quest is ended, he will turn around and walk east. I know him, too. I would like to be prepared when our paths cross."

"He might ship to China."

"I think that Kit has had enough of the ocean."

"As you said, he may find some tribe where he feels at home. He may stay there. Take a new wife. Father children."

She clutched my wrist. "Don't say that. Don't say that. How can you say that?"

"I wish him well."

Here we fell silent for a moment. We both listened to Mr. Hussey's stentorian snoring.

"I thought you were content with Mr. Hussey," I whispered, almost teasing.

"I was," she said soberly. "I was. But now I am not. You have given up Kit. He could be mine."

All that week, soon after Mr. Hussey's snores filled the upper floor like a gemshorn, Charlotte came to my chamber to tell the story of Kit. Folly the fox usually came to lie between us, and I felt we were something like characters from a fairy tale.

THE NEXT SABBATH, as we walked into town, I felt increasingly impatient with Charlotte. I wanted not to be so much in her company, for she sealed and stamped every step of the journey into town with images of Kit and her together, in a time innocent of my existence. As we walked down Orange Street, I suddenly said I would visit the Unitarians that day and walk home alone. "My aunt was a Unitarian," I explained. "I've been curious about their creed."

"You'll find them less Christian, but with little to replace it," she said.

I thought but did not say: Good. Then I shall ponder my own beliefs.

"Mostly they pride themselves on their skepticism."

"All my life," I answered, "I have been a natural skeptic." And I turned my life—is it too much to say?—away from her. My body seemed a boat, my clothes the sails, myself the captain.

IT IS A somewhat unnerving experience to enter a house of worship when you neither have a companion nor expect to see a familiar face. One feels an intruder. Almost as soon as I settled myself, however, I saw two whom I did know: Captain Ahab, with his shaggy, gray-white head, occupied a pew across the sanctuary behind me; and, just in front, was the kindly gaoler.

Captain Ahab sat with his face uptilted and his eyes closed. His brow was slightly drawn in concentration so that a line ran vertically between his eyes. He seemed the very image of a seeker; yet I knew him to be as much a skeptic as myself, and I felt, as I often had in his company, that we had something in common. He was oblivious to his surroundings.

The gaoler—Isaac Starbuck—somehow sensed my presence, turned, nodded, and smiled at me. I could not help but study the back of his head from time to time. His hair was indeed a fine cap of golden curls.

The sermon was one that saw Jesus as a great teacher, but at no time did the minister suggest he was divine, except insofar as he affirmed that all humans were divine, and, therefore, Jesus, too. What of the animals? I wanted to ask him. They have life, and their intelligence is only of a different order. Did not Saint Francis preach to the forest creatures?

I wondered if Ahab questioned in like manner, if Ahab considered the divinity, perhaps even the sanctity, of whales. The minister skipped over the animal question and went on to extol the beauty of nature, by which he largely meant the landscape. He spoke of God the Creator as an artist, and while this seemed a bit fanciful to me, I liked the poetry of the idea. As though he read my mind, the minister then considered metaphor and what relationship it had to truth. "Metaphor is a lens," he said. "Metaphor is a mirror, a magic glass by which we see what we would otherwise not see." To my amazement, instead of quoting scripture, the Reverend Mr. Peal quoted the poet John Keats:

" 'Beauty is truth, truth beauty,'—that is all
Ye know on earth, and all ye need to know."

It was a puzzling conclusion to his sermon. I felt unsettled by his ideas in a pleasant way and resolved to visit the surprising Unitarians again. I doubted that the Universalist minister had ever heard of John Keats.

In the foyer, the gaoler spoke to me politely, saying that he hoped that I was doing well, and he inquired after the Husseys. I'm sure that if he had further news of Kit, he would have given me some indication of it. Over his shoulder, I caught the eye of Captain Ahab—oh, gloomy countenance—but then, a lantern of delight—seeing me—lit his eyes and then his whole face. At that moment, the gaoler suddenly asked if he might walk home with me.

"No," I said. "No, thank you for your kindness." And I hurried out into the street. Ahab was not long in approaching me.

"And might you want a gray-haired escort along the Madaket Road?"

"I think, sir, that you have walked that road with me before now, and at a time when I was sorely in need of comfort."

"Aye."

A silence fell between us, and the Sunday sun, crisped by the breeze of early spring, bounced from our shoulders. We both knew what that night had been like: there was no need to speak of it further.

"I'm surprised to see you, a Quaker, under a gaudy golden dome, Captain Ahab."

"I grew up a Quaker. This morning I wanted change, fresh air."

"What did you think of the message?"

"I wish that he had preached on Judas."

"How so?" I felt shocked.

"It may well be that in the heart of man there is a goodness that is divine, that we are Jesus-kin. But that is only half." His face contracted and darkened. "The other half is the Betrayer, the Liar, the Murderer, the Fornicator, the Cannibal, the Prince of Darkness. And I know, by thunder, that I have kinship there. It's that half of me that wants to be called brother."

So ready was his pain, so anguished his speech, that a word leapt from me to him, as lightning might leap from one cloud to another: "Brother," I said.

"Do you call me brother, Una? You do not know me."

"I have said what I have said," I answered and turned from him and began my walk home. Neither of us wanted further conversation after all.

AS I WALKED HOME, I thought about the gaoler. Was Unitarianism the source of his civil demeanor, as Universalism was the ground of Charlotte's acceptance? Did I want him as beau? His interest was evident. No. I did not want an admirer whose work it was to imprison others, no matter how civilly. He is not his work, my fair-minded, skeptical voice suggested. I replied: He has chosen his work, though. Fairness insisted: And Ahab has chosen to slaughter whales. Yes, I answered, but Ahab is an altogether different case.

Ahab knows me, and I know him, and that transcends all else.

CHAPTER 79   Baptismal

I SAW NOTHING else of Ahab for a month, while the spring came on. Twice the gaoler walked out the Madaket Road to eat at the Try Pots. I myself now felt shy of the town that I had just begun to explore. I did not want to go back to the Unitarians—though I was full of curiosity about not so much their beliefs as their modes of thinking— lest it seem to Captain Ahab that I hoped to see him there. On the *Pequod*, I had overheard him speak of me as Spring.

I am ashamed to say that I made quick use of Isaac Starbuck when he came to the Try Pots; by chance I had a large bundle of mending ready to go back to Mrs. Macy, and I asked him to carry it for me. He promptly volunteered to walk out with a new batch. Twice I used him thus, but after the second time, I told Mr. Starbuck I must do my own walking and take care of my own business. Yet that seemingly independent declaration was devious on my part, for I knew that Captain Ahab would surely sail in the spring, the usual three months in port for restocking the ship and hiring crew now being well past. Perhaps if I encountered him while I was on my business, I would feel no embarrassment.

Since Ahab knew the way to the Try Pots as well as the gaoler, I hypothesized that Ahab had wanted nothing more of me but a passing (and parting) recognition. And for what reason did I seek out a man who was about to embark on a voyage of possibly three years? I did not know exactly. It seemed I needed to wish Godspeed—whatever that might mean—to a kinsman.

With my bundle of mended, washed, ironed, and neatly folded sailors' clothing on my back, I set out for Nantucket town. When I was within sight of the place that I had calculated to be the halfway mark,

I saw a man standing there. He neither approached nor receded. It seemed he stood there watching me. Within a few steps more, I recognized the man to be Captain Ahab. With this identification, I began to laugh. I quickened my pace and, despite my heavy bundle, half ran to meet him.

Ahab did not laugh, but there was a full smile upon his face.

"So, girl," he said. "We have mutually decided to close up the distance between us."

I do not know what devil possessed me, but I laughingly said, "Nay, Captain. I'm only bringing my mending-work to Mrs. Macy."

How dark the cloud that blighted all his smile. He turned abruptly away from me. I had embarrassed and humiliated him with my dishonesty. Quickly, I caught him by the arm.

"I did hope that I would see you. To say good-bye."

"Well then"—and he smiled again, but with only half the radiance of his initial greeting—"let us walk together."

"This is the halfway mark," I said.

"It might be a good omen that we each come halfway to the other."

My heart began to boom like a loose sail in the wind. Like Cordelia, I could not heave my heart into my mouth. I looked at his gray-white locks and thought that he was a kind of Lear, though his domain was watery and he faced his storms at sea.

"The *Pequod* sails tomorrow," he went on. "I have news of Kit to give you."

"News of Kit?" I was much surprised, even alarmed.

"It comes by way of Tashtego, who spoke to a friend of his from a tribe in Maine. Kit is better. He wintered with the Penobscot. For a month now, he has been on his journey west. He has taken the St. Lawrence as a highway, canoed the Great Lakes, gone through the chains of lakes in Minnesota that the *voyageurs* marked. He makes friends wherever he goes, and the word is passed back and back along the eastward track that he fares well."

"I am glad to hear it," I said.

"And will you wait for him?"

I considered for several moments. Ahab would not mind while I searched for the truth of my heart. I felt in myself a depth of calm, profundity like the ocean, yet floating on top a sort of nervous, superficial froth. "Friend Ahab, my heart is not hard—Kit is not dead—and yet—though I can envision him making friends, walking westward, though I know what his mind is like when it is clear—I feel neither loyalty nor bereavement—I do not understand myself in this."

"Then the message he sends back will not pain you."

"What message is that?"

" 'Tell them I am never coming back.' "

I gasped and stopped walking. Like a hammer blow to the forehead of a calf, the words stunned me. Almost I felt I would drop to my knees. And yet had I not wanted a full freedom?

Ahab stood silently and waited for me to recover myself. Finally he said, "But the words do hurt you."

"It is their finality," I said.

"That which you greatly feared has come upon you."

"I feel bereft, after all. Bereft—like a blow." I began to walk forward again. "Not bereft of Kit. He lives. Bereft of a companion."

"You must have felt that many times before?"

"Yes. It is the finality of it. That now I have no choice in the matter."

I stopped again, swung the bundle from my shoulder, and handed it to Ahab. He took it without a word, and we walked on. I did feel stricken, as though I needed all my strength, all the air in my lungs, simply to go forward. Encasing me was froth of nervousness, like a thin garment, a veil. My knees trembled. I seemed to walk like a blind person through the town to Mrs. Macy's door. He handed me the bundle.

"So then, Una, it's good-bye."

"Yes," I said, dazed, and for no reason added, "I am a married woman with no husband."

Though he did not speak, quicker than language, Ahab's eyes darted defiance. The scar! It seemed to contract, to convey an electric discharge from his brain down his neck to the trunk of his body. All his being was charged, embodied storm and power. He wheeled, like a cyclone or waterspout, and walked away.

It was no proper good-bye at all. The thought of saying Godspeed had deserted me.

Limply, I sank upon the settle in Mrs. Macy's kitchen.

"Girl, girl," she said, "you're pale as bleached linen."

"My husband is gone forever," I said.

"Now then," she said, sitting beside me and patting my hand. "So's mine. And look at me." Her forearms were covered with small freckles, very close together, yet distinct. What else did she mean for me to see?

"He'll never come back," I said.

"Nor will mine, till Christ comes in the clouds, the graves open, and the quick and the dead ascend."

She spoke of the end of the world with total good cheer.

"Look at me," she went on. "I have my own business. More close friends than I can count on fingers and toes. Who knows, for you, even—why, it could happen to me—I'm only of middle age, and strong—God may send another, better husband. Here," she said, "take off your clothes and get in the washtub. The water's warm, but far from scalding. Wash off your grief. I hear he was but a sorry lot, anyway."

Here I sniffed, preparatory to tears. She ought not criticize my Kit.

"But no doubt you loved him well enough. You have a loyal heart—anyone can see that. Still, there's nothing like a spring bath in water someone else has heated. Strip down, girl. I'll pull the curtain."

Indeed, I could not move, but Mrs. Macy pulled the curtain, stuck her finger in the water, then grasped a hot stone with her tongs from the hearth and threw it sizzling in the water. I felt the rock was my heart, gone already ahead of me into the water.

"The Indians cooked with hot stones in their water," she said. "Can you imagine the filth of it? Not my rocks, though. They've been boiled ten thousand times. Do you use hot rocks for your washing?"

"No."

"Now lift your arms, and off slides the camisole. Oh, you've nice breasts, indeed. You'll yet nurse a babe. And I'll scald his diapers for you. It's a promise. And you'll remember Mrs. Macy who on your day of woe, scrubbed you pink and pretty and sent you to town as fresh and sweet as the first rose of summer. Now the drawers. Yes, you have pretty lace trim, but my! such a hard tie-knot. Now you mustn't tie the knot so hard, oh, no. No one likes to fumble. No, he doesn't like that. Yes, you've the hips to be a mother. That's right, just step right in.

Doesn't it feel pleasant? Fold up now. I'd squat, not kneel, if I were you. Yes, then rock back and sit on your buttocks. Here's a rag to wash the upper story."

Indeed the water was so clean, warm, and comforting that when I closed my eyes in the bliss of it, only a few salt tears squeezed out.

"Now, this," Mrs. Macy said. "Glycerine and rose water." She gave the little clear bottle a vigorous shake. I saw the oil droplets inside. She opened it up and poured it all into my bathwater. "It won't be long till high spring," she went on, "and after that—oh, you've never seen the roses of Nantucket. They are a sight. Like clouds of clabbered sunset, pink sky sweetly curdled and come down to earth. They sit on every fence, they cover the sides and roofs of the houses."

I thought of the stone house with its hat of roses, at the Lighthouse.

"Sniff up," she said. "Breathe deep."

I did, and sure enough, the odor of roses and summer came to me.

"Splash it up on your breast and neck. That's right. Face too. Oh, how pretty you look. And your hair is like gypsy curls around your face. Do you want to marry a sailor again? Then you must come sit in the shop and do the business direct with them. The joy of the sailor is he's often gone—"

I must have looked shocked.

"Oh, you can come to love your own life. Alone. Have no doubt of that. The women of Nantucket have their consolations—do you know about that, dear?"

I had no idea of what she spoke. I merely regarded her apron, immaculately ironed, smooth and pristine as ever soap and flatiron could render cloth.

"Here," she said, and she displayed another vial. "Laudanum. Anybody can get to sleep with that. And this—" She went to a drawer and took out a porcelain item that somewhat resembled a pestle for a mortar. "It's from China, and it's called 'He's at Home.'"

I gasped.

"But you need not marry a sailor, if you don't like. There's that young keeper from the gaol. Isaac Starbuck. Oh, he would walk around the world for you."

I felt my face flush.

"Now are you getting too hot, dear? If you stay too long in a bath, it will make you sick, they say. We want none of that. My rose must be a healthy rose, not one with a dribbling nose. Here's a towel—just stand up and wrap it around you."

What a whirlwind of talk she was. I did feel new and clean as I stepped over the edge of her tub. What would become of me? How should I know? How could I know? I need not know.

Next, Mrs. Macy insisted that I take bread and cheese, and again I was reminded of the Lighthouse, for the cheese was tangy brown goat cheese.

"We used to add herbs to our goat cheese," I offered.

"Is that so?"

"Sage, rosemary, parsley, oregano, dill. Each has its own flavor."

"Do you not like the flavor of plain cheese?"

"Indeed, I do. But on the Island, we ate so much cheese that the variety of flavoring was nice."

"And would you have a vinegar egg? The hens are only beginning to lay again."

I smiled and gladly bit into it. The third omen from the days of the Lighthouse. Yet they had not written to me. Nor my mother. And then I knew why, with a smooth certainty, as surely as Mrs. Macy's clothes were untroubled by a single crease or wrinkle: they simply had not received my letters. Anything else was inconceivable. Given who they were, they would have answered. I could go to visit. Tell them I *am* coming back, I wanted to say. Let my message reverse that of Kit.

So when I stepped back into the Nantucket street from the home of good Mrs. Macy, I was clean and fragrant with love of myself and my life. I walked toward the harbor, as though I would take ship and go at once, though this was not my plan. Along the way, I stopped at a shop and bought paper and envelopes and borrowed the use of a quill, and I wrote letters first to the Lighthouse and all there—Uncle Torch, Aunt Agatha, Frannie, and the new babe whose name I did not know— and then to Kentucky.

What did I write? I was tempted to describe my recent perfumed bath and the egg I had just eaten, the furnishings of the shop where I sat—the immediate world defined me and swirled through my brain. Finally only these words: the date, followed by: "I am coming home. I am fine." I wrote the same note to both my homes. I signed my name *Una Spenser*, for so I felt myself to be—my own old self again. Then I sealed up the two envelopes, returned the quill, and stepped outside to continue my walk toward the harbor. There, I planned, I would find a boat bound for Falmouth or Hyannis; my letters would be my messenger doves flying before me.

I saw the *Pequod* and other outbound whalers lined up along Long Wharf, and I passed on to North Wharf, where the little barks nudged up like shoats to their sow. As though to fling the round arms of myth about me, to make my ending in my beginning, what vessel should I spy in the middle of the line but the *Camel*. Yes, there was the *Camel*, loaded and apt, who had first carried me from the Lighthouse to New Bedford. Standing on her deck was the same captain with the marvelous twin mustaches, hanging like twin awls from above the corners of his mouth, almost to his collarbones.

"Ready to go home, are you?" he hailed me, as though he had been expecting me.

I was tempted to say yes, but instead I replied, "Not yet. But my letters are. Will you take them? One to the Lighthouse, one to forward overland to Kentucky?"

"We'll send it by steamboat," he answered. "I know captains who know captains all the way to New Orleans. For me they'll leap ashore at any port." He added that he no longer served the Island, but he would find a carrier in New Bedford.

I jumped lightly from the pier to the prow of the *Camel* and handed him my precious doves.

"Come with me now," he said.

"I have to say good-bye here."

"Send letters to them that's here that you have gone. Postlude instead of prelude. You come with me."

His insistence seemed almost rude. He breathed deeply, his mustaches hiking up. "Rose, Rose," he said. "Let this vessel be your vase. I'd make you a proper husband, Una, if you be not wed. Are you wed?"

"Captain," I laughed. "You have not seen me for nearly two years."

"I know freshness when I smell it," he said. "I know sweetness and beauty. I know you. Will you have me? Are you wed?"

I saw he was earnest. "I am not wed," I said soberly.

"And you'll have me?"

"You do me honor—" (How could I wed such mustaches? Something in me wanted to giggle. I made myself be solemn.)

"—but you won't have me." His head dropped, and I saw he was truly grieved. The mustaches almost tipped his waist, so low was his head sunk, and when he raised his face the silver trails of tears ran from his eyes down into the hair of his face.

"Oh, Captain," I said softly.

"Well, I'll take the envelopes then."

"I'm sorry."

"I'll mend, to be sure," he answered and tried to smile.

"Do you have clothes that need mending?" An imp gave me an idea.

He looked at me wonderingly.

"May I borrow your handkerchief?" I asked.

He handed me a yellow one, with red spots on it. Quickly I put it in my mouth and tore a rent in it.

"Now," I said. "On the sincerity of your question to me, you must take this handkerchief to Milk Street. There you will find a widow named Mrs. Macy, who mends and launders and is equipped to tolerate a husband's journeying, and you must say to her that I have sent you to her, and she is to mend and wash and iron your handkerchief dry while you wait—"

"On Milk Street?"

"Yes."

"But, look, Una Spenser—" He raised his finger and pointed. At first I thought he was pointing to the dome of the Unitarian Church, which was the only bright spot, being high enough to catch the last of the setting sun, but then I saw the dark smoke that drifted between the wharf and the dome. We both sniffed for smoke, and there it was.

"If there is a fire," I said. "It's far from Milk Street, which is at the other end."

"Shall I really take only a handkerchief to the mender?"

"Shall I tear a sail?" I teased.

He folded the little square of cloth so that the rent was uppermost and put it in his shirt pocket. "You have sharp little teeth," he mused as we walked the wharf.

Though it was not an accusation and I did not feel stricken, I sealed my lips over my teeth. Fatigue washed my body. I felt my newness dulled. "I want to see the fire," I said and parted company with the captain of the *Camel*.

As I walked toward the fire, I felt a clear bubble of humor rise in me like a gurgling spring at the proposal of Captain Mustachio. Laughter would renew me again. What had Shakespeare written? *Thou purple-hued, mustachioed Malt-Worm?* But I would bless and not curse the *Camel* and her master, who saw and smelled me sweet, and beautiful, and worthy.

Hurrying down the street, I passed Tashtego and Daggoo, the *Pequod*'s harpooners, walking together toward the wharf—no doubt to spend their last night in port aboard the ship. But I did not see Captain Ahab. I wished that I *would* see him now that I was bathed. My father's scripture came to me: *Purge me with hyssop, and I shall be clean; wash me, and I shall be whiter than snow.* As I passed other crew members of the *Pequod*, some of them recognized me and tipped their hats or raised their hands in farewell. To each I said, Godspeed, Godspeed, and I felt forlorn to think that I was being left behind. And yet, as Charlotte said of Kit, I knew that I had had enough of oceangoing.

CHAPTER 80   🜊   **Fire**

T HE FIRE raged in four buildings, their shingles buckling and springing away from the walls. Like bursting buttons, the hot tiles shot out toward the people, who stood well back. A line of men passed buckets of water as quickly as they could. The crowd looked wild-eyed, and some neighbors tried to divert the buckets to douse their own walls or roofs, though they were not yet burning. On all our faces there was soot, and I thought of the night-burning of the tryworks, and this seemed to have the desperation of that butchery, though merely wood and not flesh burned.

The townfolk wept, distraught over the loss of their property. Then the cry went up that there were yet people in one of the houses that was blazing like a torch.

"Who? How many?"

"A child. A boy. He was asleep. An orphan, with no parent to count him."

"Who?" they asked again, as though the answer had not sufficed. "We don't know him. A child."

"But who is it?"

"*One,*" a voice whispered beside me. It was the gaoler. He pulled off his shirt (skin pink, with golden hair in the middle of his chest, like a fleece). He stepped to the bucket line and plunged his shirt down into water, then held the dripping wad against his mouth and nose and ran into the house. Now my own breath went sharp, and apprehension coursed my veins.

"Who? Who?" they called out again, as though there could never be an answer certain enough. "Who is inside?" Yet some replied, "A man!" for Isaac Starbuck did not return as minutes ticked on, and the Unitarian clock struck six. I looked up and saw how the cruel flames reflected red in the dome. "Who? And who?" voices both mumbled privately and shrilly cried.

The terror of the scene brought back the sailors in the open whale-boat, whose names and faces had returned to me when I was lost on the moor. In the flames, I saw and heard them again. Sometimes they had muttered, on and on. Sometimes a shriek more piercing than a bird cry emanated from an anonymous throat. No, that was Oscar who cried and rolled his eyes toward me. A white bird had perched on the mast, and we had longed for it, debated throwing a shoe or weaving a net to cast over it.

"Who?" I myself cried out, though I meant to ask *How long?* A velvet voice spoke naturally in my ear. "A man, a boy." *Ahab!* I thought, but the voice was that of the judge.

"No," I roared. And No, and No, and No, I screamed. Till Isaac, the gaoler, suddenly staggered out, double-headed. Peeping over his shoulder was a little black face. Isaac stumbled and Judge Lord caught the boy from Isaac's back and laid the child on the ground. The gaoler fell like a charred beam. The boy, I cried, and someone gave me wet cloth, and I scrubbed and scrubbed until I realized that he was not black with soot but that he was a little black boy. He opened his eyes, and the judge lifted him up in his arms.

A man pushed on the gaoler's chest to squeeze the smoke from him. He pushed and pushed, and, still on my knees, I heard myself saying "Again" and "Again," but the attendant stopped, shook his head, and stood up. I flung myself on the prostrate Isaac Starbuck. I drew deep breath into my own lungs and tried to force my breath into his lips and down into him, because he was human, only for that reason, and needed his life. But when I looked up from this fruitless labor, I saw Judge Lord all sooty now standing above me, watching, with the little black boy gathered up in his arms. The judge, smudged black with the soot from the child, seemed to step backward, and without turning away from me, they were absorbed into the night.

Then there was Mrs. Macy, and other women, helping me up and leading me away from Isaac. They held my hands and washed and dabbed at me. While they did this, I saw someone take a sheet and spread it over the naked chest and body of the gaoler, whose last whisper had been for the worthiness of one life, and so of us all. Then I wept for Isaac Starbuck, and despised my superiority and my hauteur.

" 'Twas he you were learning to love then," Mrs. Macy said.

"No," I sobbed. "Not nearly enough." But I did not mean as a beau.

I spent myself crying, leaned against Mrs. Macy's shoulder, so watering her apron shoulder strap that it loosed the starch in the fabric, and I tasted the sourness of the starch. I thought of all Isaac Starbuck's aliveness—his quick nod of recognition in the church; his compassionate discourse with the judge the night of Kit's liberation; his pleasure in the little sandwiches and tea we were served; the way the palm of his hand unconsciously brushed and enjoyed the nap of the velvet couch; the way he swung my bundle of mending onto a clean table at the Try Pots and smiled. Who else in Nantucket would remember his friendly ways? I had not had enough interest in Isaac to find out whom he knew.

Finally, I wiped my nose with the back of my hand as though I were again a sailor myself. My grief for Isaac was excessive. It was beyond my connection to the man. Yet those tears had washed out something of the old grief. I asked Mrs. Macy if Captain Mustachio had visited her, and she replied that she must have missed him. I let the frivolous-seeming matter drop.

Again my ear registered the roaring of the fire, and my eye fell on the unmistakable shrouded human shape lying on the ground. They were bringing up a hand wagon because the horses would not come close to the flames. Two men approached with a broad board.

"I'll go now," I said, not wanting to see the gaoler taken away. I thought, *I've missed him.* Not as a beau. I had missed his goodness, his humanity—I had failed to acknowledge those. Some were saying that Isaac was a hero, but I thought only that he was dead.

The fire continued to crackle and spread. Sparks flew so high that their red flicks mingled with the yellow stars. In the streets, the pandemonium multiplied. I turned away from it.

I walked the dark streets as though they were a labyrinth. I met no one. Eventually the human misery and the elemental fury of the flames beckoned me back. I would find a vantage point from which to view the fire. When I mounted the stairs to the South Tower, as the Unitarian structure was sometimes called, my body confided encouragement. Oh, I was a climber of stairs! The muscles had not forgotten. So easy was the ascent, I only lightly skimmed the tops of the stairs. But now I was not a girl, and I climbed to see neither clear sky and bountiful clouds from the Lighthouse nor the vast and wrinkled sea pleating itself in blue or green below the masthead. No. My mind's eye saw the inert, shrouded body, the low earth-resting sheet over Isaac. The drapery of the covering sheet.

As I climbed inside the church tower, I passed the gears and mechanisms of the timepiece and noted a circle of red around the edges of the fire-facing clock, where the fit was imperfect. The rippling and flickering of the flames could be seen even in the thin line around the clock rim.

A door led from the interior of the tower onto a railed balcony, which was situated on the square portion of the building, just above the four-faced clock. I thought fantastically that I had climbed beyond time. But my body yet made the ordinary gestures. I opened the door cautiously, in case other viewers might be standing in such a way as to be hit by the opening door, but others, it seemed, had not thought of such a vantage point.

No, not others, but one other. *One.* To that one my heart flew out. Never does a heart leap so but toward a beloved, when his face is turned, your presence unrealized. You *must* become real to him. Though you stand quietly, your heart has already leapt forward. Where the railing made a corner, a hand on each of the perpendicular rails, facing the fire, stood Ahab, speaking.

NATURE, ye term yourself. Fire, earth, air, and water. Essence of nature, ye pretend to be. But what is natural, Fire, about eating men half my age and sparing me? But I have seen the little one snatched from your glowing jaws, your deadly black breath. (I imagine him so black and small, his rescuer would not have found him except for his whimpering. A puppy? *I have visited the heart of the inferno,* that rescuer would think, *for the sake of a puppy.* The judge can put him to school here, and when I come back, I'll take him—Pip—with me as my cabin boy. How he clung to the judge's neck—tighter than barnacles to the pier, tight as his own curls to his scalp.)

No, I'll not call ye Natural, even if ye be set by lightning spark. Ye can burn naturally in the forest, or gallop naturally over the prairie like bison with collars of flame and crackling hoofs. But here ye feed on timbers torn from the forest, planed and tamed, and shaped and nailed by men. Ye take their toys one by one—so they seem from this height—toys—and my own ship *Pequod* safe beyond at anchor, another kind of toy among these stationary ones. These little houses are the hopes of men. Habitats for us naked creatures who having less of fur and feather need more of shingle and brick.

How come ye here, Fire, ravaging the homes of humans? Ye are will-less. I know it well. Leibniz claimed this was the best of all possible worlds, and so he would say, Lick away, little flames, toast all those who live on this street—it's for the best. Indeed, the next street would be worse for all. A stupid faith, this best-of-all-possible notion. Let Leibniz stick to calculus. Let him invent one that calculates human misery and holds God accountable.

This town pays for Prometheus' insolence. Yet contained in the hearth, Fire, thou art the most comforting of friends. I'll have one yet! Hearth, that is. Friend, too. Friend of my bosom. My eye seeks for her, but I cannot find her in that labyrinth. I saw her wiping the face of the black boy, and then she moved and the roof of the building shielded her from view. (The man who bore the boy from the flames— him I love, too. For he alone risked himself for the cinder boy.)

"Una," I'll shout for her. Una! Let me bay it like a solitary, shaggy wolf. Roar, Fire, you will not quench my howling till she look up, and

"Ahab Addresses the Flames"

like a visitor to the Vatican, she will look up and see not God, but Ahab in the clouds, reaching down to her, quickening her even as the Creator touched Adam.

Fire, I see thou art my brother, for with such heat Ahab rages. The fires of hell, the fires of creation—they are all one—and they burn all knotted in Ahab's bosom's heart. Burn, my heart! Burn, my town! Burn! For thy Flames are like a refiner's fire, and thou shalt purify them—

Why come these sobs?

Thou shalt purify me!—

Let not sobs come and quench the flame within till it has done its work and I am fit for hearth and home—

Let this church and its tower be my stake. Here let the demonic in me writhe into nothingness. Una!—Obsession! I fear ye more than flames!

[Here he sank to his knees, still clutching the railings, as though the church's altar had come external, bent itself into a corner where he might kneel so as to better relinquish his pride and sin.]

CHAPTER 82   Ahab's Wife

Neither alarmed nor embarrassed—for what adult has not witnessed the struggling of her soul?—I walked to him, placed my hand on his shoulder, and said, "Look ye behind, Ahab."

First his hand covered mine, his hard-as-stone hand roofed mine. Slowly he lifted his head but did still gaze upon the burning town. Then, still on his knees, he turned his head and looked up, all disbelief and wonder.

He said in a broken voice, "Art thou angel or devil?"

"Some of both. Even as you are."

"Even as I." He rose to his feet. "Ye have spoken truly. Thou art as I am, though we be female and male."

Then he encircled me with his arm, and together we stood, all calm inside, and contemplated the flames below.

"I would not have the old town burned to the ground," he said quietly, "if I were God instead of grateful mortal."

"Nor shall it."

"Una, be humble. The gods might take us down from our height."

I laughed. "Look," I said, and I pointed up toward the rain clouds blowing toward us.

"Ye have a weather eye indeed."

"All my life, I have watched the clouds."

"I remember ye stood aloft for me on the *Pequod*."

I remembered but did not confess that I had let pass unheralded one cloudy mass slipping whalelike just under the frigid water. And this was the first secret and the last that I kept from my husband.

"Avast!" Ahab shouted to the fire brigade below and pointed upward. Gradually, the people in the streets all stopped and looked up, lifted their faces to the heavens. When the first splatters of rain came down on them, they tucked down their heads, resumed the handing of buckets, augmenting the force of nature that had come to their aid.

"I would have us go back to the *Pequod*, the spot where ye were first wed."

I nodded, for I knew what was in his mind.

When we were down in Orange Street, he stopped and pointed back to our balcony. "I should have known that the same impulse that sent me up there would send ye there, too."

"As it was earlier," I said. "When we met at the halfway on the road."

It rained hard upon us before we reached the *Pequod*, but it was, for me, like a natural washing, the complement of Mrs. Macy's kind human ministrations to my flesh. And though this water was cold, the glow within warmed me like that very hearth of which Ahab had spoken.

We found our spot on the rain-swept deck—it was as though the *Pequod*, too, were getting her bath, and all her ivory fittings gleamed anew. I knew the red and black harpooners, Tashtego and Daggoo, slept below our feet in the forecastle, perhaps others as well, if they had not stopped at some dockside inn. There was no sound but the pelting of the rain on the boards and into the furled sails.

"Here," said Ahab, and the lightning flashed in his eye, though his voice remained calm. I hoped it would remain so. I did not want him to rage again. I wanted to bring him peace. He took both my hands in his flinty ones. If ever there was trust in my life, it was in him and in that moment. The *Pequod* swayed under my feet.

"Here," Ahab said, "what I did join together, I now put asunder." What he said was beautiful and true, to me. His voice was quiet and humble as rain. "And here I wed Una and take her for my bride."

"Even as I take you," I said. The course being figured and set, our kiss was the sweet, uncanny, effortless drifting toward harbor and blissful home.

"I would not spend this night on the *Pequod*," I said. Though I flouted the marriage laws and conventions without a qualm, the shadow of my union with Kit aboard the *Pequod* made me shudder.

"Nor would I have us stay here," Ahab reassured. "Wait."

He went below and came back with an oilcloth satchel full, I presumed, of dry clothes, and he brought a broad umbrella as well, though I did not realize that he owned such an item. He slid a nuptial bracelet carved from ivory over my hand. A circle of whales swam round my wrist. Ahab no more needed the validation of priest or paper than I.

I was beginning to feel cold, and we hastened ashore. With my hand through the crook of his arm, we hurried away from the wharf over the cobblestones of lower Main Street. Soon Ahab guided us to turn, and we passed the gaol on Vestal Street. We walked down Vine and on. We climbed a hill. Across the street from the judge's home, we stopped before a dark house and then stepped onto its dark portico, where I had seen Daggoo lounging against a column. Ahab thrust a key into the lock of the uninhabited dwelling. Turning to me, he explained that he had bought himself a house, and that now, thank God, he had a place worthy of his wife.

This I could hardly believe. A grand house! We stepped from the wet street through the portal. And I was to live here!

"One day I was driven to it," Ahab said, "to buy myself a hearth."

The rooms were huge and empty—no furnishings. Wood was laid in the fireplace, though, and there were candles and matches on the mantel.

"Do ye like it?" Ahab asked. The strange ordinariness of my groom's question almost made me laugh, and I did laugh, but mostly with the joy of the place and the unlikeliness of all that was culminating here. The candlelight reflected against the bare walls and flickered so unsteadily that the tall walls of the place bent and danced in light and shadow.

"All of it is for us?"

"I'll show ye."

And I followed my husband from room to room, my soul ever expanding. Our footsteps echoed through the empty first floor, where there were shelves in one room for a library, beautiful fireplaces located at both ends of the house, and along the front and back, large dark windows, unhung with curtains, reflected our candles and us when we passed. I felt a flicker of fear. The walls of the room Ahab said was the dining room were wrapped in wainscoting, and above that a mural of a whaling scene encircled the room. How strange it was to stand in a bare room as though the floor were the deck of a ship, but the painted scene was much busier with ships and whales and whaleboats than any I had seen at sea. I liked best the broad flukes of a plunging humpback whale.

As we ascended to the second floor, my fingertips trailed a curved banister of fine wood. Then again, he showed me too many rooms to count, all bare. "Ye shall furnish them as ye please," he said. And again I gasped.

At the door of one bedroom, he took out a key, and here in the bedroom there was a large, plump bed, hooked rugs, and curtains at the window. This room was as full and complete as the others were empty. He knelt to light the fire and then several lamps, till the room was bright and cheerful with the clear flame from sperm oil.

Just at the moment I felt acutely shy of asking questions—does one question the genie?—and shy before the worldly wealth implied in being married to a successful whaling captain. Ahab explained somewhat more fully that he only this morning had ordered this room to be furnished. Daggoo and Tashtego had trundled in the furniture. Then Ahab had walked out the Madaket Road to find me. I wanted to ask if he had known we would marry, but again I felt in awe and shy of the power that my husband commanded. His absolute power at sea I was well used to, but, except for the judge across the street, I had never spoken to a man of property on land. I did not question the legitimacy of our marriage, our power to define our lives. Again, in a kind, quiet tone, with none of his sea-gruffness, he told me he had been by no means sure that we would come together, but he had hoped. "My hope was like a slain whale that sinks before any harvesting—it will sometimes, ye know—but then miraculously buoys and rises again." He smiled at me. "And the prize the sailor thought was lost to him forever becomes rightfully his."

I had no nightgown, but Ahab said he would turn his back and I might slide unclothed into the bed. "It has enough of sheets and puffs to cover ten brides," he jested, and I did as he suggested. Then he went around and made sure curtains were closed, screwed down the wicks to the lamps, and turned the key in the lock. Peeping over the covers, I watched his unhurried preparations. Here was my husband, strong and happy, tucking us in for the night.

When he lifted the covers and came into our bed, I went to him with no shyness at all, but with love and purity and gladness of heart.

CHAPTER 83   A Sky Full of Angels

THE SPURT of the match woke me while it was still dark, and I opened my eyes to see my husband lighting a lamp. He sensed that my eyes had opened, and he said, still watching the flame mate the wick, that he must go early to the *Pequod*, but I flung my arms open to him and softly called, "My Ahab! My husband!" and he set down the lamp and came to me.

All was given; all was taken. And there was a rising in me and a release and a bliss in me that met the same in him and that I had never known before.

"I would have a child for your returning," I said.

"May it be so."

And he kissed me with such a mixture of tenderness and passion that I half felt myself a child, one to whom is given all love and all protection. And yet my woman's body yearned toward him, though I would not ask again, because I knew his need to embark.

Ahab took his leisure, and held me, and kissed my face many times. "If there can be but one night's dent in the marriage pillow, let us at least tarry over it." When I reminded him that I knew the ship waited, he said, "But now I'm with my love."

At times he seemed a dream to me, as we sat together in our luxurious white bed, for starched lace trimmed the linens and hung from the curtains. I had never imagined Ahab resting in aught but his rope hammock. But here plump pillows cushioned and pampered us and everything was ironed and smooth and white as snow.

The nap of it, indeed, was familiar to my fingers, and I asked my husband if, by chance, Mrs. Macy had ironed the linens. He said that she had procured them, but whether she had washed and ironed them he did not know. But I had no doubt of it.

"You did not say the linens were for me?" I asked a bit timidly. And he shook his head no. Would he, then, have had any bride, if I had not been willing? Though my goat-nimble mind thought of the question, to ask it would have been blasphemy. I knew my place in his heart, and I knew that he knew his in mine.

Then I marveled some (to myself) that I had known so little of my own course. I had been like a ship, blown about in dark and storm, suddenly finding, beyond all hope, that the dawn illuminated the port of home. And I thought back, recognizing how even aboard the *Pequod*, obsessed with the state of Kit's mind, I had always been comforted by Ahab's presence.

"I know when I first saw you," I said. "I was aboard the *Sussex*, looking through the captain's telescope. Standing at the tiller, your legs seemed wedded to the distant *Pequod*, your hands to her strong steering, and your face to the wind. I took away the telescope from my eye and you were gone, but the porthole framed the *Pequod* and the sea and sky."

"How was it you were aboard the *Sussex*?"

"Disguised as a cabin boy," I answered without hesitation. I smiled. "But I would have that story keep for another time." I was not afraid of his knowing any of my secrets, but I did not want to fill our time with a past that pertained only to myself.

"And my stories, too. They'll keep."

In the gaze that passed between us all was known, all was accepted, all transcended, as we inhabited our moment together.

"There's a room ye have not seen," he said.

Something in me shuddered. It was a sentence from Bluebeard's tale.

"And I would show it to ye before I leave."

I stepped immediately from the bed, reassured, and Ahab held a softly woven white blanket for me to wrap about myself. "Come, my lamb," he said softly.

We stood at the top of the stairs, and he handed me a wooden pole with a hook in the end. At first I thought it some equipment for whaling with which I was not familiar. But Ahab told me to insert the hook in a ring in the ceiling, and to pull. It would not be difficult. When I did so, almost like magic, a small staircase unfolded itself. Taking the pole from me, he bade me ascend the steep little stairs. Up I ran, gathering the wool blanket away from my feet, and there was a small, glass-sided room. An enclosed cupola, with its own tiny flat roof and a window facing each direction.

Dawn had come upon us. The dawn-drenched clouds suggested wings: mauve, purple, rose, gold-outlined—and the sky seemed full of gigantic beings. Though they had no real form, yet they flew and floated in their domain. "Angels" was all I could say.

Ahab joined me and said, "Aye," and stood behind me with his arms wrapped around me as we looked. For only a few moments those good angels soared as disembodied colors, swirled and thinned themselves in expansion, ever more immaterial. Ahab pointed, and I looked down from the sky to the harbor, to the *Pequod*, sails furled. A few insect-sized people moved about, and I thought the *Pequod* was like a tight-closed peony bud groomed by ants before the flower unfurls its petals. The clouds dissipated into blue.

I turned to inspect the small, glass-sided room. "It's a crow's nest made luxurious," I said. The little cupola held a rocking chair and beside the chair a brass telescope on a stand. "Here ye might watch for me," Ahab said. "Protected from the weather, here. And if there is a child, ye might have a cradle here beside ye. And if I am gone a long time, the child might look out the window at the ships and the sea."

"And I would speak of you, Ahab, of the father who loves his child from faraway waters." How fervently, how completely, I hoped that my new husband was leaving me with child! I took Ahab's hand and kissed it and watered the back of it with a few tears, and when I looked in his face, I saw that he, too, was ready to weep.

"Now," he said. "I have left money with the judge across the street, and I shall write a note of permission for ye to use it as ye will. And I will have Captains Bildad and Peleg, who are owners of the *Pequod,* call upon ye and help ye in any way they can. But they are stingy, and ye shall not be fettered by their ideas of parsimony. Nay, ye will make yourself merry in all your living and spending till I come home, and, meantime, you will write to me, and I to ye, even though we both know letters are often lost at sea. Look, Starbuck is bidding farewell to his wife and babe."

Though Ahab knew the likelihood of this event well enough to note it with the naked eye, I looked through the telescope and saw their last embrace. The child was but a knee-high bundle, but Mary's face, which I could barely glimpse inside her Quaker bonnet, was serene as any saint's, though her clothing was not resplendent.

Swinging the telescope away, I noted that the *Camel* was putting out. I hoped that my letters were not lost.

"I shall be happy here," I said. "This home—it overwhelms me."

"No, Una. I think nothing overwhelms ye. The cupola is the crown of the house, and ye in your person are diamond, ruby, emerald, and sapphire in that crown. I would not have ye overwhelmed by mere stationary boards and window glass."

I had thought to ask if I might visit the Lighthouse and even beyond to Kentucky, but with these words of Ahab, I changed my request to a statement. "I shall be happy. I know it. And likely I will journey to see my aunt and uncle, and my mother, as well, in Kentucky."

"But ye will not go to sea?" he asked me.

"No," I freely answered. And the vastness of the ocean came upon me, and the utter unlikeliness of two boats ever finding one another. The expansiveness of the ocean spread before me, not as one who has never been to sea might imagine it, but as I knew it to be, stretching day after day, and moonlight night, and black night, and star-pierced night after night, and endless swaying, and the creak of wood and rope, and the hissing through the water, and the smack of the wind taking sails. "Godspeed," I said to my husband. "Godspeed."

"May angels keep ye."

AFTER AHAB blessed me and bade me farewell, I stayed up an hour in the cupola and watched with the telescope as the *Pequod* was towed out of the harbor. Then she unfurled her sails and moved away. With the glass, I could view his expressions to some extent, and I was surprised to see the hard, captainlike lines in his face. I knew them well, since I had sailed with him, but of the softer radiance that he offered me when we were alone together I saw not a trace. And how masterfully his feet came down upon the boards! All his movement, hands and shoulders as well as feet, had the gestures of an athlete or warrior.

The three officers—Starbuck, Stubb, and Flask—were familiar to me, as were, of course, the new harpooners, Tashtego and Daggoo. A few others I also recognized, but there were many new faces among the crew, and I supposed that there was often a shuffling of crew members among the various whalers. I had seen Ahab shake hands with someone I took to be either Captain Bildad or Captain Peleg, the principal owners of the *Pequod*. This man seemed of an age with Ahab, and equally able-bodied and energetic.

I recalled an item Crèvecoeur wrote of his Nantucket visit in the 1770s: "You will hardly find anywhere a community . . . exhibiting so many *green* old men who show their advanced age by the maturity of their wisdom rather than by the wrinkles of their faces. . . ." Not that Ahab was an old man—his hair was more gray than white—and his body had a lean hardness to it, for all his gentleness with me, that carried no hint of aging. And his wrinkles were more a matter of facing into the weather than anything else.

After the ship was beyond the eastern horizon and after I had paced through my empty rooms many times and tidied my bedroom, I thought that I would cross the street (my spread clothes having dried out by the fireplace) and get some money of the judge. But who was the first person I saw when I stepped through my portico (houses of the Federal–Greek Revival style typically have recessed doorways, Ionic porticos, and granite steps, as well as the four end chimneys and squarish cupolas) but Isaac Starbuck, the gaoler, whom I had left for dead, his face and body covered by a sheet.

He was as startled to see me emerging from a fine house as I was to see him risen from the dead. We stuttered and stumbled with our speech till eventually we had communicated that when they bent his chest up to lift him onto the stretcher, he had gotten his breath again, and though weak and light-headed, he was quite all right, *and* (for *my* part) that I was now married to Captain Ahab and was a resident of the home between whose Ionic columns I was standing! The essentials having been exchanged, we said a hasty good-bye. On my part, nothing could have pleased me more than the enormous surprise of seeing that Isaac had survived and might now be hailed (I hoped) as the fire-burnished hero he was. But I knew, for his part, that the surprise of my sudden marriage—he had not asked how it came about—surely left something of an ashy taste. Perhaps he felt as had Gulliver after his travels—that he was not quite the same person nor his home the same place, upon his return.

And I felt ashamed of having seen him shirtless, the little cloud of golden hair upon his chest, in his extremity, though of course when I was a cabin boy I had seen all manner of male nakedness, which, along with the crude language of sailors, I have not tried to report in my narrative. But on Nantucket, I was a woman and a young wife who felt embarrassment. (I smile now at that self who could blush and tremble before the conventional, in spite of the terrible experiences I had survived. The time has come when taking off my own clothing is a confident, unafraid act, the most natural way to meet the waves.)

Nonetheless, I proceeded to cross the street, employ the brass pineapple knocker (deciding in the act to purchase a similar one for my home to advertise my hospitality), and present Judge Lord with the paper Ahab had left with me. After the judge invited me in (and again I sat upon the velvet sofa, this time making more careful note of items in his parlor that found particular favor with me), he went to his desk and drew out certain other papers Ahab had left with him and glanced back and forth between them, to compare—I was sure—the signatures. His surprise at finding Ahab to be a providing husband had engendered something close to incredulity.

But very soon, he looked up over his spectacles, smiled, and said, "Captain Ahab has long needed a wife and a family, and I am glad that it is you."

"Thank you." I am sure I blushed.

"And so you received word that Kit—"

"Yes, that Kit—" I began.

"—is dead," he finished. "And Captain Ahab, being due to sail, lost no time. Nor does he have time to lose, being a mature person. Even more so than I. But that's beside the point. The news about Kit came—?"

"Yesterday—oh, he's never never coming back!" I suddenly wailed. That yesterday inscribed the end of one life and the immediate beginning of another overwhelmed me.

"There, there," the judge answered. "Perhaps it's for the best. Most decidedly it's for the best. You mustn't weep. You're newly married! Think, you're just across the street. You must take tea with me, Mrs. Captain. An old bachelor like me would be honored. And, why, it will be no time—two years or so, why, maybe less—till Captain Ahab will come sailing back. Now, dry your tears. Here's a hankie."

He was so kind and so inept in his bachelor-but-dignified-judge way that I began to laugh as suddenly as I had cried. He tried to laugh along with me, but seeing nothing funny, he began to urge me not to become hysterical, but to calm myself. He rang furiously for his servant to bring us some tea. "And have you eaten, Mrs. Captain?"

"Not a bite."

"Well, then. We must get some ballast in ye—as a seaman might say."

And very soon I was eating buttered toast, followed by bacon, followed by fish, followed by oatmeal—all to ward off hysteria. And it worked very well. After a while, the judge took up business again.

"Did you read the letter that Ahab has addressed to me?"

Although it was merely folded and not even placed in an envelope, it had not occurred to me to read it.

"It says that you are to have a housekeeper. He suggests a Mrs. Macy."

"My friend. I worked for her."

"Captain Ahab says that I am to trust in your good sense about every financial matter—he has underscored 'every'—and that if it should seem you are a little extravagant at first, I am to encourage rather than discourage you! What a remarkable instruction! Well, what are you going to do?" Looking a bit like Ben Franklin, Judge Lord peered at me over small spectacles.

Now there was a question. I didn't know what I was going to do, which I said. And so I changed the subject for a time and asked about the little black boy. The judge replied that he would send him to Maria Mitchell, the daughter of an astronomer and banker on Vestal Street, to be educated in whatever way she saw fit.

"She takes both boys and girls together in her school," he went on, "and she will not object to a black child, being more liberal than even her Quaker forefathers."

"Would the Quakers not admit the boy?" I asked.

"No. Not at their meetings. There are separate black churches here on Nantucket."

"It's a bit disappointing," I said, "about the Quakers." I said it timidly, for I did not want to get in a dispute.

"They tried to make the Mitchells quit their piano," he went on.

Then I bethought myself of the family around the piano that Kit and I had noticed when we walked to town together that last time on Christmas Day. That had been on Vestal Street. The memory made me sad, and I became quiet.

I must say that at this point the judge, too, became quiet, and though he did not know the cause of my quiet, he did not try to fill up the silence, as so many would have done, but waited patiently. "I think that I will use some of the money to travel back to my old home," I said, and added, noticing his dismay, "After I furnish my new one. How long do you think it might take to furnish the house?"

"Did you know the house comes with a name?" First he told me it was Heather's Moor—for at its back, the heather-covered moor began and there were no more houses—and then he suggested that a month might be required to buy furnishings, if I was careful about my selections. "You might want to take the ferry for a short trip to Boston, to see what sofas and carpets and dishes they have there. And then come back." He was so kind as to offer to accompany me. "And Mrs. Macy, too," he added, with a bow to propriety.

To neither proposition did I give a definite answer, but I told him I much admired his furnishings.

Breakfast being over, he asked if he might be of any further service that morning. Rather to my own surprise, I asked him if he would mind to write to Charlotte out at the Try Pots and tell her the things that had happened. And to tell her I would not come out for my clothes for perhaps a week (here my eye noted my own reflection in the cherry top of the butler's table that held my breakfast), there being no urgent need of reserve clothing and I having much to do in town (I admired a scallop shell cast into the top of the handle of my silver spoon), but if Charlotte should come in, she must be sure to call on me.

I did not stop to think that the judge had not offered to serve as my secretary, but I was new to such neighbors, and it would take me a while to learn their customary limits and habits. I did know that I was glad to have Judge Lord for a neighbor, and I left his portal with some definite intentions, namely, first to visit a seamstress, and also to purchase some fabric, which I myself would sew up. To make something new, instead of mend! My head quite sang with it. Would I buy a new needle? No, my needle was too good a friend, but perhaps a silver thimble. One with an ornate *A* nestled inside, in the cup of it—for Ahab!

As I paused to look across the street at my house, a very dark-suited Quaker gentleman with a most stern countenance knocked at my door. Captain Bildad, or Captain Peleg. Whoever, he was much too somber for me this morning. I quite gave him the sly slip simply by staying on the judge's side of the street and walking toward the shops. After all, he didn't know me. I giggled with glee. Then I decided I would go give Mrs. Macy the news. And to think—I need not mourn Isaac, who, after all, was not dead.

CHAPTER 85   The Purpose of Art

COME TO PICK UP your mending? Not married yet?" Again her laundry tub steamed before the fire, but this time it was already full of sheets, and a scum of soap floated on top.

"No, Mrs. Macy." I tried to answer her first question.

"But your young man is up and about. Oh, I can see you're happy!"

"No." (He was not my young man.)

"What! Not happy?"

"No—" I struggled to correct the misassumptions of her question.

"No, again!"

"No, I mean yes. Yes, I am happy. And married."

"And a lovely golden fleece of a man."

"No—"

"No?" She laughed. "You don't think him lovely after one night."

"I only saw him this morning."

"And you had no joy last night?"

"No. I mean yes. But not with Isaac Starbuck. With Captain Ahab!"

"Captain Ahab! Well, blow me down." And she sank into the chair by the tub. "And you don't love the brave young man?"

"I'm delighted he survived." I thought how last night I had repined that I had loved him too little as a valued human being.

"And so ye regret?"

"My only regret is for Captain Ahab—"

"That's my meaning—"

"That Captain Ahab has already gone back to sea!" And here I let out a little shriek followed unexpectedly by a flotilla of boo-hoos. "I'm so happy," I sobbed, "with Captain Ahab."

"But you ain't with 'im." She rose from her chair and gestured for me to sit down. "That's just the problem. Now I've got it. You've come to the right place."

And with that she reached into her cabinet, pulled out a lumpy, clanky bag, loosed the drawstring, and poured the contents into my lap. What an array of porcelain devices! Some artfully decorated with flowers painted on the china shaft, others with ships, and male torsos ... the variety of sizes and shapes! Colors, too.

I was stunned.

"All under the covers, was it? Then close your eyes and just feel among them."

I was speechless.

"Which most resembles your captain?"

Now I erupted in laughing, and she laughed with me, and I told her, politely, that I should not be wanting such. She looked at me as though she knew much more than I, but on the point of an essential difference between flesh-and-blood and detached china, I had complete confidence. I turned the conversation to tell her that Ahab had been very generous in his leaving: I had a new house to live in, and, unless it was too short notice, I would not be doing any more mending.

"And you're such a fine seamstress. 'Tis a pity."

"Oh, I'll sew dresses for myself, and one for you, too, if you like."

"Ah my dear," she said, grasping my forearm, quite serious, "I've not had a dress made by any but myself since I was a girl."

"Would you like one?"

"A dress made for me by a captain's wife!"

"By Una, whom you employed and who can never adequately repay you for that."

"You are a dear," she said, kissing me on the cheek.

I proposed that she come with me and select whatever fabric she wished, but she said she must tend to the washing to keep on schedule, and that we would do it later. "Besides, I must sit down and recuperate," she said. "To think I really did bathe you for your bridal! And such a fortunate marriage."

So I left Mrs. Macy and commenced my shopping myself. Nantucket had so much beautiful fabric; I began to quiver as I touched it. I could have whatever I wanted. What was to keep me from buying miles of cloth?

My own good sense. I knew full well how long it took to stitch a dress. From much experience, I knew what yardage corresponded to practical ambition. So I chose fabric for two dresses and for underthings and breathlessly watched the clerk flop off yardage from the bolts, pull a thread across, straighten the diagonal, and flash his scissors through the fabric. My parcel was heavy enough that I decided to carry it home before visiting the baker's and the meat shop, for I knew I could not always eat with the judge. Yet when I reached home, there was in fact a note under my door inviting me to lunch across the street. Blithely I went.

This time the judge had me into his dining room, where places were set on a mahogany table, and he served apple jelly and crackers and thin beef soup until the main meal was ready.

"You had a caller," he said. "Captain Bildad."

"I think I noted him knocking," I said. "A rather dark captain?" I let my eye twinkle, for I felt that I had not just a neighbor but a friend in the judge.

"Indeed," he answered, with a corresponding twinkle. "He asked about your furnishings, Ahab having told him the house was bare in most rooms. Did you see some furnishings you liked in town?"

I replied I had not, though I had pursued other objects. "Where can I buy a door knocker fashioned like yours, like the pineapple?"

"Ah, that's from Boston."

"Boston?"

"Now, Captain Bildad tells me that he and his spinster sister will return and that they will personally help you buy; he is confident that all your needs can be met, with his guidance, by Main Street. He saw a black chair that he fancied for Captain Ahab."

"May I ask about your sofa? Was it purchased on Main Street?" The sofa was not a frank red, but more a cherry color—a delicious, subtle color.

The judge was chewing, but he shook his head and simply said, "Boston."

"And your lace curtains?"

"New York."

I laughed, and so did he. "Would you rather have his guidance or mine?" He was all atwinkle, and we were not only friends, but conspirators.

"I think we'd better slip off to Boston this afternoon," I said. "On the ferry."

"You need a proper chaperone. None more proper than myself." Mrs. Macy was forgotten. Besides, I knew she was busy.

AND SO it was that Judge Austin Lord and I took the ferry around Provincetown and on to Boston. We chatted the whole way, till we were hoarse. He was full of gossip about all of Nantucket and filled me in on the Coffins and the Crosbys, the Hadwens and the Barneys, the Starbucks, Swifts, and Swains, all intermarried to each other and dominating Main Street. The triplet houses, three bricks recently completed by Joseph Starbuck for his three sons, had cost a scandalous amount, the three together requiring an outlay of over $40,000. I asked if Mr. Starbuck of the *Pequod* was of that family, and the judge said certainly he was, but very distantly, the Main Street Starbucks being whaling merchants, but not actually whalers, as was the first mate, who lived more humbly out at Siasconset or 'Sconset, as the natives called it. Isaac Starbuck, the gaoler, was yet another strain of Starbucks.

We were gone perhaps three weeks. The sight of Quincy Market reminded me of how happy I had been seeing it for the first time with Aunt Agatha, Uncle Torchy, and Frannie. And how I had yet to face the terrible suspense of Frannie's illness. Then, when I admired the monuments, I hadn't known the *Petrel* existed.

In terms of Boston shopping, Judge Lord was as indulgent as ever my husband had instructed him to be. But I soon learned from a slight frown or lift of an eyebrow what my chaperon considered a good buy or a tasteful, well-made item. An expensive rug he actually urged me to buy, saying it was from India, while most people in Nantucket had rugs from China; and, further, that the pattern was rare—a kind of tree of life filled with birds and fruit. Yes, I wanted that. A tree of life.

It was a wonderful trip. Sometimes I regretted that neither Charlotte nor Mrs. Macy was there with me to share the excitement. I had written them both notes before I left home. Never again would I leave dear ones wondering what had befallen me. I knew too much now about how anxiety could wring the heart. In this mood, when I was alone in my hotel room at night, I dispatched additional letters to the Lighthouse and to my mother, telling them of my new, happy state, reminding them of what we had shared, and assuring them that I would soon come to visit.

Not only did we buy furnishings, china, and silver, but also books by the boxload. I told the judge to choose what he thought a well-stocked library should have, and I myself chose many books—often they were by authors whom I had read perhaps in a single volume, but now I swept my hands over the Complete Works of such writers.

IT WAS WHILE I was at a bookstall that I fell into conversation with the remarkable woman writer Margaret Fuller. As we stood on the sunny street, she showed me engravings of great art works—of Leonardo's *Virgin of the Rocks* and *La Gioconda*—and invited me to attend one of her Conversations for Women. Surprised by her spontaneous and intense invitation, I regarded her more closely.

Quick in her movements and speech, she had large and dreamy eyes. Her hair, parted in the middle, was the most smooth and glossy I had ever seen. Her claret dress fit beautifully, and I thought her the picture of elegance. I was glad that at least I had been in Boston for a fortnight and was not totally unused to sophisticated fashion. Because I felt timid, nonetheless, about accepting her invitation, I equivocated till I thought I might ask Judge Lord for an opinion.

He did not encourage me. But when I thought again on my own of Miss Fuller, her intensity and intelligence, I informed him that same afternoon that in fact I *did* intend to go. He but lifted an eyebrow. In some way, he seemed pleased that I had not taken his advice.

H O W W I S E I was! At Margaret Fuller's salon, women talked of magnificent ideas, of poetry and art, of science and travel. Never had I heard such discourse among women. Not one word of family or home or food or even sewing. I interjected the question did they not think that quilting could be an art form and perhaps the only art available to frontier women, and several, including Miss Fuller, quite agreed with me, though not all. "Quilts don't last," one said. *"Ars longa, vita breva."* Though I did not know Latin, I surmised what she was saying. "Nor would a painting last," I said, "if you covered yourself in bed with it. You might choose not to use a quilt, but simply admire it. Then I think it would last. My stitches would, I know." I was sorry I was wearing a dress, tailor-made, purchased in Boston, and so could not display my own fine stitches.

"What then is the purpose or purposes of art?" Margaret Fuller asked the group. And we went on to discuss the question of utility and beauty. She was very versed in German views, and often she quoted Goethe, whom she herself had translated. Very considerately, though Miss Fuller quoted fluently in German, she always followed with a translation for those of us who did not understand the language. But at one point, I could not help myself from saying simply how beautiful the German was.

"Shall I quote you one of my favorite lines? It's from a song."

We all waited, aglow. I felt so honored.

" *'Ich weiss nicht, was soll es bedeuten, dass ich so traurig bin.'* 'I don't know why I am so sad.' It's the first line from 'Die Lorelei.' But the rhythm is so much better in German, isn't it?"

We all agreed that it was. I wondered if there was some particular circumstance making Margaret Fuller herself sad, but the question seemed too intimate to ask in a chiefly intellectual discussion. Suddenly she told me I might call her Margaret, as the others did.

We returned to the subject of beauty, and our leader mentioned that some of the oldest art was associated, perhaps, with religious expression. She mentioned cave drawings, and the idea that those people had worshiped animals.

My mind began to buzz with ideas, and I remembered my question in the Unitarian gathering about their intelligence and souls—those of animals, that is, not Unitarians—and as though she read my mind, *Margaret* went on to speak of Mr. Emerson, who was dissatisfied with the Unitarians and wanted a less conventional, more philosophical worldview, which was being called Transcendentalism. And again my brain buzzed with the idea that no matter how liberal, how radical an idea might seem, and certainly Unitarianism had seemed more free than Universalism to me, one's thought could always be more free, and freer and newer still. I was so excited I could not speak, and many of us were speaking at once, so ignited were we by the breadth and flexibility of Margaret's mind.

When it was time to go, I asked Margaret when the next Conversation would occur, and I felt much disappointed to learn it would not be for another week, at which time I would have returned to Nantucket. She was interested that I lived in Nantucket and asked if I knew Lucretia Mott, but I did not. She saw I was disappointed at not being able to come again, and she kept me standing, chatting, at the door, after the others had floated like bright bubbles, though they wore winter coats, down the street. That I was from the wilderness of Kentucky also intrigued her.

I cannot begin to say how much I admired her. Though I guessed her to be only eight or ten years older than I, I associated her with my mother and my aunt, and her erudition was far more dazzling.

At the hotel, I tried to convey to Judge Lord some of the breadth of Margaret Fuller's allusions, but he was not nearly so interested as I had expected another book lover to be. "I should rather have you, my dear," he said, "describe to me exactly what you are seeing and thinking at this moment than listen to Margaret Fuller's dusty learning." A bit of me was flattered, but in the main, I was disappointed and frustrated that I could not rouse the judge with my enthusiasm. I was sure that he was wrong not to value Margaret.

The next day being our last for shopping, we arose early, but as we were going out the door, the desk clerk called that there was a note for me. It turned out to be an invitation from Margaret Fuller to spend the day with her in private conversation.

"Surely you'll not miss our last day of shopping?" the judge interjected.

"Dear Judge Lord," I replied, "please, you must shop. Buy whatever seems best. Don't spend too much, though. I would swap the whole boatload—except for the books—for this opportunity."

And what a breathless day! I think that it changed me forever, as some days do. As did the day when the *Petrel* came to the Lighthouse. "What *was* it like to live on the frontier?" Margaret asked, and how did those conditions affect thought? Might one be more bold and innovative there, and not only in meeting practical needs—but did practical needs enslave one? What was the role of fear? Did nature seem a moral guide? She said she was so interested that she was resolved to go herself to the West. "I would choose Illinois and Wisconsin," she said. "They are free of the scourge of slavery." The scourge! Yes, I thought, that was what it was. But she quickly passed on to speaking of the condition of women and spoke about the way *we* were bound in invisible chains.

When we had lunch, the conversation turned to art, and I mentioned that, much as I loved the engravings she had shown us, since they had no color, it seemed to me they falsified the art they represented. Here Margaret defended the gray engravings as yet allowing the *form* of those distant masterpieces to be available to us, even if their splendor was not. "Perhaps form is the more essential element," she suggested.

I thought, though, of the colors in the sky, and how they moved me, whether or not they assumed form, and I advanced the notion that art had both emotional and intellectual force. "Emotion may be embodied more readily in colors," I said, "while ideas might reside in the relationships of the forms to each other."

Margaret smiled; she called me "dearest Una"; she said I was a joy to talk with.

I was almost in a swoon, almost as much in love with her as I was with my husband. Yet I knew there was something magic and ephemeral about the day. After lunch we went for a walk on the Common, and she spoke again of the artificial restrictions that society had placed on women. I thought to tell her of my own life as a sailor, but I wanted to leave that life behind me. Margaret and I walked arm in arm, and she commented on historic spots and on architecture.

When we returned to her apartment, both of us a bit weary, we had tea, and I asked her if she would read some more German aloud to me. She saw this as a chance for a game: "I shall read only passages that in some way deal with a topic we have discussed during the day. And then, without translation, you must guess at their meanings." Had I not grown to feel that I could trust Margaret with all my uncertainties and questions, I would never have made myself vulnerable to committing such colossal errors. But Margaret said one might learn a language partly by guessing and intuition.

"I will give you a clue for our first passage," she said. "The word *Schicksal* means fate." Now I was ready, for we had much discussed whether women had a natural fate or only a conventional one in the present day, and I did remarkably well, many times, in guessing at the meanings of the German sentences. Much of the time Margaret's facial expression, and my growing knowledge of what ideas appalled or pleased her, came to my aid.

At length, she closed all her books and smiled at me, and I felt it was a sign that our day was over. Yet I could not let it go. "Would you not recite the line from 'Die Lorelei' for me once more?"

She did so, and then I gathered my courage and asked—for everyone needs a sister—if there was some particular instance that made her sad.

"I have spoken much," she said, "of the conditions men have imposed on women, of our deprivations, which are so unnecessary and wasteful. Of course, some men do understand this. There have also always been some men who were fair-minded and possessed imagination. I think that imagination is an important part of what makes change possible. One must be able to imagine what it is like to be a woman, or a slave, if one is moved to remove artificial barriers. To remove unjust legalities. But, Una, I have also found that even among men with transcendent minds there can be a lacking."

"What sort of lacking?"

"It is in the realm you spoke of so eloquently at lunch. Great minds may have cold hearts. Form but no color. It is an incompleteness. And so they are afraid of any woman who both thinks and feels deeply. That is perhaps the sorrow that you sense in me."

"But then, you do know why you are sad."

"I know it only by fits and starts. I cannot accept the idea. I do not accept it. I want to burst through it. I want to strike through the wall that separates thought and feeling, and let there be free-flowing commerce. I want to know a great mind among men, one in whom beats a passionate heart *and who recognizes me*."

This last part was said almost savagely. Much later I came to realize she meant Mr. Emerson. Her own passion seemed to have ravaged Margaret's mind, and she put her hand to her forehead. "There now," she said, "I've said too much. I shall have a migraine." Her heavy eyelids hooded her eyes.

I tried to thank her for the day she had given me. At first, she smiled a little weakly, and still held her forehead, but as I talked, she gradually lowered her hand. "It has passed," she said. "I've had these headaches since I was a child—from studying too much Latin and Greek. My father was a demanding teacher."

"Was he? So was mine, in his own way." I thought that the similarities in our fathers might be an element in our own rapport.

"He had me reading Ovid by age eight, in the original. Yet, I am grateful for the pains he took with my education."

"With my father, it was only the Bible. But he was exacting."

"But the Bible is among the greatest literature," Margaret replied.

I did not want to overstay my welcome. At the very end, Margaret said, "I should be glad for you to write to me. Someday I shall write a book about women. At the beginning, I shall say: 'Let them be sea captains—if they will!'"

I wanted to tell her I knew we women could at least be sailors, for I had been one, but that would be to initiate a new topic. So I went away, her glorious words singing in my mind: *Let them be sea captains*.

WHEN I returned to my house on Nantucket, I noted with a start how empty the rooms were. Restlessly, I walked about in all that walled space. It was mine, yet I had not properly filled it or inhabited it. I was eager to unload our Boston prizes and position them.

Only the bedroom was a haven of comfort. I was tired, and I lay upon the bed to rest. And I missed Ahab very much. I wondered if he would be pleased with the furniture and china I had bought. What would Ahab think of a woman captain? He was not conventional, and I did not anticipate that this idea, or any idea, would shock him. But his daring and independence seemed more spiritual than intellectual to me.

I bethought me to count the days since I was married to Ahab. And then I counted back again. Why, where were my menses? I leapt from the bed and paced around and around the house. Perhaps the emptiness of the rooms belied my own state, for perchance *I* was not empty! I stood in the middle of my dining room and enjoyed the mural of the surrounding ocean. I placed both hands tenderly on my own belly and smiled at the painted sea.

CHAPTER 86   **The Office of a Friend**

Wᴴɪʟᴇ ᴛʜᴇ ꜰᴜʀɴɪᴛᴜʀᴇ was being moved into my house (the door constantly opening to fan the flames of the four small fires I had lit in the fireplaces), while I was in the midst of directing the movers, who should walk in next—not my china cabinet—but Charlotte. She carried a small bundle of my things. I threw my arms around her. I asked the men to bring us two chairs and a small table, and we camped before the marble hearth of the parlor.

As soon as we were settled, I realized that Charlotte, in the five or so weeks since I'd seen her, had been ravaged by grief and was even now in a most unsettled state of mind.

"I received the letter from the judge," she began, "so I'm not at all surprised, and I am happy for your good fortune—"

"Captain Ahab," I interrupted, "like your dear Mr. Hussey, is quite a bit older—"

"But Kit—" And here she burst into tears. She hunched her shoulders and hung down her head and sobbed. The name of the flower "Bleeding Heart" came to mind, and I reached out with both hands to soothe her trembling shoulders. Behind her chair, the movers carried rolled rugs and boxes of china, never glancing at us.

Yes, Kit. Was I so unmoved by his situation? Then I remembered: I knew him to be alive; Charlotte thought him dead because the judge would have written her so. Indeed, I had hoped that he would pass on to her his own mistaken notion that Kit was dead, so that Charlotte would forgive my marrying Ahab. But her inconsolable pain! She was the image of my own grief at Giles's death. I scooted my chair closer and leaned my bosom into hers. I found her hand in her lap and squeezed it hard.

"Have you no grief for Kit?" she finally burst out. "I am devastated," she wailed.

I resolved to tell her that Kit was not dead, but I did not want to shock her sensibility, so I started obliquely. I began quietly, "I have news to tell you. May I?" She grew more calm and nodded assent. "Ahab and I had but the one night, Charlotte. But, Charlotte, I find that I am with child."

At this she entirely stopped weeping. "So you are to have a child!" And then she burst out crying again in a strange mixture of joy and continuing sorrow. She added, "I think I shall never have a child, for it has been months with Mr. Hussey and me."

Then I felt very bad for her.

"But I don't want to have a child," she blurted out. I saw one of the movers swing his head in our direction. "I want Kit."

"Charlotte, Charlotte," I cooed. "You must stay with me for a while. I will cheer you up. You must help me get my kitchen in order, and I will make you a dress. I'm going to make one for Mrs. Macy. Such measuring and snipping and sewing we'll have! And I'm to have a housekeeper, so we'll do no work at all but what we choose. You'll go with me to lectures, and we will have an endless gam."

"What will Mr. Hussey do without me?" She sniffled, but her crying was over. "Una, could we place a plaque to Kit in my church?"

"We can buy anything we please. Captain Ahab is very rich. Oh, Charlotte, why don't you and Mr. Hussey move the Try Pots into town? You'd have much more business if the sailors didn't have to walk down the Madaket Road. Let's do. Oh, please, let's do it. I will help you. I'm to do just as I please with the money."

At this, she jumped from her seat, threw her arms around me, and sobbed anew. I began to feel aquiver myself in sympathetic vibration with her overwrought state. Consciously, I tried to calm myself. For the baby's sake, I hoped that having her in the house would not disturb my equilibrium. I condemned the selfishness of such thinking, for this was Charlotte, who had taken Kit and me into her home when a lesser soul would have protected the peace of her own household. Though I duly prevailed upon her to spend the night, to sleep in my own bed with me, she eagerly prepared to leave, saying she would return to the Try Pots to discuss its relocation with Mr. Hussey.

I had not amended her knowledge of Kit's situation.

Might not Charlotte proceed on a more even keel if she grieved for Kit as dead and gave up the idea of him? The joy of all the society of town might make up for the loss of one Kit Sparrow, who was, at best, half a figure created by her fantasy. All the time I directed the movers and unpacked my bright silver, I mused over this question and another: What about my reputation with myself for truthfulness? Perhaps it was only self-serving not to tell her the truth about Kit.

I looked up to see Judge Lord, along with a freckled woman. She was Mrs. Macy's sister Lenora Sheffield, and the judge proposed I hire her as my housekeeper. I was glad to do so, Mrs. Macy herself having declined. Straight off, leaving Lenora in charge, the judge carried me away from the bustling to his house to take tea. Here civilization was already in place.

"And how will you arrange the books of your library, Mrs. Captain?"

"Why, alphabetically, by the author's last name," I replied.

He opined that the books should be put in coarse categories, such as literature, history, science, and art, and within the sections be arranged by date of publication. "In each discipline, knowledge evolves," he said, "and this way you will have a picture of the development of ideas. Alphabetizing is arbitrary."

I could not but agree his plan was a more rational one, though mine might be more convenient in some ways. Nonetheless, I acquiesced to his system. While we talked and ate—he had noted my fondness for exotic jams and had stocked up on them (secretly) in Boston—a part of my mind began again to contemplate the truthfulness issue.

I had not corrected his erroneous assumption about Kit's fate; nor did I have any impulse to do so. Of course, it was not an important issue to him, though it was to Charlotte. Neither had forced me to fabricate details of Kit's supposed death. And my allegiance to Charlotte, my integrity as Charlotte's friend, was for me a spiritual issue, not merely a moral one. Still, I was troubled and pondered many times if I was being honest with myself in considering the reasons for silence. I was glad their assumption of Kit's death arose from their own simple misunderstanding, and I had not compounded it with details. Perhaps Charlotte thought I was not possessed of much information.

Wondering what Margaret Fuller would say to such a distinction between spiritual and moral matters, I asked the judge if he thought there was a difference. He liked the question.

"Many churchmen would say, Una, that the spiritual is the foundation of the moral. Belief in a just God causes us to be good."

"Yet there are moral folk who are not religious."

"Do you truly think so?"

"I myself am one."

"You have an interest in the Unitarians."

"Because it is a church that grants me freedom of thought. It does not dictate my actions."

"You probably have the potential for highly immoral acts, if none of God's commandments bind you. But I believe that God's laws are the foundation for the laws of a just society."

"Do you find Moses' commandments a complete guide for behavior?"

"Of course not: Jesus added the laws of love."

I remembered that he was an enthusiastic Methodist. "Do you think that love can be governed by law? I think love is a disobedient emotion."

" 'Thou shalt not commit adultery.' The law is in place to meet that unruliness."

" 'Thou shalt not eat thy neighbor.' There is no such law." What a boldness had come upon me! "Yet all civilized folk abhor the practice. It is an absolute tabu."

"Well, I rather think 'Thou shalt not kill' takes care of the matter." He stirred his tea triumphantly.

"But suppose someone else has done the killing?"

"I think that loving your neighbor as yourself covers the case. How would you like to be eaten?" The judge looked mischievous.

"I think I should not mind it," I said soberly. "If I were dead."

"I certainly could not bring myself to eat another human being."

There was something in his smugness, his erect posture on the needlepoint seat of his chair, the unswaying stability of the room, that made me burst out at him: "Suppose you were starving. Starving unto death. And those about you whom you loved, on the very verge of death. And one of the company dies. Would you not urge your companions to take and eat? I would! I know I would! And were I the dead person, it would have been my last wish that I be consumed so that others might live." And with this declamation, I crumpled into crying.

"My dearest Una, let us change the topic. Such extremity need not be imagined. You are not in a wilderness. There is no starvation here. These issues are gruesome and hypothetical. They are morbid and Germanic. Are you quite well? Exhausted by the travel and the excitement, I think?"

I thought to tell him I was pregnant, but I was shy of such a disclosure. "Germanic?" I thought of Margaret Fuller's great interest in the Germans' thought.

"Oh, Goethe," he said. "*The Sorrows of Young Werther*. It swept Europe in morbidity. People fancied themselves too sensitive to live, if they could not have the object of their love. Werther committed suicide because his beloved Charlotte was married to another. Young people throughout Europe followed suit."

"Did we buy this book?"

"Not I."

I instantly resolved that I would write to Margaret, who, after all, was an expert on Goethe, and ask her to send the text and to comment on the inclination to morbidity as engendered by that writer. Perhaps there was in Margaret, in her essential sadness, a certain love of sorrow?

"Why do you shake your head?"

"Did I? It was at my own line of thinking. For myself . . ." I spoke slowly, for with the judge, as with Margaret, and with Ahab—though how different each was!—I could discover my thought in his presence. "For myself, I reject sorrow as essential to my being. I would pursue joy."

"It is part of your essential health." My friend smiled at me, though there was still a trace of concern about his eyes.

We changed our tea topic to the Try Pots, and I divulged my plan.

In response, the judge stayed carefully neutral. Not even the lifting of his black eyebrow betrayed whether he thought my plan foolish or wise. I rather admired this careful neutrality. And he was helpful, making various suggestions about vacant lots and their availability for building. Suddenly he said, "It would be nice for you to have your close friend at hand, wouldn't it? With your permission, I will make further inquiries."

Soon our discourse was broken off by a knock from the foreman of the movers, saying all was complete, and they were leaving.

"Would you like me to accompany your inspection?" the judge asked.

"Thank you, but . . . but I think I should like to amble my house by myself."

A S   I   W A L K E D   through my home, furnished with the beautiful objects that I had bought, occasionally adjusting a chair, lifting a curtain, or tugging out a wrinkle in a rug, I felt myself blessed beyond any deserving.

And I thought that I would not tell Charlotte that Kit was yet alive. Though it left me a liar, it left me having placed a higher value on Charlotte's happiness than on my own clean conscience. But was it not arrogance in me that made me think I knew best in the matter, that my hand at the stopcock had the wisdom to regulate the flow of truth?

The image oddly caused me to see myself as a male wizard in the midst of experimentation. And oddly that image gave way to one of Ahab, his hand on the tiller of the *Pequod*. The ship parted the waves at his will. I missed my husband.

Everything being in order, the house being left with Mrs. Macy's sister as guardian housekeeper, not to mention Judge Lord across the street and Mr. and Mrs. Hussey in residence while they directed the construction of their new inn, it was time to commence my journey to the silent Lighthouse and thence on to Kentucky.

CHAPTER 87   Childhood as an Island

SENTIMENTALLY, I wished I could hire the *Camel* to take me back to the Island, as it had taken me away. But Captain Mustachio was away. I hired a sloop to take me directly from Nantucket to the Lighthouse.

As I sailed away from Nantucket, I felt the final loosening of the bonds that marriage to Kit had imposed upon my spirit. Now I was married, but because my husband was independent, so was I. Yet I missed Ahab, and a lump rose in my throat whenever I thought of him. I thought of John Donne's poem "A Valediction: Forbidding Mourning," in which one is to imagine a compass describing a circle. The woman is the fixed point of that inverted V formed by the stance of the two-legged compass upon the paper. While the circle is drawn, the woman who is at its center merely turns in place. The man makes his circular voyage. Donne says that if the circle of the man's voyage widens to a larger radius, then the fixed foot "leans, and hearkens after it," which is true: as the circle becomes larger the compass stretches ever flatter to the page. So I felt myself to ever be harkening and leaning after Ahab as he sailed farther and farther away, even though in my case I had my own little journeys to make. In spirit, I was fixed in place, yearning, if not mourning, for my husband.

And when the voyager comes home—to complete the compass figure—the twin arms embrace; he stands perpendicular to the page, erect, his wife beside him.

During the last three weeks in Nantucket, waiting for spring as a safe time for my own travel, my longing for Ahab, my strong desire that he should see his hearth and home so beautifully and completely furnished, that he should take happy pride in my pregnancy, that he should share again with me that bed where our heads had made but one dent—all such desires had grown every day. My waist was thickening ever so slightly; in my breasts a special tenderness rapidly developed. I needed much sleep, and my appetite, particularly for the judge's jams and jellies, increased geometrically. (The judge had found an importer of the wares of missionaries' wives; hence, my jellies might be based on mangos from India, kiwi, coconut, pomegranate from the

Holy Land. From the California territory came an avocado paste that I adored on salty crackers.)

When two more weeks had passed and there was no possibility of error, I told the judge that Ahab and I were to have a child; then the judge branched into other fine foods for me—caviar from Russia, French pâtés, double Gloucester cheeses, heart of palm, water chestnuts from China. I saw him every day and ate with him perhaps as frequently as every other day.

As I sailed the open water toward the Lighthouse, it pleased my grateful heart no end that Charlotte and Mr. Hussey had decided to move to town and that I had been able to offer them hospitality at Heather's Moor. Their new tavern would be more extensive than the old one, though many of the old fixtures, including the wonderful seasoned chowder pots, were to be moved. Mr. Hussey insisted that I be given a silent partnership in the new Try Pots Tavern, which he swore would eventually bring me in a nice income. The judge himself considered the money I provided to be a wise financial investment, though I would have been happy to throw it down a rat hole for their sake.

Charlotte invested the relocation of home and livelihood with her usual radiant cheer. She seemed truly happy, and I was glad I had chosen to let stand the judge's erroneous conclusion that Kit was dead. I tried my best to examine motives advantageous *to myself* in the idea that I had become a widow before becoming a wife for the second time, but I convinced myself that *Charlotte's* welfare accounted for my choice primarily. I was not entirely pure, and to this day I feel some guilt and discomfort over the issue. But human beings are morally complex, women as well as men, and I must live with that.

During these weeks, as the spring came on, I had run up two beautiful dresses for my dear Nantucket friends Charlotte and Mrs. Macy, and I wrote twice to Margaret Fuller, who duly sent me the works of Goethe, but alas they were in German, which she bade me learn. By another route, I acquired English translations. I preferred the story *The Apprenticeship of Wilhelm Meister* to that of Werther; while Werther disintegrated, Wilhelm learned from the wonder of life, and grew.

My sea journey took but a day and a night and half of the next day. We were a little out of our way, for my boat commander perceived squalls developing on the horizon ahead, and he wisely chose to navigate around. In truth, I did not like the idea of a rough sea. While I had had no experience at all of nausea with my pregnancy, I did not want to test my immunity.

The Lighthouse appeared as vague as a stroke of charcoal, on its headland, in the misty distance, much as it had when I was twelve years old and approaching it for the first time. It seemed to me a totem of family love, insular, safe, and complete. My excitement was an evanescence all through my body. I hoped my babe, no larger than a small fish, swam in those bubbles and participated in their joy. What wonderful people they were—Uncle, Aunt, and Frannie. I adored and treasured each of them. And their new child, too.

Now I could see that the column was made of stones, and I could discern the open balcony that encircled the tower just below the lantern room. As they had approached in the *Petrel,* Kit and Giles had seen me up there, fighting an eagle. The roof of the cottage became visible when the *Cricket* hove around the headland and approached the small wharf on the low side of the Island. Goats! They still had the goats.

A wind was coming up steadily, and it must have been fierce enough on the Island to keep the family inside. Smoke came from the chimney, puffing away quickly in the wind. I wanted them to notice our arrival and come out. I wanted to see Frannie jumping with delight.

As we approached the dock, a child in brown trousers ran from the door. Not Frannie, and far too old to be the new baby, if he was a boy. Perhaps they had taken in another cousin. I felt a small stab of jealousy. I wanted nothing to have changed; I wanted no replacement by some distant kin. I felt confused by this child, who exhibited no particular excitement in us.

I stepped onto the dock, while the boy called over his shoulder, "Ma! Pa!" His adults came out—not Aunt and Uncle. My head spun with the confusion and disappointment of it. I nearly fainted and went down on one knee. Quickly the woman ran to help me up. I peered into her face, which acted as my mirror, as though I had lost my mind. Here was a pale, middle-aged woman, with smooth brown hair and brown eyes. An ordinary woman. Nothing of Aunt's fierce spirit about her. She was speaking, but I could not answer her. The captain of my sloop came forward, explaining for me, and they helped me into the house.

Here again, all was changed. The table was in the middle of the room, not with one end lodged against the window. Different rugs were upon the floor. No basket of shells sat on the hearth.

The stone walls were the same; the tower had appeared the same, but these were like empty shells, inhabited not by their natural spirits but by hermit crabs. These people shocked me in their physical beings, for not being Aunt, Uncle, and Frannie. They seemed grotesque.

Eventually, I learned that my kinsfolk had moved.

Where had they gone?

Inland. Inland. They were gone to the Great Lakes. That coastline also needed lighthouses and keepers. They had gone to the inland sea. I was invited to eat, but I could not. As soon as I had my wits about me, I told the boatman we would leave. Though he thought me not altogether well and proposed he take me back to Nantucket, I told him I had everything I needed for the trek to Kentucky, and I directed him to sail to New Bedford.

I sat in the stern of the boat. The weather was coming in on us, and an ever-thickening mist veiled the cottage and the tower. While the place seemed dreamy and unreal, I knew it was solid enough. The buildings were of stone and endured. But the soft life within, the past I had assumed was immutable and permanent, had fled like a ghost, like forgetting.

I made myself look forward. Then, like Lot's wife, I felt compelled to look back. I saw the column on its bulge of earth, like a monument on a grave. As I watched, the tower seemed to break in the center and fold itself, headfirst, into the sea.

I made no cry, for I had no faith that anything was real.

CHAPTER 88   The World of Rebekkah Swain

YOU DON'T get it back," Rebekkah Swain said to me. Like a gigantic furnace, powerful enough to heat all of New Bedford, she glowed behind the desk in a dress of red satin with a golden panel, wide as a road, down the center. "At least not the same room." Floating above the registration counter, her face seemed rounder than the sun.

On the counter sat a magnificent globe of the world, such as might have graced a rich man's library instead of the desk of the Sea-Fancy Inn. I wondered if the proprietress recognized me. Her own mixed and multiple heritage presented itself in her countenance. "And who are you now?" Rebekkah Swain asked, even as I attempted to puzzle out the essence of her identity.

"The wife of Captain Ahab of the *Pequod*. Una."

"Ahab! That volcano! Has he erupted yet?"

"What do you mean?"

She did not reply, but studied me. "So you've married him. He's old."

"I am with child."

With her hands, she smoothed her own enormous belly. There could have been ten babies lodged there, or a hundred. She smiled and continued to rub her belly. "Another baby?"

"It is my first."

"Another baby," she repeated. "And you yourself have traveled a long way." With one finger she poked one side of the hemisphere of her stomach; with the other hand, she indented the other side. "From here to here, yes? Halfway around the world and back?"

"Partway back," I replied, following her metaphor. "I'll travel over-land to Pittsburgh and then steamboat down the Ohio, to home."

"Here. Sign the book." She handed me a quill. "Wait." She turned the page. "I'll give you a clean page. It's more than most get."

"And you have a room for me?"

"For you? People have moved on. Graduated, you might say. I think a vacant room is on the ground floor now. Next to mine."

"Then I've come down in the world instead of up."

"Turn the world upside down, and you've come up." From its cradle on the counter, she grabbed the globe and inverted it. "It depends on you, how you count my meaning."

If anything, she was more enormous, this woman who had used her house as a chair. Swollen with living, she seemed. Her face and head were nearly the size of a small tub; her body was far fuller than any washtub I had ever seen. Her head, her body, and the globe seemed like three gigantic soap bubbles stuck together. They grew larger, trembling, as I watched.

"I'm dizzy. May I go to a room?"

I LAY DOWN at once, hanging my feet over the edge of the strange bed so as not to sully the coverlet.

When, as a virgin in a navy-blue dress, I last rested at the Sea-Fancy Inn, Rebekkah Swain had seemed more friendly. Now she radiated heat, glowing and glowering, ready to melt me down for recasting. Then I had imagined her protective, instructive. She had sent me aloft, so to speak, to the top of the house; she had given me a view. Now she was not quite menacing, but I did not understand her at all. She seemed unpredictable, and for all her solid flesh, insubstantial, as though she quivered at the threshold of disappearing into nothingness, as bubbles do.

I myself felt unmoored, drifting. It was my disappointment at the Lighthouse, I thought. Frannie and I had played at making the tower a kind of god. But the granite shaft had only been the most conspicuous feature of the godhead, like a gigantic nose supported, after all, by surrounding features and the rocky skull. The stone cottage, the people who dwelt there, the Island itself—they all composed the icon of my childhood. What did it mean that the column buckled and fell into the sea, that the mist shrouded all? Had I sailed irrevocably to another land? Suppose my mother was dead!

When I had left what was dear to me, at sixteen, I had scarcely considered remaining on the Island. My life had seemed *away*. Seeming, seeming—it is a world of seeming, and Mrs. Swain was right: what I had lightly left was now most precious, and my struggle was to reclaim it. Perhaps pregnancy made me dizzy. Topsy-turvy, I seemed to walk on the ceiling, my head hanging down, and I looked up to look down.

Below, with my mind's eye, which perhaps is the only true eye, I saw a sinuous river, the Ohio, brown, freighted with mud, curving through the mixed green of hardwood and pine, toward home.

My perspective floated yet upward, past clouds and through the thinnest blue. I traversed clear nothingness to a ghostly daytime moon. From thence, across the space of nothing, Earth tumbled and bounced, untethered, like a child's runaway ball. Mutating, the world took the shape of Mrs. Swain, looking like a Chinese pincushion such as sailors bring home for their wives. Bent over in a satin sheen, holding her ankles, Mrs. Swain's back, big as the curve of the world, presented itself as a stable for gigantic pins.

I gulped and swallowed myself back inside my brain, my room, where I lay fatigued, with my feet over the end of the bedstead. Sleep sat beside me and soothed my brow with the hand of a woman. Almost asleep, floating down the corridor of memory to the second floor of Mrs. Swain's Sea-Fancy, I sought the hall of women, where each had bent her eyes to her art. I could not see them; they had vanished. My fancy denied me their figures. Neither the Aleut with her cud of leather nor the Belgian with her web of lace pinned to the cushion in her lap, nor any woman, remained, but, in their empty seats, they had left their work.

CHAPTER 89   Kentucky Seasons

I FIRST SAW her bent, cultivating the garden. Even as my hired driver stopped the buggy, she straightened and peered to see who was arriving. In an instant, she knew me, dropped the hoe, almost stumbled over its long handle, and ran toward me with both her arms spreading out like wings. And I to her.

My mother! Found. Found again in all her softness and love, generosity and intelligence. Holding me. Almost, the pleasure in her face assumed the lines of pain.

Inside, the cabin was dark in the way log houses are, but I saw that her bed was covered with a new quilt, and a new braided rug was upon the hearth. The interior seemed at once both strange and familiar, and it held a strange quietness. Dangling from a peg on the mantel, a shiny popcorn popper glinted. After the driver placed my travel chest at the foot of the smaller bed, I watched my mother pour sassafras tea—we were together, yet caught in a strange medium of air and time that never stirred—watched her cut a slice from a loaf of bread and butter it for me. Two chairs were placed already facing each other across a table before the spring fire, but she moved her chair so that we were side by side and passed her arm around my waist.

"You are my Easter," she said.

Only my letters from New Bedford and those borne by the *Thistle* from the *Sussex* had ever reached either her or the Lighthouse folk, from whom she had received communications.

She fingered the ivory bracelet I wore instead of a wedding band, the circle of whales. "You have had much to do with the sea?"

"I am married to the captain of a whaler. We will have a child. He's gone back to sea, and I've come home to you to have my child."

She smiled at me a slow, tired smile. "It takes the place of the child I lost."

I held her in my embrace, and we rocked each other. With our rocking I felt that sometimes I mothered her and sometimes she mothered me, and that was how it should be.

Releasing me, she said, "Eat your bread, Una." And she straightened her back.

I asked her about Aunt Agatha and Uncle Torchy and learned that they had been yet unsure which of the Great Lakes they might settle on when they had last written to her.

"They have reversed themselves," I mused. "Once they were on land surrounded by ocean, and now their water is embraced by land."

Their baby thrived, as did Frannie. "Do you notice?" my mother asked. "I've reversed the room so that I can lie abed and see the rising of the full moon."

"I have been married before, Mother. I married Kit Sparrow, about whom I wrote you when they visited the Lighthouse."

"Kit and Giles." She rose and took a worn envelope from under her pillow. "It was the last letter I received from you from the Lighthouse."

I let it lie on the table. I did not want to clutch after the hopeful girl who had written that letter. Her disappointments made me sad.

"When did Kit die?"

"I don't think he is dead. I hope he is alive. But as a husband, he is dead to me, Mother. He became insane. I heard he's traveled to the far West. He sent word he would never return."

My mother squeezed my hand, and that was the last we said of my marriage to Kit. But of Kit himself, and of Giles, of Ahab, of Charlotte, of Sallie of the *Albatross*, we spoke freely during that spring, as we worked the earth. Through the days, we planted vegetables, picked wildflowers, cooked, sat outside before the sunny door to sew. I did not tell my mother of the hardship I had undergone in the open boat—only that we had been stove by a whale and rescued by the merchant ship.

"Stove?" she asked. "Stove?"

And this and many other seafaring terms that appeared in my speech I explained to her. I had brought the Goethe translations with me, and, to my surprise, she liked the tale of Young Werther very much. "That is how much it hurts sometimes," she said, and I knew she spoke of the loss of my father.

I sensed that she felt delicate about discussing him with me. "Religion closed his mind with a darkness," she said one night, sensing my questions. "He was not always that way. He once loved light things." She shook the popcorn popper above the embers. "Popcorn," she said. "And honey. He would guzzle honey like a bear."

Through the spring, we cultivated and planted, expanded the old garden in anticipation of even greater bounty. In the barn she kept but one cow, and once a week some neighbor would usually come by to exchange game for our excess of dairy products, or some of our eggs. Sometimes my mother swapped a few chicks for venison, saying I needed to eat some red meat, but this meat was stringy, the deer not yet having fattened very much.

Though we did not hitch the mare to visit—people came to us—I was delighted to find the same old mare in the barn that my father had had when I was a small child. She nickered and seemed to know me, and we took her out once a week just to keep her used to the harness.

"The barn was difficult for me," my mother said. And she pointed to the rafters from which his body had hung. It was not hard to imagine him darkly swinging there, where dust motes danced in a shaft of sunlight. "The neighbor men came and cleaned the floor and the stalls and the loft, and that seemed to help. They offered to take this one down and build me another smaller barn from the boards. Two offered to buy the whole place."

"You could come home to Nantucket with me. Our house is very large."

"I'll visit you. When you have your next baby. I don't want to leave my home. Not yet."

That summer we often walked the woods; several times Mother and

I walked as far as the river and baited up our hooks and fished. Sometimes a paddlewheeler would pass, and we would wave.

All the time, my baby grew within me. My body was completely at ease. I loved my roundness, the way my stomach bloomed under my apron. My mother made a little quilt for the baby, and its stitches were but half as long as ordinary. I told her it seemed that it had been sewn by an ant. I had brought delicate cotton batiste with me in the sea chest, and I made the baby seven little dresses, one for each day of the week, and each with a bit of embroidery in a different color around the collar or sleeves or hem. Sunday's dress had a purple cross-stitch about the neck, and Monday was a yellow chain running across the bottom of the yoke. Tuesday was a feather stitch, cardinal red, around the tiny sleeve cuff. Thus, I moved through the week in a rainbow, with the trim a bit lower, on the collar, the yoke, the sleeves, the waist, and down the skirt, for each day. Saturday was represented by a double row of green and blue scallops, for the sea, at the hem of the little garment. I didn't know why I did this: it pleased my fancy.

I described the *Pequod* to my mother, and she gave me the back of an old envelope to sketch it on. The preciousness of paper was a sign of how backward we still were on the Kentucky frontier.

"Though Lewis and Clark ran short of nearly all their supplies," I remarked, "when they wintered beside the Pacific, they always had plenty of paper."

"Clark's brother died at Locust Grove, down the river ten miles or so. I imagine they had plenty of paper, too." She lifted her eyebrows and smirked. "But this ain't Locust Grove."

Although my drawing was wobbly, my mother used it as a pattern to work a cross-stitch sampler of the *Pequod*. "You must hang it in your cupola," she said. "Show it to the baby, and tell him to watch through the spyglass for that ship." Under it she worked a rhyme, which she said she had heard in her Boston Quaker school. The cross-stitched verse was supposed to encourage boys to stay home and be scholars instead of running off to sea:

A Ship Is a Breath of Romance
That Carries Us Miles Away.
And a Book Is a Ship of Fancy
That Could Sail on Any Day.

I did not tell her that a whaling ship could be more like a Butcher's Shop than a Breath of Romance. It sometimes amazed me how well I knew, now, with my mother, what to say and what to omit. I was sure she did the same for me, and always had, though our discourse was unusually free. But we would not give each other pain.

Always on her face was her love for me. Even if I had only been out in the yard a few moments, when next she saw me, her face shone out in gladness, and always there was a steady radiance. Many times she thanked me for coming home to share the joy of my waiting with her.

Of Ahab I thought chiefly at night, as I lay in bed waiting for sleep. I missed him and loved him. I thought in his direction, but I did not try to write to him. The fate of letters, as I knew it now, seemed too precarious. Before I left Nantucket, I had sent Ahab a letter to tell him of our coming babe and of my pleasure in our home. Sometimes as I waited for sleep and watched the full moon sail up the window (my mother and I decided to share her bed), I imagined what might be in Ahab's letters. Certainly he would describe the sea to me and report what whales they took. I hoped that he might write of his love for me, but so much of the bond between us had traveled the path of the eyes that I did not require, with Ahab, a stream of romantic words.

Often I remembered our wedding night, the gentleness of his hard hands upon my body, the joy of our uniting. Had it been after that last time, that morning when I held out my arms to him, that his seed had impregnated me? I thought so.

I had told my mother that at the dawn after our wedding night, we had entered the cupola and angels of resplendent hues had flown around us, for I wanted her to know how I loved my husband, his mind, body, and spirit.

WHILE I THOUGHT of Ahab by night, by day those summer and fall hours were filled with the love between my mother and me. Perhaps it would have been a more ordinary time if we had both not known that at the end of the next spring, our year together would be over, and I would take my babe of five months age or so back with me to Nantucket.

When the fall vegetables were ready to gather, Mother got out her Keats volume and read his "Ode to Autumn" to me, and I loved the full sadness of the poem as never before. Especially the description of the *gnats* moved me—that such a small part of nature was yet worthy of a place in his lines about that remote English world of harvest.

Our root cellar, with its new stock of vegetables which we ourselves had not only grown but also harvested, dried, preserved, and pickled, seemed as rich a treasure house as Keats's granary. The burlap sacks were lumpy with cobs full of dried corn, and we had large jars of beans and tomatoes on the rough shelves. Against the dirt walls we had baskets of black walnuts we'd gathered in the woods and boxes of dried blackberries. We had a store of turnips and radishes, carrots and potatoes. It was a pleasure to crunch through the fallen leaves down into the ravine, to open the heavy wooden door, and to add to the bounty. When we entered the cellar, we deeply inhaled the aroma of vegetables mixed with earth. "We'll run out of room," we told each other, proclaiming the success of our agriculture.

Perhaps it was because of my own round shape that I particularly loved the apples that fall. Though my belly was not blushed with red, as they were, I seemed gaudy with joy. (Giles once told me the root of the word *gaudy*, in fact, means joy.) I ran up a lovely loose dress of red-and-gold plaid from the yardage in my trunk, and when I wore that, I felt most applelike, plump and ripening. Reaching up to the low, heavy-laden boughs, I felt one-with-the-apples as my fingers closed around them. Mother would not let me climb the ladder up into the trees, but she herself did the climbing. It made her blithe as a girl to be aloft on the ladder, though when she looked down and smiled at me, I saw many wrinkles of middle age in her skin. I told her how I had loved to climb aloft, dressed as a boy, almost a hundred feet into the air, with the ship plowing the waves far below.

In late fall, we harnessed our mare to the wagon to carry some of our apples to the press, so we would have cider through the winter. It was a merry gathering of families scattered throughout our area, and there was square dancing that night, but being so big with child, I did not wish to dance. After much encouragement from me (and from a widower who had a farm a half-dozen miles away), my mother did join the dancing. I think she rather liked showing off before her daughter.

Her feet moved nimbly and her face grew rosy and steamy. I thought of how that first night at the Lighthouse we had all danced together, and I wished that those members of the family were with us now.

We spent the cider night, all the women, wall to wall on pallets, with all the men in the barn. And that night there was much joking and singing among the women as we waited for sleep. Strangely, methought of how people might lie in a graveyard, somewhat cozy with the proximity of other bodies, but here, more cheerfully, we were a prone community of the living, of sisters of all ages, myself a woman accepted among women.

When Mother and I drove home the next day with our load of cider-filled bottles, I felt a little wary of the mare. She pulled too hard, I thought, and when she sensed that we were near home, she was hard for Mother to hold. It really made me quite angry. We had had her many years, caring well for her. Perhaps she rebelled now because my father had kept her under such a tight rein.

But there was an element to our speed that I relished. The fall colors, particularly of the maples, dogwoods, and sumac, were beyond compare, and the speed of our passage seemed to make them swirl together in a phantasmagoria. Occasionally a puff of wind would bring down a shower of leaves from a tree that overhung the road. Then we were in the thick of it! Leaves flying like colored froth. I wanted to write to Ahab about it. The speed alternately thrilled and frightened me.

We had left the barn door open, and though Mother hauled on the reins, the mare ran right in. When we got out, I saw the pallor under Mother's tan skin, and she was shaking. "That's the last time I drive Penelope till next spring," she said. "And then I'll have a neighbor take her out till she's calmed down."

Usually, once we went to bed, Mother and I did not talk. It was as though she knew I needed some time with my thoughts of my husband. But that October night, after we had pulled the patchwork up to our chins to keep out the chill, she remarked, "Listen, the mockingbird is telling us good-bye. We'll not hear him again till spring."

As I listened, I wanted to describe the bird's song to Ahab. I thought of Keats's poem "Ode to a Nightingale" and wished that I had the genius to immortalize our Kentucky mockingbird. Those who have heard both birds swear by ours as the greater vocalist. That night I felt melted by the sound. The notes were smooth-flowing as liquid and seemed individually to have the soft and fluid contours of honey. The melody was embellished with trills and flourishes; there were repeats and explorations, the tunes of other birds, especially cardinals. "Pretty bird, pretty bird." And "Look right here!"

But I dreamt of how I had battled the eagle with my bonnet and the raucous cries of that bird.

THE NEXT DAY, we began cracking nuts for our fruitcakes and mixing the batters and blending in the jam for Christmas jam cakes and measuring out dried fruits for our plum puddings. I told my mother how Aunt had filled the Lighthouse with much the same odors, in the bleak weeks before Christmas. Yes, there was a nip in the air in Kentucky, but we were by no means windswept as I had been on the Island. We saw Canada geese come down the flyway of the river. I loved it when I got to see the tired leader fall back and a fresh goose take the point of the V. Sometimes I heard the bang of guns not too far from our house.

One cold day when we knew the bees were sleeping, Mother robbed the hive in our old sycamore tree. We had buckets and buckets of golden honey. "This one was your father's favorite bee tree," she said. That afternoon a neighbor brought by a haunch of bear, which we roasted in a pot surrounded by carrots, and we ate the bear meat dribbled with honey. "The strong and the sweet together," Mother said. "It will be good for the baby." We finished supper by the fire, eating crisp apples and slices of cheese.

"I wonder, Una," she suddenly said, more tentatively than usual, "if you ever think, that if the baby should be a boy, you might name him Ulysses for your father?"

"I am not sure that it is a lucky name," I replied, and I could have bitten my too-quick tongue. "But certainly I will think of it."

"What name did you take when you shipped in disguise?" Her eyes teased me.

I admitted the truth: "Ulysses." How had she guessed?

As we lay on our bed that night, listening to the falling of the last few leaves of the oaks, I relived that conversation. Almost I chuckled at myself. My mother had penetrated my defense. There would always be a part of my father that I carried forward.

But the next day over breakfast, she apologized to me, saying it was no one's business but my own what I named my babe, Ahab being at sea. I must name him the name that came to me with his birthing.

"Our last name already being Spenser," she said, "I named you Una from Spenser's *Faerie Queene,* because I wanted you to be brave and true like Una. And you are. But the name proved prophetic in terms of *oneness,* for you are my one and only child." She brought us each another piece of cornbread from the warming oven.

"Did my father know the work of Edmund Spenser?"

"I had often thought of your father as my Red Cross Knight, he so wanted to champion God and the Good."

"How alike we think, you and I! I sometimes think of my husband, of Ahab," I confided, "as the Red Cross Knight. A whale is not unlike a dragon—a great and mighty animal, almost mythical in its power. The whale sends up a plume of water instead of fire."

"Leviathan, the scripture calls the whale. Do you think whales to be malicious?"

"Often they seemed to me as innocent as gigantic calves, slaughtered. But the black one, the one that stove the *Sussex* . . . it was darker than granite, malignant . . . intentional in its assault."

"It could not help its color."

"Ah, you are a Quaker in judging animals as well as human races. But the Quakers are a bloody lot when it comes to slaughtering whales." How delicious the bacon was that morning. I split open my cornbread and placed it inside so that the flavor would permeate the bread.

"What will we do," she asked, "if North and South part over the slavery question?"

It was the first time I had ever heard of such an idea.

"Perhaps the North will join with Canada then," I said, "and both will fight the British again."

"The mills of England run on cotton picked by Southern slaves." She poured us each another cup of tea.

I did not like to think of alliances among nations and wars that could be fought. I wanted to bring my baby to a peaceful world.

"Agatha and I used to speak of fighting against slavery," she went on.

"How?"

"Sometimes we imagined ourselves orators; other times as soldiers, if war came. We would dress in the attic as men and act it all out."

"Dress as men!"

"Yes. As you actually have done."

Suddenly I laughed to think of myself dressed as a boy, and I patted the round of my belly, which almost touched the edge of the table.

A HARD FROST came that night, and the next day we gathered persimmons. I could scarcely bend over to pick up the fallen ones, which lay among the frost-rimmed brown leaves. Our supper was a reckless gorging on persimmon pudding, on more and yet more pudding, spicy with nutmeg and cinnamon, which I had purchased in New Bedford. Despite our giddy gorging, I saw anxiety in my mother's eyes.

In another week all the hardwood trees were bare. The cedars yet held up their bushy green plumes, and the sprays of pine needles were green and crisp against the thin blue sky of the approaching winter. At night, because the elms, maples, and even sycamores down by the creek were all bare, we saw the stars caught in the fine twigs and lattices of the trees. Sometimes we bundled up and walked out a quarter of a mile from the cabin expressly to see the night sky.

"The hairnets of the trees," my mother said, "have caught the brilliantine of the stars."

"Let stars be little shining fish," I answered as we turned toward our door and warmth. "Constellations are schools of fish caught and pulled together in the nets of celestial fishermen." Later, I wrote down these pretty ideas in my journal.

Our feet on the brown fallen leaves seemed married to the earth, the way moles, rabbits, and muskrats go to earthy dens in winter. The leaves we trod were sodden, not crunchy, already losing their structure and uniting with soil. Kentucky is the middle of the middle of something Substantial—the very opposite of water. This was the forest, sprung from Kentucky earth—our house was of it, we ourselves were of it. Even the canopy of stars seemed Kentucky stars.

I N D E C E M B E R, the temperature fell and fell. The bare trees around the cabin snapped and popped in the wind. Once a limb cracked off, and when it fell against the frozen earth, it exploded. We salvaged the wood, spreading it out before the hearth to dry it, to use later as starter or kindling. Those days in December we did not allow the fire to die. Often I sat before the fireplace in a rocking chair and dozed, my great belly swelling yet more to fill my lap.

My mother still sewed, but I had no ambition for it.

Nor was there need. My mother's sewing was not for the babe but a spring dress for me. The fabric was a light lawn, besprinkled with tiny flowers, a whimsey, and I thought lazily back on how I had stood in the shop in Nantucket—a world away—and purchased the fabric. Heather's Moor seemed like something from a dream. What need, really, did I or anyone have for such a house? A cabin with a fire and a rocking chair, a baby kicking his small foot from time to time inside, a beloved mother at my side. I had brought her a silver thimble with an *S* for Spenser engraved inside the cup. With this little engine, she plied the folds of the cobweb fabric, while I dreamed and rocked by the fire, my belly in my lap. The world seemed indolent, sleepy, replete.

I fancied Ahab sailing right down the Ohio, saying he wanted to live in the woods. He came in a miniature *Pequod*. The woods were the place of rest. The ocean was too incessantly active for peace. Let my husband sail down the Ohio, while curious squirrels and deer, Indians and settlers peeked through the river birch to see a seafaring man sail home to his woodsy wife.

One night as the full moon came up, snow began to fall across her mellow face. I went to sleep remembering how it had snowed on the *Pequod* and frosted her like a floating cake in the freezing waters. And I had waited for the ice to melt on the ratlines and then climbed aloft for Ahab. How lithe and thin I had been! Perhaps that was the true beginning of our love—when together we kept the ship.

In the morning, Mother and I awoke to a world around the cabin that had gone soft—lavender in color—with snow. I saw where deer had toed their way among the old cornstalks in the garden. We had taken down a section of rails for them. The sun did not shine, and the temperature dropped again. We pinned on shawls and walked about a little, but our shoes were not high enough to keep out the snow, and our world seemed unfamiliar. Often I turned around to be sure nothing was creeping up on me.

"I wish the sun would shine," Mother said. It seemed unnatural to us both that snow should seem gloomy.

That night the wind came up, and it snowed again. I could hear the snow dashing against the shutters. Mother took out two extra quilts. The sound of the snow sweeping the roof reminded me of the water swishing against the hull of a ship. We seemed a little ship of sorts, isolated, anchored but bobbing in the elements. I was grateful for our good woodpile.

For breakfast, Mother cooked sausage on the spider, and the cooking woke me up with its medley of aroma and sizzling. She also made white porridge, sweetened with maple syrup, and in the taste of maple, I remembered the hard little pieces of Ahab's Vermont candy. All this she brought to me in bed, telling me to get up gradually. She put such logs on the fire that the whole fireplace was filled from top to bottom with flame, and I could not see the tips of the flames, but just an undulating curtain of fire.

"Now, what would you have me read?" she asked.

"Keats. 'The Eve of Saint Agnes.' "

"But it's morning, Una."

"I want to eat the language," I replied, "and feel it with my fingers." Such a richness we seemed to have together, in our cabin. I wanted rich words, and none are richer than Keats's.

"I think he must have studied Spenser," my mother said. "Do you happen to know?"

I knew only the poems themselves, but I loved this insight my mother offered, her sense of connection and influence among separate literary figures. I would ask Margaret Fuller if Keats had read the Elizabethan.

"If you were to piece a quilt," I asked, "that looked like Keats, what colors would you use?"

"I think he is beyond real colors."

What an idea! "Heard sounds are sweet; unheard, sweeter," I quoted freely from "Ode on a Grecian Urn."

We ate such a hearty breakfast that we had only bread for lunch.

In the late afternoon, the storm moved out, leaving the deep snow behind. We both sensed that again it would grow colder. In the late afternoon, the sun came out, but only long enough to set itself amidst long streaks of red. And then when the sun sank down, the temperature dropped again.

"Perhaps the river will freeze," she said, as the darkness and cold tightened around the cabin. "It has a few times. Once your father and I went sliding on it."

Now I was so big with child that it was hard to get comfortable, and night after night, I rolled about in bed. So as to disturb my mother less, I made up the bunk bed that was nailed in one corner of the cabin. After one December night of tossing and turning, I could not wait till morning, but rose before dawn and woke my mother.

"Crawl in," she said, lifting the cover.

"Feel my belly. Do you think my time is near?"

She got up, lit candles, put wood on the fire, and then felt me under the cover.

"Not yet," she said. "I think you have a ways to go."

THE NEXT DAY, the sky was clear, and the sunlight dazzled the snow so much our eyes could not stand the glitter. In the middle of the afternoon, my labor pains began, though my water had not broken.

We were happy at first. At last my time had come. The pains interested me. I still had some appetite, and my mother gave me the savory broth from the bear roast. She installed me again in the bed and even got in beside me so that we both had our broth propped up side by side, with our legs under the covers. Later, she cut an apple in half, and with the tip of a table knife, she scraped the apple. I opened my mouth, and she poked in the juicy pulp. "Not that you're sick," she said, "but let me feed you." During the night, she slept some. I could not. I tried not to squirm, for I knew she wanted me in the big bed with her, but my pain was getting worse. I willed myself to lie still while it racked me.

How many weary times was I to ask her to check my progress? How many times did she answer, "Not yet," each time her mouth more tight and grim? "It's always hard the first time, Una."

"Was I hard, for you?" Why had I not asked before?

"You were a happy little fish that came swimming out."

At length, after a day of labor, I found that I was moaning. A far-off sound, as though it came from wind-abraded rocks on a distant shore. I circled without progress on a sea of pain, and the moaning seemed leagues away.

"Is it time?"

"Not yet. The water needs to break."

"I feel I can't open my eyes."

"Just reach out your hand. Here's the cup. Wait, I'll guide you."

What was that smell? Food, again? My mother's supper. I didn't want any.

"Why is it taking so long?"

"I wish it were me instead of you."

She put the whiskey jug we kept as medicine beside the bed and from time to time had me take a spoonful. Its effect was mainly to daze my mind.

And I held her hand, felt the bones within. Saw candlelight. Registered night. Her strong hand, thin. Her face, pain for my pain, though she tried to hide it. All our happy months, let my eye catch her eye, and there was love—remember the radiance—hold that. Always. . . . Afternoon, and already? Back from the woodpile? How cold out? *Your hand's cold. Put it on my forehead. No, let me hold.* Knuckles knobby, one, two, three, four in a row.

"Una, I'm going for the doctor. I'll hitch the mare. Una, be brave."

CHAPTER 91   The Burden

WHAT HAS BEEN the hardest in my life, I have told first in my narrative. I have already told that I lost my mother, that the buggy turned over on the snowy road, and she froze. I have already told that I lost my baby. I needed to tell those terrible things first, to pass through Scylla and Charybdis early in my voyage of telling; otherwise, I feared I would turn back, be unable to complete my story, if those terrors loomed ahead.

I have told how when I was alone with my birthing pain, Susan emerged from between my mattresses to help me. And we laughed. *My mother was still alive then; my baby still a promise.* Though neither my mother nor a doctor returned, Susan was there. And later it was Susan who helped me when his weak little mouth could not suck. It was Susan who devised a sugar tit for him and gave him the strength to live and to be loved for a day. When Satan dragged me into sleep, it was Susan who held my babe and changed the cloth and did not wash it but saved the one wetting for me to see.

When Liberty died—

That moment is beyond my writing. Perhaps Susan was in the room, but I was alone, as everyone is when the universe opens its black mouth. It swallowed my babe and me, and spit me out again.

And then Susan kept the fire going, cooked, held me while I cried. She cut a lock of his red hair, swaddled the babe in burial clothes, with spices, cloves and myrrh, to keep him, and placed him in a bed of snow. And the neighbors came, while I hid Susan, to speak of the buggy overturned, my mother dead.

And all the time Susan should have fled, but she refused. I told her, that night, to bring me scissors and a needle. From every dress and cloth I owned, I cut a piece and sewed them together and made her a coat for her journey, stuffed with the thickest wadding. And I told her to bring Mother's shoes, and tacks and the hammer, for we had decided she would go over the ice. I could not get out of bed, but these things I could do for Susan, and I told her to bring me the skillet and I turned it over for an anvil so that I could hammer in bed.

My mother—it was as though she had melted into the air. When I looked up, she who had been with me in the cabin for months had vanished. And she was no more. The neighbors had her body. In some dark shed her body lay wrapped, preserved by the cold that had killed her. She lay stiff, long and cold, her hands folded over her chest, her being wrapped in strips of sheet, safe from the nibbling mouse. I could picture her thus, but it was her absence, not her death, that seemed real. The way she was not held by the walls of the cabin. The vacancy in the air. *My mother, my babe, forever dead.* If only tomorrow they would begin again to breathe.

When all the quilting was finished on Susan's jacket, I tasked myself again to sew a parallel row, with smaller stitches, inside the loops of the first quilting. And then I imposed a running rain of stitches over all the design so that the jacket grew heavy with thread. I listened to the silence of the house as I sewed.

Susan had never been taught to sew, because her mam worked in the fields. I gave her a scrap of velvet to make a small bag, which was a first project I had had as a child. I told her how as soon as she saw the tip of the needle emerge from the nap of the fabric, she was to make it dive down again, to gather at least four stitches on the shaft of the needle before she pulled it through. How we must keep the thimble on, for though it was clumsy at first, it was our friend, our shield, while the needle was our spear; how since it was too large for Susan's tiny finger, we would pack it with a fold of yarn. I pretended that life was nothing but the craft of sewing. And no, we would not sew with a double thread, but learn to pull, just so, using the friction of the thread so that the unsecured end never slipped through the eye of the needle. But how to roll a knot between the thumb and forefinger off the end of the thread, I never succeeded in teaching her—that being a gesture that takes a great deal of practice—and her knots were loose globs, wet with spittle.

"It doesn't matter," I said. "We'll hide the knot on the inside of the bag. Sewing has always been my friend," I said. "It's the way a free woman can earn her keep."

"I will be free," Susan answered. "If ice jaw open up, drag me down, I still be free." Her courageous statement settled on my head with the weight of melancholy.

"Have you ever seen the ocean?" I asked, to stir up a new topic.

"I've heard 'bout it."

"I was once a sailor." I showed her the sampler my mother had cross-stitched of the *Pequod* and the verse. "My husband is the captain of this ship." But Ahab seemed no more real to me than if he had been a man made only of cross-stitch.

"It start to soften up outside."

"Probably they'll come to get me for the funeral tomorrow."

Susan put down her sewing. She brought me a quill. "Teach me the letters of my name," she said.

I was ashamed I had placed sewing before reading and writing. I wondered if Margaret Fuller could sew at all. Susan sat beside me propped up on the bed, and we made our knees into a desk. I put my hand over hers to guide it: "The *S* is like a snake and makes the sound of hissing, the *U* is deep like a tub, and then we have an *S* again. The *A* is like hands coming to pray, the tips together, but not the heels; with a crossbar. The *N* is like a rail fence, squeezed up a bit. And there you have it, S-U-S-A-N. Snake, Tub, Snake again, Pray, Fence. And look, the same letters, rearranged, can make UNA."

"I done learned two names at once," she said, pleased.

"It's always that way. In learning, one thing always has something else in it, or leads to something new." When had I used that tone before? Beside the Lighthouse, when I had appointed myself little Frannie's teacher, and we had sat in the bright sun on the smooth shoulders of rocks. Not a tone that I liked, now, and I modified it to something less tyrannical and more appreciative of *Susan*'s progress.

Susan began at once to copy over and practice the shapes she had learned. I watched her and encouraged her. She didn't know till I told her that the letters were to sit on a line and not be flung down randomly all over the page. It warmed me to teach her, and the glances between us were of conspirators, not instructor and student, as we made the letters march along.

Between myself and my grief, I had lowered a window sash. As glass keeps out the storm, so some barrier in me separated me from the death of my mother, the death of my child. On the other side of that glass, the earth tossed like a sea, and lightning stabbed anything that raised its face from the mud. On this side of the glass, I bowed my head to sew or to draw letters, or I stretched out my hand to touch, affectionately or encouragingly, the dark skin of Susan's small arm.

Often she touched me too; sometimes smoothing my back, with the cloth of my gown between her skin and mine, but sometimes along the naked curve of my cheek. Talking little, we loved the skin itself, the envelope that held each of us.

The blackness of her skin was a particular, fascinating beauty to me. She was very black, but with different shades and textures of black. At her temples her skin seemed soft as soot, but over the arch of her brow it was shiny, like fire scale on a pot. Her throat had a purplish hue to it, like a dark eggplant, and her knuckles were more brown than black. The palms of her hands and the soles of her feet were light tan, with a pinkish cast.

On the back of her right hand stood a pinkish knot of skin, shaped just like the rosette you can crochet. I put my finger on it and didn't need to ask aloud.

"Once I was in a place, two days hungry, and I come on an owl nest, big as your pillow. I hid down beside it, and sure 'nuff, 'fore long here come Mama Owl, got a squirrel dangling. Well, I gots to have it, so I snatch and she rear back, pull with one foot, fight with the other. But I have me a little squirrel meat that day, cooked on a little bitty twig fire, seasoned with what blood dripping out the back of my hand. No need to waste."

I turned her hand over to see if the talon had pierced the palm. I saw an indentation, a pulled-in place, where the claw tip had caught flesh. When the talon had pulled back out, it had drawn the hooked palm skin after it and tucked it into the wound.

Susan's eyelids were half down and the curly lashes made perfect backward-turned black rows, almost like a buttonhole stitch. She looked like a goddess carved out of African wood and shined with oil, like a Madonna but more alive, glowing. I took her other hand to see if it was likewise crowned on the back with a pink rosette of flesh, but it was uncrucified.

I showed her the white scar that skated across the back of my hand. "I had a fight with an eagle, on top of a tower." Her eyes questioned. I added, "Over a bonnet."

Sometimes when we sat on the bed together, I thought of Chester, and how I had taught him, and how he never knew me as anything but a boy. And I thought, too, of being in the open boat. I hoped Kit was sheltered from the wilderness and weather in some hogan or tepee. As they traveled west, Lewis and Clark, over two decades before, had wintered in the earthen hogans of the Mandans on the banks of the Missouri.

When I got up from bed to walk around, I placed my hands on my womb, as though to keep from dropping something. Where I had been so full, I was empty now. And no babe to raise to my breasts, which filled and filled.

In the night my gown was soaked with wasted milk, but my body replaced that overflow, and my breasts ached till I thought I would go mad. To relieve the tightness, I cradled the curves of my breasts and tried to make milk flow, though the slightest pressure was pain. At the news of my mother's death, they had released milk. Now they were obdurate.

"You must milk me," I said to Susan, and she tried, but my nipples were as unyielding as sharp stones.

"Try your mouth," I urged.

Susan did not hesitate.

Like a kitten making a trough of its tongue and stroking, she suckled me. Tears of relief flowed from the corners of my eyes as she eased me. What could I feel when I looked down on her little upstanding braids, the back of her head, but love? And I hoped my milk was good nurture, she being run-down.

"Quick now," she said. "We bind them flat."

Though the binding was a misery when the milk tried to return, it was nothing compared to the former agony. Susan never spoke of what she had done for me, but when we cuddled together to sleep, I dreamed I was a mother cat with rows of nipples up and down my body, and she was my only kitten.

As a girl rebelling against my father's dogma, I had scoffed at Job for accepting God's consolation of a new wife and new children. But I, most Joblike, when Giles was dead, embraced Kit, and when Kit conveyed that he was not coming back, it was the messenger himself, Ahab, whom I immediately loved. If Mother and Liberty were gone, then here was Susan to unburden me of love. Not to be loved but to love lightened my load of grief and gave value and direction to my life.

CHAPTER 92   The Lantern

THE LAST NIGHT we spent together, Susan set the tallow candle on the table between us and said, "I mus' tell you how I come so far."

I nodded, for I wanted to know her story, though I had asked her nothing. I did not want to test her trust.

"You've come a long way," I said. "And from a warmer place."

"Well, there be walking," she said. "Walking aplenty. But that ain't *how* I come."

I was perplexed. She leaned her face into the candlelight, and I saw a wildness to her eyes that I had not seen before. I felt afraid that she would fabricate.

"You needn't tell me," I said quickly.

"It were the Lord," she said.

"Oh!" I recoiled a bit.

"I ain't heard the name of the Lord once in this house," she said wonderingly, "nor spoke it myself till now."

It was not I who had broken through Susan's trust; she had blundered through mine. I was shocked by Susan's religiosity. Her eyes were stretched wide so that pupil and iris burned darkly surrounded by white, and her lips were parted so that her white teeth reflected like wet ivory.

"When my mam tell me one night go, she say, 'Look over your shoulder,' and when I did, then I saw a lantern light out the window. 'It is the light of the Lord,' my mam say."

Hearing Susan's words, I felt the blood drain from my face and then a flash of heat. My mind began to heat like an ember, and my face felt scorched from that burning coal that was once my brain. "I'm not well," I said to Susan. I didn't want to be confined in the cabin with a Christian fanatic.

She got the whiskey jug and poured me some in a cup. When I drank it, my whole throat was a ribbon of flame.

"And I pass through, like I going through the wall, but through the door."

No. Stop, I wanted to scream.

"For every step I take, the Lord move on. Carrying the light up ahead. It be summer, and the road dust fine as flour under my feets and soft as pillows."

Was she going to scream at me? Try to force me to *believe?*

"When daybreak 'bout to come, he lead me off the road to the deep thicket. He shrink hisself up like a little lightning bug when the bushes be thick and low, and when I parts them, then there my space to hide in."

I felt my pulse beating in my brain. I drank the whiskey again. I was caught in the rush of it and in the flow of her uncanny story the way a person can be caught in a flash flood. You may stand in an ordinary, clear place, they say, in the mountains in Kentucky, and suddenly out of nowhere a wall of water comes for you because someplace up in the heights streams from furious rains have come together—maybe they've been dammed up in some natural way—and then they sweep down and take everything.

"I hide by day in the bush like a little child kin hide in her mama's skirt, and I travel by night. Then one daybreak I part the bushes and there already be another soul there, a little old man like a raisin wearing clothes. 'I be your guide now,' he say. And we walk many a mile. He knowed some Indians who hide us, and they be on the drive, too. One day, he say we done made it to Tennessee."

"What state were you born in?"

"I just not so sure 'bout that," she said. "I don't remember nobody ever say, when I was little, only how Shady Grove be not too far away. Luverne, they sometimes say, and Petrey and Ramar? Highland Home not too far, and Helicon."

I shook my head. I put my arm on the table and laid my cheek on it. My womb throbbed.

"Now don't be getting the miseries," she said. "Here, you drink some more of this good liquor."

I obeyed, but my face was aflame and I kept my head on the table. This was Susan, who had saved my life. Like a child, I took my thumb-nail and cut the rim of the candle so that the melt flowed through and down the side of the taper and clung there, hardening into a line of drops. When Uncle took us to Boston, I saw among religious artifacts from around the world a picture of Jesus in a shop window, and down his face was a line of blood drops oozing from the crown of thorns. There was a gush from my body, and I knew I was passing blood again, but it did not keep up.

"Then he died."

"Jesus?"

"The old raisin man. I asked him did he reckon the Lord would come back with his lantern for me, but Old Sam just stretch out his thin little arm and show me the stars and the Drinking Gourd. The last thing he say was 'The stars they jes' the same as Jesus.' "

With a jolt, I caught myself sliding off the chair toward sleep. "Couldn't you say," I asked as kindly as I could, "that Sam was your guide?"

Susan slapped both her palms down on the table and jumped up. "Then who lifted me? Who lifted me high in the tree and made the tree grow up so tall like fifty years passed so dogs couldn't catch no scent 'cause I was caught up in the clouds with the Lord?"

"Dogs!"

"Oh, yes. Dogs with teeth long as your fingers, sharp as your needle."

I sat up straight and watched Susan pace around the room. I resolved to force no more skeptical interpretations on her story.

"Love lifted me," Susan went on. She stopped pacing, stood still, and slowly raised her hands so that I might understand the idea of being lifted. "The true name of the Lord is Love." And she smiled wide. Then she brought her lips together and said, "There is faith that move mountains. That make a scrawny tree grow tall. That lift you high above the dog bite. That's what I mus' tell you 'fore I leave. I could reach in this hearth fire, reach on in there, draw out burning coal, and not be burnt no more than Shadrach, Meshach, and Abednego."

"Then do it," I said. I felt all my love for Susan fall away from me the way a ginkgo tree can suddenly drop its leaves in the night. I stood up, too, ugly and skeletal, as though pain and anger had burnt me and I stood a column of blackened bone. "Oh, Ahab," I called. "Lightning has struck me as well as thee!"

Susan ran to the fireplace, knelt, and drew out an ember. She tossed it from one hand to the other, and then she plucked out another glowing coal and another. She commenced to toss and catch them in a small circle over her lap like the stars in Betsy Ross's flag till she slowly rose up, enlarging the circle as she stood. Then her whole form stood in a hoop of flame, and she began to dance. She caught the coals against the insides of her ankles and on the tops of her feet, and tossed them up again, but there was no sign of pain or burning. She appeared to have many arms and she danced in a circle of fire.

"Shiva!" I gasped and fainted.

HAD I DREAMT? I know I dreamt of humpbacked whales that night, and how they formed a circle and blew a net of bubbles, how they lunged up through the center of that net, jaws agape, funneling the tiny sea creatures into their massive bodies, fueling whatever fires must be kept burning to warm them when they returned to the depths.

And I dreamt a Greek myth, of Cronos eating his baby.

And then it was time to wake, time for our last day together, and for the final preparations for her journey.

And my love for Susan? Returned and freshened. Our differences mattered not at all. Just as new leaves return to the branches of the winter-black tree, so was I, all aflutter with green love. Susan had lived her own story. If I lacked tolerance—*she* had not tried coercion as my father had—then I was the smaller person for it.

After the funeral, I could reenter the cabin because Susan was there, hidden in the sea chest, ready to rise up and embrace me.

"FREEDOM!"—Susan's cry came thin and sharp from across the moving river ice. At that distance, she was but a shape, a wedge, ferreting through brambles on the free side of the Ohio. Yet still she was Susan, and I knew the bite of her studded shoes into the snow, for I had tried them on, and I knew the weight of the many-threaded coat on her shoulders. I knew the soft nudge of the velvet Precious-bag against the skin of her chest, and inside the bag at the beginning of the seam the messy wattle of her sewing knot.

And, though Susan did not know it, my mother's silver thimble with a pad of yarn in its tip was hidden inside her coat pocket. During the late afternoon the last day, secretly, while she carried out our slops, I had sewn the thimble into a tiny pocket within the pocket and sewn that secret compartment shut. Some day she would feel it as a pebble, perhaps, that had worked its way into the lining of her coat. Whenever that day came, she would grow curious, explore, pull the familiar pocket wrong side out, note the seam of overcast stitches. Bemused, she would mutter, "What *is* this?" and take a blade to the line of whipstitch. Then she would spread the fingers of her right hand and slip the thimble onto her finger.

As I stood on the snowy bank and watched her go, I wheeled the ivory bracelet around my wrist. *S* at the bottom of the thimble cup was even the right initial. When Susan was out of sight, I turned back toward the cabin. The moon hung like a lantern above us both. Beside me, the river sped its freight of ice floes downstream.

Before I went into the cabin, I circled to my mother's root cellar, knowing it brimmed with the bounty of our autumn harvest. The snow reflected the moonlight so well that I scarcely felt it was night. But when I reached the place, the wooden door was broken. Perhaps a bear had found a palatial den there. But no, this was the work of men. The bounty hunters? Earlier thieves? They had not left enough food to see me through till spring. The shelves had been ravaged by deft hands with opposable thumbs. A few things were broken—a jar of cucumber pickles, an overturned barrel of dried corn. And there were the fresh droppings of raccoons who were taking advantage of the spill. Yes, I had seen their star-shaped tracks in the snow outside.

Some items had been left. A sack of pumpkin seeds, two jugs of cider, a burlap bag of dried shelly beans. The moonlight reflected eerily into the cave through the broken door. I found a jam cake deep in a keg of sugar. The spuds were all gone into thieving pockets. I determined to transport as much of the leavings as I could to the cabin.

As I lugged my basket up the slope to the house, I began taking mental inventory of what should be quickly eaten and what would serve me well while I waited for spring and the first hoot of a steamboat on the river. I knew the cabin itself was full of food that the neighbors had sent home with me after the funeral. My treasure was a large smoked gift ham. Bits of that, simmered with the shelly beans, would see me through. The cow and chickens my mother had sent to board at a neighbor's, but I could claim some milk and eggs.

Though it was bad luck to find the root cellar looted, it immediately challenged me to try to be clever, to calculate how to survive without begging. And of course the neighbors, knowing that I had no way to visit them, save walking, would come from time to time. Likely they had worked out a schedule among themselves. And each would come with some gift of food that would add surprise and variety to my table. What to do with my loneliness? Even before I gained the cabin, I decided: I would read.

THAT NIGHT, I did read a bit. I read Byron for his naughty wit. But the rimes rang dull as lead coins. I tried Wordsworth—but those lines had been too loved, by Giles and me, by my mother and me. "In vacant or in pensive mood . . ." But my heart did not dance with the daffodils. I turned the book over and stared into the flames. I thought of Susan dancing in a wheel of fire. Was I in the realm of memory or imagination? I heated cider and added to it a large teaspoon of the whiskey. Certainly I would not drink it by the cup again! I loaded the popper with kernels and held it close to the fire. The first tiny explosions seemed as hollow as they had once seemed joyful and convivial. O, the loneliness of that little thudding. But I ate the popcorn anyway. The fire had been too high, and much of it was burnt black. Such a long day, but I did not want it to end.

I wondered if Susan had found shelter in a barn or sighted smoke curling from a chimney. I had told her to look for Quaker people, somber and neat in their dress, said that they were sympathetic to slaves. I did not tell her that on Nantucket their sympathy did not extend to worshiping with people of color. In the Precious-bag was a slip of paper on which I had written my address. And she could use the money I'd given her to buy shelter if she found a town and an inn that would admit her. But tonight, she likely would walk a long way till she found a safe house, for some folk across the river would return a runaway for the reward.

I took a hot brick to bed with me so that I would feel less alone. There, though my toes burned, the grief for my mother and my baby washed over me like a cold tide. The tears ran from my eyes until I fell asleep. When I awoke, I awoke crying.

I hadn't known people could do that.

I MADE MYSELF sassafras tea, and I warmed up a pot of grits that a neighbor had left. I put a pat of butter in the center of my bowl and poured maple syrup over that. It was good, but when I reached the bottom of the bowl, I cried again.

MY DAYS were spent that way, with sudden bursts of tears. I gave in to them. The rocking chair became my place to cry. When the tears came, I hurried to the chair, covered myself with a quilt, rocked, and gave myself up to tears. These emotional storms had a natural duration, and when the time had passed, I arose, folded the quilt, left it in the chair seat, and set myself some useful task. When I grew weary, either in body or in spirit, of work, I permitted myself diversion. Shakespeare was the best, for his was a highly peopled world, and I had more than a plenty of vacant nature by opening the cabin door. Yet when Cecilia Pack rode through the snow to visit and invited me to come home with her, I refused.

I found diversion in the light, magical worlds of *A Midsummer Night's Dream* and *The Tempest*. When I tried to read *Lear*, the love between parent and child broke my heart. Perhaps my mother, trapped under the buggy, raged against the storm: "Blow, winds, and crack your cheeks." No. I knew that her thinking would have more resembled prayer than imprecation, and that her prayer would have been that I be safely delivered. She would have gone to sleep gently, her head on a pillow of snow.

And the women in Shakespeare who impersonated men! I had done that, too. Perhaps I had stepped so easily into the idea from having read him. The image of my aunt and my mother swashbuckling in the attic—Agatha and Bertha younger than I had been boarding the *Sussex*—wounded me, presented my mother's space as vacancy.

I commenced a long letter to Margaret Fuller raising the question of to what extent we modeled our lives from our reading. Remembering the story told by my Nantucket judge—I had almost forgotten Austin Lord—about the effect of *Young Werther* on the young people of Europe, I raised the question of an author's moral obligation. Surely Shakespeare had felt it, for in each of the tragedies, though the stage be littered with bodies, there was left some idea of order or hope, or the memory of some transcendent act. For Lear, it had been the rekindling of his love for Cordelia, that love rising from the ashes of remorse. Somehow they had triumphed, even in prison, because of the exchange of love between them.

And if one wrote for American men a modern epic, a quest, and it ended in death and destruction, should such a tale not have its redemptive features? Was it not possible instead for a human life to end in a sense of wholeness, of harmony with the universe? And how might a woman live such a life?

When I switched from thinking of literature to life, I abandoned the idea of capturing any idea worth communicating to Margaret. I simply stared into the fire and decided to eat something sweet. Could the narration of pain, and of what had been of sustaining value in difficult times, be in itself redeeming?

When I had languished in the whaleboat, I looked at the sky aglitter with stars and wondered if some other soul—a girl like myself—looked out into the darkness and wondered about me. Now I thought of Susan, probably still walking, but free now. Looking for her happiness. I rocked and stared into the fire.

So I struggled through my days. At the end of one week, it being Christmas Eve, I thought that perhaps I would have some neighborly visitor, but it snowed again. I noticed the thick blanket of snow so enwrapped the cabin that it was warmer inside, and I need not burn so much wood to keep it so. I began to feel like an animal in its burrow. Furiously, I read Shakespeare to feel that people yet lived and breathed in the world. Though I had cried out to him, my Ahab seemed but a myth.

I pictured him not with a lance but sitting in his captain's cabin with a shepherd's crook. The God of the Old Testament, reduced to human terms, might resemble my Ahab. Unreal Ahab had brought me a rich house and left me in it, and a babe within me. Why then was I here in the snowy woods of Kentucky, and where was my babe? A year ago at Christmas, Kit had pissed on my skirt. Not far away a piano had played carols.

I turned from Shakespeare—the plots ensnared me—to my father's Bible, to the poetry of the Psalms. Only those songs soothed my loneliness. "The Lord is my shepherd; I shall not want. He maketh me to lie down in green pastures. . . . He restoreth my Soul." Those words, that song, that, only that, promised redemption, the restoring of my soul.

And what of that promised Messiah of the Old Books, promised to be born the very next day?

What is the Lord? my still, small, skeptical voice questioned in the snapping of the fire. I wondered if I was sick, so fevered, so convoluted was my thinking. The Lord seemed to be Hope—not Faith. Susan's Jesus was her hope. But she had said the best name of the Lord was Love.

No. I am the Lord, said the fire, *this small spark, this undulant tongue, as much as the psalmist who could sing "The Lord is my shepherd."*

We are the Lord, the quiet logs emanated in their brownness from the enclosing walls.

I am the Lord, spoke the radish, lying long-tailed on the thick china plate.

How could the material world, the world we consumed, claim divinity or even kinship with humankind? I felt amused and smug in my whimsy. *Beauty is the permeable membrane:* I was startled, unprepared. Who spoke?

No one, no *thing,* spoke again.

"Jesus, our Brother, strong and good," the old Christmas carol titled "The Friendly Beasts" hummed semi-wordless to me from the bed of memory, "was humbly born in a stable rude. / The Friendly Beasts around him stood, / Jesus, our Brother, strong and good." And the bramble bush that I imagined had caught on Susan's coat as she pushed northward; with its sharp thorn it, too, claimed to partake. And the forehead of the black whale swimming toward us malevolently. *Am I not a beast, a brother?* I turned away—*And what were you to those you devoured?*—away from that question, quickly, quickly. And completely.

Yes, the simple song was right, not the fanatical preachers. Poetry told the truth, not polemic. Jesus was our Brother, and in our human kinship was our salvation. I rocked my chair toward that idea, for Christmas Eve in Kentucky. The song did not claim more. It did not ask to be believed—these fantasized animals "under some good spell" presenting their gifts of cows' hay and sheep's wool. The Christmas story asked to be imagined—never mind belief—and with imagining came the capacity for compassion.

Ah, the dove: the last gift—Aunt Agatha's verse to sing when we created our makeshift Christmas holidays, a green swag pinned to the stony tower. But why did she have my mother's voice? "I, sang the dove, from the rafters high, I cooed him to sleep that he should not cry. . . . I cooed him to sleep on Christmas morn." When my father died, Aunt Agatha had taken me like a giant baby into her lap. My mother, my child—lost—how much more I needed my aunt. I sang to myself, in a low, speaking register, there being no one there to sing to me.

Yes, the poet of the Christmas song whispered to me in the silence at the end—the singing, the telling—*yes, you have guessed my meaning,* or part of it—how life can be celebrated and can be given rest. *How else is life made real, but by story and song and fiery dance?*

CHAPTER 94   The Guide

Mᵧ REVERIE by the snapping fire ended with a knock at the door. When I tried to push it open, I found the load of snow so heavy against it that I could not.

"Pull," I called to my visitor, who heard me, for the boards registered a jerking.

"Together," I said, "on three." I counted and I pushed and the person pulled, and the door flew open.

There was no one there, just the bare place, a fan shape, carved in nearly four feet of drifted snow.

"Are you behind the door?" I asked, and I peeked around. Again no one stood there. But there was a movement under the snow. The force of the opening had knocked the visitor down and buried him completely. Where I saw the most movement and determined a head to be, I began to part the snow with my hands.

What I found in the snow was fur—animal fur—and the black leather snout of a wolf emerged, followed by blank vacancies where eyes should have been! And then I saw a swale of human hair. The snow was churning with his movements to free himself. I stepped back. From within the snow, into the clear space before the door burst the bounty hunter, the dwarf who had covered his head and shoulders with a wolf skin. His face was plastered with snow, and snow caked his beard and the fur of his cloak; but it could be no other. Snowman, wolf-at-my-door, wolf-man, his eyes were there, amber, almost golden. Kind.

"Come in," I said.

He laid his pelt before the fire. Under that he wore another jacket. I indicated my rocking chair, and he climbed up in it. His short legs stuck out like a child's toward the fire. He briskly rubbed his knees and shins with his hands. "This feels good."

Without asking, I took the kettle from the hob and poured him a cup of tea. Wolf or man, he was my first guest in many days. I unwrapped the jam cake and cut a fine wedge for him. I had no idea what to say to him. I listened to the slight rocking of the chair, curved wood stroking boards. Finally, he broke the quiet.

"You lost your baby?"

I was shocked by his directness, but the cabin had but one room, and it was clear we were alone. I nodded.

"And your mama?"

"The buggy turned over. Probably the mare was too difficult. My mother was killed." I had mentioned to the bounty hunters that my mother was away to fetch the doctor.

"You're pretty snug here, all the same."

"Yes." I felt an odd shyness with this man. He had led the pack out of the house. He had seemed to restrain their brutality. He and the Scotsman.

"I done put my donkey in your barn."

"A donkey?" I sat down in the ladder-back chair to listen.

"I bought myself a donkey with the bounty money. My legs are too short to walk all the way home. I didn't want no animal too large to handle."

"The bounty money?" I felt afraid. "But you didn't—"

"Una—" he said. He knew my name. "I did and I didn't."

He reached in his pocket and drew out a silver thimble. The yarn in the tip was gone.

"The others gave up. I had give up, too. I saw her entirely by accident. She was crossing a snowfield in Ohio, an old cornfield at the base of a hump of a hill. When you see a lone black woman like that—surely lost, traveling light—you wonder. And so I began to track her. I never knew it was Susan."

"Susan!"

"I sure to God hoped she would not climb that there hill. The snow was deep on the windward side, and it was purgatory to me to have to mount that hill. But she sees me out in the field. She knows I'm after her. Though my legs are short, hers were tired. I knew she saw that I would overtake her, and there was no place to hide. The hill was just a snow-covered hump. A nuisance in the landscape. But she struggled on. I saw she wanted to gain the top before I caught her. That was what she was trying for, only that."

"No," I murmured. "No."

"She actually waits for me at the top. Then she says, 'Little white man, let me buy my freedom.' I asked, 'How much do you got?' She opened a little bag on a string around her neck. 'I've never counted money,' she said.

"But I saw it was enough. 'Anyway,' I say, 'what else you got in your pocket?' She answered, 'My pockets be empty,' and she turns them wrong side out. At first glance, them pockets did seem empty, but being short, my eyes were close to the pockets, and I saw one has this odd little bulge. We took my jackknife and opened the seam.

" 'Una done hid her thimble with me,' she said. 'I never knew.' For some reason, I believed her. I could have cut her throat—my knife was already out—and taken her gold money and the silver thimble. Or I could have taken her money and still turned her in."

"Where is she?"

He smacked his lips on my jam cake. "I let her go."

"Did you?" I said. "Did you! That was so good of you." I jumped up. I wanted to hug him. "I'm so glad," I exclaimed. "Let me cook for you. I have beans and ham."

He smiled at me. "I'm hungry," he said.

"I thank you." I flung my hands open in gratitude. "I thank you for letting Susan go."

"I'm glad I did it," he said. "She was just a tiny little thing. She reminded me of myself."

"You know I did hide her," I said. "She was between the mattresses, but I didn't know it. She had slipped in. Then she took care of me."

"But your baby died."

I nodded.

"And you're here alone till spring."

"Yes," I said, because it was true. But I felt a little afraid. Though he was short, the power in his body was evident, like that of a compressed spring.

He watched me make the preparations for supper. I did not know what to say. After a bit he asked me if I was nervous. Again, I felt unbalanced by his directness.

"A little," I said.

"Perhaps I ought to tell you the rest of the story."

I only looked at him.

"I took Susan back to the road, and I pointed out a house I knew to belong to abolitionists. Big white square house. I told her they would help her, but they knew me, as I knew them, and I couldn't go to the door."

"How do I know that you're telling the truth?" The question blurted from me.

"Susan thanked me. She said to tell you, if I saw you, for I gained *her* trust, anyway, this string of words: snake, tub, snake again, prayer, and fence. What does it mean?"

Gladness flooded my being. "It is her name," I said. "It describes the printed capital letters in her name." I took up pen and paper and drew the letters, naming them as I drew.

"I see."

When my visitor got up to step outside, I could scarcely believe how small he was. How did such a man come to be a bounty hunter? I did not know, yet I knew there was goodness in him. When he returned, he sniffed deeply, enjoying the aroma of the ham and beans, as any person might. I wished that he had not taken Susan's money and thimble, yet he had let her go. It was more than many would have done. He did not need to be perfect to be good.

I asked him to tell me of his travels and his family. He said he was from Virginia, and there he had a wife, a son, and a daughter. His wife was only a bit taller than he was, but his children were full-sized, by which he meant normal. "My boy is six," he said, "and already as tall as me." He told me they sat on small boxes, he and his wife, and when he got home, he would buy normal furniture for his growing children. "No need they be cramped up by what fits me."

But I did not tell him my secrets. I told him only that I lived in Nantucket and would return when the river was navigable again.

"Do you want to go sooner?" he asked.

"I would if I could."

"I could take you out. You could sit the donkey, and I would lead. I would do it for a fee. You'd be safe."

"I think we should wait till the melt."

"Let part of my pay be a place to sleep and food, till the thaw."

"I must ask you," I said. "Will you deal with me honorably?"

"You'd be safe. I'd take you as far as you needed to go. To Cincinnati, I think. You can take a coach from there."

"I would like to see the donkey. Tomorrow. Tonight you can sleep in the bunk in the corner, but you must not cross to my side of the cabin till I am up."

"Done!"

I felt happier. I did not want to stay in this cabin where I had had so much sorrow. The food supplies would run low before the steamboats came. Living in a corner with some other frontier family seemed unbearable. In Nantucket, I had an ample home, if I could but get to it.

As we chatted on into the evening, I felt that I was right to trust the dwarf. Nevertheless, that first night, I slept dressed and with a butcher knife under my pillow. As I lay in bed, I swallowed my tears for my child and my mother, lest the dwarf hear me and come to comfort me.

I HOPED Susan had found shelter in a stable or house. I could not know her story, but she had one, as surely as I did. Perhaps some omniscience, with stars for eyes, saw her walking, knew her mind. My life and that of Susan, though I could not tell her story, were surely a parallel that made loneliness in the universe impossible.

"Merry Christmas," I called out to the dwarf, as I sat up on my elbow to blow out my candle. In the dark, in a nice, male voice, he called back the same to me.

CHAPTER 95 🜚 Getting Started

For the next few days, the weather seemed too cold for me to inspect the donkey. During this time, I took woolen blankets and sewed them together, shaping shoulders for a smooth fit, for a long cloak. So that I could wrap it over my knees when I sat sidesaddle on the donkey, I made the cloak quite full. I joined a hood at the top, and then I stitched myself a muff as well, since the dwarf would lead the donkey for me and my hands might as well be warmly lodged. I sewed rapidly and almost carelessly, for I wanted to be ready to leave at the first possible moment. I felt like a hare pursued by the hounds of grief. Faster, faster, I urged the needle. *February*, I promised myself. *We'll leave by February.*

Of course we could not take the sea chest with us, but I made a roll of a few clothes to carry behind my saddle. I could make new clothes in Nantucket. In the center of the roll, I placed the spring dress my mother had made for me. I left Liberty's little clothes in the sea chest.

When it was warm enough to walk to the barn, I visited the donkey, who was white and named Milk. She was as docile and willing a little beast as though created just for me. She had large soft eyes, and long ears like a rabbit's. She was so small I almost hesitated to sit upon her, but the dwarf, whose name was David Poland, reassured me her back was strong, and I weighed less than a hundred pounds.

Once a day, after picking our way across the yard around melting clumps of snow, David saddled Milk, and I sat upon her inside the barn. He led us for turns for half an hour or so, so that we might all be accustomed to each other. *This is the barn where my father hanged himself,* I could have told David, but chose not to. Instead I listened to the soft placement of the little donkey hoofs on the dirt floor. The bad weather lingered into March. When my neighbor Roger Pack checked on me, he was relieved to find David with me and trusted him at once. At night we played cards, or I read to him. I taught him chess.

I did not understand David, but I grew to like and trust him more every day, as we waited for the final thaw. What I did not understand about him was his readiness to do hideous work, such as bounty hunting, or any other job—guiding me to Cincinnati—if there seemed to be a profit in it. I asked him once, and he said, "Like any man, I must support my family. I am an opportunist. I look for opportunity, for I am quick-witted, and I make more money that way than I would in any steady employment."

"But you are far from your family."

"So is your sea captain, Una, far from you."

As David led Milk and me about in the barn, I asked him if he thought a woman could be a sea captain, and he replied, "Why, I don't know. I don't know nothing about the work." But he had not laughed, and I liked him for that.

After discussing it with David, I decided that on our way out, I would stop at my neighbors', where we had had the cider-pressing and dancing, *and where they had kept my mother's body in a shed*, and leave Roger Pack a paper authorizing him to sell my farm. He would send the money, through banks, to Nantucket. And the sea chest.

When the day came that the snow was gone and the ground drained enough of runoff for David and me to commence our journey, I let the hearth fire sink to ashes, and I pulled out the latchstring. I put a small sign on the door welcoming any who needed shelter and giving the name of my neighbor, should anyone wish to buy the property. Then I climbed up on Milk, and with David leading us, we started our journey through the wilderness.

We had gone only a mile when we met my very neighbors coming to call. Cecilia sat on their mule, with one child fore and two aft, and Roger had packsaddles full of food draped over his gelding. It was a pleasant meeting on the road.

We decided to go back to their place, and for a while we were a little caravan on the road, like Chaucer's pilgrims. Each of us, too, I thought, had a tale, though for their children the stories lay mostly ahead. Short and bitter, unjust! had been the story of my Liberty's life.

I tried, as we sat by their hearth, to be cheerful, but my tongue was slow to bend to sociable chatter. David seemed to sense my discomfort, and he told stories of horse races in Virginia. When he was a boy in his teens, he had been much in demand as a jockey, being so small and light. Sitting on the floor with his back to the fire, he scarcely rose above the height of the children who sat around him. Like an elf king speaking of a faraway land, he described the horses—colors, markings, dispositions—and their owners and jockeys with such language that we all had picked our favorites by the time the races began. My eye fell upon his small but chunky hands, and it was easy to imagine him guiding a racehorse. The children of the family adored David; indeed, they were *enchanted* by him and his stories and the curiosity of his own diminutive person. Sometimes as he spun his stories he called a child by name, as though the story were just for him or her.

Nonetheless, I was glad when it was time to set down the pallets, and I wrote the short legal document, witnessed by David, authorizing Roger Pack to sell my farm.

CHAPTER 96   🜨   **Forest Murmurs**

T HE NEXT MORNING, David and I had gone but a mile when I felt the weather warming, and I pushed back my hood to free my head to the air. As each day passed, David leading Milk in a northeasterly course, I could feel spring creeping along behind us. She, too, needed a guide, I thought. Often I glanced back on the trail to see if greenery was in pursuit. After a week of progress—we had slept at a cabin with a family named Mackensie—when I came out the door, I saw that spring had caught up with us in the night, and her net of green was flung over the brown grasses and the bare twigs of the trees.

Along our way, people were surprised to see us—a young woman on a white donkey led by a dwarf—but they were unfailingly hospitable. One little girl asked me if I was a preacher lady. She was disappointed to learn that I was only a traveler. "Bet you could preach," she said. I told her I was a seamstress, and I could show her how to make some fancy stitches if she liked. So I asked David to lend me the silver thimble he had got from Susan. I took out some bright floss and showed the child how to pull the six-ply apart into two-ply, and how to make cross-stitch, and feather stitch, and seed stitch, and French knots. She loved the French knots the most and laughed out loud when she saw them, like miniature popcorn. I, too, laughed aloud, for the first time since Liberty died.

I told Carol she might decorate her collars and cuffs with such stitchery, and while she stood there, still and solemn, I slowly circled

"Forest Murmurs"

her, embroidering a pretty scallop trim for her collar. Of course her mother had a needle, but I gave the sweet girl two twists of floss, spring green and daffodil yellow, to make things pretty with. As I was about to remount Milk, I noticed that Carol's eye fell on my puffy muff, which dangled from the saddle horn. I gave it to her and told her she might embroider flowers on it so that whenever she looked down at her hands in winter, she would remember spring.

David and I left the Falls of the Ohio–Lexington Road to cut north toward Cincinnati along the old Buffalo Trace. Once we passed a small band of Choctaw Indians. Four braves stood along the path, with their arms folded over their chests. I followed David's example and did not look at them, except with the corner of my eye. They were immobile as tree trunks, and both we and they pretended the other did not exist.

Once we passed a family whose skins were gray. Gaunt and hungry-looking, they sat beneath the long golden fronds of a willow tree. Their hair was dirty and matted, and they scratched as though they had lice. The gray hue to their skin was caused by a layer of dirt and grime long left undisturbed; it had spread out evenly over their faces and necks and hands, like a gray envelope. A little bright-eyed boy ran out from the group toward us and asked if we had any food. I placed a package of biscuits into his gray hand. When I looked back at them, the willow fronds curtained them off.

The greenery that had started out as mere dots and dashes, which at a distance looked like a hazy net hanging over the earth, now broadened into real leaves and blades of grass. These were not palms, of course, but there was jubilation in the spring that made me think of Palm Sunday.

I felt now at perfect ease with David and Milk. As the weather grew warmer, I preferred that we stop by ourselves, instead of buying a bed in a cabin. David would erect a little hut from saplings over which we flung a tarpaulin and before which we'd have a warming fire. With Milk tethered nearby, we boiled corn and threw in bits of the sacred ham. After supper, by the flickering flames, I sometimes read from my mother's volumes of Keats or Wordsworth. I had brought along only two books, but I had placed the others in the sea chest, and asked Roger Pack to send the chest to me, when he could, by paddlewheeler. I thought that I would put the books from home in a special place in the Nantucket library, by themselves on the mantel.

David found the poetry almost as impenetrable to his understanding as if it were written in a foreign language. After each line, whose meaning had been clear to me since childhood, he would say, "Now what does that mean?" After my exegesis, he would ask that I read the line again, and even then, sometimes, the words did not fall into meaning for him. Occasionally I would turn the tables on him (as Margaret Fuller had done when introducing me to the German language) and ask him to guess the meaning. Such answers were often painfully askew, though we dealt only in English.

"I get part of it," David said once, "but I need you for digging out the deeper meaning."

These smoky evenings were as pleasant as anything could be. My strength was not entirely with me, though, and I continued to ride on Milk. David took it on himself to rehabilitate me, and once in the morning and once in the afternoon he would ask me to walk a bit.

"Do you think Milk is tired?" I asked.

"No," he said. "But I be. I'll just ride a bit myself."

During such times, I led. Once we passed a foot peddler with David up on Milk. As we passed, the peddler muttered, "My, what a beard on a child!"

I began to giggle, and when I looked up at David, he was smiling broadly, too, all his nice white teeth showing between his mustache and beard. I recalled noticing his teeth—he had smiled slightly and continuously as he spoke—when he told the racing stories to the Pack children.

There was something about David's being small and yet a full-grown and strong man that I came to like very much. I could rely upon him, but he never assumed the stance of dominance so common in men speaking to women. Yet he was not shy, nor even particularly gentle. Once I saw him hit Milk sharply on the nose, when the donkey had insisted on cropping a particularly juicy-looking bunch of grass by the wayside. David's fist was as authoritative with his world as any man's, but he being small, his hand and fist were also smaller. He was normal in every way, a friend.

To my senses, the spring sang both lullaby and reverie. I was both soothed and alerted by what my eyes saw and my ears heard and my skin felt. Merely breathing the fresh air wafted on us by the surrounding sweet gum and maple, the creekside sycamores, was a pleasure. My hands felt fresh in the moist spring air. Sometimes Milk's feet crushed mint or chamomile, and my nostrils feasted on that natural perfume. My menses had not reestablished themselves yet, and I traveled like a young girl free of sexuality. I absorbed every beautiful detail of the Kentucky forest. Here I was in harmony. And the steady clip-clop of Milk's hoofs and David's high, reedy whistle were all a part of the enchantment.

I thought of the storm at the Lighthouse that had blinded me and how beautiful was the world when I could see again. In childbirth, my own life had hung in the balance, and now I had it back again. I lifted my chin and sucked in life, heavily, with both nostrils. When crows cawed, I would caw back at them, and when cardinals rolled an ornamental note, the tip of my tongue trilled reply.

I hoped that David was as happy as I was. I knew that I was neither kith nor kin to him—indeed, I paid him to guide me—but still I hoped the forest magic spoke to him. For my part, I could not imagine a more perfect companion. The first time I mocked a raucous crow, David merely turned his large head, glanced back over his small shoulder, and grinned.

The last night we camped, he unpacked the wolf skin and laid it out for himself to sit on. How benign that flat head looked now, as it lay on the ground. The vacant eyes were mere wobbly holes, the shiny nose an innocent. I sat across the little fire from him with the sapling lean-to, like a scoop, to catch the heat at my back.

"The river's clear of debris," he said. "You could take a steamer now, if you like."

"Yes."

He leaned around the flames to hand me something. It was the silver thimble.

"If ever you see Susan again, give it back to her for me."

"And her gold?" I said mischievously. I stuck the thimble on the tip of my middle finger.

"Well, I must have that."

I leaned over and tapped him in the middle of the forehead with the thimble.

"Shall I pay you now?"

He nodded, and I counted out the agreed-on sum, which he promptly pocketed. Then he stretched himself on the wolf skin, straightening out his short legs quite the same way a man with long legs straightens his.

"You watch me all the time," he said, "to see if I am different."

I only nodded, for it was true.

"I've told you a lie or two."

"How so?"

"The woman with the children. She's not my wife. She's my sister."

"But you make your home together?" I did not want to think of David's not having a home. I cared little that he had lied. He nodded affirmation. Sensing that he had a story to tell, I asked him how it was that he and his sister had come together in their living arrangement, and were the children his sister's or his own?

"I would never marry nor risk the chance of children. I would not bring another dwarf child into the world to face what I done faced. But she did. She's a bit taller, like I said. And a full-sized man was the father of George and Martha. He liked my sister's littleness well enough. He could pick her up with one hand if he wanted to. Shake her till her ears bled."

He looked at the campfire rather than at me as he spoke, and the shadows of the flames rippled across his face like insubstantial whips.

"I found a wolf cub and gentled it, in secret. But it was to do my will. I trained it like a hunting dog. When my wolf was full-grown, I sicced it one night on Norman—that was his name—when he was near to home. My sister found him in the morning on the path, his throat tore out."

My earliest image of David, when I was in my labor, came back to me, how he had scuttled about my cabin trying to sniff out Susan, how on all fours he looked under the bed, how when he stood up he had seemed a magic beast, as much wolf as man. I said nothing, but sat quietly on my side of the fire, looking at him. *Throats? I could tell him something of that. Captain Fry rose up, stood in the whaleboat next to the clumsy cleat, his sword in his hand. The hilt came down on Chester's curls, the tip lost not a moment lodging under the captain's own ear.* I looked at this small man beyond the campfire, lying on his side with his head propped by spread hand, forearm, bent elbow, and said nothing. After a moment, he raised his eyes to look into mine as he spoke again.

"I told her and the kids that I would kill the wolf that killed their father. So I took my rifle, went into the woods. I called my wolf, and when he come to me, I killed him. This is his pelt between me and the ground."

That he had killed the innocent wolf, obedient to his training and his nature, shocked me more than his human murder. The smoke from my father's rifle as he stood in the doorway had drifted back into the cabin when he shot King.

"My ways might not be as powerful or bold as a normal man's, but I swear the man deserved to die. Once I asked him not to mistreat Nora, and he just sneered at me. 'You gonna stop me?'

"I did stop him. There is ways to compensate. The weak of the world should remember that. Your Susan, she compensated for her weakness with gold. Once money and death was invented, the weak only need to use their wits.

"When I dragged the bloody wolf to the door, Nora and her kids took me as a hero. I was a hero, for I killed Goliath, but not the hero they thought."

Again I said nothing, but I felt for this small man, and I hoped that the gaze between us conveyed some sympathy, for I didn't know what to say. *I have not spilled blood, but I have drunk it.* I could have said that. After a moment, he averted his eyes, stared again at the flame, and spoke even more softly.

"So perhaps it's not so hard for me, after all, to be gone from home. She's only my sister. Perhaps it's harder for your Ahab."

"He's sailed a long time by himself. Many years."

"There's no man leaves his wife, I'm sure, but what jealousy gnaws him. Is she faithful? It eats him every night."

I offered the counterpart anxiety for any sailor's wife: "Ahab sails the South Seas. He has gone there before. He has lived there before, with the women, yes, long ago, and he came ashore and hunted with the savage warriors." I did not say, *Why do you suppose my husband speaks of himself, in the midst of domesticity, as 'cannibal old me'?* "But Ahab would not take an island wife now. I trust that."

David said nothing. He poked small wood into the flames.

"Was it true—you told me that you wanted to go home and buy normal-sized furniture for the children?" I prodded.

"Yes. There's no reason they should be cramped sitting on a little box that fits me."

"No Procrustean beds?"

"You'll have to explain that."

I did, and our conversation grew lighter, but all the time I told the myth of Procrustes, I was picturing a short-legged table and little chair where David sat when he was home. Diminutive furniture for the murderer. Well, he'd said boxes. No doubt he had had a diminutive rifle to point at his faithful wolf. Did he think he might dispatch the wolf within, his own rage, by pulling the trigger in the actual world? And on a brute, who was his friend. I knew better: that I was then, beside the campfire, the Una who had been cannibal in the whaleboat; and ever would I be the same. *There is no exorcism or expiation,* I could have said. But I would not tell him my own story—how strangely it had come about that fate had provided a fine home for a cannibal.

"Let's eat the last of the jam cake," I said.

When I handed him the larger portion, he said, "But I'm the smaller person. I don't need as much."

" 'Reason not the need,' " I quoted Lear's statement to his unfeeling daughters. "Besides, I know how to make another jam cake, when I'm home in Nantucket. And you don't."

"You're a person," he said, "who makes me think about things. From being around you. I don't mean the poetry. It's you yourself. Always taking things in. Always thinking. I like the way you think."

His sentence made me gasp. So had another little person, just his size, but young and girlish—Frannie—so had she once said this to me. Suddenly I missed her terribly. I wished that her words could call her back, that she could sit here by the fire, in the freshness of the Kentucky spring, listen with David and me to Milk cropping off the grass. Speak whatever was on her own innocent and inexperienced mind into this flickering circle.

But I did not speak what was in my own heart. I had told Charlotte my horror, but she was another woman.

"Because I'm around you, I think new thoughts," David said.

"What were you thinking?" I asked.

"About the big and the small. It's occupied my mind much of my life. Walking along today, I thought how there was ways of being big and small that had nothing to do with size."

"Well, yes," I said. But it surprised me that the idea was only now occurring to him. Such a simple idea, like the nugget of truth in a homily from some backwoods preacher.

"Take you," he went on. "It's your nature to be tolerant. I am a murderer. But you swallowed that right down. It wasn't hard for you in the least. But for me, it's hard to be tolerant. I can't tolerate the idea that somebody stupid or somebody with a black skin is as smart as I am."

"Yet I'd say Susan knew how to buy you."

He threw wood at the fire, and the sparks shot up like a fountain. "That sticks in my craw," he said. "And your toleration makes me feel small. I feel the size of an ant alongside you."

I felt ashamed of my own reticence. "Perhaps I am tolerant of murder because I know what I myself am capable of."

"No, I think tolerance is in your bones. You might be able to do certain things other people can't do because of it. Things most folk would call outrageous. Like travel with me. Few women would do that. But you say to yourself, 'There's nothing wrong with it. I'm willing to take a chance with him. I want to go home.' And so you're off. You don't even care what your husband might say about it. You might not even tell him."

"Sometimes I don't tell things. Then later I feel I was a coward." I wanted to tell my history, but I felt cut off from it. The loss of my child, the loss of my mother—those were worse and more immediate horrors.

"There aren't many rules for you. That's the thing. You decide."

"I think there might really be some rules."

"Think there might be! Most preachers would rise up out of their graves to hear you say that. You don't go to any church at all, do you?"

"Well, I've tried the Universalists. And the Unitarians."

"Universalists?"

"They say you're saved no matter what you do. God loves his creation universally, and he won't destroy it."

"So their God loves me?" I nodded. He continued, "You believe in the eternal life?"

"I don't know. I hope."

"God damn it, Una. You're as slippery as an eel."

I laughed and asked him if he'd ever eaten eel.

"River eel."

"In the ocean, there are eels like giant sea serpents. Sometimes boats go out to the Pacific from Nantucket to hunt them, like whaling boats."

"Which do you like better, the river or the ocean?" he asked but didn't wait for an answer. "The ocean is just there. It don't go noplace. It just comes to shore and goes back. Just bounces up and down. People have told me. But a river—now that has some direction, some purpose. It gets someplace. You can ride its back better than riding an elephant."

"I'll bet the people you talked to had only seen the ocean from the shore," I said. "There are currents in the ocean. And winds."

"Somebody told me the Amazon River holds its own in the ocean. A hundred miles from its mouth, you can let down a bucket in the ocean and get fresh water. I love that idea. See"—he got another wind—"that's a big idea. Ideas are just like people. They can be big and they can be small. That's a big one."

"Why is it big?"

"It makes a shiver go down my back. That's not all." He sat up and crossed his ankles in front of him. "It's an unnatural idea, unexpected. You wouldn't think it was possible. Impossible ideas—those are the big ones." Then he fell silent for a time.

His enthusiasm was like that of a child suddenly allowed to speak his piece. He seemed naive. Was I arrogant enough to be amused by him? Yes, a little. But so must it have been for Margaret Fuller when I told her my naive ideas about the nature of art. But Margaret had received my ideas and responded to them with substance, not with these effortless Socratic questions of why? and what? I could not give to him as Margaret had given to me. But did he want me to? No, I thought. He wants me to listen.

"I'll tell you something else, Una." Now he spoke with a note of defiance in his voice, though more quietly than ever. "When I go home, my sister and I will sleep in the same bed. Oh, we'll put up the bundling board while the children are still awake. They have sweet snores, like little piglets, and when their little grunts get going, then we take up the board, and lie closer. Sometimes it's her head on my shoulder, sometimes it's mine on hers. What's the harm in it? It's not like husband and wife. But once, months after I done for Norman, she took the palm of my hand and laid it on her breast. She don't mind a little touching. Nor do I." As though to hide his face from me, he pressed his body and face against the earth, his forehead on his forearm. After a bit, his voice muffled, he continued, "But we know the limit. Then sometimes it's best if I leave home for a while. Travel about." He paused. "Someday I'll come home, and she'll be married again. I know it's bound to happen."

I dared not move. So fully had he revealed himself, so trustingly, that even to twitch would have been sacrilege. When I made no reply, he stretched himself out again on the wolf skin. He looked into the flames for a while, and then just once, but long and intently, at me. Again, I made no response. He rolled to his back and closed his eyes. At length, I heard him snore, himself somewhat like a shoat.

I retreated farther back into the lean-to and wrapped myself in my cloak. By day I had no need of it now, but it was good to have at night. David had a supreme sanity. Nothing was twisted or dodged. Murder—yes, justified, in the circumstance. Incest—no, the necessity for it was not so great that it could not be denied. What would David say of the lesser crimes—bigamy, adultery?

Along the trail, David had stopped to carve his name on the smooth gray flank of a huge beech tree. Other travelers had left their names or initials there. I said the tree reminded me of an elephant in its girth and color. After he carved *David Poland,* he had walked around till he had arrived at a respectful distance, placed the tip of his knife against the bark, and asked if I would have my name engraved there.

"Yes," I had answered. "Una Spenser." I was surprised, for that was no longer my name. But I let what I had said hang in the air, uncorrected, till it was cut into the tree. "And put up Milk's name, too," I added. "Milk Donkey." He laughed and did so.

Our names were not very high up, since he was small, and all the other names seemed to float in a spray above us, as though those people were our thoughts.

"Would you put my baby's name, too?"

Without having to be reminded of the word, he merely nodded, and close to my name, he began the *L* of Liberty. The tail of the *y* he drew down long so that it touched the *U* of Una.

AT BREAKFAST, David was quiet, and so was I. Sadly I mounted the sidesaddle—perhaps my last ride on Milk's small back. We knew we were very close to the ferry crossing for the Ohio. "Perhaps it's beyond that crest of cedars," he said. "I'm not sure." Maybe neither river nor ferry exists, I thought, but we plodded on. We were drawn toward our goal, and yet we dreaded it. At last we came to the top of the bluff, and through the donkey's long ears I saw below us not only the landing, but a steamboat with red paddle wheel ready to depart port. Even as we watched, the whistle blew and a puff of steam drifted up.

"Hurry!"

"Hold on tight," he called back, and we started down the red-clay gully. Milk sat back on her haunches, and we half slid, half fell down the incline. The dwarf leapt from side to side in our gully, sticking a bit against a side, and then with his small legs rebounding. Like a spring, he compressed and bounced from side to side, pulling Milk's reins and encouraging her to sit and slide in the central trough. I did hold on, as tightly as I could, and we raised a great cloud of red dust as we descended. Even as we slid, even in the rush and dust of all that, I thought, *I have not been as honest with you as you were with me.*

At the bottom, we were full of our triumph and excited. The steamboat was as pretty as a bridal cake. I dismounted and felt strange and short as we walked toward the landing. I was sorry to be covered with dust.

"Lean down," David said.

When I bent over, as though he had read my thoughts, he wiped my face with his handkerchief. I could have whispered to him, *You are not alone in your infamy*, as he cleaned my face. But without my having spoken, the handkerchief was gathered back into his hand, stuffed into a pocket. Quickly, he turned to unstrap my roll from Milk's rump. "Get out your ticket money," he told me, and leading Milk along on the dock, her feet clopping on the planks, he escorted me to a man who had emerged to accept my passage.

With my ticket in one hand, David looked up at me and offered to shake hands. I sank down on my knees on the boards of the dock and insisted on embracing him.

"David, I meant to tell you last night," I whispered. "Then I grew afraid. I was afraid you would not tolerate what I have done in my life." I could feel the eyes of the ticket-taker watching us curiously— a woman down on her knees whispering in the ear of a bearded dwarf.

I pulled back to see what impression my words had made; the triumph left David's face.

"I wanted to respond to your—your *trust*," my whisper whisked on, "but I could not."

David's face infused with beauteous hope, he looked across the narrow space at me, his lips parting in surprise. Lovely as art, lovely as Susan showing me the indentation in the palm of her hand. What was that hope?

"I am a cannibal," I whispered. "In the strictest sense of the word." *No matter if it be in a loving face, when lips reveal teeth, when your lips reveal teeth, I think, "How strong? how sharp?"*

"How?" he asked, looking straight across with his amber eyes, level, into my eyes. They were the last part of his face to lose the sudden softness I had seen.

"At sea. In an open boat."

He seemed stunned. I stood up, stepping awkwardly on my hem.

Suddenly, before I got my balance, he embraced me, around the thighs, as a child might hug his mother. He looked straight up at me, his beard pressed against my dress. "I forgive you," he said in his mellow male voice that seemed to blend God and nature. His short arms were strong as tongs about my legs.

"And I you," I replied.

Then I crossed the gangplank.

STENCILED on the white-painted side of the boat, in red letters outlined in gold, was the name of the paddle wheeler: the *Lorelei*.

David Poland and I had had our good-bye, and I did not prolong it by standing at the railing. When I got inside, I sat down on the nearest chair. I could feel the great heart of the boat, driven by steam, thudding under my feet. How many times, I asked myself, must I tell and be forgiven? Charlotte, David. My own heart thudded in time to the engine. Not my friend Judge Austin Lord (too much of mischief and high jinks in our gossip), not Margaret Fuller (too high in seriousness and philosophy), not my mother (for us had been communion, and communication was lesser). How was it the heart decided whom to tell? My own physical heart rushed away from the moment of my telling David. I thought of Coleridge's Ancient Mariner, with his glittering eye, compelled to tell his guilty tale to the wedding guests, to anyone. I was not like that. Yet sometimes, as with Charlotte and David, my soul would have shriveled if I had not confessed. And to Ahab? Ah, he knew. He knew without having to be told.

The sound of wood gliding through water came to my ears—I was leaving Kentucky—and I thought of the Ancient Mariner's message: "He prayeth best who loveth best all things both great and small."

I should have quoted that to David when he was sharing his ideas about big and little. It was not transfer of coin that connected us, but life, and our need for compassion. I felt stunned, as though I had kissed him full upon the lips, so intense was the intimacy of our parting.

The *Lorelei:* Appropriate for a riverboat. Margaret Fuller had told me that along the course of the Rhine River, they had named a dangerous boulder the Lorelei.

David was standing on the dock, probably puzzling over the name of my boat as she worked her way upstream against the current.

Ich weiss nicht . . . I don't know why I'm sad. I'm going home.

CHAPTER 97   In the Cupola

NOT WISHING to frighten the housekeeper, I knocked at my own Nantucket door. What a glorious sound—the heavy brass pineapple, clunking against its plate.

The door was opened almost at once, not by my yellow-haired housekeeper, but by my former employer, her sister.

"Mrs. Macy!"

"No," she said, but I ignored her reply.

"Mrs. Macy, how wonderful to see you! And where is Miss Sheffield?"

"Not with us anymore."

"You don't mean she's died."

"In a manner of speaking, Miss Sheffield don't exist."

"Mrs. Macy, what do you mean?"

"I'm not Mrs. Macy." She beamed.

"Why of course you are," I said, beginning to feel anxious. She and her sister did resemble each other—both covered with freckles—but *this* was the laundress.

"You can't expect us at home to sit still just because you go traipsing all over the country," she said tartly.

"But who are you except Mrs. Macy herself?"

"The upshot of it is, Miss Sheffield is now Mrs. Hussey of the Try Pots, and I am now Mrs. Mustachioed Captain. Just like you!" She laughed and drew the shape of imagined mustaches under her nose.

"Ahab is not mustachioed! But you've married the master of the *Camel*!" We both laughed, and I proceeded to hug her well. Even with my arms about her good neck, I grew sober and drew back. "But what has happened to my friend Charlotte of the Try Pots? to Mrs. Hussey?"

"There's a new Mrs. Hussey, and she was the old Miss Sheffield."

"What has happened to my Charlotte?"

"Well, that is a story you need to sit down for. I hope it won't be upsetting to you. It wouldn't upset me. No, not with a captain for a husband, which is what I have. And what you have. Don't be forgetting that. But come sit in the parlor before the fire, and I'll bring you some China tea."

I sat down on my silk-upholstered parlor chair as though I were sitting on a basket of eggs. Did all these fine things belong to me? Perhaps they belonged to Mrs. Macy now. She seemed to be in charge. And I was filled with apprehension.

When Mrs. Macy reappeared carrying the tea tray, I asked her forthrightly: "Charlotte has not died?"

"That I can't tell."

"Mrs. Macy—"

"No longer Mrs. Macy—"

"My dear friend, certainly you can tell if a person is dead or alive?"

"It's usually easy enough, yes, if you're looking at the person. But even there a mistake can be made. We made it—you remember—after the fire, and we thought Isaac the gaoler to be dead, but in fact, he got up and is the father of a fine, golden-haired boy— Oh, Lord," she said, "where is your baby?"

Here I bit my lip, and tears of both grief and frustration swam to my eyes. "My baby died."

She grabbed her apron to her eyes and instantly had a cry. I sat waiting, as though, again, I were stunned by my own news. Finally, she peeped over the top of her apron—I had never seen it so wrinkled—and said how sorry she was. She soon followed up her heartfelt condolences with hope: "You shall have another sweet babe. Make no mistake about it. When Captain Ahab comes home, we'll keep him here till the deed is done, even if I have to swim underwater and bore holes in the *Pequod*."

I sat quietly. She sniffled a few times, drank some tea, and then continued, in quite a different tone.

"About Charlotte Hussey. She told me once that she had loved Kit Sparrow, what was your former husband, from the first moment she saw him, though they were both but children. Then when the news came back the *Sussex* had been stove by a whale and all hands lost, she married Mr. Hussey, the first Mrs. Hussey having died of natural causes, and I was as glad as any to see Charlotte pick up her life and go on. Then you and Kit came back, married. You know how that was."

I nodded, remembering the first time I had seen Charlotte's merry face materialize from the steam of the chowder pot, and her amazement at seeing not a ghost, but a living Kit.

"I really don't know how that was for Charlotte," Mrs. Macy went on. "I expect no one knows, unless maybe she told you, seeing as how you were friends. She was a dear girl, and she never placed blame where it was unwarranted."

"Was?"

"I only mean during the time I knew her. She's gone now."

"But, please. What do you mean by gone?"

"Well, Mr. Mustachioed Captain of the *Camel*—I should call him Robert Maynard now, and I am Mrs. Maynard, if ever you should wonder what to call me—he arrives at Straight Wharf with a letter addressed to Charlotte Hussey, and clear as can be the return name on the envelope of Kit Sparrow. Not usually running out to Nantucket, and being all unfamiliar with the populace here, he—Captain Maynard—asks where to find Charlotte, and whoever that was he asked sees the return and says that Kit Sparrow is dead. So they take the letter to the judge.

"Now I can't say under what law he acted, but Judge Across-the-

Street he takes it upon himself to open the letter and read it. Then Judge says not a word to anybody, but he sends for Charlotte Hussey. What was in that letter exactly, I do not know. None of us knows. Except the man over there across the street, and his lips are sealed."

A slight smile crept to my mouth. I could have bet Mrs. Macy— Mrs. Maynard—that before sundown I would know.

"Go on," I urged.

"Well, that night, slick as a greased pig, Charlotte Hussey disappears. My captain claimed that somebody came down and put her on a little sloop. He thought it might be the judge, but the judge is the Judge Lord, not to be questioned, and you're the only person I've even told what Captain Maynard told me. This is an island, Una, and the talk can twist round and round till there's a whirlpool in the washtub. That's not good for Nantucket, and I tell Captain Maynard that this is my home, though he may come and go as his work takes him, but I won't have my home all stirred up over something he might have seen."

"Where did Charlotte go?"

"Well, nobody knows. At least nobody tells. A couple of months pass. Poor Mr. Hussey is crying into the chowder so bad no salt is needed. And he's run off his legs, for the new inn is three times as busy as the old place out Madaket Road could have ever been. About this time, another letter comes, shipped from Boston, but no return address on the outer envelope. It's addressed to the judge.

"He opens it and calls a group into his parlor to hear what it says. It's from Charlotte—"

"She's alive!"

"Well, at least at that time. I've not seen her since. She may be dead now, and that's why I can't say straight up if she's alive or dead, murdered by Indians. But the letter, like I said, is from Charlotte, and the judge reads aloud that Charlotte says she is gone forever, and that the judge is to grant Mr. Hussey a divorce for desertion! If that don't beat all." She finished her tea.

"I wonder what the letter from Kit said."

"I wouldn't hurt you for the world. You were as sweet and faithful to him as a woman could be. But you see, they had all that growing up together. Well, nobody knows, except the judge, but some speculate that Kit asked Charlotte to come to him someplace out beyond the Great Lakes, and she's done her best to find him."

"It seems possible," I said, shaken. "Mrs. Macy—Mrs. Maynard—forgive me, but I need to rest."

"Well, there's just a bit more." She stood up. "I introduced Mr. Hussey to my sister, your housekeeper, and he married her. They say her chowder tops even Charlotte's, and hers topped the Mistress Hussey's before her. Not trusting your silver and fine china to just anyone, I moved in myself to keep house."

As quickly as I could, after expressions of appreciation, my brain dizzy with Mrs. Maynard's recital of how names and identities had shifted, I retreated to my room, which was sparkling white and cozy as it had been on my stormy wedding night. My own room! I did get it back, despite Rebekkah Swain's pronouncements.

As I lay on the bed, I thought *he* had wanted her instead of me. A bitter tear squeezed from each eye. Kit could have sent for me. But I was married now, and I would not have wanted to leave Ahab or my home to live with Kit among the Indians. But Charlotte chose it. I was sure she had. Then let her choose it, and let him choose her!

I would miss my friend, though. Had she guessed that I knew all along that Kit was not dead? Probably not.

Did the judge guess that I had misrepresented the facts? I heard Mrs. Maynard slip out the front door, and, rather faintly, I heard the brass clap from across the street of the judge's pineapple knocker. After perhaps ten minutes, scarcely time at all either to rest or collect my thoughts, my own pineapple clanged away, and I wearily sat up, put on my shoes, straightened my hair, and went to greet the judge.

He was all smiles and happiness to see me, but he immediately exclaimed, "How tired you look!" and asked if he should return later. "I've brought you a basket of jams," he quickly added.

How elegant he looked! Like a younger Benjamin Franklin, I noted again, bald dome but his straight side hair fell only to his jaw and not his shoulders. Austin Lord wore gray trousers and coat, cut from cloth of such tight and expensive weave that the color had no power to proclaim its drabness. And he wore a quilted vest of sky-blue silk, crossed in front by a silver watch chain. He was slimmer.

I escorted him to the dining room and put down place mats and dishes for us. How unfamiliar these dishes were. Haviland china bedecked with flowers and ribbons. I felt almost afraid of them.

"I saw some Irish porcelain-paste dishes when I was in Boston," he said. "They are so thin they make this look like frontier crockery."

"These are dainty enough," I said shortly.

"Mr. Hussey has twice brought me money—your return on the Try Pots. He prospers, Una. And you with him. But the business would have gone to rack and ruin if he hadn't remarried."

"My dear friend," I said, and I actually reached my hand out to him. "Don't fiddle-diddle with me. Mrs. Macy—the new Mrs. Maynard—has half diddled me to death with her equivocations and misunderstandings. In heaven's name, what has happened?"

"Kit wrote to Charlotte. He didn't ask her to come, but she determined to travel west. There was no stopping her. Finally, I gave her some money—some of mine and some of yours, since you have prospered so handsomely—to help her travel—and I wanted a financial collaborator in speeding them west. Who better than you?"

It pleased me that the judge used his position so freely, in behalf of friendship.

"Kit's letter was mostly a sweet reminiscence of their childhood together," he went on. "Charlotte took the letter with her."

"And she herself has written back. Has she found him?"

"Well, not exactly."

"What do you mean?"

"She didn't write back."

"Mrs. Macy—Maynard—said there was a letter to you, from Charlotte."

"Try this guava jam, Una." He put a smear of the ruby stuff, quite seedy-looking, on a biscuit and waited for me to try it.

I did. "Delicious. But do we have something less fancy—domestic strawberry?"

"The best. Made from the plainest Quaker strawberries."

"I discern that you are rather proud of yourself. And not over jam exotica. What news was in the letter Mrs. Maynard said you received from Charlotte?"

His face turned red. "My dear, no one reads me as you do. I am delighted that my dear young neighbor has come home. Also, Una, I'm very sorry about the baby."

"My mother died, too," I said petulantly. I felt like a child who was not getting her way fast enough.

"Oh," he gasped, and then stammered, "So sorry . . ." He waited a moment, then went on, "Well, the letter. I wrote it myself, to myself."

"You did what?" I could only stare; he blushed all over his bald head. "Suppose she returns, no Kit at all, and her husband has gone and married the third Mrs. Hussey?"

"Well, Charlotte did leave Mr. Hussey. She *should* have sent such a letter. She should have legally released him. He was crying so hard—"

"I know, that the chowder needed no salt. Mrs. Maynard told me."

"Una." He was suddenly serious. "If you could have seen Charlotte that night. She was a woman on fire. There is absolutely no doubt in my mind that she will look forever for Kit. Never again will she believe that he is dead. She would have to see his body herself."

My head whirled. "She might not be able to tell, even then. You can't always, you know." I remembered Isaac Starbuck, apparently lifeless, lying on the ground before the burning house.

The judge regarded me anxiously. "She said that you had a husband, that you were going to have a baby. She said that you would not begrudge her Kit." There he stopped, for he was truly curious about my reaction.

"She's right." I looked at my judge and smiled.

Austin Lord was my friend; he respected my judgment in spending my money and in deciding to travel as I wished; but he was the judge in Nantucket and not just "my" judge, as I liked affectionately to think of him. As we allowed a pause in our conversation, I contemplated him. His wealth and power were like polish on his being. He glowed with it. When I first came to him, I had been poor and my husband had been an outlaw and insane.

"So what are you thinking now?" he asked me as he sipped his tea.

"How is it," I asked, "that we have become friends? My station was abject. I came to you with a plea. I suppose had Ahab not, by chance, bought the house across from yours, we would not have become friends."

"That was my good luck. I am grateful for it."

"And so am I."

There was comfort in his largess. He was a kind of protector.

"It is partly luck," he went on, "that we have become friends. But that first time you sat in my parlor with the gaoler, there was nothing abject about you. You had your purpose, your wish. That alone saves any human from abjectness. You wanted me to let Kit go. Did you get your wish? Yes. In the old fairy tales, it is the strength of the wish that transforms life. The wish is itself the magic wand.

"And you already had a suitor, Una. You were blind to this, but half the unmarried young ladies in Nantucket—at least the ones whose families were not wealthy—were spellbound by the gaoler's kindly nature, his easy strength, and his golden hair."

"Knowing that Kit is yet alive, will the town count any children I and Ahab might have to be legitimate?"

"Only one person has asked me this. Can you guess who it was?"

"The Unitarian minister?"

The judge laughed. "No, Una. He is probably the most liberal and humane person in Nantucket. After, perhaps, William Mitchell."

"Mitchell?"

"The scientist? The astronomer who sets the chronometers? No."

"Who, then, asked you?"

"Think a moment. There is a clue in our most recent discourse."

"The gaoler."

"Exactly."

"Mrs. Macy—Maynard—has just told me he is married and has a golden child."

"When he asked me, I told Mr. Starbuck I had pronounced Kit legally dead, and your marriage to Ahab was as legal as any marriage, and your children as legitimate. I told him I was the absolute civil authority in the matter."

"Are you?"

He did not deign to answer. As I looked at him, he seemed to grow larger. I put my hand on my forehead.

"Una, I think you should go back to bed. But you have found home essentially intact. There is nothing here that has the power to stop your world from spinning at the same rate that you left it. You have jumped off and back on the turning top. The power of the law has kept it so, like magnetism or gravity."

"Ahab divorced me from Kit." I gasped, for I had not meant to tell him. "And then married me to himself."

"Ahab did not think Kit dead?"

"No."

"Then he is as powerful as the law."

"He took me aboard the *Pequod*, and there on the spot where he had married Kit and me, when we were all far out at sea, he divorced us. And took me as his wife."

"You have left one outlaw for another."

"Ahab loves me in a way Kit was incapable of. And I him. Kit's vision was double, always ambivalent and double. Ahab's vision has a piercing singleness to it. I am his single choice."

"This divorce by captain's decree, and the marriage, then—they were what you wished?"

"Yes, I wished it."

"And you thought you had no power!"

"I feel weak enough right now." Indeed, the room seemed almost in motion. The painted waves on the walls—while I focused on the clean-shaven, polished skin of my bald judge—seemed in my peripheral vision to sway.

"I meant to make your homecoming light, with crumpets and sweetness."

I reached my hand across the table to him. It was a broad, shining mahogany board, and only our fingertips could touch. "No," I said. "The conditions of home needed to be clear to me."

"Well, they are also much clearer to me."

"I've troubled your conscience?"

"No. But you have astounded me. You and Ahab." He fidgeted in his chair. "I had not reckoned his power, in his own lawless way, to be as great as mine. It's a little unsettling."

I tightened my grip on his fingertips. "I do respect the law," I said. (Why, having just put my own history into an honest light with him, did my lips so soon bubble out a partial truth?) "You have been a wonderful friend to me," I added, with all my heart.

He returned the squeeze. "Then very soon we shall settle again into our cozy, neighborly way. I shall introduce you to the Mitchells—a family you will enjoy."

"I'd like that."

"Good. Now you should rest." He released my fingers and pushed back his chair from the dining table. The painted ship over near the corner seemed to move. It was coming closer to home. The judge spoke yet again: "Let me leave you with an abstract question."

"Yes?"

"You say that Ahab married and divorced you—"

"Divorced and married—"

"Quite right. Married, divorced, married. That he divorced and married you on the same spot on the deck of the *Pequod* where he had earlier married Kit and you."

"Yes. As nearly as could be told."

"And that makes a kind of rightness and order of things, doesn't it?"

"Perhaps. In some symbolic but nonessential way."

"But consider if it really was the same spot, or a thousand miles off the mark?"

"Scarcely that. How could it be?"

"You and Kit were married far out to sea. The *Pequod* moved away from that place, even while you were wed. What is the nature of a spot, a place? Can it remain the same? Is it adequate to give a place only a local definition? Ought it not be global?"

I smiled, pleased with the question. "This is a new line of thought for you."

"While you were away, I spent a good deal of time with the astronomers, with William and his daughter Maria Mitchell."

AND SO I climbed the stairs toward my room with the happy thought that Nantucket, for all its smallness as an island, had yet new and interesting people with whom I might make an acquaintance. I hoped that Charlotte would find Kit in the wilderness, since she wished it so ardently. I would miss her. Kit seemed scarcely real to me. Nor the horror in the whaleboat. Sorrow for the loss of my mother and child was covering all of that—a new sediment.

I did not stop my climbing with the second floor. I climbed to the third level, to the cupola. There I picked up the brass telescope and swept the horizon for the sails of the *Pequod*. From that line, my eye traversed a zigzag path across the ocean, coming closer with each sweep, scanning the waters for my homeward-bound Ahab. At length my telescopic vision, unrewarded, came to harbor.

How dear a place it was. I could see the gestures and expressions of people disembarking, pleased they had come to port. I put down the spyglass, and the harbor moved away from me. Now the scene was landscape instead of portrait. The ships and wharf seemed a size to hold in my hand. Dear home, beautiful home.

CHAPTER 98   To Summer

FROM THE CUPOLA, I came to my room, and then BLAM BLAM BLAM went the pineapple again, and when I dragged myself again to the front door, there was my third set of visitors. And a set they were, that is, a pair: Captains Peleg and Bildad. Two stern old Quakers, Bildad carrying his Holy Book and Peleg a small black satchel. No bearers of sweetmeats, these two.

I bade them sit in the parlor, and I was glad to see that Mrs. Maynard had carried off our cups and plates before she quit the house. She wished to move back to her own place now that I was home.

"We've come to see ye at the very first possible moment," said Peleg.

No, I thought, *you've been preceded twice.* There was something perverse in me that made me want to contradict whatever truth these righteous people presented.

"As we were instructed to do by our friend, thy husband," added Captain Bildad.

"Blast ye, Captain Bildad," put in Peleg, "we would have come to see the lady in any case, instructions or no."

"He fears ye dead," Bildad went on in a dolorous tone.

"Yet she's all as sweet and pretty with black curls as she was before she ever voyaged to the wilderness."

"She's drawn and pale," intoned Bildad. He sat very upright on my flowered sofa, with his hands, lest they be contaminated by colorful chintz, resting on the black cloth of his trousers.

"I'm but back from my travels."

"We know," Peleg said, "and we've come to call, by our own inclination as well as by the request of Captain Ahab, communicated by letter, to deliver letters to you at the soonest possible moment. And they are here in my satchel."

"You'd not give them all to her at once?" Captain Bildad turned harshly to his partner. "She's wan and sickly."

"Oh, no," I spoke up for myself. "I'm quite well. You have letters?" I felt swept with joy, that tide quite replacing the sluggishness of fatigue.

As Peleg reached inside the dark satchel, which he had set at his feet, Bildad grabbed his hand. "No, ye don't!" Bildad ordered. "Have ye forgotten the ways of the sea so soon? When a shipwrecked sailor washes ashore, a-clinging to his board, do ye thrust a whole cask of biscuits down his throat? Nay, ye careless devil! Ye ration! Ye ration! Look at her. Shipwrecked if ever I saw a shipwreck."

Peleg looked at me anxiously. "Hast thy life been hard?"

"I would much appreciate and be grateful if you delivered my husband's letters to me from your satchel." I spoke as politely but firmly as I could, yet I was shaken.

"Resign thyself to tell the truth," Bildad said. "Where did thy ship flounder? Where was she stove?"

"Thou, Bildad!" Peleg roared. "Her journey has been by land!"

"I speak all metaphoric," Bildad said serenely, peering at me through his spectacles and crossing both hands over his chest. "And Mrs. Captain knows it well."

"Thou shalt not torture her with piety," Peleg said warningly. "We'll have no talk of what is good and what is best, of what is meet."

"Thou shalt not kill her with too much joy. I see thy soul, Peleg, sinking down in the fiery pit, a murderer of innocence, a persecutor of Mrs. Captain, who is a lamb of sweetness and resignation."

"How do I persecute her?"

"With too much joy!"

"Blast ye, Bildad—"

"No need of profane words. Impatience is thy sin. Prodigality—"

"Prodigality of biscuits! Blast ye, I mean letters. 'Tis thou wilt kill her. Look, she's likely to faint with wanting of her rightful letters, which Captain Ahab commissioned us to bring so that when she came home she should not be alone! And I'll give them to her, if ye bite my hand for it!"

But lank Bildad, though the satchel sat at Peleg's feet, bent himself as fast as a trunk lid could close and snatched the satchel into his own lap. "It was never my intent not to give her something," Bildad pronounced sanctimoniously. "But thou shalt not kill her with too many biscuits." He slowly reached his hand into the satchel and drew out a precious envelope. I recognized Ahab's handwriting, large and flowing with crests and valleys like the waves of the sea.

I sighed with happiness and held out my hand. Very grateful, I took my letter and pressed it to my bosom.

"Now, brother Bildad, old shipmate," Peleg said, quite appeased, "we must cast off and leave her to her reading."

The letter felt like a dove at my breast.

As they stood up, I said, "Please, how many letters are there?"

"We have received three," Peleg answered in a kindly voice. "In a few days, I shall bring thee the second."

"After thou hast had time to masticate and safely digest the first," Bildad explained, persisting in his biscuit analogy.

I walked with them to the door, still cradling my letter against my throat.

In a quiet, confidential tone, Bildad inquired, "Thou wert where? when thy boat was stove?"

"Kentucky."

"How many lost?" Bildad murmured.

"Two."

"God bless ye and have ye in his holy keeping," old Bildad mumbled, as they left.

I flew up the stairs, pulled back the white covers, and ensconced myself in my plump bridal bed. My hands shook as I opened the envelope, and upon reading his greeting words—"Una, One, My Dearest One"—a great scoop of feeling swooped me up.

Una, dove and eagle, I could quote thee Shakespeare, "Let me not to the marriage of true minds admit impediments," but I think we are not of two minds, but only one. And I think marriage is too tame a word for the union that we have known. Also, I must dismiss "impediments." We have cast aside any impediment by the force of our own will. Notice I do not become inconsistent and say "the force of our own wills," for our will, like our mind, is one. Neither ye nor I would name the ocean as an impediment. Oh, no, it is the great flowing connection, second only to the air itself, participating in our unity. Why our souls were forged in the same smithy, deep in the bowels of the earth, I cannot know, but you and I, Una, are made of the elements named by the ancient Greeks—fire, water, air, earth. Those elements and their myriad manifestations are not impediments but minions; they do our bidding and will transport our thoughts to one another and finally be the means of our reuniting.

I cannot admit impediment, for it would drive me mad. If there were any real thing that kept me from my Una, then I would destroy it. All things are means by which to come to thee, are angels of facilitation—else I would name them devils and send them to the pit of hell. Ah, old Bildad liked to talk of the pit of hell. I used to ask myself what need he had of that. Was not the loneliness of this earth enough of hell?

I have felt my power before, but now, loved, loved, I could sail this ship into the heavens, harpoon the moon. Do you think I rave? Do I frighten my Una? It is only that I have never been complete before, never felt the stretching out of my completeness. I am full of life, not madness. Surely at this moment, I am not restless in my cabin, forever peering out the portholes, but held in your blessed arms.

The last morning, when ye opened your arms to me—poetry fails Ahab, for the comparison may not please thee. But, yes, I have known that rapture many times in the hunt. In the hunt there is a kind of marriage.

Was I with thee before the world began? Will I be with thee after death? Our union is too perfect to think that it can be rusted by time.

And so if Shakespeare has not adequate language to tell thee of my love, what use the ravings of old Ahab? Ye know all that I might say. So, then, if I cannot tell thee of my love, let me tell thee of my labor—for we have had a bridegroom's luck.

The first whale the Pequod saw—'twas Daggoo who sang out—was shriveled and sick, very nigh unto death. Perhaps ye did not whale long enough to know that there can be treasure in such animals. But any experienced whaleman knows—AMBERGRIS, at $200/lb. Baleen oil is at 33 cents a gal., and sperm oil at 88c./gal. The case oil, the finest lubricant known to man, so light, slick, and slippery, is at $1.38/gal., but ambergris, the fixative in the finest perfumes, is at $200/lb. And I saw a great whorl of it, a spot like a healed scab where a tree has lost a mighty limb, a little in front of the side fin. Not that the whale had lost his fin.

No, the ambergris forms very much as the nacreous pearl forms in an oyster. Ye know that the chief diet of the sperm whale consists of giant squid, which the whale fetches from its lair in the greatest depths. The squid's body was never built to survive at any other pressure, and when the sperm whale ascends, the squid, clamped between the toothed lower jaw and the bony sockets of the sperm whale's upper jaw, explodes. And the sperm whale feasts. But sometimes the horny beak of the squid lodges all indigestible within the whale. There's impediment! The whale cannot disgorge the final sword of his foe, it festers its new scabbard, and despite the whale's internal bandaging of the irritant with a material that is rather golden and cheeselike in texture, the whale dies. It is that cheeselike glob that can be extracted, through floating surgery from a whaleboat drawn up beside the leviathan, which is called ambergris.

Yet, for all my joy at recovering this treasure, for like any new groom, I would bring to my wife all my worldly treasure with the determination that it should ever increase, there was little challenge in the action. But let not Ahab turn up his considerable nose at luck!

Later in the day, we gave chase to another sperm whale, which we took, and the try-pots burn now, even as I write.

—Hark, Una. Faithful Starbuck has just now appeared to say that the Coriander, homeward bound for Nantucket, is in the offing. We are off the Cape Verde Islands. He himself has a letter for his wife, and he asks that he might take one of the whaleboats and deliver our letters to be relayed home. I said, "I'll go myself, and thee with me!" Though this page be but brief, it is the flag and ensign of a bounteous love.

Ahab, Captain, the Pequod

BAM! BAM! BAM! The pineapple again. Had I dreamt, or had I read and slept? All exhausted, I crept, half clinging to the stair rail, down toward the front door. There stood Aunt Charity, the sister of Bildad.

"Thou art pale as a ghost," she said. She held the other two letters, one in each hand. "My brother and Captain Peleg came to me swelled up and proud as peacocks that they were managing thy business so well. 'Ye intend to ration her letters?' I asked. 'I have never been married, nor ever even hoped to marry'—I said to them—'but I am not lacking in imagination. Do I not fill up thy boats with all the goods of the land that anyone could ever imagine having need of at sea? Yea, I do. And has imagination ever been found wanting in me? Has anyone ever said, "O, if Aunt Charity had but imagined my need of beeswax with which to coat my bunion"— Nay, for I did imagine bunions, beeswax, and blister powder. And now only the slightest consultation of imagination on my part tells me'—I informed those old bachelors— 'without doubt that all her letters must be delivered, and I shall surely do it.' "

With that she clapped me on each cheek with the letters, followed by two little kisses, soft as butterfly wings, in the same places, then put the envelopes tenderly into my two hands, and left. I walked into the dining room to surround myself with seascape.

Una, of my Heart,

We have rounded the Cape of Good Hope, and so now the continent of Africa hangs pendulous between me and thee. Has ever a captain been so impatient for a voyage to end? I hope this letter finds thee happy with thy mother, or that this linen page, now swept with my hand as I write, will be waiting, in Nantucket, for thy return. May this be a happy day for thee, dear one. I know only that for thee it is an autumn one. My restlessness is unbounded, and that seems the only thought or feeling that I have to communicate to my beloved. I pace as unceasingly as the waves slap the bows of the ship. My feet and legs want mountains to climb, and, lacking that, I sometimes mount the lookout myself. Air seems the better connector than water now, for it can sail quickly toward India and skirt China, easterly blow over the Pacific, whirl up the North American coast to the Arctic cap and then southward, inland, to find thee. If air from Canada plains touches thee now, it is my breath. Many times, aloft, have I blown it easterly to navigate the atmosphere in search of thy soft cheek.

Words I have few of—and no passing ship has brought me any words of thine—but feeling festers and boils in me like something molten. I cannot really write, but I will send this attempt to write, when next there is opportunity.

Bridegroom's luck, indeed: we have taken a second treasure trove of golden ambergris.

Ahab

And the third letter:

Una, whose second name, this night, is Luna—

Starbuck, noting my impatience this evening, said merely that it was hard to be far from home. "Why have I created a hearth only to abandon it?" I asked him, for the anguish broke out of me. He told me that when his loneliness was almost beyond bearing he meditated on the evening star and thought of Mary.

There being a large, shining moon tonight, she instantly took my eye, and I thought Una, Luna. The words were very beautiful and soothing to me. The whole night became lovely to me, and I will describe to thee how the prow of the Pequod *turned back the water in silver scallops. Small, phosphorescent fish were jumping to starboard, and they seemed a marine reply to the blurry Pleiades.*

—More he wrote, for this was a long letter, when he took up pen and put it down and took it up many times. He had hopes for our baby and wishes for my health and safety; to my mother Ahab had penned greetings both polite and sincere. But the best of the letter was the closing:

We have taken ambergris yet a third time, as though we lived in a blessed fairy tale. The hold is nearly full of oil as well—and we may take another whale or two as we sail home. Yes, home! for it is in my authority to say we set sail for Nantucket, and I have done so. With three caches of ambergris we shall not lack for profit. This letter will be saved and sent ahead when I spy the fastest of Yankee clippers; and before midsummer I shall greet thee, wife.

W<small>HAT MAGIC</small> there was in the word when it named all that I would be! Mother, daughter, neighbor, friend—I let go of all those names, except my own, for that of wife. I drank the word as though it were wine. Every night as I pulled up the coverlet, I let myself have one sip, "Wife," and I fell asleep intoxicated. For breakfast, before I broke my bread, I murmured "Wife" to myself and smiled down at my blurry reflection on the mahogany tabletop.

Twice a day I climbed to the cupola and swept the sea with my spyglass. I visited that little glass-sided room upon awakening, and then again during the last light of day. My impulse was to run aloft every hour, but I would not allow it. I kept my house as though my husband were there so that when he did come, every household task would be practiced and perfected. All day I cooked and cleaned, and occasionally I purchased some new item from town. When housekeeping work was done, I read or sewed.

I had the judge to many a meal, and also the sweet, practical, imaginative Aunt Charity, and good Mrs. Maynard since her captain was usually away, so I did not lack for company. Some of the richer citizens from Main Street came to call, but I had not known them when I was poor, and I did not encourage them now. I wanted my world, even the people I knew, to be intact for Ahab. I did invite each month Mr. Hussey and the new Mrs. Hussey, who was far less refined than my dear Charlotte, and each month he brought to dinner a small bag of gold coins which he said was my share of the Try Pots earnings. "That it is," Mrs. Hussey would boom out, "to the penny!" I always served them beef, knowing they must be saturated with chowder.

From Margaret Fuller, I received a few letters and also an invitation to visit her in Boston, which I declined, as I did not want to miss Ahab's return by so much as a day. He must find his wife at home. But I promised Margaret that after Ahab set sail again—alas, I knew that was inevitable—I would promptly visit her.

My judge did insist that I make the acquaintance of the Mitchell family, and I have been forever glad I did. "Word of the *Pequod* would come up from the wharf," Judge Lord said, "in plenty of time for you to scurry down, or to wait at home, if you can contain your eagerness." If Margaret Fuller was the preeminent woman of letters with whom I was ever so fortunate to make a connection, Maria Mitchell became the preeminent woman of science.

CHAPTER 100   The Mitchells

To BEGIN our acquaintance, my judge invited me across the street for dinner to meet Maria Mitchell and her father, William Mitchell. I had had time to stitch up a new dress of sprigged chintz, but my handiwork could not have been of less interest to either Maria or her father, despite the elaborate smocking of the bodice. Her dress was a fine, rich brown, simply made, and I immediately commented, "What a lovely silk, Miss Mitchell."

She said quietly, "We wear the silk, Mother and all of us at home, so as to avoid the cotton."

"Why is that?" I queried.

Her father put in, "The Southern slaves pick the cotton for our textile industry. We don't wish to be a market for what begins with slave labor." His tone was one of sad information but with no reprimand aimed at my own cotton frock.

Then they both exclaimed over the bounty and beauty of the dinner table.

Before us on the judge's platter sat a white mound of baked scrod, seasoned with paprika and cracker crumbs, garnished with new peas and new potatoes, and surrounded by many side dishes of squash, cabbage, radishes, and the like. I had furnished a twelve-egg pound cake for our dessert, capped with a sugar drizzle, and the judge had placed it on a cake stand with a pedestal to honor my culinary creation. He and I sat at the ends of the table, set with the Irish china he had seen in Boston, so thin I feared breaking it with a fork. (Never had I met a man so fond of pretty china as my judge. He seemed to have an insatiable appetite for it—as though the plates themselves and not what they presented could be eaten! I knew that his cabinets were stuffed with large sets from the Orient, from England, from France, and beautiful blue-lattice-marked plates and dishes from Russia. But on that night, it was the newly acquired Belleek.)

William Mitchell pleased me; he seemed the essence of an ideal father. Kindly, comfortable, and above all reasonable, yet he had an ability to identify sympathetically with his listeners. Maria said he had been a wonderful teacher for her, and he returned the compliment by saying that of all his eight children, she was his most apt student.

"She sets the chronometers for the captains, when I am away," he said, taking a large helping of fish. "And has, since she was twelve years old."

Knowing from my own days as a sailor how essential that instrument was in determining longitude, I understood that she had earned the trust not only of her father but of the captains as well. I myself had never used the instrument, and when I asked her to teach me how, she promptly said she would be glad to do so and that I must visit her the next day at Vestal Street. Since the invitation was issued so early in the meal, while I was still helping myself to the peas, I felt Maria to be of an open and trusting nature.

"We shall soon be moving from Vestal Street," Maria went on, "to the Union Pacific Bank, where Father has a new job, but I prefer that you know me in the place I think of as my natural habitat."

Her voice was rather deep in pitch, and she, like myself, had naturally curly dark hair, but hers was neatly smoothed on the sides and defined in sausage curls in the back. As the evening progressed, I noted an evenness and quietness in her manner that seemed almost too even to me: a young woman brought up in the Quaker tradition. But her father had a sparkle in his eye, and his conversation roamed freely over matters of education, the slavery issue, the Quakers and the Unitarians, his weather records, and his correspondence with other scientific men up and down the coast and even in England.

"Have you become something of a naturalist, living in Kentucky?" Maria asked me in her even, well-modulated tones.

William seemed curious about what I could tell him of my life in the forest, while Maria wanted me to share my observations of nature. She had much less curiosity about me in any personal sense. Yet I began to want her as a friend. I'd not known anyone like her.

I told them I had not only lived in the heart of the continent, in Kentucky, but also on a lighthouse island.

"Compare the flora and fauna," Maria quickly said.

"Did you take notes on the weather?" her father asked. Then they both laughed at themselves, and my judge and I joined them. "The Scientists in Pursuit of Data," Mr. Mitchell murmured.

"Well," I replied, attempting to perform, "you might think that squirrels have a prodigious memory to bury their nuts and then remember where they are and come back to dig them up. But in fact, squirrels just dig in a place where it seems likely nuts are hidden. Squirrels dig up nuts hidden by quite different squirrels. I noted it during the years when I was nine and ten."

"Brava!" exclaimed the judge.

"How did you keep the squirrels straight?" Maria asked. "Did you tag them?"

"No. If you look closely, each is an individual. Like the humpback whale—if you look carefully, each whale has distinctive markings on its flukes."

Maria's eyes glowed as though she saw in me a kindred spirit, but, alas, I really had very few naturalist observations to make, unless they had bearing on surviving in the wilderness. I told them that one must not put in a garden close to a black walnut tree. At least not tomatoes, cabbage, or radishes, as some substance from the walnut roots would poison the vegetables.

"I notice the weather," I went on, "and respond to it. On the frontier, the weather is sometimes the only news. Sometimes it is a matter of life or death." I saw again the great drifts of snow that had nearly covered the cabin only some half a year previous. I thought of my mother's body trapped under the overturned buggy and of her freezing. Such was not the stuff of dinner conversation. "But I have never made a systematic notation of the weather. I wrote a paragraph describing the recent Great Meteor Shower."

"November twelfth through thirteenth, 1833," Mr. Mitchell interjected.

The judge said, "The uneducated thought it a sign of the end of the world. The entire firmament blazed with meteors for hours. I myself felt uneasy."

"Visible from sixty degrees west in the Atlantic to one hundred degrees west in the Great Plains," Maria said, "and from Lake Superior to the southern shore of Jamaica."

"Where were you, Una?" Mr. Mitchell asked, and we went on to compare our whereabouts during the shower. Although we four had not been acquainted at that time, now in reference to the event it was as though we shared an experience. It made us cozy.

William Mitchell then mentioned the Annular Eclipse of 1831—"The superstitious believed that just such a darkness had engulfed Egypt in Bible times," he said. Then he spoke of the Luminous Arch of 1827, about which he had given a public speech, bits of which he now rehearsed for us, to the Philosophical Institute: "I first noticed it about ten o'clock. It was a well-defined, radiant belt extending itself from the east to west, of the most brilliant magnificence. Its center passed the bright star Deneb in the constellation of the Swan, at fifteen minutes past ten; by twenty-five past ten the western extremity passed the bright star Arcturus in the constellation Boötes."

"How did the arch move?" I asked.

"With a slow and majestic motion toward the south. There was a quick undulating motion of its component parts comparable to the rippling surface of the sea, in a steady wind."

We sat in silent admiration as his words conjured up the awe-inspiring arch of light. I myself was thrilled with this history of the Nantucket skies, and Mr. Mitchell, moving ever backward in time, I noted, in his celestial history, obliged my taste for the sensational by then describing the comet of 1825 (the tail being some twelve degrees in length and split into five branches) and the "Great Bright Comet" of 1811, with two tails, one of which grew to a length of seventy degrees.

"How long is seventy degrees?" the judge asked.

With a sweep of her arm, Maria pointed her outstretched fingers toward the horizon and then swung her arm up, remarking, "Forty-five degrees of a circle," and then continued beyond. In her sudden gesture, a salute to measurement, there was such spontaneity, such unconventional desire to instruct, such speed, perhaps even haste to make clear the point, that I determined I should have a very interesting time coming to understand her nature.

"WAS IT a success?" my host wanted to know after the Mitchells had left. Alluding to Maria, he suddenly held out his arm in the horizontal and swung it up to a salute of seventy degrees.

"Indubitably," I replied.

"You liked them?"

"It would be lovely to have Mr. Mitchell as a father." I knew I would have grown up with a less romantic and tempestuous nature if he had directed my education. Yet I liked myself and did not wish to be Maria.

"And what of the daughter? Can she be a friend for you? She knows so much! You're about the same age. Both with such exceptional minds."

"What a connoisseur of young women you've turned out to be!" As to what Maria might come to mean to me, I was uncertain, but Charlotte's absence had left me with a vacancy.

CHAPTER 101   Vestal Street

AT VESTAL STREET, in the small, gray house, the natural sweep of Maria Mitchell was much more evident than it had been when we sat in the judge's stiff dining chairs. Almost as soon as I arrived, the solar system came tumbling down the steps with a great wooden clatter, the planets being represented for instructional purposes as an assortment of proportionally sized wooden spheres. Maria grabbed the largest one, aimed for her brother, and said, "Here, catch Jupiter," and sent the ball flying. Her younger brothers and sisters were all around her in a web of affection.

The mother, Mrs. Mitchell, I saw only in passing. She, as well as all her daughters, was indeed dressed in silk. She seemed to be a strong woman, but to have no exceptional intellectual leanings; Maria apparently took after her father in that respect. The mother was on the way to bed for a nap, having been up much of the night with a sick child.

"A mother of eight puts in more night hours than an astronomer," Maria observed, with grave regard for her mother.

"But you were up all night, too, with the stars, weren't you?" a little sister asked quietly.

"But I'm much younger," Maria responded. Then I noticed the tracery of dark circles under her eyes. "Let me show Una my office."

Maria's office turned out to be nothing but a closet, literally. It had only width for a desk, each side of which abutted a wall of the cubby. Before the desk there was depth for a chair, and three bookshelves were conveniently mounted on the wall above the chair and desk. The outer wall, to the left, was filled with a window, which would have provided excellent reading light in the closet.

"It's great advantage," Maria said, "is that it has a door that can be closed." She gestured to a sign that currently hung on the inside of the door but could easily be hung on the other side facing the hall (and the younger siblings). The sign read: *Maria Mitchell is busy. Do not knock.*

"It's as cozy as a first mate's cabin," I said. "More so. I have always had an admiration for well-fitted small spaces."

"Above the bank, I shall have a whole room of my own."

I saw that the papers on the desk were covered with mathematical calculations.

"What are you figuring?"

"Father and I have reviewed the calculations that tell us Halley's comet should appear again this August."

"Comets are predictable?"

Her eyes glistened. "Some are. Halley's is. It will not come again for another seventy-six years. This is our only chance to see it."

"Yes," I said slowly. "We'll likely be dead in seventy-six years."

"It will be another century—1911 and then again in 1986 and 1987."

"An unthinkable distance—1987—in time," I said.

"Not at all," she laughed. "Astronomically."

"How far does Halley's travel?"

"Beyond the farthest planets. Then it turns around and comes back, loops the sun, and leaves again for outer darkness."

I was silent a moment, and then I observed that "outer darkness" was a Biblical phrase, the place for outcast sinners.

Maria just laughed again. "How I should like to ride a comet to Outer Darkness!"

Now I laughed. "I can see you—an astronomical witch with a new broomstick to ride."

"I fear I will have to content myself with my telescope as a broomstick. Will you watch for Halley's with us?"

"Yes," I answered, but I knew that if my husband was home my nights would be spent in our conjugal bed. When she took me to her rooftop observatory, a platform with railings such as many houses in Nantucket had, I remarked that she could use my cupola for observation if the weather was bad.

"The cupola has a solid roof," she said. "And if the weather is bad"—she smiled—"you can't see through the cloud cover anyway."

I felt embarrassed for my lack of logic. "I like the airiness of this," I replied, gesturing toward the neighboring roofs. "The openness." Indeed, I did feel much more a part of the green treetops and the surrounding houses than I did in my little well-roofed, window-sided room perched in the center of my house. Maria pointed out a patch of mulberry trees, for silkworms had been imported to Nantucket and they fed upon the mulberry. She pointed out the factory where the silk was unwound from the worms' cocoons and woven into cloth. But my cupola had a better view of the harbor.

As we two women stood there, queens of the scene, I blurted, "Your life seems somehow so . . . successful."

"I am doing exactly what I love to do."

How blessed, I thought, for a woman to know her path so well. My investments were so much in people, in Ahab now, and before that in Kit, and in Giles. In my mother and my father.

"I had a stormy youth with my father," I said.

"My father and I are much of like minds. But I do not always succeed. The judge asked me to take Pip, the black child rescued from the fire, into my school. I did so, for a week or so, but he was miserable and so was I. The judge took him away."

"You don't think his blackness had aught to do with it?" I asked boldly, thinking of my Susan and her eagerness to learn to sew and write.

"Not at all. I have taught other black children with success. But Pip can scarce sit still. Only dancing and banging on his tambourine truly please him. He wants to go to sea."

"Perhaps Ahab will take him."

Again we fell silent, filling our lungs with the sweet, green air.

"Do you not count your own life a success?" she asked.

"I'm happy," I replied. But I didn't know if I counted that the same as success. Because I wanted her to know me more personally, I added, "Last winter, in Kentucky, I lost my baby and my mother."

She put her arm across my shoulders and squeezed me. "I am sorry," she said. She said nothing else for a while, but with her arm across my shoulders, I breathed again, and I could not help but rejoice in my own aliveness. When she spoke, it was to inquire if I had other kin, and I told her that I had failed to reconnect with them.

"There is a registry of all lighthouses. It may not be current as to keepers, but you can write to each."

Then I knew Maria was, indeed, a friend, in response to my need. Grief seemed a dark storm cloud that was moving off, released, behind my head.

Maria fixed us and the children an efficient lunch, during which time she was much at their disposal conversationally. They were apparently in the habit of asking her questions so that their educations might be advanced as they ate. She was not the least bit dry or pedantic in her answers. Sometimes she mixed in legend and fable. In answer to the question "How was Nantucket formed?" she replied that once there had been a gigantic sachem. When he walked on the beach at Cape Cod, his great weight made his feet sink deeply, and his moccasins filled with sand. Disgusted, he pulled the sand-filled moccasins off and flung them into the sea. One became Martha's Vineyard and the other became Nantucket. "Now," Maria asked, "how else do you suppose Nantucket might have been formed? Think also that we are in a line with the Vineyard, and with Block Island, and even Long Island."

After that geological topic was discussed, one of the children fetched a fossiliferous rock. We all stared respectfully at the tiny stone skeleton in the rock. "An autograph of time," Maria called it. It pleased me that she looked not only to the heavens but also to the earth. These children, and Maria herself, seemed so preoccupied with the outer world that they left their inner feelings to take care of themselves, and the Mitchell brood all appeared to prosper with the regimen.

As I walked home that June afternoon, I reflected that I, too, had been very happy in the midst of their curiosity about observable phenomena. But what of the inner life and what of the dark issues of our time—of slavery, of the position of women, of temperance, of the crisis in religious belief? William Mitchell had spoken as an ardent abolitionist at the dinner table, but he mainly invested his time in science. Maria seemed content merely to focus on what she herself wanted to do. Perhaps that was as good an answer as any to the question of the status of women.

At home, I climbed up to the cupola, though it was yet midafternoon, but I took my writing box with me and commenced a letter to Margaret Fuller. As soon as I stuck my head into the glass enclosure, I felt the intensity of the boxed-in heat. Quickly I flung up the sashes of my windows in all four directions, and at once the breezes cooled the space. Still, because of the opaque roof, the cupola did not feel so free and open as Maria's roof walk. Yet it was very comfortable and pleasant.

Before I commenced to write, I took up my own brass telescope and scanned the seas for the *Pequod*. I saw one, two ships, their sails beautifully luffed by the wind. Like two swans, they approached Nantucket. But neither was the *Pequod*.

I opened my letter to Margaret by describing the scene—I always enjoy receiving a letter when the writer locates himself or herself in a definite place, and I like to know if there is a cup of tea at hand, or how the light is falling in the room or beyond the window. Such descriptions transcend the barriers of time and space and give reader and writer the illusion that they are together. After fixing myself in space and time, I wrote Margaret something of the judge's dinner party and of my subsequent visit: "Maria of Vestal Street is something like a Vestal Virgin, attending the fires of Science."

While the subject of fathers had only passingly interested Maria—probably because Mr. Mitchell was so satisfactory—I brought up the issue to Margaret, who like me had been oppressed by hers. A far less balanced man than William Mitchell, Margaret's father had been bent on stuffing her mind—with literature and the arts rather than science—and he often kept her up so late learning Greek and Latin that his instruction became a form of torture. Unlike William Mitchell, he had had no sense of play or spontaneity about him. Even as a child Margaret had had terrific migraine headaches, and she often dreamt of drowning in a rising sea of blood.

Then I wrote, "I have considered the difference in the ambience at the Lighthouse, when I was a member of that family, and the ambience at the Mitchells'. We at the Lighthouse were more intense and inward, though we, too, were happy. Perhaps our inwardness came from the isolation from other people and from the exposure to the weather. When the value of that haven on the Island, of my aunt, uncle, and cousin sweeps over me, I wince, for I have failed at contact."

My letter to Margaret seemed heavier than I had intended, for my initial mood had been buoyant. Happy to make a new friend in Maria, I had vivaciously approached writing a letter to my old friend. But my mood had changed, with the thought of my losses, as though a cloud had passed over the sun.

Indeed, a cloud had passed over the sun. I looked to the northeast and saw storm clouds on the horizon, moving swiftly inland. The color of the sky drained from blue to gray. A hard breeze rushed through the window and scattered my papers. Quickly, I put down the opposite window, except for an inch. Soon I partially closed all the windows. Still the air puffed in, fresh with excitement, and I saw a crack of lightning run vertical down the sky. I counted the seconds till the thunder and judged the storm about ten miles off. The cupola was topped with a lightning rod, though I would not linger long enough to risk being blinded again. But here was the advantage of an enclosed cupola: a safe seat for watching the approach of a storm, if not the storm itself. The whole sky above the ocean was a roiling gray mass, and the sea changed color to match it. It seemed to spread out at the same time that it blew shoreward. I picked up the telescope to have a last look, for that day.

There she was! There at the far seam of gray water and gray sky, her white sails filled, running before the storm: the *Pequod*! "There she blows," I yelled, as though my husband's ship were a long-sought whale. But it is the happiest and most excited cry I know. My heart beat against my eyes. Yes, there she was. With a small twist, I fine-tuned the telescope. Unmistakably the *Pequod*, surely Ahab! The lightning blazed all the way down to the sea betwixt him and me, and I saw the three masts dancing with fire—St. Elmo's fire—like three lit candles. Thus sailed home my fiery Ahab, in power and in glory! She rode deep, as I knew she would, well laden, not counting the three magic cheeses of golden ambergris.

Could Ahab, with his glass, see me, or at least my little glass house? He would not look. His hand was surely upon the ivory tiller, but in his mind's eye, he saw me. Let me die, if that was not true! My Ahab, my captain!

Every second she plowed the high gray hills and the deeper gray troughs closer toward home. I could see the spray, white and feather-like, off her prow. How the shape of her filled me! I could not put down the glass. Her wooden sides, the decking, the masts, the sails— every part was bent to the proportion and shape that said *Pequod*, husband, home. How truly, how recklessly, she came.

Surely there was no heart on the ship that did not unrestrainedly urge Ahab on toward home. Certainly Starbuck wanted every risk taken, and Stubb with his pipe clamped in his teeth was muttering encouragement. Even Daggoo, whose home lay on the other edge of the Atlantic, sympathetically caught the scent of home. "I smell meat," I could hear him say to Tashtego. And the noble Tash longed for home, marred as it was by the history of his people; even Tash urged the storm-driven ship toward this place where once his fathers walked in pride and plenty.

My heart left off excitement and went serene. I thought of my white bed, still almost bridal, and how in the hush and lamp glow of the room I would open my arms to my husband. There was peace. There was peace. But it gave way to a new anticipation, as though all the excited waves churned within.

The *Pequod* came on and on, cutting across the waves. Dear Ahab used the energy of the storm to speed her home. He was glad for the storm! His outward demeanor would be calm, his face set and hatchetlike, but I knew, I alone knew, of the soft glowing within, of Ahab's manly eagerness for home and hearth and wife. I heard his voice.

BLAST WINDS! and spank these sails as though they were the flanks of horses and could with mightier effort on their own part draw me faster, ever faster, to my wife, my child, my hearth, my home. Let the spirit of Ahab leave his body, hover behind the sails, spend itself with huffing! Why not? Is not the spirit naught but wind? How often have I wondered it! When breath leaves the body, is that all there is of life? Can breath itself become rarefied, float upward toward the heavens, and yet retain something of the deceased's own character? Breath, life! let them both flee from me if soon I do not hold my Una, my One, in these two arms! And we three—we two—make one— there's Unitarianism!

AHAB: There's Brant Point—Stubb! Stubb! Look yonder and ye see
    your twin in that stubby beacon.
STUBB: I see it, Captain! My very image, had she but a pipe to
    clamp, and had she but teeth to clamp the smoking pipe, and
    nose to savor smoke, and face to support the nose, and body,
    and two short legs!
AHAB: Don't quibble, man. Shortness is all!
STARBUCK: Well spoke. It's shortness we want. Shortness of time, till
    home.

I'll speak no more to them. They'll guess what's in my heart. Starbuck, a married man, half knows. But they're underlings, and I'll keep them apart from Ahab. And who is not an underling in this world? For Ahab, only Una is equal. Only Una. Our child? I dare not count that chick till I hold him in my hand. We'll have another downy one to companion him. How my loins leap toward it! Una shall be my underling this night. None wishes it more than she herself. She is my true bride. Agony, agony aches me. How left I with only that one dent in the marriage pillow?

How is it but the one letter found me? The letter of the Annunciation, I call it. Not worn as some men might in a pocket across the heart, but stitched into a pocket of my own devising as near the loins as devising can devise.

Ah, wind and waves, ah, worthy vessel—I am telling thee farewell. I go to my true wife now. Thou hast been but a mistress, a seducer who has led me away from the wholesome bread of home. Yet I thank thee, wind, waves, and vessel, for thy company.

CHAPTER 103   From Cupola to Wharf

H OW THE RAIN dashes these windows, obscures not only *Pequod*, sea, and wharf, but all outside, all obliterated in rushing gray rivulets down the glass. How smug I am—confident in my estimate of her speed. Ahab has but married another sailor boy in me! He waits for no pilot. I can leave cupola for wharf in five minutes, no sooner. I'll wear men's oilcloth—perhaps he will mistake me. No. Not that.

But he thinks I have a babe to show him. Why have I not written otherwise? To have told him with such a space between us would have been crueler than this childless homecoming. Did I fear his stopping with some island maid? Not once. I do not know why, but it is his wife that my Ahab loves, and on her alone will he beget a darling child. We'll have another. Every fiber of my body tells me so. To want a child, to want the visitation of one's husband—this day they are the same sweet ache.

So, descend. Carefully.

So, to the bedroom. Whiteness, purity.

So, my arms into the oilcloth coat, my fingers brushing the coarse weave of its backing.

So, the umbrella; I squeeze its narrow ribs, spiny within the furled cloth.

So, storm, wet streets—I raise the canopy of umbrella—and to the wharf, and Ahab.

THE WHARF MEN were making ready, all abustle with ropes, wheelbarrows, and wagons within the downpour. No sign of either Peleg or Bildad. But in the bustle, on the far end of the wharf, stood a figure who seemed the projection of myself. With her face turned toward the water, she stood wrapped in oilcloth, hers with a hood, and an umbrella spread over her head. How could it be that I myself was already there, waiting for the *Pequod*? I felt superfluous, redundant. I determined to approach myself. My heart beat fantastically, for how does one address such a usurper?

"You, there!" I called.

She turned, and the face was not my own. Mary Starbuck. As though to assert her own identity, she pushed back her hood, her head still protected by the umbrella, and I saw golden-haired Mary. Immediately, I felt ashamed, for not once had I made an effort to go out to 'Sconset to see her.

"Una," she said, "I've meant to come to see thee."

I laughed. "And I you. When did you sight the *Pequod*?"

"An hour and a quarter ago. My neighbor brought me . . ."

"You and Mr. Starbuck must come home with us to Heather's Moor. We've room aplenty." I thought of them together at the other end of the house, another couple reunited, the double of our bliss.

With a sudden gust, the wind caught my umbrella and tore it out of my hands. It blew into the water and floated upside down. A wave swamped the fabric bowl, and the umbrella sank rapidly, the crook of the handle being the last part, leaning at an angle, that I saw. Open to the wild weather, my hair and head were instantly drenched and the rain ran inside my collar. With such wind, the *Pequod* would wait at the mouth of the harbor.

"Come under my shelter," Mary called. "Mr. Starbuck will be all eager to see our son. I must decline thy invitation." The gray waves broke against the pilings, sometimes dashed our feet with spray.

"Mary," I said, as though we were intimate friends. "Captain Ahab does not know. Our baby died." My teeth began to chatter with nervousness as well as cold.

"Shall ye go back home, then? Ye be all ashiver. Shall I tell him for thee? Send him to thee at home?"

One of the wharf men ran up with a new, very large, strong-ribbed umbrella. "Here's another, Mrs. Captain."

"No," I said to Mary. "No. He would weep to have no welcome."

The *Pequod*, half shrouded by mist and rain, hovered beyond the harbor. The anchor was released, the chains rattling. The ship itself seemed to shudder and beat as though it were a great, gray heart. To our surprise, an eager whaleboat from the *Pequod* lowered, Tashtego and Daggoo riding it down. Ahab leapt over the gunwale and slid the ropes, followed by Starbuck. Strong Tash, an eagle feather twirling atop his black hair, bowed his back in rowing and made the boat his arrow, and Daggoo pulled beside him.

"Tell my husband I've taken chill," I said. "Tell him I'm home. Tell him our babe is dead." I bolted from the wharf. I ran like a child afraid of her father.

Mary's voice echoed behind me. "All will be rightly done," she said, her voice chiming sweet as a small bell through the wind.

I felt that I had deserted not only my husband but my better, braver self. If I climbed into bed and waited him there, he would find me almost as he left me on our wedding morning. Then, in the beating of my two feet I heard my mother's words: *Be brave.*

Be brave, be brave, be brave. My own feet spoke to me until I turned around and ran back to the wharf.

I saw Ahab's head and then his shoulders and chest come up over the edge of the wharf as he climbed the ladder. I ran for him as fast as I could, and by the time he stood at the head of the ladder, I was in his arms. Had he not been a strong, well-rooted man, the rush of my arrival would likely have carried us both backward into the water.

He stood as unyielding as a cliff against the onslaught of the sea and held me steady.

All movement ceased.

Like a double-trunked tree, we stood rooted to the wharf—so rooted that Mr. Starbuck had Tash row to another ladder so that he might meet his Mary. When I heard her soft cry behind me, I knew that they, too, had come together. I turned my head and saw the two of them walk down the wharf, arm in arm, under her umbrella.

Where my second umbrella had landed, I had no idea, and the rain streamed off both Ahab and me till finally he said, "Home." Someone placed the umbrella in his flinty, reddish hand, and we, too, moved side by side. He steered us along, with an occasional fond glance down at me. I could not take my eyes from him. I wanted to stand, facing him, on his shoes, as children do when learning to dance.

WHEN WE GOT to our door, Mrs. Macy-Maynard emerged, saying, "For all it's being June, I thought you'd like a bit of fire to dry you out."

My husband and I merely nodded. I could not speak to any but him, but I'm sure she felt our thanks. The parlor fire was the picture of home, and before it she had set the tea table. What? A second good fairy, vigilant and provident, had visited, for on the tea table were the judge's creamy, thin Irish dishes, and dainties that all bespoke the goodness of home: hot, fragrant bread, cranberry and huckleberry jam, fine slices of beef, a pat of goat cheese, a small basket of Nantucket apples. But Ahab and I could not eat for a long time, for embracing one another.

Those things that I had thought would be difficult to say were somehow said without effort. "Safe in the bosom of Abraham" I remembered my father singing once, but I was safe in the bosom of Ahab. I do not know where he learned his kindness—known to all as an unapproachable, moody, hard, and forbidding man, most of his life spent at sea. Now his face had the soft glow reflecting the hearth, not the demonic burning from the try-pots. When I asked him how he had learned his kindness, he replied, "At thy knee, Una," as though he had been *my* child.

Finally, we ate, and his appreciation of the food was very great. I was surprised that he seemed quite as charmed by the dishes as the judge had been. "Ye can almost see through it," Ahab remarked, holding his teacup toward the fire. "How wondrous delicate." Then he turned and looked long into my face. "Never till this moment, in my home, beside my dear wife, have I felt so strongly that there might be a God, and he might be good."

I kissed him again.

"Thy lips are sweeter than the berry," he said. Then he put his hands on my shoulders and held me at arm's length. "My eyes need to drink thee in."

Gladly did I take his gaze, and gladly return it, too. My Ahab, healthy, comfortable, his soul a sweet glowing. Yet this image is linked to the next homecoming.

OUR SON, Justice, is there, a boy of four. Ahab is carried through the street on a stretcher. The white whale has taken his leg. Half out of his mind with pain, he yet holds my hand while they carry him home. "It's bleeding again," Ahab says to me. He is wrapped round and round in blankets, for it is a mean October wind. He is like a cocoon on a stick. When we breach the door, Justice is holding Mrs. Maynard's hand, afraid, but Ahab calls the boy to him, kisses him, and then says, "Aloft, aloft," and they carry him up to our bedroom. No longer bridal white, but the patchwork is cozy as a Kentucky home, greens and reds of the Christmas season to come.

Let not the nightmare come to me so soon!

Let me spin instead the idyll of Ahab and Una, those summer months in Nantucket when he returned intact from his first voyage after our marriage! Let me sing of dinner parties and picnics. Let me remember our white chamber all lit with whale oil lamps, and the tiny cheerful fire in the grate. Goose down and ironed linen. The fragrance of lavender. Ahab and Una joining as husband and wife.

AT THE JUDGE'S BOARD, my husband and my friend Maria Mitchell honored each other with much courtesy and information, for Ahab was not lacking in lore of either stars or seas, both that which he had experienced and that he had found in books. Let me tell how Ahab gave the judge an enormous wooden trough, bought off Africa, for a fruit bowl. How he discoursed with the judge on the law systems of the Polynesians, and the ruin the well-meaning missionaries had wrought on that culture. Was there no subject on which Ahab could not discourse? No. All tastes and interests of others he cordially accepted. Let me tell how people stopped me on the street and asked if it was true: three caches of ambergris! How Ahab insisted that we accept the invitation of the Gardners, and how the old banker said, "Ahab, never have I seen anyone so improved by marriage!" And Ahab but chuckled in his throat, though I saw the fiery glance shoot from his eyes like a harpoon as soon as Mr. Gardner turned to admire Mrs. Coffin's lace jabot.

Afterward I asked Ahab if *he* felt himself much changed and if he liked such drawing-room discourse. "I think *ye* like it," he answered. "And I will bridle up my tongue, or unleash it, in whatsoever way suits thy world." But he seemed more himself when we had Captains Peleg and Bildad to dinner, with Aunt Charity.

She told the tale of the letters and how she had had to pry them away from the caretaking captains, and Ahab laughed and said she was an angel of mercy as well as of charity. Old Bildad was so astonished by Ahab's demeanor that he must have said a dozen times in the course of the evening, "Thou art changed, Ahab. Thou art changed." Each utterance more dark than the one before.

I would savor that first homecoming, be ever nourished by the idyll of *that* homecoming. For then it was that our marriage bed knew no limits, and I became pregnant with Justice. Together Ahab and I walked the moors and the meadows, and with sheep grazing in the distance we lay down among the violets and clover, the curly-cup gumweed, the heathers and heaths, on mosses and lichens, and studied the sailing clouds, took our bliss in the sunshine.

"So it is among the brown island people, when they mate," Ahab said. "Why not us?" Those picnic spots were secluded enough. No one knew but the sheep and omniscient clouds. Often we sat down with our picnic basket, lavishly stocked by the judge's jam and jelly cupboard, and with those sweets we had breads, cold meats, cheeses, fruit, and often a flask of wine. How Ahab loved these fresh, dainty foods! I sat with my skirt over my legs, but after we had eaten, Ahab would pull back my skirt to my knee, and always I smiled fully at him. We lay back in one reclining—remarked some—quietly—on the clouds, but not too long of chat—and then he would come to me. My welcome was that which the eager earth gives the sun when she turns round each day to greet her fiery lord.

One time we shed all our clothing to wallow and lounge in sunlight, and then I saw the scar like lightning that traversed from his temple to his heart. I traced it with my finger, but I did not ask whence it came. Of our pasts we seemed to know all we needed to know. Nothing was concealed, and though nothing was overtly revealed, all was known. In guilt and in forgiveness we counted ourselves equals, and always had. The sun himself envied us.

Our joy at night by lamplight and candlelight was no less than when we made the sunny moors our bed, and once in his eagerness Ahab asked if we might not lie together on the carpet before the parlor fire.

How well we loved, too, to sit in our library, both reading, occasionally reading aloud a paragraph or two, but neither attempting to instruct the other, and then with the beginnings of fatigue for either one of us, that person remarking, "Might we go upstairs soon?" and the reply "As soon as I finish this page." Then our clasping hands and climbing up. Or almost equally pleasing was to come home from some entertainment, to mount the steps directly, wordlessly, urgently, to help each other with buttons and hooks, fall into goose down, and glory in our privacy.

Our friends remarked, "Ahab grows younger every time we see him." They would add, "And you, Una, also go backward in time. You yourself will soon be but a babe." And here I would blush for fear that they alluded to my ambition for an infant.

When the third week of July rolled around, but no menses for Una, I thought my hopes fulfilled and confided as much to Ahab. His eyes spoke the soft love of his response; his lips said, "But if thy menses come yet again, then I shall enjoy thee in thy bloody time as well as now." Yet we both felt we had got our child. In our marital bliss, we ceased not, but modulated to the key of celebration, of triumph, of tenderness and brimming gratitude.

At this point, fearing his departure and his yearning for the sea, I asked my captain if he would take me out in a small boat, toward the old Lighthouse of my youth. He rented a beautiful sloop, easily handled by two, and one bright and bonny morning we sailed southwest. Once away from Nantucket, I put on boy's clothes, for the fun of it. We flew before the wind. "Ye have made me sail for the sheer pleasure of it, Una!" Ahab exclaimed, his long gray hair billowed back from his brow. "If ye have secretly harbored a harpoon, throw it overboard and let me not lay eye upon it."

In early afternoon, we spied the Lighthouse, upright, rising against a slight haze. "I've seen it," I said. "Now I would turn back."

"Not gam, not put in?"

"Nay."

"But let's tarry a bit in these waters," Ahab said. He trimmed the sails. While the sloop drifted, he made sweet love with me, my eyes often resting on the gray shaft of the Lighthouse in the distance. I felt a completeness, my girlish self united with the woman and mother-to-be.

After our fill of love, when we sat on the deck, eating our grapes, our fresh-sliced crescents of apple, our bread and cheese, the sparkling little waves all around us seemed to laugh and clap their hands in glee. We entered Nantucket harbor just as it was aglow with sunset, a pool of gold.

BY THE THIRD WEEK of August, my menses had not appeared again. Mrs. Maynard declared me surely pregnant and that she would not be obliged to swim underwater and bore holes in the *Pequod*.

The last week of August, William Mitchel reported that with the telescope he had spied Halley's comet and invited us to come to watch. "To think," he said, "that to my knowledge no man has seen it for seventy-six years!" But our nights were too precious to Ahab and me for that kind of stargazing. Now, we sat up in bed and talked and talked.

As a young man Ahab had traveled occasionally on land, as well as by sea, and he wanted to share those sights of the Norway fjords and mountains with me. "Their churches are wooden and humble, made of beams and staves, like landlocked ships," Ahab said, "for they seem to know the Spirit dwells not there but amongst the rocks of the high mountains." When he spoke next of the old cathedrals of France, I knew that the questions haunting him before this voyage were those concerning the spiritual. When he spoke of Mont Saint-Michel beside the Normandy coast, on an island joined to the mainland by a single road, and that road covered by the tides twice a day, it seemed natural to me that for him a holy place might ultimately be haloed by water.

"I've felt that way," I said, "about my Lighthouse on the Island. There height and air spring upward from the rock—"

"The rod of Jesse," he interrupted.

"—and water surrounds."

He went on to say that for him the most holy of man's constructs was the cathedral of Chartres. "I saw Chartres rise, a small mountain itself, out of a wheat field on a plain. Inside, stone ribs, like those of a mighty whale, arched over me. I felt myself swallowed, like Jonah, and within that sepulcher of stone wondered, might I, too, find salvation?

"On the floor," Ahab continued, "twists the pattern of a labyrinthine path, like entrails. Pilgrims travel it on their knees to the central place, the navel of goodness. It is a shrine that acknowledges it is a dungeon"—my husband set his jaw even as he spoke—"but the stone walls are pierced with light shining through thick glass of unnatural, intense saturations of red and blue. This was a man-god-stained light," he concluded, "that made me gnash my teeth—so much did I want to act upon it and for it to act upon me."

Here I touched my husband's brow, and my fingertips remembered the try-pots, and I thought of the hot butchery of the business to which my husband was about to return, after this idyllic summer.

"Might you not stay home?" It was the first time I had asked such a question.

"Una, why burns this room so brightly? Whale oil. I bring light to the world. If it is not the colored light of Chartres, still it is a pure and useful light."

"Think of Prometheus."

"Punished for his hubris. But I wage an honest battle with the deep. I do not steal from the gods."

"Sometimes I fear I have stolen my happiness from the gods, for my life with you is beyond my due."

"Then let us smile and lounge while we may," he said, strangely bemused, suddenly relaxed. "For they will have it back again. In no corner of the earth have I found a happiness that lasts."

"Nor an unhappiness!" I said.

"Well spoke!" And Ahab smiled again, that rare, sweet cracking open of his face. Often a chuckle would break from him, but his grim lips seemed usually disconnected from the muscles that made for smiling. His smile honored me, and I have treasured it.

"I have seen," he spoke again, "the cousins of those colors at Chartres, of red and blue, in the petals of little alpine flowers. Their stems are thin and wiry, and they dance their colors on the high mountainsides the world over. They are much the same in Switzerland, or Vermont, or the foothills of the distant Himalayas."

So we talked our nights away. My dozing to sleep was with the blue and red of swaying flowers. But I dreamed more deeply that night of stony, time-gnawed Chartres; I was inside the vault, crawling on bloody knees, but no window and no light pierced those lofty white-dark ribs.

That morning I found some spots of my blood on the sheets. Mrs. Maynard said it meant nothing at all, yet Ahab stayed on, well into September, to be sure that I would not miscarry. "Fear not," he said. "I shall not leave thee with an empty womb." Those days he cuddled me and brought me treats and books, and even, when I asked it, hummed a lullaby for me.

When he was assured that all was well, there being no more bleeding, Ahab prepared to sail. Little Pip was deemed too young to go as cabin boy, but in the presence of Captains Peleg and Bildad, the judge, and Maria Mitchell, Ahab promised that if Pip would wait patiently and be obedient, he would go on the next voyage. Like a whirling dervish, Pip beat on his tambourine and danced for joy, till Ahab caught him and sent him outside to the pavement (where there were no Irish teacups about) to do his spinning.

"PRETTY SHIP, thee hast thy ballast within thee," Ahab said to me.

"Do not kiss me, but smile at me once more," I entreated for our good-bye on the wharf.

"Let time be a pleasant wind, Una, in thy sails." Long his gaze at me, and long my eyes on him. "Send thy thoughts of me to the moon, Una, and Luna will beam thy serenity back to me. Every night we will see the same moon. But write letters, too."

"I shall use my eagle quill till it is short as a sewing needle."

Then, Ahab smiled at me. But he could not stop at that and took me again in his arms. I trembled, as alpine flowers do against their mountain.

MY HAND on my belly, only so slightly swelling, I stood on the dock and waved my Ahab off. Then I rode in a buggy with Mary Starbuck out to 'Sconset, and we stood on the sandy beach and saw the last of the *Pequod* rounding Nantucket, far out to sea; finally its sails blended to a single white handkerchief against the sky, and then a dot, and then gone.

Mary asked if I should want to spend the night with her at 'Sconset, but I said I wanted to return to town. And I invited her to visit me soon, and she returned the invitation. Superficially, I had not gotten to know her very well. Ahab seemed to feel that he saw quite enough of Mr. Starbuck at sea. The toast of Nantucket, we had visited 'Sconset not once. But I did know Mary anyway, profoundly, from that day in the rain on the wharf when she had seemed my double.

When I got home, Mrs. Maynard opened the door for me. "My captain is away tonight, too," she said, "I thought I might spend the night with you. Here's a hot toddy for you to sip."

Gladly did I share the parlor with her, she knitting and I sewing. We were pleasantly and cheerfully at work, but as I heard the clock bong through the night, I could not help but think how many strokes of that hammer would fall before Ahab came home again.

Shortly after ten, Mrs. Maynard and I were both surprised by a late-night knock at the door, which I opened to an excited Maria Mitchell.

"Halley's comet's visible tonight to the naked eye," she said. "Come see it."

Mrs. Maynard declined, but I put on a wrap and hurried out with Maria. A number of people were coming out of their houses and pointing up. "Don't look yet," Maria instructed, as she and I walked beyond the houses to the old mill hill. "Wait till we get to the top." From the crest of the hill, with the sound of the creaking timbers of the mill at my back, I viewed the celestial visitor, a beautiful bright streak in the sky. I wondered if Ahab was watching it.

"Come home with me," she urged, "and see it also through the telescope."

"The Comet"

I did not want to leave Mrs. Maynard alone too long, but I hated also to disappoint my excited friend. "Some night, soon," I promised, "I'll come at night and watch with you through the telescope."

"Would you?" She clutched my arm.

"Maria," I said, "you are overwrought. I've never seen you so stirred."

"If you would but watch at night with me sometimes!"

"Indeed, I promise."

"There is a prize," she confided. "The king of Denmark has offered a medal, a gold medal, to the first person in the world who discovers a comet with the aid of a telescope. No one has ever done so. Every night, with the telescope, I watch for a comet no one has ever seen before."

"But that would not be Halley's comet," I said.

"Oh, no. It must be a comet never before seen, and one first seen with a telescope," she reiterated. "I think if any new celestial object appeared in my field of vision, I would know it was new. I've learned the known sky so well now. Father thinks I am ready."

"Perhaps he will make the discovery." I pulled my shawl about me and gazed reverently at the comet I had never viewed before.

"I think not. I think it will be I, for Father is not so ardent as I."

"At least I will look at Halley's comet with you some night," I assured, and Maria assured me in turn that the phenomenon would be visible for many nights.

As I walked home, I thought of how the comet was traveling past, even as Ahab was traveling away. My child would not see such a sight till he was an older man than Ahab was now. And our lives would be gone. I glanced up to see that bright spark again, but the tops of dark buildings obscured the view.

I wonder if Maria's life was less content and complete than I had thought. If she was not the first to spy a new comet telescopically, would it be a great loss to her? Perhaps she would discover another, if not the first. A Nantucket woman to win the gold medal from the king of Denmark! A woman in her observatory on top of a bank. Would they even let it count? I decided to ask Maria exactly how the king's announcement was worded.

When I entered the parlor, Mrs. Maynard said that comets had ever been heralds of disaster and that she wished I had not looked at this one on the night of my husband's sailing.

"But it's there," I said, "whether I look at it or not."

She announced that she herself did not ever intend to even so much as glance at Halley's comet.

CHAPTER 106   🐚   Frannie's Letter from an Inland Lighthouse

W HAT HALLEY'S COMET ushered in, despite Mrs. Maynard's misgivings, was a blessed connection reestablished at last. Having stopped at the post office, Maria appeared at the door again the next morning (her eyes as dark-circled as a raccoon's from late stargazing) with letters from Frannie and Aunt Agatha.

Dearest Una, cousin and friend of my childhood,

Mother says I am not to write to you because you are not to be trusted. Father climbs up the tower when she talks about you that way, but he says nothing. Butch is now four years old, which is the age I was when you came to the Island Light, and I always remember how kind you were to me and how you played with me, and I try to be as good to Butch.

Butch is not so isolated here as I was, since we are on the mainland and there are farms not too far away. It is as though my childhood landscape has been turned wrong side out, with the land surrounding the great water instead of the sea encircling the island.

I hope you do not think too bad of Mother. She was worried to death. We all went to New Bedford looking for you. Captain Maynard said he did not know anything about where you had gone. He said he had not taken you to the boardinghouse to wait for your mother as he was supposed to do, and Mother reached out and grabbed down on one of his mustaches. She was furious, and I have never seen her so angry before or since. However, she is angry with you because she said you betrayed her trust. She says it is a Sin to leave home and leave your loved ones behind to worry about you. Father said that he had never heard her speak of Sin with a capital S, and she said that it was Warranted (I could hear the capital W in her voice) because you had not been considerate of the people who loved you most and you had thought only of what your own heart told you to do.

This is part of why I write to you. I wonder what you think now, many years later, of that issue. But I have to say you must not write the answer to me, for Mother would then know that I have disobeyed her by writing to you. Perhaps I too have betrayed her.

I do not want to go to sea, but I want to travel west. Perhaps you could write here without referring to this letter, but give me some advice. I don't think you have forgotten what it was like to be young. I am now twelve years old, but I know that my maturation has not been as rapid as is probably normal. Still, you left your Kentucky home at twelve and left us when you were sixteen.

I want to travel west because I believe that Kit is there. I heard from a young man who comes to help clean the lens—we have only the old type here, not a Fresnel—that a strange white man among Indians passed through the town. Why do I think it was Kit? For one thing, the description, but also, it is what he said. They asked him why do you, a white man, travel with Indians? Kit answered, "My skin may be white, but my heart is red." Do you remember when he said that at the Island Light? I remember everything Kit ever said. Then he said it about black people and attending the black church in Nantucket—that he felt at home there because his heart was black. It has to be Kit.

I was surprised that you and Kit did not get married. The letter we have from you referred to the fact that Giles had gotten killed in a fall from the masthead. It did not tell what had happened to Kit. You said that you were expecting your second child, that you were married to Captain Ahab, and that you were rich and happy. I am sure letters have been lost. That is all I know about your life, except that the first baby died, and your mother died in the wagon accident. I am truly sorry you lost them.

My mother cried and cried for her sister. She said that was your *fault too, that when you betrayed us by running away you started a long chain of consequences. Father quoted, "As in Adam all die, so in Christ are all made alive." It made Mother so mad that she burst into tears, because she could see the parallel bad logic. Even I could see that it was wrong to blame you for every bad thing that happened to any person you knew.*

I know that I do not want to upset my mother by leaving. She doesn't deserve to go through that again. I would like to convince her that I am smart enough to take care of myself, even in the West. But at some point, everyone must become independent, I think. I found out recently that Mother's father did not want her to marry my father! And he is, as always, the best father in the world.

You are the best friend I ever had. I do forgive you for worrying us so much. I cried every night for a month when you left. Finally, your letter came, explaining what you had done. But we had already been missing you so terribly. I guess, like Mother, I am a little mad at you about that. But I still trust you and love you more than anybody almost.

Frannie, your devoted kinswoman

CHAPTER 107   **An Angry Letter from Aunt Agatha**

Una,

Frannie has confessed to me that she has written to you for advice. My heart sank like a diving bell. Why does she ask you for advice? You who betrayed not only me but all of us at the Island. We had been entrusted by your mother with your care. Do you have no concept of the anguish you caused us? First, for love of you. Yes, we loved you. Loved you as though you were our own child. You were a gift to us. We longed for another child. You were so bright. So in need of a fatherly love such as Torchy freely gave you. Your own father's mind had turned black with religion. Torchy was the keeper of the light, of enlightenment, of tolerance. Surely you felt that when you were here.

And my love for you! Little sister you seemed, part woman and part child. Insofar as you were not my child, I loved you the way a teacher might have loved her student. Your qualities stood objectively before me. I appreciated and admired you. I took pride in who you were and who you were becoming under our guidance. Let Frannie find a model in Una—*that was my thought.* I hoped my own child might aspire to your honesty with yourself, your ability to puzzle about large issues, your generosity and care for others, your self-reliance and inventiveness, your unstinting commitment to do your share and beyond, your brave vivacity.

But where was your honor? Did you not think it dishonorable to sneak away?

I cannot account for your thinking on this matter.

If I prayed to God, I would give thanks that Frannie has had a sense of honor, that she felt guilt over having written to you. Her disobedience has gnawed at her for five days. It has not been two hours since she confessed to me.

Three days have passed. Torch and I have talked much of you these three days. Of your grief when we heard your father was dead—the night of the bonfire on the headland, while the lens was being installed. How you struggled earlier with your homesickness and we tried to make you merry at Christmastime. How you visited with your parents in New Bedford—you were fourteen—but were happy to come home with us and climbed to the top of the lighthouse as though you were lord of all you surveyed. It was the midpoint of your stay. Torch and I spoke of your great anxiety, after Boston, for Frannie when she was ill. How you were bewildered by the arrival of not one but two eligible young men in the *Petrel.*

It is enough that I have told you how I felt and suffered. To be free of this, now I have another need. And that is to tell you, or at least myself, that I forgive you. I do believe that you wronged us. But my rage is over. I wish you every happiness.

I know that you would not give bad advice to my daughter. Torch agrees with me.

And so I end with another wish. First that our letters do reach you. Second that you will respond. If you do respond and then hear no reply from us, know that your letter simply did not reach us. Write again. We wish to claim our Una. My words begun in anger and anguish have ended in good wishes for you. We hope you will want to claim us.

Your Aunt Agatha

CHAPTER 108  **Letter to an Inland Lighthouse**

Dearest Aunt Agatha, Uncle Torch, Frannie, and Butch,

First and foremost, I beg you to forgive me for the pain and anxiety I caused you by my precipitate leaving. At the time, I did not think of it as running away. But, as an adult, I can easily imagine the anguish it caused all of you who loved me. I am heartily sorry. I ask forgiveness.

I am especially grateful to you, Aunt Agatha, for arguing with yourself about me and for finding an abiding love in your heart as well as the justly deserved anger. If I have learned to be honest with myself about the nature and origin of my own feelings, it is due in no small part to the example I had before me in you. My gratitude also to Uncle Torch and to Frannie for their love and faith. Dear Butch, I have long wondered what kind of boy you are and hoped that someday I would know you.

Frannie, I believe you should content yourself till age sixteen. We will all exchange long letters till that time. Then I will send money, and a guide to bring you to Nantucket, if Aunt and Uncle approve.

With all love,
Una

CHAPTER 109 🐚 The Minister in the Woods

In October, I thought how I must now keep my promise to Margaret Fuller and visit her again, before the winter set in. I made the crossing alone, on the *Camel,* with Captain Maynard, who was a little huffish with residual embarrassment over having once proposed to me. But such standoffishness did not trouble me. Mrs. Maynard had very much wanted that her husband be selected to transport me; of course, I never told her that Captain Maynard had once approached me with a marriage offer. I occupied myself with reading from my old volume of Wordsworth.

Although I had sent Margaret a note of my intention to visit, when I reached the city I found she had not received it, and, in fact, her housekeeper said she had gone to Concord, to visit with Mr. Emerson, Mr. Hawthorne, and Mr. Alcott. It excited me to think of Margaret among three famous men. Concord was nearly a day's drive away by coach, but having come so far, I determined to go on. The housekeeper fed me, noted that I was pregnant, and advised me not to go, but I did it anyway. I left my larger bag in Margaret's Boston apartment and took only a valise.

After hours of jouncing through the autumn countryside, a new coachman had me exit the coach too soon. Through inquiry at the crossroads, I learned that Mr. Emerson's house was but on the other side of the forest and that if I took the footpath through the woods the walking would be much shorter than going by the road. The path was fairly clear, and I might walk there in less than an hour. Scarlet and gold with the fall colors, the woods beckoned me.

There was no such forest on Nantucket, and the Concord fall display of hardwood forest thrilled me and reminded me of the crimson dog-woods in Kentucky. I felt scarlet come to my own cheek in an attempt to fit in with the autumn splendor. As I walked along and the trees grew more dense, the light became more muted. I relished all the color about me and loved the great thickness of the tree trunks and the pleasing shapes of the oak and maple leaves. I thought of my passion with Ahab, and the flamboyance of the colors engulfing me seemed an emblem of ardor.

Squirrels were about, and their chattering and the scurrying of their little feet pleased my ear. At one point, I thought I heard a larger animal moving, but I did not see him.

I stepped over a little stream, using the flat creek rocks for stepping-stones, and then I seemed to be in a somewhat different realm. The moving water of a stream has a freshness that the ocean, for all its inspiring movement and size, can never suggest, and I was glad to baptize the tips of my shoes in the gurgling water. Beyond the stream, the woods were cooler, and again the light seemed to dim. There were more evergreens here, and I saw fewer squirrels, but I could hear birds in the upper boughs. To my surprise, I heard the hoot of an owl, which is not common in late afternoon.

Then I came to a branching of the footpath. My informants at the crossroads had said nothing of a fork in the path, so I felt disconcerted. Perhaps I had already taken the wrong path. Still, my heart was light, I was not very tired, and being alone among the sort of trees I had known as a child made me feel I had traveled back a bit in time. I would linger in the timeless zone. My baby, still so small, rode comfortably within me, and my shoes and clothes were perfect for the walk. The valise had grown heavy, and I considered abandoning it at the fork. The valise was not worth the weight. I could borrow nightclothes from Margaret when I needed.

Thinking that most folk would choose the right path, I chose the one on the left hand. *I do as I please,* I thought, and a lovely thought it was. The feeling of independence that accompanied me when I was on the road with Milk and David came back to me; but now I was more independent, for I traveled by myself and on my own feet. And I was blessed with four months of loving between Ahab and me, and the fruit of that love within my body.

Again I heard an animal, perhaps a fox or badger, perhaps as large as a wolf, move to my right over the crackling leaves. All such creatures would be shy of me, a human, and I felt more curiosity than fear. A great scolding of jays and mockingbirds occurred in the trees. Just so had I heard them squabble in Kentucky, for their territories are mutually exclusive.

Then I saw a man coming toward me on the path. He was well dressed, all in black; I took him for a minister at once, but he had an odd black veil over his face.

"Good day," I called ahead so as not to startle him.

"What's this?" he replied.

"A traveler, like yourself," I answered.

"But you are alone in the woods, my good woman?" There was a sternness about him that I did not like. He seemed to be critical that I was where I was, but he himself was alone in the woods.

"Aye. I seek Mr. Emerson's house. My friend Margaret Fuller visits him."

"Farther on," he said. The veil swayed. I assumed he was not Mr. Emerson.

"My name is . . ." And then he stopped. "Can you guess my name?" What a sudden whimsy, for a man so encased in blackness!

"Nay, sir." I was amused that he would want me to guess. "Mr. Alcott?"

"Not in the least."

"Mr. Hawthorne, then?" I spoke a bit impatiently.

With his identity tendered (though not acknowledged), he rattled on, "Where do you come from? Shall we sit and talk? It's not every day that I meet an unattended woman on this path." While he spoke, the lightweight veil puffed about on his face, but he made no effort to remove it. Perhaps, I thought, he's blind—he had spoken almost as though he had no sight, or perhaps he was disfigured. The eternal zone of solitude, nature, and childhood airs being violated, I hesitated to take time to talk.

He went on, "Let me assure you, I come from Mr. Emerson's house, and I am a friend of his, and I know your friend."

"I would be obliged if you would point the way to Mr. Emerson's."

"What is your name?" Again, his voice had the chill and authority of an Inquisitor.

"Una."

"That is not possible. I plan to name my daughter Una, named from Spenser."

"And so, sir, was I."

"And have you read Spenser?"

"Of course."

"Then I see you are, indeed, a friend of Miss Fuller, part of her coterie. Please, you must be tired—if you don't wish to retreat to a fallen log, let us stand here in the path a bit and swap philoso-phies."

"Philosophies! I would but learn the way."

"Your face is flushed"—he was not blind—"and you are with child. Chat a bit."

I sighed. "Because I am pregnant"—I said the word boldly, and he stiffened—"my feet may swell if I stand still. Let us walk toward Mr. Emerson's house and chat as we go."

"But I was going the other way," he protested. "This will take me back along the way that I have come. I don't wish that."

"Then point the way."

"I will walk back partway," he conceded.

And so we started off, slowly, through the brilliant woods. We both were silent.

"There is a particular reason I don't wish to return to Mr. Emerson's house."

"What is that?"

"We have quarreled. Your Margaret Fuller and I have disagreed."

"To disagree is not necessarily to quarrel," I answered.

"She is exasperatingly opinionated. She is too vivid, too bold and tenacious, too instinctual!" He thundered these words as though he were behind a pulpit instead of treading on the fallen leaves through the woods. "Even Mr. Emerson says that she is addicted to the superlative. 'The grandeur of this fall is unmatched by any other.' 'The crimes against the red man and the black man are the greatest possible national sin.' 'The body is the most wondrous gift bestowed by God on man.' " He mocked her with his tone of voice as he pretended to quote my friend. Yet she did hold such views.

"And what is your opinion of her opinions?"

"Jesus Christ is God's greatest gift to sinners. The body embodies and perpetrates Original Sin. It is the very vessel of the devil."

"I think not," I said coolly. "Are you a minister?"

"Nay. I am a writer. 'Nothing from America has yet to match the literature of mighty Europe'—she says that, too. She reads German and French, Latin, and even some Greek as though they were English."

I smiled, for I recognized my own envy of Margaret's erudition in languages. I said nothing. Here was a man who resembled my father, philosophically, but I did not feel intimidated. He amused me, whoever he was.

"What do you write?"

Here he apparently quoted a sentence he had written or intended to write: " 'I built a cottage for Susan and myself and made a gateway in the form of a Gothic Arch, by setting up a whale's jaw bones.' "

"What a pretty sentence! It touches me, beyond its internal charm and coherence, in two quite strange ways."

"What associations does it set to resonating?"

"My husband is the captain of a whaling ship, and he sometimes brings home ivory artifacts. And Susan. Susan is the name of the best friend I ever had." Here I would very much have liked to be able to see the expression in his eyes, to have some clue to what degree of respect he was willing to grant my private associations. I would have liked to talk about my dark sister Susan to this black-clad man. Perhaps we were all congenial beneath the outer layers.

"But when you speak of the intrinsic coherence of my little sentence—what are you thinking of?"

I sighed. "Recite it again."

" 'I built a cottage for Susan and myself and made a gateway in the form of a Gothic Arch, by setting up a whale's jaw bones.' "

"Oh, I do love the sentence," I said.

"Please, speak! Just ramble on as you like. I won't criticize whatever you say."

"Well then, I like the concepts. A cottage for two people—especially one built by one person for the other—is as cozy and contained as can be, but straightway you give the place a gateway and the outer world is admitted, after all. Then you surprise me by moving from humble, domestic architecture to a term used for the great cathedrals of Europe—the Gothic Arch. But then comes a totally surprising idea: the Gothic Arch is made of whale's jaw bones. There's nature, most unexpectedly and grandly evoked. If man has produced Gothic architecture, well, nature has produced the whale."

"Perhaps now you're straying into associations with your husband's domain?"

"Anyone knows that whales are mammoth. That no greater creature exists on earth and that man has had nothing to do with creating that wonder."

"I grant your point. You do speak impersonally about the sentence itself. I thank you."

"I have not finished. But perhaps man is not ascendant in your sentence after all, for the whale is out of his element, rendered useful inland by man. Ah, but the bones suggest death, and in that, man is very much a part of nature, his cottages—or cathedrals—notwithstanding."

"Has Margaret instructed you in literary analysis? But you are not only more concise than that long-winded, superlative-addicted lecturer but more precise, too."

"I grew up at the knee of a mother who loved poetry, and I have tried to understand not just what it means but how it achieves its meaning, all my life. Your sentence gleams like poetry."

"Go on."

"I wanted to speak of the sounds in the sentence. Please say it again."

" 'I built a cottage for Susan and myself and made a gateway in the form of a Gothic Arch, by setting up a whale's jaw bones.' Proceed, please."

I confess I felt a bit heady with the writer's attention. "Well, from the first hearing, I noted what a nice phrase 'Susan and myself' is. Because there's an *s* right in the middle of *Susan* and in the middle of *myself*, the two seemed linked, a sort of internal congeniality. And then *Susan* is so *s*-rich in herself, and the last phrase, 'setting,' et cetera, starts with an *s* and the last word ends in *s*—*bones*. Then there's the middle phrase, 'made a gateway in the form of a Gothic Arch.' The *m* of *made* is tied back to the *m* of *myself* that ends the first phrase—"

"Are you a musician?"

"No. And *made* and *gateway*, both have long *a*'s in them, and *gateway* and *Gothic* both start with *g*, and the *o*-sound in *Gothic* ties it back to the *o*-sound in *cottage*. And so it's all knit together, the three phrases, so well. Oh, that *b*-sound in *built* right at the beginning and the *b*-sound in *bones* at the very end—I suspect that helps to contain the whole utterance."

"We will stop and talk," he muttered and took me by the wrist. "I cannot walk through these hideous colors and talk of deep philosophy. Let us turn to that."

All amusement left me. Never since my father had a man held my wrist by force.

"I will talk," I said, "only if you let loose my wrist."

He dropped my wrist. I noted that beneath the dark cloth his chest was heaving. "Why do you wear the black veil?" I asked softly. "I am not used to speaking to a man alone in the woods who covers his face."

"But you are not really afraid, are you? You are of the tribe of Margaret."

"I am her friend, as I have said."

"How rightly I call you a tribe. There is a pagan element in your souls. You trust nature when you should trust God."

"It is somewhat easier, rather more scientific, to trust what you can see rather than what you cannot see."

"Many of the forces pondered by scientists are quite as invisible as God."

The visible, audible world surrounding us imprinted itself continually upon my senses, while he talked. It was good to stand still in the woods and not simply move through them.

Yet, I would keep up my end of the discourse for a while: "Those invisible, scientific forces have measurable, observable effects."

"Some would say that all of your nature is the measurable effect of God."

"But you would not?" I could not see his face, for the veil hung from the hairline of the forehead down to his mouth, stirring constantly and slightly with his breathing and speaking.

"Nature is not good enough to be purely the work of God. The pilgrim fathers felt that the devil lived in the deep forest, with the savage Indians. The body in all its lust is as natural as animals are natural. Even a man of God could be corrupted in his admiration of the female."

"You said that you are a married man, that you have a daughter who bears my name. Do you not think the marriage bed a holy place?"

Here he covered his veiled face with his hand. "I am not yet married. I speak of a daughter who is ethereal, potential. Yours is the very question that torments me. When I saw you coming on the path toward me, I thought, *I must speak to her.* You seemed yourself full of color, a cousin of these scarlet trees. Your ripening body said that you had been one with nature. The very way you trod the path said that you were unafraid in the woods—even though, I learn, you were uncertain of the path. There is about you a terrible well-being."

I saw a tiny chickadee light on a twist of bittersweet vine. How light the bird, for that thread not to break under its weight. "How completely you observe in a glance," I said. Although the gloominess of the man repelled me, I felt that within him imagination shone like a star.

"Carnality is surely the enemy of the spirit," he said. "But Margaret Fuller disputes that. It is an irony, for despite her careful, nay, fashionable dress, she herself is repugnant, with her eyelids ever fluttering up and down, her long neck like a serpent's."

"Sir! Her neck reminds me of a swan's. She is my friend, and I think her beautiful. I will go at once if you wish to insult her."

His chest heaved in a long sigh, and he stepped back. "You are conventional in your loyalties," he said. "You cannot brook an honest opinion."

I thought of Giles and Kit, determined and hurtful, in their honesty.

"Honesty, like any inclination, can become a ruling passion, a monomania almost," I said.

"Greek ideas—balance, tolerance, moderation. I think the world did not know true passion till Christianity."

"And in its name forever have the Moor and the Jew been slaughtered!" I felt myself growing passionate. Whether he was minister or writer, his smugness offended me.

"I see overweening pride in you," he said.

"I see confusion, darkness, repression, and cruelty in you!" My face felt on fire. "Go your way, and I'll go mine."

"You speak in clumsy allegory," he murmured.

I started down the path, boiling with opposition. Over my shoulder, I called back, "May your daughter Una more resemble me than her natural father!"

It was this last sentence that rang in my ears. But I had not gone far before the splendor of the woods dissipated my anger, and again I felt amused. But now I laughed at myself instead of him. I had engaged in an absurd as well as heated exchange.

Why did he wear the black veil? I mused. Then I speculated—it was to filter, to strain out, to obscure all this glory.

WHEN I REACHED the home of Emerson, I found that Margaret, too, had gone off in a huff, taking the coach. Mrs. Emerson supplied me a room for the night, but I did not see the great man more than for a moment, when he said, "Two of my guests have shot off from here like Independence Day rockets. I hope you find good repose."

Some years later I heard Mr. Emerson speak at the Atheneum in Nantucket—I found him very thought-provoking, though not more so than my own minister—and I was sorry that he had not wished to engage me in conversation that night when I stayed at his house. Perhaps his other guests had exhausted him.

IN BOSTON, Margaret was again not at home. She had apparently gone to the Alcotts' instead of returning. I returned to Nantucket. The Indian summer of October being brief, I did not try to see Margaret again, but we corresponded.

THE ODD AFTERMATH of my encounter with the phantom in the woods was that I received a package and a note from David Poland. He said he had found a valise at the forking of a path in the Concord woods, where business (of an undisclosed nature) had taken him. He recognized the volume wrapped in clothing to be the Wordsworth that had been my mother's and was herewith returning it, though not the valise, thinking, too, that the nightdress was not precious to me—I could easily stitch up another—"probably quicker than making jam cake"—and postage was dear.

David wrote that he had hoped to catch up with me, and he had chosen the right fork of the path in pursuit. At times he had thought he heard human footsteps far to his left, but he could not see me.

What a pity! I thought. I would very much have liked our paths to cross again. I wondered if he would have had the pelt on his shoulders, and if I would have mistaken him, at first, for a wolf. In his letter, David mentioned that a minister had come along as he was opening the valise and offered to purchase the nightgown from him. David had accepted the money—characteristic!—which I did not begrudge. But that my intimate garment had fallen into the hands of that dark man made me color with shame.

CHAPTER 110   The History of Snow
and Restlessness

IN DEEP WINTER, in January, when new snow had freshened already deep drifts, when Halley's comet had turned round the sun and was headed back to darkness, its tail blown out before it, then a profound restlessness came upon me.

I had had Christmas with the Unitarians, and a very satisfactory celebration it was, not insisting on the exclusive divinity of Jesus, but allowing all births to be miracles, all babies holy. It suited me in my pregnant state. The minister had spoken of animals and angels in a way very congenial to my own sense of human beings. During the service, I admired Isaac, the gaoler, who was also a Unitarian, and his family— now two girls, his own little sisters (with golden ringlets and wicked-merry dark eyes), his wife, the toddler, and a new infant. Toward me he always had a friendly smile, but he never attempted to chat, though we both felt that we were friends.

And then the congregation had a shared feast. How well Unitarians cook! and savor all the good things of this life! The minister's recipe for plum pudding was one he had gotten from his mother in Maine, and half the church had turned out to mix and pour the batter in its forms, to watch the ovens, to cool and wrap the puddings till Christmas came.

Despite the satisfactions of the season, with its aftermath and the deep snow came my own dissatisfaction. In a fit of whimsy, I asked Pip to build me a snowman behind the house, and he did so—three great balls, topped with an old hat and a parsnip for a nose. Next I gave Pip a broomstick and took one myself, and together we knocked the snowman into powder. Pip said, "Pip hate to be your boy, Miz Una, you pack a wallop like dat." But creating and destroying the snowman was a quixotic whim. And it did not satisfy my restlessness.

ASSUMING my new wool cloak, edged with wolf fur, I walked carefully through the snowy street to visit the Mitchells at their apartment in the rear of the Union Pacific Bank. Maria being out at a lecture, Mr. Mitchell sat down with me for a bit of conversation. "What is the history of snow here on Nantucket?" I asked him.

A thorough meteorologist, he immediately turned to his record books. "How long it has been," he said playfully, "since someone has asked me such an important and fascinating question." He could not have been kinder to me if I had been one of his own daughters. I wished I had been.

William Mitchell was only beginning to age, and he had about him a natural peppiness; aging, in him, seemed to have added zest for every fact. Zestfully, he embedded his spectacles over his nose; zestfully, he placed his ledger on a round table; most happily he drew up two chairs to the table for himself and me. He had a fine, smooth complexion and a beautiful resonant voice, which Maria had inherited from him. Both had the ability to look you unflinchingly in the eye and to monitor not merely if you were paying attention but how much of what they said was actually penetrating the consciousness. Mr. Mitchell did not expect perfect absorption in his listener, but if one let her mind stray too often, he would politely change the subject to one less taxing in detail. Detail, detail—how the Mitchells loved it, and if numbers attended the detail or constituted its bulk, then they were among the happiest of mortals. No, I was not of this family, after all.

"Well, not so long ago, we had a fine old-fashioned snowstorm, hmmm. . . ." He perused his records. "January eighth and ninth it was, to a depth of two feet, three feet in the drifts. Continuous snow with winds."

"How deep are we today, officially?"

"But six inches, though it will snow again about midnight. We're getting more moisture, you see, to feed the ravenous nuclei upon which condensation depends."

I ventured that Maria would not like to lose another night of telescopic inquiry to bad weather, but William was not ready to be diverted from the History of Snow. "The Great Snowstorm was in January of 1831, not merely locally, but all along the Atlantic. Three feet deep in the groves, four feet in other places. Very fine sleighing, and the harbor was frozen out to Brant Point. I do remember the sleighing. We were all like children again. Let's see. . . ." He flipped the pages. "Three severe snowstorms in the winter of 1829 with a shipwreck, perhaps a foot deep in places, but because of the terrible wind, some places left bare—so it is with money, eh, my dear? Prodigious heaps of it in some places, others quite barren of that commodity. . . . Do you get a bit sleepy? Next big event, going backwards of course, was in 1806— somewhat before your time, I believe, my dear. Una, have you thought of acquiring a cat? We have an extra one someplace here about."

"Cat?"

"Shall I walk you home, dear? Maria won't be back for another hour, I'd guess."

"Whatever shall I do with my restlessness?" I wailed.

He peered at me over his half-glasses. "Well, we shall walk it home." He unhooked the glasses from behind his ears. "You shall crawl into bed. Is Mrs. Maynard there?"

"No."

"At any rate, you'll sleep well and awake tomorrow refreshed. Now come along."

CHAPTER 111   🐚   **Altar Rock**

WILLIAM MITCHELL was quite adept at predicting the weather—at least three more inches came down during the night—but woefully wrong in his prediction that I would awake refreshed. No sleeping position was comfortable. And then I remembered that it had been so when I was pregnant before. I determined that I would go for a fine walk, perhaps all the way to 'Sconset to see Mary Starbuck— seven miles or so—and spend the night with her. I pulled on woolen stockings, determined to try the hike.

In brighter spirits, I set out into the bright morning. Yet I felt gay with purpose, and the sparkling of the snow invigorated me. The children of the town filled the streets with their snow forts and snowballing of each other. Once I had passed the town, the road was hard to discern, for no one had walked out.

As I walked on, my merry mood was replaced by a more solemn one. Occasionally I passed a house and saw other human beings, but much of the island was draped in snow, and I felt my smallness in the unbroken fields of white. At length, I saw the rise of hill atop which I knew to be Altar Rock. Except for the cliffs at Sankaty, north of 'Sconset, it was the highest point of the island. I do not know why, but in an instant I decided to change my destination to Altar Rock. Perhaps I knew I was growing tired, and I had scarcely traversed half the distance to Mary's house. So I began my climb.

The slope was gradual, like the back of some giant beast. I thought of David's pursuit of Susan in Ohio up the snow hump of a hill. As I climbed the snow hill, I found myself praying for Susan, praying that she lived in freedom and that life had brought her many good things. Not Susan but Mrs. Maynard would attend this next birthing, and no doubt the judge would produce the doctor at the very moment if he should be needed. I thought of Susan emerging from beneath my mattress and smiled.

How bleak the climbing of that last, futile snow mound must have been for Susan. *That* was alone. And yet she used her wits, and the money had been enough. When I gave it to her, I had wondered why I was giving her so much. I had not thought it necessary for her journey, but it had been a way not to pay her—for that could never be done—but to honor her. And where was David now? For him, too, I prayed, as I struggled to climb the hill.

When I paused to pant, I saw two field mice running hard over the top of the snow, and then the shadow-wings of a hawk. But I think I was too imposing an upright for the raptor to stoop, and I waved both arms at him. Yet I knew that the hawk, too, had his rights.

Bigger than any whale, the slope rose skyward. Suppose my babe should die again? But he would not. He would not. My legs churned in the snow, and I thought of the froth that billows up around a whale swimming on the surface, and the flakes of foam that fly back continuously from the prow of a ship. I plowed and struggled upward, my feet and legs cold to the shins. I would attain the rock; I would attain it. Was it in homage to Susan and her struggle that I first decided to climb the hill?

Whence comes this pilgrimage? I mused. Surely a futile act. I might as well scrub the stone floor of Chartres Cathedral with my knees. I should not have let my restlessness drive me to punish my body this way. Yet I could not turn back.

When I reached the top, I dropped to my knees; I placed my elbows on the rock and looked out over the vast white sea of snow. Only the distant hawk violated the silence with his scream. I knew why I had come. My pilgrimage was not for Susan or for David or even for my unborn babe. I sank to my knees in the snow to pray for Ahab.

God of strange and extended whiteness, God of heights, who lurks around the crow's nests of ships, who circles the tops of lighthouses, who inhabits the high crags of Norway, God of frost and nothingness, love thou my Ahab!

When I turned the knob on the door of my own home, I was very tired, and my restlessness was gone.

CHAPTER 112   Mothering

IN MY SNOWY BED, I dreamt Giles Bonebright falling, and from his shoulders sprouted long hawk wings, mottled brown and tipped with white, the feathers deconstructing and scattering for their own soft fall. Mother and I stood at the rail and watched the feathers rocking like little cradles on the water. In each small, curved feather—they must have been breast feathers—yowled a tiny, inch-long babe. A hundred of them afloat, crying in unison. "Another baby," said the voice of Rebekkah Swain from a rumble deep in the earth. Foam, white as milk, lapped into the cradles, nourishing the babies, then swamping their little boats. "Susan!" I cried out, and awoke.

IT WAS IN April, standing on the seashore, admiring the foam white as milk, when my fluid broke. I let my waters fall on wet sand, stepped back to see the sea come in. I fancied our water—the babe's and mine—uniting with the big sea where Ahab yet rode the *Pequod*. And then I walked calmly homeward.

Mrs. Maynard attended the birthing, which was in my own bed, and not in the birthing room, since there were no other children present to be disturbed; the labor lasted but six hours. My second child was born about seven o'clock in the evening.

His skin was softer than rose petals, his eyes the blue of forget-me-nots. His breath! I put my nostrils in the way of his exhalation so that I might inhale his discarded sweetness. The living weight of him in my arms! He was a miracle, as all babies are. But he was the miracle of Una and Ahab, of a blessed marriage. His black hair was but a fuzz over his head. His arms and legs seemed to have the beautiful, strong form of Ahab's arms and legs, but the eyes! They seemed to be my own eyes looking back at me.

Maria Mitchell kissed my forehead in a manner that suggested a seal of approval. She presented a little white silk dress, embroidered with a comet.

"Read the motto," she said, "embroidered on the hem." She stood by my bed, her hands on her hips.

It read in cursive: *We are kin to stars.—M. M.*

I smiled but questioned her. "How can we living beings be kin to what is lifeless?" Maria never objected to any question.

"Only in an elemental way," she answered. "Most basically." There was a hint of irony in her voice. "That's all." She paused and stroked the golden threads of the star she had embroidered on my baby's shirt. "Or metaphorically, if you prefer. Stars have their births, agings, and deaths. Their journeys."

And then she inquired about my comfort. Since she had attended her mother after the births of the seven younger siblings, she knew much about my state of both mind and body. That data told her I hungered to hear the baby admired and myself encouraged. While tending both those needs, she picked up the small silver disk sent up while I was still occupied in labor by the affluent Absalom Boston, the black man whom I had not seen since I first set foot on Nantucket.

"His boardinghouse prospers," she observed, "even if his venture as a whaling captain was an economic disaster."

"He was a captain?" I had never imagined a black man in that position. I was surprised at my own surprise. Certainly Margaret Fuller's idea that women might be sea captains was no more startling.

" 'Justice,' " Maria read. "Did you know the medallion is engraved with the word *Justice*?"

"Mrs. Maynard," I asked softly, "you do think my babe will live?"

"I have never seen a more alert or robust child. Unless illness or accident befall him, his own dear body is as sturdy a vessel as soul could hope to sail in." How much alike in shining expression were the faces of Mrs. Maynard and Maria.

"Then I shall name him Justice, for he comes to balance the loss of my frail Kentucky baby."

"What was that baby named?" Maria asked.

When my lips tried to form the word, a lump stoppered my throat and I could not speak.

Mrs. Maynard answered Maria's question for me; she named the dead babe and rushed on to speak of the living one: "Oh, this Justice is a prince, a king!" she declared. "Just look! He listens to us. And look at the little boat the Indian brought him." She held up a tiny birch-bark canoe.

We heard the flap of the brass pineapple knocker, and Maria crossed the room to look down at the stoop. "It's the Husseys," she said.

Mrs. Maynard joined her at the window. "Oh, a pot of white flowers! I must go down and bandage up the knocker. Don't stay long," she added, instructively, to Maria.

But I made her stay long enough to listen to my thanks, again, for the baby's embroidered dress, for I knew Maria hated to sew. Indeed, she viewed the needle to be no less than a ball and chain for women. (We disagreed on this, I having found independence through my needle.)

I slept with my babe by my side. There he was, contained by his own soft skin, breathing, his heart beating beneath my fingertips. Thus assured, I fell asleep, and in my dream I drank milky chowder from crocus cups, presented on a silver circle reminiscent of the moon.

I NEVER TIRED of teaching my babe or tending him. Every moment I felt that if his father should appear, my happiness would overflow. Time was defined by the skills my child acquired. His first word was *big*, and he used it as a synonym for *beautiful*. My new dress with large flowers on it was greeted with cries of "Big, oh big!" His feet were ones that loved to dance, and if I put him on any new surface, he knew it by dancing on it. He loved all exotic foods, which he ate without hesitation, particularly my imported jellies made of guava, mango, and pomegranate; his little hand approached an open jar as slowly as a starfish and disappeared into the rim with an inevitable calm.

Before he was two, he applied physics to our various chairs; that is, by grasping a leg close to the floor he found any chair could be levered up and over. When Mrs. Maynard saw him pitchpoling the chairs, she said, "Una, you must yell at him when he does that," but I could not bring myself ever to raise my voice at him. I did explain about the fragility of chairs, and he ignored me till he had dominated them all.

Once, he was perhaps two and a half, I entered the chamber painted a sunny yellow, while the real sun poured through the window, to see him smile, open his eyes to the happiest of worlds, and ask, "Mother, what is death?" The truth was that I had already wondered and dreaded when he would become acquainted with the idea, but still I was unprepared for it to enter so abstractly. I pointed out the difference between what moved and what did not, and said that people and all that lived—plants and animals—might change and become still and that to become a mere thing was to die. "Some people believe," I added fairly, "that there is an invisible part of us that goes on to live without a body, but we cannot know about that."

Each time he returned from Boston, the judge brought Justice a gift, but he seemed rather ill at ease with my child, as some old bachelors are, while others are the most comfortable of substitute fathers.

"Children are not quite civilized," I remember his saying, as though he feared for his china.

"Of course not," I replied. "If truth be known, neither am I."

Sometimes the judge suggested we go to a lecture or some festivity and leave Justice behind; Mrs. Maynard's report was that he usually slept through our absence. But as he grew older, I noted that Justice did not count it just that he should be left behind, and so in the spring when Justice turned three, we took him with us to the sheep-shearing festival.

Outdoors, Judge Lord was, indeed, less tense, and Justice was full of delight at the animals and loved plunging his hands down into their oily wool. He loved, too, the rough texture of their horns, and I told him about my old friend Liberal who liked to challenge the Lighthouse.

In great curly curds, the wool fell from the sheep, who emerged from the shearing pen naked and shivering. All of this fascinated Justice, as I knew it would. "Cottage cheese, cottage cheese," Justice chanted at the billows of wool. But his best delight was the boy in the woolsack, who pranced on the wool and packed it down.

Later a stranger from the Vineyard suddenly appeared with Justice by the hand. "He was in with the animals, petting and playing."

I snatched him to my bosom, but Justice held out his arms to the judge, who took my boy clumsily to his chest.

CHAPTER 113   Chowder Swirls

SUCH WAS the full and shining face of joy. And on the backside—sorrow. Not the loss of my babe. Not that. But darkness and loss all the same. No ship brought a warning word of the mishap in the Sea of Japan. That first moment!—I was ravaged by the sight of my husband, in terrible pain, raving, on the stretcher. I had not seen him for more than four years, but letters had reached me. I had waited patiently, happy in the mothering of my child.

Spinning a tale is sometimes like stirring a chowder. Steam and mist will rise up, different particles are whiffed from the broth. When Ahab came home still bleeding, his soul raging, it was the Husseys' chowder, fortified with sweet butter, for which he had the best tolerance. The hard time, Ahab's homecoming while Justice was still a little boy, swirls up from memory.

DURING THE NIGHTS I was tortured as well as Ahab. I thought of the long white shape that, as a girl dressed like a boy in the rigging, I had seen sliding like ice under the frigid northern waters and how I had not cried out. Had that lookout's betrayal led to this bloody stump, the face contorted in pain, the fever that left only to come again?

"Fedallah," he said in his delirium. "Bring me Fedallah," and he scribbled on a piece of paper where I might find an old and hair-turbaned Parsee.

"My husband asks you visit him at night," I said.

"My master summons," he replied mysteriously. "My old master calls his servant at last."

But this Bombay man seemed far older than Ahab. I found Fedallah in our bedroom one night. I never knew how he got in; he had emerged like an evil vapor through a crack in the flooring.

As I entered, Fedallah brushed past me. "Let him find his way out," Ahab said. As I watched the fire-worshiping fiend leave, walking on two feet, I would have cut his leg away from him, if my husband could have used his parts—withered, yellow, and old though Fedallah was. And it seemed I had seen a future Ahab projected in Fedallah's haunted, plotting eyes.

When Starbuck tried to visit, Ahab said, "Tell him I'll see him aboard the *Pequod*, the day after we sail." The Parsee had fanned the flame of vengeance in Ahab. He was tortured with obsession as well as pain. Ahab asked, during those first weeks, to be moved to the birthing room so that little Justice would not hear his groans. While still at sea he had been fitted with various ivory legs, but the wound was not sufficiently mended, and the appendage had chafed and torn the flesh again. The small room was kept dark, at Ahab's insistence, though I tried to convince him that air and light would better pro-mote healing.

"You'd best send for the minister," Mrs. Maynard said, nodding toward the room.

"He's getting better. He's not dying. Don't say that."

"Something's dying in that room. Something like a human soul."

How the fear cramped me! Was Ahab to go the mad way of Kit?

As though my friend had read my thought, she said, "It's not his mind, my dear. Best send for the minister."

But the next day, when I glanced toward the birthing room, I saw Ahab standing in the doorway. He leaned against the doorframe; one leg extended a certain distance, wrapped in linen, and ending in emptiness, but he stood. Justice saw him, too, and retreated up the steps. It was the first time he had ever seen his father upright.

"Disheveled Ahab," I said merrily, as though I had been expecting him. Then I went to my husband and kissed him, and he returned the kiss. His cheek was gaunt, and pain had left its print on his brow, but there was affection in his eyes.

"Papa," Justice said, peeking around the corner. He was then four years old.

"Come to me." Ahab jumped one-legged to the nearest chair, sat, and patted his knee. "Come, sit. I have but the one knee to offer thee."

Justice came promptly to his father.

"Be careful not to bump his hurt," I cautioned.

"Aye, son. Ye might start it to bleeding, for it bleeds sometimes even if the sheet rubs it."

"Where is thy other leg?" Justice asked, immediately using the Quaker speech in addressing his father.

"Like Jonah, it is in the belly of the whale. And what do ye think it's doing there?"

"Resting and getting well."

"Nay. All day and night, between which there is really no distinction in that dark belly, the leg kicks the whale—else, in thunder, it be not Ahab's leg."

"To punish the whale."

"Aye, lad. And the rest of me shall, next voyage out, pursue the monster with our ship and our harpoon. Dost know Tashtego, the Indian? And Daggoo, the black tower? We shall all pursue Moby Dick."

Suddenly Ahab threw back his head. He gazed beyond, it seemed, at the offing, and had forgotten the little lad on his knee and his wife who stood by. With his lifted, outlooking gaze, Ahab had the mien of a weathered god. What sight did he envision? His arm quivered involuntarily, and I thought, *He is striking the whale with his lance.* Finally he muttered, "Now back to thy nap."

Justice jumped down and ran up the stairs. After I helped Ahab back to the birthing closet, I found Justice waiting for me at the top of the stairs.

"Take me higher, so I can see the *Pequod*."

Many afternoons, in the cupola, his nose against the glass, Justice worshiped his father's ship.

CHAPTER 114   The Birthing Room

I STOOD OUTSIDE Ahab's door to listen to him breathe. Rapidly, pantingly, like a man at hard labor, he gasped the air and spat it out. So savage his breathing was, I thought his teeth grasped air and gnashed it into his lungs. I heard myself whimper, as though I were nicked. No leak of light escaped from under the door; darkness sealed the seam. *Not Kit, not Kit again.* My knees weakened, and I feared I would buckle in prayer before his closed door.

He must have heard my whimper, for he said, "There is a kind of divinity in madness. You have it in you. The password's 'Madness.' "

"Madness. May I come in?"

"Aye," he whispered. And then more to himself than to me: "My wife makes me say *Aye*, when I would never say the word again. *No, in thunder. No!* But not to Una. No, for her, Ahab says No to No. Come in."

I saw him on the narrow bed. Disarrayed. New blood on the bandage of the stump.

"Ye must close the door," he said, "and abide with me in darkness."

I closed the door and waited in the Stygian gloom.

"Speak, goblin."

"No goblin. Una, your wife."

"There are only goblins here."

"Then I am a goblin." I could see nothing at all. One line of light behind my heels. "Let me stay."

We were silent a moment, he on the bed, I standing. I heard him moving in the covers.

"I've made a place," he said, so gently I trembled. He patted the bed. "Here, wife, come sit beside me." My hand found his hard-as-brick hand, and I remembered how he had comforted me on the moor merely by taking my hand.

"I would not be afraid to die"—the truth blurted from me—"if I held your hand." Like a vise, his clamped mine and took it to his lips.

"I would kill Death," he murmured, "before he could take ye. No, I'd not wait like Orpheus and then try to harrow hell. No, I'd stand before Eurydice. No death for ye, Una." And he kissed my hand and fingers again. His breath was hot. He began to pant, and a groan like a low surf filled the room.

"Let me touch thee, and heal thee," I implored.

"Ah, Christ visits in the darkness." His tone bit like vinegar in a wound.

"No, as a wife. I would soothe you as your wife."

He held my hand even tighter, took my fingertips between his lips. "Beyond the visible," he murmured, "the whale has dismasted me."

I leaned over him and kissed his face, but he became still as a corpse. I sat erect again. A gasp like a sob escaped him, and my chest heaved with sobs I stifled as best I could.

"Una," and again his voice had the quality of the purest, quietest brook in the woods. "I would tell ye a thought of mine." He hesitated.

"I would listen."

"There is a tragicalness in being human. In the mere being—"

Yes, I wanted to say, *but that is only one way. There are many ways. We choose.*

"Because," Ahab went on, "we are imperfect in strength and power. Without that, choice is an eyeless socket. The promise that man was given dominion over the beasts, the fowls of the air, and the fish of the deep is a false promise. There are secrets God keeps from himself. Perhaps his omnipotence is a sham. We need the Zoroastrian model, or perhaps the Parsee's. The wounds of Christ speak of his compassion for humanity, but what message would my wound impart? I have the spark of an idea. In this dark hole, I've seen a spark of Reason in the chaos of Unreason."

Again he hesitated, then mused, "Is this fear of Una I am feeling?"

"Fear of me?" I felt the cube of blackness around me.

"Two brave fingers can snuff out any spark. Ye have a mind stronger than any thumb and forefinger. I would not have ye snuff out my little idea. It must be fanned into a flame, a conflagration. Remember, we stood above time, at South Tower, and watched the world burn."

"It rained."

Ahab sighed. "And so ye'll not listen?"

"I'll listen." I fastened my eyes on the slender light burning under the door. I had promised silence, acquiescence.

"Man perishes, but so long as he breathes he insists on dealing with all Powers on an equal basis. If any of these other Powers choose to withhold certain secrets—why we err, suffer, die—let them. That does not impair my sovereignty in myself; that does not make me tributary."

Ahab stopped. I was forbidden to cross his speaking, nor would I extinguish any consoling idea. He listed to my silence.

"No addendum?" he asked. Then he mumbled to himself. "He has astonished me. But I will yet astonish him." He paused. "Astonish. What's its Latin root? *Tonare:* to thunder. There's thunder in astonishment." He turned his mouth toward me. "That lance of light—it blinds me."

"I'll cover it." I reached to the foot of the bed for an unused blanket.

"Go out," he said. "Leave me to think, dear One. Cover the crack from the outside."

As I obeyed, I wool-muffled out the light and sealed in his words: "Madness is undefinable—it and right reason extremes of one. *Ego non baptizo te in nomine Patris . . .*"

CHAPTER 115   **The Leg**

W E S O A K E D the tender flesh of the stub in seawater to help it toughen and callus. My pride when he could bear to be fitted again with the ivory peg! My pain to see it there, more permanent-seeming than any real leg, it and the generations of ivory legs to follow. Ahab could walk again, but how angrily he trod his world! That he had once been whole and competent and now was imperfect and clumsy all but brought despair. Anger, it seemed, was his only antidote to despair. Not love. Not even pride in Justice.

As soon as he could, he stalked the beach. "If I see water, I am *there*," he told me. "I am about my business. In the white foam I see the forehead of Moby Dick."

I begged to walk with him.

He replied, "Revenge is ever solitary. Isolating." He looked at me as though I grew strange and remote.

But ten days before the *Pequod* was to sail, he fell on the rocks and was brought home bleeding again.

"Carry him upstairs. To our bedroom," I directed.

Treacherously, my heart rejoiced: now he could not sail. Not on schedule. I could try again to calm, distract, dissuade, persuade—beg—him to be content that he was alive.

The bleeding of the stump bloomed like a rose through bandage after bandage.

"Stanch it," he cried. "Stanch it with fire!"

Mrs. Maynard, horrified, backed up against the door.

"Throw wood on the fire," I ordered, and I set the poker in it.

She fluttered about the room, her hand at her throat. Seeing her consternation, Ahab said calmly, "Leave my wife and me alone."

She was glad to flee.

As I pressed a pad to his wound, Ahab and I watched the glow of the metal.

"It's white now," he mused. "White as Moby Dick." I could not move. "Now!" his voice rang. "Now!"

And I grabbed the iron and rolled its hot tip over the flesh, searing and sealing the rawness.

That roar—myself, not Ahab.

When he was better, I begged him to wait at least till the New Year, a mere week later, but he would not. He said, "How do ye know I will improve? I may fall again and be utterly wrecked, my vengeance never accomplished." He spoke propped up in bed. I thought his head seemed grateful for the soft pillow behind it. He was beautiful in the white bed, his head framed by the lace of the pillowcase.

"If ye did not try to walk upon irregular rocks or the beach—"

"Ahab will go where Ahab decides to go, Una." He did not speak unkindly, but patiently, for he loved me. I am sure he loved me then. "Note this." He reached in the pocket of his nightshirt and held up a slender glass tube, closed with a cork. " 'Tis sand of Nantucket. I scooped it up just before that minion of Moby Dick betrayed me."

"The whale's minion?"

"The leg! the leg!" He pointed to the spare one, a disembodied bone, standing in the corner. "I do not trust the ivory. 'Twas the devil-cousin of this bone that betrayed me. My head dashed against stone? driftwood?—found senseless, brought home senseless."

Stem the tide—the rage of Ahab would not be stemmed. He had no wish to harm me, but I was battered by his raging. Bruised into quietness. His finger shook as he pointed at the new leg standing in the corner.

" 'Twas the shaft that bruised the groin—it was my splintered leg has sent me back groaning to bed for these last days before my leaving. It did not pierce the groin—no. But mocks me freshly to incapacity all the same. Yes. That incapacity that so gores my spirit. But here's Nantucket"—he waved the vial again drawn from his pocket—"though Moby Dick send me to the ocean floor, I shall triumph—remember that—for I shall be buried in Nantucket soil."

"Ye could have a wooden leg!" I exclaimed. "Ye could pursue every whale but Moby Dick."

"Nay, nay." He contemplated the vial of sand. "Moby Dick is the King of Dragons, Una. Too many Nantucketeers—he has devoured too many of us."

"Let some younger knight take up the battle." I could have bitten off my tongue to say such a thing. Nights he lay beside me, he had muttered, *Injury or age?* and I had kissed his face slowly and more slowly till he slept.

Now he looked at me. Now his face softened. "My girl-wife," he said quietly.

I stepped toward him, my tears ready to fall.

"Stay." He held up his hand. His gaze moved back to the ivory leg in the corner, a virgin leg, yet untried. "No, it is ivory, bone of his bone, that will carry me to revenge." Suddenly he raged again, "What is revenge but extravagant justice?" He did not look to me for answer. He opened his own jaw, curled down his lip, showed his lower teeth, became what he hated—the sperm whale. His body grotesquely lunged itself upward as far as it could, as leviathan heaves itself from water to air, yet twists its body, eyes its adversary. "Moby Dick! Vanquished! Dead!" Ahab sank back into his bed, his gaze still fastened on the leg standing in the corner.

I stepped between him and the bone.

"Ahab, husband." My voice shook, not with fear of him but with fear of failing to persuade him. Only the words of my father came to me, " 'Vengeance is mine. I will repay,' thus saith the Lord."

"Yes," Ahab said, exhausted by his passion. He closed his eyes. "I will repay."

Something like the smile he had always reserved for me rippled over his lips.

CHAPTER 116   Christmas Eve

IN THE SWIRLING FOG, on Christmas Eve, I walked with Ahab to the wharf for his third voyage since our marriage. Each step forward was agony to me, a hideous mistake. Ahab's ivory leg tapped on the stones, and the sound rang and echoed in the street.

"Well, it is not the sound of a coffin hammer," Ahab said. "Not mine. Perhaps it bespeaks a coffin for Moby Dick."

"He is but a beast." I envisioned the long, Arctic shape—now made of ice, now pale as the mist around us. Such a mist could conceal a white whale, could conceal the *Pequod*. Let us be lost in fog; let us wander lost till reasonableness be found.

Ahab's whisper was like the release of angry steam. "Dismasted, I am. Unmanned. I leave ye as I swore never to do, unless ye wished it, with an empty womb." Ahab leaned heavily on my shoulder.

"We have our Justice. He is enough." I heard the whine in my voice and replaced it with firmness. "I am happy and complete in him and in you."

"Well, I shall have a second kind of Justice. Not with any woman. With the sea. She shall open her thighs and yield up the whale to me. By thunder, she shall."

"Aim your harpoon at your own obsession," I urged. There was the great gray hulk of the *Pequod*. "Fragment this monomania." Firmly I grasped him round the waist. Would that my arm were a monkey-rope, that whaling device that insures the man on the cutting stage from slipping off into the jaws of the sharks.

He said nothing, but his hard hand squeezed my shoulder.

"My husband, I shall pray for you," I said desperately.

"What, religious?" He glanced down at me. The fog obscured objects ten feet away, as though they were shrouded in a whitish veil.

"Nay. But I cannot help my prayers for you. They tumble out. They are but ardent hopes and wishes."

The golden-haired gaoler materialized from the mist, tipped his hat to us, and tried to pass.

"Hold, man," Ahab said. "You look to be a man without a grudge. How can that be, when Ahab's heart is all grudge and malice? Tell thy bright secret, for ye emerge from this mist and fog like some bright thing."

"I go to fetch Mrs. Maynard. My wife is about to deliver our fourth child."

"Heaps of gold, heaps of gold," Ahab muttered bitterly. "Give me your hand, man. Nay, not to steady me. Hand in hand. A man to a man. Ye spoke of your wife. Look beside me. Here is a wife! Mark her."

All bewildered, Isaac looked at me, refused evasion in his gaze.

"Not now," Ahab said. "For later. Come, Una."

The ghostly mist and fog thickened as we approached the water. Tap—tap—tap, we walked, and I heard many feet about us, strangely furtive. Suddenly Ahab reached out and grabbed a shadow. "Fedallah," he hissed.

"All is as you have instructed," the man replied and twisted away into the pale darkness.

Ahab took no further step. "Tell the boy, wife, I will yet come again to rock him on his horse, and I will play with him again from my chair. Don't let him forget me. I'll come again to dance and dandle him between two strong hands." Ahab smacked his palms together. "Tell him good stories of me, whitewashed stories, of cannibal old me." He nodded toward a whitish wall of mist. "Yon group of yellow men— I would speak to them."

"I see no group."

"There, scurrying in the fog. My special crew. My secret crew. I shall pack 'em in the hold."

"Not the forecastle?" I could detain him with questions. There were thousands to be asked.

"We'll part now, Una." He sighed as though he were fetching up words that were known but needed to be uttered. "My infirmity has embarrassed me; know that my heart is yet a man's, and I love thee and cherish thee."

"And will you look at the moon, the benign, serene moon, and ask Luna to mirror your love to distant Una?"

"Aye, aye. I did that before. I'll not forget thee. Nor thy fresh bread, dainty dishes, juicy berries." Here he grappled me to him—not the fond and loving embrace I had known before, but a desperate clenching. "Moby Dick slain, I shall return to you not a whole man, but more than I was, avenged, puissant, all puissance." He hurried on in his speech, his lips in my hair, his voice the rumbling of his thoughts. "But Una, if the bitter time comes when it would be best for thee to forget me, do it."

I did not try to contradict him; he regarded his own mood and thought as law. The tears came to my eyes. I reached up in the white mist to kiss him. "Peace be with you."

I pulled my cloak around me—winter was full upon us—and walked homeward in white confusion. I berated myself: I should have spoken better. I pictured my heart upon a platter. If only I could have rightly presented him my heart. Would it have given me the power to convince, gladly would I have eaten my heart. Let my mouth gush with blood if that were a lubricant for language. As my feet came down on the paving, I bit my tongue to punish it, till it bled.

I SLEPT but ill that night, alone, while my husband slept cabined, his ship at the wharf. I dreamed of a medieval castle bedecked with pine and holly. Before a roaring fire, a minstrel played the lute and sang carols, but his music was deadened by a great pounding. A battering ram assaulted the castle door. I ran down stone steps to the door, which, at that instant, splintered, with a rush of water, and the mighty head of the white whale broke through.

It was not yet six in the morning in Nantucket and there was no sign of dawn. Mrs. Maynard came. I dressed, donned my wolf-trimmed cloak, and hurried down to the wharf. The white mist continued to hang about the streets, and I was cold. I saw the *Pequod,* still at the wharf.

"Avast," I heard someone call out, but it was not to me. Vaguely in the fog, I saw three men, one detaining the other two.

"Going aboard?" the first one asked.

"Hands off, will you," one of the men replied. His back was to me, so I heard his words only spottily. But he and his companion were, indeed, about to board the *Pequod,* their traps being already aboard, apparently. In a jaunty, defiant manner, the sailor spoke of venturing to the Indian and Pacific oceans. *He has no idea,* I thought, *of those vast immensities of water.*

"Ye be going thus, be ye?" The lone man seemed to mock the adventurer and his silent companion. "Coming back afore breakfast?" The speaker was Elijah, a crazed wharf man who fancied himself a reincarnation of his biblical namesake.

"He's cracked, Queequeg," the sailor said. "Come on." The sailor's voice was hearty, but it had the veneer of civilization to it.

Then I glimpsed the face of the man addressed—Queequeg, not the speaker—and that visible face was shockingly inscribed with tattoos, a South Sea Islander. He carried his harpoon. *The natural complement to Daggoo and Tashtego—a triumvirate of pagan harpooners!* This harpooner and his well-spoken companion started to move off toward the

Pequod, but Elijah halloaed them again. I heard the sailor repeat, "Never mind him, Queequeg, come on."

The two men did walk on, but Elijah continued to speak to the mist: "Oh! I was going to warn ye against—but never mind—it's all one, in the family, too." (I felt jolted; did he know I was at hand?) "Sharp frost this morning, ain't it? Good-bye to ye. Shan't see ye again very soon, I guess; unless it's before the Grand Jury."

"Sir," I called to him. "What warning would you give those men?"

"Mrs. Ahab, ain't it? All in the family, ye too? Ahab boarded last night. I saw ye kiss on the street like a harlot. Well, I should think ye'd know."

"Know what?"

"The cabin door's locked from the inside. I tried it. He'll not let ye in, or any Christian soul. I heard him gnashing his teeth in there." Elijah had a cruel pirate face.

"I only came to see the ship. I've had my farewell with Ahab."

"That ye have."

I drew back from Elijah and went home for breakfast. Mrs. Maynard and I played with Justice till late in the morning. Then once more, I put on my cloak. I would see the *Pequod* once more, if not her captain.

The *Pequod* had been hauled out from the wharf and waited in the harbor. Aunt Charity was coming off in a whaleboat. Soon she stood with me on the wharf and watched as her brother Captain Bildad and then Captain Peleg appeared on the ship's deck. Peleg's words to the first mate carried over the water: "Now, Mr. Starbuck, are you sure all is right? Muster all hands, aft here—blast 'em! Captain Ahab is ready—just spoke to him—nothing more to be got from shore, eh?"

Charity whispered in my ear, "I took Stubb a nightcap—he's my brother-in-law, ye know. And an extra Bible for the steward. I've ransacked my mind for what else might be needed, but truly I'm content. They're well supplied." She clasped her white hands over her black cloak and leaned back into her heels with satisfaction.

Bildad took his position as harbor pilot, and Peleg swaggered and swore about the deck as if he were commander: "Man the capstan! Blood and thunder!—jump!" and the crew sprang to the windlass, fitted the handspikes, and began to weigh anchor. I saw Queequeg was among those at the handspikes, and also the sailor, his face concealed by the slouch of his hat, who had companioned the Polynesian. Unfortunately, that slouch-hat sailor paused in his work, and Captain Peleg's foot delivered a swift poke to his rear.

"Is that the way they heave in the marchant service?" Peleg roared. He pronounced the word *marchant* the better to express his contempt. "Spring, spring and break thy backbone! I say, all of ye—spring! Quohog!"—I had heard the Polynesian's name to be Queequeg. "Spring thy Scotchman, spring Green Pants, spring your eyes out, Quohog!"

To those he kicked, I thought ruefully, "Merry Christmas."

Pip was running about the deck, peeking over the rails, for Ahab had kept his promise, despite his black and narrow mood, to take Pip as a cabin boy. After Ahab had learned to walk on his ivory leg, he had interviewed Pip, to see if it was still his inclination to go a-whaling. Pip had been steadfast, but after he left that interview with Ahab, his whole little body had shivered like a struck tambourine. He whispered to me, "Cap'in Ahab done been saved from fire, like Pip. Cap'in Ahab done been tied to the stake. Who cut him down? Pip don't know."

This primitive appraisal of Ahab had smote my heart: I had had so little balm to offer.

My bruised heart felt wrapped in chains and anchors, lay strangled in the deep.

Followed by the small sailboat—to bring back Bildad and Peleg— the *Pequod* seemed to shrink as she left me. A carol chant silently recited itself:

I saw three ships come sailing in,
come sailing in, come sailing in;
I saw three ships come sailing in,
on Christmas Day in the morning.

But it was a worthless charm. My eyes beheld, that Christmas Day, but one ship, sailing out.

THAT VERY DAY, even though it was Christmas, Justice spent an hour in the cupola, watching for his father's return. I could not dissuade him. I told him clearly it would be next Christmas and beyond before his father would come back, and there was no hope in watching for him. But the boy had something of his father's—and his mother's—stubbornness about him.

I thought that I would let him exhaust himself with the vigil, and during the days that followed, he often went aloft. I myself did not return to the cupola for a fortnight. When I did, I found the boy in the room so forlorn in his watch that I told him he might bring up his rocking horse and whatever other toys he liked, and that I myself would use the room to sew in. With light coming in the windows from every direction, it was an excellent place to sew, though too small for laying out cloth and cutting. Throughout the spring, Justice and I were good companions in the cupola. After a few months, I preferred that small, light place to any other room in the house.

Sometimes I would raise a window, lean out, and think, *No matter how far away Ahab is, I am now two feet closer.* And to get closer still, I would hurry down from the cupola to walk the wharf again, my eyes leaping to the horizon, seeking with a shrewd, focused gaze the shape of Ahab's ship. Those days, I scarcely wanted our boy to grow, but to keep him unchanged at each darling moment till Ahab would return. I thought cheerful words to myself: *He has survived a thousand lowerings.*

My skeptical self countered: *But this time he goes with only one leg.*

The hopeful, loving wife and mother, watching our young son playing with his ivory toys, added: *Ahab knows well the limits of the ivory leg. On the* Pequod *he fits it in a pivot hole when he would steer. And in the whaleboat, there's a notched place in the prow for him to wedge against, and the hull of his whaleboat is double-sheathed to withstand the pressure of the timbertoe.*

But I wished he would not go into the whaleboat.

I felt it my *duty* to be calm and assured for the sake of our son. Ahab was beyond my help, and though I had spoken of praying for him, no prayer burst spontaneously from my lips. My constantly serene behavior did, after a time, soothe my inner self. I remembered the strange evenness I had seen in Maria Mitchell, at our first meeting, and attributed to her Quaker upbringing. So during Ahab's third voyage, I made something of a Quaker woman of myself, in placid manner and even temperament. My greatest joy, after mothering, was my sewing, and while I stitched, my mind lay smooth and quiet.

Thus not only spring passed (with Justice's fifth birthday), and summer with its little outings, but fall and winter and spring again. As each season turned, I wrote a letter to Ahab, and sent it by whatever ship was at hand.

My son continued his watch at the window for his father through all these seasons. In the warm weather, we spent our hour in the cupola in the morning, with the sashes up. In cooler seasons, we climbed aloft in the late afternoon when the room had had time to collect and multiply whatever warmth of the sun came there, and we left open the trapdoor so that heat from the house rose up. Thus we kept tolerably warm, or cool, as the season required.

The cupola was like a miniature or a sampler of the house, offering a roof over our heads, windows, and a doorway of its own though the door was in the floor. Now it was as imaginatively stocked as if Aunt Charity had provided: holding my sewing basket, a little standing bookcase, an ivory stool (the duplicate of one Ahab had taken on the *Pequod*), a lap writing desk (equipped under its lid with extra paper, quills, ink, sand, and blotting paper), pillows, a small rug, a quilt or two, a basket of snacks, a corner full of toys. Once I wrote to David Poland, at his sister's, that my cupola and my house provided material for a meditation on little and big, with the small really holding the heartbeat of the large, though its space was only a fraction of the volume bound by the whole house.

THE SPRING of my son's sixth birthday, I glanced out to see something of a commotion on the wharf. The whaler the *Jeroboam* of Nantucket had returned. Justice did not remark it, but I told him, our hour being almost over, that I had bethought myself of a pressing errand and needed to go down, and he should go across to the judge's when he finished his sea-watch.

Shouting through a horn from the deck of the anchored *Jeroboam* was a man who styled himself Gabriel, after the archangel, and his news was of the Second Coming of the Shakers' God. Except for Gabriel, the crew of the *Jeroboam* were not to be seen. What made the hair on my arms rise up was that Gabriel proclaimed the Shaker God to have embodied himself as a great white whale—Moby Dick! Gabriel was alone on the deck, having ordered the hands below, once the ship was in the harbor.

Quickly I worked my way through the crowd to the edge of the wharf to hear whatever he might say of Moby Dick. Gabriel was a short man enveloped in a long-skirted coat, the skirts of which he occasionally grasped and flapped up and down. The effect was not one of heavenly wings but of a deranged man vainly trying to fly. His yellow hair and the complete sprinkling of his face with freckles made him resemble the third Mrs. Hussey, but I did not imagine such a lunatic could be kin to that sane and forthright genius of the chowder pots. The archangel professed himself to be the possessor of certain vials and seals, within which lay an epidemic that could be unleashed on the town, as it had been on that very *Jeroboam*. At this I saw Isaac Starbuck, who stood a distance from me, shaking his head in disapproval.

"Bow down, ye sinners of Nantucket"—Gabriel raved—"for the Second Coming is at hand and perdition for all who—"

His words were drowned out by the thumping down of knees upon the wharf. "Thou," he said, pointing a finger at me, for I was among a few conspicuous for not having bent the knee, "blasphemer! Beware the blasphemer's end!" His pointing finger moved from me to the water, as though to show me my death by drowning.

"For shame! Thou jabbering humbug!" It was Captain Peleg from the back of the crowd.

"This woman's husband pursues Moby Dick. Dost deny it?" he asked me, all the while pointing at me. "At the bottom of the sea! With one beat of his flukes, Moby Dick hath sent him under."

Ahab lost! A storm of white passed before my eyes, and my knees buckled, even as I strove to stand upright.

With my collapse, he trumpeted, "Behold, Mrs. Macey, wife of the drowned blasphemer, how she sinks to her knees!"

Mrs. Macey? No. Not I. My husband pursued Moby Dick, but he was not Macey. I struggled to regain my feet and felt the helping hand of the gaoler under my elbow.

"This be not Mrs. Macey!" the gaoler shouted.

Had I not been faint with relief, I would have giggled.

Another woman, who had dropped with the congregation to the injunction of their priest, slowly rose. "I be Mrs. Harry Macey," she quavered. I knew her; she was married to the brother of Mrs. Maynard's second husband. He spelt their name with an *e*.

"Dead. Harry Macey. Dead and in the fiery pit!" Gabriel pointed to the deep, and presumably beyond.

"Flukes and flames!" shouted Peleg. "Where is thy captain? What hast thou done, mutineer, with Captain Mayhew?"

While this conversation was occurring, the gaoler unloosed my arm, quietly untied a dinghy from the wharf, and began to row out to the *Jeroboam*. Like any Nantucketeer, Isaac handled a boat expertly, and soon, while Gabriel raved about vials, seals, and epidemics, Isaac climbed a rope, hooked his knee over the rail, and approached the archangel from his rear; the summer sun glinted on Isaac's golden curls.

"Who art thou?" Gabriel blurted in surprise, and then, know-it-all that he was, he answered his own question. "The Archangel Michael comes to assist me! Together we bind this town with seals given by the Shaker God himself, the White Blot!"

"I am not the Archangel Michael," Isaac responded loudly, "but the town gaoler, come to take you to gaol!" And with that, in a single, practiced gesture, he clapped the archangel in the wrist irons which could always be seen and heard jangling from the gaoler's belt.

Another dinghy, manned by Captain Peleg with a crew of four, was on its way to the ship, and soon the hatches were opened and the sailors and captain of the *Jeroboam* released. Straightway, the gaoler and Gabriel, accompanied by Peleg, returned from the ship. The folk on the wharf appeared not at all shamefaced at how easily they had been bamboozled. As spontaneously as they had succumbed to prophecy did they recover from it. But not all were left unmarked by the return of the *Jeroboam*.

Mrs. Harry Macey, with two women friends to comfort her, stood sobbing and anxiously waiting for Captain Mayhew to come ashore. Regrettably, Captain Mayhew affirmed that Macey, burning with reckless energy, had given chase, and had succeeded in landing one iron (insufficient!) in the white whale. With his lance poised, Harry Macey had been dashed from the boat and to his death by one fast, fanning motion from Moby Dick.

As Gabriel was escorted past me, he said, "I *do* know thee. Thou art the wife of Captain Ahab!"

"I am." But I was not then afraid. One right guess out of two tries was not a winning percentage, I thought, for prophecy.

"Now thy husband is a postman," he jabbered. "I gave him a letter to deliver to Mr. Macey. A moldy missile addressed by yon weeping woman—yon right-well-weeping woman—and there shall be gnashing of teeth."

"What do you mean?"

"The letter bag. Her letter to him was in the *Pequod*'s letter bag, should *Pequod* cross with *Jeroboam*. Thy husband tried to foist it off on Mayhew, but I sent it back, on a boat knife, to Ahab. 'Twon't be long till Postman Ahab will go the way of Harry Macey."

Here Peleg gave the Archangel Gabriel a forward shove. "An all-fired outrage," he said. Then he applied his foot to Gabriel's backside, though Isaac did not wish his prisoner so treated. "Flukes and flames!" swore Bildad. "I'd keel-haul thee, angel, if thou wert mine!"

A bit shaken, I watched them go. Standing beside me, I realized, was our own local madman Elijah, who regularly haunted the wharf. Elijah spoke to me quietly, and all the more sinisterly for that quietness. His face was a blazing red. "Thou knowest, Mrs. Captain Ahab, perhaps of the old prophecy of the squaw Tistig? Not mine, but I have foreseen it, too. Tistig said that Ahab's name would prove prophetic. The wicked King Ahab of the holy Book of Kings, she had that referent in mind. That dogs, too, would lick Ahab's blood. Who are the dogs of the sea, Mrs. Captain, but sharks?"

I walked away, but I was afraid for Ahab, forked by prophecy. And afraid for myself and for Justice.

CHAPTER 119   ✺   # The First Part of Ahab's Third Voyage After His Marriage

LATE THAT AFTERNOON Captain Mayhew, a most reasonable and responsible-seeming Quaker, came to call on me at Heather's Moor. Though Harry Macey's letter, impaled on Gabriel's boat knife, had been returned to the *Pequod*, Starbuck had tossed aboard the *Jeroboam* a bag of several letters, which Captain Mayhew laid out on my parlor table: three for sailors' wives, one from Mr. Stubb to his wife, one for Mary Starbuck, and one skinny envelope for me.

"How fared my husband?" I pressed his letter to my throat as though to give it voice.

Captain Mayhew answered, "He pursues the white whale. That much of the mutinous madman's tale was true."

"In what style does my husband pursue Moby Dick?"

"Moby Dick can be pursued in only two possible styles." Captain Mayhew had a quiet, sensible bearing. A short white scar sat atop one cheekbone.

"They being?"

"Either ignorantly, foolishly— That were the way of poor Harry Macey. Thy husband is no fool, but full of cunning."

"Or? The other way?"

"Madly."

Standing in the double doorway of the parlor, with arms folded across his chest, was my lad of six. "Madly? What do ye mean by madly, of my father?"

Captain Mayhew glanced at me, but answered, "I think thy father is a brave and skillful captain. Perhaps he pursues Moby Dick too hotly."

"I thank thee for thy answer. But, please, tell me, what ye mean by *hotly*." Justice's speech was that argot of Quaker and sailor usage that he had heard from his father, but that he never spoke to me.

"With too much singleness of purpose. Too much ardor. Let me pass, lad." And with that Captain Mayhew walked by Justice and out the front door.

Justice crossed the room to me.

"What is *ardor?*" he asked me. He squeezed my hand.

"It is passionate feeling, great love."

"My father pursues the whale because he loves him? That's not true, Mother. He hates the whale." I was startled by my son's logic; it seemed far beyond his years. He spoke like a man of the law—ah, he was borrowing logic from the judge. "How is it, then, that Captain Mayhew said my father pursues Moby Dick with too great love?"

I retreated to the sofa of the parlor and patted the seat. I tried to put my arm around my son, but he would have none of it.

"Thy father—your father—loves not the whale, but he loves the idea of revenge. That is the part of himself that he most loves now, that part that would punish the whale for taking his leg."

"Moby Dick is a thief."

"Aye, and he has stolen away more than thy father's leg from us."

"Could he not forgive the whale?"

"He burns in his heart for revenge. 'An eye for an eye and a tooth for a tooth.'"

"But Moby Dick has no leg."

"Thy father requires his life." I saw Justice's brow knit—so like his father when he was gathering thunderclouds—beneath the dark curls on his forehead. For the first time, he made me think of Chester, the little cabin boy, and his father, the good captain, who hoped to die to save his son. The waters of grief rose up in the well of me.

"Moby Dick's whole life?"

"Your father feels the whale has ruined his life."

"Ruined!" At that the boy's face contorted with pain, he gasped one mighty, shuddering sob and threw himself into my arms. I could have bitten off my tongue.

"It is a temporary feeling your father has. Once he has killed the whale, your father will feel whole again." I rubbed the boy's back and felt it grow more still and then more stiff under my strokes. Was I hardening my son by passing on to him his father's passion for revenge? "Of course, your father's life is not at all ruined," I went on. "How could any person be ruined when he is loved the way you love your father and the way I love him? Do you think it's possible to have a ruined life when you are so beloved?" I waited for his reply.

"I don't know." His words were muffled against me. He hesitated, then added, "Moby Dick has such a big life."

I smiled, relieved to hear him speak childishly. But I thought of the tons of blood in that great body, and how it would incarnadine the sea all around if he was slain. I had hoped that Ahab would have a change of heart, that he would forgive the whale, or forget his hatred. Ahab's life was as intact as he wished to perceive it. "Yes," I answered my son absently, "whales are enormous." But I wondered, if Ahab did prove victorious, then who would Ahab be?

Presently I reminded Justice, "Captain Mayhew delivered a letter from your father."

"Let's go up to the cupola to read it," he said, sitting up.

I hesitated, for I did not know what grown-up news it might hold, but I agreed. "I shall meet you there, but first a trip to the privy for me."

I hastened down the path, and could not help but notice how nicely the berries, which Ahab loved so much for their juicy freshness and purity, progressed. Enough daylight came into the privy for me to be able to read, but, never lacking for oil, we kept a lamp there, and sulfur matches in a tin canister. Ah, the luxuries of the rich. In that clear glow, I seated myself and read, nay, devoured:

Dearest Wife, my One,

Sunset, and beside the ever-brimming goblet's rim, the warm waves blush like wine. There was a time when even as the sunrise spurred me, the sunset soothed. No more. This lovely sunset light—it lights not me; all loveliness is anguish to me, thine most of all, though most beloved, since I cannot enjoy it. My high perception responds to the ethereal beauty the eye brings the mind, but I lack the low, enjoying power. Damned in the midst of the soft blush of Paradise! Good night—good night, my wife!

But not good night, for I would share with thee what can be shared in language. The diver sun—slow dived from noon—goes down; my soul mounts up! Though she wearies with her endless hill.

Moby Dick, a hump like a snow-hill. There my soul needs to climb. There I shall find ascendancy. Sovereignty! Remember, I whispered that word to thee in the birthing room. My human sovereignty! the same in the face of animals, angels, absent gods. The idea was born and grows into a giant—but that's enough. This letter—the first one home—let me comfort thee and reassure thee.

*There was a prophecy—I told thee not—that I should be dis-
membered. Aye—I lost this leg. But I now prophesy that I will
dismember my dismemberer. Now the prophet and the fulfiller of the
prophecy shall be one. That's more than the great gods ever were!
Forgive me. Rage breaks out like a fire that dies only to leap up
again.*

*My pipe, Una. One evening, I lit my pipe at the binnacle lamp,
as was usual for me, and called for my ivory stool. "How now," I
finally asked myself after a time, "this smoking no longer soothes."
My pipe having been so long my companion, I spoke to it. "Oh, my
pipe! hard must it go with me if thy charm be gone!" and I threw
it lit and hissing into the sea. It was a thing meant for sereneness.
And that is beyond Ahab's grasp.*

*Una bade me look to the moon for sereneness, but I know there'll
be no moon tonight. The phase is wrong. Let me think of Justice.*

*Tell our son that some bright days Ahab feels like a farmer who
has spent his days among inland wheat fields. "What, wheat fields
in the ocean?" our son will ask. "Yes. Let me tell thee where." (Now,
dear wife, assume my voice while reading to our son.) In this first
part of this third voyage that I have taken since thy mother and I
were married—aboard the* Pequod *we were married, whilst she stood
at anchor in Old Nantucket harbor! didst thou know that, son?—but
leagues thence, on this voyage, from the Crozets, northeastward, the
sight of wheat fields was to be seen.*

All around the Pequod, *as though the ship were an innocent
farmer's house, glowed meadows, an expanse of ripe and golden
wheat.*

*And if we were the farmer's house, then where were the machines
to harvest this great bounty? Oh, they were there. Such prodigious
mowers, too! The mowers were the Right Whales.*

*Whales! my son exclaims. Did ye sing out? Nay, for though they
are the Right Whales for many to hunt, they are the Wrong Whales
for us. Now there's a riddle. But easily solved. For the* Pequod
*mainly pursues the Sperm whale, whose oil is of the finest and most
profitable sort, not the Right Whale, who is the right whale for some
because he is easier to catch. (Though I admit I have sometimes
topped off an almost brimming ship of sperm with kegs of lesser oil.)*

What appear to be meadows of ripe wheat surrounding the Pequod *are in fact meadows of brit, the tiny animals that the gigantic Right Whale must have to live. Do you know the kinds of whales, my son? The sperm whale is a toothed monster, but the baleen whale has a kind of mustache inside his mouth—sailors speak of it as a wondrous Venetian blind. So the Right Whale, like a threshing machine, opens his great mouth and with the fringy fibers of his mustache filters the water (which flows back to the sea), leaving bushels of brit to nourish the whale. The sound of this harvesting operation is a grassy, cutting sound, and where a whale has made a swath through the gold, ye can see the blue of the ocean.*

It has been now some weeks since I contemplated that pastoral scene. Dear Wife and Son, do not think that though Moby Dick draws me on, I do not feel thy gentle tugs pulling me back.

Dear boy, if up till now ye have had but a vague idea of the varieties of whales, ask thy mother to be thy encyclopedia. She has herself hunted whales, and they her. Look now at the ivory bracelet carved with whales that she wears as my wedding token. Put thy finger on their midget backs, and ask her to tell thee of their true size, habits, dispositions, and uses. Let her read thee the whales as though they were the runes of old.

Ahab

Captain, The Pequod.

In the cupola, I read of the *Pequod*'s encounter with the meadows of brit to Justice. He thought it pretty—I asked him so—but he said he would prefer his father describe a chase to him. "Then you must write to him yourself and tell him so," I said.

"Yes, I should learn to write," he answered. "It's time to learn to read, too." He looked serious, but pleased and brighter. He glanced about and suddenly knit his brow. "We will have my lessons up here."

That dark imperialism! I saw the stamp of my own father in his grandson's brow. And Ahab's stamp, as well.

T HAT NIGHT I could not sleep for anxiety about my husband.

Was there not a moon tonight?

I left the bedroom and climbed to the cupola. There she was, with the cross of the mullions quartering her face. I sat in my rocking chair, then rose to open two windows a crack, so the cooling night air could visit me. Soon I adjusted a shawl around my shoulders. I rocked and watched the moon. I tried to make my mind as blank of worry as her blank face. Eventually, the moon rose above the roof of my little cupola, and I could no longer see her. Yet I rocked and rocked, incessantly as the sea herself.

When I awoke it was morning, with the sunlight streaming in and heating up the cupola.

To my surprise, Justice was not in his bed. I had just dressed and was about to look for him when Justice with Captain Mayhew appeared at the door.

"I couldn't find you," the boy said, half sobbing. "I went to the wharf. I thought you might have gone to sea and left me."

"I tried to tell the boy his mother was no sailor," Captain Mayhew explained.

"He doesn't know, does he, Mother?"

"Well, here I am," I said. "I went up to the cupola to watch the moon and fell asleep."

"He is a fine, bright lad," Mayhew said. "I've stuffed his ears with tales of whales and ships."

"I shall go with Captain Mayhew as cabin boy," Justice said with horrible cheerfulness, "if my father doesn't come back."

Turning to go, Mayhew said, "Mind your mother, boy. I won't have a cabin boy who doesn't mind his mother."

"And what has happened to Gabriel?" I inquired.

"The judge says he's too mad to hang, and the gaoler has taken him out to Quaise with the other poor, mad folk."

"My father is not poor," Justice said. "He's very rich."

"Hush, Justice. It does not do to brag."

Captain Mayhew looked up. "It's as fine a house as any in Nantucket. And beautiful inside." He sighed. "I invest in oil," he said.

"What whaling captain does not?"

"Not that sort of lubricant. A new kind of oil, oozed from the ground, lying about in pools over the bogs in Pennsylvania."

"Pardon me, Captain Mayhew, but it is unusual for a sea captain to turn landward for his profit."

"Yes, Mrs. Captain, but someday the whales will all be dead, hunted to extinction by the likes of Captain Ahab and myself."

Justice made a darting motion with his arm. "Let Moby Dick die first!"

AFTERWARD, I crossed the street to visit the judge.

"What is this new oil that Captain Mayhew speaks of?" I asked.

The judge shook his head. "A sad business," he said. "No one wants the stuff. When you burn it, it billows noxious black smoke."

"I fear Captain Mayhew's taken a loss, then."

"Did Captain Mayhew discuss his business with you?" Austin Lord wished to tease me.

"Why not?" I said, with something of my old sauce.

"Well," the judge began, scratching the side of his nose thoughtfully, "you scarcely know Captain Mayhew. One does not discuss business with casual acquaintances."

"Do you think Captain Mayhew will stand a heavy loss?"

"He has already stood a heavy loss, my confidential friend. Now he insists on throwing his money down a sinkhole."

"Confidential, of course. Why is that?"

"The project is undercapitalized. He got into earth oil too soon. There's no technique for transforming it into something that can be used in lamps. There will be, no doubt, someday. But Mayhew is already living at Absalom Boston's boardinghouse."

"I should like to invest some of my excess in Mayhew's earth oil company."

"Too risky. I advise against. Strongly."

But despite my friend's objections, I made the investment, and substantially. Perhaps I could tide over Mayhew's enterprise; he tided over my son's need for a father, for a few days.

THOSE WERE RESTLESS days and nights for me. My son was taking beginning steps into the broader world. Not only did he go every day to visit the wharf—he soon made friends with many of the mates and crew, and occasionally a captain, for Ahab's sake, would chat with him—but, as he had proposed, he quickly learned to read and write. His first laboriously written sentence was a simple demand to his father: *Tell me about A Chase ye have made this voyage.* I was glad for all of Justice's progress, yet it made me uneasy.

Many a night I kept a moon watch. I saw her through all her phases. My physical tides became tied to her, and when she was dark, and her gravitation pull was added to that of the sun behind her, then my menses were pulled from me. When she circled around to the other side of the earth and her face was fully lit, there was a ripeness and readiness to my body. Sometimes I thought of Mrs. Maynard's porcelain devices, but such things repelled me. I did not merely want my sex to soar; I wanted the entirety of Ahab, body, spirit, and mind. During the full moon, I thought of farmers throughout the great plains of the West, of Indiana and Illinois, and how they planted corn and wheat when the moon was full.

AS THE DAYS, weeks, months, years passed since our parting Christmas Day, and as we received no further word from Ahab after that delivered by Captain Mayhew of the *Jeroboam,* nor came any ship to port that had seen him, a kind of cocoon spun its slow self around me. Oh, I could still chat amiably, about nothing, with the judge; and the Mitchells would occasionally tell me some interesting fact, but those facts were no more than pinpricks to a determined sleeper. My letters to Margaret were dull, and she wrote back to me more briefly than she had at first. Her observations about her "Summer on the Lakes" seemed intense, but oddly impersonal, and in fact it turned out that she soon published a book of that title, and some of the very phrases and sentences of her private correspondence to me could be read there. I do not know exactly why that disappointed me. Perhaps I should have been thrilled. Only in church did I find some enlivening of my spirit. My minister never failed to say words that seemed to reach down in me and quicken something vital that might lie dormant otherwise.

I thought of the fog and mist that Christmas Eve when I had told my husband farewell on the cobblestones of Nantucket. There had been strange movement of feet; there had been Fedallah, whom Ahab had reached out and grabbed into our ken. What had been shrouded by that immaterial whiteness? It seemed inside me. It had stopped my throat like cotton and kept me from crying out warnings to my husband and from making enough entreaties to right his mind before he sailed.

He had used my shoulder like a crutch that evening. He would board the ship under cover of darkness so that none of the crew would see him come a-limping down the street. *Stay, husband, stay,* my heart pleaded, even then, with the ship emerging before us in the mist, and something like cotton muffling my spirit.

Now there was a numbness to my life. My son grew. He prospered, for he was eager to learn everything that might fit him for a life at sea. My friends were kind and patient with me during this period, but it was as though they stood on the other side of a many-layered veil.

Once Maria and I were sitting on the same side of the table in the dining room when she said, "Turn your telescope upon the moon. You could map her face. Galileo was almost burned at the stake for saying the face of the moon was blemished with craters."

"Really?" The bit of history interested me. I wished something would burn away my dull anxiety. "Where was the heresy in such science?" I asked.

"The moon, being a heavenly body, was supposed to be perfect, reflecting the perfection of God's creation. The church would not brook Galileo's observation of irregularity on its surface. The observation of sunspots was also a threat to their system of belief."

"Surely only a few crackpots would dispute so irrationally?" I poured out tea for us both and told her this was not China tea, but Darjeeling, from India.

"You assume a time as reasonable as our own. Galileo was invited by the Pope, the very head of the church, to recant."

"Truly?" I was incredulous that a person could rise to such power as a Pope and yet be so foolish, even in a distant time.

"When Galileo refused to recant, the Pope said, 'Show him the instruments of torture.'"

"And?"

"Galileo recanted. Now you can use the telescope safely to map the craters of the moon."

I smiled at my loving friend. "I doubt that I shall ever travel there."

She returned my smile, yet persisted. "There are *mares*, seas, on the moon, albeit dry ones, as well as craters." Her eyes glowed over the rim of the teacup. "And one of the seas is called Tranquillity."

I gazed into Maria's face and saw nothing resembling tranquillity but a face where passion had been transformed into scientific curiosity.

"Do you still search for your comet?" I asked, putting my arm around her.

"Oh, yes."

She waited for a lover she had never seen.

CHAPTER 121   🌑   Letter from Susan

Dear Una. I pretty sur you be real surprised to see how good I write. And to get this letter. How do I aim to mail this letter. Well, I am at your house again. Been north for quite a while. When I got back here, I seed your note saying Welcome Traveler and also how Any business can be conducted by your neighbor, so I just now put your name and then care of him on this envelope. Figure next traveler will take it to him. As I doesnt dare. It dead of winter here now. Just like it wuz when we both here. Good fire going in the hearth. But I be thinking Whoa, Susan. Back up and tell Una where you ben and how it wuz and why you here again.

Where I ben. Maybe four or five days after I lef you and we shout Freedom, I look behind, see I be followed. I knew who. Wolf-man bounty-hunter you told me about. Had to be. I could see the wolf snout point up over his head, and his beard, and him so small. I saw he wuz gaining, but I move fast as I could. Snow everywhere. I says to myself Just get on top of that little snow hill in the middle of the cornfield. But time I got up on the noll, he caught me. I wuz so scared that I split off and part of me just hung up in the air and watched. But I wuz able to think what to do, anyway. I bought myself free with your money.

You might wonder how I got the time to tell all this. Trapped in the snow again, here at your house. Me and my friend who was resting here. My friend, he say it must be ʒero outside. I get to my friend later. Snow near bout to the knee outside, but we warm in here.

Once the wolfman wuʒ out of sight, I call out to my part left hanging, just a air shiver-self like ice crystals. Self she come on through sunset air to be with me, and I start on.

Come deep dusk and the night wind, I know I got to find a place to stay. No house in sight. I start down a little rise and I stumble. I roll down the hill till I a white snowman. Then I have to bust out of all that snow. I done rolled off a little creek bank. Well, I start digging me a cave under the little overhang. I make me an ice cave. Once I get inside, I block up almost all the front opening with snow and ice.

I go to sleep for a while. Dream I home, warm on the porch, got a sugar cane joint in my hand. Purple case all peeled back, me chewing and sucking on the good part till it limp. It flop over on my hand like a little white mop head. I wake up.

I wake up hungry in the ice cave, safe from the wind, take off my mitten, grope till I get into my napsack. Touch cornbread with ham bits. Potatoes gone. Still got some honeycomb in your little tin box. I feel around, put my fingertips under that little curled lip, hinge the lid on back—honeycomb just waiting. All sticky. I can't see much in my ice cave. Jus feel and taste. Doorwall gray with dawn light. I scoop up snow for thirst then I kick and bust out. All bright daʒʒle.

I walk on some more. Peddlers pick me up in they wagon and I stay warm in a little tiny room inside the cart, got a little stove even. Her name wuʒ Judith and she got a black cloud for hair and silver-rim eyeglasses. She stay in the warm room while her husband drive on through the cold. We kin hear the horse feet, so soft, wind moan. She give me some hot tea and it wuʒ in a clear glass set in a silver cup-holder. She got stacks of dishes in there. Every plate with a silver rim. Silver buckles on harnesses. Pile of silver money on the table— everything all snug in that little moving room. They drive on to some friends of theirs and that woman had a baby while we stayed there. I learn some mid-wife from Judith. I felt good for Emma, but I felt so sad thinking of your baby. We stayed there a bit.

One night Judith told my fortune and it was a black Jack and a red heart Jack, and she say that Coming and Going may be the same thing, far as I wuz concerned. It upset me.

Spring come on. Judith and Abraham drive off with the cart, me up on the box between them. Cart wuz yellow with red curly cues, and they give Emma and Paul a little baby cradle painted the same yellow with curly cues on the head hood. But soon they need to drive west and I got to walk north, but it spring now.

One day I go to sleep under a apple tree covered with blossoms. I chose that tree. You never saw so much pink blooming as that apple orchard and I just wanted to be part of all that pink. Little white girl woke me. She was dressed all in pink check gingham. Her folks wuz mighty nice to me. I did a few chores, stayed there several months, on through the summer.

The woman picked up with my reading and writing where you left off. She wuz teaching little Molly at the same time. I must brag on myself because my teacher did. I didnt let on that you already started me out and I already got the hang of what it all about, how you sound out the letters. Sometimes I jus spell the way it sound. I know better. That I ought to always write was and not wuz, but if Im thinking about what it is I want to say, I forget the spelling. I can spell just, not jus, too, when I think about it, but I dont want this to be full of blots and cross-outs, so I let mistakes stand. Guess I ought to told Mrs. Anderson I already had some learning but I just bout to bust with pride when she brag on how quick I catch on, and I end up not ever telling. When we read out of the Bible once I get a few words I know what got to be next. Mrs. Anderson say I just about grade eight in reading.

In one lesson, we was learning the names of shapes. She point out circle, like the lids on the stove, and lines that run parallel, and rectangle like the bed. Then we came to triangle, and go look at the rafters, but I be thinking Triangle, triangle, that what this family be. Three parts. No real place for me. And it weigh on me. It weigh on me so I miss my mam. Weigh like being a slave. They wuz good as could be. But I dont fit into they shape.

One night Mr. Anderson showed us a comet in the sky up over the barn. I took it as a sign. Like the light of the Lord which led me this far. Next morning I in such a hurry to go, I dont even say *good-bye. But I write a note. My first letter to anybody. It say Thank you for your kiness.*

Next place I stayed was with Shaker folks. And they invited me to move right in. Already one old black woman staying there. When I walked across the yard, she rake behind me. Rake out my footprints. She say she dont ever want to own nothing, but if she was young like me shed get something for herself. She didnt even own the rake.

I stayed on a bit. They wuz wonderful dancers, but men and women all separate. No kind of marriage at all. I think This here some kind of idolatry spite of all they say about Jesus. They got twin stairsteps all in a spiral like they done twirled off the fingertips of God. Staircases so pretty they scare me. Belong in heaven, not this world. Everything so neat and well-made. Chairs hanging on pegboard all around the rooms so cant no dust hide under chairs.

Then I learn they got overseers. Two women two men live in high rooms looking out over everybody else. They see you do wrong, lazy or grouchy, got envy, het up, anything—you got to confess. Or they confess for you. I dont want to live my life watched. I ben watched.

They give me a nice oval basket, sausage and bread, a little patty-pan with the cake still in it. Walked north till I come to big water. My heart about broke. Nothing there. Nothing but water and sandy beach. I think this be the ocean you told me about. I taste it, but the water be sweet. Is this why you left your mam and all you know I ask myself. To come to this. This was the wilderness and the dessert. Nothing but sweet water and too much of that.

Then I see a trunk bobbing along on the waves. Here come something for me. Thats what I told myself. That place wuz such a disappointment. It was nothing. Wasnt nothing there meant anything at all to me. So what if it be freedom. It Was Nothing. I put my hopes in that trunk just jigging along out on the water.

Fore long it washes up and I step out on the wet sand to grab a handle, pull it in. Didnt have any lock and I opened it right up. I thought Wouldnt it be great if this trunk full of hot bread. Now I knowed that couldnt be, still I hoped. Mighty cool wind off the water.

Trunk was full of two printed books and lots of hand-written pages. These books said on they cover Faust, on one, and Wilhelm Meister, on the other, and when I open them up, I cant read a word. Now I know I can read. Finally it come to me they got to be in some other language. But the loose paper handwriting was in English, but it wasnt a good hand—just dashed cross the page so you had to go slow to make out a letter. I made out one whole sentence. It said *Of all the Greek myths that of Orpheus and Eurydice is the sweetest I know.*

I dig on down in the trunk but it was wet and the ink was smeared. Looking for some little something to cheer me up. At the bottom, the words was all washed off. They wuz just pale blue pages. I picked one up. Like a square of sky. I held it up, all tender and wet, and it matched the sky.

Made me mad as a hornet. I kicked that trunk over. Then I dragged it out to the water. Same water, always moving. Same blank nothing sky. Not even a cloud for me to look at it. Why *this place* hurt me so, I asked myself. Nothing here for me, I answered myself. Now, I thought, if my mam wuz here—

Thats when I knew my path and the meaning of Judiths fortune cards. Yes, I knew the way. I wuz going back for my mam. I thought a sentence *Of all the folks, love for my Mam sweetest I know.* So I have started back. Winter has caught me here for a while.

Im thinking about you Una. Im hoping this letter find you. I hope that your heart is cheered. I sur did hate to leave you by yourself, but I had to go. You musnt try to find me. Dont forget me. My friend stirring. This be the morning we leave. I got to stop. I aint afraid cause I scaped the jaw of death crossing back over. Another chance, I write you all bout that and my new friend. I will find a way to write to you again for I have copied down the name of your neighbor to send in care of. The reason I dont have the address you wrote down for me it blew away while the dwarf took the money. I still got Libertys hair curl. Hope you dont mind I take a book cause I might not ever see one down there. It say *Nature Ralph Waldo Emerson* on the cover and I ben reading it.

Susan Spenser, if I can borrow your name
as it was writ in an old book.

   The *Samuel Enderby* of London
Puts in for Repairs at Nantucket

PRECIOUS PERSON, precious letter! So Susan had looked freedom in the face and found it sterile. But I hated to think of her traveling south. *Don't, don't!* She had written not a word of the danger or of fear. She could not accept freedom when those she loved were left behind. But still I wanted to shout *Don't*. The Shakers must have been at South Union, Ohio; the great body of sweet water, where she found only a trunk of books and papers, might have been Lake Erie. I thought of her eagerness to learn, of how much she had already learned from kind Mrs. Anderson. And Susan had loved me enough to write to me. I felt alive again.

For a week, scenes from that time with Susan came back to me frequently. And I was pinched by anxiety about her passage south. Then I received another letter from Ahab, delivered in a roundabout way and not directly by the vessel to which he had first transferred it. It was a gloomy letter, full of forebodings, and since Justice was playing down at the wharf when I read it, I deemed it best not to share the missive with him. Apparently, his father had not received Justice's request for a rousing description of A Chase.

"Pip has twice leapt from a whaleboat. Pip's being left alone in the vast ocean, with no ship in all the circle of his seeing, cost the little black boy his senses. So even did Lear have his fool," Ahab wrote. "Pip is a hundred times more dear to me now, and me to him."

I thought how in my extremity, Susan had become so dear to me—a shadow self—so kin she had seemed. But Susan had kept her wits, even when the dogs were barking behind her.

Ahab wrote, too, that Queequeg (the tattooed harpooner I had just glimpsed in the mist that Christmas Eve) had decided to die and had had his coffin prepared. Eventually Queequeg rose up from his tomb (Ahab queried, "Is his savage, incised face the true face of Christ?"). The *Pequod's* life buoy had filled with water and rapidly sunk when it was sent after a sailor who had fallen at sunrise from the fore masthead. Ahab noted that the sailor swallowed by the deep was the first man who mounted the mast to look for the white whale in the whale's own particular ground. "At last we have reached those grounds of the Sea of Japan," he wrote, "where I lost my leg, and where I shall find my revenge."

What needed my boy to hear such news of fear unto madness, of death and revenge? And soon enough, by spring, we had other troubles come sailing in.

I sat in the parlor—it was unseasonably hot—sometimes fanning myself, sometimes crocheting on a white, fleecy coverlet—I knew not for whom, it was about the size of a baby's blanket, the combination of air and yarn cloud-soft—when Justice burst into the room, pulling a sea captain by one wrist. The sleeve of his other arm, I noted at once, hung empty.

"I do apologize, madam." He spoke with an English accent. "I be Captain Boomer of the *Samuel Enderby*—"

"Mother, he has seen my father! He has seen the white whale!"

"Is it true?"

"Show her!" Justice commanded.

From within the slack fabric of his coat, he produced an ivory arm, ending in a hideous ivory hammer! I gasped and all but fainted. I was glad I was already seated on the sofa.

"It's a startling sight, madam. Not meant at all for ladies. I do apologize." His words were clipped, British. "But then my life is spent at sea, and there's need there to occasionally hit something."

"I know," I managed to murmur.

"Tell her!" Justice commanded, his eyes wild. "Spin her the yarn!"

"So like his father he is. He said the very words to me, that I must spin him the yarn of how I lost my arm, though I never got the companion tale of how he was missing his leg."

"Shall I bring you tea, or a cool lemonade?"

"Nay. We have but put in, and there's much I must oversee. But the lad here, Ahab's son, such insistence! I confess I am surprised to find myself swayed—even by such ardor. But here I am, and so let me spin the yarn, even as I did for Ahab."

"Please do." There was something about Captain Boomer, or perhaps his English speaking, that made me want a polite manner and proper introduction. "I am Una, the boy's mother, Mrs. Captain, as you have no doubt surmised."

Captain Boomer bowed and commenced his tale.

"After we spoke the *Pequod*, Ahab came riding up and over the bulwarks of the *Sammy E.* on our blubber hook, landed on the capstan head. Seeing his appendage, I held out my ivory arm, and he his ivory leg, and it was as good a handshake between comrades as flesh itself ever pressed. We crossed our ivory like fencers unashamed of whatever rapiers we possessed." Captain Boomer heaved two bushels of air into his lungs. "But it was with Moby Dick we had both already fenced.

"Ahab seemed full of joy to meet such a brother as I. 'Aye, aye, hearty!' he says. 'Let us shake bones together!—an arm and a leg!—an arm that never can shrink, d'ye see; and a leg that never can run. Where did'st thou see the white whale?—how long ago?' I answer, 'On the Line, last season.' 'Twas the first time, madam, I'd cruised on the Line, and of the white whale I was ignorant. Amongst a pod of four or five whales, he bounced up as though he owned them, a great whale with milky-white head and hump, all crow's feet and wrinkles—"

"Moby Dick," the boy breathed reverently.

" 'It was he, it was he!' Ahab exclaims. 'And harpoons sticking in near his starboard fin?' I add. 'Aye, aye—they were mine—my irons,' cries Ahab, boiling with joy. When I tell Ahab that the white whale runs all afoam into the pod and goes to snapping my fast-line, Ahab says, 'Aye, I see!—wanted to part it—an old trick—I know him.' "

"My father knows all his tricks, all of them!"

"The white whale was the noblest and biggest I ever saw in my life." Captain Boomer jumped to his feet. "And I let the old great-grandfather have it." He pretended to throw with the arm that ended not in a harpoon but an ivory hammer. "Next instant, in a jiff, blinded I was by foam and the whale's tail straight up like a marble steeple inclined to fall. Another instant, the boat is splintered, all chips, and I am hooked in the arm by the barb from the second iron, and down the watery ladder to the depths I ride, towed by Moby Dick." He sat down again on our sofa and spoke quietly. "Yet an arm is but human flesh, and I too puny a fish for such a fisherman as Moby Dick, and the hook tore down the length of my arm and out, and I rose to the surface.

"I told this tale to Ahab, my ship's surgeon, Dr. Bunger, standing by and verifying all that I said. But Dr. Bunger is a joker as well as a surgeon, and he made light of my missing limb, much to the annoyance of Ahab, who wanted only more information. Had I seen the whale after my loss? Aye, I told him, twice. I allowed as how there would be great glory in killing Moby Dick, but I says to Ahab, 'Hark ye, he's best let alone; don't you think so, Captain?'

"Ahab knows I am meaning his ivory leg, but he answers most strangely, reasonably and yet at the same time flinging reason away with both hands. I only have one hand now to throw away reason myself. So when I say Moby Dick is best left alone, Ahab answers, 'He is. But he will still be hunted, for all that. What is best let alone, that accursed thing is not always what least allures.' He said that the whale was a magnet for him, and he asked, 'Which way heading?'

"Before I can reply or fling some one-handed reason back into his face, Dr. Bunger notes Ahab's agitation and goes to joke about it. 'Bless my soul, and curse the foul fiend's,' Bunger says, and making like a dog, he snuffs around at Ahab—"

"Snuffs my father!"

"And Dr. Bunger says, 'This man's blood—bring the thermometer!—it's at the boiling point!—his pulse makes these planks beat!' and Bunger takes his lancet from his pocket and approaches Ahab's arm as though to relieve him of too much hot blood. 'Avast,' roars Ahab. And any man would describe his sound that way. It was a roar such as a lion might make. 'Avast,' roars Ahab. 'Man the boat! Which way heading?' And then when I ask of the Parsee, 'Great God, what's the matter here?' that ancient pedestal-for-a-turban slides over the bulwarks, brings round the boat, and Ahab commands my men to lower him as he came, astraddle the hook."

I sit in silence a moment, and even Justice is quiet.

"There's no more to tell," Captain Boomer said. "And I should return to my ship."

"May I visit you, sir, to hear it again?" Justice asked, all politeness.

"Aye, lad. I'll tell you again, if you must have it. I'll introduce you to Dr. Bunger. He's a jolly one. He'll make you laugh."

THE AFTERMATH of the story of Ahab conveyed to us by the *Samuel Enderby,* put in for repairs, brought no lightness to Justice. The next day Justice went down to the wharf, which was all abuzz with the latest news of Ahab (a native son and thus of much interest), told probably not so much by Captain Boomer as by the crew (who all witnessed Ahab's froth for the whale, adding that Ahab's own crew resembled a pod of yellow Manila tigers, even possessing long cat whiskers) and embroidered by Dr. Bunger, who struck me, even indirectly met, as a foolish fellow to offer Ahab's arm his lancet.

On the wharf, Elijah, who despite his prophetic hauteur also listened to the gossip, stepped into Justice's path. He had never before accosted the boy. Perhaps he had not known his identity, though many remarked his resemblance to Ahab, notwithstanding my dark curls on his forehead.

This scoundrel Elijah began to degrade Ahab. He called him a vile sinner and the brother of Beelzebub and other such nonsense, and it so upset Justice he burst into tears. Then Aunt Charity came along and quickly saw what the problem was. She heard Elijah say, "Thy father shan't come home. He lodges at the bottom of the sea with the White Devil Whale. He likes it there."

"I'll have no such jabbering nonsense told the boy," Aunt Charity said, and she backed Elijah to the edge of the wharf with her wrath.

"Jezebel, Jezebel," Elijah began on her. "A consort sure for the wicked Ahab."

Charity, her maidenly honor besmirched, shoved Elijah off the edge of the wharf. He sank like a stone. Not so much as a bubble arose. When Charity saw what she had done, she screamed, "Run, Justice, run for help, lest I've drowned the devil."

Help came speedily. Many sailors were about, but none came speedily enough. Charity had indeed drowned the devil.

HIS DEATH was not so sad as the aftermath. Though Judge Austin Lord quickly settled the matter as an accident, Charity went about for weeks and months entirely dejected. She had never meant to take a human life. All her days had been devoted to making life more comfortable for her fellow creatures who went to sea. People said she spoke of herself most unforgivingly many times at the Quaker meeting. All who knew and loved her spoke most reassuringly to her. Certainly I did, for it was in her trying to protect Justice that the accident had ensued.

Out of concern for Charity, some of the lethargy and suffocating numbness, as it had in response to Susan's letter, left me. But I was even more shaken by my concern for Justice. The old crackpot's message that Ahab would not return greatly disturbed the boy, for Elijah had commanded among the children a certain mysterious power.

"But my father shall come home!" Justice declared to me. "I shall make him!" For hours and hours each day, he retreated to the cupola, his eyes fastened on the sea, his brow furrowed in concentration. Here was young Ahab willing a thing to be so. And I thought of Kit willing the sun to stand still.

One morning I stood in my son's way, at the foot of the stair.

"Mother, I will go up," he said, and brushed past me.

It was anguish for me to see his state of mind—both defiant and terribly afraid; sometimes his eye flashed at me the way I had seen Ahab's eye flash at others (but never at me). I could not soothe my son's terror at night, nor interest him in wholesome activities in the day. I asked many folk for advice—my friend Austin Lord advised me to be patient, that the melancholy was natural and would naturally run its course. But they did not know Ahab a fraction so well as I did, and they did not know how Ahab's blood, at least partly transmitted to Justice, could seethe with intensity and singleness of purpose, undiluted by time.

One day the judge sent for Justice to come visit him, by himself, and the boy reluctantly crossed the street. I knew the judge was trying to help, though I could not imagine in what manner he might be able to do so. Yet Justice came home all smiles.

"He has such chocolate, Mother, as you've never eaten before. He has cherries and nuts and raisins, all dipped in chocolate. There's light chocolate and dark chocolate—that's the best. The dark is a little bitter. I love the bitterness. Here—it's pecans inside, and caramel."

Not every day, but many days, the judge unpredictably sent for Justice and gave him candy. Eventually the treats expanded to my beloved jams and jellies, and finally we were invited to a dinner with the entire Mitchell family. The younger Mitchell boys, as clear-headed and balanced as their oldest sister, soundly ridiculed any idea that Elijah's prophecies were anything but humbug. It was an excellent tonic, provided by my friend the judge.

Nonetheless, that night Justice returned to the cupola, though it was too dark to see the ocean. "I want to think strong thoughts," he told me. I thought again of Kit's rhetoric, and a hand seized and squeezed my heart. "I'd like to be alone," Justice added, but gently.

A week later the Mitchell boys came to visit us with a large gray dog. Not a pup, but a creature over a year old and beautifully schooled to sit and shake hands. Justice was much taken with his obedience. "He's not a dog," Justice said, "he's a prince."

"You could name him Pog," Billy said. "That's a combination prince and dog."

"His real name is Fog," Michael said, "but that's so near to Pog he'd probably come."

"Here, Pog," Justice called, and the dog came, wagging his shaggy gray tail.

"He's so big," I exclaimed admiringly. I had not owned or wanted a dog since my father shot King.

"Maria says he's part Irish wolfhound. They're the tallest dogs. They guard castles."

"Maria says you'll have to walk him a long way every day because he's so big."

"*I* should walk him?" Justice questioned.

"He's a present!" the boys all exclaimed. "We want to give him to you."

Justice patted Pog's head quietly. "That's nice," he said. "But I don't think I could keep him. I need to be in the cupola."

The Mitchell boys exchanged disappointed glances.

"I couldn't walk him enough," Justice added.

"Well," Billy said slowly, "if you ever do want to walk him, you can. Just come over."

AS THE WEEKS passed, Justice seemed gradually to be a bit better. He was quieter, at least seemed less angry. But he spent many, many hours in the cupola, even in the heat of the day. When he came down, his face was unnaturally pink. One day he asked me, "Mother, couldn't you have asked Father to stay home? Did you ever think about doing that?"

"Indeed, I did." I felt myself accused of negligence. "He looks for the white whale with the same persistence that you watch for him."

The boy smiled ruefully.

'Twas then that the pineapple knocker fell against the brass plate, and we opened the door to Mary Starbuck and Jim her boy, some few years older than Justice. When Justice learned that Jim, too, had a father aboard the *Pequod*, he took a great interest in him, and they went up to the cupola together.

No sooner had they left the room than Mary said frankly, "Una, the boy's not well."

"You heard of Elijah's drowning off the wharf?"

"Yes, and his poisonous prophecy as well. I've come to give you advice."

"Oh, please," I said. I nearly wept in response to her practical sympathy. The braided coronet across her head gleamed in the sunlight.

"There is a cottage close to us at 'Sconset, for let. I think you should rent it for the summer. The cottage is humble, but I'm sure you'll like it. And I am sure that Justice will do better away from the town and the cupola. I think you should also rent a pony or horse—the boys can care for it and ride it."

I had to laugh. "Mary, your plan is so well thought out, so complete. I will love being your neighbor."

"It's time we were friends." She smiled in a lovely, wise way.

The boys came rattling down the steps. What a healthy sound!

"It's too hot for me up there," Jim announced casually. "I don't see how he stands it."

"Mother," Justice asked, "did you know that 'Sconset sees the ships come in long before we do?"

"And you can go up on the roof walk, if you like," Jim said. "It's open and breezy up there."

"I'd like us to go to 'Sconset," Justice said.

"So we shall!" I replied, thinking: All the better that Justice believes it to be his idea.

GIDDY WITH ADVENTURE, we four clip-clopped out the Mile-stone Road, straight for 'Sconset. Our good spirits were contagious even to the mare, and she pranced along. It being a distance of, Mary said, something over eight miles—I had thought it shorter—we stopped about halfway to have a picnic. The boys clamored to go to Altar Rock, and so we left the main road to drive north to the foot of the highest hill. As we tethered the horse, I could not help but remember the winter day I had climbed this hill—a snow hill like a whale hump—to pray for Ahab. How cold and restless I had been.

But now it was good summer. That very boy whom I had carried inside me now walked beside, and we were adventuring genteelly with friends. The air was fragrant with the blooming heathers and heaths. After we had eaten and Mary and I had sipped some ruby port, I let my eye circle the summery land that lay all about us like a favored skirt. Centered in this landscape, the goodness outside and inside seemed almost enough.

When we arrived at 'Sconset—what a bright booming of water! It burst against the shore with the joy of free running. The horse tossed its head and nickered.

Across all the distance from Portugal the water rushed to us, and still it snorted and billowed, indefatigable, and sent flashing plumes into the sky. With the sky-splashing water, fountainlike, plumed with joy, my spirit climbed higher and higher. Lifting my hands above my head, I clapped them together, rippled my fingers like fringe tasting the air. And so did Mary and Jim and Justice clap their hands above their heads and tickle the sky. From our seats in the stopped buggy, we mimicked and saluted the sea.

The sea, the sea defined me!

Excitement and fresh resolve almost made speech impossible, but I had to tell Mary—and as soon as the boys had slid out and begun to run the beach, I spurted, "I shall live here all the rest of my life!"

She smiled and said nothing. Perhaps she was incredulous at the absoluteness of my declaring.

"Not for Justice," I said. "For me. Whether he wills it or no."

I could hardly contain myself. I wished to return immediately to town and tell the judge that I must buy the property that was now for let. And I would buy two ponies as well, one for each of the boys, and have a stable built. But I bit my lip, for I did not want Mary to think that I had taken leave of my senses.

"Don't you want to see the houses?" she asked.

(Houses, of course! We must have them. But it was light and sky and spume of sea I wanted to buy!)

"Mine is over there." Mary pointed. Her plain, gray cottage was caught in a mesh of roses.

What could I do but gasp, and then weep a bit, joyfully. "It's like the house on the Lighthouse Island. Like home."

"Yours is up there." She pointed to a somewhat higher bank, where there were several houses. "Yours is the small one closest to us, set back from the road. The one of that group closest to the beach." A tall hedge stood between my cottage and the neighbors beyond so that I was curtained from the houses to the north.

"There is no house between you and me," I said, pleased, but I also felt a bit disappointed, for my house was not bedecked with roses, as Mary's was.

"It doesn't take long to grow a quilt of roses," Mary said. "Our houses are almost twins."

So they were, both of gray shingles in the typical Nantucket manner, both with roof walks. Mary's yard had a low stone wall like a loose necklace for the cottage.

"I built the wall," she said. "With my own hands. It's a windbreak for the ocean breeze, to protect the flowers in the lee."

"It's a beautiful wall. Without mortar. The Shakers in Kentucky build walls thus."

"Shall I tell you how I laid its circumference?" She shaded her eyes with her hand, regarding her work. All the time the sea surged and tossed, and its wildness sang a counterpoint to me, under Mary's gentle words. "For the first voyage when my husband was gone," Mary went on, "I placed a stone, one for each day, on the ground. He was gone almost three years, and the bottom course of stone numbers one thousand and one, laid end to end."

"And did you tell yourself a thousand and one stories?"

"No. I sang myself to sleep. The buggy is borrowed from the last house in the group. We'll drive there and walk to see your place."

MY PLACE! Because I had discovered and chosen it myself? A place in the middle way—not so small or crude as a one-room cabin in the woods of Kentucky; yet a place far from being so grand as even one floor of my house in Nantucket. In size and convenience my place reminded me again of the stone house on the Island.

When we entered my house, the space seemed to have been waiting for us. On the ground floor were a large room for keeping and two smaller rooms; one was a bedroom with a double bed made up with a white candlewick counterpane, but the other room, unfurnished except for sunshine, jutted out toward the ocean and had windows on three sides.

"I envy you this room," Mary said. "It is the only house at 'Sconset with so much glass and view. In winter, it must surely be cold."

But the sunny room shared the fireplace with the main room; I bent and looked through the opening back into the main room. I hoped that the empty room might be warm enough in winter, for here I would have my books, my desk, my sewing cabinet. Before the hearth I imagined a braided rug, dyed with cranberries like Mr. Starbuck's on the *Pequod*, but larger.

Upstairs, two small rooms were tucked under the eaves, each with a large window in the end. When Mary and I climbed the narrow steps to the roof walk, I saw that the platform embraced the chimney and extended out a way over the gable of the sea-view room. I could sit here in winter with my back against the chimney and look out to sea.

The inside walls of the house were finished with a soft gray plaster. The two bedrooms upstairs were so small that they would hold little more than a bed, a chest of drawers, and a chair, but the downstairs bedroom was somewhat larger, the keeping room was spacious, and the window room was beautifully proportioned as well as large and full of light.

"The house is unusual," I said. "Built in its own style."

"It suits you, doesn't it?" Mary asked.

"I love it already. It crimps a bit, here and there, but it expands just where space is most welcome. A wise little house."

Justice liked only the big keeping room, at first glance, and announced that we would both sleep in there, or in the window room, and I decided I would humor him on the point. "When we know the house better," I said, "we may want to rearrange."

As we walked back to the Starbucks' cottage, we crossed a little dell which would be just right to shelter the stable I intended to have built. It would be halfway between the boys, and far from the neighbors without stables. The buggy people at the end had also considerably built their stable north of the settlement. "Except for the man next door to you," Mary said, "these are summer people." She added warningly, "They all say the wind is too strong out here in winter."

"It wouldn't be too strong for me or Jim," Justice asserted.

"It's not," Jim replied.

Our visit was entirely happy, and when Justice and I returned to town, we were both itching to be at 'Sconset.

WHEN I TOLD Mrs. Maynard of the migration to 'Sconset, she said, "There's nobody there. It's a wasteland." And my friend the judge was not at all pleased to hear that we were moving. "Just rent," he counseled. "That's all Mary ever suggested."

"I am going home," I said. "And home is at 'Sconset. I want to buy it free and clear. I want a stable big enough for winter chickens, a nanny goat, and four horses."

"Four!"

"Who knows? Mary and I may take up riding."

"What about this house?"

"Rent it for a year, rent it for five years. Sell it."

"Oh, no." The judge grew pale. "I am sure Ahab wouldn't want you to sell it."

"No, I suppose not. He loved this house." I glanced around the pretty parlor. "It was the only one he bought. But now I must do what's best for Justice and me."

I decided the furniture I owned was far too polished and elegant for 'Sconset, so I bought new furniture, all made by folk living on Nantucket. I ordered new china, though, from Boston; each plate had a large scallop shell in the middle. Pointing at the catalog illustration, I explained to the judge, "The shell is the sea's handprint. I don't want ever to forget, even at the supper table, that I am next to the sea—the sea, the glorious sea."

And so it was, after two impatient weeks, we rode with three wagons full of furniture out to Our New Home, the lumber for the stable and the animals to arrive later. The judge came with us and watched dolefully as the rented furniture was carried out and I had my furniture placed first here and then there. I did bring to 'Sconset Ahab's and my polished cherry bed.

In the late afternoon, when the judge said he must return to town, he suddenly took both my hands in his at the door. "My dear neighbor, you have no idea how lonely I shall be without you across the street."

"You must come to visit often," I said, seeing his pain.

"I think you have done right. I see the boy is happy here." He peered down at me through the spectacles bridging his long nose just over his nostrils. "I've left Justice a new box of chocolates. I hope he doesn't forget me."

"Of course not."

"I've often thought, Una, how well you named him. What is justice but some combination of singleness of vision wed to compassion, of Ahab's intense focus and of Una's quick heart? And I like to think, too, that in his name there is an honoring of my profession, if not my person."

CHAPTER 125   The Hedge

WHEN I AWOKE in the morning, I ran to the high back edge of my yard. Below me were three narrow bands, one of small trees, one of nodding sea grass, and one of sand, then the ocean. I registered her sheer size—another Giant to live beside. She took my breath and gave it back again. Deliriously happy, I stood and admired her fluid expanse, her great light-reflecting surface, the air above her, the incessant sound of breaking waves, till I had my fill.

When Mary had pointed out my cottage from a distance, I had noted the tall, wall-like hedge between my house and the next. It attracted my curiosity. The privet hedge was perhaps eight feet thick and sixteen feet tall—a virtual fortification composed of small, green, oval leaves and their twiggy stems. I couldn't begin to see through it. I wondered if I chose to hurl my body into the mass whether I would pass through. I thought not, for I would be caught by the twigs and held suspended in the hedge, like a bug in amber.

So I walked along the hedge, amazed at its bulk, sheared into a perpendicular face and squared off at the high top, until I came to an opening. Something like a pointed Gothic arch had been carved out of the lower five and a half feet of greenery. Above the passageway, the top of the hedge was still perfectly knit together. I entered this hedge's opening, and with no trouble at all walked into my neighbor's yard.

Here was a garden! A world of purple, pink, rose, and white flowers—hydrangea, cosmos, rose of Sharon—and in the middle an enormous green sperm whale. He was fashioned of privet, but not at all angularly. In him all was fluid curve and beveling, from the bulging forehead to narrowing torso to spreading tail and flukes. And from his forehead sprouted a perfect green plume of privet-spray. I could see only six inches or so into the creature before the density and multiplicity of leaves became impenetrable to vision. By no means did the size of this whale rival that of a flesh leviathan; this was a garden whale. Yet in comparison to myself, he was impressive and overwhelming.

He had no expression, though I have never seen a real whale that was not able to project by some facial means and bodily gesture an attitude toward himself, his world, and his assailants. Here all was a green, vegetable blankness.

Around the base of the privet monster, hundreds of white cosmos tossed their airy heads, somewhat resembling the foam of the sea. Then the collar of flowers became a ring of bubbly blue hydrangeas, mixed here and there with a purple rose of Sharon shrub, and the outer ring was dotted with rosebushes and other rose-colored flowers, so that the whole effect was that the green whale swam haloed in a sea reflective of a sunset palette.

I had never seen anything quite so charmingly artificial. The whole yard was walled in by the mighty privet hedge. I felt as though I had entered the labyrinth of Crete, which held in its center not the Minotaur, but a bull whale. Whether he was captive or king, and how he regarded his green self, I could not tell, for as I said there was a blankness about the sculpture. Beginning to feel myself something of a trespasser, I slipped back through the hedge to my own grassy yard.

From the back edge of my own yard, I descended a set of wooden steps lying against the slope down to the beach. From the foot of the stairs, a path passed through some stunted apple trees, bearing misshapen yellow fruit, and led me through scrubby white pine trees. Then the path parted sea grasses for perhaps twenty feet and stopped on a lip of sand where the beach sloped more abruptly to the sea. I stood on the lip of sand before the broad water. And so began my habit each morning, not only to acknowledge the sea from my house and yard but also to go down to her, to commune with her close at hand, intimately.

I SEE IT NOW: the first morning on the beach at 'Sconset, the waves roll in on long diagonals. The water builds and builds to a steep, high crest and then folds in the middle into a high line of foam which quickly dips in front and spreads on each side in a widening scallop. Rolling in, the wave scampers itself into a flowing, milky apron of white. How densely white this froth, more cream than milk! And behind this turbulent flounce of white, from the backside of the translucent crest, floats a broken net of thin foam, patterned like a mosaic.

The mosaic is lifted by the next long, unbreaking roll, which passes under it without disturbing the netting, only stretching it here and there. The ceaselessness of the whole greeny-gray and startling-white drama of it! The casual constant, unmonitored crashing goes on and on, like the pulse of a body. So it was and so it is.

THAT RESTLESSNESS lay open-faced before me. With the sea there was no secret longing for change, for at no moment did it even pretend to hold still. Why did people speak of the *eternal* sea? An unwanted answer rose up from my own depths: perhaps because all her heaving and sighing were endlessly futile.

I decided to waken Justice and to cook him an egg.

CHAPTER 126

🐚 Journey Toward the Starry Sky,
in Present Tense

IT IS A SPLASHING, spanking surf tonight. Earlier, there were fists in it, and the water pow-pounded the shore.

Sometimes it is pouring, pouring, as though there were two oceans—one continually pouring into the beaker of the other, and back and forth between them a watery juggling. Whose hands hold those beakers?

Sometimes it's the swish and swirl of it and the whistle of the wind, many pitches at once, like a mouth covering ten pipes on a harmonica, this wind breathing right at the window glass. And now the slight rattle of wood against wood, of the movable window against its frame.

Now I imagine roses in the surf—bushels of roses being emptied headfirst against the shore. In the morning I will find heaps and heaps of them in a long row that stretches for miles along the 'Sconset beach. Their imaginary stems will lie across and over each other weaving their own pattern of stemmy X's, and the heads of all the roses will lie sodden and limp as clusters of red rags.

Sometimes I can hear the ocean jumping—I mean there is a discontinuity; it gathers itself and then a leap—silence—and a landing of heavy water. Like an athlete leaping forward, there is a takeoff—the wave pushes off from the other water, lifts its feet entirely into the air where I cannot hear it, and lands. Ha! Water "lands" though water falls back into water.

Here Ahab would say I quibble-fiddle with the language. Oh, where is Ahab tonight? Here at 'Sconset I listen, listen (in the night what good are eyes?), for the sound of wind in canvas far at sea, or the special hissing water makes when parted by a ship's prow, but all I hear is the sound of black ocean wringing its hands over and over.

So I will walk the roof walk and look for Ahab. If the try-pots be burning, I can see him far out in the sable Atlantic. Probably this is what has happened: they were almost to Nantucket, and there was one more whale. The *Pequod* was already rich as an autumn honeycomb, every cell brimful of oil, sealed and stored in the hold. Once I was like a cask of grief storing myself there, just a girl hiding from my mad young husband, but then the sea sent up its strangest flower, the droplet-bushy exhalation of a whale, and there was calling from the masthead, then excited feet on the deck, lowering of boats, and the chase. A victorious chase, and there was the chaining-in of the great carcass, snugged beside the ship like a natural, fleshy shadow for the artificed boat (with its delicate, noble construct of masts and lines, of layered decking, of internal staircases and ladders, fitted drawers with china knobs, and closet doors). All this I imagine again to justify the try-pots, surely burning now out in the darkness like two red eyes of a moving sea monster.

Oh, the constant rhythm of the sea in the dark—its patient, long application to shore, like a lover coming into her and into her, ponderous with age and experience, heavy and full of groaning love.

Though it be night, I could see the *Pequod* out at sea, if the try-pots burned.

I'll just arrange the lamps—the whale oil lamps—along a path through the room leading to the stairs. Now one on the bottom stair . . . now one on the top. I look back and find them pretty, each with the wick turned low, steady-burning glowworms to show Justice the way, if he should wake up and miss me. His logic will follow mine, and he will know I'm on the roof. How strange that he should so urgently miss his father, when he can scarcely remember the father who danced him and told him stories, whose ivory leg Justice smoothed and petted as though it were a sleek white cat. Justice spoke as he stroked— "Nice leg, good leg. You *are* a good leg to serve beneath my father." Well, here's the lighted way, Little One, if you would follow me.

And here's the creaking hatch to the roof walk.

TO MY PLATFORM I carry no lamp, for it would ruin vision for distance. There is Mary Starbuck's house. She has a wisp of smoke in the chimney. Probably before the hearth she has made Jimmy's pallet, for he has had a cold in his chest. There's a water-filled iron pot, herbs swimming on the surface, bubbling in the embers, to help open his breathing. I imagine Mary's sweet face in the fireglow too dim to sew by, but she crochets a line of lace to ornament her underdrawers, where it will be safe from the eyes of all the Quakers, save one. Her fingers know the stitches; the hooked needle, like a shining harpoon, darts down to pluck up the thread. Her fingers know, and she does not need to see. She has learned how to wait better than I have. But then she has never been to sea, cannot begin to imagine the vastness of that ever-shifting bend and bulge of water.

Now I must look beyond Mary Starbuck's faith and patience to the blackness beyond. I hear the roaring of the sea. With my eye, I can discern neither where the sea meets the shore nor where it blends with sky. Perhaps, erroneously, I am looking for a boat in the sky, since sea and sky are indistinguishable. But those beacons are stars, not try-pots burning. No one can calculate the distance to stars, Giles said, with the yardsticks we now have.

In crow's nests, I have been a skilled lookout, and I know how to sector out the world, how to ever so slowly turn my head, how to alert the sides of my eyes, which see motion better than does the direct gaze. Still I gaze and gaze, and the ocean twists and rolls as usual. There's booming always and the sound of spray rushing in the air.

Ahab, my captain, my beloved; Ahab, again, I call out to you. My spirit rushes over the water searching, searching for the *Pequod*. Is there not even a plank of her left floating? A drenched scrap of sail washing along just under the surface of the water? Remember when I looked for icebergs for you?

My eyes have swept all the way to the south. Now I retrace, but lift my gaze the breadth of a thumb, closer to those constellations that hang low over the water.

When I stand here in the day, there are friendly clouds to tease me, but this night is moonless, cloudless—only black and stars. That liquid black, the sea, runs in to me, sighs and retreats. His roar has become a groan. Oh, the effort of heaving himself! Does the human, heart-driven pulse sometimes wonder if it will ever get to stop? So much more must the mind of the sea suffer from travail.

I look again. My eyes burn with blackness. Oh, I would penetrate it. Let my vision encircle the globe till I find one old, ivory-clad whaling ship. And there my lover, white-haired, ivory-legged, but a true lover. Let his brain not be boiling with revenge on that dumb beast. May all the embers be under try-pots, and none in Ahab's breast or mind. When he pivots on the ivory leg, even at this great distance, my spirit circles round like a falcon on a tether.

What was that snap? What is this centerless flight? I'm hurled through space! I fly tangent, away, out from my center. Now I look frantically.

Back and forth I swing my head. No boats at sea. None. Nothing but blackness. The harness of discipline is cast away; all unsystematic, all impulse, I cast lances-of-gazing hither and yon, left and right, near in, as though the *Pequod* were beached, and out far into the domain of stars. Why have I chosen this unyielding night to look?

I AM STILL. For the first time, I know. If I were a lighthouse whose beam could bend to embrace the curve of the earth, I know I would not find him. There is no use to look out.

I feel it in my face. My mouth has settled at the corners. Resignation. There is no use to look out.

But I will stand here awhile. I could be wrong.

My bones are weighing me down. Here, my fingertips feel the splintery top of the railing, the rough grain of the wood. Ahab is gone.

But is he gone? I only know that I can no longer wait, looking out for him. Still I stand and face the dark.

What is this force that tilts up my chin? Why does my gaze climb up a ladder of stars? Why do I no longer look out, but up? Up! And there the heavens blaze and twinkle. In this moonless night sky, the endless stars declare ascendancy.

With my face up, I drink and drink the black goblet, the universe.

Like funeral cloves are these stars, spiky and spicy. Like cloves in an orange, they are the preservers of the skin and of the black flesh of space.

Oh, Starry Sky, can you hear this moaning of the earth? Let the sea be our voice, our loudest voice. It speaks to every dark corner of you, Star-studded Sky, as we spin and turn through space. The sea is moaning to your blackness and to your bright fires. Might some warmth, some comfort, from you kiss the cheek of earth, light if not warmth sent unerringly over distances too great to measure.

And yet when I blink, I seem to collect configurations of stars— perhaps it is to know them. My eyelids slide down, followed by a smooth, lubricated lifting, and there you are, Starry Sky, no longer out there, but through the lens of my eye brought home into my head. Into the brains of all and any beings who lift their faces and open their eyes.

The Roof Walk and the Starry Sky

There is the great journey yet to be taken. Let my mind be a ship that sails from starry point to starry point. In my brain, I feel those cold black spaces containing nothing. I approach a pinprick of light closer and closer till it is a conflagration of such magnitude that I am nothing. And yet with my mind I caliper it with contemplation.

Where is my place before this swirling ball of star mass, edgeless and expansive, without horizon? Where is my place, when I know that this is but one of ten billion? Here the categories crack. *Beauty*—that gilt frame—burns at its edges and falls to ash. *Love?* It's no more than a blade of grass. Perhaps there is *music* here, for in all that swirling perhaps harmony fixes the giants in their turning, marches them always outward in their fiery parade.

That I can see their glory, that is my place. That I have these moments to be alive—and surely *they* are alive in some other way. Perhaps it is only *being* that we share. But something *is* shared between me on this rooftop and them flung wide and myriad up there. What was the golden motto embroidered on the hem of my baby's silk dress? *We are kin to stars.*

I reach my hands toward them, spread my fingers and see those diamonds in the black *V*'s between my fanning fingers. To think that I could gather them into my hands, stuff them in my pockets, is folly. But I can reach. It is I myself, alive now, who reach into the night toward stars. Their light is on my hands.

Their light is *in* my hands. I gasp in the crisp air of earth and know that I am made of what makes stars! Those atoms burning bright—I lower my hands—why, they are here within me. I am as old as they and will continue as long as they, and after our demise, we will all be born again, eons from now. What atoms they have I cannot know. I cannot call their names, but they are not strangers to me. I know them in my being, and they know me.

Little scrap, little morsel, the stars sing to me, *we are the same.*

THAT NIGHT of truth and stars, I tried to sleep lying on the roof walk. I wanted my friends, the stars, to grate over my body. Oh, I went down into my house first, to get covers. I was not so ecstatic a star-gazer as to forget how to conserve my human warmth.

Descending to my house, through the trapdoor onto the top step where my lantern waited, I seemed to enter the Essence of Snug. Up there, the denizens were fearless and bold, but we mortals have our warrens here, and they are worthy. Our walls have been plastered and smoothed by human hands; our light emanates from lamps of lung-blown glass; the flame dances on a wick woven by human devising, and the flame consumes sailor-harvested oil. These small globes of light, in scale and warmth so like gifts of human love, illumine everything interior: the walls of my house and all its precious contents.

My child.

My table. The blank page, the glass lip of the pot of ink, the white shaft of my quill pen. The soft chevron of feathering attached to this eagle shaft.

Once Tashtego's fingers grasped this feather, slid its tip through his straight black hair, along his scalp. How much space has interceded between those fingers and this feather hovering over the page? Place defined all; not time, but place, I thought. *Where* was Tashtego who had given me a feather? If I knew where, what need of time? And Daggoo with his golden-hoop earrings? Did they sit adrift, slack-armed, in some whaleboat, as I had once done with Kit and Giles, and was Ahab with them?

No. Not even their images persisted; less substantial than mist, Tashtego, ebony Daggoo, inscribed Queequeg, dismasted Ahab—they disappeared into darkness.

I saw only black ocean rocking itself, blank of boat.

And yet I could not weep. This knowing—what was its character? Too quiet for tears. No storm here. An inland sea. Contained. A wide, quiet pool of unverifiable knowing.

There did seem a small boat upon that sea, but that boat was myself. It was this house and all that was in it, and I was alone at the tiller, reading the stars.

Though I had descended the lamp-lit steps from the roof walk down into my house that night, I needed to go back with my blanket, to lie flat, cocooned from the night air, to contemplate that endless void and the stars that navigated it. So I left the world of Snug, climbed aloft, a humble height this time, and laid myself down to the sky.

I laid myself down, the small tooth of a gear, in all that wheeling universe. And yet I was a part. The inner sea, right-sailed, had wholeness to offer, and this, this vastness—it let me partake of harmony.

Thus, I felt and thought and loved and yearned till daybreak.

And what was the residue from my stay in that dark furnace? The morning after that night, peace inhabited me and intimations of distant joy.

CHAPTER 128   More of Morning: Tashtego's Feather Makes the Letter *S*

S IS THE SOUND of the sea. Her surge and suck, her spray and surf. Sometimes she seethes. She knows the sound of smooth. With her *s*, the sea marries the shore, and then there is scamper and slush in the sand. With curling *s*'s the sea rises to stroke the side of her superior, the sky, who loves and meets her in the *s* of spray, spawned in liquid and air.

Will I someday send my son to the sea? Will the ships and sails call to the heart of Justice my son, seduce his soul just as they have my husband? Let him go. Let him set sail as I have, as well as his father. But I think the journey there is bounded by the spherical size of the globe. Circumnavigate this globe, and you but return to the place of your departing. The bigger journey is up there. Though now it is morning, and my eyes and ears are full of the surge of the sea.

S-s-s, the first sound my mother taught me.

And suppose the universe itself is but some greater globe where it is possible to travel through rather than on its curving surface. Or suppose that—that we are only on the surface of a dark expanding globe—then where is the journey to the place that is limitless? I find it within. Last night I found it within me—independent and single. No, I do not unmarry Ahab. But I marry myself. I take my fate as within. Would that I could give this thought to Ahab. His singleness of purpose is all fastened on the white whale. Yet I do not think that in his most extreme moment he forgets his wife and child. I know that there is a part of him that longs for us, for home, for Nantucket.

He sees us in the mirror-eye of Starbuck, whose heart is with his wife and child. Yes, Ahab can see all that is human and relenting in Starbuck's eye. Yet, my imagination tells me he looks in Starbuck's eye and looks away. His gaze roams the horizon for a slash of foam, for a low and bulbous cloud that resembles the white whale. He fixes his own heart to the tip of a harpoon that is ever seeking the heart of Moby Dick.

Without his heart, I fear that Ahab my husband is but a standing ash. Such a column is all powdery, and frail. The breeze blows against him, and he is scattered. So I sit at my window, open a bit, in 'Sconset. Does this breeze bring me some small atom of Ahab? Is he scattered in the sea? Do his cells brush boundaries with whatever is left of my ashy father, or rub against an enduring shard of calcium from Giles's bones?

How one we surely are with one another. And one with all that fiery burning scattered through the endless night. Such an idea surely brings peace. Is it a form of worship? I feel that I should walk to the beach and randomly select a grain of sand. That grain I should enshrine at home and call my god. In its impenetrable complexity, there is surely enough to fill my mind with wonder.

My boy is stirring in his bed. I shall put three turtle eggs in a pot of water and boil them for our breakfast and cut two thick slices from the loaf Mary gave us yesterday. I will spread that fragrant bread with a good smear of clear rose-hip jelly that Mary made from the fruit of the sea roses. I will call her pet nanny goat to come stand in the door and let me milk her on the threshold. Yes, Justice is stirring under his quilt, a lasting gift from Mary, a quilt pieced in triangles of sea green, pale blue, and storm-cloud gray, bound and bordered in the tan of sand. He straightens his leg, he turns his face my way, though his eyes are yet closed, so that when he does open them he will see my eyes of love. Fitting for a child, fitting for the father of the child!

For me, this morning and every morning and may it ever be all my life, my eyes are greeted by the surprising, ceaselessly rumpling sea. And every morning my heart will rise to meet the sea, which is what we know here on earth of infinity and change.

What is the word for where the sea meets Una? There are my origin and my immortality.

CHAPTER 129   The Neighbor Beyond the Hedge

SOMETIMES the past returns as present—at least those moments that never leave us do. All happened as I thought it would: my Justice awoke to his day. But before my son opened his eyes, he smiled and came close to laughing. When his eyes did look into mine, I asked, "Why are you happy?"

"I dreamt I got it at last," he said.

"Got what?"

"My father's watch."

And I went and fetched it from the mantel. He took the pocket watch in his hand and kissed its face and rubbed the smooth silver back of it against his small palm. The grooved winding knob on the stem he rotated between his chubby thumb and forefinger. Looking up at me, his face was ashine with delight and gratitude.

While Justice and I breakfasted on turtle eggs, a question formed in my mind about my neighbor's hedge. Many houses on Nantucket boasted a handsome hedge that divided them from their neighbors or shielded them from the dust of the road. Perhaps some were cultivated to sieve the sea wind, as well—I don't know. But few hedges, I thought, had carved through them a Gothic opening so that one neighbor might pass freely into the garden of another. I wondered if on the far side as well as on my side the neighbor had cut a door.

"Have you seen the neighbor's privet whale?" I asked Justice. "Would you like to go with me into his garden?"

"Couldn't we build houses on the beach?"

Clearly my boy already had plans for his morning. I agreed to play with him, and he agreed to my plan as well. When we reached the sand, he was dismayed that all his building of the day before had been washed away, he having been unfamiliar with the reach of the tide at 'Sconset. His eyes overflowed, and he bit his lip to keep from sobbing.

"Look," I said, kneeling down. "It's soon rebuilt," and I scooped up sand in my hand.

Justice made no move to help, though I constructed one little castle and began another. "Help me," I said encouragingly.

"No," he said. "When you've built them all back, then I'll build again. I had fifteen."

I stood up and put my hands on my hips. "I'll not reconstruct the world for you, child. There's no fairness in asking that of me."

"Then I won't," he said.

"And I won't either," I replied.

He kicked the sand and sent a slur of it toward the water. Then he ran to the ocean and stamped on the edge of it that was washing to the depth of an inch deep onto the shore. Far from me to tell him not to splash his clothes! He could wear them sandy. Still, I thought he was a foolish lad. Neither I nor Frannie had ever stamped the water.

"Water feels not a thing," I called. The wet sand clung to my fingers, and I brisked them together. I saw I would have to walk to the water to rinse them. This I did, being careful of my shoes and standing a distance from my splashing child. But while I bent over, clutching up my skirt in one hand and washing the other, Justice charged at me like a little bull from the sea. I lost my balance and fell shoulder first, wetting my whole side, into the water.

Now I was angry. "You imp," I said, and Justice ran for the wooden steps. I was after him in a flash, and being much-longer-legged and angry to boot, I caught him by the shoulders and hauled him off. Then I dragged him to the water—oh, he struggled all the time—and forced his body down into it—not his head. The water was cold, and he resisted me so thoroughly that I was drawn down into the water in my attempt to dunk him. I began to feel ashamed as we struggled. My clothes became sodden and full of sand; my hair fell down and the length of my braid was dunked into the sandy water as well. Justice had not a dry hair or thread on him. I feared for the leather of our shoes.

"Let's stop, let's stop," I pleaded.

"I win," he shouted.

"Very well, you win. But let's stop."

And so we waded to shore, I breathless and embarrassed, he still sullen despite his triumph.

At this moment a large black dog bounded up and barked at Justice, who suddenly grew stiff and still with fright. I walked slowly to my son and took his hand. "It was time to go anyway," I said and led him toward the stairs. Now the dog barked more furiously. I put Justice ahead of me and told him to keep going. The barking stopped. Halfway up the embankment, I turned to see what had become of the dog. He was sitting below, a large stick of driftwood athwart his mouth, wagging his tail.

"Look," I said. "He only wanted to play."

Quick as a minnow, Justice darted past me and down to the beach. He took the stick and flung it across the sand, and the dog ran to fetch. So all our fright was turned to fun, and I could see that Justice thought himself honored to be chosen to play by the big dog.

Sometimes the dog ran so hard to the stick that his braking almost covered the trophy with sand, and then he dug energetically for it, though sometimes he was inaccurate as to the stick's position and his digging only tossed more sand over it, and then there *was* a mighty digging. I stood at the foot of the steps and watched all this, and of course I was glad that Justice had found a friend. I resolved that the next day I would go and call on Mary and have some adult companionship of my own, though I did not want to make a pest of myself now that I had moved to 'Sconset.

Justice came to me and asked what we should name the dog.

"Alpha," I said, "for he is the first dog we have seen here."

Up trotted a second black dog, smaller, but in both color and shape the sure mate of Alpha. "Omega," I announced. She dragged a strip of sandy carpeting, and with a snap of her neck, she unfurled it like a huge question mark in the air. Alpha jumped for the end of it and caught it in his teeth, and then the two dogs ran off together, sometimes stopping to play tug-of-war with each other. But the strip was like a banner between them, and while no writing inscribed it, I felt that they proclaimed the joy of having a mate.

I felt weary, and I called to Justice that now it was my turn to choose our activity, and we must inspect the neighbor's hedge—thus I hoped to save my boy from the sense that his dog friend had abandoned him for another. He came with alacrity, a gritty, sandy little boy, but pink-cheeked from his play with the dog. I myself felt a mess, and the damp and dirty skirt clung against my knees and chafed them. We passed beyond the wind-dwarfed pines and misshapen apple trees, up the hillside steps, and into our yard; then through the opening in the hedge to the garden of our neighbor.

Justice was utterly delighted with the privet whale—"You should have told me!"—and immediately he began to dance around it and to look for a pretend harpoon that he might assault it. The yard being scrupulously free of debris, my son was reduced to make-believe, but he cocked his arm and threw airy darts at the vegetable whale and shouted in a kind of whisper-shout. Just so had Chester played in the moonlit whaleboat.

Meanwhile, I circled around the fantasy to the opposite hedge and walked its length, finding no opening. With this unbroached wall, I found satisfaction. The garden was not open to anyone, but only to those who had the good taste to rent the cottage that Justice and I now occupied. It was as good as a formal invitation. I fantasized a friend.

I sat upon a little wooden bench whose back was placed against the wall, closed my eyes, and sucked in through my nostrils the odor of honeysuckle, which grew on a shallow trellis on the sides and over the bench. I hated to move, for any shift in my posture brought me in contact with the unpleasant, gritty garments I wore. I hoped that this tussle on the beach with my son was not the harbinger of many tussles to come.

But was it true that I waited no more for Ahab? Had not something irrevocable happened in my soul on the roof walk atop my cottage? Yet, for Justice's sake, I appeared the same—serenely, hopefully, anxiously waiting. But had I not given him his father's watch? Surely that was some sign to him. My honeysuckle reverie was interrupted by Justice's rush to me and his declaration.

"Mother, there is a shed here full of wooden women."

Bluebeard's Garden, I thought, but I said, rising, "Show me."

Justice led me to a shed with a glass window. When I peeked in, indeed, I did see two dozen or so carved wooden women. Some were completed and beautifully painted; others were carved but bare of paint. Still others had only rough approximations of a human form, and some were still encased in what was no more than an impaled upright and leaning tree trunk, either stripped of bark or brown and rough. It was a workshop for making figureheads for ships.

Before I could say so, a masculine voice said, "You must be my new neighbor."

I spun around, shy to be caught peeking, and sodden as well, and explained that we were the wife and son, Una and Justice, of Captain Ahab of the *Pequod.*

The man asked courteously if I would like to see the figures. I replied that I had fallen in the water, and that I needed to go home, but the figures were beautiful and striking.

"Well, you must see them later," he said, "when I return from my trip. I keep the workroom padlocked, and you will have to wait till then."

Justice glared at the man, though I half wished my son would rudely ask what I dared not: where was our neighbor going, why, and when would be the return? But Justice was uncertain of the woodcarver and said nothing.

He was a man about the age of Ahab, from looking at his face, which lay in folds. But his hair was jet black, almost preternaturally black. Perhaps he was two decades younger than Ahab, then, for all his care-carved face. The man was not at all strong and muscular, as Ahab was, but thin and tall. His hands were covered with nicks and scabs and small white scars, which I instantly deduced came from slips of the chisel while he carved.

"I have two of them ready to sell," he said.

I do not know why, but I shivered. It was as though he were a slave trader. "Do you keep some of them?" I asked.

He shrugged. "I have some warm water," he said. "Let me show you."

He led us around to the back of the shed. Fastened to the roof was a large black tank, with a funnel and pipe fitted to its bottom. There was a stopcock device at the end of the tube. "Let me rinse you both," he said. He turned the stopcock, and water showered out. As he put his hand in it, I followed suit, and found it warm. There was no fire to heat the tank; merely the sun had warmed the water in the reservoir. Gladly, I stepped under its spray and called Justice to me. Together, we stood there turning in the warm water and rinsing away the sandy grit and clammy temperature.

"Now," the neighbor said, turning off the water. "Run home like rabbits through the hole in the hedge."

I took Justice's hand and we ran home, Justice dropping my hand as we neared the opening and running through first, laughing, ahead of me.

WHEN WE CAME to our own green, we saw that Mary Starbuck and her son stood at our door. Mary held a cloth-covered basket in her hand, which my nose soon told me contained hot rolls. She laughed out loud to see me, and she teased that no sooner had I moved to 'Sconset than I had gotten into trouble.

When we were all dry and changed and the boys had gone outside to play, Mary and I sat beside the hearth and chatted. I felt wonderfully fresh and happy. 'Sconset, I told Mary, was far better in its simple isolation than town with its bustle. I had never lived in a town before Nantucket, and, I claimed, if I had more people about me than could compose the crew of a ship (about thirty on a whaler), then I grew restless.

"No, Una," she said, "you are a person who can adjust to anything. If you prefer 'Sconset, it is only that you choose it."

Always, I have felt uncomfortable with such a remark—it implies I have no true core, no essence—but I knew Mary did not mean to imply that I was lacking. She must have seen the shadow pass over my face, for she reached out and took my hand.

"I meant only that you are always your own true self. Every time I see you I am but more impressed by that."

"I spent the night on the roof walk."

"Did you look for try-pots burning at sea? I used to. But now I sleep through the night. I looked this morning," she added. "Nothing."

"I felt that they were not coming—ever." I hesitated to tell Mary this, but as I wanted her as my true friend, I did not wish to hold back.

"I have sometimes doubted, too," she said.

"I seemed to know that they would not return. It was not doubt I felt."

"Still, it was your revelation," she said. "Not mine."

"Have you not felt it?"

Now her eyes filmed with tears. "Every day I feel it with more certainty. With me, it is not the revelation of a night's watch. But every day my soul fills with the same knowledge, slowly, as some wells slowly fill with water."

"You have concealed it well."

"As a mother should," Mary answered. "But I think such concealment is not becoming to friendship."

I felt my nostrils flare, as though I were a cannibal catching the scent of meat. I spoke as gently as ever words have passed up my throat and through my lips. "What else would you tell me, Mary?" But on my tongue I tasted blood.

She reached for my hand—her fingers were warm from her teacup, now set aside—that familiar gesture that is the prelude to confidence.

"When I was a girl of twelve"—her eyes searched my face, how vigilant, how knowledgeable, their movement—"a man in Nantucket lured me into the mill. He was very short, scarcely as tall as my shoulder, and I mistook him for a younger boy. He had no beard. He showed me silver coins. He opened his hands so that there was one in each palm like two large silver eyes. He moved them back and forth like demon eyes that seemed located in a face that could grow as broad as a giant's, or very narrow. It was daylight, but in the mill it was like dusk, yet somehow beams of light fell on the coins so that they glowed. These I could have, he said. 'If you take off your drawers, lie on your back, spread your legs, and make no sound.' "

Mary repeated the words like a horrible four-part litany. *Take off your drawers, Lie on your back, Spread your legs, Make no sound.* I felt my own lips moving after them as though what had been the experience of Mary, my sister, was now included in my own history—this outrage, this rape.

"And so he had his way with me. For money. Any prostitute is my sister."

"Believe that I am your sister, too. Not in this particular. In another way. More heinous." But now was not the time to lay my story atop hers.

Silence breathed on us, and then she added, shaken, frightened, "I could not have told anyone of my shame if I had felt Mr. Starbuck was yet alive." Our gaze was a bridge of shared truth. "How will we live without our husbands?" she asked.

Not just her words but all her sweet face, stunned and puzzled under the cornet of crossed braids, inquired of me. I squeezed her hand. I swear there was nothing callous in me. Only strength, which seemed to increase geometrically. "Very well," I said quietly.

CHAPTER 130   🐚   **The Roar of Guilt**

THAT NIGHT, though I was weary with the day, I took to the roof again. Some constellations were known to me—like lands I had already visited—and these I sailed past. Some stars hung in splendid, isolated brightness, and these, too, I tried to look beyond. Were all the stars the same size? My fingertips rested lightly on the wooden rail. I could not know if stars were equal to each other, but if they were, then the dim ones must be far and farther away, and toward those reaches I hurled my soul.

A palm of lightning smacked the sky. I felt the rise of the wind. Soon the sea would begin to roar and rain would sweep landward. A harpoon of lightning flung itself from the sky into the sea, and then the crack of it came walking more slowly to my ears.

The night was rising so black over the ocean that darkness had obliterated half the stars. The sea was roaring like a pride of lions. I thought of Ahab roaring shame into vengeance. I imagined lions caught in the sand-tossing surf, their tawny manes all tangled in froth and foam, their sharp-toothed mouths open and roaring.

And in their own ravenous mouths, I saw my own, in the whaleboat. I saw my hand holding a grisly present toward my gaping mouth. *If thy hand offend thee,* my father would have quoted, *cut it off!*

I held my hand up between me and the night. My right hand, the one that held the needle and my livelihood. My pleasure in writing as well as in sewing. Could I not sacrifice the other hand, less valued? But it was the right hand that had offended.

Again I looked at it. At my narrow wrist. There was the place to bring down the hatchet. Could I? Of course I could. Hesitation was no longer a part of my soul. There was only decision and action. Of course I could. Yet time was mine, to contemplate and decide.

What I saw was a good hand, an articulate wrist, capable of bending and turning. *Holy the Body,* the stars chirped softly like little chicks running under the shadow of hawk wings.

No. It was a hand that could yet do much good. I would not mutilate or diminish my power. I pulled my blanket higher on my neck. I let my hands clasp each other over my belly. I felt the sweep of wind over my face and watched the darkness take more stars.

When I went downstairs to bed, I dreamt turbulent dreams, like the roar of the surf, of wolves swimming in the water alongside lions and sharks and eels and other predators of the deep—squid and octopus, and in their tentacles they held sailors, some of whom had been with Giles and Kit and me in the whaleboat. When I awoke, I was biting my hand, and I sleepily promised myself that I must make it be a good hand, and nevermore would it cause harm to any human being. I would not feed my hand to guilt.

Then a great hunger came over me, and I got up and went to my cupboard. There I had a beautiful fillet of cod that I had cooked in cornmeal during the day. The tips of my fingers on touching the grainy coating seemed to have tastebuds on them, and I wanted the fish so unmistakably that I lifted it up and ate it. The cooked fish was bliss on my tongue. I went back to bed thinking that humankind philosophizes by need.

How lovely it is to sleep amidst warm quilts next to a smooth plaster wall with the roar of the surf in one's ears and a full stomach.

AT LEAST once a week during the summer, Austin Lord drove out to visit, often accompanied by Mrs. Maynard. Taken by Mary, Judge Lord claimed she had a medieval simplicity about her that painters should adore. "Has anyone ever asked if he could paint you?" the judge inquired.

Mary laughed. "No, but the woodcarver asked if I would sit and lean forward as the model for a ship's prow."

"A discerning man," the judge commented. "What's his name?"

"Robben Avalon."

"Did you sit for him?" I asked. I thought that I would very much like to have been asked.

"No. It's too close to idolatry for my Quaker husband. I don't think Mr. Starbuck would have liked it."

"But would you have liked it?"

She laughed a little while she thought of the answer. "No, I couldn't have enjoyed doing what might upset Mr. Starbuck."

"Would you have accepted the invitation, Una?" the judge asked.

"Yes," I said frankly, amused at myself.

Now Austin Lord laughed. "I thought so."

The summer passed without our seeing the woodcarver again.

I spent many nights, but not every night, on the roof walk. I did not go there to look out to sea, but to look up at the starry sky. I liked it best when there was no moon: Luna was a bittersweet mirror for Una those days. Sometimes when I looked at her I ached with hope that Ahab, too, saw her shining face. But I did not believe that was true. In the dark of the moon, the heavens aglitter with stars, I gradually made my peace, lived through and beyond a slow grieving.

Throughout the summer my spirit sailed those spaces between stars, much as it had that first night at 'Sconset, and while it did, something like a taproot also went down from me, and I knew myself to be at home. Always this expansiveness and this rootedness grew.

One night while I sat cross-legged on the planks, my back resting against the chimney, I heard Justice climbing up the steps. He quietly asked if he might sit with me.

"You're watching the stars, aren't you, Mother?"

"Yes."

He sat awhile, silently, beside me, cross-legged, looking up. Finally he said, "Sometimes I think my father is not coming back."

I waited and said, "But we remember him, even if he doesn't. We love him the same. And we're all right, aren't we?"

"The Perseid meteor shower is next week—" he said.

"Mid-August, already."

"—and the Mitchells are coming out to watch with us."

"That's good." I put my fingers in my son's curls.

"They say they can't see as well in town because of all the lamps and lanterns. But I thought light helped us to see. They say it's 'good and dark' here."

Together we watched one spark skate across the sky. "The town lights are like a reflective screen. They bounce our seeing back to us when we would see beyond."

"Mother, when summer is over, let's stay here."

"Yes," I said. "I want to stay, too."

CHAPTER 131   The Return of the *Delight*

WHEN I AWOKE, the sea ran white and virginal. Not just its lacy foam, but all the expanse of its fabric was white, reflecting a white sky overhead. Where the muted sun glittered through his white veil, the white sea modulated to a satiny silver that glistened and blinded my eyes. On each side of this strip of silver lay spangles and bright flakes of light and white blankness. Occasionally, where the morning breeze disturbed the blank surface, the white sheet lifted toward the palest hue of green—as though the warp were still of white threads but the woof ran pale green.

My eyes were at feast on it when the line of the horizon was suddenly punctuated by the yet-white, but dully so, silhouette and mass of a ship, a whaler. She was not the *Pequod*, for this image was not congruent to the one stamped in my heart. (Turn the *Pequod* to any angle, stern or aft, starboard or larboard, at any intermediate angle, and I know her. All variations of her shape and rigging, if a hundred be not the right number, then a thousand variations, hang in the gallery of my memory. I could not mistake her.) This ship was another, but she hove toward Nantucket and she was a whaler and perhaps the bearer of *Pequod* letters or sightings.

I shook Justice and told him I was running to see Mary, and he might come down as he liked. As I ran along the path, my nanny goat frolicked by my side, and I took it as a good omen.

I knocked softly at the window, knowing that Mary's head lay just beyond the curtained glass, and called her name. When she drew back the curtain, I saw her sleepy face and tousled hair. I but pointed to the sea, and she leaned forward, looking, and then sprang up in a swirl of white nightgown and, to my surprise, pink ribbon. Ah, she was no plain Quaker for her husband, I saw. As she stood in the door, her gown showed itself to end in layers of lace from her knees to the ankles, as though she stood in sea-foam.

"It's the *Delight*," she exclaimed, "though I have not seen her for five years. We are her home port."

"How do you know?"

"She's built with shears." These were broad beams which crossed the quarterdeck at a height of a few feet above a man's head. Shears were used to lay whaleboats athwart.

Mary stepped back inside the door and reached up for the brass telescope, where it always hung between large hooks, as a shotgun might hang in a Kentucky cabin. When she held the instrument to her eye, concern passed over her countenance, and she said, "She sails sadly."

"What do you mean?"

She handed me the glass, and I looked for myself. All was tidy aboard, but two whaleboats were missing. Usually the ship's carpenter could refashion what was stove, and rarely had I seen a ship with less than its full component. Observing further, I saw that the number of men on deck was sparse, and those that were there moved slowly. Indeed, they did seem sad, as though they hesitated to bring home sorrowful news.

"Yes," I said. "I see."

"Do you see the captain?" she asked.

"He stands very still at the wheel."

"Yet a captain may bring news of a captain," she said.

"And I see the first mate, too," I replied. But the sight of the man was not reassuring. He was gaunt and stooped. I handed her the glass.

"It would only be their own sorrow that weighs them so," I said.

"One of us must go to town, and one stay here with the children."

"Do you wish to go this time? It's been a long time since you were in Nantucket."

"I would rather stay," Mary said. "We know that this is not the *Pequod*. Hereafter, we will take turns."

A sleepy-faced Justice had followed me. Now he took my hand. "Mother, do you think the Mitchells would still give us Pog?"

"I'm going to town. I'll ask. They can bring him for the Perseid, if they want to."

THE ROAD between me and the wharf seemed not to exist, nor the time between the farewells at 'Sconset and the moment I stepped from the harbor dinghy into a loop of rope so as to be hoisted to the deck of the *Delight*. When I introduced myself to the captain of the *Delight*, I thought, *Ironic name!*—for he appeared to be the captain of Sorrow. This hollow-cheeked captain started as though at an apparition when I told him I was Captain Ahab's wife.

"You've seen the *Pequod* then?"

"Aye, and that old, wild man."

"What of my husband, sir?"

"I baptized your husband with death or resurrection. I don't know which."

"What do you mean?"

"When first I beheld the *Pequod* at a distance, he was aloft, hatless, risen high in a basket, keeping lookout himself, as though he had no trust of the usual lookouts."

At this my heart constricted in guilt, for I myself had betrayed such a lookout trust, and my betrayal had been at the sighting of an almost immaterial Moby Dick. Yet Ahab, by means of this mechanical basket contrivance, had flown aloft again! and a spark of happiness for him dashed across the dark field of my apprehension.

"On the end of the rope," the captain went on, "he had Starbuck, and just such a mate I'd want on the end of a pulley rope."

"What of Ahab?" I insisted.

"He stood on his vessel and I on mine, but I showed Ahab the salvaged skeleton of our whaleboat, up there"—he pointed back to the shears. "Naught but boat bones. Moby Dick, I told him, and worse than a mere stove boat has been the monster's work. 'You sail on the grave of four of my men, gone down alive and dying,' I told him, as very soon I must tell yon weeping clutch of wharf women. I must tell them after you have your portion.

"I pointed your husband's gaze to my deck, where lay a shroud inhabited by the fifth dead man. 'And all of those lost,' I said, 'were Nantucketeers like ourselves.' Even as Ahab and I stood talking at our taffrails, I with my trumpet, he only with his stentorian voice, my sailors were taking the last stitches in the canvas shroud, sealing shut the sides.

"Ahab's anxiety was only that I might have killed the white whale afore him—now, Ahab's good wife, I see the darkening of thy bright countenance—but I told him no harpoon forged would ever do that.

"Angrily, he defied me—let me finish the tale for you. Over there, on the wharf, they want different characters in the cast. Ahab snatched his harpoon and brandished it about. 'Look ye, Nantucketeer; here in this hand I hold his death!' "

Ah, in this captain's tale, I heard Ahab, I saw Ahab!

" 'Tempered in blood,' Captain Ahab shouted. 'Tempered by lightning, to be triply tempered in the hot heart of Moby Dick.' "

Though I trembled in all my being, I shivered out my question. "Was he mad, then?"

" 'Tempered in blood, tempered by lightning, to be triply tempered in the hot heart of Moby Dick where the white whale most feels his accursed life!'—those were the last words I heard him speak—'accursed life!' "

The captain of the *Delight* averted his eyes from mine, as though he was ashamed. He added quietly, "But my last words to him were 'May God keep thee, old man,' and then, the last stitch having been made and the body placed on the plank, I began the funeral words 'May the resurrection and the life . . .' But Ahab sailed away. Yet we splashed him with the bubbles from the sea-struck corpse." The captain seemed to fetch a sigh from the very depths of the ocean. "Perhaps ye know, Mrs. Captain, did I baptize him in that splash of bubbles with death or with life?" Still he would not look at me but continued to gaze at the decking of the *Delight*. "Now I have five more tales to tell, and each of them ends in certain death."

"So you do not know what became of my husband?"

"That is all I know of him—with certainty. Don't ask for more report." He turned away from me. Was he so anxious to disburden himself to the women waiting on the wharf that he had no civility for me? He muttered as he turned from me, "What I heard with my own ears and saw with my own eyes. That's all I'll tell ye." Then he stopped, as though he remembered one last sight, and looked at me. "And the last I saw of the *Pequod*—at the stern, for the life buoy, hung a coffin."

"I thank you for your telling."

AHAB ALIVE! and still pursuing the white whale! Closing, perhaps, on the whale! Ahab possibly alive! But what was the sequel?

My dinghy deposited me among the fearful women. I did not need to say that some crew had been lost; their only questions were who. On my walk to the Mitchells', to ask about the dog, I passed Aunt Charity, and she, too, as the captain had, startled to see me.

"Am I so infrequent a visitor in town as to startle you?" I asked gaily, but she merely nodded, tucked her head down, and hurried on. Perhaps she already knew that the *Delight* brought news of death. Captain Bildad probably had gone out with the pilot boat.

Mr. Mitchell was not home, but I conversed with Maria in their apartment above the bank. Like me, she thought that one could not draw any *certain* information about Ahab from what the captain of the *Delight* had told me. I stayed perhaps an hour with Maria—she said they would be happy to deliver Pog to Justice, since they had several other dogs and they had hoped to give him away, he being the largest of their dogs, with the most extensive appetite. I remembered to inquire of my patient scientific friend how her search was going for a telescopic comet, but she had no news. I saw no hint of despair in her face, such as one sees in the faces of wives of sailors who have been too long at sea. Maria would wait trustingly through all eternity, if she could, for a comet to swim into the ken of her telescope.

"Will it not be a relief," I asked, "to come out to 'Sconset and see dozens of meteorites?"

She laughed and ducked her head. "Of course it will be a pleasure to see you."

I thought she dissembled a bit; she really did not want to leave her lover for even one night. I almost teased her thus, but remembering her maiden state, decided not to embarrass her. All the time I was taking an interest in her work and in Justice's dog, my heart beat quickly with possibility—Ahab, my lover, my husband, yet Alive!

Next, I went to call on Mrs. Maynard, whom I found with Captain Maynard, and she was crying. Before she saw me, I heard her snuffle, "And I once thought him an old warthog!"

"Dangerous as Vesuvius," her husband replied.

Then they both saw me. Mrs. Maynard jumped up. "Land sakes, there she is, poor Mrs. Sparrow!"

The appellation gave me a turn, but I smiled and said, "I have not been so called for a long time."

She entreated her husband, "Oh, leave us, leave us." He seemed quite ready to do so, twirling his right-hand mustache as he went. "Oh, my dear, the captain of the *Delight* has confided to the captain of the *Camel* the most dreadfully disturbing news!"

"I have spoken to him myself," I answered. "Five crewmen lost."

"But Captain Ahab!"

"Last seen well, but in pursuit of the white whale."

"Oh, no," she said. "Oh, no."

"Yes, fiery and eager."

"That was not how he was last seen."

"But the captain of the *Delight* took particular pains to say that was the last he saw of the *Pequod*."

"Yes, but not the last heard. Not the indirect news. And what *Delight* heard later, he has confided to another captain—my captain—and it is most dreadful." She sank into her chair and sobbed.

Oh, slow wit that I was, I was yet amused by this latest round of miscommunication. She reached out, took my forearm, and drew me into the chair beside her.

"Not the last heard, dear Una, for on his way back, *Delight* had a gam with another captain, who himself had had a gam with Captain Gardiner of the *Rachel*—"

"The *Rachel* is also of Nantucket."

"Aye—and he said—"

"But that is too far removed a hearsay!" I cut her off; I was alarmed.

She gathered herself together, stopped crying, smoothed her starched apron, and said, "You must listen to what I have to say."

I nodded, terribly afraid.

"Captain Gardiner of the *Rachel* lost his son. He crossed paths with the *Pequod* and wanted to charter her for two days to help him find his son, gone, in a whaleboat. Ahab would not."

My gladness sank to hear of this heartlessness of my husband to a man whom he knew, a father. It would not be Ahab to so lose his humanity, without his own soul writhing and anguished. But alive! My heart did not dive to the coldest depths.

"Then someone else has seen Ahab," I said hopefully.

"The *Pequod* herself, shortly after meeting the *Rachel,* was stove by the whale—"

I was stunned. Like the *Sussex.*

"Stove and sank—by Moby Dick. Listen! One man only surviving. Picked up later by the *Rachel* herself. Picked up from off a coffin used as a life buoy."

"He was?"

"He was not one of ours. No one's heard his account firsthand. We do not know his name. They say he sailed for South America."

HOW I WALKED back to my buggy, I do not know. Mrs. Maynard was beside me. I put my hand on the dashboard, ready to spring up, then stopped and said to Mrs. Maynard, "I cannot go back without something more definitive. I must go see Captain Peleg."

Mrs. Maynard kindly went with me, hurrying to keep up. We were not surprised, when we went in that owner's parlor, to see huddled there with him—all three in deepest black—Captain Bildad and his sister, Aunt Charity.

"I could not bring myself to tell thee," Aunt Charity said. "Forgive my passing you in silence."

"Is the *Pequod* lost then?"

Captain Bildad slowly rose from his chair, the patriarch of the group. "The *Pequod* has gone down, Captain Ahab gone, Starbuck gone. Stubb, Flask, every Nantucketeer, every Vineyardman, every man, gone."

"Save one?" Mrs. Maynard amended.

"Save one—a fellow of former marchant experience."

"Quohog by name," said Captain Peleg.

"Nay, that name was the infidel harpooner." Bildad shook his head quietly, but produced no further name.

I stood listening, incredulous. "Are you sure, Captains? Are ye sure of it? I have my son to tell, and Mary Starbuck and her son." My eyes were burning dry, but every internal organ gushed tears.

Captain Bildad walked slowly to me, and slowly he put his arms about my shoulders. "Shall I come with ye, to help ye tell it?"

"Yes," I said. "Yes."

I AM SURE that as soon as Mary saw me drive up with the black-clad, somber Bildad at my side she knew.

He called the boys to him and, with a hand on each of their shoulders, told them their fathers were lost. Then he quickly said a prayer. "Come to me, lads, if ever ye need," he added, departing. "Perhaps there's a bit I could do to help ye, if it comes to that, ever. And ye'll have my prayers. Till the crack of doom."

The boys fell into each other's arms, and over them, Mary and I leaned inward, making a tent.

MY SADNESS at this final, stunning word was more for the other three than for myself. I but gave up false hope, hope I had harbored for only an hour, above the Union Pacific Bank, talking with my friend. Before that, I had known for some time that Ahab was dead. I had accustomed myself to that knowledge.

I tried not to imagine the awful final moments of Ahab's life. I did not care to know the name of the survivor, or to milk the captains for any details of frenzy, or blood, or suffering, they may have heard. I had known none of that, nor needed to know of that violence, when my grieving had begun.

I think things went the hardest for Starbuck's Jim. Justice had made an intuitive connection with my own resignation and with the spiritual life that was becoming not only my solace but my definition. But Jim, though a steady, sympathetic lad, had not listened to the intuitive messages that had informed the rest of us. Some Quaker elders came out to talk with Mary and Jim, and their conviction gave the boy a sort of tortured comfort. He felt that his father was in a better place, but he could scarcely bear the loss of him.

The Unitarian minister and several members of that congregation—

a party of three buggies with perhaps twelve people—soon called on us. Two of them were Isaac the gaoler and his wife, Betsy. They did not bring their children, but she was pregnant again. As always, the sight of them was a bright thing for me. We had little to say to one another, but I was glad that they had come and I told them so.

I invited Mary and Jim to meet our church friends, as she had invited Justice and me to meet hers. Even the members of this group of people who only slightly knew Mary could scarcely keep their eyes from her. I saw then that she was a bit above the average in height and that this lifted her gleaming head more into the light. She and Isaac and Betsy, who was also fair, looked like three angels, Mary in our midst and those two together at the periphery. Mary Starbuck's hair, I irrelevantly noted, was more silvery and metallic in quality than the softer, golden curls of Betsy. I do not know why these visual matters preoccupied my mind. Somehow beauty was more consoling than conversation.

CHAPTER 132   **The Perseid**

That day we learned of Ahab's death, my minister asked on behalf of the Mitchells if they should postpone their coming. The meteor phenomena would have an impressive decrescendo for a full two weeks, but Mary and I decided that the Mitchells should come as scheduled at the peak of the shower. It would help the boys to have company, and there would be much distracting talk of unimaginable numbers.

The tone of our scientific party was subdued, of course, and we all felt sensitive and careful about our human fragility. Twice, I saw dear Jim run off over a sand dune (we had our watching station on blankets on the beach) for a cry—both times shortly followed by a compassionate Justice, and then by two or three of the cheerful Mitchell boys.

Having retold the story of Perseus, for whom the meteor shower was named, Mr. Mitchell suddenly mentioned Chartres Cathedral. He said that at the center of the penitents' labyrinth, inlaid on the floor of the cathedral, was a mosaic of the head of Perseus, who had slain the

Minotaur of the labyrinth at Crete. I wondered if Mr. Mitchell had confused Perseus with Theseus, but I said it was odd to have a pagan figure as the endpoint for devout Christians, traveling on their knees. More strange—I did not speak of it—to have an image of Chartres, originally in my mind through Ahab's words, embellished by Mr. Mitchell.

"Perhaps those medieval Christians were less narrow than we think," Mr. Mitchell offered. "Perhaps the cathedral designers knew the old myths also carried light for humans."

"I sometimes thought of Ahab as a Prometheus." Yes, I could speak of him. "Did you know that as a young man, he went to Chartres?"

"Ahab was a visionary," Mr. Mitchell said. "He fought metaphysical battles in a physical world." He added, with feeling, "I thought you were a lovely pair of birds."

OUR LITTLE TRIBE spent that night on the beach. We counted—forty, sixty, eighty—meteorites and watched them slash the sky. Mr. Mitchell pointed out that they all emanated from a central station in the dark. He said they were the residue of a burst comet.

As I tried to sleep, the ceaseless crisscrossing of the waves made a lattice of sound in my mind. I hid beneath that sound. Before sleep took me, I turned on my stomach and wept into the sand for my Theseus, slain by the beast, because he could not find his way out of the labyrinth of revenge. I thought that the name of the needed thread was forgiveness.

I wished that my beloved could have heeded the words of my father, reciting: "Love your enemies as yourself, bless those that curse you, and forgive those who trespass against you."

Before dawn, I was called from sleep by Justice. Without rising, I held out my arm to him, and he lay beside me with his head on my shoulder. I held him close against my body, and the prince-of-a-dog, Pog, came and lay close to him on the other side. Never have I felt such gratitude to a beast.

I myself needed to love a beast—never so desperately as that night when the stars skated over a black night. A beast had stolen my beloved.

Aﬀter the Perseid meteor shower of August, we entered into a quiet time of grief and into the routines of our lives. Justice and Jim were much to themselves outdoors. They learned to swim and to manage a small boat. When summer turned to autumn and the winds began, sometimes they rode the horses along the beach and came in rosy-cheeked, but strangely silent. I remember the boys were always tearing their coats, and we reset sleeves, sewed many buttons on, and stitched new bottoms into pockets. If they were fighting, they never did it in our view. Jim was older, but Justice was more compact and quick. Their garments seemed equally ripped. Mary and I had little of chatter as we sat by the hearth through the fall and winter, knitting and piecing quilt tops. Sometimes I wondered if Mary had unspoken blame to lay at my feet, since Ahab had been captain of the ship on which her husband was lost.

Both the gradual coming on of spring—signaled by the greening and then the pinkening of the rose canes that lay atop Mary's cottage—and a definite event marked the end of our mourning. At shearing time, Justice and Jim were still small enough to fit inside the woolsack but large enough to have the requisite weight for speedily packing down the wool. When they both asked to be taken to the spring shearing, I remember rising up from my chair and stretching.

"Then you won't have to oil my shoes," Jim said to his mother. Since the news of his father's death, Jim's face had had a strained whiteness, a tautness as though some structure under the skin might snap. It seemed so to me now—as though he were starving and asking for bread instead of for a diversion.

"They say it gets terrible hot inside," Mary answered with a gentle smile.

"We can stand it! We can stand it!" Justice insisted. He began to jump up and down on the spot to demonstrate his stamina. Here was practical energy, ready for purposeful harnessing.

"Well, of course," I said, taking over the decision. I looked at Mary. "Why not?"

She stood up, put her knitting in her chair, yawned and stretched. "Why not?" she echoed.

When we reached the shearing pens, a festival atmosphere made me glad we'd come. From the back of a wagon someone sold baked goods with dips of preserves. I saw Abram Quary with a rack of smoked fish tidbits and, remembering his kindness to Kit, made it a point to buy and to compliment him on the flavor. "Smoked in apple wood?" I asked, and he made one swift nod down. Many families with boys had come, as we had, so that the boys could pack down the wool, and their mothers and sisters had come as well with picnic lunches. Captain and Mrs. Maynard had driven out with a whole load of boys belonging to their neighbors. Boys who owned more than one pair of shoes carried them along in hand as they ran to get in line.

Already-shorn sheep, pink and bleating, were running around in their pen. They corkscrewed into the air and skipped, light without their winter wool. One gleeful little girl pointed at the fleshy sheep with one hand and covered her mouth with the other. "They're naked, they're naked," she giggled. On the other side of the shearing floor, the unshorn sheep milled about in their pens. Really, with their fat paddings of wool all about their bodies, they scarcely seemed to be the same species as the skinny, bare animals.

The woolsack, perhaps twelve feet long, was held up within a tall wooden frame, against a high platform. Ladders made it possible to mount the scaffold. With a pulley system at one end, loose wool spread on a canvas square was hoisted up by the four grommeted corners to the platform. A stuffer-man threw the wool into the woolsack. And inside the woolsack—we could see the long white length of it pulsating as we approached—a boy jumped up and down to pack the wool for shipping off-island. As he pounded down the loose curds of wool, the lanolin penetrated and waterproofed the leather of his shoes, which would be put away for winter wearing.

The boys vied to see who could pack down the greatest weight of wool into the volume of a standard bag, and each bag was weighed and labeled. A new hoop, perfectly round, hanging on a peg, would reward the boy this year whose legs packed the wool most tightly.

The long white sack gyrated in its rack, and boys yelled encouragements. "Harder! Faster! Hurry! Let me, let me, if you can't!" Justice and Jim hurried to get in line. Packing down the wool was hard, hot work. As a boy tamped the wool and new loose wool was thrown down the open mouth of the sack, he rose higher on what he had trod. At the top, he grasped the frame for balance as he danced. Suddenly Justice returned to me.

"What is it?" I asked my son.

He crossed his arms over his chest. He looked at the woolsack with a hard, appraising stare. "It resembles Moby Dick," he said. Then he ran back to Jim and whispered in his ear. Jim seemed stricken. The other boys in the line were practicing their leaping, challenging each other for the highest vertical jump, but Justice resumed his quiet, calculating stance, arms crossed over his chest, hands hidden, and Jim imitated him.

When Mary and I approached the boys, she asked enthusiastically, "Do you think it will be fun? Don't you want to practice?"

"We will win," Justice said.

"I will win," Jim said.

Justice did not contradict him. "For now, we save our strength," Justice said.

Too small for a whole whale, to me the woolsack more resembled the head of a whale, which might be bailed for the case oil. And here was oil again, but innocent. No planking awash with blood. The shearers were experts and the pink skin of the sheep was only occasionally nicked and bloodied. I looked at the tent and picnic tables, sniffed in the festive atmosphere.

"I think it's like a whale's belly," Justice said, nodding at the long sack. "We'll be inside."

Jim nodded in agreement, his pale face stretched with tension.

"We must leave them to it," Mary said to me and took my elbow.

We walked to the shearers and watched a sheep come through the chute. One man with small shears trimmed the tags from around the eyes and ears. Next, a nearby man, sitting on a short stool, up-ended the sheep between his knees and began to cut loose the cloud of fleece. Beyond him, the woolsack jerked and trembled from the exertions of the lad inside.

"A boy could make himself sick jumping so hard," I said to Mary.

"They're strong boys," she said. I wondered she had not seen the strain in Jim's face. Perhaps she had not noticed Justice's remarks.

Wearing the red-checked gingham dress I had made for her some years before, Mrs. Maynard came to chat with us. As I always did when I saw her in this dress, my eye followed the tucks down the bodice to be sure I had sewn them perfectly straight. Of course, it had been easy to keep the lines straight with the checks as a guide; still, I always enjoyed their perfection. "Kit's mother used to bring baking to the shearing," she said. "It beat this." She thrust a curl of cinnamon roll into my mouth. I expected the familiar taste and texture I had learned from Kit, but this bread was heavier and had not been made with enough butter.

I watched Jim put Justice ahead of him to mount the platform. A load of wool was dumped into the flaccid sack, and Justice dropped out of sight on top of it. Quickly whole snowloads of the creamy, curdy wool were thrown down on top of him. I could tell that he used his hands to brush it off his shoulders and send it to his feet. His knuckles made little bulges against the side of the bag. I was pleased that he had a steady pace to his stamping; there was nothing of frenzy and all of method in his work. Sometimes his knees bulged the sides of the bag. His head was a long time emerging at the top of the sack. His black curls, wet with sweat, stuck to his forehead; his cheeks were flushed. He grasped the struts of the framework and danced himself higher and higher out of the sack, like a puppet on strings. Best of all, his eyes were merry.

Soon I knew why: his bag was the heaviest so far.

As Jim leapt into the bag, for his turn, he drew up his knees and thrust his legs down with the utmost force on the pile waiting in the bottom. Mary's back was turned, and I began to debate with myself whether I should share my anxiety with her. Not now, I decided. There's nothing untoward about zeal. But I didn't want the boys to exhaust themselves. So thorough was Jim's tamping down of the wool that some of the boys grew impatient and taunted him to speed up. Jim's head emerged pink and grinning. Excited and determined. His fair hair was dark against his scalp. He stamped on the wool as though it needed to be crushed and killed.

Jim's bag topped Justice's in weight. They stood at the back of the line together, each happy in the accomplishment of the other, picking off stray strands of wool from each other's sleeves, stooping to touch each other's lanolin-soaked shoes.

When I saw my minister, the Reverend Mr. Peal, arrive by buggy with his wife and an older woman, I went over to greet them. Learning the older woman was his mother, I complimented her on her recipe for plum pudding, which I had so enjoyed from the church Christmas baking. She was a bit deaf.

"I live in Maine now," she said, "but I grew up here on Nantucket." Like her son's, her cheeks formed defined curves at the corners of her mouth, as though all she said were spoken into parentheses. "The recipe has come home when it came back here with my son." She was obviously proud of him.

I told her that I and my son lived at 'Sconset, and I pointed Justice out to her.

She gasped and then blurted, "He is the very image of a boy I knew. A boy who grew up here and went to sea as a cabin boy."

"Mother," the minister intervened, "Una is the widow of Captain Ahab."

"Ahab dead!" Her eye fastened on Justice as though he were Ahab and could not possibly be grown and dead. "I scarcely knew him," she went on, "but I watched him, on just such a day as this. He jumped in the woolsack. Ahab won the prize that day."

"You must watch Justice then, too," I said. And I invited her to come meet Mary and Mrs. Maynard and sit with us at a table under the tent. Although I tried in all ways to be sure she got a friendly homecoming at the shearing, I longed for her to tell me about Ahab— what he had been as a boy. While I waited an opportunity, I watched the boys at their work and worried to see them emerge each time with fatigue on their faces. Not only their shoes but their clothes were soaked with wool oil.

"I'm afraid I've ruined my pants," Justice said at one point, eating some of Abram Quary's smoked fish "for strength."

"And what of your shirt?" I added. When I poked him, he oozed.

"Ruined, too," he said. The word *ruined* held nothing but happiness for him.

After he went back to his jumping, the elder Mrs. Peal said, "He has your quick smile. He's not like his father in that."

"You said you didn't know Ahab well."

"I was probably five years older. I think I was fifteen and about to marry and move to Maine when I last saw him. It was sheep shearing, and he was about ten years old. But he was not easily forgotten."

"No."

She took my hand. "I can't tell you much of him. He was poor. Your boy has his eyes. Not his smile, though."

"What kind of eyes?"

She released my hand. "We used to say such eyes could see into the waves. See the hidden things."

Jim—again triumphant over Justice and all the others—came and threw himself down on the ground next to his mother's chair. She held him out a glass of lemonade, and I could see that Mary was beginning to worry. The pulse in Jim's neck beat at a gallop. "I don't think Justice can tie that," Jim said, panting. "Nobody *else* can. That's for sure." When Jim went back to the line, he sat rather than stood in place. He laid his forearms over his knees and rested his forehead there. Justice stood beside him, his arms crossed over his chest. The hectic was in Justice's cheek and his dark eyes snapped sparks. I thought of our first day at 'Sconset, when Justice and I had wrestled in the surf and he would not quit until I said that he had won the struggle.

"All these years," Mrs. Peal went on, "I remember his smile. Ahab's smile. It was so slight."

The description was a needle in my throat: how I had treasured Ahab's faint smile. Just a line of a smile it had been. So special and rare.

"When they gave him the prize," she said, "he smiled so faintly. I was surprised. I thought he'd show more pleasure."

"What was the prize?" I asked.

"Oh, I know he was glad to get it. Ahab and his mother were poor, and it was a silver coin nailed to a pole. Where the hoop hangs now."

My eye traveled to the shiny circle of the big hoop. But I knew it was not the hoop that either my or Mary's boy coveted. They wanted a victory over the sack itself. They wanted to dominate it—that whale-like memento of their fathers.

"There was one other thing I remember about Ahab," she said. "I don't know I should tell it."

"It will not hurt me," I said. "I'd like to know what I can of him." I spoke with false calm. *I knew him all, I knew him all,* my inner voice protested.

"He was said to be a boy who had broken a promise."

"No," I said. And I was offended. Despite the reassurance I had just offered. Ahab had not broken a promise: not to me, not to his son. Nor as a child. Ahab had been Ahab.

"I don't know," she said. She sounded tired and sad. "They said that he had broken a promise to the Indian woman Tistig. He had promised to catch her a fish one day and instead he had gone sailing. She was like an adopted aunt to him—a friend of his mother's. For pure pleasure, they said, he went off sailing."

I felt a smile of satisfaction forming on my face. What was a promise? A way to enslave the future to the past. I was glad a poor boy had seized a chance at pleasure. I thought that I would teach Justice to sail.

"They said," Mrs. Peal concluded, "that Tistig cursed Ahab. I don't know for sure if it was over a broken promise. Or why she would do that."

JUSTICE DID TIE and slightly top Jim's standing record, but as my boy's face rose above the top of the woolsack, his pallor was evident. No longer ruddy, he was as pale as the wool itself. Still he tramped down the fleece. To lift his leg, to cock his knee, to thrust down—it was all will. He did not smile. He looked older as he swung onto the platform. I rushed to the foot of the ladder. When he stepped back from the last rung, he looked at me and then to Jim. "This was the last for me."

Jim nodded.

I felt smitten with shame. Justice had considered my anxiety and quit. Jim swung up the ladder for his turn.

"Oh, son," I said, almost trembling.

Suddenly he smiled at me. Some of the color returned to his cheek. He looked long into my eyes, as his father used to do. He took my arm and walked me away from the group. "I wanted Jim to win, Mother. He needed it more."

Now I smiled down at him. Justice had made his own decision. "We'll see," I said, proud of my boy. When Jim won, we all were glad.

That night as I went to sleep, I knew that I had won, too, and my trophy from the sheep shearing was the image of Ahab as a boy. I imagined him holding the prize coin between his thumb and finger, flashing the silver beauty of it.

When I told my confidant the judge about our day, he asked me if I knew that in England judges sat on a pillow of sorts called the woolsack. "Suggests agrarian origins of civilization, doesn't it?" Then he added that he, too, had seen Ahab as a young person.

"You never told me," I said.

"I was about ten, and my mother had sent me down to the wharf. A whaler was being towed out. Somehow I knew it was the first voyage for the cabin boy, who was Ahab. I suppose he was thirteen or so. He stood at the rail and waved."

"What else?"

"Not much. He wore a red cap."

CHAPTER 134   Letter from Margaret Fuller,
from England

My Una,

"*I accept the universe*"—*that's what I told Mr. Thomas Carlyle, in London.*

And that renowned writer Thomas Carlyle replied, without a shred of understanding, "Madam, you had better." 'Twas then, dear Una, I thought to write to you, for you would grasp immediately the great distance that I have come in my psyche in order to accept that which I can neither control nor alter. For me to say I accept the universe is to say that I am at peace with myself.

And with Mr. Emerson. What a height of mind is there! What a negative depth, a bottomless abyss, of heart is there! I accept both— his assets and his abysmal deficiencies. He, not unlike Mr. Hawthorne, is distrustful of what the body has to tell us. He knows not the rapture of the physical. How then, I ask, can either of them thoroughly respond to the sublime in nature? Show them a moun-

tain—show them Mont Blanc—and do their bodies thrill to know it? To know it biblically with their whole being, with the thighs, with the lungs, with the quickened nostrils consuming the crystalline air in great gulps. They know not great gulps of anything! They are too restrained. They fear passion, though Emerson can write that marriage is surely true to one's nature for only a time, that marriage is mortal and should be accorded a death of its own when it no longer serves the spirit.

Yet he fears passion! When I visited him once in Concord, having had much correspondence with him, and looking so forward to the feast of the eye upon him, for the genuine physical ear to thrill to the vibrations actually issuing from his throat and not to the "voice" that we accord the written word, to even the odor of him! (yes, for he like any animal hath an odor! oh, for a poet, an American male who would sing of this as well as of the bright abstractions!), when, in short, we came before each other IN OUR BODIES, *at Concord, then he assigned me to a room. He assigned Waldo, his little son, to be postman, and he proposed that we write to one another! I controlled myself till I trembled with indignation. Yet I acquiesced. I would have me* near *him, if not quite* with *him.*

Yes, Una, Margaret must settle for near. Why? My breath would scorch him! He cannot stand up to the flood tide of passion! He cannot weather even the forerunning, tumultuous clouds of an electric storm!

I have done with all that restraint! I wrote him that I felt like bursting through the wall, plunging through the barrier between us! And he was only alarmed. I have fled the prudery of America. I shall embrace the wiser sophistication of Europe. I shall rebel. This I mean most literally, for my next stop is Italy, where I shall play nurse to the troops. The nationalist feeling there is necessary, for only if the parts combine to make a whole can the yoke of the French, the Austrian, the last of that great Hapsburg Empire which outlasted even the ancient Roman empire, be thrown off forever. And I shall be there with my eyes open and my ears open, my woman's hands ready to nurse. And to write! Yes, to write, write, write. Horace Greeley begs for more and longer Tribune *articles in every letter I receive from him.*

Let the Transcendentalists manufacture their own nothing. But I leave them in peace, wishing them well. In the political world, not the philosophical, I find my analogue. I, like Italy, rebel. I, like Italy, shall throw off tyranny and create my own being.

You, Una, understand this. I passionately embrace your life. For what I am doing by dint of will and intellect, you have done most naturally. You create your own being. You trust your body, you send your spirit voyaging; you think. You are the American woman, an Eve more fittingly named Dawn, new and brave.

Brave—how truly that rings upon my ear as your epithet. But why? I know not. Yet because I trust myself, because my impulse is naturally spontaneous, even holy, yes that, I know that brave *is the very word for Una.*

Suppose you never receive this letter? Yet you will know my feeling for you. Do you read the Tribune? *Have you seen my articles? I tell all that I see, but I do not tell all that I feel. That requires a willing ear. Indeed, I think we cannot access our truest minds unless we direct ourselves toward some sympathetic and admired reader.*

You will marvel at my energy! You wonder now: why has she not mentioned headaches and illness? I feel them not! This old air, this Europe, reassures me. Here Margaret is not so shocking. They have known George Sand, after all. They have had great women before me. But Carlyle! The author of Sartor Resartus *(The Tailor Retailored, if thy Latin be not at hand), the creator of the great iconoclast Teufelsdröckh (Devil's Dung, if thy German hath not progressed), plays the pedant with Margaret. "Madam, you had better!" Who is he to say? Has he climbed Mont Blanc? Ah, that Byron lived! I would seek him out. We would go a-soldiering together. You know he died helping the Greeks? Yes, for you do know your Byron and Wordsworth, though I think you have too much a tendency to divorce the works, as though they were worlds of their own, from the lives of the men who made them.*

Ah, but let me slow my headlong pace, and think more particularly of the mind of Una, for it is consistent that you emphasize "La Belle Dame sans Merci" and not John Keats, that you love "Tintern Abbey" and care little that much of it was taken from the journal of poor, crazed sister Dorothy. For you, Una, look at creation and divorce it from the creator. You look at the sublime, feel it as such, but think not of the Sublime.

Yet, let me slow not only from gallop to trot, but from trot to walk. This is your way. This is your own exploration of the path that is both divine and leads to the divine. And it is as good as mine.

Ah, Carlyle could not modulate my egotism, but you, the thought of your thought, brings me to a humbler plane. And it is the way of women. We allow each other our individuality. We do not insist that we dominate or control. How well Carlyle understands freedom for his characters, how poorly for his fellow mortals. And now I pity him, for he is bound by his own self-importance. It constrains him, pitiably. Carlyle is himself a part of the universe that I accept.

Yours very truly,
Margaret Fuller

CHAPTER 135   ⚜   # Letter from David Poland, Virginia

Dear Mrs. Una,

I come to New Bedford with a new posse to take back an escaped slave. His master apprenticed him to learn ship caulking. He was able to learn it. But he took advantage and disguised himself as a sailor and escaped.

I am writing to say that he has become a respectable man in New Bedford. They are very kind to slaves and runaways there. I hope your friend Susan made it to New Bedford.

When I talked to this man he told me the story of his life as a slave. It was funny, how stupid his masters were sometimes. I laughed with him. I decided not to try to take him. I gave him the equal of the money that I took off Susan, which you gave her. To help other slaves. I wonder if I am becoming an abolitionist. I thought you would be glad. I know I am through with bounty-hunting.

Yours, David P.

Dearest Aunt Agatha, Uncle Torch, Frannie, and Butch,

I have moved from the town of Nantucket to the eastern edge of the island, known as the town of Siasconset or 'Sconset. I live simply, but I have been left very well off by Captain Ahab, who died perhaps a year ago—we do not know exactly when the Pequod *went down, stove by a white whale. We have lived with the news for several months. I think often of you. I wish again to ask forgiveness for the pain I gave you. With the loss of Ahab, I understand afresh that love is the sharpest lance. Again, now, in grief, I am flooded with gratitude that you have forgiven me.*

I am thinking of Frannie. I am remembering her restlessness. I honor the patience she has shown these years. I am remembering, too, my promise to her that someday she would be invited to travel and to live with Justice and me. Butch's time will come, too, when he is a big boy, if you wish it.

The messenger who brings you this letter and the sum of one thousand dollars in gold is a man to be trusted—David Poland. His short stature should not make you think of him as dubious in any way. I wrote to him, in Virginia, asked him to come to Nantucket, gave him this letter and the money, and sent him to you.

As you see he has fulfilled this mission. Neither David nor the money has disappeared between Nantucket and the Great Lakes. When I left Kentucky, it was David who guided me out. I rode a white donkey named Milk, whom he led. You see that he still has Milk, and is probably this minute giving Butch a ride on him!

I send the money because I have it and as a way of thanking you for the four wonderful years I spent with you. Money can never repay you: you gave me a family when my own could not keep me.

I do remember what it was like to be young, Frannie. My proposal is that you come and live with me for a while. I propose, dear Aunt and Uncle, that you allow and trust David Poland (whom I have already paid) to escort Frannie to Nantucket. I feel that Fran-

nie and I have much to talk about, and that I can introduce her to the broader world in a safe way. And her presence will help our lives to heal.

With abiding love to all of you, and gratitude,
Una

CHAPTER 137   # Letter from Margaret Fuller, from Italy

Precious Friend, dear Una,

The guns are booming beyond my hospital window where, on the sill, I put down the iodine bottle for a moment to write a few lines to you. Una, I know you have seen madness and death, but you have not seen war, nor even its aftermath. The sheer number of destroyed men before me is completely overwhelming. I dash the tears from my eyes—tears are useless—so that I can see to help. The doctors work tirelessly, cleaning, stitching, amputating, bandaging, and I try to keep up, to make their work lighter. I have ever hated to sew, even cloth, but yesterday I sewed up a bleeding gash in a man's arm because there was no one else to do it.

Let Emerson see this! He would faint. I have fainted, at first. But now I put on the whole armor of Compassion. It flinches not, it cannot allow cringing from wounds of the most horrible sort. If Emerson could see this, I think that he would put all of his mighty mind to the teaching of one lesson: we must not kill one another.

And yet, when Italian children starve under the yoke of foreign domination, is not that a reason for self-defense? Surely it is only self-defense to strike back then? I do not know. Not even Jesus is clear on the matter. He wants us to turn the other cheek, yet he says that he comes not to bring peace but to place a sword between us. It is the Old Testament whose beautiful words give me hope for a future time, when swords are beaten into ploughshares, and spears into pruning hooks.

Ah, the trees beyond my window, the beautiful olive trees of which the Italians are so rightly proud, have been pruned and shattered by bursting mortar shells. We have taken this city. The fighting, the booming that has punctuated every sentence of this letter, sometimes more often than that, is off in the hills beyond the city.

The city of Rome! I have seen the Colosseum, where men brutalized men more than a thousand years ago, for entertainment. I have seen the domed pagan temple, the Pantheon, where men aspired to something beyond their brutish nature. Una, in its stone floor there are holes, slanted like nostrils, to carry off the rainwater to drains beneath the paving-stone flooring, for the apex of the dome is, by design, an open circle, open to the sky! There is a structure to worship in! Not like St. Paul's of London or St. Peter's in this great city, both temples closed to what lies beyond their own hemisphere.

When I summered on the Great Lakes, I grew weary of hearing folk debate the issues of Trinity and Unity. All such dogma stands in the way of the true religious spirit. That spirit must be open, I am convinced. It must admit light, air, and, yes, even rain.

Una, there is a soldier here who loves me. His name is Ossoli, and by him I shall have a child. I am fulfilled. He is noble of spirit and in title, though not wealthy. My mother would find him wealthy, you would find him so, for his soul is not only rich but generous. I do not know what Emerson would think of him, for Ossoli is not a man of letters. But neither my passion nor my mind frightens the spirit of my beloved. He finds me beautiful. How difficult it is to see him march off, past this window, each morning, to the hills, toward the sounds of guns!

But my babe is safe within. For him, I would gladly die. Sometimes I dream of dying. I am swimming in a sea of blood, and I have no corks to keep me up.

May all things go well for my Una. If you were here, we would nurse together. Since you are not here, I look at the shattered olive trees and see, over the tops of them, the broken, curving wall of the Colosseum. Time, mere time, has crenellated it in places. Is not time foe enough for us mortals? Why do we hasten each other's deaths, when all our rationality and all our religion should combine to extend life and to make it lovely?

> *To know you has made my life more lovely.*
> *Margaret*

CHAPTER 138   The Judge's Invitation

My dear Una,

    Of course nothing pleases me more than to invite you and Justice to stay at my house till your cousin Miss Frannie and her interesting escort arrive. Let me be so bold as to suggest that you stay a week or so here in town after she arrives, too, so that she can make the acquaintance of some young people her own age. Without doubt there is a William Mitchell child of eighteen or so who will provide most reasonable companionship and a bridge to other young Nantucketeers.

    I am thinking, too, that perhaps Mary Starbuck and son Jim would benefit from some time in town, especially since they might be unnecessarily lonely in 'Sconset during the three weeks that we plan to have you here. Bring them, too. And of course that remarkable dog, Pog.

> *Yours truly,*
> *Austin Lord*

    P.S. I shall tell your renters across the street that you are coming into town and may wish to inspect the property. They keep the windows shiny but are too boring for extended conversation.

Just as you directed, dear, the Camel *puts in daily at noon at New Bedford to see if Our Travelers from the West have arrived. By that I mean, of course, your young cousin and her guide, let there be no misunderstanding. I do* not *mean Kit Sparrow and Charlotte Hussey!*

What preparations the judge has had me make for you! He has separately commissioned Captain Maynard to purchase an unheard-of quantity of jams and syrups and chocolates at every port o' call. I have aired mattresses and ironed linens for every bed in the house, for ye shall fill 'em up, what with the four of you from 'Sconset, plus Frannie and David P. The judge was so taken with your stories and description of the little man that he has ordered made an entire set of bedroom furniture just his size, which he intends to give him as a present, to be shipped by sea (the Camel, *of course) to Virginia and then overland to the dwarf's home. I had to stop Judge Lord from having a window cut in the wall that would be just the right height for the small fellow to see through! We are abustle.*

The judge himself has checked into a schedule of lectures and parties, for he intends you shall be fully entertained. He has even asked Mr. Mitchell if any astronomical events are to be observed during your stay. My dear, I think Judge Lord half intends to keep you here. I mean FOREVER. *I mean* with *him.*

But I would not stay forever, if I were you. It would be a pity for you to have to look across the street every day at the house where you and Captain Ahab made a couple. And besides, I have never seen you more blooming. The seaside agrees with you and with the dear little boy. There is no doubt of that. You have no need to couple up yourself again, and I advise you to stay clear of any such arrangements.

Yours,
Hilda Maynard

P.S. I have been sent to the butcher to tell him to save bones for the dog! Judge has asked me to make a Kentucky jam cake—Lord knows why, but I haven't the faintest idea how. Would you make one, dear, and bring it with you?

P.P.S. We are to have a most festive dinner the second night Frannie is here. Everyone is on standby—the Mitchells, I mean, and we have invited the gaoler because he is so much alone since Betsy's death. You knew that, didn't you? Her fifth childbirth, and the fever took her, last March, and the little one, too.

CHAPTER 140 🐢 **Preparations**

LEAVE THIS surf-song for town! Yes, tomorrow I must. Since the *Delight* came in, almost a year ago, I have been into Nantucket but once for each season. Mrs. Maynard's preparations! Her caution! Why should I marry the judge? He is an excellent friend as he is. Let friends increase! I have had enough of husbands. Justice and I are complete, and Frannie will make us but more complete.

How this dress hangs on me! I have grown thin walking by the sea, looking at the stars. And my hair curls as wild as a gypsy's. Well, I have been a gypsy of the sea. And worse.

Ah needle, ah thimble, dear friends. Here I sit and sew in the window room, my bedroom now—Justice and Frannie will be upstairs, each with a window. But I! Oh, I am greedy for light and windows. And I have them. My library is my sewing room and my bedroom. With quilts for curtains, the room is warm even on a cold winter's night, and I burn wood—dear though it is—as I please, during the day, curtains wide open. The judge says I shall burn up my fortune heating this room, but I don't care.

What a tool is a needle, so bright and quick, so obedient and willing.

Town tomorrow. This scene of water and sky, the coziness of my room, the colors of my quilts and rugs, the books, that lamp with the egg-shaped alabaster bowl, will have disappeared; and this contentment as well? Where we choose to be, where we choose to be—we have that power to determine our lives. We cannot reel time backward or forward, but we can take ourselves to the place that defines our being.

The idea abides with me like faith. I will be happy to return to this *place* where domesticity marries the cosmos.

And how will I find Frannie to be? May I make her as welcome in my home as she made me in hers. Oh, little dancing dot on the Island, oh, glad child of four, it was your joy that sparked me to life.

CHAPTER 141   Frannie

W HEN I GREETED Frannie at the wharf, my eye recoiled from her corrugated cheeks, for I had not remembered Frannie as disfigured from the smallpox, though I knew its mark was pitted into her face. But I had remembered only her beautiful spirit, not the disfigurement. She registered my recoil, I know she did, and accepted it as a response I could not help.

When she drew back from my embrace, her face shining, she said again, "Una, Una, Una. I am so glad to be here." The simple words conveyed all, and I could not speak in return for the stoppage in my throat.

I dropped to my knees and embraced David, just as I had when we parted at the steamboat, but this time without reserve, and with his short arms, he returned my embrace without embarrassment. He and Justice were friends at once, with Justice asking to see the wolf skin.

Frannie was slight, as though in her frame as well as on her face she carried the blight of a terrible illness survived. I had not thought her especially small when I was sixteen, but I saw on the wharf that she would be forever slight, as surely as David would be forever short. They were perfectly comfortable with one another, and, indeed, Frannie had a sense of sureness about her that her letters to me had not conveyed in the least. I remembered that, after all, she was Agatha's daughter, and never has there been a woman more self-reliant than my aunt.

But David contradicted that hypothesis with this speech: "See what I've made of your cousin? She was a mouse till she traveled with me for a guide. Now she's a proper girl, ain't she? and not her mother's mouse."

Frannie laughed and said she was just the same as always, and in many ways she seemed so to me. "But it was a wonderful journey," she added, her eyes shining at David. I remembered my own healing journey through the Kentucky forest with the diminutive guide.

Frannie was quieter than her mother, but there was nothing shy about her. Assurance—yes, Frannie spoke with assurance, but quietly. I did not need to worry about making Frannie feel welcome. She came to me with the conviction that she would be in the right place.

JUST AS THE JUDGE and Mrs. Maynard had planned, we had our grand dinner, Mitchells and all. Around Judge Lord's table, beautifully elongated with leaves and bedecked with silver and china as for a wedding, the talk turned to the slavery question and the rights of women. I was surprised to see the extent to which David's sympathies had enlarged. It seemed an issue on which he and Frannie saw eye to eye.

"I understand Lucretia Mott is from Nantucket," Frannie said.

"We are famous for our independent women as well as for our intrepid whalers," Maria answered. She had already invited Frannie, almost as soon as she met her, as she had done with me, to visit the rooftop observatory one night. I instantly fantasized a scene in which by accident Frannie, not Maria, discovered a comet telescopically.

"And we are famous for our schools," William Mitchell put in.

"And for our wealth," Mary Starbuck said, with dancing eyes.

Somehow she seemed so unworldly, her comment made us all laugh, even the gaoler.

Both Frannie and Mary made efforts to draw Isaac, the gaoler, into the conversation as much as possible. Judge Lord had seated Isaac between the two women, so that on his left was a woman whose face was all light and beauty (though I knew her history had not left her unmarked) and on his right was a young woman whose face was pitted and furrowed by her past illness. (Though lonely, Frannie had had a much more sheltered and fortuitous life than Mary.) I admired how Isaac spoke to each with the same courtesy and interest. In truth, anyone surely would look past Frannie's skin to her spirit after five minutes of conversation.

I was surprised to hear Frannie ask Isaac a question that had often troubled me, when I first knew him. "Does it not prey upon you," she asked, "to turn the key upon another soul?"

The judge (I was seated to his right) interposed: "What would we do without gaol? We would all be the victims of criminals. People in gaol are not innocents."

"Which I believe," Isaac said. "But nonetheless, it does trouble me at times."

Mary said, "They will want a lighthouse keeper at Sankaty in a few months. You could go there, if your present work troubles you."

I chimed in then, urging him to consider a move. In terms of the liberality of his nature, Isaac reminded me of Uncle Torch, who had found the lighthouse work so congenial. Of course, Isaac would be a pleasant addition to our little community at the east end of Nantucket Island.

Frannie told Isaac how I and also she, for a longer period, had lived at lighthouses. "It's a more authentic experiment in self-reliance," she said, "than Mr. Thoreau's at Walden. If you are in charge of the place."

Maria Mitchell spoke of the interesting fossil beds at Sankaty, and the judge offered to put in a recommendation for Isaac with the government. We sounded like a colloquy of blackbirds, each putting in his note. But I did not know how Isaac Starbuck could manage his four little children alone at the Lighthouse, unless one of his younger sisters came back to help.

After the roast beef, the question of how we should occupy ourselves arose, and the judge said that the next evening the abolitionists were having testimonials from former slaves.

David showed a great interest in this, seconded by Frannie, and I, too, felt drawn to attend.

WHEN WE WENT to that meeting, I was disappointed to see that all the speakers were men, and I said as much to Frannie, who ardently agreed. But David was bouncing with excitement. "It's him," he said, pointing to a young black man with chiseled features. "The one I let go. It's Frederick Douglass."

"Is it?" said the judge. "He's in very distinguished company. That's William Lloyd Garrison, the famous orator."

I wondered if the black man knew anything of Susan and determined to ask him at the end of the meeting. He started off his speech at the podium rather haltingly, but then, as a backwoods preacher would say, the spirit came to him, and he became one with the audience. Drawing upon his experiences, Douglass made us laugh and cry at the spectacle of man's inhumanity to man. He thrilled us with how he physically defended himself when he was sent to a "slave breaker." Even as he spoke in Nantucket, he could have been snatched up by a bounty hunter and returned to his master. David sat up on his knees, the better to hear and see. He was very excited that someone he had singled out as extraordinary was a featured speaker in a lecture hall.

Frederick Douglass was exceptionally fine-looking, with a splendid timbre to his voice and very natural and expressive gestures. All of that combined with his narration to mesmerize us and to fill us with a smoldering indignation that such a speaker could be owned, as property, by any other human. It was on this idea that Garrison focused as soon as Douglass sat down.

"Is this a man or a thing?" Garrison thundered.

And the audience responded, "A man!"

"Is this a man or chattel?" Garrison quizzed. (Even the *question*, that Garrison would frame it so, pointing at the handsome black man, embarrassed me.)

And the reply roared, "A man!"

And all the other dignified speakers rose in turn to thank and compliment Frederick Douglass. The image of my mother ripping the bounty posters from the side of the steamboat came to me many times that evening, and with the image came a surge of pride in her action. While I felt myself stirred as never before to do something practical— money, if nothing else—about the outrages of my time, when I looked at Frannie, I saw that she was aflame with it.

Frannie turned to me and said, "I have been in Nantucket for two days, and I have found my life's work."

When I tried to approach Douglass, such a press milled about him that I despaired. At that moment, I was approached by a somewhat familiar face.

"I am your neighbor," he said.

"My neighbor?" I felt confused. The judge was my neighbor.

"Your neighbor at 'Sconset. Perhaps you have moved away? I'm just off the ferry today."

The woodcarver! Yes. Tall, thin, a lined face, graying, tight curls. "I have forgotten your name," I confessed.

"Avalon. Robben Avalon. I carve figureheads for ships."

"I remember that well enough," I answered. "You showered me with warm water."

"And I remember that. Have you moved back to town, then?"

"Nay. I own the house at 'Sconset. I have had a barn built, and I shall never leave."

He looked at me curiously. "You were trying to speak to Douglass?"

"I wanted to ask him about a woman, a former slave, Susan Spenser. She went back to the Deep South to get her mother."

"I will squeeze in for you, and bring you word."

"I'm very eager to hear."

"What age is Susan?"

"A little younger than I."

"But I can't guess your age," he smiled.

He disappeared in the crowd. I watched him carefully. His body, thin as a whittled stick, was well suited to slipping between people, scarcely disturbing them. His dress seemed odd to me, though he wore ordinary trousers and a shirt. Then I realized they were exactly the same shade of charcoal gray, almost black. They flowed together, bottom and top, in a way that accentuated his leanness.

When Robben Avalon reached Douglass, I could see Douglass shaking his head in the negative, and I knew the request was fruitless. Douglass glanced around as though to locate me. When his gaze swept over me, I felt an electric sizzling of my nerves. I felt that I had been looked at by a great man.

Soon Mr. Avalon returned to confirm that Frederick Douglass had not crossed paths with Susan, and David Poland came up to us. He and Mr. Avalon shook hands in a rather serious manner, David reaching up and tall Mr. Avalon leaning down. "David and I are old friends," I explained. "He has guided my cousin here all the way from Wisconsin."

"I'm back from a trip myself," Mr. Avalon answered.

"Where you been?" David asked. Was there a trace of sneer in his voice?

"Italy."

"Amidst the revolution?" I asked. "I've received a letter from a friend there."

"I stayed only briefly. Then I went to Greece."

"Foreign places," David said. "On the other side of the Atlantic."

"Both Italy and Greece are on the Mediterranean, actually."

"Slave trader?" David seemed ready to bristle.

"Not at all. A slave trader would be an unlikely member of this audience, wouldn't he? I went to see the marble statues." He nodded toward Frederick Douglass. "None were so striking as that former slave, a living man. I'm a woodcarver. I wanted to see the art that survived all the politics and philosophy of Greece and Rome."

"Art!" David exclaimed incredulously.

"Excuse me, please," Avalon replied and moved off toward Douglass again.

"That's a strange fellow," David opined.

I looked down at him and smiled. He seemed to forget that to some he might appear to be a "strange fellow." I liked the woodcarver.

One of the great, good things about the electrifying effect that such a speaker as Frederick Douglass can have on a group is that it causes the people to speak to one another. Even the judge, jolted from his judicial reserve, had joined the knot of men: I saw him turn to introduce himself to Mr. Avalon. Soon the judge was much more animated than I usually saw him—perhaps Mr. Avalon had chanced, after mentioning marble statuary, to speak of porcelain.

LATER THAT NIGHT, when the lights of the town were low, Frannie and I accompanied Maria to her observatory atop the Union Pacific Bank. When Frannie peered through the powerful telescope at the moon, she mused quietly, "Her face is pockmarked, like mine."

"And yet she shines," Maria said.

The moonshine lay on our shoulders like epaulets, on the curve of our skirts arcing from our waists, on three women standing on a railed platform built over a roof.

THE VERY NEXT AFTERNOON, Frannie went off to an abolition meeting, and every day thereafter. I became afraid that she would not want to return to the quiet and isolation of 'Sconset with me when there was so much reformist fervor in town, and I said as much to Austin Lord. "Let her stay here, then," he said. "She is quick and tidy in her habits. She can be my second housekeeper. A judge needs an assistant housekeeper."

When I asked Frannie, at the end of the week, how she was disposed, she replied, "I long to be with you, but the meetings are here. Let me visit 'Sconset and see how my ardor for the work fares there. If it lasts."

By the work, Frannie meant abolition, not housekeeping.

Her answer seemed a sensible one to me.

FRANNIE WAS DELIGHTED with her room above the sea, and she enjoyed all the pleasantness of nature, but she had no passion for it.

Our best times were when we sat on a blanket, watched the waves, and talked. When we were girls together, we had gotten along splendidly, accepting each other simply as the children of the family, and at 'Sconset we both felt happy again to be kinswomen. Frannie took fine responsibility for herself and for the household, so I had very few extra duties because of her. Instead, those household chores that I did were made lighter by her help and conversation. But I knew that these charms of sea and shore, of familial intimacy and cooperation, lacked excitement for her. She had experienced all this before.

For myself, I continued to savor everything, those days when Frannie first came to 'Sconset. My delight was to see only people I loved with all my heart, and animals as well! Our horses, goats, chickens— Pog the dog above all other animals! Sea, sky, sun, stars! The vegetation around me, my house, my stable in the dell, the things that inhabited my rooms with me—why should such simple items be enough? But they were. And every day the flavor of them grew sweeter and more nourishing. I loved the turning of the day to night, the slower turning of summer toward late summer and toward fall. Love of the passage of time and of all of us caught in time's flow evoked in me a deep movement, like the largest waves that start deep down in the ocean and roll inexorably to satisfaction.

The Woodcarver's Studio

I visited Robben Avalon for a tour of the wooden women almost as soon as we returned to 'Sconset. When I complained that they had no expression, Robben replied that expression could not be seen at a distance—only the larger form of the sculpture.

"Still, they are incomplete," I said, hoping my honest response was welcome. "I think that their facial features are too typical. Was it that way with the Greek statues?"

"As the civilization became more decadent, they sank to realism—wrinkles and warts. In the most classical period, everyone was idealized." How pleasant he looked as he spoke. He did not mind my questions.

"And you prefer?" I asked.

"The ideal. And you?"

I did admire his work. It was a most strange experience to walk among these figures. Some seemed like dryads with only a face materializing out of wood. For others the upper torso leaned out at me, and I might touch a woody shoulder or cheek. Many were in various stages of being painted, and I loved the vividness of the colors, which had an extra depth to them so as to longer withstand the salt water. With the completed figureheads, the colors were sealed under shiny varnish. Such ruby reds and emerald greens—as rich and mysterious as jewels! But the faces of the women, even of the completed ones, were disappointingly lacking in expression.

"I prefer the real to the ideal," I answered, but I also felt real admiration for his work. And I believed I had been granted a privilege in being admitted to his studio.

"I would be interested in sculpting the actual features of Frederick Douglass," Robben Avalon added, with pleasant quickness. "In him, the ideal and the real are conjoined."

"As they are in Mary Starbuck."

He did not reply.

This conversation with Robben Avalon reminded me of ones I had had with Margaret Fuller about the nature of art, but in this case, Robben was himself an artist. As with Frederick Douglass, his statements were of particular interest to me because of his own experience. I thought of Margaret's saying I preferred the poem to the poet, a preference that gave, finally, but an incomplete picture of the poem, and decided she was right. Or at least I was inconsistent, for it was not the actual words that made me prefer Douglass on slavery to Garrison, or Robben Avalon on art to Margaret Fuller, but my knowledge of the history of the speaker of the words.

Of my own history, to Robben, I had no desire to speak. He knew, of course, that I had been married to Captain Ahab, and he had died. Yet from the beginning and in all my long future with Robben, I felt, oddly, that despite my reticence he, like Captain Ahab, thoroughly knew me. He knew me artistically, intuitively, without a factual history—the contours of my shape. He knew who I was, without the clutter of details. And, so I discovered, I knew him intuitively, too, or at least knew what seemed his essence.

I knew him to be lonely, something of a misfit, passionate, joyful about his carving and his garden; a person of integrity and concern for justice, a man spiritual but not religious, seasoned with a dash of pride, or even arrogance. Save for the defect I have mentioned, I thought Robben's work quite wonderful. Like the judge, he was a perfect neighbor, I felt, and soon-to-be friend.

A FEW DAYS after our return to 'Sconset, our townfolk began to come to see us. I was surprised, however, to note one day Austin Lord's buggy not stopping at my house but continuing to my neighbor's. That the judge and the artist had much in common surprised me. Yet, there was the judge's buggy passing me by and stopping at Robben Avalon's wooden hitching post (a beautifully carved horsehead). The judge's horse reached out his neck to sniff the impostor horse, and I called Frannie to watch. The real horse, finding no familiar scent, tossed his head and rolled his eye. We both laughed.

"Una," Frannie said, watching the judge and Robben heartily shake hands, "I do feel restless here."

"Return to town with the judge, if you wish," I said, smilingly. "This is a decision that conveys no hurt to me, if you wish to make an arrangement with the judge. I am not your gaoler."

"No," she replied. "But here comes the gaoler."

"Sure enough," I reported aloud. "In a borrowed buggy, full of children. Look, he stops to visit Mary Starbuck."

I turned from my window. Suddenly it seemed odd for my neighbors on both sides to have visitors while I had none. For the first time, I felt lonely at 'Sconset.

"Let's cook," Frannie said energetically. "We will smell so good that they'll all come running." She picked up a bowl, filled it with apples from the barrel, and immediately began to cut them up. I put water to boil, got out cinnamon, cloves, nutmeg, lard, flour, sugar, salt, saleratus, vinegar, and all the other things for apple pies. We both laughed happily. How easy it is, we thought, to make a decision, to implement a remedy, to act.

Ah, it was the we of us—Frannie and Una, Una and Frannie—so beautiful was our accord as we turned to the making of apple pie.

"You know," I said, "I have never found Hamlet convincing."

Frannie laughed out loud at the unexpected nature of my pronouncement. Then she asked, "Why is that?"

"All that hesitation. A person would either kill the king or go to another country."

"Hesitation is more natural for some of us than it is for you, Una."

"What is your favorite play?" I asked.

I was surprised to find that Frannie was nothing like the reader of literature that I was. That difference made no difference at all in the harmony of our spirits. May every woman have such a kinswoman or friend. Frannie had read *Hamlet,* but no other Shakespeare.

"What I like is for you to tell me stories," she said. "Someday you must write it all down."

"Do you think so?" I asked. I was stunned. "I have enjoyed writing down a few thoughts. I do it when I want a moment to live forever."

"Not philosophy," she said. "Not about time or stars. The things you've seen and done. The people you've met. You describe people very accurately, I think."

Again, I felt as though I had been jolted. I stopped my cooking preparations and sat down at the table.

"Frannie, what an idea," I said.

"Don't you love reading? How is that so different from writing?"

I said nothing, but my mind seemed to hold the night sky streaming with fast-moving constellations. I was dizzy with it.

"Go now," she said. "Right now. Take your quill and paper, sit on the sand, and write."

"I believe I could." I felt stunned, mesmerized.

I did exactly as she told me to do.

WHEN I SAT upon the beach, I wondered where I should begin. I had thought before of Sir Philip Sidney's muse's injunction: Look in your heart and write. But I could only look at the sand and the waves and the bright sky. Finally I picked up one grain of sand, and I wrote the little description of putting it in my mouth that I have included near the beginning of this long narrative that you now read.

That was all I could do that day. I stayed there on the sand, on that mild, blue day, a long time. Perhaps, I thought, I have made this solitude and peace for myself so that I *can* write. Is such a prerequisite to writing? Surely not for all, but perhaps yes, for me.

While my quill was poised in the air, not writing, I formed my first principle as a storyteller. I will not be governed by time. Time does not march; it swirls and leaps. Time is a dancer, not a soldier. And the second: adherence to fact is slavery. Think how Shakespeare distorted, compressed, rearranged historical events in his history plays. Such license would be mine, if I wrote. When I pieced a quilt, I did not place the pieces in chronological order, the oldest in the upper-left-hand corner! A pleasing design, color, beauty—could those be my business?

Spangled, *spangled*—as I looked at the sun on the water, that is what I thought, and it seemed a good word to me, a chosen and accurate word, such as fiction might admit. And I thought of other words that I had loved for their truth and beauty.

BY THE TIME I had climbed the steps to the edge of my yard, the odor of cinnamon and cooked apples, the fragrance of piecrust, reached my nostrils. I hurried. Seeing the pies on the table, I exclaimed, "Ah!" and then laughed, for all around the table, some sitting, some standing, were Austin Lord and Robben, Mary and Isaac, assorted children, and Frannie with the knife in her hand, ready to cut.

Tнат dаy, as he ate Frannie's pie, Isaac's heart was strangely warmed. Frannie did leave 'Sconset to work in Nantucket town as the judge's housekeeper (and to attend to what she had identified that remarkable night as her life's work), and her residence in the town made it possible for Isaac to see her often. Their religious and political views were compatible, both being Unitarians and abolitionists, and Frannie loved his four golden children.

Because of Frannie's distaste for his work as gaoler, Isaac did apply for and eventually secure the job at Sankaty Light, and then he begged Frannie to marry him and to live at the lighthouse with him and his family. She accepted the second idea—to live at the lighthouse with him—but not the first. I would have predicted it would be the other way around, because she was truly devoted to the abolitionist cause, which centered in the town. Perhaps I had spoken to Frannie too convincingly of the bondage I had felt to Kit, once I was married to him.

"Would you marry again?" she asked me.

"Whom?" I replied, startled.

She only smiled.

Frannie wrote to her mother about the arrangement with Isaac she wished to make—to live with him at Sankaty but not to marry—and Aunt Agatha replied that though her own marriage had been exceptionally happy, of course the marriage of her sister (my mother) had been troubled, and that Frannie should make her own decision about the institutions of chastity and marriage. It touched me that Frannie wished so much to spare her mother any pang or anxiety that she would consult her on such a delicate question before she herself took action. (Frannie's frank consultation gave me a pang of old guilt.)

The matter of the distance between Sankaty Light and the Unitarian-abolitionists on Orange Street Frannie addressed by asking me to buy her a fast horse, which I did. Soon (after a number of falls into the sand of the beach) Frannie rode pell-mell, astride, past the cranberry bogs and scrubby heath, down the road to town, whenever she had abolition work to do. Frannie made no pretense at marriage, even when she became pregnant. Though Mrs. Maynard had a fit of protest and both Mary and I cautioned Frannie not to ride, pregnant, at such breakneck speed, she ignored us. Her child was a healthy girl, and Frannie named her Liberty, in memory of my own lost child.

ONE SPRING DAY, about a year after Frannie's baby was born, Justice and I were picnicking on the beach when suddenly we saw dolphins leaping out of the ocean not far offshore. One, two, three, four, five gray bodies arced into the air. They challenged each other, leaping higher and higher, and then disappeared altogether when Frannie and the five golden children came through the sea grass toward the beach.

Frannie was sitting astride the horse, the baby at her bosom, with the two smaller Isaac Starbuck offspring riding fore and aft. The two older stepchildren led the horse. They were such bonny children and the horse was so willing and nice that I thought I hardly ever had seen such a surprising and pretty sight. None of the children wore hats and their golden hair sparkled in the sunlight. Baby Liberty's hair was a different hue from that of the other children, having something of Viking red mixed with the gold, the inheritance from her red-haired grandfather. For all of the pleasure and happiness radiating from Frannie I could not help but notice how rough her visage was amidst all of the petal-smooth children.

I went to take the baby so that Frannie could dismount, and Justice held the horse's head. "Look out to sea," Justice told the children. "The dolphins are breaching."

"We saw you through the spyglass," Frannie said. "We decided to intrude."

"Welcome intrusion," I said.

Frannie said, "I am pure joy today."

At that moment Liberty began to whimper.

"Give her back to me," Frannie said. "She's not quite finished her lunch. Untie the basket. I've brought goodies for all of us."

She seated herself on our blanket and nursed her beautiful baby. For us, she brought slices of Kentucky jam cake. "Your receipt, Una," she said. When I tasted the cake, it tasted exactly like mine. I thought of our mothers' shared plum jam, and vinegar eggs, and other receipts. Our connection continued theirs, and with baby Liberty at her breast, I felt that love could spiral down the decades. My heart was heavy with longing when I thought of having another child myself.

My son had taken to the baby almost as much as I. When she'd finished her lunch, under a discreet fold of Frannie's blouse, Justice asked to hold her. He tucked her up against his chest just the way Frannie had held her, as though he, too, would nurse the baby.

Looking into her eyes, Justice said, "She loves her brother, doesn't she? Yes, she does," laying claim to his cousin with the logic of his heart.

But soon baby Liberty wanted her liberty and toddled off to join her half siblings on the beach. I was surprised that Justice was content to stay with Frannie and me, but he watched the baby with an unself-conscious smile. "She's partway between being a baby and being a real child," he pronounced.

When she plopped down on the border of wet sand, Justice saw immediately that an incoming wave, though small, would be enough to topple her, and he ran to lift her up before I could shout to the other children.

He raised her up to sit on his shoulder, while the ocean ran around his ankles. She waved one hand gleefully, pleased with her perspective atop the boy-tower. Their two heads conspired in contrast—black and gold.

Just then, a slick gray body arced into the air far out to sea, like a gray crescent moon. We watched as three other dolphins, close in, breached and continued to cavort. How heavily they slapped back into the water. From her shoulder seat, Liberty smacked her little palms together in response to the dolphins.

ONLY WEEKS LATER, the child had toddled into the sea, despite the watchful eye of her mother and her four half sisters and brothers, and drowned.

The oldest Isaac Starbuck child came riding on the fast horse, and Mary and I went in the buggy as rapidly as we could. We feared that Frannie would throw herself from the cliff, so Mary and I took her from Sankaty to stay with us at 'Sconset. We were completely vigilant, taking turns watching her door all night. Only Justice was admitted to the room. When I looked in, he sat beside Frannie's bed holding her hand. His face was like a weeping wall. His swollen lips contorted silently. None of us could have been the least prepared, and my heart was wrung for Liberty and for Frannie and wrung again for my boy's anguish. Justice had to bear what I would have borne, so many years ago at the Island Lighthouse, had Frannie died of the smallpox.

Frannie refused to see Isaac or any of her stepchildren, which I thought was unfair and unfortunate, but Frannie's extreme state of mind was not to be argued with. She screamed at the mention of Isaac's name. I was about to write to her mother to come when Frannie became calmer and announced she would move back into town. She said she could never bear again to live at the lighthouse, or with Isaac and his children. Since she and Isaac were not legally married, the decision was available for Frannie. Still struggling with grief, my heart went out to Isaac and the injustice dealt him. For a time, one of his sisters came to help him.

In town, Frannie kept house again for the judge, until she exchanged letters with the antislavery league that resulted in her attaching herself to travel with Frederick Douglass's party.

My cousin and I have the indissoluble link of shared childhood between us, and we keep up a regular correspondence. She is always alert for any news of Susan, and I am grateful to her for that as well as for a thousand other kindnesses. But never again has there been the bliss of connection between Frannie and me that I felt the day we watched the dolphins. Of the many interesting observations Frannie has written to me is this one, of Frederick Douglass: "He does not look at my skin, my face, and think 'disfigured,' any more than I look at him and think 'black.' No I think 'Great Soul' and 'True Warrior' when I listen to him address the crowds."

Each in our own way, we sought relief from our loss. I took Justice up on the roof walk, where I did find for myself consolation and connection. But Justice merely gazed across the darkness to the lonely Sankaty Light.

Gradually, over months, his grief lessened, and he and Jim spoke enthusiastically, to my dismay, of going to sea someday soon.

AFTER THE PUBLICATION of his book *The Narrative of the Life of Frederick Douglass: An American Slave,* Frannie helped the Quakers raise money in America to purchase Douglass's freedom. She also worked on his newspaper *The North Star,* in which he wrote: "Right is of no Sex—Truth is of no Color . . ." Frannie attended the first women's rights convention in the United States, with Aunt Agatha, in 1848 at Seneca Falls, New York, where Douglass demanded that women be given the right to vote.

SOME SIX MONTHS after Frannie left the Sankaty Light—to take up *his* history—Isaac began to call again upon Mary Starbuck. Neither she nor I had any doubt that he was courting her. Mary had always had a shining serenity to her countenance, but now she began to shine with life renewed. When the proposal came, she accepted.

They were married in the Unitarian Church, to which Mary transferred her church membership, and I thought there was no emblem more appropriate than its golden dome, presiding over the beginning of their life together.

With the *height* of the lighthouse, her new home, Mary fell in love as much as I had done at age fourteen with my Lighthouse tower. She loved, too, the service to the light, and the fidelity that it required. She had had no desire to stay in the home that she had shared with the first Mr. Starbuck. The cottage was a house, I told Mary, with its low stone wall, that seemed married to the land. I told her that a lighthouse is married to the air.

I was truly happy for both Isaac and Mary (she had not even to change her last name, since it was already Starbuck), but now I felt much more alone, since my neighbor to the south was gone, and her house stood empty. Increasingly, Justice and I turned to our neighbor to the north, Robben Avalon, for company.

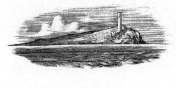

CHAPTER 144   🜚   What Has Proved to Be
a Last Visit

JUDGE LORD rode out to visit with Justice and me, and with
Robben, every three or four days. He took over the horse I had bought
for Frannie, saying that if she could learn to ride, he could. But he was
really too big for her "lady's" horse, and I persuaded him to write to
David Poland to purchase him a Tennessee walking horse and to bring
it up from the South.

David not only brought the horse to Nantucket on the ferry but
also rode the animal out to 'Sconset himself. As we watched his approach, David seemed as small as a monkey atop the tall animal. I
noticed David's teeth shining in his beard in a big bow of a smile,
whether with pleasure at seeing us again or in self-conscious amusement
at how he looked aboard a Tennessee walking horse, I could not tell.
The animal's running walk was a marvel to see coming down the road.

Judge Lord hurried to meet them and actually held up his arms to
David, as though he were a child, to help him dismount, so high up
he sat, at fully sixteen hands. And David jumped into the judge's hands
without embarrassment. I saw, in general, that David was much more
easy with all aspects of himself and his life than he had ever been
before.

"It's the furniture," he explained to me one night by my hearth.
"That and my house. I have a world I'm normal in."

"I have a roof walk," I replied.

He smiled and nodded, knowing my explanation would come later.

David would take no pay from the judge for his trouble of delivering
the horse, though I urged him to do so; he insisted that the miniature
furniture had already paid him enough. His sister had, indeed, remarried, he said, and he had built himself a small place of his own. It was
literally small—everything to his scale. I liked to imagine how someone
lost in the Virginia woods might feel that he had stumbled into fairyland
when he came to David's little house and how when bearded David
himself emerged such a person might turn tail and run. David stayed
at my house in the upstairs bedroom across from Justice.

It comforted me to have David in the house. I liked to see him and

Justice standing together, one a bearded, short man, the other a curly-headed, beanstalk boy, talking to each other with the respect of equals. So we all are—equals—I mused, and what does stature, or skin color, or age have to do with it?

To my surprise, after their gruff beginning at the Frederick Douglass Atheneum speech, Robben and David now got along very well. Robben requested David to serve as a model for him, and David said Robben might do the sculpture, if he would do it at my house instead of in his studio.

Robben agreed, and so we all got to see the image of David emerge from a short cypress stump. Day by day we watched Robben chisel and carve a remarkable sculpture, about half David's real size. He was seated in a chair with a high back. Not on David's head, but in an incision in the chair back, Robben carved a suggestion of a crown. David's short arms and legs were represented accurately and proportionately, but they were scarcely to be noticed. It was the face, the expressiveness of the large eyes, that drew the viewer. It made my heart sing. With this piece, Robben passed into creating or suggesting emotion and intellect of an individualized nature in his figures. And yet, there was something unmistakably idealized or romanticized about the figure that rendered it not false but more true to the vision of the carver.

"You like it, Una," Robben said, "because I am absent from the figure. This sort of work requires the artist to give himself to his subject. It's a Keatsian aesthetic—a negative capability."

But I thought there was a union of subject and artist in the carving.

David spent long hours happily contemplating his smaller artistic self. Near the end of David's visit, we spread a blanket for a celebratory picnic at the edge of the grass. The guest of honor was the statue of David, seated permanently in his chair, a centerpiece for the bread and meat, while we all lolled about on the blanket. We were all there— Mary and Isaac, all the children, the judge, and Maria Mitchell and her father.

At the picnic, Robben asked David what we should do with the sculpture.

"I'd like you to make me a drawing of it," he said. "Can you do that?"

"Yes," Robben answered. "A quick sketch would be best." And he asked Justice to run into his house for pencil and paper.

"After that, I'll have the drawing," David said. "I'd like to give the sculpture to Una and let her keep it close to her hearth, as a decoration."

I was surprised. But moved and pleased. "Our first conversations were by the hearth," I said. "In Kentucky, when you came to my cabin the second time. That was a rocking chair, though."

"That makes no difference," David said firmly.

And of course he was right. Again I thought, that night as I lay in bed, of how David surprised me in his ability to evolve.

WE INSTALLED the icon at the hearth—David was very satisfied with it—and he said he planned to leave Nantucket soon. "Now if I never see you again," he said to me, "you will have a way to remember me and think of me."

CHAPTER 145   A Song

HIS WORDS haunted me. I did not believe that I would not see him again—why shouldn't he come to Nantucket again, having done so twice?—and yet David's words had the resonance of truth. I felt more pain at parting from him than I ever had before.

As soon as David left, I went to Robben's studio to talk about the sculpture. Robben said that his little wooden piece of a small American person named David Poland was in some ways a response to the grandeur of the standing, marble figure of Michelangelo's *David*. He said that the idea that he was claiming his own territory and that he had a right to his own vision had come to him as he worked, not from the outset. "But doing the piece has changed me, Una," he added. "And changed what I want to do."

With my heart thudding like a mallet against my breastbone, I told Robben I had taken up writing, at Frannie's encouragement on the apple-pie day. "I have sailed between Scylla and Charybdis, right at the first," I said.

"What do you mean?"

"The two hardest things in my life have been the deaths of my first baby and of my mother." Suddenly I was overwhelmed with grief. I covered my face with my hands, peeked through my fingers, and blurted, "Robben, in all the universe, there is nothing so dead as a dead baby!" I erupted in sobs. Through my spasm, I heard my friend crooning, "Una, Una." Eventually I calmed myself and continued, "I wrote about them first. I was afraid that if I saw them looming in the distance of my narrative my courage to move forward would fail me."

"The death of the second Liberty," he observed gently, "would not be much easier to tell. Or Ahab's." When I made no reply, he continued, "Every week I will cook you a pie—tasty as Frannie's—to remind you of your commitment." He winked at me and added that he was an excellent baker.

He was indeed, and his creations over the following weeks were not only delicious, but very pleasing to the eye. There was an intensity about Robben's mind, a keenness—though it was tuned to an artistic rather than a scientific pitch—that reminded me of Giles, and, of course, the baking reminded me of Kit. I have already said that in his understanding not only of my moods but also of who I was, he resembled Ahab. In short, I found much of what I had loved in other men in him. While I developed for him the most ardent friendship, I experienced none of the physical excitement that had drawn me to both Kit and Ahab. Still I began to feel a physical restlessness.

One lonely night—Justice was away at the Mitchells'—I went up on the rooftop, looking for solace in the stars. I wanted to feel again that I was a part of some large entity. Under Maria's tutelage, I could easily map the sky now, but I only wanted the glitter. With my hand on the rough chimney, I dwelt among stars, and my heart became quiet and happy. It was no philosophical idea that brought peace. With the stars, as had occurred that first night on the roof walk of my new home at 'Sconset, all of my inward activity grew still. I resolved into Being. No longer Una, I was one with all that was.

Then, strangely in the air, I heard singing. I knew that voice. It was Mary Starbuck. She sang the old Shaker hymn " 'Tis a gift to be simple; 'tis a gift to be free." And I knew that she was standing at the top of the Sankaty Light, singing. Her singing floated like filaments through the universe.

Out at sea, I saw the fire from a whaler, her two try-pots joined in the distance to make a blazing red spot.

CHAPTER 146   A Squeeze of the Hand

EVERY DAY, I knocked on Robben's door, or he on mine. I felt a happiness at our being merely in the same room that transcended any specific language. Strange it was that as I used language, as I shaped it into re-creations of people and places, I also felt its inadequacy. It could serve to describe the past; it could not capture what I presently felt.

Sometimes I wrote in the woodworking studio while Robben chiseled. I liked the sound of his tool moving into the wood, the thunk of the mallet. When he sharpened the chisels, even the grindstone on the metal pleased me. "It zizzles," I told him. "Sizzles?" "No, zizzles my nerves."

He was carving a bust of Frederick Douglass, working in a deep ebony, which he said was a very hard wood, and it was quite beautiful. I asked him why he had made it slightly larger than life. "Because Frederick Douglass is slightly larger than life," he answered. And I felt deep satisfaction in his answer.

"And why did you make David's statue smaller than he is?"

"I was a relative beginner then. But still it was right. To show that it didn't matter."

One day when I was wandering the beach, looking at the clouds, I wished that Robben could chisel a bust of Ahab. But of course he had never seen him. Perhaps it was for me to embody Ahab—in words. I looked at the clouds and saw Ahab's visage there. I was surprised when I went inside that Robben promptly asked me if I would like him to make a bust of Justice. Of course I said yes.

So I would have a version of my Ahab, for Justice resembled him, but restored and idealized. And I smiled, for in the Justice bust I would also have the bust of myself, which long ago I had wished that Robben would want to make.

"The boy's curls are like yours," Robben said.

"His face is much like his father's."

"I love doing the hair of Frederick Douglass," he said. The cross-hatch marks did make the wooden hair look crinkled, like Douglass's. "My own hair feels as I would imagine Douglass's to feel." He put his left hand into his hair. "I've always thought I was partly black." He continued to chisel away. So matter-of-fact! An idea that would certainly scandalize most! My body flared.

I put down my pen, walked to him, and held out my hand. "Robben," I said, and smiled.

He stopped still, his mallet poised above the head of the chisel. Many expressions passed over his face. I saw alarm. I saw a flicker of sadness, for me. I saw a warm affection. Slowly he put down the tool. Slowly he held out his hand to me. I took it.

He waited a moment, then said, "Tell me, Una, truly. How does my hand feel to you? Now?"

"It's cold," I said. "It's a bit moist." I laughed, for the description did not sound complimentary. The flare of romance was already settling back into friendship.

"Yes."

"It's very dear to me," I said quickly.

He squeezed my hand. His remained strangely cold and lifeless. "There is nothing I admire more about you than your honesty," he said.

What was this warmth in his face—warmth without passion? He looked more heated when he sculpted the wooden breasts of masthead figures. What was this kindness in his expression? Ah, behind it—so like Giles!—a plea for understanding.

"What is it?" I asked. "We are friends," I added. "Tell me what is in your heart."

"Be my friend forever," he said fervently.

"I will."

"There is only one hand for me. Another friend has come to me. I never expected it."

"A soul mate?" I asked.

"When I squeeze that hand, and the squeeze is returned, then my hand is warm. Then my hand is home."

He squeezed my hand again, and again I felt the cold dampness of his.

"Whose hand?" I asked.

"You can guess, Una. Guess."

I found myself smiling.

"My two best neighbors," I said. "The woodcarver and the judge."

But I went home soon, strangely shaken.

CHAPTER 147   Una Preaches to the Waves

WHAT AN EMPTINESS in the house! Justice away. I glanced at the hedge. *Be my friend forever,* he had said, and meant it. *Yes.* But what was I to do with that flare of feeling that comes when a woman loves a man because they are woman and man?

Robben and the judge. I knew of such practices, of course. I knew of my husband Kit with Giles, our friend. When I was a cabin boy, I knew that sailors, in the absence of women, sometimes bodily loved one another.

I left the house and walked down to the beach.

The waves reared and curled and then came crawling to me. How much I admired the deep C in that curl, like a little cave! And the mobile glassiness of the green water. And what was that on the horizon but a whaling ship? No more, no more did Mary or I keep watch for particular ships. I wished it were night and Mary might sing to me.

The water hunched and poured itself. Poured and poured, my ears greedy for the sound.

Do some preachers preach to warm their own hearts? Did Saint Francis preach to the animals of the forest to justify his own speaking? No. For he loved the animals, even as I loved the waves.

Ah, Waves, what do you know of eternity? As much as any force on earth? Down the eons you have poured your cups, twisted up your water-spouts, heaved your great flanks. You have sobbed and sighed, sparkled and laughed, alternately slammed flat our puny structures and caressed and cradled us in your sweet rocking.

What do you have to teach us? Your capacity to vary, your ability to endure? Your ceaseless energy. The force of you comes ashore and dies there. Yet comes another. Froth, foam, bubbles, nothing.

How, O destructive Element, can I abide the days of your coming in, coming in, coming in? Because you are no single thing. You console with your eternal arch and spew, even though you smite us. You provide the bounty of your myriad fishes, whales, eels, clams, shrimp. But above that you offer us your beauty. You are energy made beautiful, and what are we ourselves but energy? We live by our inner tides and cycles. Our blood is salt, even as you are. We, like you, must always heave and move; may sometimes sparkle, may luxuriate in ourselves. Waves, you are a pattern that fills all the available space. Like stars.

Ah, Waves, you tell me what I am and what I may yet be.

CHAPTER 148   🐚   **The Great Fire: June 1846**

W HEN I RETURNED from my meditations, I found upon my table a steaming apple pie. I looked out the window and saw that the judge's tall horse was hitched to the lovely carved horsehead on its post. Robben had told me that he had created the head after having seen an etching of the four horses over the portals of St. Mark's Church in Venice.

I sat down, cut the pie, and enjoyed one piece after another till the pie was half gone. It offered a satisfaction. I made myself a cup of tea and looked about me.

This was my home. I paced into my own room, which was the part of the house I loved most. Out its windows, I clearly saw the hedge, and the Gothic opening carved in it. No closing gate at all. An entry, ever available to me; a garden of whimsy and color for me to enjoy, and adjacent to the garden, also open to me, the workshop of an artist.

I accepted my small world, on the outermost rim of Nantucket.

But what was that whiff of scorch? Not the pie. I'd eaten half, and it was without flaw or blemish. I sniffed about and found the odor everywhere. In the air!

With that realization, I went out to the road to look toward town. There it was, unmistakable, a smudge of smoke in the air. It was not try-pots. Unless you line up a few hundred try-pots. Even so, this was a fire for far too great a rending.

I hurried over to Robben's.

"The town! Is it burning?" I asked them.

The judge stood up as though making an official pronouncement. He leaned forward to extend his arms and long fingers so that the tips rested just on the tabletop. I thought of an illustration of a mangrove jungle tree reaching down its roots.

"The fire started last night about eleven o'clock at William Geary's hat store. Everyone said that a good jet of water could have quenched it, at that point." He straightened up and clasped his hands behind his back. (I heard the skin of his two hands rasp together.) "Two of the private fire companies answered the call—I have long said we should have a *public* fire company—and they commenced to quarrel. Quarreled about who should have the honor of extinguishing the blaze. They argued till it was beyond either of their controlling, or both put together, or them plus every other bucket, hose, and cistern in the town."

"Is much lost?"

The judge smiled ruefully. "Property, not lives."

I thought of the fire Ahab and I had watched from the Unitarian Church.

"My church?"

"Safe. And Maria Mitchell saved the Methodist Church. They were blasting the buildings. It was next, but she made an observation about the convection currents at the head of Main Street and refused to move from the steps."

How heroical my picture of her there, armed with Science.

"But her observatory next door was destroyed." He added, "They'll rebuild."

"Our homes?"

Robben interjected, "I thought this was your home, Una."

The judge dropped his head. "You have to be told. Both destroyed."

I gasped.

Surprise gaped at my feet. An abyss of surprise. But I felt no dismay. I did not fall.

Still, they waited for me to recover before speaking.

I paced the room. Then stopped to hear what was next.

"I have been persuading the judge; he must move here," Robben said.

They both looked hard at me. Robben has told him, I thought, that I know something of their liaison.

"The warehouses on the waterfront burned, loaded with whale oil," the judge began, recounting again the conflagration, watching me carefully. "The fire was so hot there, not even cinders remained this morning. When the casks burst, the oil poured onto the water, too, and the harbor was a cauldron of flame. Sodom and Gomorrah, people said. What think you, Una, of Sodom and Gomorrah?"

"I am glad you have left that place," I said. "Here"—I waved at Robben's flower garden, and the green whale swimming in its midst— "is the very place to make a second Eden. At least, I've found it so."

CHAPTER 149   **Reflections on a Wreck**

OF COURSE, the judge lost all of his beautiful furniture and china in the fire, as well as his home. The contents of my home were also destroyed, but most of all I hated to think of the little cupola sinking down into flames. In the high cupola Justice and I had created a comfortable localness of feeling. Now my son was so well situated at 'Sconset he scarcely blinked when I told him that the house, much of the commercial district, and even the wharf had burned. "I'm glad we live here, aren't you?" was his pragmatic comment.

I did not burden him with the financial loss, which was great, for the judge had failed to renew the fire insurance on both his place and mine. Likewise, William Mitchell had failed to renew the insurance on the Atheneum. I couldn't think of two living men whom I trusted more; they, like the rest of us, were only human and prone to error.

Fortunately for me, everything at 'Sconset was completely paid for. I had even paid the taxes for the next twenty years. And the Husseys' Try Pots Tavern did not burn. It did a booming business, and every month I received a benefit from my original investment. Thus, we had spending money for new expenses, and I had no need to skimp. While the pillow of excessive means was gone, still my head rested comfortably enough at night. As for Ahab's other assets, I determined not to touch them so that Justice, when grown, might receive his inheritance intact.

The judge did move in with Robben (whose masthead figures sold well in New Bedford and Sag Harbor on Long Island—Nantucket building fewer ships than in the 1830s). Despite the additional financial loss, Austin Lord gave up his judgeship and, quoting Voltaire ("Cultivate your garden"), proposed that he tend a vegetable garden to be located in my back lawn. It would go a long way toward feeding us all, he felt. From life in Kentucky, I knew a great deal about raising vegetables—a beautiful golden squash blossom came to mind, morning-open, golden and five-pointed as a star. I promised to instruct him the next spring, and as the summer waned, the two men taught me to swim in the warmed waters of the Atlantic. The judge also offered to tutor the boys, which benefited me as well as them. Often I sat in on their lessons.

I wrote letters to Margaret Fuller and to Frannie and to David, but he had fallen completely silent. I imagined David in his gnomish home in Virginia; I pictured him rolled up in a white quilt I had given him—why had I given him a quilt in bridal white?—rolled up like an insect in a chrysalis. In a chrysalis, I knew, an insect could melt its organs into a primordial gel and totally reconstitute into something new. Something beloved for its beauty and grace.

Would that I could!

Sometimes I looked at the small wood statue of David in the chair at my hearth and thought of his words that the sculpture would remind me of him, should he never see me again. Yet he was so resourceful and plucky, so capable of change, that I did not worry much about him. And the carving was beautiful and I never tired of its company. Occasionally I rubbed it with oil to keep the wood from drying and splitting.

To appease my restless spirit, I proposed that I go to sea with the boys, but for a practical purpose. It was my idea that we commence serious fishing from a small boat. Though Jim and Justice were accomplished sailors, everyone agreed that I was the best fisherman among them. No wonder! Not only had I been a-whaling, but Uncle Torch and I had done just such fishing from a small boat. I wrote Uncle Torch about the fish we caught, and he replied with accounts of vast lake fish; Aunt Agatha and I exchanged our thoughts and fears on those issues which so much concerned Frannie and Frederick Douglass. Agatha's own emphasis was more on the voteless status of women than on slavery. We were all progressive in our thinking, and our particular emphases overlapped. For myself, pacifism seemed the most fundamental, if not the most immediate, issue.

Sometimes at night after a day on the water, I thought of the wonderful day when Ahab and I had taken a small boat, spied the old Lighthouse in the distance, but not approached it closer; instead, we had loved each other in splendid isolation on the sea. I thought of this not to torture myself but to celebrate the joy we had had together.

Austin Lord insisted on building all by himself a small smokehouse for the fish. He said such a structure could be very crude—just right for his building skills. Justice told me he imagined the judge's crooked and dark smokehouse was where nightmares lived in the day. I looked at my son sharply, afraid he might suffer from hideous dreams. He understood my glance, shrugged, and said, "Mother dear, it was just an idea. I thought you'd like it." And I did.

So we sowed seed, cultivated the garden, fished, and smoked our catch. Just such independence had we enjoyed when I lived on the little Island with Uncle and Aunt Agatha. Again, my life seemed to come into balance. But I do not know what I would have done if I could not have taken Justice with me out in the boat, open to sun and clouds, incessantly rocked by the sea. And restlessness was answered by my serenity at night as well as by its expression in the rise and fall of the water.

Sometimes I looked at Justice's turned shoulder as he dropped a line into the depths and thought, *I could have named you Giles, or at least given you that name for a middle name.* Sometimes, as we rocked on the waves, I looked at my son's black curls and thought, *I could have named you Chester.*

I asked the judge once if he missed his refined life, especially his bone china, of Nantucket town days. "Not a whit," he answered. "And Robben is willing to experiment with pottery making."

It was a very happy summer. The judge would say, "Here we have pleasure and peace, Una, instead of property."

Both Justice and Jim treated me with new respect for my instruction in boating and fishing; sometimes I felt that they treated me as though I were a man. Though I had stitched myself some sailor pants, this troubled me a bit. Certainly, I was turning brown from the glare of the sun above and off the water, and my arms were lean and muscular with rowing.

The earth wheeled round the sun to autumn, and the harvest of the garden was a lovely success. Mary came and we put up and dried and stored the bounty. As we peeled and boiled and stirred with our long wooden spoons, I could not help but compare my brown and stringy arms to her pink womanliness. So had my mother and I worked together, and after Mary left, with several large boxes of produce carted home to Sankaty, I missed both Mary and my mother—the kinship and intimacy. The grief was not sharp, but the absence located itself in my throat so I could not swallow well for weeks. Ensconced with nutritious bounty, I could hardly eat; I thus lost more flesh. For the boys' lessons, the judge constantly ordered new books, which I devoured, but they failed to plump me up. At least I couldn't swim or fish or walk while I read.

On the last morning in September as I walked the beach, I came to a large fragment of a ship washed ashore. Rammed into the sand, the shattered prow could have come from the sky as likely as the sea. Once I'd found on the shore a storm-driven blackbird, dead, with its ivory beak plowed into the sand; though the bird had half rotted, one tattered wing was held up stiffly. Just so, this wrecked prow, twisted into the sand, still held up a sweep of hull, like a wing. I paused and contemplated what was not the *Pequod*.

Ahab's ship was not so lucky. Locked in the cold depths, the *Pequod* rested in profound darkness. Perhaps festooned with glowworms; perhaps a school of tiny phosphorescent fish swam through her wounds. Or did she still wander, though submerged—a shadowy ship drifting waterlike within the deep currents of the ocean? Like Coleridge's Ancient Mariner, did she ceaselessly roam? I saw Ahab and his ship becoming water, their old shapes mingled into movement.

Standing on the sand, I stared at the wooden wing, and the wreck stared at me, till we each had told our stories. And my restlessness dissolved.

That night, as I climbed the stairs inside my home to the roof walk, I thought fleetingly of its other name, the widow's walk. But when I emerged on the platform, the glittering road of the Milky Way stretched from one side of the night dome to the other. In such a swarm of light, I was not alone. Perhaps some other being on an unnamed planet looked out across the spangled void and imagined me. And on my own planet, where was Susan? Eyes lifted, lips parted, also enjoying the riches of the Milky Way? I thought of its Japanese name, the Celestial River, and how all of us lived in the glory of its current.

CHAPTER 150   **During the Pleasure Party**

W E   H A D   A L L been invited on the night of October 1, 1847, to a pleasure party, given by the Mitchells at their apartment in the Union Pacific Bank. Now that the town was quite restored physically, many people gave parties to try to heal the social wounds left by the selfishness unveiled in the Great Fire. The large-familied Mitchells could not house all of us from 'Sconset, but the judge was to stay there; Justice and I were housed with Mrs. Maynard, and Mary and Isaac stayed with friends from the Unitarian Church. Robben Avalon volunteered to do the lighthouse duties and keep track of Isaac's four children.

I admit that I had fussed over my dress. Nothing suited me, and it made me angry. Finally I ripped out the inner seams of my sailor trousers and contrived to turn them into a skirt. I sewed four brass buttons onto the front to insist on the association with sailor's clothes. Then I asked Mary if she had any spare lace and made with it a blouse so frothy and frilly that I looked as though a wave had just burst around my neck and shoulders. I thought of Daggoo's splendid gold hoop earrings and asked Robben to carve some wooden ones and gild them. It was quite a costume, but I didn't care. It was what I wanted to wear, and the Mitchells' party was just the place to allow such a getup.

So I came in like a sailor who had been too long at sea and sassy as a gypsy.

Maria hugged me warmly and said, "If my dusky skin could glow like yours, I wouldn't spend my life as a spinster."

It was a surprising statement from her, and I laughed out loud. "I love you when you're droll," I told her and hugged her again.

She grew confidential. "These large parties please my father very much, but I intend to slip up to the observatory later. You can come, too, if you like."

"But I want to see people. I see stars aplenty at 'Sconset."

"Not with this power of telescopic magnification," she insisted. "Or with lecture."

As my dear Maria spoke, my ear was gathering in the sounds of the party: many voices, perhaps twenty or more, speaking at once. A sound human and happy. Sociable. The accidental mixture of vowels and consonants suggested a small stream running or a breeze in high leaves—the slurrying of a prow pushing through water.

And the sight of them? Beautiful, all beautiful, men and women. Clothes of an interesting and fashionable cut—purple and jade—why, I hadn't even known what fashion was anymore! Jewelry on the women, and fine buttons on the men. I twisted the ivory bracelet on my wrist and watched the whales circle round. Why, I felt shy!

What to say to these people? "You should have seen Pog this morning barking at the waves. We thought there might be a shark out there." They didn't even know Pog dog. "Is beauty enhanced or adulterated by utility?" But I did not see a Margaret Fuller among them. These were mostly people I knew, at least to some extent. Ah, some strangers. But what to say to them?

William Mitchell, like a kindly father, swooped down on me. "Come, Una," he said. "You must meet the junior Walter Folger. He's invented a clock that tells time from second to century and also registers the phases of the moon and tides and locates the sun."

I had sometimes thought that my judge resembled Benjamin Franklin, but the junior Walter Folger looked just like him. (In fact, a maternal ancestor of Franklin had been a Folger of Nantucket.) Walter Folger immediately began to talk my ear off with gears, counterweights, pendulums, escapes, and other innards of clocks, while William Mitchell beamed and deserted me, he having assumed that I was now as royally entertained as he had been a quarter of an hour before. Just as I began to be interested, Folger's wife came and put her arm through his to lead him off; she had caught the gist of his conversation. "Why, sometimes I almost wish he didn't know any more than any husband," she said.

Following her father's lead in introductions as well as in science, Maria promptly appeared with a dear friend of hers, the elderly and mathematical Phoebe Folger.

Of Mrs. Folger, Maria said, "She taught navigation to her husband, and he became, in consequence, the captain of a ship."

"Do you know Lucretia Mott?" the old woman quaked. "You look as though you should."

"I think that my cousin Frannie has met her," I replied, "but I have not had the pleasure."

"That's right," she said, "it would be a pleasure for you to know her. Don't you have on sailor's breeches?" The question was sharp, but it smacked more of approval than disapproval.

"I do, indeed," I replied. "And I have a right to 'em, having sailed and fished all summer."

"I should say you do," she stated. "Lucretia told me once that when she was a child she saw a woman flogged here in Nantucket. Can you imagine that?"

"Why was she flogged?"

"You know, I can't rightly remember. I believe they thought she was a witch, or some such." At that Phoebe suddenly cackled so hard that she herself somewhat resembled a witch. "Can she calculate?" Phoebe asked of me, turning to Maria.

"Una is much interested in science, but she is more qualitative than quantitative in her approach."

"Humph!" Phoebe sniffed, and I thought she was going to turn away. "That young man wants to meet you," she announced. "He's a sailor, too." With a crooked finger, she beckoned to one of the strangers to come to us. But he did not come. "I'd like something to eat," Phoebe said, put out, and Maria politely guided her to the table.

I followed along; but though the man had not obeyed the summons, he had glanced at us, and I thought for a moment that I recognized him. As the evening moved along, I joined a circle which he was entertaining with sea stories. Maria had long since assumed her "regimentals," as her sister called them, taken a lantern, and climbed aloft to the observatory.

"The last time I told this story," the sailor said, "I entertained some young dons in Lima with it. A priest was passing by and they made me place my hand on his Bible and swear that it was so. Is there a priest about? I believe there is nothing like swearing a story is true to whet the imagination."

We all laughed. Several people urged him to begin. Already in his manner I had noted a strange smoothness. There was no doubt he was a skilled narrator, but there seemed something dark and rough beneath that smoothness.

To my surprise, I asked, "And does a good swig of rum also unloose the tongue?"

"It did that night," he answered, looking directly at me. "Do ye have any?"

Again the group laughed. William Mitchell supplied him with a large snifter of brandy. He swirled it in his hand and then drank a deep gulp of the stuff. "No temperance folk here? Usually where there's abolition, there's temperance."

"Tell the story," folk urged.

"Well, let me ask, do ye believe a dumb beast can be sentient?" When there was no answer, he rephrased his question. "Do ye believe an animal can sometimes have a sense of justice?"

"Aye," someone answered, "for I've seen a mistreated horse scrape off a master with a tree limb."

"Good," the storyteller answered pleasantly. "But might that not have been a coincidence? Good masters are also scraped off, I think."

"I knew a man whose fighting cocks turned on him and ripped him to shreds," Isaac said.

"Better," our speaker said. "But perhaps they had not selected him particularly and would have vented their wrath on anyone who came to their enclosure."

"His wife was standing beside him, *pleading* with him to give up his cruel practice with the birds," Isaac said melodramatically. "And they didn't touch her."

"Bring him the Bible," the sailor called. "Bring the Bible and have the man swear to this cock-and-bull, or I'll not believe it."

Nor did anyone else believe it. But we admired Isaac's quick and logical imagination.

"No," the judge said stoutly. "Animals know nothing of justice. That requires rationality and impartiality."

"Then you must hear the story that I heard faithfully, from the crew of the *Town-Ho*."

"By all means," William Mitchell urged. "Another brandy?"

"Aye. To sip, not to quaff. Imagine the *Town-Ho*, a whaling vessel like to scores ye have sent to sea. And aboard are men of all types, some brought up to the sea, some reformed farmers. Even preachers. Some have whaled before, but many have not, it being such a hard business that men come in and out of the trade as though it were a revolving door. Some men may have shipped a merchant ship a time or two, and then decided to try whaling. I myself was such a one."

"On the *Town-Ho*?"

"Nay. Another ship. But that's another story. This very *Town-Ho* had the usual assortment of men, good and bad. One good and handsome man was Steelkilt, who'd learned sailing on the Great Lakes. One mean-spirited, vengeful fellow, lacking in natural respect for his fellow creature, was Radney. But the unfortunate circumstance was that Radney was over Steelkilt.

"The *Town-Ho* had a leak, stabbed perhaps by a swordfish, so the pumps were much put to use, and because Steelkilt was the strongest as well as handsomest man aboard, he was much put to the pumps, and pumped with all his heart and inspired others to, as well. He did it with hearty goodwill, I tell you, sure as if I'd seen him myself, for I know his type.

"But when he finished his Herculean labor, this Radney sees him no sooner seated and panting than he orders him to sweep and scrub the deck. Now I ask ye, ye being a sea-wise town, whose job is that, rightfully?"

"The boys," I answered quietly.

"Indeed," he said, almost winking at me. "The boys can do that light work, and they do do it, every blessed evening. Why, I've seen the boys wash down the deck in a typhoon, so well established is the practice."

"Did Steelkilt obey the order of his superior?" the judge asked.

"He did not."

" 'Tis mutiny." Judge Lord enunciated the law on the matter.

"So it is, and to mutiny it led. But not at first. Steelkilt refused, but he did it as one gentleman to another who had made a mistake. There was no defiance as such in his voice. He spoke rationally and well. This very calmness enraged the ugly Radney, and he grabbed up a hammer and shook it beneath Steelkilt's nose.

"Now Steelkilt was not the man to be threatened. As I have said, he was the strongest and most athletic man aboard, and you would likely not find his match among the crews of twenty whaling ships. He was an extraordinary man. Golden-haired and as fair as your liar-and-inventor of cock-tales there"—he indicated Isaac, who blushed as the crowd laughed. But I thought, *Now he has put this Steelkilt before them palpably, for they need but gaze on Isaac to see in the flesh the very appearance whom he would create in words.*

"Steelkilt warned him, 'Shake that hammer not one more time, or ye shall regret.' But Radney did threaten again, and while he brandished his hammer, Steelkilt drew back his fist, which Radney could not see, and delivered such a blow as drove Radney's jaw back from its sockets, with blood bursting from his nose."

"Now when is the animal coming in?" It was Phoebe Folger's quaking voice.

"Too much blood, eh? Yes, this be a pleasure party including ladies. I'm not in South America among the young dons; let me remember that. Quickly, to the animal. Can ye guess what animal this story leads to?"

A silence fell, and then I said, "A whale."

"Indeed, a whale. But let me quickly run over the steps before 'Enter the Whale.' Mutiny followed assault. Steelkilt and his sympathizers against the captain and mates. Steelkilt and sympathizers locked below-decks. Steelkilt and sympathizers hung among the yards and flogged. Enough of that, though. And eventually, Steelkilt and sympathizers restored to the crew, when from the mastheads it comes, 'There she blows,' but no ordinary whale. No, it is the white whale, and the captain of the *Town-Ho* is determined to have the glory of his taking. Now quickly, listen, for Radney is mad with the desire to kill the whale, Radney, who has wronged Steelkilt, and who is it the white monster dashes from the whaleboat? One man, only one man?"

He paused, and though we all knew what the answer must be, we would not say it, for we had our own woe of Moby Dick, of the *Jeroboam*, the *Delight*, and of the *Pequod*. We were silent.

The storyteller supplied the answer. "It was Moby Dick who served as jury, judge, and executioner. It was the white whale."

"How could the whale possibly have known?" the judge replied. "It was but a coincidence, as you yourself pointed out in the tales of horses and fighting cocks."

People laughed politely and began to turn away. I saw Mary Starbuck pale as a ghost. Involuntarily she put her hand on her belly, and I thought, *They're going to have a child together.*

"Young man, I suspicion you could tell your own tale of Moby Dick," Phoebe quaked.

"Nay," the man answered. "What if I could? That is not a tale for a pleasure party. Especially not one at Nantucket."

He glanced at me, and I saw in his eye that which was identifiably familiar. He was the sailor whose eye I had encountered in the passageway of the *Alba Albatross*, the merchant ship that had plucked Kit and Giles and me from the open boat. I saw him only once, when, directly before leaving that ship for the *Pequod* and marrying Kit, I had gone to Sallie's cabin to get a few items of clothing, to leave a gift under her pillow of tatted lace.

But that was not the only reason for familiarity. Then, in that short gaze in the passageway within the *Albatross*, I had thought him the most interesting, the most unfathomable man I had ever met. *Memorable*, he had become, in a glance. Yes, lifting a brandy snifter in the Mitchells' apartment of the Union Pacific Bank, Nantucket, it was the merchant sailor of the *Albatross*. My heart quickened within me, but like the rest of the group, I turned away from him. In an instant I felt his hand on my shoulder.

I turned, and he said, "I know you. You were the captain's wife's friend on the *Albatross*. Plucked from the sea."

"Yes," I replied. "I am now the widow of Captain Ahab."

He blanched to a shade more pale than Mary. "I shipped with Ahab on his last voyage," he said.

"That is not possible."

His gaze unfocusing, the storyteller seemed haunted.

"I was the one left, the one picked up by the *Rachel,* the one buoyed up by the coffin."

"What is your name?"

"Yes," he said. "I'll proffer you a name. Ishmael."

CHAPTER 151   ☀   **Celestial**

AT THAT MOMENT, Maria Mitchell squeezed my elbow. "Una, Una!" she said urgently. "I must speak to you."

Never had I seen her so excited. In her excitement, she did not notice that I had received a shock.

"I have seen it," she said. "Through the telescope. I think that I am the first person in the history of the universe to have done so."

"Seen what, Maria?"

"I have discovered a comet telescopically. My endeavor—all these years!"

Now I clutched her in return. "Maria!" It was all I could say at first. Not triumph, but fulfillment irradiated her features. "Are you sure?"

"I am as sure as I can be. I'm going to ask my father to look. Would you come, too?"

And so the three of us ascended to the rooftop. For sixteen years now, the king of Denmark's gold medal prize had been offered to him who found a comet telescopically. As we emerged onto the rooftop observatory, my senses thrilled at the dark open air, the vast sky in contrast to the closed, bright room below, crowded with humans and the voice of the handsome sailor.

Without a word, Maria looked through her large mounted instrument. It was as long as a broom. Then she turned to her father. With his eye to the telescope, he studied the night sky carefully, consulted charts, looked again.

"It is an unrecorded comet," he said. "But we should check again tomorrow and perhaps for a few more days before we announce it."

"Yes, of course," Maria said. But I had never heard her speak with such fervor. I wanted to run downstairs and herald it to the party.

They had me look through the telescope, and I, too, saw the small dot of light with a hint of a stubby tail, that traveler who swam into our ken from some immense distance. To think that I, no scientist, but only a friend, might be the third person since time began to behold it. "I feel like Noah seeing the white dove," I said. "What strange joy it brings."

My joy was twofold. What I beheld humbled and awed me. At least as important: the victory of my beloved friend; she had watched and waited and won. I softly asked, "Will you proffer it a name?"

All night I stayed with Maria, and we watched till the pink light of dawn obliterated the comet, and the pleasure party below was long since over.

CHAPTER 152   A New Friend

W HEN I ARRIVED the next morning, red-eyed and sleepless, at the home of my old friend Mrs. Maynard, she said, "They told me you were to be on the platform with Maria Mitchell till dawn, so I wasn't worried. But mercy! you look a fright!"

With that she put me to bed and promised to stand guard like a dragon. Nonetheless, when in the late afternoon two callers appeared, she woke me up. "I won't have done it," she said, "but one of them is Phoebe Folger, and who knows when she's going to suddenly die."

Phoebe's hearing was keen, and she promptly said, from the next room, "I have too much to do to die, my dear." And she and Maria, who had been enlisted as a kind of backup, were upon me.

In a manner clearly preliminary, Maria asked, "The house next door to you is still for let, isn't it?"

The intrepid Phoebe Folger took over: "I have in mind to take all the Mitchell children there and Mrs. Mitchell for a seaside holiday before the weather turns." She spoke in a hoarse, conspiratorial whisper. "I do it so I can be next door to you. Now the question is, my dear, if you intend to visit me, and perhaps help Mrs. Mitchell a bit with the children from time to time?"

"Father and I feel we would benefit from having the house to ourselves," Maria said, self-consciously mysterious.

"How I used to hate being interrupted in my calculations," Phoebe said. "I can sense something very important is afoot, but they won't tell me." She paused to inspect Maria's visage for clues. Finding none, Phoebe went on, "They need peace and quiet—I'm sure of that. And I'd like to live as close to the sea as I can for a time, before I die."

"The house stands empty," I said. "And nothing would please us more than to have you and the less scientific Mitchells as neighbors."

"Very good. We'll come." Phoebe spoke and acted without hesitation. It was as though she had said, "One plus one is two. Definitely." She added, "We'll drive in a buggy alone so we can talk."

THUS IT WAS we caravaned back to 'Sconset. As we traveled, Phoebe told me she had been born a Quaker, but she saw that the Unitarians suited her better philosophically, and she intended to change when she came back from 'Sconset. I was startled that a person with such a long history among one group might in old age have new thoughts and take action. My admiration for my new friend increased.

She had arranged that she and I ride in one buggy to 'Sconset and that Justice and the Mitchell family (minus Maria and her father) come along behind. In a succinct manner, Phoebe told me something of her long mathematical studies and personal life. I had thought that Maria stood alone among Nantucket's women, but here was Phoebe Folger, who had not only preceded Maria but encouraged her.

"You know," she said, returning to the issue of religious affiliation, "the Quakers have disappointed me in the question of the Africans."

"How is that?"

"To get his daughter in the white high school, Absalom Boston had to file suit against the town."

"I know Absalom Boston," I said. "When was this?"

"Two years ago. You see, dear, there are disadvantages in isolating yourself so completely from civilization." Her voice teased me. "His daughter was seventeen, when he filed in '45, and she didn't get admitted till last year. And Eunice Ross. In '40, Eunice Ross was seventeen. She graduated from the African School on York Street and passed the entrance exam for the all-white school. Did the Quakers stand up for her? No. They worked against her. Oh, they're all for abolition, but that's faraway justice. They might look to effect justice closer to home."

"Did you attend Frederick Douglass's talk?" I asked. We could hear children jabbering behind us and their pleasant laughter, but how wise she had been to isolate us. The horse clopped along nicely, and Phoebe held on to a beautiful, tightly woven oval basket in her lap.

"Indeed I did," she answered.

"And?"

"Well, it was magnificent. What did you think?"

"The same. My cousin Frannie works with him."

"Does she? I remember seeing both of you there. You so pretty and alive, and she terribly pockmarked, poor child." She sighed. "It must be difficult for her."

"She had a child who died. Drowned at Sankaty."

"That's something I didn't know," she replied.

We fell silent for a few moments, until Phoebe asked, "Tell me, what do you think of the afterlife?"

I was a bit nonplussed. I had no idea what she thought, but I knew that the question must be of greater interest to someone of her age than to me. But our conversation had been completely honest, and before I could speak, honesty and tact had joined hands in my answer. "I have no faith at all," I said, "but sometimes I have hope."

"I rather think," she replied, "that total annihilation is the most comfortable position."

I was shaken. The horse clopped on. The children laughed behind us.

"When I die," she said, "I don't expect to see any of my loved ones again. I'll just become a part of all this." She waved her hand at the surrounding countryside. "That's all right with me."

"Sometimes I think the spirit may continue in some way," I said, "after the body's death, might know other spirits, might be happy. I like to entertain the idea. I don't know."

"Time is something of an enemy," she opined, "for us mortals. And yet I love it"—she fluttered her fingers in the air—"I love this moment, and it's a child of time."

"At the party," I said, "there was a man—the man—the only man who survived the wreck of the *Pequod*. I had heard of him before. He floated on a coffin till the *Rachel* picked him up."

"I thought as much," Phoebe said. "He told the Steelkilt and Radney story. The 'Moby Dick as god of justice' story. That Elijah, whom Charity drowned, had some such theory."

"No, it was Gabriel, from the *Jeroboam*, who believed that."

"But Charity drowned Elijah, didn't she?" How cold-bloodedly she repeated that fact!

"Yes."

I did not tell Phoebe that I had seen this Ishmael some years before. I did not tell her that once, in an awkward moment, I had looked so deeply into him that I had concluded his eyes held an unfathomable profundity, and that I had remembered him, in some buried way, all those years.

"I've avoided knowing—I haven't wanted to know—about the last moments of the *Pequod*," I said. "I don't want to have it in my imagination. But now I could talk to him—the survivor. I could settle how it all happened."

"Well, you don't have to."

"No, I don't." I envisioned the gaping maw of Moby Dick, the sockets in the upper jaw where the lower teeth housed themselves. His great mass. Bloody water. "But perhaps it's something I should try to settle."

"It may be."

"Do you have an opinion?"

She slowly turned her body toward me, to look at me. It was the first time that she had spent the energy to twist herself toward me, though I had felt her eyes shift toward me as she spoke. I glanced at her. "No," she said slowly. "You'll decide. I can't tell you whether 'tis best or not to settle the *Pequod* with the sailor's account. That'll be fine, Una, whatever you decide."

I laughed. "You will make a good Unitarian, Phoebe Folger."

"I expect so."

"But who was Ishmael, anyway?" I asked. "In the Bible?"

"An outcast. Somebody who lived on the edge of things."

I glanced at her. "As I do."

"No. You come and go. Sometimes going out, sometimes coming in. Like the waves."

"What became of Eunice Ross, when the Quakers kept her out?"

"She's in now. She was twenty-four years old, but they let her in, with Boston's daughter."

I refused the request from the vehicle behind to stop at Altar Rock, not wanting to prolong the journey for Phoebe, and we clopped on to 'Sconset. By the time we arrived at the sea, I was full of admiration and affection for one very old Phoebe Folger, mathematician, philosopher, and advocate of social justice.

CHAPTER 153   A Sermon Overheard

MRS. MITCHELL, being used to cooking and keeping up with her children, really required very little help from me, and she quickly told me that my job for the seaside week was to entertain Phoebe Folger. As this arrangement suited Phoebe and me as well, all fell into place in a way that seemed almost predestined.

I had not expected to make a new friend, let alone a friend who was a very old woman who had lived in Nantucket all along, but she somewhat filled the vacant place left by the demise of my own mother. Phoebe was more outspoken than my mother, and I associated her with Great Affection, rather than with love, but still my tie to her was fully rewarding.

Although she was a little tottery, one day Phoebe insisted I help her down the steps so that she could walk directly on the beach. Descending was a strain for her, and she suggested we stand in the shade of the fragrant pine trees before we expose ourselves to the sun again.

When I said we might sit down, she said pleasantly, "No, I'd rather stand. It's too difficult for me to get up off the ground." What a sensible person she was. "I once promised myself," she went on as though she had read my thoughts, "that I wouldn't be one of those tiresome old people who refused to accept help when they needed it. Or one who talked about her aches and pains all the time. But I won't get into unnecessary trouble, either. I know what I can do."

The ocean rumpled itself before us, and a few pale clouds hung on the horizon. It was a bright day, but not so hot as to threaten, and besides, we stood in the shade. The shadow of a spray of pine needles danced on Phoebe's cheek. My hand reached for my own cheek: so long ago my father left the print of his hand there; and there my husband Kit violated my visage, no, sought to displace my identity, with his assaulting hand. I had hidden in the *Pequod*'s hold, among the barrels of harvested whale oil. The massive ribs of the ship had curved around me as though I were Jonah inside the whale.

Phoebe and I inhaled the sweet fragrance of pine resin. I felt enormously happy to be there with my new friend. Seaside, with Phoebe Folger, I felt this was a world that gave back as well as took.

Then she surprised me by telling me about her daughter Nan, a bit older than I, who had died. I was much moved by the story. A cancer had killed her, but Nan had had some episodes of derangement as well.

"I know the pain of it for you," I said. "My husband before Captain Ahab became mad."

"And did he get over it, too?"

"No, he never did."

She stepped forward on the path into the sunshine; the pine-spray shadow slid from her cheek. She looked back over her shoulder and smiled. "Now, let's go on to the water. I want my shoes off, if you'll help me."

If she was something of a mother to me, I was something of a daughter to her. I supposed Maria Mitchell had been, too.

"You know," Phoebe said, lifting the hem of her skirt above the water, "Nan was not very mathematical or science-minded, but she was interested. Like you."

AFTER OUR RETURN from the beach, Phoebe was tired enough to ask to lie down to rest, and I took the opportunity to go visit Robben. As I knew the judge was still lingering in town, I thought Robben might enjoy some company. I let myself in without knocking, and then was surprised to hear a male voice speaking:

"Consider the subtleness of the sea; how its most dreaded creatures glide underwater, unapparent for the most part—"

(It was the voice of the storyteller from the pleasure party. It was Ishmael.)

"—and treacherously hidden beneath the loveliest tints of azure. Consider, once more, the universal cannibalism of the sea—"

My heart constricted. Did he know my secrets as well as Ahab's?

"Consider, however baby-man may brag of his science and skill, how forever and forever, to the crack of doom, the sea will insult and murder him, and pulverize the stateliest, stiffest frigate he can make—"

The man was preaching a sermon, not to the sea, but about the sea. I heard no word from Robben, the assumed but out-of-sight audience for Ishmael's lecture.

"Yes, foolish mortals"—did he imagine he addressed a multitude?— "Noah's flood is not yet subsided; two-thirds of the fair world it yet covers. And wherein differ the sea and the land?"

He paused as though he expected Robben to answer, but I knew that Robben was enjoying this philosophical run of rhetoric and would not reply.

"Consider all this; and then turn to this green, gentle, and most docile earth; consider them both, the sea and the land; and do you not find a strange analogy to something in yourself? For as this appalling ocean surrounds the verdant land, so in the soul of man there lies one insular Tahiti, full of peace and joy, but encompassed by all the horrors of the half-known life. God keep thee! Push not off from that isle, thou canst never return."

With that I noiselessly turned and fled through the Gothic Ach into my own territory. Too much this man traced the path of my own life. Oh, it was done all abstractly, but too accurately, too closely.

My vegetable garden was already plucked over, but I distractedly found myself walking among the bent stalks, the leftovers of the harvest. I kicked a clod of soil. I got a hoe and chopped away at the row, though it would not want weeding till the earth had traveled halfway around the sun again.

This is stupid, I told myself. And then I claimed to myself that despite all, I was glad that I had left my particular, insular Tahiti. Where would Justice be if I had not? Nor would I have had any of the friends who were so dear to me. I was sure Phoebe Folger would not offer such conservative advice as Ishmael. (But then she *had* been born on Nantucket and never left.)

I threw the hoe down among the dry stalks and passed again through the arch in the hedge. Robben's flowers were yet radiant, and I would enjoy them. I inspected the docile green whale, and walked around the circle of his flowery pond.

Whales! One black, one white—how they had stove my life! And yet, unlike Ahab, I could not blame them. What were they but the largest life-form? Were they our own animal self inflated like the pig's bladder turned balloon? Nonetheless, I preferred this pretty green fellow. This bloodless, vegetable, well-pruned artifact. His spout and he, all privet, all one. Oh! Here came Robben with Ishmael in tow.

"Una," Robben called. "Meet a new friend, Ishmael."

"We've met before," he said, as they walked toward me.

Suddenly my bad temper was gone. "Twice met," I said and smiled at the sailor. "You are a wonderful narrator." (All our sensibility is surely tied to blood, not vegetable juices.)

"I would suppose that you yourself have a story to tell," he answered, his pontificating manner all evaporated.

Robben said, "He's writing a book of his experiences. Ishmael wants to understand all that is possible to know about ships and whales. Mrs. Maynard sent him out to interview me on masthead figures. He came to Nantucket to interview Captain Pollard, whose *Essex*—"

"And I have given him a foretaste of my thoughts on the sea—as they may appear in my book, more or less."

"Do you like her?" I asked.

"The sea or Mrs. Maynard?" Robben put in puckishly.

I laughed. "That's just the sort of confusion Mrs. Maynard fosters."

"I did not expect to see you again," Ishmael said. "I think that you must surely have a gloomy association with me. At the party, when you found out I was the survivor, you quickly turned away."

"Do you like the sea at all?" I repeated. His answer was important to me.

"No one who knows the sea—no, let me say more narrowly, more close to my own experience: no man who worked a whaling ship did not both hate and love the sea." His countenance grew contracted and dark. I had seen Ahab draw into himself in just such a mood. "When we kill her mightiest creature," he mumbled, "her great, oil-saturated baby, surely we show that we hate the oceanic mother."

"Did you know my husband well?" My heart quailed. I did not know how far I wanted to pursue the subject.

"As I said, the last voyage of the *Pequod* was my first one with Captain Ahab. In the beginning, he was quite mysteriously removed from all of us. We sailed on Christmas Day—"

"I remember." Even to Ahab, even then, that had seemed an unfortunate, sacrilegious gesture.

"And only after the weather moderated did Captain Ahab come on deck."

"He had had a fall," I said. "He was not entirely well. Before he left, the ivory leg splintered and gored him."

"So I came to understand."

We all paused. He seemed to look at me for permission to continue. Again, his eyes bewitched me. I must have granted assent; I do not know what my own countenance said.

"So after the weather was better, Ahab was much on deck—"

"I hope there were beautiful days."

"Days as lovely as a Persian sherbet, held in a great glass." Another pause. "And Queequeg—"

"Queequeg?"

"Yes. A friend as dear to me as though we were a married couple. Our acquaintance, our appreciation, began, in fact, with the renting of the same bed at the Spouter-Inn. Queequeg."

"Then this is the fourth and not the third time I've seen you. I saw you going aboard with Queequeg, in the fog, accosted by Elijah."

"Whose prophecies all were true. . . . Did I know Captain Ahab well? Queequeg and I often heard him speaking to Starbuck or Stubb, the carpenter, the cook, Pip. He rarely spoke to me, for I was the greenest of the green at whaling. As green as yonder green fellow." He gestured toward the centerpiece of the garden.

"But sometimes I heard him speaking to himself. It may be impudence in me to say so, but yes, I think I knew him well. I think I knew him as someone connected to myself, as though I were a man on a monkey rope—you know the device?—and he held the other end."

"Whatever possessed you to go a-whaling?" Robben asked his

guest. And I was grateful to Robben, for I had heard enough, for the time being.

"Well, I had been several times in merchant vessels. I wanted not just to cross the ocean like an errand boy, but to live with her, to live upon her heaving breast, to know her creatures, not to consort with some silly merchandise in the hold. I had no money in my purse, and I had a melancholy in my head."

How melodiously he spoke. Whole paragraphs rolled from his tongue.

"Whenever I find myself growing grim about the mouth; whenever it is a damp, drizzly November in my soul; whenever I find myself involuntarily pausing before coffin warehouses and bringing up the rear of every funeral I meet; whenever I feel like deliberately stepping into the street, and methodically knocking people's hats off—then I account it high time to get to sea as soon as I can. Which of you has not sometimes felt that way—half in love with death, senselessly combative, restless, and what do you do with yourselves then?"

"I've walked. Sometimes in deep snow, to unpredictable destinations."

"I grab my chisels and mallets and a block of wood and have a go at it."

"Sometimes," I added to my declaration, "I have climbed aloft."

"Ah, a very philosophic perch," Ishmael put in.

"Sometimes I sew, or read, or even write," I added. "Or fish."

"You have too many resources. I can go to sea or, like Cato, throw myself upon my sword. But I don't. At least not so far. I quietly take to the ship."

"You can also write your story," Robben said mildly.

"Ishmael," I said, "you have an unusual name."

"My name is David Pollack."

"David Pollack!"

"Yes. Is it so remarkable a name?"

"I know a David Poland. He is a very dear friend."

"Well, then, the name augurs well, though I would seem to be an informal, bastardized version of your friend. I call myself Ishmael, and I ask that you do also."

H E STAYED a few days at Robben's house, during which time my tongue wagged like a bell clapper, right and left. To the south a new friend, female, old, wise, a kind of dispassionate mother. To the north a new friend, male, of my own decade, a whaler, a seeker, the survivor of a wreck. I rebounded between them—and it was a joyous clanging of that clapper, my tongue, for they both listened as well as they talked. And always in the background was the sound of children let loose, self-sufficient, ordering their own small society with minimal interference from adults. How would any one of them have remembered those October days on the sand? What would Pog have said of his multiple playmates, the bright and cooling weather?

But then the south house fell vacant again, and Ishmael, too, returned to the town. Robben must have felt my loneliness, for he and Judge Lord appeared with a hot pear flan. I was in my own window-faceted room watching the sea, but I smelled the flan and heard them enter into the main room and the scuff of chairs on the floor. How comfortable to have separate neighbors, but all our houses open to one another. I imagined them seated at the table, the pie upon it, waiting patiently; and when I entered the room, all was just as I had envisioned.

"We have a proposition, Una," the judge said.

"And?"

"To come to the point," he smiled, "Robben and I have decided to travel together to Italy and Greece."

"How fine!" Then the north house, too, would be vacant? The distant flashing light my closest friend? The summer people were already gone. No house in 'Sconset was inhabited.

"And we want to take Justice and Jim with us," Robben said.

"You may think them contented children—" Austin said.

"We think they may run off to sea, otherwise. Probably you did not notice. The day after Maria's comet—the judge said you were sleeping late—they spent that day at the wharf, interviewing captains. The judge received a visit from Captain Mayhew—"

"The *Jeroboam*?" I asked. "The *Jeroboam* was in port?" Would they all come back, again and again, but not the *Pequod*? What of the *Samuel*

Enderby? I heard the clack of ivory, of Boomer crossing his bone arm with Ahab's whalebone leg.

"The same *Jeroboam.* Mayhew said he had given Justice a promise long ago to take him—"

"By all means, he and Jim must travel with you two instead. Believe me, I know too well what can happen to cabin boys." I thought of Chester, whose curls resembled Justice's. "I know it far better than either of you. I will never be able to thank you enough if you will take them."

"And Jim's mother?"

"I will speak to Mary. I can tell you already, she will be exactly of my mind. But I don't know about the expense—" Here I felt awkward, for if I had had my old resources, there would have been no question of Jim's expenses. "Mary and Isaac would not have so much, I think."

"There was another reason for Mayhew's visit to me," the judge said. "He had a good report. His investments in the new earth oil have done well. I looked into yours, Una, the investment of yours that was meant to bolster his. My dear, you are, if not rich again, at least prospering."

"*Kerosene* is the name of the new god," Robben said.

They stayed a bit longer, and we all chatted happily about their prospective voyage, but when they left, I could already feel the emptiness on both sides of me. The furniture seemed like Shakespeare's bare branches, "where late the sweet birds sang." In my mind's eye, the two houses beside mine hulked like ghost ships, drifting and derelict. I put my head down next to the pretty pear confection. The savory, fruity heat from the pastry warmed my forehead.

To my surprise, I felt a hand on my shoulder and looked up into the gentle eyes of Robben.

"You feel we're all deserting you," he said.

I sat up and wiped away the tears. "No, Robben. I want you to go. If I came, it would be no adventure for Justice."

"You have your writing, Una."

"And I can visit in town, occasionally."

"And Ishmael will be here."

"Ishmael?"

"I forgot to mention. I've sublet my house to him. He's a bit of a wild one. You won't feel uncomfortable having him next door?"

"Next door?" It was as though the Frost Wind—strange, fresh, inevitable—had come down from the sails to blow around my body.

"Phoebe got to him first and told him he should sublet Mary's house, but when he heard mine was falling vacant, too, he said he preferred to share the hedge with you."

"The hedge?"

"Well, it's some kind of dividing line. A sort of bundling board between yards." Robben's eyes were merry. I put my hand in his gray curls and tugged.

CHAPTER 155   Recitation by Beach Fire

O NE MILD, moonshine night on the 'Sconset beach, after we had laid down our picnic basket and our quilts and gathered driftwood for a future fire, I watched Pog cavorting in the sand. The dog picked up sticks with his teeth, pulling up the half-embedded ones and bringing them back to our collection. Again, as I had done many times, I admired the shaggy creature. I thought of my old friend David, who had come to me in wolf skin.

Pog wrestled another sand-encrusted stick up from the beach. A zaggy stick. He carried it delicately, his lips curled away from the sand, his ivory teeth gleaming. We—Ishmael and I—sat on our quilt and watched silently. Angular and heavy, the zaggy stick tilted out of balance. The dog persisted, dragged the stick to me with one of its ends trailing in the sand. When I took it from him, I saw it was not wood at all, but glass. It was the mark lightning can make when it strikes the beach and fuses the sand particles into its imprint. I thought of Ahab—the zaggy mark on his face.

The moonlight touched the tips of the waves with silver, and, as I had done many times alone, I walked to the shore, took off my clothing down to my camisole and drawers, and entered the water.

"Can you swim? Can you swim?" Ishmael called after me, as though I had taken leave of my senses. He followed me to the hem of the water, then shed all his garments and threw them inland so that he could overtake me, for I swam out without hesitation.

I glanced over my swimming shoulder to see his long naked legs and body, the head cloaked with hair and beard, as he stood on the sand.

When I heard his shout, I looked back again and saw his long arms snaking over the water. He was smiling. I let myself swim too fast, trying to show off my prowess, but I knew when it was time to turn around and how to monitor my endurance. But he had not caught me before I turned. He chose to tread till I reached him, and then we swam back together in the face of the retreating tide. On the return, I fancied my companion to be Poseidon, so easily did he breast the waves.

"Who taught you such swimming?" he asked me. "You're at home in the water."

"Sweet Robben, whose house you inhabit." (But I had little extra breath for talking.)

"I'm a hermit crab then." The hair of his mustache and beard, studded with droplets, parted in a smile. He swam a few strokes side-wise, like a crab.

"No."

But I could not say what I meant. I tasted the salt water on my lips. My body felt cold, but I kicked on, sure that the necessary warmth would well up within me.

As we swam, Ishmael said for me to look, and his finger came dripping up out of the water to point. Porpoises were leaping, their bodies an arc of phosphorescence.

They came close to us and surrounded us with their big bodies, but never touched us. The thudding of their bodies, returning to the water, shook the air, and the vibrations through the water vibrated us. Our bodies were as slick and unfettered as the dolphins, but only they were phosphorescent, fiery green, crimson, silver, in their leaping, traveling circle. Amidst those cold fires we swam to shore.

We quickly dried and dressed ourselves, and he struck a sulfur match to light the driftwood. I shall always remember the spurt of the match, like a small star exploding, white-hot in the center. The flare of the tinder, nestled in the tent of driftwood. We lounged, propped up, looking into the flames, with quilts under us and the soft sand for mattress under that. How comfortably, how companionably, we lounged at ease—just so had I rested by a campfire in Kentucky with the first David. Was that Milk the donkey chomping the spring grass? Here, too, at 'Sconset, was campfire ease. Ishmael spoke as softly as the flamy tongues tasting air, as the liquid tongues lapping against the shore:

"When I was floating atop the coffin—Queequeg's coffin-become-life-buoy—sometimes as the waves rocked us—I say us, for I was wedded cheek to wood, and I and the coffin were one as surely as death and life are one, as surely as we are one"—he glanced at me, did not touch, spoke on—"I heard within that hollow a lightly sliding noise, a movement as though something shifted, sledded within, over the planks. I listened for diversion. And that long night, also to divert by touch, my fingers explored the minutiae of my buoy-world.

"This finger"—he held it up—"following the tarry seal between lid and side, discovered eight inches of fresher slickness, a place where the line of oakum and tar had been broken and resealed. There the tips of my fingers glided all night along that dark, short track where the hardened tar became softer, less baked. Long days of hanging in the air, from that time the ship carpenter caulked and converted the closed coffin into buoy, had stiffened the rest of the seam into something impenetrable. The buoy had hung in the stern like the heel of a shoe.

"A coffin for a heel! The *Pequod*'s heel it had been, the last of us shown to the *Samuel Enderby*, and finally to the *Rachel*." He mused silently, then continued speaking into the flames.

"Along eight inches, perhaps six, my fingers traveled, wondering, along the seam of softer tar." He rubbed his fingers back and forth over the stitches of the quilt, as though to relive that time.

"Till I concluded they had broken the coffin seal to slide something flat and slight inside, and it moved there now. *Slip-slip*, I heard the cargo when I laid my ear to the wood. Some wafer, I thought, some sustenance.

"Before morning came, I, like a ship's rat working the corner of a cracker crate, gnawed the coffin corner nearest my mouth. I had hardly to move my position for my teeth to find purchase on an angle of the boards.

"I gnawed on, splinters between my teeth, splinters working like needles into my gums. The taste of tar was like black blood in my throat—why should I alone survive!—the sharks swam round, *their* mouths padlocked, it seemed—till there was a chewed place big enough for hand and wrist to enter. So I groped within, like a midwife blindly searching out her prize.

"When ocean tilted just so, a paper slid against my fingertips. So thin a sustenance! But what else but paper could have entered that coffin's vacancy by so narrow a passageway?

"Whose words writ on that strangely hinged paper? I thought how I must coax an eye to open to a slit, for my eyes had sealed themselves. My pupils acknowledged daylight, sometimes pinkish, sometimes yellow, as through a veil. Floating stomach-down on the swaying coffin, in one hand I clutched the paper, with the other I took a finger and massaged an eyelid till moisture came and unglued the crusty eyelashes.

"I rolled on my back—which took some care, for I did not know if I should roll accidentally off my sanctuary whether the sharks might not count me prey, or whether, indeed, I would have the strength to pull myself aboard again onto the coffin—I read, and then slept like Beowulf on his bier but with this thin crisp of paper pressed against the salt-stiffened cloth covering my chest.

"I dreamt seabirds were ripping away cloth and then my flesh. They swooped down on me again, as I lay upon the box. I dreamt I was a string of bones in human form, clutching a message not its own. The harpies would ride me at times, their claws encircling the curve of a rib.

"But it's not Ishmael's dream you would hear. Whose handwriting? No doubt you wonder, dear Una, if Ahab might yet speak to you from beneath the waves through those words I pried my lids apart to read? Or if good Starbuck had mailed a final missive penned during those last days? For your nimble mind thinks, who but Ahab or Starbuck would dare to broach the sealed, life-buoy coffin? Insouciant Stubb? He had the nonchalance but not the imagination for it. So, was it Starbuck's or Ahab's hand had slid words into the postbox life buoy?

"Both. For there had been two pages posted there, separately. And those sheets had found each other. In extracting one, I extracted both, Ahab's and Starbuck's pages melded along the side as inextricably as their fate. My fate, you know. 'Twas to be picked up by the *Rachel*."

"Can you read the letters to me?"

"Nay, Una, but I can recite."

"I START WITH STARBUCK'S, but his words are mostly of Ahab. They give the portrait from the outside:

"*Mary, I looked in at him among his charts. Yet not among them, for his head was down, exhausted, and he slept. The charts but offered thin pillow for whatever raged within his skull, his old hair all splayed in disarray.*

"*I thought of murder. I had thought it before. I had thought it all my life, so long concealed but mutinous now—to murder authority, to strike and topple, though I willed my knee to bend, though I commanded my hand to serve. To serve God had been my devotion! Would I strike God? Had all my piety, my devout and earnest desire to ever obey the laws of God and those who spoke with just Authority, come to this? Was not this the fated heresy in our Quaker faith, we who sat on our benches without minister but equal to each other?*

"*Am I so utterly lost? An assassin! of him who has the right to command not only me but also all the* Pequod's *precious human cargo to follow him to the depths.*

"*And when I go there—for we shall know the cold depths—what will save me then? I would go home, home, not there. But God will be there waiting—let Ahab make no mistake about that—and He will read the treachery of my heart. Go there—I will—before I lift my sword to Ahab's heart or gun to his head. Yes, Starbuck follows Ahab, not murders Ahab. And sunk to that cold place, though hand be unsullied with violence, must I, Mary, show a murderous heart to God?*

"*This prayer perhaps I'll make before the Throne: That Thou knowest murder was in my heart, even the hottest desire for murder, yet knowing, ye forgive! I did not strike. Mary would forgive! Mary!*

"Writ to Mary! To be known, all in all, by Mary."

"Where are those pages?"

"The beak of a nightmare seabird swooped the white pages from my hand as though they were flat slices of Lebanon bread."

"But spared your flesh."

Before he began the second recitation, he worried his lip, glanced anxiously at me. Then began Ahab's words:

"*Una, the monster flies before me—a hump like a snow-hill he will appear! A hill I must climb. We will beach the whaleboat on his back. What if the act be futile! It is my will, my will, most futile folly or fated* victory, or I am not Ahab. I know the loss of thee, Una—I know and yet I pursue—for I've seen my wife and child reflected in the eye of Starbuck, that mirror of humanity. And yet I am compelled forward! I will give chase as long as time requires till I see that miracle-swimming white hill-hump caked with snowy age, and him I will mount!

"But I see thy figure, Una, already ascended to the crest. How now? Thou art dark as a cinder! A candle with a black flame! Burnt like a widowed Hindee? Black? Thy feet in snow? Even thou art rendered all paradoxical! Is even my Una finally undecipherable? That thought is greatest torture, worse than the hot harpoon of revenge that embedded itself here! Here where I smack my palm, and again, as though to awaken a human—a husband's—heartbeat.

"Nothing walks in my chest, no steady, human, home-turned, determined plod."

Unhesitating recitation! That profundity I had glimpsed in the merchant sailor's eye. A reservoir of words. Ishmael continued speaking for Ahab.

"So, quietly I will fold this page and slip it into the tarry slot. Starbuck has shown me the way. Would that he could show me the way back to Nantucket, to thee. But he lacks the language for it.

"And I! I have the picture that draws me on. A hump like a snow-hill! Moby Dick! I shall add my stature to his height! Ahab, not Una, let me picture there. Though legs fail, my hands, like mitts of flintstone, will pull me to the summit! Leviathan! My hands are harder than thy flesh! Leviathan! I shall make thee bleed, even as my own manly blood poured from my leg as from a funnel-spout! Moby Dick! When I top thee, THEN, let my punishment begin, for I embody the great Lie: Hate, revenge, my wounds—they are greater than Love. Together let us, like a mountain—higher with Ahab's added height than you ever reared before—be brought low.

"Brought low, we'll storm the shadow valley, we'll harrow the depths . . . these depths . . . whose mere surface lies before me now and all about me. What depths lie below—layer after watery layer of increasing cold. And the floor reached, into what valley do water . . . whale . . . Ahab . . . fall then? And who will exalt the crevasse that on the ocean floor opens itself to step yet again toward unthinkable depths? And who will exalt that valley?

"But I will lift up my eyes, for now.

"See how all womanly the ship glides through the waves, her skirts lifted? So might my Una run toward me through the shallow waves.

"See the towering sails filled with the breath of night. 'Tis speed, I think, that thrills the body into spirit. 'Tis beauty."

CHAPTER 156   🐚   # Letter from Susan, Forwarded

Dear Una,

I am home. And have been home for many a day, week, month, two years, I think. Again, I hope and long for freedom. But I am home. Did you get my first letter? Are you well?

I still have Nature, the book I borrowed. It been my grammar and my speller. I've taken the sentences all apart so that they are just a string of words. I've learned them all. Now I can put them back together to make my own meanings instead of those of Mr. Emerson, the author. I want to write my story for you, Una, up to this point, because you taught me my first letters. If I could, I would write to Mr. Emerson who has given me so many words. Thoughts, too. Now I take a back-stitch and go back a little before where I left off last time.

As I retraced my journey to the north side of the Ohio River, I prayed it might be froze again, for I doubted my ability to transcend were it not. More than froze, it was completely still and filled over with snow. At both banks, the snow curved up in drifts, so that the river seemed more like a trough of snow. A long swale. Nothing there but me and all that white snow glittering in moonlight, just a sickle moon, and starlight.

When I stepped off the bank, I sunk up to my chin, but my feet landed firm. I held up my basket, had my tin honeycomb box and the patty-pan in it, and commenced to plow across. Moses parting the snow. Going back to Egypt, though. That snow lying on the river ice was light as white feathers. I stopped in the middle and looked back at the furrow I made. Whole world was quiet, quiet. Got to the other bank and the ice rotten. I felt my foot going through, tried to hold on but might as well try to grab a cloud. When my shoulder hit, that thin ice just crack open. I knew I was swallowed up. All alone, nobody to help me. Whole land shout, "One basket-toting, home-sick, Mam-sick, blackgirl—she nothing." Shout, and echo, too.

I don't know how Nature did it, but she speeded time for me. When I look up through the cold water, I see the full moon. Must have been Moon didn't want Earth to swallow me up. Moon pulled me out. I brought my face up out of that ice water. I felt the freezing against my scalp soon as I came up. My feet on slippery mud underneath, but I slip and I claw, I break back ice like a loose tooth till I get to firm. Run! That's what my bones told me.

I knew I must run all the way to your cabin. I have to tell myself Lift knees, Push feet! Over and over. My clothes freezing. I made myself run. I drive myself like no whip in hand driver ever drove nobody. Faster, faster. Feet like cold flatirons. Lift knees, lift. Dress froze stiff on my thighs. And there it was. Smoke in the chimney. I burst in. Half dead.

Well, there wasn't any Una there, but there was Daniel, running north. He build up the fire, wrap me in warm blankets. We get acquainted, and I make a long story short. He never forced me, but one evening when he was sitting in the rocking chair, I just climbed up in his lap because I wanted to. Wasn't too many nights till we sharing the bed.

Maybe a week passed. He begged me to run back north with him, but I explained I had to go back for my mam. I see a new kind of owning, the way he look at me. Man owning woman type of owning. What I didn't know for a long time was I was carrying his child with me. I said good-bye to Daniel standing in the snow on the riverbank. Hole in the ice still marking the spot where I went under, just a little skin of clear ice over the water. We tried to fork up my basket with my tin honey box you gave me and the patty-pan the Shakers gave me, but we couldn't get it. Daniel chose a new spot, put down logs in case the ice rotten all along. Then he walked peaceful as could be over the river. Got in my old track where the snow still rumpled. Stars watched with me, Daniel climbing the north bank, *gone into the snow and woods. Last sight, him slipping round tree trunks.*

I walked south. Met the Spring and then the Summer. Folks helped me again, and I saw some I couldn't help but would have if I could. A great drove of Indians walking west. They had dogs to pull their loads, hardly any horses. I saw a family stop, dig a hole, bury a child, knees to chest. I listen to the mourning song. Torn from the side of suffering *was what I thought. The line walked around them while they buried by the trail. I was hid under a mountain laurel. Knees pulled up to my chest. Finally the family fell in with the line, walked on west. I cried.*

I planned what to say if I was caught. "Please, oh do please, take me home. I was stole away." But I wasn't caught. Everything looked right to me, farther on south I traveled, the kinds of trees, the bushes, the slant to the sunlight. It was all way too pretty, I thought, couldn't be all bad. One night the lightning bugs came up to meet me. One other night, though, I see this glowing that was too big for lightning bugs, and I wondered Baby Haints. All in a cluster, pale and bleary. They bobbed and swayed a little in a group. Scary, but I had to see what. When I got closer, I see this was a gourd vine over a blackberry bush. Those little gourds had whitish ends, and the ends reflecting moonlight. I decided to stop there, sleep under that glowing—you can find little rooms inside where blackberry canes curve over.

In the morning, hanging in the vine was a pair of shoes.

"Who left these shoes here?" I say to the woods.

"I did." I see an old black man sitting on the ground, head screwed sideways, cheek on his knees, grinning.

"Haint?" I ask.

He shook his head No.

"Who?" I asked, and I wanted to laugh, like all this a big joke. "Why?"

"And how?" he said, mocking at me. "And when?" He had a high-pitch cracked voice.

I wanted to hear him talk, so I just kept my peace.

"I, the Shoeman."

"You got many customers in these woods?"

"I gib away," he said. His voice sink down so deep and muddy I could hardly understand him. "Bout here, long this stretch, where shoes gib out. I gib anybody a pair of shoes, if he need them. Them soles is polly-wally wood."

I unhooked the sandals from the vine, slipped my foot onto them, nice shaped foot bed, tied the laces threaded through the ends of leather straps. "They fit."

"Girl, you think I make something don't fit?" Voice all high. "I measure your footprint." Voice sinking low. "But you headed the wrong direction." Voice at the bottom, thick.

I told him I was going home. He just shook his head. He didn't say no more. I look away, I look back. He gone. Nothing but space where he was. But he didn't take the shoes.

When I walked the last mile home in the dark, a mockingbird commenced to sing. I knew that was a bad sign. Seemed like he followed me. I wanted holy quiet. But that bird just kept shooting off his mouth. When I looked in the window, I see a candle and a woman sitting at a table, sewing. My mam worked the field, she didn't sew. I saw she squinted her eyes, and my mam never did, and I saw she was stout, and my mam never was, but it was my mam.

The window was swung open on the side hinges and I just ducked down and stood in that little wedge space between the glass and the opening. I breathed home air. Saw children sleeping round the room, big quilting frame. Saw her skirt hem resting on the floor. Head bent.

She didn't look up, but my mam said, "Is that you?" still sewing. "Susan?"

Una, it was my mam, and she knew me without looking.

Oh, I sat on her lap, and she told me get the buttermilk pitcher, get the cornpone off the shelf, and it had her own handprint over the pone top. I knew she watched me stretch up to the bread shelf, and she said, "You come home to born a child into slavery!" Her words just burst out. Mean as sparks.

I said, "I come for you."

"Look here," she said, and she pulled up her skirt. I standing there with the pitcher in my hand. Where they should have been a foot was only a stump wrapped in rags. "Now you grow me a new foot while you grow that baby. Maybe then, we run."

My heart broke. "You want me to kill 'em?" I said. My voice

"You want me to kill 'em?"

sunk low like a growl I never heard. I heard the mockingbird sing, too, Una. So shrill. Like it want to scream but not got the throat for it.

She didn't answer me straight. "I try to run. They catch me. Take my foot."

I cried myself stupid, on her lap. "Sho. Lets think about killin em." She rock me, spoke it over and over, like a lullaby song. "Lets think, lets think." I listen to the children sleep. Some my own kin, some she must of been keeping. "Lets think bout it." Finally I breathing with the younguns. My mam told me to get in bed, over against the wall. She said she was so stout now couldn't anybody see over her to see me. I got in, and then she used the ladder-back chair to help hop. Three hops. And her way too heavy to hop at all.

When morning come, my anger was melted down to sorrow. For her. Night melted me. I don't know how. I don't know why. Only a sorrow lump left. Grief was for me, too, cause I couldn't leave her.

I did what I had to do, her standing in the door calling "Wait now. Lets talk this over. Lets plan." I went through the quarters to the overseers house. Knocked on his door. I looked at the ground like I was ashamed. Orange tigerlily blooming by his step. Door opened, I mumble so humble never looking in his face, "I was stole away, sir, but I done found my way home."

He knock me down. "Reckon I best brand you," that's what he said, "so nobody won't steal you off again. Get up." I follow him inside his cabin.

He sat me on the three-legged stool by the fire, heated up the branding iron till it was white, and sunk it in my cheek. His wife gave me a wet, cool cloth, folded in a square. Walking home, there the mockingbird. Hopping in the dust. He see me, he jump quick into air, two white fans spreading out of his two wings. My cheek with an oak leaf. Burning. Burning bad. For Thousand Oaks. The name of this place where I am. But you mustn't use it for address, lest I be beat. I find you someday, Una. When freedom come. If you could buy us all, I would pay you back. And I got a baby. When she was born, I say to my mam, "This baby's name is Liberty." I named her for yours. I shamed to born her to slavery, but that name helped, so I could smile a little.

My mam say, "Lets name her Liberty Lee, and we'll jus' call her Lee. Time being."

She smiled so big, and so did I. So would you. All sneaky. We will have freedom, and we will have it right this time. I have no doubt. My faith is firm. My mam called in the children and holding up my baby girl to the sun in the window she said to all them what I say to you, "This is the day the Lord hath made. Let us rejoice, be glad in it."

My girl is growing, and sometimes I whisper other names in her ear, magic names whose meanings I don't know. "Orpheus Eurydice," I whisper, for she is the sweetest life I know.

In love and hope abiding,
Susan Spenser Oaks

Susan's letter had been held for me at the Mitchells', and I could not help but explode into tears there in their apartment after reading it. As soon as I could speak, I consulted with Mr. Mitchell about how to find Susan, for her letter mentioned Thousand Oaks plantation, but not the state. Mr. Mitchell's reference books supplied me with the names of all the counties in Mississippi, Alabama, and Georgia, and Maria and I immediately began to pen letters to the sheriff of every county, saying only that we were trying to locate kin who were staying at a farm called Thousand Oaks. With great urgency, we wrote letters for three days, and then I came back to 'Sconset.

CHAPTER 157   🐚   **The Roof Walk**

ONE NOVEMBER NIGHT, I felt so anxious that I knew I must walk the widow's walk. I left the trapdoor flung open to the pit of light below, and I wore a blanket around me like an Indian to swaddle myself from the breeze. I grieved for Susan. For my own innocent baby, alive three days; and for Frannie's. For Susan's Indians, moving west. *Susan, be safe.*

What are your houses, dear readers—if ye exist as other than wisps in my mind—but platforms to lift you up? Walk above your house, and the heavens are open to you. Let what might seem like roof for your head become floor for your feet.

The wind wanted to blow me clean. How I had loved the wind when aloft at sea, and how, with sails, one could fly before such a wind! I clutched the flapping blanket under my chin. Smeared by the wind, my vision bleared the stars. I loved the wildness of it all. *Among you, among you*, my spirit sang.

I thought of my boy and of Jim, of my friends Robben and Austin as dear to me as brothers, all of whom were now someplace on the ocean. I did not feel afraid for them, though, ironically, they sailed in a ship named the *Liberty*. It tormented me to think of Susan waiting for help. Worse was to think she'd run again, was captured, parted from her child. Sold. Killed. And she had appealed to me.

But gradually my pacing brought me calm. The vastness of the heavens seemed a haven for all of us. Surely Susan was somewhere. *Be safe*. And I thought of Margaret Fuller's letters from Europe, of Charlotte and Kit, and of Frannie's letters, of Aunt Agatha and Uncle Torchy tending their lighthouse. We were not fragments, or if we were fragments we were in-gathered. I stood still and felt them all gathering home. If my mind called their names, they seemed with me. I felt us all in-gathered by the glittering universe.

Alone on my platform, I knew myself to be in motion, though I stood still. My motion was rooted in the earth and its journey. Not just my house, but the world itself was my ship traveling airy waters which rarefied beyond air into sheer blackness. And beyond and all about me in deep black nothingness were sources of light, they, too, moving. What a rushing, what a rushing we all made, like this Nantucket wind, immediate, crisping my cheeks and ears. And none left behind, nor could they be. We are embraced even before we can embrace.

I heard footsteps, which I knew well, pass through the house. From the first night in my bed, we had known the depths of each other; my body had whispered to me as his had to him: This is marriage. It needed no courtship.

I heard his feet on the stairs, and his dark form emerged from the light below. "November in your soul?" I called.

"Nay," he answered, "this November's external, where it should be."

When I turned back to the star-bright sky, he came to stand behind me, wound arms around me, knotted me close to him with clasped hands.

"In a few weeks, we will rejoice in the hearth," he said.

"Do you mind we write the same book?" I asked. *The Star-Gazer* seemed to be my title.

"Think of the mighty Cathedral of Cologne," he said, "left with the crane still standing upon the top of the uncompleted tower." He paused and then went on, for it was ever Ishmael's way to extend a thought. "Think of the Cathedral of Chartres. Think of its two towers. They do not match at all. Built perhaps a century apart, or more; but without both spires, our Chartres would not be Chartres."

The pulse of me beat against his hands knotted over my stomach.

Unself-consciously he mused on, "Small erections may be finished by their first architects; grand ones, true ones, ever leave the finishing to posterity. My whole book is but a draft—nay, but the draft of a draft."

I said I felt the same about my book.

Ishmael added humorously, "Oh, Time, Strength, Cash, and Patience!"

The wind enwrapped us both, with whirling, invisible arms; its fingers plowed our hair. I covered his human fingers with my own, and we were quiet awhile. With our faces uptilted toward the stars, he said, "And what do you think, Una, of these heartless immensities?"

"That we are a part of them, and they are a part of us."

Epilogue

W E A R E N O T legally married by even so liberal an *institution* as the gold-domed Unitarians, but united by our natures. Each day and forever we choose to be husband and wife as surely as the spangled sea meets the land before me, as surely as the ink flows from my sharpened feather to meet the sun-washed page on my desk.

We may sail again, taking Felicity—our daughter—with us, when these books are done. I would gaze at those disparate spires of Chartres, with Ishmael beside me. We would see Margaret's pagan Pantheon in Rome and the pyramids in Egypt and the Nile, where the spiritual may yet be found in cyclic floods and vegetable forces.

Last year, in 1850, Margaret died, drowned with her husband and small son, just off New York's Fire Island. Because I knew from her letters that she was bringing a trunk of manuscripts, I went there, walked the beach, hoping at least to salvage the part of her spirit committed to paper, but I found it not.

As I wandered the warm sand of Fire Island, the birds circling above, I met a man and a boy of five, who spoke to me, amazing me by his spiraling sentence—"My name is Henry James," he told me, "and I shall always remember this day when Father and I searched for the trunk of Margaret Fuller, who is known to me only by her writing (perhaps someday my flesh, too, or yours, shall be represented only by marks on a page, or scratched letters like those I saw in Rome on the stone wall of a catacomb, where I also saw a picture of a fish incised in the stone, and I wondered if it were a great fish?)—and I shall remember the essence of Margaret Fuller without volition on my part, the same way I shall remember that hawk who cries overhead and this desolation of flatness." He was a blessed boy—a prodigy—and I wanted to weep at the marvel of him. The period at the end of his spoken sentence, though invisible, seemed like a speck to me, like a bird flown so high that finally it was only a diminishing dot.

Survivors of the shipwreck reported that Margaret refused to try to save herself, but I cannot believe that. They say she sat on the deck, her back against a mast, her long hair streaming over her shoulders. My heart shrieks against that! She would try, *we* would try. Certainly Susan and I would try. But I have not yet heard again from Susan, or of Susan.

Next door, in Mary Starbuck's old home, I have a school—have I not wanted to be a teacher since I was a girl—called First School, where I teach young women sent to me by Frannie. My students lived but recently in slavery, and they share their stories with each other, and I teach them how to read and write and sew, even as I began to teach Susan. Their first letter is an *S,* as my mother taught me. *S* for snake, for sea, sand, sun—look out the window. And sometimes I tell them, my voice almost choking, that *S* is also for Susan and for School, which I began to honor her.

Amidst fundamental learning at First School, strange questions are also welcome. A girl of twelve, her skin the most lovely hue of milky brown I have ever seen, looked up from her stitching and asked me, "Is time an orphan?" Later, when I took her to the night sky, I waved my pale hand at the glory and said, "Time lives here. Far away and near as us, on this platform."

Now I see Robben next door, pruning the green whale. We enjoy much interaction and discussion among us, visiting with the Isaac and Mary Starbuck lighthouse tribe and the Mitchell clan, and Phoebe from town, as well as new friends. Justice and Jim study and board in town with William Mitchell.

Our friendly discourse is not always reassuring. We, like other folk of this midcentury decade, look at the North and South and wonder if there will be war. To Ishmael I have trotted out an old idea—if civil war comes might we not sail west, to the farthest reaches, into that territory not a part of the United States, for I would not be party to any national solution to either slavery or states' rights, or, indeed, to any political problem, writ largely in blood.

I look north along the coast, and I can just make out the clot of students from First School standing on the Sankaty cliff, with the light-house behind. The judge is with them; he became an expert at the potter's wheel, once he learned to abide the gray slurry on his hands, and he teaches these former slaves that craft. Today they are recreational together. They are all launching kites from the headland before the lighthouse. Maria Mitchell is with them, no doubt discussing air currents. At this distance, I see the kites as bits of color rising up like glad-flung confetti.

I shall call Ishmael, point toward the Sankaty headland, then read aloud this last writing, believing that he will like my own wind-flung confetti—words streaming from my hand. Each day and forever, by the ticking of the mantel clock and by the dark wheeling of the cosmos, we have given time a home.

FINIS

Acknowledgments

AHAB'S WIFE is dedicated to John C. Morrison, my husband, who sailed with me throughout the voyage of writing this book, while writing his own book in physics.

Karen J. Mann, Lucinda Dixon Sullivan, Robin Lippincott, and Susan Johnson read every draft of *Ahab's Wife,* making innumerable valuable suggestions and offering constant encouragement. Without their generous help, both I and the book would have floundered.

For their very detailed, insightful, and heartening response to the third draft, I must express deep gratitude to Neela Vaswani, Julie Brickman, Jody Lisberger, and Judy Himmelfarb; and to Nan Goheen and Marcia Woodruff Dalton for their work on the second draft; and to Daly Walker and Bill Pearce for critiquing the critical opening chapters.

For their encouragement at the outset of the project or along the way, I thank my brothers John Sims Jeter and Marvin D. Jeter, and my friends Nancy and Bernard Moore, Richard M. Sullivan, Roger Weingarten, Mark Pollizzoti, Alan Naslund, Lynn Greenberg, Elizabeth F. Sulzby, Patricia and Charles Gaines, Melissa Pritchard, Dennis Buchholz, Rob LaFreniere, Luke Wallin, Mary Gordon, Maureen Morehead, Bret Lott, Christopher Noël, Linda Beattie, Kay Gill, Nana Lampton, Kay Lippincott, and Lee Salkowitz. A special thanks to Ann Marin for sharing her office with me, in the spring of 1996.

My gratitude to Leslie Daniels and Joy Harris, of the Joy Harris Literary Agency, and to my editor, Paul Bresnick, and my publisher, Michael Murphy, at William Morrow and Company overwhelms me.

And with loving thanks to Flora Naslund and Marty Kelley and to Debra Morrison and David Rizzolo, Paul Morrison, David Morrison, Sara and Michael McQuilling, and Ryan Morrison.

I also thank the Kentucky Foundation for Women for an Artist's

Grant and the Graduate School of the University of Louisville for a Completion Grant, which allowed me to lighten my teaching load by a course one semester and also helped to cover travel and research expenses to whaling museums at Nantucket, New Bedford, and Mystic. I also thank the University of Louisville for granting me a one-semester sabbatical leave of absence from teaching during which I worked on portions of this book.

About the Author

SENA JETER NASLUND grew up in Birmingham, Alabama, where she attended public schools and received the B.A. from Birmingham-Southern College. She has also lived in Louisiana, West Virginia, and California. She received the M.A. and Ph.D. degrees from the University of Iowa Writers' Workshop. She is the author of the novel *Sherlock in Love* and the short-story collection *The Disobedience of Water*. Her short fiction has appeared in *The Paris Review, The Georgia Review, The Iowa Review, Michigan Quarterly Review,* and many other journals. For twelve years, she directed the Creative Writing Program at the University of Louisville, where she teaches and holds the title Distinguished Teaching Professor. Concurrently, she is a member of the M.F.A. in Writing faculty of Vermont College. She is coeditor of the literary magazine *The Louisville Review* and the Fleur-de-Lis Press, housed at Spalding University, and has taught at the University of Montana and Indiana University. A recipient of grants from the National Endowment for the Arts, the Kentucky Foundation for Women, and the Kentucky Arts Council, she lives in Louisville.